Lucifer's Drum

To Dana~
With abiding thanks
for your friendship and
admiration for the person
you are.
Love,
Bernie

P.S. Check the Acknowledgments

BERNIE MacKINNON

Also by Bernie MacKinnon:
(publisher Houghton Mifflin)

The Meantime
Song For A Shadow

ISBN: 0986077402
ISBN 13: 9780986077401
Library of Congress Control Number: 2014908395
Pine Badge Press, Memphis, TN

To my mother and father, for all the best reasons

Author's Note

THE SPRING OF 1864 remains America's bloodiest season ever. In early May, Ulysses S. Grant led his army into northern Virginia, touching off a titanic clash with the army of Robert E. Lee. Tens of thousands died. Despite major Union successes in the previous year, the three-year-old Civil War seemed destined to grind on indefinitely, and many stunned Northerners wondered if all the sacrifice had been for nothing–if it was time to just let the South go.

Pro-Confederate "Peace" Democrats, or "Copperheads," would dominate their party's election platform later that year, and it was widely believed that Abraham Lincoln would be denied a second term. Secret Copperhead organizations flourished, agitating against the war, the draft and Emancipation. Gold prices soared, threatening financial chaos. European observers sounded death knells for the American experiment in liberty and unity. But for the battered Confederacy, too, conditions were growing more and more desperate, even as its dream of independence burned brighter.

Into this teetering hour rode Lieutenant-General Jubal A. Early. In the first half of summer, he marched his sizeable Confederate force down the Shenandoah Valley and across the Potomac. He then sped it toward Washington, D.C., imperiling that weakly garrisoned city and throwing much of the North into panic. Surely the sack and ruin of its capital would prove too much for the Union. Surely this grand-scale humiliation would break its will, bringing final victory to the South.

What happened next remains one of the great "what ifs" of history. Early's legendary raid provides the pivot for this work of fiction, which includes other real events and several real characters, along with many invented ones.

Major Civil War Events To Late Spring, 1864

1861

April 12. South Carolina's bombardment and capture of Fort Sumter triggers war. By end of May, eleven Southern states have seceded to form the Confederate States of America under President Jefferson Davis; Maryland, Kentucky and Missouri threaten to follow.

July 21. First Battle of Bull Run (Manassas, Virginia). Union troops under General Irwin McDowell routed. In August, General George B. McClellan given command of main Northern army, now called the Army of the Potomac.

1862

February. In West, Confederates surrender Forts Henry and Donelson in Tennessee. (First notable victories for Union General Ulysses S. Grant.)

March 9. Off Hampton Roads, Virginia, first-ever battle between ironclad vessels—the *Monitor* (Union) and the *Virginia* (Confederacy)—ends in a draw.

April 6-7. Battle of Shiloh in Tennessee. Grant repels strong Confederate attack.

April 26. Union navy spearheads capture of New Orleans.

April 5-July 1. McClellan's Peninsular Campaign, culminating in Seven Days' Battles. After coming within a few miles of the Confederate capitol of Richmond, McClellan withdraws in the belief that he is outnumbered.

His army is in fact significantly larger than General Robert E. Lee's Army of Northern Virginia.

May-June. Confederate General Thomas J. "Stonewall" Jackson raises havoc in Virginia's Shenandoah Valley, winning a string of victories and evading Union pursuit.

August 29-30. Second Battle of Bull Run (Manassas). Union troops under General John Pope badly defeated by Lee.

September 17. Battle of Antietam near Sharpsburg, Maryland. Bloodiest day in U.S. history. McClellan checks Lee's invasion of the North but loses chance to destroy Confederate army. Lincoln sacks McClellan on November 7.

October 8. Battle of Perryville, Kentucky, ends Confederate General Braxton Bragg's invasion of that state.

December 13. Battle of Fredericksburg, Virginia. Union General Ambrose Burnside launches massive frontal assaults on Lee's position and suffers heavy defeat.

December 31 & January 2. Battle of Stones River near Murfreesboro, Tennessee. Union General William S. Rosecrans defeats Bragg.

1863

January 1. Lincoln's Emancipation Proclamation declares freedom for all slaves in Confederate-held territory. Northern recruitment of Negro troops begins in earnest.

May 1-4. Battle of Chancellorsville, Virginia. Outnumbered again, Lee soundly defeats Army of the Potomac under General Joseph Hooker. In accidental shooting by his own troops, Stonewall Jackson is mortally wounded.

May-July. Black Union troops first begin to see heavy action, fighting at Port Hudson, Louisiana, Milliken's Bend, Mississippi and Fort Wagner, South Carolina.

July 1-3. Battle of Gettysburg, Pennsylvania. Army of the Potomac under General George G. Meade stops Lee's second invasion of the North. Like McClellan, Meade fails to follow up the victory; Lee's badly damaged army escapes.

July 4. Vicksburg, Mississippi falls to forces of Grant after a siege. Confederacy now split, with Union in full possession of Mississippi River.

July 13-16. New York City Draft Riots. Union army conscription sparks worst civil disturbance in U.S. history. For four days, largely Irish mobs burn, loot and kill before authorities restore order.

September 19-20. Battle of Chickamauga in northern Georgia. Bragg inflicts heavy defeat on Union army under Rosecrans, who is then replaced by Grant.

November 24-25. Battles around Chattanooga, Tennessee. At Missionary Ridge and Lookout Mountain, Grant's army defeats Bragg's, which retreats into Georgia.

1864

March 9. Grant made general-in-chief of all Union forces, though Meade retains direct command of Army of the Potomac. General William T. Sherman will lead federal push into Georgia.

April 12. Battle of Fort Pillow, Tennessee. Confederates under General Nathan B. Forrest massacre much of bi-racial Union garrison following its surrender. Both sides are committing atrocities with increasing frequency, but Fort Pillow becomes the most notorious.

May-June. Grant launches campaign against Lee in northern Virginia. In the Battles of the Wilderness and Spotsylvania, he suffers losses so great that the government delays their publication for weeks. At Cold Harbor on June 3, Grant's frontal attack on Lee's position ends with no gain and massive carnage. Still he pushes his army onward in an effort to outflank Lee, whose strength is also seriously reduced. In western Virginia, the struggle for the Shenandoah Valley continues. While its rich farmlands help supply Lee's army, the Valley's configuration—running southwest to northeast–makes it a natural invasion route for Southern forces. In much of the North, momentum gathers for peace and for recognition of the Confederate States. This is championed by the Peace or Copperhead faction of the Democratic Party, which will soon nominate George McClellan for President. The fall election campaigns promise more dirt and acrimony than ever before.

Table Of Contents

PART I

A Copperhead's Fate

Self-esteem: An erroneous opinion of oneself.
• AMBROSE BIERCE, THE DEVIL'S DICTIONARY

1

Northern Shenandoah Valley
June 6, 1864

GIDEON VAN GILDER had left his dignity far behind, like an expensive top-coat forgotten in haste. He did not mourn its loss–had not mourned it even at the last roadside inn, when he started awake and spied his stricken face in a shaving mirror. Now, huddled again inside the rocking coach, he could think only of escape. Escape–southward, southward by moon and carriage light, along this road so rough that it threatened to break the axles. Up the hill-haunted Shenandoah lay sanctuary, some haven behind the booming, gargantuan battle lines. Only there could he know rest once more. Rest, and perhaps the luxury of pride.

The lump of the derringer beneath his vest was small comfort–he had never fired a pistol in his life. At times in the jouncing blur of his journey, he had found himself gripping his cane between his knees like a talisman of dubious power. More frequently than ever he yelled at his hunchbacked coachman, calling him a sausage-eating monkey or a deformed German half-wit. The coachman said little.

Awaking from a fitful doze, Van Gilder realized that the coach's rocking had ceased. He shuddered as he blinked out of the window into a mass of tall black shapes that hid the moon. He heard a ragged breathing sound. After a disoriented moment, he identified the sound as that of the horses and the obstruction as a stand of pine. He shifted to the other side and elbowed the door open. In the carriage lamp's glow he discerned the misshapen form of the coachman. He was carrying two pails down an embankment, headed for the ripple of an unseen creek.

Van Gilder drew a breath to holler, but in the dark his voice came as a hushed rasp. "Kirschenbaum!"

Maintaining his balance on the slope, the coachman made an awkward turn. "Horses are tired, you makes them run all night. Tired like me, sir. I get vater."

"Do it, then, imbecile! But no more stops!"

The hunched form started to turn away, then hesitated. "Herr Van Gilder?"

"Get the damned water!"

"We gets closer to the secesh."

"Yes!" Van Gilder hissed "Yes–and I've paid you! Get the water!"

"I did not know I must take you five days and now all night. And we gets closer to the secesh."

Though still hushed, Van Gilder's voice began its climb toward full fury. "Fool! I know where we're going! I've paid you!"

"You pay me more, I think."

In the rippling stillness, one of the animals snorted. Van Gilder sputtered a curse. "Three dollars more, when we reach the place!"

"Ten."

From the creek, a bullfrog let out a deep "bong" sound. Van Gilder thought of the derringer–wishing, thwarted. This time he spoke in just a murmur. "Ten, when we get there."

"I thank you," said the hunchback, who resumed his descent.

Dense with cricket noise, the warm, still air pressed in on Van Gilder, worsening his agitation. He took up his map, rattled it open and lit a match. In the match's flutter he followed the black line of his route to the town of Strasburg, marked by a tight circle. Twenty-five miles to go, more or less. He blew out the match, folded the map and again peered outside.

"Kirschenbaum!" he called in a hoarse whisper.

From the embankment, the hunchback's laboring form reappeared with the pails, slopping water. Kirschenbaum began watering the first pair of horses. When they got to Strasburg, Van Gilder thought, he would stick his derringer in the face of this insolent moron. Then he would drop a single coin at his feet and tell him to get out of his sight forever.

"Van Gilder!" came a deep-throated call.

Van Gilder jerked upright. For a crazed moment, he could neither move nor think nor breathe. Then, blindly, he began fumbling for his derringer.

"Don't fret," came the voice. "I am here to see that you pass safely through our lines."

Van Gilder stopped pawing at his vest. Shaking, he leaned slowly out the side. He saw Kirschenbaum standing motionless, staring past the back of the coach. From that direction he heard a crunch of pebbles, very close. How–how could anyone have come upon them with such stealth? Leaning out farther, he forced his head to turn. Out of the gloom, the shape of a horse and rider emerged. The man wore a military cap, cape and double-breasted tunic, its brass buttons winking like sparks. With the oil running low, the lamps cast a meager halo about the coach–and as the stranger entered it, his uniform proved to be Union blue. He held a revolver and the reins in one hand, an extinguished lantern in the other.

Van Gilder gazed, open-mouthed as the intruder guided his mount forward and then halted–a bearded, powerful-looking officer, the right side of his face hidden by bandages. In an attitude of dutiful ease, he slouched in the saddle, his revolver held loosely away. His one visible eye peered down at Kirschenbaum, though it was Van Gilder whom he addressed:

"Major Henry Spruce, Army of the Potomac, currently on detached service. I am your official escort–to assure that you make your rendezvous in Strasburg. That you do so without being fired upon by federal pickets, who perhaps know a traitor when they see one."

There was something odd about the major's low-in-the-throat intonation. Still gaping, Van Gilder fidgeted with the buttons of his coat. "How did you know . . . ?"

"For reasons that are plain enough, our government has observed you closely for some time. We welcome your decision and wish to aid you in carrying it out. The Union is well rid of you, don't you think?"

Van Gilder's ire stirred, eating through his fear. "And I, sir . . . *I* am well rid of the Union!"

The major passed the lantern down to Kirschenbaum, who distractedly placed it in the coach's boot, along with the empty pails. Holstering his weapon, Spruce dismounted with a grace unusual for a man his size, let alone an injured one. His whiskers were cinnamon brown and the bandages new, with no trace of dirt or blood. The horse complemented him entirely—a sleek black stallion whose forehead bore a patch of white, like a chipped diamond.

Spruce held his palm out to Van Gilder. "I'll take your piece, for now."

Van Gilder hesitated, teetering between caution and resentment. Then, with a quivering hand, he reached under his vest, withdrew the pistol and gave it up.

The major stuck the weapon in his saddlebag, from which he then took a bundled hitching strap. Unfurling it, he fastened one end to his horse's bridle ring and the other to the coach's roof railing.

"What are you doing?" Van Gilder demanded.

Spruce took out a little sack, then placed his booted foot on the coach's step plate. "My mount can trot along behind. It'll be daylight soon, and I don't mean to be picked off when your secesh friends see us coming." He signaled for Van Gilder to move his legs. "You're stuck with me for the last few miles, good sir."

Van Gilder budged over.

The major glanced over at Kirschenbaum. "Drive on."

"Ja, sir."

The hunchback hoisted himself up to the driver's box as Spruce climbed in.

At the sound of the lash, the vehicle lurched, rocked and continued along the rutted road. Van Gilder's heart still thudded. Longing for daylight, he averted his gaze from the major who sat opposite, one hand playing with the cord of the window blind.

"A Concord Coach," said Spruce. "You do travel in style, don't you?"

Van Gilder granted himself a look, taking in the holstered revolver, the bayonet in its leather scabbard, the broad shoulders with epaulettes. Spruce had not seen fit to remove his hat, under which tufts of cinnamon hair protruded. However noxious, his military aspect made him a known quantity, nudging Van Gilder toward sullen acquiescence. Still it unsettled him to sit facing a man with half a face. Then Van Gilder noticed the one pale eye looking straight at him.

"You will pardon my appearance," said Spruce. "This little addition to my features was made a few weeks ago at Spotsylvania, courtesy of one of your fine compatriots."

Van Gilder cleared his throat. "A misfortune I would have wished to prevent. As with this war."

Arms crossed, the major gave a shrug, barely detectable amid the jarring of the dim coach.

Van Gilder felt satisfied with his own response. Beneath the lingering shock, he was settling down. He reached for his cane. Holding it firmly, he raised his double chin and tried to meet Spruce's eye. Instantly his stomach tightened again. Even in this gloom, the look on the rugged, half-concealed face seemed too knowing.

Van Gilder struggled for an airy tone. "Through your lines, eh? I didn't think there were lines to speak of in this region."

"Your information is faulty, sir. Like your politics."

Van Gilder managed an authentic glare.

"The Valley's in federal hands," said the major. "General Hunter's on the march." With a hint of smile, he reached under his cape and withdrew a flask, which he uncorked. "It helps the pain as well as anything," he said, and took a quick swallow.

Van Gilder's tension eased a bit. The coach bumped along beneath him, headed toward safety. He would make Strasburg, albeit with an unwelcome companion. "So you're all they sent," he observed.

Spruce chortled. "Ho-ho! First you're indignant that we knew your movements–and now you complain of insufficient escort? Thanks in no small part to you and your kind, our forces are fully engaged throughout Virginia. We can scarcely spare men for duties so . . . minor." He took another swallow, then wiped his lips on his cuff. "My regrets, sir, but one loyal convalescent is all we can afford you."

Looking out at the bumpy darkness, Van Gilder sneered. "In truth, Major, you're more than enough."

Spruce let out a comfortable sigh. "I reckon I'll suffice."

Van Gilder sat back. He didn't need to look at Spruce again. For him, in these cramped shadows, the scales had balanced. Patience had never been his strong card, but he could stand the presence of a tippling bluebelly for a while. So long as it meant asylum in the great gray bosom of Dixie.

"But come, Van Gilder–credit me with restraint. I've been told of your career and yet refrained from calling you any number of names. Treasonous dog, reptilian Judas, Copperhead scum . . . "

Van Gilder straightened in his seat. His face grew warm as he forced a glare into Spruce's lone eye, and for a moment he became the self that he fancied best: champion of states' rights, arch-foe of miscegenation, battler of the tyrannical federal serpent. "Then credit *me*, sir! Credit me with the ardor of my convictions! The prospect of despotism and half-nigger infants may not worry you. The plague of freed black bucks robbing honest white men of their livelihoods may not concern you. But for my part I've endured intrigue, vilification and all manner of devilry for merely wishing peace. Peace, Major! An end to the wounds and killing! Your face, sir, would be whole now if my words and those of my fellow believers had been heeded!"

Holding a hand up, the big officer looked into his lap and slowly shook his head. "And you have many words, I'm sure. I cannot hope to match their eloquence, certainly not at this late hour." The hand fell. "In fact and at heart, I'm a humble soldier. Besides, I've heard the Copperhead gospel so many times it makes my senses fog. So let's simply enjoy the ride, eh?"

Van Gilder looked down at the major's boots and smirked. Spruce's voice was as odd as the man himself, sounding as if he had a pebble in his throat or needed to burp. Now it throbbed with false conciliation, its owner taking refuge from Van Gilder's impassioned tongue. Whiskey was rapidly dulling this warrior's spirit. The man had just pleaded for mercy, after a fashion, and Van Gilder supposed he might soon be hearing maudlin tales of a wife and children left behind. This was by no means the sort of exit he had planned, but at least he would depart Northern soil on a note of moral victory. Miraculously he was no longer afraid.

"You do well enough, Major," he said, "–for a humble soldier. Though you rely on snideness overmuch."

"War hardens us overmuch, Van Gilder." Spruce took another nip and then reached into his little sack, from which he produced a silver folding cup. "I propose that this trip be made not in the spirit of rancor, but in recognition of opposing ends achieved at a single stroke." He raised the cup, its rim glistening. "For you the South opens its grateful arms, while the North may now turn its intrigue and vilification upon other worthy targets. This journey, sir, is celebratory."

Van Gilder leaned forward on his cane. He sniggered. "You propose that I drink with you, Major Spruce?"

Looking thoughtful, Spruce lowered the cup, then used it to push back the brim of his hat. "I . . . I propose that we honor the one objective, the one prayer we find mutually agreeable. To this sorrowful conflict's end."

Van Gilder arched an eyebrow.

Spruce raised the flask and the cup, poured two fingers' worth and offered it to Van Gilder. Sneering at the cup, Van Gilder let Spruce's hand hold it there for a moment, vibrating with the road. Then he took it. He could humor a jabbering Unionist fool. Perhaps he could even squeeze the man for an answer or two–answers that he could impart to Richmond officials, when he told them how outrageously sloppy their agents were.

"Not that it matters now," Van Gilder said, "–but how were my movements made known to you?"

Now it was Spruce who smirked. He drew his hat down till it hid his eye. "Let it just be said that the government has its ways. More than either of us can know."

Van Gilder shifted position, frowning at his drink. After all the tense planning for this contingency, his Southern friends–maybe even Cathcart, his most trusted–stood guilty of some idiotic lapse, the exact nature of which he would probably never know. The thought made him sullen once more.

Spruce held the flask up. "To war's end!"

Van Gilder squinted at the hat's brim, hoping the major could feel the heat of his contempt. "To peace!" he declared, and downed the liquor.

Smacking his lips, he gazed out at the night again. In the deep black of the east he sensed the Blue Ridge Mountains, soon to be fringed red with dawn. Sooner than that, this road would join the Valley Pike, taking him through Winchester and on to Strasburg. Surely he was in Virginia by now.

The coach slowed as it started on an uphill grade. Through the door seam came a breeze, clammy on Van Gilder's face. He was perspiring. He realized that he had dropped both the cup and the cane and that his fingers had gone limp. As he turned his head, the fear began–a quiet explosion of cold, all over.

On the seat beside his companion he saw the corked flask. Next to that lay the major's hat, upside down, the cinnamon wig like some dead creature in its hollow. And he saw the man watching him–fingertips together, elbows out, cape spread. A man of shadows–half-faced, dark-maned, somehow larger than before. Van Gilder knew the patient mannerism of the fingertips. He knew the lone steady eye, the barely visible scar along the scalp. And when the voice came, the true voice, he knew that too–smooth and distant yet horribly intimate, as in his nightmares.

"How do you feel, Gideon?"

Van Gilder understood at last that fear had been a presence through-out his life. Fear of many things, played out in bluster and vitriol. But the terror that struck him now dwarfed the sum of every fear he had known, quaking him in a tide of nausea. His eyelids fluttered, but if he blacked out it was only for a few seconds. In his swimming vision he beheld the half-faced specter, waiting there. Van Gilder could not move. His lips emit-ted a low whine.

"Nothing fatal," said the voice. "The cup was coated with a substance derived from the glands of a large Caribbean toad. Hard to obtain, but within our means. It will simply . . . hold you in place."

Wide-eyed, his insides bucking, Van Gilder strained against the near-complete paralysis.

"It was easy, mind you. I just had to wait, watch, trail you for a bit."

Van Gilder stared, choked.

The fingertips parted, then came to rest on his knees. "And if you could speak, Gideon, what would the words be? A plea, I suppose. But you recall our last session and what passed between us then. A whole year ago–could that be?" Reaching out with his index, he flicked Van Gilder's hair beside his right ear. "A covenant broken is a kind of death." His caped bulk leaned forward, looming. "It is death. Death, precisely. With death as its only atonement."

The coach started down a grade, speeding up with a clacking of wheels. Blood thumping in his ears, Van Gilder fought to breathe. For an instant, horror transported him back to the night that he had entered into the contract and doomed himself–a howl within his memory, unfathomable. Then he returned, though the howl could not break free. His eyes bulged at the one pale eye and he knew that he was in hell–a cramped, dim, rock-ing hell prepared for him alone, with the darkest of angels presiding. The specter looked down, contemplative. Next to his upended hat sat a jar full of clear fluid labeled "Formaldehyde." Then, with that casual elegance, he drew his bayonet. If Van Gilder's soul had harbored any small hope of reprieve, it died now. There would be no reprieve, no mercy.

The dark angel sighed. "Gideon–your atonement begins."

2

Near Winchester, Virginia

Nathaniel Truly regretted ever speaking with the telegrapher. Now all he could think of was his son. With the thought came a series of images, all too vivid–Ben and bayonets, Ben and artillery shells, Ben and head-stones–grinding at him like a crosscut saw. In his work for the U.S. War Department, Truly's talent for concentration made him productive–but this lengthening vigil, here in the seat of the covered wagon, seemed to have sapped it. Despite the softness and stillness of the hour, he ached with dread, his hands worrying the reins. Once more he tried to focus, staring a short distance up the Valley Pike. By the wooded crossroads stood four gray-clad figures, phantoms in the mist of daybreak.

He cleared his throat. "The trouble with this bunch is they're too damned well-fed. Last real johnnies I saw were prisoners from the Wilderness–scarecrows all."

Slouched beside him, Captain Bartholomew Forbes of the Military Information Bureau gave a shrug. "They're the best specimens the Harper's garrison had to offer."

Truly glanced at him. "Must say, you make a fine-looking Reb yourself."

In his Confederate cavalryman's garb, complete with saber and black silk cravat, the young Bostonian did appear every inch the genuine item. Unsmiling, he shifted his wooden leg and yawned. Truly understood his colleague's mixed attitude toward the disguise, but Forbes' melancholy had been obvious since his arrival last night at Harper's Ferry. It was the last thing Truly needed. It occurred to him that Forbes' route had taken him past Sharpsburg and the Antietam battlefield, where his missing limb kept company with so many others.

Forbes had once allowed that his wounding took place not in the battle proper but in a skirmish the day before. An added touch of injury, Truly thought–to be unable to say, without qualification, that it had happened in the great clash of hallowed name. Truly remembered the guns of that day–the titanic sound if not the sight of them. A civilian scout then, he had listened from safety in the rear, endlessly glad to have been spared the fuller experience.

He pulled up his battered slouch hat and scanned the horizon. The sun had cracked the Blue Ridge, banishing the fog, spreading rose-colored light across the woods, fields and pastures. It sparkled the nearby spring and the more distant Shenandoah River. For this moment, with the lowing of cattle and the dense nattering of birds, the Valley wore its splendor as if neither men nor wars existed. But the reflection brought Ben back to mind, and the Ferry telegrapher's news: more action at Cold Harbor. Again the sawblade of images, cutting deep. Truly had endured similar instances, hearing of battles in which Ben might be involved. Where was his fortitude this time? He reached into the pocket of his mud-splattered coat, drew out a plug of tobacco and bit the end off.

"Tobacco this early?" Forbes said.

Chewing, Truly gauged his partner's tone for any hint of blueblood disdain. Recognizing his own irritable state, he gave Forbes the benefit of a doubt. "I reckon it's relative. The day started awful early." Both the dread and the irritability receded a bit–enough to let him wonder, as he often had, at the contrast between Forbes and himself.

At twenty-six, Forbes was his junior by two decades–lanky, dark-haired and clean-shaven, with the even features of an archangel, while Truly was short, bowlegged and ruddy-haired, with an untrimmed mustache and a face seemingly hewn by a dull chisel. But the differences did not end there. It was Boston versus Missouri, mansion versus cabin, store-bought versus homespun, bachelor versus widower, Harvard versus books-by-campfire. Nothing about it should have worked. Confronted with such a partner, Truly should have felt the preemptive scorn of which he had been guilty in other situations, while Forbes should have equated his lofty birth with lofty virtue and behaved accordingly. Truly even wondered if those who had arranged the sporadic partnership had been less than sincere–if by this very choice of men, higher-ups had sought to subvert the stated goal of inter-organizational good will. If so, they were disappointed. Over three protracted cases, so far, the pair had worked as an effective if peculiar engine, oiled by mutual regard. For this, Truly could only credit some fortunate alchemy, some factor well beyond his grasp.

It had been uncertain whether Forbes would even make it here in time. His hasty trip up from the main front, following Truly's out-of-nowhere request, had doubtless left him jarred. Truly decided to let him doze, but presently it was Forbes who spoke.

"I've picked a name for myself. When Van Gilder arrives, I'll be Captain Luther McKendrick, 17th Virginia Cavalry. Luther was the name of my family's coachman. McKendrick was our chimney sweep."

"Dandy," said Truly. "And I'll be . . . Aw, heck–Mister Jones, Rebel spymaster. Whatever sounds impressive."

"More impressive than that, I trust. So we give him hearty congratulations from Richmond . . . "

Truly spat, nodding. "We rain praise on his sorry hide. It's likely that somewhere south of here, Reb operatives are waiting to spirit him away, so we'll pose as them. We'll tell him we had to change the rendezvous point because of Yankee patrols. The uniforms should put him at ease, and he'll be grateful to see us in any case. We'll offer him food and whiskey, promise him an audience with Jeff Davis himself."

"And you're reasonably sure he's coming this way?"

"Reasonably. I just figured the Valley was his best bet for escaping South. It's full of Reb sympathizers, so our hold on it is shakier. And he does seem headed in this direction. Manfred's been wiring in whenever he can sneak away to a telegraph office, and I've had his messages relayed to the Ferry. Yesterday's was from Chambersburg–it said Van Gilder would likely make him drive all night, poor fellow. But if the Valley's their destination, they can't help but come through this crossroads."

The fog had now thinned considerably and made the crossroads more visible, along with the glade and the four bogus Rebels. Propped against a tree, one of them looked up from whittling. Truly's mind too was clearer, clamping onto its purpose.

Prime fact: Gideon Van Gilder, owner-editor-publisher of the *New York Comet-American*, an influential Copperhead newsrag, was apparently hightailing it for the South–reasons yet unknown. Prime object: take advantage of this baffling occurrence–head him off, fool him, learn anything he might know about current skullduggery in the Peace Movement. Any other questions–and there were many, God knew–would have to wait their turn.

"Well, I read that file you gave me," Forbes said.

"I hope I boiled it down enough," said Truly. "Didn't want to swamp you with particulars." He noticed that the whittling private had left the glade and was ambling toward them. "You've spotted something, soldier?"

The private reached the wagon and gave a sleepy salute. "No, sir." Pudgy, with small whimsical eyes, he stroked one of the horses as he spoke. "Major, the boys and me was wondering if Reb partisans might be nearabouts. It's said they've been down this way a lot."

Truly turned his head and spat with emphasis. "Most of 'em are busy hounding General Hunter's supply trains up the Valley. They're Hunter's problem today, so don't fret."

The soldier nodded vaguely.

"But if they did surprise us," Forbes said, "we're certainly dressed for it, aren't we?"

The soldier stopped stroking the horse's neck. He chuckled as Forbes' remark registered. "Yessir. Come to think of it, that's right." Looking up at Truly again, his face sobered. "But, Major–what if one of our own cavalry patrols was to show up and take us for true johnnies?"

"Ah–a man who thinks from all angles!" Truly got rid of his chaw. At times like this, his job felt clownish. Not beneath him, by any means, but more ridiculous than he liked. "Well, in that case we'd take two brilliant steps. First, we'd surrender. Then I'd show them your Union-blue duds in the wagon here, as well as my War Department credentials." He winked at the soldier, who still seemed deep in thought.

"And sir–if a civilian was to come by . . . ?"

"Simple! If he wishes us well, we detain him. If he's alarmed at the sight of us, we detain him. In fact, any civilian who happens along, we detain–until our little errand here is done."

The soldier nodded at his boots. "Yessir. Thank you, sir." He saluted, started away and then turned on his heel. "Sir?"

"Oh, good!"

"Whoever it is we're waiting for–they're coming soon, you think?"

Truly stroked his rough chin. In every single man, he believed, a sneering bully resided–and eyeing the soft-featured face with its look of drowsy petulance, he felt his own bully stir. He had felt it with Ben, on occasion. And as with Ben, he was restrained just enough by a boyhood memory–of kicks and punches in the saddler's shop, of his master's bellows and foul breath. "Private—as you perform this patriotic duty, why not compare it to digging latrines? Or charging cannons, maybe."

The soldier stood there a moment, looking as if he might ask something else. Then, with a smarter salute, he turned and tramped back to his three friends in the roadside glade.

"Sleep secure, O Union of States," Truly muttered. Reading a suppressed smile on Forbes' face, he felt suddenly grateful for the inquisitive private.

"I can't half blame him," said Forbes. "About the Rebs, anyway. How many times has this vicinity changed hands?"

"Enough so these boys'd be used to it, I would think."

"Not these ones." Forbes hoisted himself down off the seat. In his laborious gait, he began to pace around. "I'd wager their fighting experience is limited to blackflies."

Truly sat back and looked at his pocket watch. Barring a wrong turn or a lost wheel, Kirschenbaum and his erstwhile boss would arrive quite soon. "Now, as regards the questioning . . . " Whatever Kirschenbaum had been unable to find out, he explained, they would goad Van Gilder into volunteering—such as his contacts within the Peace syndicate, and any election-related mischief being planned.

Eyes down, Forbes stretched his arms wide. "Has the man really been worth all this attention?"

"I believe he has. By himself he'd be little more than a political nuisance, another boastful rapscallion. But given his position, he's had truck with those quieter, shadier types whom we must take more seriously. For me he's served as a window on the whole Copperhead scene up there." Truly blinked at the still-misty road. "Tell you, though, I'm powerful curious about why he's turned tail, and why he anticipated having to."

"Did he fear arrest, for any reason?"

Truly shook his head. "There was no sign of that being an especial threat, from either civil or military authorities. In New York you practically have to fly the Stars 'n' Bars from your rooftop to get charged with sedition, what with the feeling there against the war. Heck, maybe it's a private and unrelated matter—dangerous creditors, say. Except I understand his paper's making a tidy enough profit."

Forbes stopped pacing. "Secondarily, then, we'll want to pump him for why he took flight?"

"You bet your papa's nightshirt we will! Nothing that Manfred has sent me explains why a prominent Copperhead in a Copperhead stronghold would drop everything and skeedaddle. Not by boat or rail or other public means, but by private coach, as if there's some extra fear of pursuit or interception. It's confounding, all right."

"Major! Sir—this could be it!"

The soldier who had called was waving to them, gesturing up the road that joined the Pike from the northwest. Truly hopped down. "Well, Bart—now you finally get to meet my German hunchback."

"And his employer," said Forbes. "Lord, I feel I know the fool already."

They started toward the crossroads.

"McKendrick," Forbes muttered. "Captain Luther."

"Jones," said Truly. "Mister."

"Nate, for God's sake—pick a decent name."

In the glade they joined the four counterfeit graybacks, all of whom stood staring up the road. A quarter-mile off, a black coach with a four-horse team rattled toward them, its twin lamps extinguished, a lantern burning faintly on its long pole. Truly made out Kirschenbaum's hunched figure in the driver's box—his brown vest and black wool cap, his bristly mustache. When this was over, he thought, he would solidly reward the little German, though for now they would have to quell their mutual greetings.

Forbes adjusted his hat. "Now remember, boys—smile, but keep your tongues still. One Northern accent could spoil it."

A buck-toothed private grinned at him. "Ah'm from jest over Bull Pasture Mountain, sir. That ain't so north."

The pudgy whittler spoke up. "And ain't you from Massachusetts, sir?"

Forbes eyed him. "I know dialect, soldier."

Truly stepped to the middle of the road and watched the coach draw nearer. He noted the horses' lather, the dipping of their tired heads. Predictably, Kirschenbaum too looked tired.

Forbes turned to the buck-toothed private. "Soldier, what's your full name?"

"Tom Withers, sir."

"Nate, your name's Tom Withers."

"Dandy."

The coach was some forty feet away and slowing when Truly caught Kirschenbaum's eye. In his gut, something twanged like a bowstring.

Reaching the glade, Kirschenbaum brought the team to a halt. Forbes led the way to the muddy-wheeled coach. Lagging, Truly kept his gaze on Kirschenbaum, whose urgent return look held some question.

Forbes stationed himself by the vehicle. Pointing at the pudgy soldier, he spoke in a fair Dixie drawl. "Open the door for Mister Van Gilder."

All eagerness now, the private skipped to the door, grasped its gilt handle and yanked it open. No one stepped out.

"Mister Van Gilder!" Forbes called.

The soldier stuck his head inside. He recoiled, stumbling backwards. "Sweet JESUS!!"

Bounding to the coach, Truly peered inside. His vision took a few seconds' adjustment to the dark interior, but instantly he caught a queasy odor. Then he saw the body.

Seventeen years ago, just after the Battle of Molino Del Rey, Truly had come upon the corpse of a Mexican boy-soldier who had been shot, clubbed and bayoneted more times than even war could justify. What he saw now was approximately as bad. Seated but listing against the coach's other side, the body was that of a corpulent middle-aged man with a bald crown, wispy blond hair and muttonchops. His high collar and green frock coat were soaked almost entirely with blood. Gore covered the floor-board and the plush seat. A black hollow gaped where the man's right eye should have been. The remaining eye bulged at Truly, as if all of the victim's dying terror had concentrated there. An ear and the tip of the broad nose had been cut off. Two fingers of one hand were missing. The cheeks had been sliced upward from the corners of the mouth, creating a grin so ghastly that Truly had to look away. Finally, between the open flaps of his coat, the man had been carved open in a vertical fish shape, exposing the pearly breastbone and spilling innards.

Truly took a slow backward step. Bumping someone, he turned around and saw Forbes there, staring at the corpse. Truly recalled that his partner had survived the howling carnage of a barn-turned-hospital at Antietam. He could count on Forbes' steadiness. Behind Forbes, three of the soldiers stood ashen-faced while the pudgy one stood shaking against a tree, hands cradling his stomach.

Truly shut the door. "Bart," he murmured. "Sit 'em down. Let 'em settle. I'll think of something to tell them." With his skin still prickling, he moved around the horses and approached Kirschenbaum, who had just climbed down.

"Manfred–who the devil did this?"

Kirschenbaum blinked at him and then at the coach. A look of foreboding crossed his haggard face. "What, Major?"

Truly placed a hand on his shoulder and leaned close. "The man in there's been slaughtered like a harvest hog." Kirschenbaum stared, his lips quivering. He started to turn but Truly held him. "Don't look."

"Major . . . !" Kirschenbaum pulled his cap off. "I . . . We was stopped by an officer! Major Henry Spruce, he gives his name."

"A Union officer?"

"Ja! Mit a bandage on his face."

"Go on."

"He. . . He hitches his horse in back and gets in mit Van Gilder. He says he knows Van Gilder is going to Strasburg and he will escort him to there. Major, I thought he was maybe part of your plan!"

Truly stepped back, took a big breath. "Part of someone else's plan, my friend. Someone with a strong interest. And mad too, I reckon."

Clutching his snarled black hair, Kirschenbaum gesticulated with the cap. "This Spruce, he tells me drive on, so I drives on. Then three mile back there he put his head out and hollers to stop. I stop, he gets out and takes his horse, says proceed to Strasburg. He tells me, 'Eyes will be watching you, so do not stop till you get there.' And I am thinking, 'What is this?' But I do what he says . . . Major, I am so sorry!"

Truly patted his arm. "Whatever this is, none of us saw it coming. Go sit in the wagon and we'll finish up here."

Kirschenbaum gave a bewildered nod, put his cap back on and stumbled toward the wagon. The four soldiers were seated on the roadside grass while Forbes loomed over them, his jaw set hard.

Truly gazed at the coach. Dangling from its pole in front of the horses, the lantern flickered out, sending up a puff of black smoke.

3

Near Cold Harbor, Virginia

ANOTHER RED DUSK, the day's heat lifting. From the darkening battlefield, an isolated moan or cry could still be heard; anyone ignorant of its source might have taken it for an owl's call. Yet no one paused to listen, least of all Robert E. Lee.

Having inspected some earthworks along the front, General Lee conferred briefly with his chief of staff and rode back to his tent. Seated there by lamplight, he felt himself aging. Strain, sleeplessness and a week-long bout of diarrhea had depleted him, just as the month-long carnage had depleted his magnificent army—mangling its ranks, claiming some of its top commanders. Stuart was dead, Longstreet and Pegram badly wounded. Hill remained sick, Ewell exhausted and unstrung. Jackson was of course long dead, the most gaping absence of all. And Lee, beneath his gray-marble stoicism, sensed that he was not quite the man he had been.

The Union assault had come at dawn on Friday, June 3rd. Outnumbered as ever and fighting with their backs to Richmond, the Confederates had delivered a repulse so quick and devastating that they themselves had trouble believing it. A decisive outcome at last—except that Grant, by all appearances, refused to admit it. With a hard turn of mind, Lee kept his sharpshooters in place, demanding a formal flag of truce before Union litter bearers be allowed to gather their wounded. Two days of sunbeaten stalemate followed. Out between the opposing lines, the sounds of agony peaked and then grew fainter. Yesterday Grant had sent an aide with a ceasefire request; Lee had restated his demand. Only today—Monday—had

Grant agreed to a truce flag, though it was unclear whether he had gotten Lee's reply yet. In all likelihood, any surviving wounded would be spending another night on the field, ungathered.

The General barely gave it a moment's thought. There were orders to issue, dispatches to read and send. From western Virginia had come news of another enemy thrust into the Shenandoah. Sure to turn eastward, it threatened Lee's rear and, more immediately, his supply base at Lynchburg. To its defense he had just ordered two brigades under Major-General Breckinridge.

Lee summoned an aide, who confirmed that Breckinridge had received his instructions and would be on the move by daylight. The noble Kentuckian had joined the Army of Northern Virginia but recently, having crushed the enemy's last Valley campaign in mid-May. Injured in the fighting three days ago, he remained unable to ride, but had assured Lee that this would not hamper his performance. Lee donned his spectacles and began writing a message to Major-General Beauregard at Petersburg. Then the aide returned. Begging Lee's pardon, he announced that Major Norris of the Signal Bureau was here to see him. Irritably Lee nodded assent.

When the major entered and saluted, Lee found himself dismayed at his own reaction. A man of proud yet respectful bearing, William Norris had a trim copper-brown beard and deep-set intelligent eyes. As chief of the Signal Bureau, he oversaw functions that were vital to the Confederacy—the ferrying of spies in and out of Washington, the smuggling of mail to and from the North, the cobbling and channeling of secret intelligence. But his smart, clean appearance stirred in Lee an emotion that he had long sought to deny—the fighting soldier's resentment toward the non-fighting class.

"Yes, Norris?'

"Genr'l, I am just arrived from Richmond, where I met with President Davis and Secretary of War Seddon."

"You have a communication from them?"

"Not written, sir. Memorized."

Lee peered up at him, then gestured to a chair near his writing desk.

Norris pulled the chair up and sat, placing his hat on his knees. "Genr'l—please understand that I would not have interrupted you for anything of lesser import."

"I assume as much, Major. Proceed."

Hunching in, Norris spoke in a softer voice. "From a trusted agent in Washington, we have learned of a plan to help bring about the seizure of that city."

After thirty-four grim days on the defensive, mentally and literally under assault, Lee experienced a moment of disorientation. The shock of Norris's words sunk in. "That extremely *well-fortified* city," Lee intoned.

"True, Genr'l–although Grant's campaign is reportedly sapping it of men."

"This . . . plan of seizure–does it perhaps involve a secret partisan force within Washington?"

"We have sympathizers aplenty there, sir–but no. It would involve an attack by a sufficient number of our troops."

Shock became annoyance. "Norris, we are hard-pressed everywhere. In addition, the federals have retaken the Shenandoah and are menacing our rear."

"The President and the Secretary appreciate that fully, Genr'l. And they would not presume to dictate a specific action. At the same time, they share your concern about our current defensive posture–a most necessary posture, for now, but one which allows a numerically superior foe to wear us down. Their message is that both political and military considerations argue for some kind of move against Washington. Whether or not this is also practicable will of course be left to your judgment, in which the greatest faith abides. But such an operation would draw pressure off your main front here. And should you deem it wise to aim higher–that is, to attack the city and perhaps tilt the war back in our favor–a plan is in place at the Washington end."

Lee removed his glasses, rubbed his eyes. "Extraordinary measures will be called for, sooner or later. But assuming that I could detach enough troops for this purpose, what does the plan hinge upon? Specifically?"

Norris lowered his voice still further. "A Yankee traitor, sir."

Treason–antithesis of the soldierly ideal. Keeping a somber gaze, Lee recoiled inside.

"A lieutenant-colonel," Norris added. "One whose actions, properly timed, would leave Washington at our mercy."

Lee drew a weary breath. "One wretched man. That seems a rather flimsy thing, Major, on which to base a gamble so large."

"I would be thinking likewise, Genr'l, were it not for the agent whose plan it is. I call him 'trusted'–but 'exceptional' is the more apt word. He has spent most of the war in the city. The intelligence he has sent us has been of rare quality, overall. Extremely valuable, on several occasions."

"Even so, the best of men overreach themselves." (How well Lee knew that grievous fact.) "I fear it will take more than this to convince me."

Lee did not know how to interpret the hesitation in Norris's eyes, the subtle droop of his shoulders. Was this all? Could the major have already run out of persuasion?

"Well, Genr'l . . . The agent has formed a connection with a small group of individuals. People of certain means and abilities. They have been of crucial help in the past, as they would be in this case."

"Sympathizers?"

"Of a kind, sir."

Lee eyed the major.

"I know the fine results of this association," said Norris. "But of the people themselves, I confess my knowledge is sketchy. This agent is more solitary, more secretive than most. Still, other men in our network have had periodic contact with him, and it is through them that I've learned what little I know."

"And what would that be?"

Norris looked down at his hat. "These associates of his are well invested in the Confederate cause, Genr'l. Yet they are of a . . . a mercenary stripe."

Lee's gloom turned heavier. "Their services are paid for?"

"In this case they would be, Genr'l. Quite a lot, too, considering the particular service."

"Tell me, Major—what else might describe such characters?" Having subsided, Lee's annoyance staged a counterattack. "What 'means and abilities' do we speak of? Are we perhaps consorting with criminals? Murderers, even?"

Norris appeared stung, sitting up a bit straighter. But he replied in the same tone of reverence. "Genr'l, sir—I cannot rightly say. I will allow that these folk are not the sort we would have chosen to be linked with. But their interests are linked with ours, and apparently they have been effective. In my own small capacity, I can afford no standard but that. I only need think of the odds against which the South has struggled, and struggles yet. That, and the ruthlessness of her enemies."

Between the tent flaps, Lee saw that darkness had completely fallen. He stroked his beard.

"Sir, I only bear the message," said Norris. "Whichever way you decide, I am certain that the President's confidence goes with you, along with that of the entire Confederacy. But as you yourself observe–extraordinary measures are called for."

Norris was right, of course–no victory could be called pure. In warfare, however much God held sway, only the savagery was pure. And Lee realized that he would be better off not knowing certain details. Regarding the major, he suddenly appreciated Norris for his professional restraint, for revealing no more than his burdened General needed to know. This evasiveness was not impertinence but tact, a keenness of insight.

A long moment passed before Lee spoke. "We would need to maintain as much secrecy as possible."

"Indeed, Genr'l. For that reason, all related written materials will be destroyed. The President, for his part, will do his utmost to keep all reference out of the newspapers. Once you select a commander, you could tell him as much as you wished or as little as he required, with the caution that he must not advise his subordinates until the proper time. Courier and telegraph communication would be kept minimal."

Lee nodded. "And should Providence bear us to the gates of Washington, I assume that some coordination with your man would be necessary?"

"Not much, sir–although, that small part would be a vital one. Just prior to the assault, the commander would be contacted and instructed by our agent, who will go by the name 'V. Grayson.'"

From his desk drawer, Lee took a sheet of foolscap and tore off a small square of it. He penciled the name, then folded the scrap and put it in the drawer.

Norris repeated that the decision of whether or not to proceed was Lee's alone. Meanwhile, the Signal Bureau would be keeping both him and Davis apprised of the Northern capital's vulnerability. Lee said that he would give it the most serious thought. He got to his feet and Norris followed suit, looking invigorated. Lee thanked him, then dismissed him with a nod.

Seated and alone again, Lee let the conversation echo in his mind. Already it had an unreal quality, as if Norris had been an apparition. Lee would have chosen a different apparition. Trained from birth in the dour acceptance of God's will, he nevertheless missed Stonewall Jackson, his greatest subordinate.

Beyond the tent flaps, night gaped. His left hand had come to rest on his Bible, fingertips lightly brushing its tooled-leather hide. Caught between hope and dismay, he realized that, even more than Jackson, it was the old feeling of certainty he yearned for. "Traitors and mercenaries," he muttered. So it had come to this.

4

On The B&O Railroad, Northern Maryland

EASTBOUND, LURCHING THROUGH the night.

They had caught a freight train out of Harper's Ferry, consigning themselves to an empty boxcar that smelled of stale foodstuffs. Huddled in a corner, Truly let the train's rhythmic juddering lull him away. He saw Rachel and himself at the Missouri homestead shortly after their marriage. Seated together atop the big flour barrel, they were looking over the field at dusk and he was telling her about the time he met Chief Black Hawk. Compared to Rachel, he had always been the talker. In the vision, their feet dangled well off the ground, like children's feet. And though they had fancied themselves a man and woman back then–working the frontier, proving themselves against it, doing what they were supposed to–they may as well have been children. Then a change in the train's motion woke him up. Shifting his back, he pondered the fast-fading image. War and much else, he thought, had rendered the past a dream region peopled with child-folk, pretty figurines whose hopes, answers and expectations seemed unbelievable now.

From the dimness close by, Truly heard the thump of Forbes' leg as he too stirred. To his left, a lantern outlined Kirschenbaum's blanketed form. A corked, partly consumed bottle of schnapps–Truly's welcome gift–lay by the sleeping man's head on his duffel sack. The train had slowed, the car yawing as wheels scraped underneath. Truly guessed they were at Point of Rocks and turning north from the Potomac, following the Monocacy River. Even with a smooth change of trains in Baltimore, they would likely not reach Washington until tomorrow afternoon. Since the Ferry, Truly had been fluctuating between bafflement and worry, between thoughts of Van Gilder in the coach and Ben at Cold Harbor.

Near his hand he found the document he had written out yesterday for Forbes. He yearned to find in it some overlooked bit of fact, anything that might direct his heated guesswork. Holding the pages toward the lamp, he again started from the top:

<u>Gideon Van Gilder</u>: Born New York City 1820, son of rich Knickerbocker family. Through 1840's and 50's squandered inheritance on speculation. Kept afloat by relatives and other connections. Series of ventures included acquisition of New Jersey newspaper, The Springfield Trumpet. Source who I questioned years later said he seemed to develop taste for that business, though he lost paper in Panic of '57. (Note: All this earlier history I got from former acquaintances of Van Gilder, prior to Manfred's employment with him.)

<u>1861</u>: At start of war became partner in munitions firm. October–In Washington trying to wangle contracts when associates cut him loose, having found him skunk-like. Around same time, heard that New York Comet-American (small, stable, moderate Democrat paper at the time) was coming up for sale. Rushed to see owner J. Howland but reputation got there first. Refused by Howland, went fuming back to Washington. December–Howland found dead in office. Frail old man of modest habits, yet seemed to have drunk himself to death. Then Van Gilder appeared with signed papers of ownership. Had gotten Comet-American on mighty generous terms. Also, for transaction Howland had not used regular attorney but one of ill repute, named Nash, who at inquest swore his client was of steady mind when he signed.

<u>1862</u>: With war picking up, interest in case faded fast. Revived briefly in February when attorney Nash's body found floating in harbor. Under Van Gilder, Comet-American took Copperhead editorial turn. Big jump in sales, given much of NYC's opposition to war, and despite unlettered state of new "readers"–famine Irish, mostly, who fear free Negro labor. Van Gilder became rising star in Peace Movement, boosted by attacks on him in Republican papers. In some of his broadsides, made other Copperhead leaders sound meek by contrast.

<u>June-July '63</u>: Van Gilder dropped out of sight for a few days. Returned in unsteady state, with bandaged ear. Claimed Unionist thugs assaulted him but I doubted this–any thugs so inspired would have long since enlisted–and guessed it to be an ordinary street crime. Late in July, one Adam Cathcart arrived at paper, started writing column. Seemed not to have known Van Gilder beforehand but in no time they were best of friends–dining together, swapping observations, cussing the Union. Odd because close friends were what Van Gilder notably lacked, and because he customarily treated employees as serfs. I theorize Cathcart came recommended by someone high in Van Gilder's esteem.

<u>July-August '63</u>: NYC Draft Riots. In editorial Van Gilder cheered not only street lynchings but burning of Colored Orphans Asylum. To his martyred outrage, military shut him down for a week. At this time I arrived to assist riot investigation (a fool's errand which I'll relate some other time), fixed on Van Gilder, gathered intelligence on him and decided he deserved extended look-see. Placed Manfred in his employ. Manfred soon friendly with Comet-American staff, from whom he learned much of preceding information. Learned too that Van Gilder, since purchase of paper, had been making solitary trips to Washington, allegedly to meet with congressional Peace Democrats and discuss national policy. Had him followed each time he came down–once in late August, again late November, again late February. Each time, he did meet with one or two Copperhead bigwigs. Also stopped at high-toned bordello on city outskirts. Nothing about it to imperil Union, but strict quarterly basis of trips puzzles me still.

<u>Adam Cathcart</u>: Since he hails from District of Columbia, probing his background proved easy. Family of Southern roots and sympathies, living mostly in Georgetown. Father owns textile concern in which Cathcart was involved, until sudden switch to journalism and New York. In Cathcart's desk, Manfred found notebook jottings on things beyond the political: estimates of troop strength in NYC, details on state of harbor defenses, speculation on number of Gatling guns available for riot control. I then had agents tail Cathcart through city, but he was never observed meeting any suspected Rebel contact. Wondered if Richmond was keeping Cathcart in reserve for some subversive scheme. Decided that until such scheme came to light, would not arrest him and needlessly tip our hand.

<u>Deeper riddle</u>: Cathcart was playing some kind of double game on Van Gilder. One day he approached Manfred in stables and presented him with a bucket of beer, then began to ask personal questions about Van Gilder, his own boon companion. Asked if his friend ever spoke of his visits to Washington–also, if he ever received visitors from that city. Manfred said truthfully that he knew nothing of this and Cathcart left disappointed. He had been doing the same with other staff members, wheedling for something behind Van Gilder's back. Soon after, while emptying waste bins, Manfred found Cathcart rooting through correspondence in Van Gilder's desk. Cathcart startled but recovered himself and handed Manfred coins, asking him not to tell the boss. Question: If Cathcart was so interested in Van Gilder's D.C. trips, why not invite himself along, using kinfolk down there as pretext? Conclude that Van Gilder must have insisted on going alone–that his secrecy held firm, even with his supposed chum.

Truly's reading was interrupted as Forbes came clumping into the lantern light. Forbes had shed the Rebel attire for a brown civilian suit and a black felt hat. Kirschenbaum muttered something in German as he turned his head, sending his schnapps bottle rolling. Attempting a lighter step, Forbes moved to Truly's side and slid down into place, holding his leg out straight. "How's your friend?" he asked.

"Don't think he's sleeping too well."

Truly thought of Van Gilder's hasty burial in the woods above Harper's, his mutilated carcass stuffed into an undersized pine coffin. Next-of-kin would be contacted and directed to the remains. From the carriage floor, Truly had retrieved a number of items: a cane, a matchbox, a wrinkled map, a bloody handkerchief, a blood-flecked hat and a silver folding cup scented with whiskey. In the shadows of the car's other end, these now sat in a box next to the dead man's trunk. The trunk contained only clothes and a strongbox, with impressive wad of greenbacks in the latter. The business of the money rankled Truly. A few bills from the dead man's savings would never have been missed, least of all by Secret Service chief Lafayette C. Baker, who would surely pocket the whole amount at the first opportunity. Brooding on it, Truly glanced over at Forbes, whose family wealth and rectitude surely barred such lowdown thoughts.

Forbes nodded at the page in Truly's hand. "I meant to remark–you never told me you were part of the riot probe."

"Disgust can bind a fellow's tongue," said Truly, banishing the money from his mind. "But yes–half of Manhattan was still smoldering when I got up there. I'd come to help the boys in our New York office–except, after a week of botched leads and false arrests, it was plain they couldn't have properly investigated a catfight. The one good thing that came of it was meeting Manfred, when he damned near ran me over. He was a hack driver. Those fellows get to hear and observe plenty, but Manfred was a downright sponge. I used up a whole notebook listening to him, trying to penetrate his accent. He'd come over in '57. Kept all kinds of books in his hack for idle moments, learning English. So when it came time to plant someone with Van Gilder, he was the very man. Van Gilder had a fellow working for him, an all-purpose drudge; some money, liquor and other persuasion got this man to plead ill health, quit the job and recommend Manfred as his replacement." Getting to his feet, Truly stretched and then, like a stormbound sailor, lurched his way to the boxcar's secured door. He leaned against it and held his face to the seam, letting the breeze cool him. "What I'm thinking of now, though, are those healed scars around Van Gilder's ear and neck–his injuries from a year ago, we may assume."

"Allegedly at the hands of patriotic thugs," Forbes said.

"Right. They had the same artful quality as the death-cuts, but were clearly meant to cause only pain. Ever hear of a street tough wielding a blade like that? Part surgeon and part Michelangelo? And it strikes me that quite soon afterwards, Adam Cathcart joined the paper's staff. Coincidence, maybe–but maybe too there's a connection."

Truly made his unsteady return to the corner where his gear lay. Sliding back down between his companions, he picked up the pages, tilted them lampward and read on:

New Year's 1864: Since Cathcart seemed to have no Rebel contact in NYC, I wondered if he might have one in Washington area, to whom he could report on visits home. Manfred managed to alert one such visit. When Cathcart arrived at D.C. rail depot, had agents ready to tail him. He met up with cousin James, fellow bachelor who works at Patent Office. They called on family in Georgetown. Then they hit series of saloons, plus brothel in Marble Alley. Kept it up next day, then sat for double por-trait at photography shop, after which Cathcart staggered back to NYC. Wondered if James might be secret contact, but inquiries turned up noth-ing suspicious. By looks of it, none of this amounted to spit.

<u>April 16, 1864</u>: On this day Manfred drove Van Gilder home as usual, found young gent waiting outside house–long-haired, highfalutin, likely of Dixie planter class. Van Gilder startled to see him, told Manfred to wait while the two went inside. They soon came back out, Van Gilder giddy with excitement. Told Manfred to take visitor to rail station, where fellow boarded southbound train. Over following days, Van Gilder's moods wavered more than usual, between good cheer and ill-tempered anxiety. Manfred caught fragments of ongoing discussion between Van Gilder and Cathcart. Seemed the former was seeking plan for safe haven outside Union, pressing latter to arrange it fast. Cathcart pushed for explanation but Van Gilder was vague: "Adam, it's just a precaution. One can never tell what this government might do to a man in my position." Federal agent at Niagara confirmed request made for Van Gilder's possible asylum in Canada, which Confederate agents discouraged. As part of courtship with Irish community, Van Gilder had endorsed Fenian Revolutionary Movement, advocating attack on British possessions in Canada. This and some choice remarks about Queen Victoria made him persona non grata up there. After this refusal, Manfred overheard him demanding "a Southern route" instead.

<u>Mid-May to present</u>: I went to chase smugglers in St. Mary's County. Left word for Van Gilder to be tailed as usual on his next Washington trip, due at month's end. Returned June 1 to find two wire dispatches from Manfred. One on May 28 said Cathcart, not Van Gilder, had left for Washington the day before–too late for us to shadow his movements. One on May 31 expressed surprise that Van Gilder had stayed put in New York. Had scarcely read these when third message came in, from somewhere in central New Jersey. Said Cathcart had returned to NYC and Van Gilder, after brief talk with him, had taken flight–also, that Cathcart would be back in Washington sometime next day, bearing letter from his friend to unknown party.

Pondering, frustrated, Truly would have read the chronology once more. But Kirschenbaum had begun to stir beneath his blanket, his hump like a capsized dinghy.

"Another thing about Cathcart," said Forbes. "A Copperhead newsrag seems an awfully brazen place to stick a Rebel agent."

"True, but then there's that proverb: if you want to hide something, hide it in plain view." Truly set the pages down. "It hardly needs saying–I'm itching like a hound to question Cathcart. Him, and whoever the letter was meant for."

"And to see the letter itself," Forbes said. "Did you get further word on any of that?"

"None." Truly swallowed his anxiousness. He would have lingered in Washington to supervise Cathcart's arrest, had it not been for a lamentable misunderstanding. Kirschenbaum's first message *en route*–hastily sent, no doubt–had failed to mention Van Gilder's means of travel; Truly had wrongly assumed it to be the railroad and, fearing that the Copperhead would outdistance him, left for Harper's Ferry. "Well, my orders regarding Cathcart were clear enough," he told Forbes. "I specified the same agents who tracked him at New Year's, to be led by the same lieutenant. I can only trust that all's well." He watched as Kirschenbaum sat up stiffly. "How are you, Manfred?"

Squinting, Kirschenbaum rubbed his eyes. "Good schnapps. Bad sleep."

Truly took an apple from his coat pocket and gave it to Kirschenbaum. Then he slid his canteen over. With thanks, the German took two swigs before sliding it back to Truly.

"Manfred, can you guess at all why Van Gilder didn't make his regular trip?"

"Nein, Major." Sitting cross-legged, Kirschenbaum scratched his head. "On the staff there was wonder about it–and disappointment. We looked forward always to him being gone. But no one knew why."

"All right. Cathcart, however, did go to Washington. Was anything said about that?"

Kirschenbaum crunched into the apple. "To one of the reporters, Cathcart says he is going down to help celebrate his cousin's birthday."

"Cousin James again, most likely. And high revelry it must have been, since Cathcart didn't return till the first of June."

"Ja. That day he comes back to the *Comet-American* and goes to Van Gilder's office. Soon Van Gilder hurries out with his friend following, looking confused. Van Gilder is shaking, his face white." Kirschenbaum said he then drove the pair to Van Gilder's house, where the Copperhead began packing. To Cathcart's exasperated questions, he replied there was no time to explain. Van Gilder begged that Confederate agents be there to receive him "as planned." He also implored Cathcart to hand-deliver his hurriedly scrawled letter. Looking at the address, Cathcart grumbled that he had just returned from Washington and was tired–he would head back down there tomorrow. Then he left, shaking his head. "Van Gilder yells for me to get his trunk," said Kirschenbaum, "and so we are off."

"Yes," said Truly, "–on a trek that would tire Hercules and confuse the angels."

Kirschenbaum chewed his apple. "Major, I have never seen a man so frightened. Always reaching under his coat to touch the pistol. Giving false names at the inns where we stop. Each night he pays me a dollar and promises more so I will not leave him."

"You managed damned well," said Truly. "But this Major Henry Spruce stepped in, armed with knowledge of Van Gilder's escape plan. His facial bandages suggest a disguise–which would have been necessary, if his victim knew and feared him. So he bluffs his way into the carriage, then murders Van Gilder in such a way as to cause maximum pain and terror."

Forbes shook his head. "Remarkable for any number of reasons–for the planning involved, especially. Plus he made no attempt to take the money, though he could have inferred that Van Gilder was carrying a large amount. To me, that indicates a singularity of purpose. And beyond that, there's the cruelty–a combination of savagery and precision. The assassin left behind several items but not the victim's severed parts. He took them like trophies."

Grimacing, Kirschenbaum put his apple core aside. He made a sign of the cross.

Since the hunchback had heard no screams, Truly speculated whether Van Gilder might have been drugged, thinking of the cup found on the carriage floor. He also wondered aloud why a killer so devilish would spare Kirschenbaum, the lone witness.

"Why indeed?" said Forbes. "Let's imagine, then, how it might have gone had we not intercepted the carriage. It arrives at the rendezvous point in Strasburg, where Reb operatives make the discovery. Southern newspapers seize upon it as fresh proof of Yankee barbarity."

Truly nodded. "Further muddying the truth, whatever it is. On the other hand, let's hope that Major Spruce is not, in fact, a crazy rogue officer but an impersonator using an alias. I'd prefer to think our ranks were free of such a man. Still, I'll order a search of the army rolls."

Kirschenbaum yawned. With clumsy movements, he lay down and pulled his blanket up.

"All right," said Forbes. "Looking elsewhere—I'm thinking of the late Mister Howland and the circumstances under which Van Gilder bought the *Comet-American*. Might the killer be some vengeful member of the Howland family? A son?"

"That might be worth looking into," said Truly. "But I recall that of Howland's two sons, one's long dead of cholera and the other's prospecting for silver out in Nevada Territory."

With a sigh, Forbes slouched lower. "Then I'm out of ideas, for the present."

"So am I." Truly pulled a knee up, jouncing as the train started down a grade and gathered speed. "Once we reach the capital, we'll interrogate Cathcart. Then, with luck, we'll have grist for more questions."

"But there's one more that we can ask right now," said Forbes. "How, on the face of it, does this fit into your work or mine? How would we both justify pursuing it?"

"The South's involved somehow—through Cathcart, at least—and that should serve well enough for the time being. But let me go ahead and state the plain truth."

"If there's anything *plain* about this, I'd be grateful to hear it."

"Well . . . In calling you up, I didn't really stick to the formal arrangement."

Lowering the brim of his hat, Forbes proceeded to quote the original directive. "'In those infrequent cases where matters of military and domestic intelligence or counterintelligence run together, Major Truly and Captain Forbes shall be assigned to work in collaboration, thereby ensuring the free flow of information between their respective bureaus.'" Forbes gave a drowsy smirk. "Gosh Almighty—it does seem you've stretched the terms a wee bit."

Truly gladdened, realizing that he would not have to explain. In contacting Forbes, he had simply sought out the best partner he knew, better than any within his own organization. "So are you game for this thing?"

"Oh, I'd say so. My curiosity's up. Furthermore, I'm in Colonel Sharpe's good graces."

"Fine. And lately I'm in Baker's."

"For how long, though? Your relations with him are a touch mercurial, aren't they?"

"Fair to say. But if I dress it up right in my report, he might approve our joint investigation."

Having fallen back to sleep, Kirschenbaum looked like a burrowed goblin, his humped shadow dancing against the timbers. Forbes fell silent, long enough for Truly to think that he too had nodded off.

"How is Annie . . . er, Anna?"

Forbes had no doubt been working up to the query about Truly's daughter, wanting it to sound casual. Truly smiled to himself, then sighed. "She's well–but unfortunately, still stuck on Lieutenant Chadwick."

"Dear God!" In the brief quiet, Truly could feel Forbes blushing. "Uh . . . I beg your pardon. I . . ."

"Bart, the one thing I can't pardon is your failure to get there before that blockhead, that pampered jackanapes who inflicts himself upon my door most days of the week. Don't ask me where he gets time for soldiering, if that's what you can call garrison duty. I just wish his damned elbow would heal so they could ship him out."

"No, no–I'm sorry . . . Well, then–how's Sapphira?"

"Hard to tell. Once the smallpox scare ended, they didn't need her at the Contraband Hospital, so she started teaching colored children. That does seem to have sparked her."

"And Ben?"

"Until his last letter he was stuck at Bermuda Hundred on the Appomattox, with the Tenth Corps. Now he and half of his regiment have been detached to the Eighteenth Corps and sent to Grant."

Forbes looked up. "At Cold Harbor?"

"Right."

Truly appreciated his partner's silent response–a frank silence, not an awkward one. With Forbes, he would be spared the kindly reassurance that a civilian might have offered. Back at Harper's, the last Cold Harbor bulletin had struck an eerie telltale note. Beneath the neutral facts about brigade position and such, a single vague reference to battle losses lay trapped like a miner, its cries muffled. Only disaster or something like it could have spawned those lines of telegraphic jabber, entombing what none dared acknowledge.

Early in the war, one of Truly's clandestine trips to Richmond had taken him through Cold Harbor. Now he tried to recall how the place had looked. He tried to picture Ben there amid the embattled legions but then stopped himself, surrendering his brain to the mesmeric rumble of the cars. Then, with a shudder, he saw Gideon Van Gilder's death-grin and the lone staring eye.

5

Washington, D. C.
June 7

IN THE HUFF and hiss of the crowded railway station, Truly picked up a discarded copy of the *Washington Evening Star* and began reading about Grant's worst mistake. The story related the events of Friday the 3rd, when fifty thousand troops had struck across open ground at Cold Harbor. Launched against strong Confederate earthworks, the attack had been swiftly aborted with no gains worth mentioning.

The new warfare. Like a moving storm, it kept shaping and reshaping itself, intensifying, leaving bigger bone-piles at record speed. This time it had consumed several thousand men in under half an hour. The paper featured other worthy items: the ongoing suspension of prisoner exchanges; General Hunter's progress up the Shenandoah; the National Union convention, busy with Lincoln's re-nomination in Baltimore. But the Cold Harbor news held Truly motionless, wondering about Ben and thinking at the same time about Grant. What sort of man had the inner makeup to blunder like that and yet keep going?

Hovering at Truly's shoulder, Forbes broke the silence. "Any mention of colored units?"

Again Truly's eyes combed the paragraphs. "Don't see any."

Forbes turned to Kirschenbaum, who looked on in curiosity. "The major's son is a lieutenant with a Negro company."

"Ja?" After a pause, Kirschenbaum put on a reassuring tone. "These, Major, I hear are being used mostly for guard and forage and other such things, not fighting."

"So they say."

Despite the disproportionate use of Negro troops in dull non-combat areas, they were in fact seeing action with greater frequency and in all theaters of the war. But Truly did not bother to modify Kirschenbaum's statement. Nor did he point out that Richmond had threatened to execute all captured officers of colored units. Nor did he mention Fort Pillow, Tennessee, where in April a combined white and Negro garrison had been mostly massacred after surrendering.

Van Gilder's belongings had already been loaded into a waiting hack, whose liveried Negro driver kept stealing looks at Kirschenbaum. Leaving the paper on a bench, Truly decided that he would walk home. He gave Forbes a few bills, enough for his and Kirschenbaum's lodgings. Forbes offered to stop at Treasury and have Van Gilder's things stored–also, to find out about Cathcart's arrest.

"Ask my favorite clerk about it," said Truly. "He'll know."

"I will, if he lets me get a word in," Forbes said.

As his companions climbed into the hack, Truly shouldered his duffel and started away.

Not far up New Jersey Avenue, Truly stood aside for a file of scrawny Confederate prisoners, their guards motioning them along with bayonets. They were headed to the station–bound, most likely, for the teeming squalor of Point Lookout on the Southern Shore. On the captives' weathered, bearded faces, Truly saw the familiar mix of pride and foreboding. He caught sullen glances from a couple of them. Measuring his own reaction, he was relieved to detect no hate, none of the deep burning. To him, these tattered men were still other people's sons and brothers. Inevitably he recalled the letter that he had received some months ago from a female cousin in Missouri. Enumerating kinsmen who were serving proudly in the Southern ranks, plus two who had perished, she had wished him "the warmest little corner in h—l." He could not, as yet, return the sentiment, but knew too well how that could change. Overnight, from the bitter seed within, hate's poison flower could sprout and bloom.

When he reached his small frame house on North H Street, buoyant piano chords greeted him. The music ceased and Sapphira emerged smiling from the parlor, her muslin dress all the whiter for her dark skin.

"Father, I never know when to expect you!" Taking his hat and coat, she eyed the latter's caked mud with distaste.

"Why aren't you gone teaching?" he demanded.

The smile fell away. "I lost the position."

"What?"

She explained that the camp school had been absorbed by a newer, larger one that was already well-staffed. "Besides that, they said I wasn't stern enough with the children."

Truly sighed. "Well . . . Petty minds always find an excuse, don't they?"

"That's what Reverend Cass said. I'd never seen him angry before."

In the parlor he got a glass of whiskey and settled into his armchair. Over on the piano top lay another copy of the day-old *Evening Star,* and he had the weird sensation that it had followed him. He averted his eyes to the mantelpiece. In the vases that flanked Rachel's portrait, he noticed fresh marigolds. From the portrait, his wife's clear steady gaze reached out to him.

Sapphira sat on the piano bench. "Anna got a letter from Ben."

Truly stirred. "Dated when?"

"The First, she said."

He took a longer sip. "What did he say in it?"

"I don't know. Anna took it with her, since she was preparing to go out."

"With Chadwick?"

"Of course."

"Dear God!"

"You did permit him to call here in your absence."

"Just as I'd permit a dentist to yank a tooth–yes. Tell me, what's Chadwick still doing with the Veteran Reserves? Is he that slow a healer?"

"It was a severe break."

"Well, when he does get around to mending, he should avoid horses for the rest of his life."

"He's with the cavalry."

"You're just full of rebuttals–aren't you, missy?"

Suddenly she got to her feet. "On a different subject, I just remembered something." She left the parlor and returned holding a note in one hand and a hatbox in the other. Giving him the note, she took the lid off the box and revealed a black bowler inside. "It came by courier this morning."

Puzzled, he eyed the hat and then read the note:

Dear Nathan,

This is to congratulate you for your excellent work in St. Mary's County, but you may also take it as a respectful suggestion. It was reported to me that in your last audience with Secretary Stanton, you wore your signature trailblazer's chapeau and were slow to remove same. Nate, though I too am a man of the "rough and tumble" frontier, I must urge you to take your current station into account, to acknowledge that we serve men of refinement and consequence and must therefore avoid all dubious impressions in matters of custom, appearance and courtesy. What fits in the wilderness does not necessarily fit in the halls of government. Accept this gift and wear it with pride. Once again, good work!

Your devoted servant,
Col. L. C. Baker

"Ah, Lafe," Truly muttered. "Next thing, he'll start going to church." Slowly he crumpled the note and dropped it into the hatbox. "Saph, does that Irish muffin boy still come around?"

"On occasion."

"Next time, give him this hat with my compliments."

"Father, it's a fine hat."

"Then maybe he'll sell more muffins. So—are you going to play something for me?"

With a sigh, Sapphira placed the hat by the newspaper on the piano and retook her seat. She shuffled through the sheet music while Truly sipped his drink, mumbling oaths about Baker. At length she began a moody, mid-tempo progression—and as the notes climbed and tumbled, his gaze moved from her precise fingers to her intent brown face. A memory came to him from several years ago, when they were living on the outskirts of Chicago. One morning, to his annoyance, he had discovered Sapphira's chickens squawking and unfed. After a quick search he found her talking with a skinny colored boy, the servant of a neighboring family. The boy tore off across the field, leaving Truly and Sapphira to stare at each other.

In that moment, which could not have lasted as long as it felt, Truly saw that the wary little girl that he had plucked from a New Orleans auction block was no more. In her place stood a slender young woman with skin the shade of a thrush's wing—one whose fuller beauty had eluded him until then, like that of a foreign song. At random times since, he had wondered if anyone else could see that beauty or see it in quite the same way, even as it struck higher and higher notes—in the line of her chin, in the luster of her eyes and the slope of her thin shoulders, in her voice when she dreamed aloud of Paris. Her reveries of crossing the ocean to Paris charmed him, except when they made him think too much. Then they pained him, reminding him of just how he had failed her.

Sapphira knew something of what awaited her beyond the lace curtains of home. In the presence of white strangers, moreover, she knew enough to hide the truth of her nature like a smuggled gem. Yet too often, of late, Truly had noticed her long-limbed grace turn to restlessness. Just as often, when her fingers swept the keyboard, he had heard something adamant, a rush of yearning within the melody. And he knew that in a passive sense, at least, he had done much to foster these yearnings, with barely a thought to their long-term consequence. Therein lay his guilt. Unsettling enough that a girl's longings could stray so far from the warm confines of the hearth. How much more unsettling in the case of a colored girl?

He realized that she had stopped playing. "Don't recollect if I ever told you, Saph—I got that piano from an official of the Illinois Central, for a job I'd done. Just a whim of mine, in lieu of the usual fee. But you turned it into the best investment I ever made."

"As you have told me, several times." Her hands slid into her lap and she muttered thanks. Compliments often flummoxed her. "Father . . . when Reverend Cass sees you next, he'll likely ask if he may take me for a ride or a stroll sometime."

Truly stroked his mustache. Cass, like Truly, was a widower and Sapphira's senior by many years. Yet he was a fine figure of a black man, courtly of manner. In Truly's contrarian universe, preachers of any color ranked somewhere between sutlers and pickpockets—but in conversation, he had found Cass mercifully free of sanctimony. "Well, he has been a real friend to you. I give my consent—you can tell him yourself, if you like."

"He said that he would observe custom and call at the kitchen door."

Truly took another swallow of his drink. "Anyone worthy of our dear girl's company is worthy of our front door. Besides, I reckon the neighbors need something new to whisper about."

A faint smile came to her lips, then faded. "He has been a good friend—but he's so somber, most of the time. Like Captain Forbes. Strange to say, but I can't help the comparison."

"Forbes?" Truly chuckled. "Bart was born old, I suspect. Speaking of which, we're paired up again . . . " Tensing, he caught himself. But she was already giving him a curious look.

"Are you? And how does your work go, Father?"

In his mind's eye, the image of Van Gilder's body flashed. "Oh—same as usual. Humble and humbling, though not in ways the Good Book would sanction. Play something else, would you?"

Clearly disappointed, she began a new progression as the big coffin clock struck three. He listened, finishing his drink. A female household, he thought—unprotected, left to fend for itself. What kind of paterfamilias was he? Drowsing, he stared across the room at Rachel's portrait, the marigolds like beautiful sentries. Then he nodded off.

A rapping at the front door awakened him. Stretching, he smelled roast fowl and heard Sapphira's voice in the hall, greeting Forbes and offering to take his coat and hat. Then Forbes shambled into the parlor. Truly started to rise but the Bostonian motioned for him to stay seated.

"You're in time for supper," Truly said sleepily.

"Unplanned," said Forbes, "but appreciated." He took the settee. From his distracted eyes, Truly guessed that he was wondering if Anna might appear.

"Have a drink, Bart?"

"No—no, thank you . . . Well, Kirschenbaum is ensconced upstairs from me at my usual boarding house. And I met up with Octavius at Treasury."

At the mention of his industrious clerk, Truly sat up straight. "What did he tell you?"

"Even more than expected. First of all—in the written instructions you left before going up to Harper's, you requested a specific trio of agents to tail and arrest Cathcart, right?"

"Correct. The same ones who tailed him that other time, and so would recognize him when he stepped off the train."

"With a Lieutenant Heatherton in charge?"

"Yes—one of our abler boys. Why do you ask? What happened?"

"It seems that Heatherton was sent up to Morristown, New Jersey earlier that day, on another assignment."

Truly squinted. "Who got the duty, then?"

"A fellow named Bliss."

"Bliss?!" Jerking forward, Truly hissed the name. "Bliss, as in 'Ignorance Is?!'"

"Octavius said you'd be less than pleased."

Forbes related how Cathcart had been followed from the railway station to West Third Street, where he stopped to greet a man. At this point, the over-eager Lieutenant Bliss had sprung, arresting both men and taking Cathcart's letter. It soon appeared that the second prisoner—a meek Belgian carpet-dealer—was innocent in the matter. Under questioning, he pleaded that he was just a business acquaintance of Cathcart's father and knew the son but slightly. This was quickly verified and the shaken man released. As for the letter, it was addressed to Congressman Ezra T. Underhill of Maryland.

"Underhill," Truly murmured. "A Copperhead, I suppose?"

"Oddly enough, no. According to your office's congressional file, he's of the Democratic middle—the Constitutionalist faction, so-called—supporting the administration's war measures while criticizing it in most other areas. But he's changed his colors a couple of times. Before the war, as an attorney up in Westminster, he served a term in the state legislature and dabbled in the late lamented American Party. But he was elected to his first congressional term as a Constitutional Unionist and then reelected as a Democrat, shifting with the political breeze in his district. He's up for a third term this fall."

"And I wager he'll get it," said Truly. "Sounds like his weathervane's working just fine. So do you reckon Cathcart was on his way to deliver the letter?"

"Maybe, but not to the congressman. Underhill lodges at Brown's Hotel, nowhere near West Third. What's more, Cathcart was headed north—away from the Capitol Building, where he might have found Underhill at work. It brings to mind the double game that he was playing on his friend Van Gilder. I'm thinking that Cathcart had a Washington contact after all, and that he was en route to him with the letter."

Truly thumped the chair arms with his fists. "Until a chance meeting and our fidgety Lieutenant Bliss ruined our opportunity to find and arrest said contact! Lord help me!" He got up and stalked out to the hall, where he snatched a tobacco plug from his coat pocket. He returned to the parlor. "Damn him! If I ran this organization, his next assignment would be in the Dry Tortugas! And damn me for not seeing to it myself! If I hadn't been in such a tarnal rush to get up to the Ferry . . ." He went to take a bite of tobacco, then paused to glance about the room. He stalked back to the hall threshold. "Sapphira! Where's my spittoon?!"

"Anna hid it somewhere," Sapphira called. "You know she doesn't like you chewing."

He returned to his chair, dropping into it with a huff. "Not even a master in my own house." He lay the plug beside his empty glass. "You don't have the letter with you, I suppose?"

Forbes shook his head. "Apparently Bliss still has it. And Octavius, as we speak, is trying to track the fellow down. If he's not at his boarding house, there are two or three nearby saloons that he frequents."

Truly drew a ragged sigh. "Well–assuming that Bliss hasn't lost the damned thing, we'll read it and question the Honorable Mister Underhill about its contents. But not before we've thoroughly interrogated Cathcart."

Forbes sent a pained look to the floor. "That won't be possible, Nate. Not right away."

He explained that Bliss had failed his instructions in yet another way, hauling Cathcart not to the Old Capitol Prison but to the county jail–closer by, but outside of War Department authority. Whereupon the District marshals who ran the jail had misplaced Cathcart, mistakenly shipping him out with a group of common criminals.

"To where?"

"Albany."

Truly was quiet.

"The penitentiary up there," said Forbes. "You may know that the District has an arrangement with the State of New York. With Washington's jails full of enemy troops and assorted Rebel suspects, somebody else needs to house its regular criminal population."

"Which will soon include me, if I can't keep from strangling Bliss. So . . . what you're telling me is that Cathcart came down from New York and was arrested, only to be sent back to the very state he started out from. Except farther north."

"Yes. But listen–Bliss, to his meager credit, did send an urgent wire to Albany demanding Cathcart's return. We'll get the fellow back, all right. Just not as fast as we'd wish."

Truly settled, drumming his fingers on the chair arms.

"But from what Duke told me," Forbes said, "Cathcart won't be an easy guest. He was quite a handful when they grabbed him, and at the jail.

He only admitted what he couldn't deny–his political bent, his friendship with Van Gilder. Beyond that, he sounds like a candidate for thumbscrews. And speaking of candidates, I stopped at Brown's on my way here; the desk clerk said Congressman Underhill's not in Washington."

Truly gave a stiff smile. "Well–everything's coming together wonderfully, I must say. So where would he be? Home, courting votes?"

"No–at the front, courting votes. He left this morning and won't be back till at least Saturday. Gone to strut for the correspondents, to pose with any battle-scarred Maryland boys he can find."

Truly frowned, thinking. "You know . . . I've a mind to run after him. If he has something to hide–and hang me if he doesn't–it would be good to catch him outside his element, off guard."

Forbes shrugged. "I'm keen to do it, if you are. Once we get hold of the letter, we can take the night ferry, or any transport that's headed south."

A realization came over Truly. "And while we're at it, I could visit Ben!" Suddenly, mindlessly, he felt certain that Ben was alive and unhurt.

6

Near Cold Harbor, Virginia
June 9

CONGRESSMAN EZRA UNDERHILL was a short man with a coon-like darkness around his eyes. But he had a good handshake and a knack for small talk and kept himself well tailored. For some people, he even held a certain charm. Upon introduction he would straighten up, cock his head slightly and give his lipless smile, as if not only pleased but fascinated. His speech could be soothing and avuncular, accompanied by nods, with none of the righteous bark that characterized his speeches to the House. This personable mask had helped him weather the upheaval of his riven border state. After Sumter, it had cushioned his shift from advocate of Southern placation to upholder of "the Constitution as it is and the Union as it was." It had seen him to a second term and would surely see him to a third, facing a token Republican challenge. Currently it served him in meeting important constituents, in the polite acceptance of bribes and in dealing with military officials who viewed all Democrats as suspect, especially the Maryland breed.

Yet there was one grievous flaw for which he could scarcely compensate, no matter how he tried. Away from his district and away from Washington, beyond the immediate reminders of power and position, he grew wobbly. Like a rich man's son discovering that Creation did not revolve around him, he became sulky and pensive. So it had happened on this reluctant journey.

On the schooner trip around the peninsula and up the York River, he had been sick to his stomach. Overnight, at the West Point railhead depot, a card game among some rowdy Indiana troops had robbed him of sleep. In the sway and rattle of the morning train he found himself, along with his friend Wakefield and his secretary Ives, crammed in with those same smelly Hoosiers. A sergeant demanded to know the contents of Wakefield's cases. "Camera, ye say?! A camera and sech takin' room from honest soldiers?! We orter throw it all out the side, eh boys?!" Underhill's stiff announcement that he was a United States congressman distracted them from this threat, though not in the way he had hoped. Pressing him hotly, the sergeant raised a foot and demanded to know why Congress had not mandated the hangman's noose for manufacturers of rotten army shoes. "Look at it, will ye? Barely worn, and splittin' like the Red Sea!"

While Ives cowered and Underhill stammered, Wakefield managed to save the situation. "That's outrageous, Sergeant. Congressman, look at that shoe—disgraceful! Come, boys, what else? You won't get a chance like this again soon."

Underhill then had to feign interest in the litany of growled grievances, from worm-infested rations to ill-fitting bayonets. Then they pulled into White House Landing and the train would go no farther, due to a rumored cavalry raid up the line. Leaving the soldiers to laugh and curse, Underhill sought other transportation. Ives turned up an old sutler who forced an extravagant fee for taking the trio in his wagon—"Must charge ye for the cases as well, sirs."

Now, in this encampment that seemed the size of a small nation, Underhill felt even less significant, with no shield against further indignities. The heat did not help and neither did the booming artillery, too close for his taste. The first officer they met, a major, received them with polite phrases but no smile and looked distractedly at their War Department passes. Maryland volunteers? Yes, there was a regiment somewhere hereabouts. A conveyance? Yes, he supposed a wagon could be found for them. The major left with Ives tagging after him.

Underhill stood gazing across the grassy terrain to some woods farther off. Behind him, Wakefield dozed in the shade of a lone tree, his cases stacked nearby. Underhill decided that not even a good friend should snooze while he suffered.

"It's the last time I'm doing this, Miles."

Wakefield stirred, then spoke in a dreamy drawl. "What did you say?"

"Nothing we accomplish here could possibly justify what I'm having to endure. The delays, the insults . . . "

"Well, Ezra . . ." Wakefield yawned. "Voters appreciate an official who takes on the common man's discomfort. Coming here this way shows you have the plebeian touch."

Underhill clasped his hands behind his back. Glad though he was for Wakefield's companionship, he resented his stoicism. "Maybe so. But after this, never again."

From the west came a deep rumble, thunder on a hot cloudless day. Underhill flinched. Some passing soldiers glanced at him and smirked.

"Miles, you don't suppose the Confederates would start up now?"

The photographer took a moment to answer. "As I understand it, random shelling occurs even on quiet days. But we're far back enough, I think." With the slowness of one born to Southern heat, Wakefield rose and walked to Underhill's side. He stood several inches taller, with fine features and a dashing sandy-brown mustache. For an instant Underhill realized how much his friend's admiring attention meant to him. Without that deference, he would have felt rankled before such a man—handsome and erudite, at ease wherever he went. The contrast made Underhill brood once more upon the railcar incident—how naked he had felt to the soldiers' low mockery.

"I wish to God I'd gotten that sergeant's name. The Indiana delegation will hear from me when I get back."

Wakefield sighed, fanning himself. Turning stony, Underhill guessed what he was thinking but trusted that it would go tactfully unspoken. Ives and Wakefield had suggested that Underhill join a party of other representatives. But he had rejected their advice, unwilling to share berth space—or newsprint space—with a gaggle of self-satisfied Republicans.

Farther to the north, another cannon boomed. Then the sound of approaching whoops and hoofbeats made both men turn, and from the front's direction came a mounted gang of soldiers. In their midst rode a dapper civilian whose grim, worried face marked him as the object of ridicule. Others in the camp stopped to jeer as the passel rode by with the unhappy civilian, upon whose back a placard declared in black letters, "Libeler Of The Press."

As the riders bobbed into the distance, Underhill called out to a strolling private—"Soldier, what was that about?"

The soldier paused, wiped his brow and grinned. "Genr'l Meade don't like newsmen, is all—'specially them that print lies. They just took that feller on a tour of the front lines, with the Rebs shooting. He's lucky that sign ain't his eppy-taph." Winking, he doffed his cap. "Something to think on, gents."

The private strolled off while Underhill gazed sternly after him. "Well—that's a pretty piece of work! If they've banned the journalists, what's the use of my being here?"

Wakefield swatted a mosquito. "I doubt they're all banned. From Meade's headquarters, maybe, but not Grant's."

Taking out a handkerchief, Underhill mopped his forehead. "Yes—we'll go to Grant's headquarters. I'll announce my purpose and then we'll visit the Maryland men—who are, I trust, of better stock than these."

"That's the way, Ezra. That's the man I know." Wakefield put his hat back on. "Truth be told, I've been concerned about you."

"This little expedition would affect any man."

"I was speaking of the past few weeks. You've been agitated, but unwilling to say why."

Underhill looked off. "It's a pressured season. The war as it is, the elections coming . . . "

"Ah, well—we'll do some good for you here. We'll find those boys, maybe even a few from your district, and then we'll make some pictures. Nothing like a picture to move people and convey your sentiments. Those ones we made on the Antietam battlefield—people looked at those and wept, remember? What's more, they voted for you."

"They did, yes." Calmer now, Underhill tucked his handkerchief away and walked to the tree's cooling shade. Sitting against the trunk, he took out his notes and began looking them over. "Miles, would you go see what's keeping that damned clerk of mine?"

WAKEFIELD WANTED TO look directly down at the congressman, to let Underhill glimpse something in his face. He resisted the urge. In the heat, time seemed to liquefy and dribble away. From the distant woods, his eyes found a road running north over the tent-covered ground, then picked out a white steeple. He wondered if common people still worshipped there, seeking fortitude amid the guns. Inexplicably this mattered to him. Then the moment turned solid once more and he ambled away, reminding himself that someday this would all be over–sooner, perhaps, than anyone thought. He had to believe it.

He encountered the soldier who had spoken to them. In his shirt-sleeves and suspenders, the private was seated against a wagon's wheel and writing a letter, using his mess kit for a surface.

"Good day to you again, soldier."

The private shielded his eyes, looking up. Though young and fair, he had one of those angular faces that needed aging to look just right. "G'day," he said–less sociable now, maybe annoyed at the interruption.

"Just wanted you to know I'm no news hound," said Wakefield. "Nor is my companion back there. He's a congressman."

Beneath his hand, the soldier smirked. "That's worse, I'd say."

"Yes. Especially when it's him." The soldier chuckled. Instantly Wakefield liked him, as a prisoner likes any face but his torturer's. "Well– I've interrupted you, so . . . Lord, how long have you boys been stuck here?"

Letting his hand fall, the soldier squinted. "Nine wondrous days."

Wakefield nodded. "Must seem like forever. When Grant decides to move, though, you'll notice the signs."

The boy shrugged. "Reckon so. 'Cept I was just writin' my mother– ain't seen nothin' that says we're set for any new adventures. Not just yet."

Nodding, Wakefield pressed a boot heel into the grass. In Grant, he reflected, the Union not only had a fighting commander but a highly secretive one. "Yes, well . . . War's ninety per cent tedium, isn't it?"

The private gave a lazy smile. "Today, I'd say it's near a hundred per cent."

Wakefield smiled, then tipped his hat. "Take care of your mother's son."

"Doin' my best, sir. Thank you."

Wakefield felt better as he wandered off. From the exchange he had gained nothing except a little good will, enough to counter Underhill's effect on him. That would do for now.

7

Two Miles South

SINCE MARYLAND UNITS were few, Underhill proved easy to locate. Still, it had required contact with a series of brusque officers, and the experience left Truly soured. At the front, Secret Service men were regarded as maybe two notches above the enemy and only one above war correspondents. Catching a sullen look as he offered his papers, he reflected that common cause sometimes meant virtually nothing. Even neutral terms such as "detective" or "intelligence operative," let alone "spy," evoked the image of a cold, base, ruthless being. Concealed like a dagger, submerged like a torpedo–an instrument of dishonor. Forbes could at least identify himself as a soldier–but Truly, with his Washington credentials and only nominal rank, bore the full taint his department, that great meddling octopus. When honest fighting men looked at him, he imagined they saw not only an expert in duplicity but a loathsome tendril of government.

From a near distance, he and Forbes watched Underhill pose with a group of volunteers. A camera sat on its tripod near another contraption–a raised tent-like structure on collapsible legs, its flaps largely hiding the stooped photographer within. Backing carefully out of it, the tall shirt-sleeved man held a plate holder which he then loaded into the camera box.

Controlling his impatience, Truly took the wrinkled, folded letter from his pocket and read it once more. Blots and cross-outs marked the hurried script–yet even in his panic, Van Gilder had taken pains to word it just so:

Sir—

From a disinterested source (my friend Mister Adam Cathcart, who has delivered this to you) I understand that our young squire, for all his airs, has completely botched the information upon which our safety and our chance for freedom rested. How he managed this stupid miscalculation, seconded by yourself and the others, is of no consequence to me. Given my distance from Washington I decided to rely upon your collective judgment, but my trust was misplaced. I am at this hour attempting to put myself beyond the reach of retribution. Yet the nature of our keepers leads me to wonder if any sanctuary can be found.

I therefore call upon you, whose means and prominence are unique among us, to recall your role in this business and do whatever might stop the impending wrath. I am essentially ruined, bereft of all but my life, though that too may well be forfeit. I am, moreover, under no illusion that my welfare worries you in the least. Yet I can think of four other personages, yourself included, whose welfare also hangs by a thread. Please do or say anything—the promise of larger payments or private favors, any concession that will stay the blows. Once settled, I will try to contact you from hiding and inquire about the outcome.

Yours, G. Van Gilder

Despite the letter's fear-and-secrecy refrain, an appalled sense of betrayal burned through. More specifically, terms such as "keepers," "payments," "wrath" and "retribution" suggested blackmail. Blackmail or extortion, directed at a five-person group that included Van Gilder, Underhill and this airy "young squire." The latter individual, Forbes had offered, could well be the secret visitor who Van Gilder received in April. That visit's purpose, it seemed, was to impart some "information" which later proved false—disastrously so, by the sound of it. On this false basis they had, after mutual consultation, tried to free themselves and then come to grief. So much for safety in numbers.

No more could be presumed, save one thing. Since Van Gilder referred to his comparative distance from Washington, it seemed that his fellow victims—and the "keepers" too—lived in or near the capital.

Truly returned the letter to his pocket.

The photographer called to the soldiers—"Just another moment, boys. This'll be the last one." They huffed, joked, shuffled their feet. Stocky and well-attired, Underhill smiled as he spoke with a sergeant. To one side stood a slight, fidgety civilian—Underhill's secretary, one officer had said.

"I didn't know congressmen had secretaries," Truly said.

"Generally they don't," said Forbes.

Truly grunted, his mood still recovering. Far off, another big gun resounded.

The photographer unscrewed the lens cover and put it aside. Stooping, he hid himself under the camera's black-cloth hood and made some adjustment. Then he reemerged and picked his hat off a travel trunk. "All right, then," he called. The men bunched closer together, Underhill looking nobly steadfast in the middle. The photographer ducked back under the hood. "Straighten up now, boys—this is for the kinfolk." Both of his hands reached out, his left covering the lens with his hat while the right gripped something on the camera's side. Then he pulled, removing a thin black panel. He took his hat away. After a few still seconds, he replaced the hat over the lens and slid the panel back in. "Thank you," he said. "You just might see yourselves in an engraving afore long. Check your illustrated monthlies." Truly detected a fair Southern drawl in the man's speech.

The group quickly dispersed, the congressman shaking hands on all sides. Extracting the plate holder, the photographer repaired to his tent-like contraption.

"We should be direct but genteel," Truly said.

"Gentility with directness—yes," said Forbes.

They walked toward Underhill, listening as the congressman wished a soldier well—"and I'll certainly tell your papa that we spoke."

"Congressman?" said Truly.

Underhill looked up. Despite the smile, he looked haggard. "Sirs?"

They doffed their hats. "Major Nathaniel Truly, at your service—and this is Captain Bartholomew Forbes." For simplicity's sake, Truly said they were both representing the War Department.

Underhill's smile thinned. "What may I do for you?"

"Well, there's a distressing matter at hand, which we believe you could help resolve."

"My willingness to help is a proven thing, gentlemen."

"It concerns . . . " Truly threw a glance to the secretary a few yards away. Observing the exchange, the cowed-looking young man did not approach. "It concerns, sir, a threat to yourself and perhaps others. A physical danger."

Underhill frowned. His dark-circled eyes went darker, shifting between the two of them.

"Your safety is our main thought," Forbes interjected.

"Your meaning, please?" said Underhill.

"Word has reached us that there are criminal pressures against you," Truly said. "We would like to offer our protection—the least we can do, given your steady support of the war."

Underhill stepped back. "What is this? Yes, I support the war effort—for my country and my district, not the administration you represent. Now would you please decipher this babble of yours?"

Inwardly, Truly said good-bye to any chance of getting on Underhill's good side. Behind the congressman, curious soldiers had begun to listen in. The secretary hovered a little closer, his face full of timid alarm.

"Congressman," said Truly, "you need to tell us about Van Gilder."

Underhill's thin lips parted as words tried to form. In his gaze, shock warred with outrage.

"Your acquaintance, Gideon Van Gilder," Forbes said. "Please tell us about your association—and, if possible, why he fled New York for the South. If we're to help you, sir."

Staring at the ground, Underhill took another step back. "Van Gilder? The Copperhead publisher? I . . . I know of him, of course, but . . ." His gaze snapped over to his secretary. "Ives—see about getting us a wagon!" The man scurried off. Tight around the mouth, Underhill glared at his questioners. "I'd have no association with such an individual! None!"

Truly looked straight into Underhill's coon eyes. "It's an unlikely connection, all right, especially for a man of your caliber. But you need not be destroyed by it."

"Politically or otherwise," Forbes added.

"I told you, I have no dealings with the man! I don't know him! And I tell you further that this insult will not go unreported!" Reddening, Underhill jerked up a fist and shook it. "I know how you blackguards work! Lies and intimidation—that's your style, and more than once I've complained about it to the House! So now, in return for my criticism, you're here to . . . to flummox me with some stupid, fraudulent allegation! Out of spite!"

Swapping a look with Forbes, Truly reached into his pocket. "It is in your vital interest to read this. Once you have done so, kindly give it back."

Smoldering yet clearly shaken, Underhill took the letter and unfolded it. As he read, his shoulders stiffened and then his face drained pale. The letter quivered in his hands. Reaching out, Truly pinched it by a corner, and the quivering fingers let go.

"Sir–we beg you." Truly tucked the letter away. "We are discreet. Tell us . . ."

"Congress will hear of this," Underhill muttered.

"Van Gilder is dead," said Truly.

Underhill went stone silent, still paler.

"Not only dead, sir, but mutilated. Carved open. An eye plucked out. Other body parts taken. Worst sort of death you could imagine, really."

Truly watched each detail land like a blow. Underhill sagged, his eyes dimming.

"Congressman," Truly went on, "–tell us why this happened to him. And why he was racing south at the time. Tell us about the tie between the two of you and the others. Only then can we shield you from whoever . . . "

Doubly haggard now, Underhill shuddered. "Leave me."

"Think about it, then. Contemplate poor Gideon. We'll come see you again. And if you decide to . . ."

"LEAVE ME!!" Underhill bellowed.

The onlookers stared. In the press of blue uniforms, the photographer stood idly wiping his hands with a rag. He caught Truly's eye for a second, then looked away.

Looking back at the congressman, Truly tipped his hat. "As I was saying–should you change your mind, my office is at the Treasury Building. Good-day."

The pair headed back toward their mounts. "Gentility with directness," Truly muttered. Stepping around the photographer's tent-like structure, he nearly tripped over a large open case beside it. Catching himself, he glimpsed a label affixed to the lid, hand-printed: M. WAKEFIELD PHOTOGRAPHY, with a Washington address underneath.

He fell in stride with Forbes, shaking his head. "When he read the thing . . . Heck, I've seen cannons with less recoil."

"Like he'd been hit with a spade," Forbes said. "As frightened as Van Gilder was."

"Yes–even with our pledge of protection."

They reached the hitching rail. On the promise of their prompt return, Truly had secured a light-footed pair of bays from the Cavalry Bureau–Vermont Morgans, complete with saddlery.

"So what could make him shake like that, yet keep his lips sealed?" said Forbes.

Truly looked back toward the camp. He spied Underhill–still agitated, wiping his brow with a handkerchief–in close conversation with the photographer. The taller man turned his head, gazing in the agents' direction.

Forbes went to untie his horse. "In any case, you're free to hunt for Ben now."

Gladdened at the reminder, Truly mounted up. Soon, across a field powdered with buttercups, they were riding north toward the Union right, where the colored regiments were said to be concentrated.

Forbes wondered aloud if, being down here, he should report in to Colonel Sharpe. Leaving the thought unfinished, he gazed off, his handsome face turning solemn. Truly guessed his thoughts.

"You were down here two years back?"

Forbes nodded. "I believe that's Gaines' Mills over there. Where I first heard the Rebel yell."

"You know, early in the campaign I could've waved at you from the Confederate side."

Forbes eyed Truly. "Do tell."

"During the standoff at Yorktown, I was on the far bank of the Warwick, disguised as a sutler." It occurred to Truly that whenever he spoke of the Peninsular Campaign and its bloody, stupid, colossal waste of bravery, he ended up regretting it. But it was too late now. He told Forbes about his eventual race for Union lines–abandoning his horse and wagon and paddling across on a hollow log. Then, dripping wet in Pinkerton's tent, telling the intelligence chief that previous estimates of enemy troop strength were far too high. "We outnumbered *them*, for God's sake, and not by a little! Magruder was staging the pageant of a lifetime, marching his johnnies 'round and 'round so we'd think them a vast horde. But no . . ." A cannon boomed in the west. "No–Pinkerton wouldn't hear it. My report conflicted with the others and . . ."

The two of them jerked their reins as the ball's arcing banshee moan bore down, becoming a scream. Their horses reared. Forbes yelled something.

8

Four Miles North

FIRST LIEUTENANT BENJAMIN Truly, Company F, Twenty-second United States Colored Infantry, crossed the road and entered the lush green field. There he paused. His head and his purpose were clear but he wanted a minute of solitude, time to let his pulse settle. "Cold Harbor," he thought–hell, it had to be over ninety degrees. Then, scanning westward, he recalled sights from the week just past: Confederate guns belching murder and the shattered regiments drifting back, faces dazed beneath their soot; ambulances full of wounded and then wagonloads of dead, like debris from a wrecked armada. No colored units had been sent in, and Ben watched it all with a mixture of twisting guilt and gratitude.

The month-old campaign felt more like a lurching halt of time itself. Like God's own guillotine it had severed the legions from the world that sent them forth, cut them off more effectively than torn tracks or flooded streams or snapped telegraph wires ever could. A million miles from girls and gardens, from parents and children and parlors, from the tame concept of hours and minutes, it had stranded them, cast them into a filthy titanic womb–a womb wherein men were not born but killed en masse, killed at the clock-proof speed of dreams. The most experienced veterans–fewer and fewer of whom survived–muttered that it was like nothing they had ever known.

For Ben it was certainly unlike Chancellorsville or Rappahannock Station or any battle he had seen. Yet he could scarcely believe that he had ever belonged elsewhere, least of all in the peaceful realm of home.

Sapphira's last letter had reflected an impossibly sane and gentle plane of existence, Annie's an impossibly frivolous one. The newspapers he tried to read were blocks of hieroglyphic, impotent to convey what none could truly convey. Out here death gaped as big as the sky, its own blank reason for being, with Sunday school notions of grace long since trampled like clover.

From back across the road, in the wood and on the rise, he felt eyes watching him. Aware that he could not let himself appear hesitant, he resumed walking, looking around, hoping to intercept the forage party. He veered toward a dale near which he had sighted them. They had to be new recruits, he thought–fresh arrivals, unscathed as yet. Only a bunch of greenhorn imbeciles could have taken amusement from a prank so low. Then, as the ground began to dip, he looked to his left and saw them coming–a slovenly group of four, armed with sticks and emerging from some brambles. He stepped behind a big bush and waited. Among them loped the gangly one who had been identified from the distance. Carrying two dead rabbits by their hind legs, he was yammering to his comrades, becoming audible as the group neared:

"Last time we was there I was ridin' this Dutch gal, and right in the middle of it I look up and she's got this (chortle, chortle)–this little saint statue with candles on the sides. And the candles, they're stuck in these empty whiskey bottles . . ."

They were just a few strides away now. Ben stepped into the open. "Ho, there!"

The four stopped in their tracks.

"Greetings, boys. I'm bringing thanks for the soup my men were sent yesterday. Very neighborly, it was. Real act of kindness. Say, what state are you all from?"

There was a quick exchange of glances, with muted smirks. "Pennsylvania, sir," said one of them.

Yes, Ben thought–greenhorns, probably from the reserves brought up since the failed assault. Scruffy but with little of the weathered look, none of that stony cast. "Well, thank the Lord for fighting Pennsylvania men! Anyhow, boys–my problem is locating the man whose idea it was to send that cauldron over. Want to commend him, shake his hand. So who and where is he, eh?" He eyed the gangly one with the rabbits. "Soldier?"

The man averted his eyes. "Sorry, sir, I can't recollect . . ."

"Come now, Private—we know it was you and one other who brought it over and scurried off like bashful missionaries. My boys spied you from camp just now and said there was no mistaking you, with that walk of yours. It was you, all right. So tell me whose generous thought it was—unless it was your own. Was it your own, soldier?"

The man looked alarmed. "No, sir! No, no . . . "

"Then cough me up a name, Private. When someone's good to my men, I don't take it lightly."

A stout younger private looked at the rabbit-holder. "Lucas, weren't it Mitchell? Seems to me I seen him send you and Price off with . . . "

"Mitchell!" Ben said brightly.

"Uh . . . " The gangly one looked at the ground, poked it with his stick. "Yessir, I guess that's right. Was Quartermaster Sergeant Mitchell."

"And where might he be found?"

The stout one piped up again, clearly glad to resolve things. "Think I last seen him down that way, sir." He pointed. "Near them trees by the branch, with Corpr'l Price."

"Well, good! Thanks a heap, boys. I'll let you get to those rabbits now."

Passing looks, the four went on their way as Ben went on his. From behind a stand of trees near the branch, he noticed a plume of smoke curling skyward. His blood was at low simmer. He smiled to himself. Once when he was ten, his father had quietly compelled him not once but thrice to go back and renew a fight with a larger boy who had stolen his mouth harp. Bloody-nosed, Ben had done as he was told, hating his father even after he finally pummeled the boy's head and retrieved the harp. Since then he had come to see the truth about frontiersmen, fathers included—that their solutions were often blunt and simple because they had to be.

Nearing the stand of trees, Ben spotted the sergeant and corporal tending a still. From a large kettle over the fire, an angled length of pipe ran to a keg on a stool. Affixed to the keg's spout, a shorter length of pipe dripped the elixir into a vat. The beefy sergeant stirred the vat with a long wooden spoon while the small, fair corporal squatted below him, measuring out some dark fluid from a bottle. With their giddy conspiratorial looks, the pair seemed oblivious to Ben's approach, but he lightened his step anyway.

The sergeant put the spoon aside, then dipped a bowl into the vat and sipped from it. "Argh! Good! Yep, we'll have ourselves a bellyful afore we give the boys a holler."

Reaching the shade, Ben watched them a moment longer.

The corporal rose, then spoke in a yapping voice. "That's enough bark juice, I reckon. I'm-a bottle some o' this for later. Then we can . . . "

"Ho, there!" As Ben strode out of the shade, the two flinched. "Sergeant Mitchell?"

The swarthy, thick-featured man gazed at Ben, eyes darting from his face to his epaulettes. "Yes, sir?"

Shedding his tunic, Ben lay it on the ground and rolled up his shirtsleeves. He extended a hand. "Lieutenant Ben Truly. Just wanting to thank the fellow what sent my boys that cauldron of soup yesterday."

Mitchell blinked, glancing at the corporal. He placed a limp hand in Ben's and Ben squeezed it hard.

"Thank you, Mitchell!"

"Well, sir . . . Uh–" Ben caught the barest flicker of a smirk. "We had some left over."

"It was a damned fine gesture." Putting his hands behind his back, Ben sized up the sergeant. Like most men, Mitchell stood a few inches taller. He looked to be thirty years old or more. Ben smiled at the corporal, then at the vat of o-be-joyful.

The corporal gave an anxious giggle. "Guess you caught us, sir."

"Oh, never mind. Good times are scarce, and soldiers need 'em."

Mitchell seemed to relax some. He motioned to the brew. "Want a sample, Lieutenant?"

"Oh no, no. I won't keep you but a moment. So tell me, Sergeant–how long have you been a quartermaster?"

"Got the promotion two weeks back, sir."

"And how long in the army?"

"Late last year."

"Picked up a nice fat bounty, I bet."

Mitchell looked quizzical, then cold. "There was an enlistment bonus, sir. Nothin' wrong with it."

Ben stood there smiling, saying nothing. The corporal fidgeted.

Mitchell dropped his gaze, tugged at his belt. "Well, sir–if it's fine with you, I think I'll try our batch again."

"Go right ahead, Sergeant."

Mitchell hesitated, then squatted at the vat. He dipped his bowl and took a long slurp.

Ben walked over and crouched beside Mitchell. A loamy scent rose from the concoction, filling his nose. He sighed. "Have to tell you, we appreciated the soup a darned sight more than we did the stones in it."

The sergeant dribbled some brew onto his knee. He glanced at Ben, then at his companion. Awkwardly the corporal had started gathering up some empty bottles.

"Stones, sir?"

Ben stared at the vat. "Lord, this stinks. Is that a bug in it?"

Mitchell looked. "Don't see one."

"Yes, Mitchell–stones. Or pebbles, really. Lots of 'em. One of my men broke a tooth."

The sergeant gave no response and Ben eyed him. Mitchell chuckled faintly, his gaze searching for his friend's, but the bottle-laden corporal had his back turned. Ben's stomach felt like knotted rawhide.

"Lieutenant," said Mitchell, "I can't say as I know 'bout that."

Ben nodded. "I'll say it, then. You know. You know because you did it. But just tell me, Sergeant–what's your view of colored troops?"

Looking edgy, Mitchell wiped his pug nose. "Don't go out of my way to view 'em."

"Your opinion, then."

"All I can tell you . . . I see things different from you, is all. Sir."

The corporal's bottles clinked. Dropping one in the grass, he bent to get it.

Ben stared at Mitchell, who squinted in the direction of the branch. Ben let the moment pass, pass, crawl, till finally he took his eyes away. "Well, I've said my piece." He got up, stretched. "Good day to you."

Mitchell remained in a crouch, unmoving.

Ben took a stride, whirled and sent his boot full-force into Mitchell's buttocks. With a guttural cry, the sergeant pitched forward into the vat, capsizing it.

"The batch!!" cried the corporal.

In shock and fury, drenched in liquor, Mitchell glared up in time to receive a foot to the jaw. He struggled to rise, groping for Ben's legs. Ben sidestepped and was on him, throwing punch after punch to his head and adding a kick to the chest. Mitchell fell back, rolled and tried to get up, knocking the keg off its stool. Ben grabbed the stool by a leg and crowned him with it.

Through bloody lips, Mitchell let out a moan. Ben stood breathing over him and then leered at the gawking corporal, who hugged his bottles as if they were all he possessed. "Lord, that stuff stinks."

Ben's cap had fallen off. He put it back on, then slung his tunic over his shoulder. Starting back across the field, he felt his sweat run and fancied a dip in the branch somewhere. He crossed the road, passed through the wood and started up the rise toward camp. Mingled shouts drew his gaze and he saw two men of G Company mounted on the high "horse" beam, paying for some infraction. Hanging on tight, they were waving their caps at him. On the ground below them, several others were doing the same, hopping and hooting. He trudged on. When he next looked up, he beheld Captain Isaac Langstaff several yards ahead, seated atop his speckled gray stallion. Langstaff watched him come.

Slowing to a stop, Ben saluted. The captain didn't budge. Barrel-chested and bewhiskered, Langstaff had served eight years in the regular army before switching to the Colored Infantry and achieving his present rank. He still spoke with a strong Scottish burr. "Ye're outa uniform," he said.

Ben pulled his tunic on and buttoned it. "Your pardon, Cap'n. Army duds don't take Virginia summers into account. Could I trouble you for some water, sir?"

Langstaff took his canteen from his saddle and passed it down.

"Thank you, sir." Ben guzzled.

The captain's left hand brought up a field telescope, waggling it like a great cigar. "Quite a show, Lieutenant. I dinna know ye were a pugilist."

Ben wiped his mouth and handed back the canteen. "My pappy was a frontiersman, Cap'n."

"Truly–there's more t' bein' an officer than popularity."

"Your pardon, sir, but I didn't do it to be popular. Morale suffers when you leave a thing like that alone."

Langstaff removed his cap, wiped his broad forehead. "'Twill positively plummet, then, if ye're court-martialed."

Ben looked steadily into the captain's sun-beaten face. "Is that what'll happen, sir?"

"Ye shoulda gone the official route."

"Your pardon, Cap'n–but I would offer that retaliation is most effective when swift, which the official route never is."

Langstaff pressed his lips together. "When the major hears from the commander 'cross the road, and I hear from the major, I'll tell him I'll take severe measures against ye–so long as like measures are taken against those rascals over there."

"I'm mighty obliged, Cap'n."

"And for the time bein', Lieutenant, learn t' be less familiar with the troops."

Ben felt scalded. "Cap'n, if you're referring to that time back at Bermuda Hundred, I was using a spare hour to teach them the game of baseball."

"Truly, ye will listen. Keep yeerself above the frivolity. Later ye'll reco'nize the value, 'specily with these raw young bucks shoulderin' muskets instead o' cotton bales."

Ben knew he had to submit quickly. "All right, sir. But there's an unrelated matter we need to address."

"Aye?'

"Our standing order has been to clear brush, and the men have been hard at it. They've collected more than their share of cuts and bee stings, all within range of Reb sharpshooters. Just this morning a private in G Company . . ."

"Got nicked in the leg–I know. What air ye askin'?"

"That we use the rest of the afternoon for target practice. We've had precious little of that or much drill since April. In the ranks there's talk of Fort Pillow and what the Rebs did there. The men pray to fight, and who knows when the chance might come?"

"For us, a fight's an unlikely thing in the near days."

"As far as we know, yes. But they want to feel ready, sir, and that's a fair expectation."

Langstaff squinted at the sky. After a moment, he gave the slightest nod. "Assemble your company and notify the others. Pick a safe spot."

Ben smiled. "Done, sir!"

"Truly, ye make me talk too much." Langstaff pulled at the reins. "Come, Culloden."

As the captain rode slowly away, Ben saw Young and Tucker a little farther up the grade, standing side by side. Corporal Sabbath Young, ample in the belly, grinned at Ben despite his swollen cheek. Platoon Sergeant Flavius Tucker stood poised and solid, chestnut-dark, wearing a look of muted pleasure.

"How's your tooth, Corporal?" Ben asked.

"Doctor yanked it, sir." A laugh pumped up from his chest. "We begged up a pair 'o field glasses so's we could watch. Dang, sir, that was some good thrashin' . . ."

"Yes, well–back to things as they were." Ben straightened his cap and looked at Tucker. Though he had been with the company since day first, Tucker's quiet, cryptic ways still caused men to step well around him. Among those in his platoon, his decidedly un-cryptic way of delivering orders commanded obedience. "Sergeant," said Ben, "–we've been granted time for target practice."

Tucker stood straighter. "Yessir."

"Praise be," said Young. "Shootin' time!"

"Somewhere down in the meadow," Ben said. "Go notify the other sergeants."

Ben returned their salutes and watched them head for camp–Young's gait jaunty, Tucker's purposeful. His knuckles smarted pleasantly. Recalling Tucker's expression, he wondered how the approval of a Negro sergeant could feel this good.

CARTRIDGE PAPER LITTERED the grass, and the smell of gunpowder was the smell of time well spent. Out in the meadow, four man-sized boards stood evenly spaced, one for each platoon, each with a whitewash circle on it and peppered with holes. F Company had some godawful shots, as well as a few excellent ones–but if Langstaff permitted, a few more practices would make these men a unit to be reckoned with. Their traded grins bespoke the reminder: they had not joined to just dig graves and clear brush.

Ben eyed each of the platoon sergeants: Reddick, the pious farmer; Armstrong, the quiet cobbler; Parrish, the bricklayer with the droll tales and smallpox scars; Tucker, best of the lot, the husky centurion from Canada. Ben had yet to learn what trade he had plied there.

Marching them back to camp, Ben ordered every rifle cleaned and stacked before mess call. As they fell out, Young begged to demonstrate his progress with the company mascot. Ben agreed and Young led him to the T-stand where the hawk was perched.

"There he be, Lieutenant! He hangs on yer arm and don't snap. Eats his mice and what-all else ye give 'im."

Sable John's alert yellow eyes suggested a warlord reborn as a hawk, one that didn't so much perch as preside. A knot of men gathered around him.

Junie, the drummer boy, gazed through the steel-rimmed spectacles that Ben had finally procured for him. "And Lieutenant, he takes no skeer from the guns."

"Junie boy," said Young, "–hand me that mouse."

Junie picked up the dead field mouse by its tail and passed it to Young. Dangling it, Young glanced at the bird and then at the tall private named Prince. Said to be a true African and nearly as dark as the bird, Prince bore deep lash marks on his back and shoulders. His height, reserve and limited English sustained the rumor of his royal lineage, prompting small acts of deference from the others. Young offered him the rodent. Prince hesitated but then accepted it, holding it gingerly toward the hawk. The beak lunged as Prince jerked his fingers back. Gobbling the mouse, the hawk flapped its velvety black wings.

Young laughed. "There, look at him show off!"

Just then Ben saw Tucker coming.

"Yes, Sergeant?"

Glancing at the others, Tucker spoke low. "Lieutenant, your father's here."

Ben's mouth fell open.

Tucker pointed. "Over that way, sir."

Ben left the group. Passing between two tent-rows, he saw his life's most familiar figure loping toward him. Joltingly out of place, smiling through that weedy mustache–a bantam, leathery, bow-legged, slouch-hatted mirage. Somehow his father had crossed the million miles.

"Surprise inspection!"

They joined in a backwoods embrace, all claps and jostle, until Ben noticed his father's dirt-caked clothes.

The major slapped his hat against his leg, sending up a dust-puff. "Near miss with a Reb cannonball. Forbes is still trying to calm the horses."

"What in blazes brings you?"

"Official matter–but there's time to visit. Where's your tent?"

In the tent Ben sat on his cot, giving his father the lone chair.

"So how's Saph, Pa? Her letters sound restless."

"She has her humors. Usually she takes them out on the piano–you should hear her nowadays. Oh, and Reverend Cass wants to court her."

Ben mused on it, unsure of how he felt. He reminded himself that Sapphira, by his father's reckoning, was just a year or so younger than his own age of twenty-three. And why shouldn't a pretty colored girl attract suitors?

"And Annie–how does she fare?"

"Anna now, Ben. At this late date she has announced that she wishes to be called Ah-na. She seems pleased with the work she's doing for the Sanitary Commission. Mainly, though, she spends her time at levees and cotillions, accompanied by . . . "

"Chadwick?"

"The very same."

"Dear God."

"Yep. What's more, she's gone and hid my spittoon." The elder Truly sighed. "I was starting to despair of finding you around here."

"Just before the big assault, they moved us up from White House Landing. Probably guessed they'd be needing more gravediggers."

"Hm . . . From what I've read, they did."

Ben told of men going in with squares of paper pinned to their backs, stating name and regiment and where to ship the body. For three days and nights after the assault, moans and wails had carried from out between the lines–pleas for water, mostly, growing faint. But the Reb sharpshooters would not budge and the ambulance wagons just stood by. Some dispute over truce flags and protocol, they learned later–Lee and Grant swapping messages back and forth. On the second night, with Tucker, Ben assembled a volunteer party and sneaked out with a couple of litters. They brought back two men who lived and a third who did not, being partly disemboweled. When truce terms were finally settled, there were few wounded but plenty of corpses left to gather. Several of the men got sick on burial duty.

His father nodded, looking at his knees. "Any talk about another flanking march?"

"Talk runs every which way. Me, I don't think Grant will repeat a mistake like this last one."

"Well, hang it, I hope not!"

"But we're not accomplishing much here. He'll have to pull off something pretty soon, something trickier than before."

His father looked around the dim little tent. "Don't see your rock collection anywhere."

Ben shrugged. "Had to leave it back at Bermuda Hundred. I can't rightly tell the men to travel light and still be lugging a sackful of rocks about."

"Ah–the tribulations of wearing shoulder straps."

"I'm getting used to it, Pa. What rankles me is all of this fatigue duty. It wasn't till mid-May that we finally got our shipment of Springfields and threw away those relics we were carrying. Plus, there's the pay issue. What are colored troops supposed to think, getting ten dollars a month while white ones get thirteen? They always get the short end of the stick."

"You expected they wouldn't?"

"Well, next time you see Stanton, please urge him to make it right."

"Ben, you can't conceive how little pull I have with our Secretary of War."

"The President, then."

His father chortled. "Seems everybody and his brother has met the man. But whenever I stop by the departmental telegraph office, they tell me he's been and gone. Anyhow, I've read that Congress is close to settling the pay business."

"Fine. Then they can move on to the question of colored officers. Did I tell you, Pa, that we've been without a second lieutenant since before the campaign? The one we had came down with malaria and they haven't seen fit to replace him. If it was mine to do, I'd promote Tucker in a blink–he's the one you met. But there's this blockhead policy against it."

The elder man held his hands up. "If fate ever lands me and Abe in the same room, I'll sure enough state your case. Of course, after November he could be headed back to Illinois."

Ben looked out through the tent flaps. He heard a man telling a joke, others already laughing. The sunlight had turned a riper gold. He smelled smoke from the portable cooking stoves. "We'll see what the summer brings, I reckon."

His father sat up. "Well . . . I should go find Bart. We need to turn in those mounts."

Ben didn't want to move. He wanted to keep talking. "Greetings to Bart. Fond wishes to Annie. Tell Saph I've sent her a letter."

Outside the tent, they shook hands.

"Vaya con Dios, Ben."

"See you, Pa."

Ben watched him lope away, past the curious glances of the troops. By tomorrow, the visit would feel like the fragment of a dream. Then Ben recalled his thrashing of Sergeant Mitchell. His father would have loved that story–how could he have forgotten to tell it?

9

Two Miles East

SPRAWLED BESIDE FORBES in the cart, Truly stared back down the road to the horizon, a band of burning ruby. Across the darkening terrain, hundreds of campfires already winked like lightening bugs. Ben was back there. At dawn, he and the rest of Grant's great, battered juggernaut would awake once more to rolling cannonades.

The teamster handling the reins had a boy at his side, about ten years old. The boy held a homemade banjo across his lap, and his tuneless picking mingled with the creak of the wheels, the clop of the horses. Though fighting a headache, Truly somehow did not want the boy to stop. He heard the father speak softly–"Eddie, don't be bumping my arm with that." Shifting the instrument, the boy resumed picking.

"Nate," Forbes said, "–if you don't mind saying . . . "

Truly leaned in.

"Did you quit Pinkerton's service, or were you dismissed?"

"I never told you about that?"

"Only that you were with him years before the war. And that you left on unlovely terms."

A rut in the road jarred them. Truly braced himself against the side. "I joined his agency in its early years, in Chicago. I left him twice, to be truthful, but the first time was on good terms. That was in '58. I thought I'd try a life of writing and lecturing, but that little romance bit the dust afore long."

Forbes gave him a surprised look. "You've written things? Books?"

"A humble memoir, was all. If you're curious, I'll dig you up a copy sometime. Anyhow–when hostilities broke out and Pinkerton went to work for General McClellan, he made me an overture. I accepted and came east. For Anna and Sapphira, the move was an adventure. And Ben was already on his own in Wisconsin, soon to enlist. But for Rachel, I'm afraid the uprooting did more harm than . . . " Truly paused, his headache still threatening. Frankness was pulling him where he did not wish to go. "My trouble with Pinkerton, and his with me–it came to a head on the Peninsula. He declared that I'd never understood the chain of command. I declared that I understood this particular one–chiefly, that it was forged by a damned imbecile. So that was that. To my mind, I quit, though he would surely tell you otherwise."

Truly got out his tobacco and took a bite. "Not that it made any difference. By year's end, Little Mac was dismissed and Pinkerton gone with him. And I'd found work with Baker. I didn't care about his reputation." Or about much of anything, he thought. Just two months a widower, he had wanted to take on something big again, to lose himself in it. "In Lafe's view, my strife with Pinkerton marked me favorably. They'd been bitter enough rivals, at least in the counterintelligence area. Still, I vow to you–those two could have hatched from the same egg."

The cart bumped along. Encompassing it, crickets lent their brittle chorus while the boy plucked his banjo. Over the high grass, black swallows dove and skimmed like evening sprites.

Truly spat over the side. "Once we're back in Washington, I'll have Octavius go digging for fact, rumor and gossip on our congressman. It's the sort of task he'll like."

Forbes yawned. "Another public man with dung on his shoes. And who else? And how did they all step in it?"

Truly rearranged his gear, trying to get comfortable. Between chews, he began to recite. "'Vice is a monster of so frightful mien/ As, to be hated, needs but to be seen.'"

"Shakespeare?" Forbes asked.

"Pope . . . 'Yet seen too oft, familiar with her face/ We first endure, then pity, then embrace.' I think it's Pope. Or Swift, maybe. Heck, I forget."

PART II

The House Of The Emperor

Tolerance of vice was a strictly masculine attitude. Ladies, hermetically sealed in their virtue, might not even recognize its existence, and were permitted only a glacial unawareness of their fallen sisters. But, by 1862, if they ventured on Pennsylvania Avenue, they met on every hand the gaudy courtesans, promenading with the officers or lolling in their carriages.
• MARGARET LEECH, REVEILLE IN WASHINGTON

10

Brown's Hotel, Washington
June 11

LOOKING AT THE night outside, Miles Wakefield assumed a half-seated pose on the window sill. Then he looked at the congressman. Wan and disheveled in his cushioned wicker chair, Underhill stared into the flames of the fireplace. Abruptly he got up and went to the stand by the window. Pouring himself a glass of claret, he knocked over his portrait photograph.

Wakefield reached out and righted the picture. "Can't you tell me about it, Ezra?"

Glaring, Underhill took a greedy sip. "Is it not obvious? Bad enough to find myself on a wretched excursion like that–but then to be accosted by a couple of War Department knaves!"

The photographer nodded. "They were insolent, all right–the older one, especially. Still, when they showed you that letter . . . "

Underhill dripped claret onto the rug. "A dirty fabrication! A smear which I don't choose to dwell upon!"

"You seem to be dwelling upon it. At least tell me about this man Van Gilder."

"Miles–please!" Underhill tossed back the drink. Drawing a sleeve across his mouth, he put the glass down with a sharp rap. "They're attacking my reputation, trying to connect me with men of low character! I tell you now that it won't work–but please, these questions just echo the insult!"

Despite his heated words, the congressman's voice trembled, as plaintive as a dog in a thunderstorm.

There was a light knock at the door and Wakefield went to answer it. Horace Ives stepped in, carrying a leather pouch. He gave Wakefield a sallow-faced smile which then vanished into his usual expression, pinched and wary.

"Ives—what the devil took you so long?" barked Underhill.

"Beg your pardon, Congressman. I needed a change of clothes. But I brought all of your notes, as you wished."

Wakefield reached for his hat. "Gentlemen, I'll take my leave."

Clearing his throat, Underhill put on a solicitous tone. "You won't be intruding here, Miles. In fact, I'd value your counsel. I consider this to be the most important philippic of my career."

Wakefield looked at the door. "I'm honored, as always, but I can look at the draft once you're done with it. Just now I'm weary from the trip."

Sullen now, the congressman poured himself another claret. Ives took a sheaf of papers from the pouch and handed them to Underhill, who dropped back into the wicker chair.

"Tomorrow, perhaps," said Wakefield. "And Ezra—the trip was fruitful, whatever the unpleasantness. You'll see the pictures as soon as I've developed them. I'll be offering one or two to the magazines for engravings."

Underhill stared at the fire. "Yes."

Ives sat at the writing desk, his eyes baleful. "Good night, Mister Wakefield."

"See you, Horace."

Wakefield left them to their separate miseries.

As he descended to the lobby, facts and questions tumbled through his head. The federals had Cathcart—of that he was now certain—and he would need to take precautions. Keep his shop closed, for one thing, and spend less time there. But it was the letter that nagged him the worst. At Cold Harbor, he had felt like running up and snatching it from Underhill, right in front of those agents. What did it contain? Maybe the answer to why Van Gilder had taken flight—although, in the end, it had done the wretch no good.

Outside, Wakefield paused in the shadow of the columned portico. Again he reflected that he had not always been a man of malice. But since coming to this vain, skewed, hemorrhaging city, he had spent too many nights alone, tasted too much of humanity's rancid parts. He had lost something. However much trouble issued from this turn of events, and however urgent the questions, he deeply enjoyed Underhill's fright. True hatred had infected his blood and made him into this sort of man, one who could relish another's torment while feigning friendship.

A short distance down Pennsylvania Avenue, he signaled a Negro hack driver. Despite his relief at leaving Underhill, Wakefield felt a touch of queasiness as he climbed into the carriage, knowing what company awaited him. Still it was best that he deliver the alarming news in person.

WITH THE NOTES spread in his lap, Underhill droned and drank to the scratching of Ives' pen. "Now read it back," he said.

Ives held the papers toward the lamp. In his dry, hesitant voice, he began to read. "'I say as well, my honorable countrymen, that our brave population cannot withstand another season such as this, though indeed one gapes before us like the pit of Hades itself. As a Democrat of proven allegiance to the Union and the Constitution, I reaffirm that allegiance, yet must decry the blundering of a leadership which trumpets a divine preordination of victory while heaping fresh sorrows upon common folk and shame upon itself. In the name of its supposed contract with Heaven, it has unchained the Negroes and, in doing so, chained itself to an absurdity which galls the most loyal heart–the notion that God-fearing white citizens must now give way to the tide of the darky franchise.'"

Sipping his glass, eyes deep in the fire, Underhill let the words drift from his hearing until they became a grand aural blur. Not even Ives' delivery could stay their majestic ebb and flow. The congressman pictured himself delivering the speech before chastened or reverent colleagues in the House. In a life of tedious corruption and facade, the chance to speak from pure conviction was a gift that made his eyes moist. And the liquor's caress worked other magic. Settling the protracted shudder in his breast, it called forth a wave of defiance. He was a United States congressman, a power in the land. Whoever crossed him would face the manifold resources of that power.

Ives read on: "'Further, fellow patriots, how can we continue to call upon their valor and devotion, after such sacrifice, while building before their appalled vision a future whose black uncertainties . . .'"

Yes, Underhill thought–a man of consequence could always defend himself. By official channels or hidden ones, he could strike or obstruct the most lethal foe. He had only to think and plan.

"'For what man can so sacrifice for a future wherein he, his wife and his little ones confront a peril far worse than that which he sought to prevent? A nation in which . . . '"

Underhill watched the flames. Besides, he thought, this had not been Van Gilder's first violation of the pact. It had been his second–and, if the insolent Major Truly were to be believed, his last. Perhaps the matter would end here, with only one death–a warning to him and the others. Still, he had to think. He tried to do so. Then, with a crackle and a spray of sparks, the firewood shifted. Underhill flinched, spilling claret and scattering his notes.

11

Treasury Building

BETTER THAN MOST examples, Lafayette Baker's career reflected both the chaos and the expedience of wartime. At first a solo agent attached to the State Department, Baker had been transferred to the War Department but ensconced at the Treasury Building, where he began to build his own Secret Service. The term "domestic security" came closest to describing its nebulous role. In late '62 it had undergone its most significant growth spurt when Lincoln removed General George B. McClellan as the Army of the Potomac's commander. The general's loyal civilian friend and hireling Allan Pinkerton also quit the scene, taking with him his detectives and his voluminous records. Baker's organization expanded to fill part of the consequent void, chiefly in the area of spy-catching and other counterintelligence work– while the newborn Bureau of Military Information, attached to the Army of the Potomac, concerned itself with the movements of Lee's army.

Yet the limits of Baker's authority remained vague and his activities scattered, ranging from the pursuit of smugglers and bounty-jumpers to the ferreting-out of profiteers and counterfeiters, to the raiding of saloons and gambling hells around Washington. He called his service the National Detective Police, a name that Truly scorned as half-baked and preposterous. With a colonel's commission and the title of Special Provost Marshal, Baker ruled a staff of only modest size but also a thriving network of informants throughout the North.

Truly's drab little office suggested nothing of such power. Neither did the sight of Octavius Duke, slumped and snoring at the cluttered rolltop desk. As Truly and Forbes entered, the latter remarked on the room's stuffiness and raised the window sash. The noise awakened the clerk, who twitched upright and fumbled for his spectacles.

"Just as I thought," said Truly. "Saturday night, no less, and here you are!"

Duke smiled up, pink-faced, still fiddling with his specs. "Welcome back, sirs."

Though of Forbes' age, Duke had a schoolboy's voice and an older man's body, soft and squat. A ripple of ginger hair crowned his otherwise sparse head. His pronounced upper lip gave him a smile like a pie scallop, while his magnified green eyes flashed delight or anxiousness by turns. His small hands seemed always in motion.

Quickly gathering his paperwork, he moved to relinquish his chair but Truly told him not to, pulling up a rickety stool. Forbes leaned against a bookcase by the desk.

"Sapphira told us your message," Truly said. "Something you learned from your police friends?"

"It hardly qualifies as information, sir, but it might be pertinent." Duke shoved his chair back so his gaze could include both listeners. "You see, when I learned that Van Gilder's letter had been intended for a Congressman Underhill, that name kept scratching at my memory. Then, just after you left for the front, it came to me–I'd heard it from a policeman named Bob Gilchrist. I wanted to confirm the recollection and find out more, but lately I hadn't seen Gilchrist on his rounds. So I went down to the Fifth Precinct station house. It turned out that Gilchrist had left in May and would not return. Consumption, unfortunately–he never did seem well. But another officer recalled Gilchrist confiding the same thing to him, about an incident in which Congressman Underhill somehow figured."

Hands flicking, Duke described an encounter with Gilchrist on the Avenue, about two months ago. The policeman appeared glummer than usual, and when Duke pressed him, he allowed that he had stumbled upon a bizarre affair that involved a girl's death by drowning; a confrontation had somehow resulted, between him and a congressman named Underhill. Out of discretion or plain disgust, Gilchrist would say no more.

Truly frowned. "Well, in light of the congressman's cussedness, a visit with Officer Gilchrist would be in order."

Hopping from the chair to the desk, Duke plucked a slip of paper from a pigeonhole and gave it to Truly. "He and his wife have rooms on North C Street. He may be too sick to talk—but if not, you should find him receptive enough. And if you please, pass along my best wishes."

Truly looked at the address. "Very good, Octavius." He sent a meaningful smirk to Forbes, who arched an eyebrow. Forbes had expressed wonder at Duke's role as unofficial police liaison—specifically, why said police had not yet tossed him off a bridge. Aside from the history of rancor between the police and Baker's detectives—a situation that was only lately being smoothed over—there was Duke's penchant for babble. Yet over the months, individual officers' regard for him had passed from tolerance to amused tolerance to amused affectionate tolerance—a process helped, no doubt, by his frequent gifts of coffee, pastry and tobacco. In this way, under Truly's guidance, he had been able to circumvent the territorial squabbles, trading information on suspicious people and activities within the District.

Duke listened intently as they described their encounter with the congressman. He informed them that he had sent another telegram urging the prisoner Adam Cathcart's return from Albany. It had elicited a response from the penitentiary promising a quick sorting-out of the matter. Truly rolled his eyes. Duke added that he had spent hours looking through the available army rolls but had yet to find a major named Henry Spruce.

"Well, you can stop wearing your eyes out," said Truly. "Instead, I'd like you to nose around for anything murky in Underhill's past, any rumors or questions."

"Certainly, Major."

"He has a secretary named Ives—he's one possible source. If you're game for it, find out where he spends his free time and approach him there. Strike up a friendly conversation."

Duke blinked with excitement. "I'll do that, Major. And thank you for your faith in me!"

Truly caught Forbes trying to suppress a smile. "But listen, Octavius—try other avenues first. And work on your subtlety, all right?"

"Subtlety—yes, sir."

Truly tilted his stool back against the wall. He yawned. It would be good to sleep in his own bed tonight. Pondering Duke's story, he flicked the slip of paper against his knee. "A drowned girl, eh?"

12

Boarding House, North C Street
June 12

"WE'RE SORRY TO disturb you," Truly said. "And on a Sunday."

"No matter," said Robert Gilchrist. "My wife will be gone to church presently."

On a narrow bed beside an open bay window, the policeman lay with two pillows buttressing his head. Blood flecked the blanket below his chin, and the eyes in his pale boney face bore the shine of illness. Despite sunlight from the window, most of the room remained dim.

"Octavius sends his greetings and best wishes," said Truly.

"Well, send him mine," said Gilchrist. "He's an odd duck, but we're fond of him at the station-house."

Gilchrist's plain-faced wife appeared in her shawl. Truly and Forbes rose from their chairs but her stern eyes looked past them.

"I'll return straight after service," she said.

"Tarry if you like," her husband said. "It's a fine day out there."

Her gaze turned to the agents. "Gentlemen, you won't keep him long?"

Forbes bowed. "As briefly as possible, Mrs. Gilchrist."

They retook their seats as the door shut behind her.

"A good woman, my wife," said Gilchrist. "These days she has a bone to pick with the Almighty. My only gripes are with mortals." Grimacing, he jammed a handkerchief to his mouth. The shuddering cough made Truly want to move his chair back, but he checked the urge.

"Our questions concern an incident that occurred about two months ago," he said. "It involved Congressman Ezra Underhill of Maryland."

Squinting, Gilchrist spat into his handkerchief. "Under . . . Yes. Ohhh yes."

"We understand that you had words with him while pursuing facts in a girl's drowning."

Closing his eyes, Gilchrist took a slow, cavernous breath. "On that writing desk behind you, there's a small blue book. Please hand it to me."

Truly got the book and brought it to Gilchrist.

"Regulation diary of my rounds," said Gilchrist. "My sergeant never thought to collect it." Opening the slim volume, he glanced at Truly. "Although, if you'll pardon my saying, I don't see how this business could pertain to federal security."

"It might well not," said Truly. "But we have to probe the possibility."

Gilchrist started thumbing from the back, past blank pages that would never be filled. He stopped near the middle and read in silence, then closed the book and lay it on the blanket. "On Friday the fifteenth of April, about four in the afternoon, near Franklin Square, a colored hackman drove up to me in an excited state. His story was a muddle at first . . ."

Not long after mid-day, Gilchrist told them, the hackman had transported a young gent from the St. Charles Hotel to some establishment on the northern outskirts. The fellow told him to wait. Heading inside, he stopped to pass pleasantries with an older man who was on his way out, accompanied by a young lady. That pair left in a private gig. A while later the Negro's passenger hurried back outside, telling him to drive after the couple. Apparently the older man had mentioned driving to the Eastern Branch. The hackman sped there, where they found the couple's gig in a secluded spot. Then they found the man curled up on the riverbank, wailing that the girl had drowned. The younger man got out and belabored the other, urging him to his feet and getting him into the gig. They raced off against the hackman's protests. The Negro was alarmed about the girl but also because his passenger had neglected to pay. Not one to be cheated, he followed the two men for a few miles but lost them in the city. But he'd heard the young delinquent tell the other man that they needed to go to Brown's, which the Negro took to mean Brown's Hotel.

Gilchrist gave a harsh, hollow cough. "So I had him take me there. The hotel barkeep confirmed that two gents had arrived a short time ago and gone up to see a tenant–this Congressman Underhill. That confounded me even worse. The barkeep added that Underhill had just sent a hotel messenger racing off somewhere. I had a steward take me up to the congressman's rooms, and through the door I heard a discussion in progress. I caught fragments of it. Something about 'our liberation' and 'the time is come'–a younger man's voice, excited. Then someone else said, 'Go over it again'–Underhill's voice, as I soon discovered. Beneath this I heard a third man–sobbing, it sounded like. Then I knocked. The congressman called, 'Archer?' and I said no and identified myself. I heard silence and then a curse and found myself facing the fellow. At first he tried congeniality, but that turned to anger when I insisted on entering. Inside I saw the other two. One was a haughty pup, your rural gentry sort. Long hair, long nose, planter's clothes . . . "

Forbes cast Truly a look. "Our young squire?"

"Did you get his name?" Truly asked.

Again Gilchrist flipped the diary open. "Peavey," he said at length. "Jonathan Peavey. As I recall, he announced that to me like a damned European prince."

"And what about the other fellow?" said Truly.

"He was in a bad state–seated, face buried in his hands. A tall man in his mid-to-late thirties, I'd say. Well-dressed, though his pants and boots were mud-stained. I asked his name but Underhill interfered, demanding to know my purpose. Questions about a reported drowning, I said–and the seated one let out a loud moan. I started interrogating Peavey but once more Underhill was on me like a terrier, threatening to have me dismissed from the force and all that for my impertinence. He and I were shouting at each other when a fourth man arrived, and this one I recognized. Detective Quentin Archer–I'd seen him a few times at the station-house."

"A police detective?" said Forbes.

"One of the handful on the force. And I remembered that Underhill had called his name when I knocked. I started to explain, but then I had one of my prophetic coughing fits. In the midst of that, I saw a look pass between Archer and Underhill–they were well acquainted, it seemed to me. Archer asked me my name, then said the matter was now in his hands–a real skewing of procedure, I can tell you. He stressed the need for delicacy and that I should not discuss it with anyone, including my sergeant. In short, he told me to forget about it."

"That must have stuck in your craw," said Truly.

"It did. Especially later, when I met a Second Precinct officer who confirmed the drowning–boatmen had fished a girl's body from the Eastern Branch. Despite Archer's instructions, I did grumble aloud–to my wife, of course, and a few colleagues. And to Octavius, apparently. But at Brown's that day, I didn't protest. Archer has a reputation for competence and also for piety–Archer the Preacher, I've heard him called. Sounds like mockery, I know, but he is respected. He played a key role in the breakup of that thieves' ring in the Center Market area. Besides that, any mere roundsman like myself would hesitate to defy the detective squad. Their duties include the inspection of station-houses and monitoring conduct on the force. Even the cleanest of us act careful around them."

"So it ended there?" Truly asked.

Gilchrist shut his eyes again, his breathing like wind in an empty bottle. "Not quite. I told that Peavey brat what he owed the hackman–in fact, I think I might have boosted the amount a little. Archer told him to pay up and he handed me the fare, smirking. And he said, 'Champion of African wage labor, are you?' Damned puppy. But right then, the troubled one looked up and I saw his face. Red-rimmed eyes–light blue, they were. And he had one of those pointy beards."

"An imperial?" said Truly.

"Whatever they're called. Neat and pointy, with twirly ends on the mustache. I never did get his name, or the dead girl's. But as I left and shut the door, he started to blubber again and I heard Peavey say, 'Lieutenant-Colonel, forget the little harlot! Tell them what we both saw!'"

Forbes sat up. "Lieutenant-Colonel, you say?"

"Yes. Though he was dressed as a civilian."

Of the establishment where all of this had commenced, Gilchrist knew neither the name nor the exact location. But referring to his diary, he identified the hackman as one Simon Hodge.

In Truly's mind, the details of Gilchrist's testimony ebbed for a moment, and he thought of how the man's wife had eyed him. He recalled Rachel's last days, her stunningly rapid decline. "That's plenty for us to use," he said. "Listen, is there anything we can bring you?"

Gilchrist coughed. "Thank you, but the Policeman's Fund is sufficient."

The pair got up and put their hats on, then put the chairs back in place. Taking the diary, Truly returned it to the writing desk. "This was especially good of you, Officer, considering the past friction between your force and ours."

Raising the bloody handkerchief, Gilchrist hacked and sputtered. "Well, sirs–for me, partisan squabbles seem a bit foolish at this point. Besides, when you first got here I expected something more unpleasant."

"How's that?"

"I thought you might have come to haul me off. To the pest-house at Kalorama, I mean." The policeman sent Truly a shiny-eyed glance. "Anyone tries that, I have my service revolver under the bed here. I'm a good shot."

Truly felt a sudden heaviness in his chest. "I believe I'd do the same. Thank you again." The agents turned to go, but a gesture from Gilchrist stopped them.

"Come to think of it, I do have a request," he told them. "If you get to the bottom of this–and if Gabriel hasn't blown for me yet–please come back and tell me what the devil was going on."

"You have our word," said Truly.

"I'd be grateful. Good day, sirs."

Outside, Truly and Forbes stood amid the clangor of church bells.

"And the next day in New York," said Truly, "a man of Peavey's general description met with Van Gilder."

Forbes glanced at his note pad. "If Peavey was picked up at the St. Charles, that could be the hackman's regular spot. Shall we go there?"

"Well, on the chance that the fellow's a churchgoer, let's find ourselves an eatery first."

Headed toward Delaware Avenue, they speculated about the lieutenant-colonel.

"A fairly high rank," said Truly. "–with responsibilities to match, let's assume."

Forbes nodded. "Consider that and consider the apparent fix he's in, being part of this errant group. Under the thumb of Lord-knows-who."

"Yessir–the imagination starts to travel, all right."

13

West Of Cold Harbor, Virginia

Lɪᴇᴜᴛᴇɴᴀɴᴛ-Gᴇɴᴇʀᴀʟ Jᴜʙᴀʟ Aɴᴅᴇʀsoɴ Early, Army of Northern Virginia, reined his horse and observed the religious service in progress. A stone's throw to his left, beneath an elm copse, a chaplain held up a Bible and declaimed to a shabby congregation of troops seated on the ground. In their worn faces Early read degrees of attention and inattention.

Sundays–for Early they always brought Jackson to mind. Jackson, the pious warrior prince, Lee's oddball genius partner and the Confederacy's brightest bolt, who had thundered up and down the Shenandoah vanquishing bluebellies and lifting Southern hearts. Stonewall Jackson, a year and a month dead, shot by his own troops at Chancellorsville amid the night's confusion. Lee must feel it too, Early thought–the exalted gray spirit of Jackson looming above, saying "fight on." So many of his victories had been won on the Sabbath that it had become a joke, and to some a crowning proof of God's favor. What would this army have accomplished by now, had he survived? And if he was watching, what did he make of all this miserable defensive warfare? There were few fellow commanders living or dead who elicited Early's respect–but of those who did, only Jackson could move him to humble tears. The others would trigger a crossfire of comparisons in his brain, his ability versus theirs, and a dark resolve to surpass them. Meanwhile, it was he who had been honored with the command of Jackson's old corps, the Second.

The sermon was winding down, the chaplain's voice falling in somber cadence–" . . . that He will guide you, boys. That He will open His Kingdom unto your souls and give you the courage for victory." Early supposed that it helped morale, but he preferred the uplift of enemy body counts and prisoner tallies. Jackson, while pleased with Early as a divisional chief, had lamented his irreligious nature and specifically his profane tongue.

Early noticed one soldier look his way and then nudge the man next to him. Through the group there ensued a ripple of stolen glances and stiffening backs as the chaplain's voice rose, competing vainly with Early's presence. Early knew well that it was a distinct presence. And today he had spurned his customary civilian suit for a splendid new uniform, including his white slouch hat with black ostrich plume. Though known in the ranks as "Jubilee"–soldiers could never resist playing with a good name– little about him seemed to warrant that joyful sobriquet. With his black beard streaked gray and shoulders hunched from rheumatism, he seldom smiled. In his days as Franklin County prosecutor he had put his inquisitorial stare to frequent use, like a brandished fire poker, and that stare still served him well.

He continued down the road at a canter. A major cavalry fight raged to the northwest at Trevilian Station–but Lee's summons had implied something unrelated, something of greater scope. Musing on it, Early spurred his horse toward Lee's camp, now visible beyond a stretch of wood. He spied Lee long before he reached the tent-cluster. With aides standing attentively near, the kingly figure sat in the shade on a displaced church-pew, his white head bowed. An aide gestured; Lee looked up to see Early's arrival. As Early dismounted, an orderly hurried over with a salute and took the reins. Lee dismissed his retinue and stood up. Despite his marble dignity, he was odd to look at in one respect–short in the legs, big in the torso. His gray frock coat appeared newly pressed and his boots polished, his beard trimmed. Still, Early saw the toll of six weeks' hellish fighting. Lee's roseate face betrayed an inherited condition, but his drawn look and the folds beneath his eyes told of ceaseless mental strain.

Early swept his hat off and gave a leisurely salute.

Lee nodded. "You left your staff behind, Genr'l?"

"Didn't fancy I needed them, Genr'l. And I liked the chance to ride alone."

"I understand. Well, then, how's my bad old man?"

"Older, sir. But bad as ever, I reckon."

Given Lee's nine-year seniority, the "bad old man" tag was mysterious, though Early never cared to puzzle over it. Lee motioned to the bench and they sat together. After so long and so much, there was a warm famil-iarity between them, if not an intimacy. And with a number of Lee's main subordinates dead or incapacitated, his affection seemed to focus on his fellow Virginian.

"Presently we'll go to my tent and the map table," Lee said. "For the moment, I can tell you that your prime objective is Lynchburg. Hunter's force is reportedly nearing the town and the depot there, threatening our rear. I've already sent General Breckinridge with two brigades and he should arrive Thursday, but dispatches indicate that this won't be enough. Speed is paramount. From Charlottesville you can take your corps west by the Orange & Alexandria line and arrive a day or so after Breckinridge. The two of you should stay in close touch. Top command is yours, of course—but with proper coordination, you may be able to trap Hunter and destroy him."

Early nodded. "That would give great satisfaction, Genr'l."

"Now, you will find Breckinridge a fine man and an able soldier . . . "

In Lee's glance, Early felt a quiet demand for reassurance. Quarrel-some by reputation, Early had trouble concealing his frequent disap-proval of fellow generals. But Lee need not have worried. Early had met Breckinridge and found him disarmingly cordial and good-humored, as well as competent. "That's my assessment of him too, sir—but I am a mite surprised to hear his name. Didn't he end up under a dead horse, some days back?"

"He did. But thank God, he seems to have overcome the injury. His knowledge of the region is sound. I'm sure you're aware, it was his vic-tory last month at New Market which provoked this latest invasion of the Shenandoah. Now—" As Lee sat back, a note of restraint entered his voice. " . . . your combined force will have a second purpose. For this, however, the decision of whether or not to proceed will be yours alone."

Once the enemy force was disposed of, Lee said, Early should assess the condition of his troops, as well as any related developments. If these cast his position into doubt, he should speedily rejoin the main army. But if the outlook proved better—and if he deemed it worth the gamble—he was to march north down the Valley, destroying what bridges, rail crossings and other facilities might aid an enemy counterstroke. The people there had suffered much and would no doubt be grateful to see him. Apart from disrupting Confederate supply lines, Hunter's men had burned and plundered and committed other outrages.

Early listened hungrily. Back to the offensive, he thought. Once more he would be a dog unleashed.

Lee cleared his throat. "As for our main front here, I'm uncertain of what Grant will try next. Beauregard seems to think it will be against his position at Petersburg, but I need more information. Like us, Grant has suffered great losses. Unlike us, he is being reinforced daily. You may therefore wonder at these orders I'm giving you."

"I certainly don't question them, Genr'l."

Fixing a tired eye upon his subordinate, Lee smiled a little. "A more cautious man might. But this is a time for daring, and that's one reason I've chosen you. You see, Genr'l–if the variables still permit, you are to move beyond the Valley. To seize Harper's Ferry, cross the Potomac and then swing southeast."

Early blinked. "Toward Washington."

"Correct. Given the enemy's fretfulness about his capital, your menace ought to draw off a sizable number of Grant's men–more than enough, I believe, to justify the danger. Or, make him launch another wasteful assault like the last one."

Early's hands were clenched. "Genr'l–if I'm to menace the city, how far do you wish that objective pursued?"

"As far as Providence and your own judgment allow. You know my faith in you."

Lee had ordered all pickets tightened–but to avoid detection, Early would have to march out well before dawn. President Davis, who knew of the plan, would endeavor to keep any references to it out of the newspapers. Secrecy and surprise mattered here, if ever they did.

"Yet we will be in sporadic contact," Lee said. "By courier when necessary, by telegraph when practicable. I will follow your progress and offer suggestions, but you'll have wide discretion on the specific use of your troops."

"To the point, Genr'l, of a direct attack upon the city?" Realizing that it had come out sounding too sharp, Early added, "If that appeared feasible, I should say?"

Lee stared toward his tent. "You will agree, I trust, that it would take a considerably larger force to capture and hold Washington. And that with Richmond itself at risk, such numbers cannot be spared."

Early's heart fell. "To capture . . . ? Yes, Genr'l, I'd have to agree. God-a-mighty, though–to breach the perimeter! To have just a few hours' freedom within the city, showing them the same scant mercy they've shown us! A day of reckoning, sir, before the eyes of the world!"

Lee took a slow breath. "Such visions . . . They have a cyclone pull–the sort that could bear a commander's mind away. But that mustn't happen, Jubal. Remember, I want very much to welcome you back here, eventually, with your legion intact." In the distance, artillery sounded. Lee's stare drew back and turned upon Early. "There is information which I will now impart to you, something I've saved for fear of overemphasis. From Richmond has come word that Washington's fort system, for all its supposed impregnability, is in fact being drained of men by Grant's campaign. A secret agent is keeping us apprised."

In Early's gut, an electric current began.

Lee's expression hardened. "Now, with your mind firmly in the saddle, I will tell you that this same agent informs us of a Union officer there, a lieutenant-colonel, who has been . . . compromised." His lips expelled the last word like a maggot. "Exactly how this individual might help us is yet unknown, but I'm told he could prove quite valuable. Should your mission proceed favorably enough–that is, should you find yourself nearing the city against weak opposition–the agent will contact you with a detailed plan. He will use the name . . . " From an inside pocket, Lee took out his eyeglass case and a folded scrap of paper. He donned the specs and unfolded the scrap. "V. Grayson," he said.

"V. Grayson," Early muttered.

Lee handed the scrap to Early, who put it in his breast pocket.

"So, Genr'l," said Lee, "can you blot out this particular vision for now? To focus upon more immediate challenges?"

"Consider it blotted, Genr'l."

"Good. Much will have to go well for you first. Then and only then will this last thing become something more than whimsy."

"I understand."

"And Jubal–whether you get that far or not, Northern morale is said to be sinking, and your thrust could sink it further. The moment is crucial. Sooner or later, a general is forced to view the broader field of action. The political field."

Lee was referring to the Yankee elections, now less than five months away. When the Northern Democrats convened, their peace faction was expected to dominate the platform. A major Southern success would boost them at the polls, deepen resistance to Lincoln's draft, drive up the price of gold, increase the clamor for a negotiated peace. Plus, the rest of the world looked on. France or England or both might finally tilt toward recognition of the Confederate States.

"But how much more convincing it would be," said Early, "to blast the very seat of Yankee government!" Catching himself, he quickly added, "Still, Genr'l, for this operation I'll call upon the courtroom Early. I'll be judicious."

Lee gave him a look of approval. "Right. First, Lynchburg–then we'll see."

From the east came the throatier rumble of a big Whitworth gun. Lee glanced in that direction. With the sun glistening on his eyeglass rims, he looked like a battered oracle–creased and shrunken, still magnificent. Out in the bud-flecked meadow, a wagonload of coffins bumped along.

Lee sighed. "Well, let's go work this out over the map table."

It was mid-afternoon when the two emerged squinting from Lee's tent. Signaling for Early's horse, Lee wished his visitor godspeed. Early saluted like a palace guard and mounted up.

Once on the road, Early dug his spurs in and brought the horse to a full gallop, even as the sunlight dazzled him. He burned with purpose–incandescent purpose, the kind that Jackson would have called sacred. Praise be on this Sabbath, he thought.

14

Pennsylvania Avenue

FROM HIS FALLEN gaze, it was clear that Simon Hodge found the events of April 15th an anxious subject.

"I thought that all was done with," he said. "Day after, I heard they pulled the young lady outer the river. She gone and drowned herself."

"That much we know from Officer Gilchrist," Truly said. "He was helpful, and we were hoping that you could be helpful too. There are things only you can tell us."

On the iron-columned porch of the St. Charles Hotel, a uniformed attendant opened the door for a gentleman and signaled the first hack driver in line. Hodge kept his molasses-dark face averted. "Your pardon, sirs–I gotter move up a space." He flicked his reins, advancing with the file of black carriages along the curbstone. Truly and Forbes moved with him.

"You needn't fear," said Forbes. He offered a greenback from his pocket. "Besides, once we've gotten some answers, we'll be needing a ride."

Adjusting his high hat, Hodge eyed the bill and then took it. "Well–seein' that, sirs, I'll give up my spot here and take you 'cross the way."

Truly and Forbes climbed in. Guiding his team in a U-turn, Hodge bumped across the cobblestone and the omnibus tracks and drove a short distance down the Avenue's dingier side. They passed honking geese and snuffling pigs, braying peddlers and dirty squealing children. With the Capitol Building in view, they halted by the Botanical Garden enclosure and Hodge got down. Facing Truly, he stood with his hands behind his back.

"Now," said Truly, "let's start with the young gent you transported from the St. Charles that day."

"He was at the hotel every few months, sir. None of us hackers liked to take him–but a fare's a fare, and I took him a couple of times. Planter sort, he was–high-and-mighty, strict of tongue, ruffly cuffs, soft-lookin' hands. I had to remind him to pay me and he done it with a hard look, like he wasn't used to payin' a colored man."

"And where did you take him?"

"Same place each time, sir–way up the Seventh Street Road and just past Piney Branch, to a place they call the Emperor's House. Run by an old French lady."

Truly's eyes widened. "La Maison de l'Empereur."

"You know it?" Forbes asked.

"Remember the bordello where Van Gilder would stop on his visits down here?"

"Well, well."

Relaxing somewhat, Hodge flashed a smile. "That's not what they call it out there, sir. To them what partake, it's a gentleman's club, a place of finer ladies and civil high talk."

"So I've heard," said Truly.

"Bein' that far, it's a good fare. Oe'r the past few years I took a good number of gents out there and back. Men in commerce and gov'ment, with more to spend than most."

"And on that particular day, what happened when you delivered this prince to the gentlemen's club?"

Hodge tensed again, taking a breath. "He told me to wait, like he done those other times. And like those times, I had to tell him I needed the first part of the fare right then, if I was to wait. He put the evil eye on me, slapped the money on the seat. Then he stepped out and a tall skinny man . . . " Hodge made a pinching motion under his chin. "–man with a pointy beard, he come out with a small lady on his arm, just a young thing in a pink bonnet. A child, almost. And seein' this man, my gent smiled at him. A mean sorter smile, the kind you give somebody who you goin' to laugh at once his back's turned. And he did a low bow, actin' all fancy. 'My dear Lieutenant-Colonel!'–that was his greeting."

Upon hearing this, Hodge said, he realized that he had seen the bearded fellow on another occasion. About a month earlier, on a slow evening, he had driven a fare out to the Emperor's House and been paid to wait. He was thus waiting outside when this man drove up in a gig and got out. Hodge saw that he was in uniform. "Top army–shiny buttons, polished boots and all. He had a bouquet in his hand, so I figured he was sweet on some lady in there. Anyhow, that's why I recollected him when I heard 'Lieutenant-Colonel' and seen him with the little damsel, only this time he was in reg'lar clothes."

"So your passenger stopped to talk with this man?" said Truly.

"Just for a bit, sir. I heard the lieutenant-colonel say he was takin' this young lady for a ride along the Eastern Branch. Seemed to me he was right proud to be with her, pretty as she was. But those two men was tryin' hard to be polite–you know, a lot of after-church type words that don't mean much."

Hodge recalled the girl as looking frightened, stumbling along as the lieutenant-colonel took her to his gig. They left as Hodge's passenger went inside. Some time afterward, the young gent came racing back out in an excited state. He ordered Hodge to fly off after the mismatched couple. "It's a long stretch to the Eastern Branch, sirs, and he cussed me the whole way, even though I worked the horses awful."

Hodge told of finding the gig by the reeds and the lieutenant-colonel seated nearby, his clothes muddy, wailing that the girl was drowned. "Afore I knew it, him and that ruffle-cuff is tearin' off in the gig and there's Simon without his fare. Well, sirs, I didn't come all that way to get cheated, so I tore after 'em. With my two horses to their one, catchin' up was easy. For a mile or so I was right behind 'em and hollerin' like blazes and them not stoppin'. Then, when we come into the city, a cart blocked me and I lost 'em. But I 'membered hearin' the young one say to the lieutenant-colonel 'bout goin' to Brown's. So I hunted up that policeman and he went and got satisfaction for me, God bless him. And that's all I have to tell."

Truly nodded, stroking his chin in thought.

"Where should I take you now, sirs?"

"I've a little errand at the War Department. First there, then the Emperor's House."

15

Seventh Street Road

EVEN BEFORE THE Boundary Street intersection, the city gave way to woods, fields and orchards. The hack trailed a cloud of yellow dust, the area having seen three consecutive weeks without rain.

Earlier, at the War Department, Truly had telegraphed a plea to Lieutenant Heatherton in New Jersey, where that agent still toiled on a counterfeiting case. Truly had explained his lack of confidence in the men of Baker's New York office. Promising reimbursement, he asked that Heatherton make a trip to the city and gather correspondence, financial records and any other pertinent material from Gideon Van Gilder's home and office, then ship these by rail to Washington.

At the same stop, Truly had helped himself to a smuggled two-week-old copy of the *Richmond Examiner*. Slouched under the canopy, he read a front-page editorial blasting the "devilish Yankee ban" on prisoner exchanges. He skimmed a series of short items: a gloating assessment of Northern casualties at the Wilderness and Spotsylvania; praise for the ladies' auxiliary and their service to Southern wounded; black-bordered death notices; an updated list of rationed foods and household items. Truly concluded that the Rebel capital was an even less comfortable place than when he had spied there for Pinkerton. Near the back of the paper, a cartoon titled "General Questions" showed Lee, nobly resolute, holding a club over a dazed Grant on all fours. "May I have another, sir?" Grant was asking, while behind him a splay-footed Negro soldier pleaded through huge lips, "Kin ah go home now, Massa?"

Turning to the last page, Truly began skimming it. "Be damned!" he cried.

"What?" said Forbes.

Truly read aloud, competing with the rattle of the carriage. "'Word comes that among C.S.A. officers captured in the Beaver Dam vicinity is that esteemed son of Virginia, Brig. Gen. Gustavus Adolphus Dinsmore. Washington sources report that the general has been placed in the infamous Old Capitol Prison.'" Lowering the paper, Truly chuckled. "Snakebite Dinsmore! That old dog–he was my captain on the march to Mexico City. Small world, eh? I wonder what he'd think of me now."

Forbes gave only a pained look, shifting in his seat. His leg was bothering him.

"Let's turn around," said Truly. "We could get you some laudanum."

"No, no. It will pass." Leaning down, Forbes stroked his wooden shin. "Strange, these ghost-pains. Who'd have ever thought that poplar could throb?" He sat back. "You were going to tell me more about this place we're calling on."

Truly glanced once more at the *Examiner* notice, his joshing mood well past. The thought of Dinsmore carried other associations, other memories from which his mind recoiled. Clearing his throat, he folded the paper and lay it on the floorboard. "If memory serves, La Maison was purchased seven or eight years back–purchased, mind you, not rented–by a Frenchwoman whose name escapes me. It has kept up a steady trade, even with all the wartime competition. The periodic police raids have never touched it–due partly to its out-of-the-way location, I think, plus the fact that it draws no riffraff. As Hodge said, its management is pretty selective–not only about the clientele but about its stable of girls, who get fine clothes and special training. Word of mouth bills the place as an outpost of manly sophistication, where a gent might proclaim how refined his vices are. At a price well above the going rate, of course."

"A vanity magnet, then," Forbes said. "Somehow I'm not surprised it would draw the likes of Van Gilder. Or this Peavey character."

"Or Underhill," said Truly. "My guess is that their mutual acquaintance began at La Maison. It's the simplest explanation for such an unlikely crew coming together."

"Well, it seems their current trouble started there too. Whatever Peavey and the lieutenant-colonel saw that day, it seems to have set this whole affair in motion."

"Right. Which leads me to think–however lofty the airs of this place, the occasional viper is bound to slither through its door. One smart and dangerous enough to ensnare these others. He could even be a regular patron."

The hack bumped across a bridge spanning Piney Branch, its rocky bed all but dry. Still in some pain, Forbes gave a slight grimace. He called to Hodge's erect back. "Are we nearly there?"

"Coming up on our left, sir."

In a moment, as they passed a pear grove, a yellow-brick mansion with a wide lawn came into view. Another coach with a liveried Negro waited by a row of empty hitching posts. Trading a nod with his fellow driver, Hodge pulled to the head of the walkway. Forbes got out with discomfort. Truly passed Hodge another bill, telling him the wait could be as long as an hour. Stepping down, Truly took in the sight of the wide two-story building. Few houses in the District–and no bordellos, not even those of Marble Alley–boasted as many grand features: a white-marble main portico with fluted Doric columns; a stately paneled door with a stained-glass fanlight on top; tall, fancy-curtained windows with lintels of carved gray stone; a three-part hipped roof of brown shingle, with two tall chimneys and a row of dormer windows; flanking pavilions whose yellow-brick facades matched that of the central one, each with a balustraded balcony.

As the pair started down the walkway, Truly saw a curtain flutter in an upstairs window. At the front door, he yanked the bell-pull and they removed their hats. The door swung wide. Before them stood a heavy, buxom, fair-skinned young woman in a green crinoline gown. Smiling brightly, she greeted them with a pronounced German accent.

"Vel-kom, sirs! You please come in, ja?"

Following her brisk green bell-shape, they passed through a vestibule into a grand hall, varnished and expensively carpeted. There she turned to them, still beaming.

"Gentlemen–you have letters of reference?"

Absorbing the opulence, Truly let his partner respond.

"No, Miss. We're here on an official government matter. May we see your proprietress?"

"Madam Ravenel . . . Oh, sirs–she is not vell today."

Truly spoke up. "Would you please ask if the lady might still receive us? It is important, and we'll keep her as little as possible."

The woman hesitated, then curtsied. "I vill ask." With a swish of petticoats, she hurried up the wide staircase.

"Reckon this is our day for bothering invalids," Truly muttered. "Not very gallant."

Forbes appeared more at ease, no longer pained. "If there's one thing that exceeds my gallantry, it's my hatred for pointless trips."

Gazing toward the staircase, Truly noticed a circular black object mounted on the supporting beam. It was a large military drum. Adorned with a rigid white eagle, it lent a jarring, forbidding touch to the overall splendor. "Queer choice of ornament there."

Forbes looked, frowned, then glanced elsewhere. "The shields are a bit much."

Lining both sides of the hall, the decorative shields terminated at two opposite entryways. Truly advanced a few steps and peered into the adjoining space on the right. It was a parlor furnished with teakwood chairs and sofas, their cushions covered in lace antimacassars. Slanting sunlight enlivened the plush colors: crimson brocatelle draperies, gold-and-garnet wallpaper, royal blue carpeting with an angel-and-flower motif. A harp stood in one corner and a spinet in another, next to a closed side-door. On a mantel over the big fireplace, a vase of fresh lilies paid homage to the room's centerpiece, which hung just above it–a portrait of Emperor Napoleon I. Inserted between the buttons of his coat, the conqueror's hand looked almost casual, though his obsidian gaze bespoke the mind that had leveled Europe and now measured the viewer's worth.

"Bart, do you think that's an original?"

When Forbes didn't answer, Truly turned and saw him peering into the opposite space. Truly crossed the hall and joined him. This room was much larger, stretching far toward the rear of the mansion. Beneath sparkling brass chandeliers, chairs and small tables were neatly arranged, along with decanters, cigar holders and Argand lamps, as well as various gaming articles–card decks, faro boxes, roulette wheels. On a straight line from the entranceway stood a polished saloon-counter with a long rectangular mirror behind it, revealing well-stocked shelves. There was a majestic old coffin clock, an incongruous bookcase of bound volumes, a half-naked statue of Venus or Aphrodite. On the walls, the heads of a boar, a bear and a stag alternated with ornately framed portraits of legendary Frenchmen–Voltaire, Charlemagne, Richelieu, Louis XIV. Above another imposing fireplace, a passable likeness of George Washington presided.

Truly gave a low whistle. "You've seen more fancy interiors than I have. What do you think?"

"I'm from the Puritan capital of America," Forbes said. "Just setting foot in here pretty well ensures that I'll roast in the Afterlife."

"Reckon you'll have me for company."

From the staircase a female laugh echoed, followed by two pairs of feet coming down. A well-attired man of Truly's age descended with a much younger woman on his arm, dressed in white taffeta.

"Ah, the weakness of the flesh," Truly muttered. "Speaking of which, I'm out of tobacco."

"Pity," said Forbes.

The couple breezed by. As they exchanged parting niceties in the vestibule, Truly noted an Irish lilt in the girl's voice. Then the German girl reappeared on the stairs. "Sirs," she called, "–Madam will see you for a little."

Forbes made use of the banister as they followed her up, passing under the big black drum. In a corner of the middle landing, a bust of Napoleon's Marshal Ney frowned on its pedestal. At the top of the stairs, a circular stained-glass window tinted the blue carpet red, green and gold. Their crinolined escort turned right, leading them past a series of closed rooms and a stooped Negro maid who was feather-dusting the baseboard. Near the hallway's end they came to a paneled braid-trim door with a leonine coat-of-arms carved into it. The girl knocked gently.

"Entrez," came a withered voice.

The girl opened the door. Entering, she motioned for the men to follow.

In a large bed with a gold-tasseled canopy, an older woman lay swathed in purple linen. She wore a ruffled white nightgown. Her hair, grayed to a deep ash color, tumbled in such volume that her head looked unnaturally small. From a bedside chair, a balding, bespectacled man with a large nose stood up, holding a medical bag. He addressed his patient in graceful French.

"Merci, Docteur," she replied.

Exiting, the doctor gave the agents a cold look, spurning Truly's nod.

The old woman dismissed the German girl. With a small bow, Truly introduced himself and Forbes and took out his credentials, which she waved away with a thin hand. "Gentlemen–I am Yvette de Ravenel. As Ursula has informed you, I am not the robust *jeune fille* of years past. But do please seat yourselves." Even through the barnacled crack of her voice, her English was nimble, with enough accent to charm an American ear.

Truly let Forbes take the doctor's high-back chair and drew up another one for himself. Up close, the woman's face surprised him. The sharpness of her eyes, lips and jaw line made him guess that she had once been exquisite, and he tried to picture the drawn, webbed mask as smooth and full. With the pull of age, her features had passed some critical point—sharp to hard, striking to harsh. Beauty had collapsed inward, or so he imagined, settling to an ugliness of like degree.

"We're awful sorry to impose," he said.

"Worry not, monsieur. Ursula said you are with the government, which rather mystifies me."

"A complete explanation would be a lengthy one, and we don't wish to tax your graciousness. We are pursuing facts in the death of a young lady who was in your charge."

Madam Ravenel closed her eyes. "Our poor dear Briona."

"And her last name?"

"Kibby, monsieur. Irish and a recent immigrant. She came to us only in January."

Ravenel said that when her health allowed and there was room for a new girl, she would travel to the Baltimore waterfront and greet the immigrant ships. This was how she had met Mademoiselle Briona. "A lovely girl—lost and destitute, like so many. Yet I choose carefully what girls to bring here, those in whom I detect the seed of something finer."

"That would surely follow," said Forbes, "given your select membership."

Eyeing Forbes, she seemed to probe him for flippancy. In her calm, sloe-eyed gaze, Truly sensed a force that belied her body's frailty, and for a moment she could have been Napoleon's aging daughter. "It is true," she said, "that La Maison de l'Empereur caters not to the rabble. It is for gentlemen such as yourselves. Familiar visitors are welcomed as members of a club might be—but they may bring friends, or provide them with letters of reference. Yet we have no 'membership' in the formal sense." She closed her eyes. "As for les jeune filles, they come here willingly enough, knowing that a cruel path awaits them otherwise. They are penniless and bewildered, yet aching with promise. And yes, they are pretty—especially after I have fed, clothed and instructed them. Doctor Dubray sees to their health as he sees to mine. They are cared for. And they are exposed to a culture they would never ordinarily see, yes? There are thirteen here now, but we have had as many as twenty. When one of them asks to leave, she is given money and a wish of *'bonne chance.'*" The dark empress eyes blinked open, straight at Truly. "I pretend not to be a missionary, Major. Yet consider the fate of these girls, if Madam did not discover, guide, protect."

Wearily insistent, her digression had taken Truly off guard. A moment passed before he resumed questioning. "On the fateful day, Miss Kibby reportedly left with a lieutenant-colonel. Though dressed as a civilian, he had been seen here in uniform at least once before. Who was this man? Can you tell us?"

"Alas, no. Though we are select, many men call here. And age erodes the skill for names and faces. I am told that this lieutenant-colonel visited previously, in uniform, but I have no memory of him. Not from that visit and not from the afternoon of Briona's death, as I was confined to bed." With bony fingers she began to massage her temples. "Among our guests we have had more than a few *hommes militaire.* And it is known that they, like other patrons, sometimes think it best to give a false name. Whatever the case, for them we make an exception and require no letter of reference. Out of respect for their patriotic sacrifice."

Truly frowned. Seldom had he gotten so thorough an answer, and never one that so thoroughly squelched his line of inquiry.

Forbes jumped in. "They say he's a tall man. Tall, with an imperial-style beard."

A few of the young ladies had described him thus, Ravenel said, but could add nothing more. When he had asked that Briona be permitted a ride with him, Ursula delivered the request to Ravenel. "Ordinarily, I only grant such requests if the patron is known to me. But this time, God forgive me, I thought–this is a Union officer, a man of honor and responsibility! How could I have foreseen?"

"Can you venture a guess," said Truly, "as to why Miss Kibby reportedly looked frightened as she left with him?"

From under her purple sheets, Ravenel produced an embroidered handkerchief. Daintily she dabbed the end of her long nose. "Briona was a timid girl, though I am sure she would have blossomed eventually. It was her first time out with a stranger, away from the house, and perhaps the simple prospect of this alarmed her. Whatever the case, I misjudged, and will blame myself forever."

"The police called her death a suicide," Forbes said.

Ravenel gave a tired nod. "This is true. And who am I to scorn the conclusion? Who knows what desperate sadness lay hidden in the poor girl? But I can tell you this, monsieurs–" Like a desert gust, her voice abruptly rose. "To the care of this dishonored lieutenant-colonel I entrusted Mademoiselle Briona, and he will pay for his failure! Should I or anyone of La Maison ever again see him, we will direct you to him forthwith! He will be held captive for you, even if I must place the sword of my glorious dead father to his miserable heart!"

"We'd sure thank you for that," Truly said. "Madam, can you recall the name of the investigating policeman?"

"Detective Archer. In the past he has come here on official duties, asking about men wanted by the law. Plainly we cannot keep out all disreputable types–so in this we have cooperated with Archer, and helped him to catch some of these criminals. When he told me of Briona's fate, I was desolate–and as helpful, I fear, as I am to you now." She dabbed an eye. "I saw to her proper burial. No girl of mine shall rest in a pauper's field."

Thinking, Truly slouched, his gaze lost in the purple furrows of the bed sheets. "Madam," he said at length, "–what is Archer's attitude toward this house of yours? Or rather, what do you sense it to be?"

She sighed, tipping her hands. "If you mean does he approve of us, Major, I can tell you he does not. As a religious man and an officer of the law, how can he? I once received a kind of sermon from him on the subject. In my life, however, I have come to value such frankness of opinion, especially when combined with a willingness to compromise. Perhaps I flatter myself, but I believe that Detective Archer appreciates this same quality in me. He is no simpleton. Whatever his misgivings, I believe he sees La Maison as a better alternative to the filth and peril one finds in the city."

Truly glanced at Forbes, then back at Ravenel. "We too value your frankness, Madam. But we're mighty keen to find this lieutenant-colonel, and must therefore ask a bit more of you. Tell me, isn't it customary for female establishments like this to have a male guardian at hand?"

"That guardian would be Monsieur Monroe. He is also our groundskeeper–but like me, unfortunately, he is not what he once was. He is still strong enough but suffers from rheumatism, and this affects his disposition. Though Doctor Dubray has tried to treat him, I may soon be forced to replace him with one younger and healthier."

"Whatever the case, we would like to question him. Also–however shy Miss Kibby was, she no doubt had a friend or two among the other young ladies. A confidante."

"True, she did–Mademoiselle Fannie O'Shea. They came over on the same boat. As a matter of fact, I discovered them together."

"If you please, we would like to speak with Miss O'Shea also. And Miss Ursula. And do I understand correctly that Doctor Dubray lives as well as works here?"

"He does. Antoine is an old friend and associate."

"Him too, then."

"Very well. But you should know that Detective Archer questioned all of us at the time, and at some length. Would you pull that cord, Major?"

She gestured toward the bell-pull, which dangled to one side of the headboard. Truly pulled it and Ursula soon materialized. Ravenel told her to fetch the other three people and she scurried off.

Waiting, Truly paced to an open window that overlooked the rear grounds. Below he saw a stone well, a rose-studded arbor and a flourishing garden. Farther back and proceeding from the right, a carriage house, a stable, a smokehouse and a row of rude sheds bordered the curving tree-line. It took Truly a moment to recognize the sheds as slave dwellings– grim novelties nowadays, as the institution had been banned from the District in '62. Out of one stepped Doctor Dubray, buttoning up his fly. La Maison de l'Empereur was an eminently practical place, Truly reflected. Swords had not yet been made into plowshares–but here, at least, slave sheds had been made into privies.

He turned in time to catch Ravenel watching him. Closing her eyes, she gave a delicate yawn. "Life is too full of sorrows," she murmured.

Presently Ursula came back. On her heels, curtsying, was the girl in the white taffeta dress. Ursula said that Monroe and the doctor would be there soon.

Ravenel spoke. "The pair of you will answer these gentlemen's questions as best you can."

Truly looked at Ursula and then at Fannie O'Shea, a slim pixie with auburn sausage curls. Her eyes were both direct and demure, like the smartest girl at a spelling bee. "Now, I know that nearly two months have passed and that Detective Archer questioned you at the time. But what can you tell me about Miss Kibby's escort?"

Fannie's eyes darted to the bed. "What I recall, sir . . ."

They were interrupted by two heavier sets of footsteps coming down the hallway. The door bumped open and Dubray strode in, looking rankled. Standing by the women, he clutched his lapels and sniffed. After him a taller man in jean pants, suspenders and a slouch hat made a plodding entrance. Truly had expected that Monroe, despite his specific duties, would bear some mark of his employer's worldliness. This big, shabby man did not. He stood apart from the others, his hat tilted forward so that it hid the upper part of his face. His mustache was unkempt, his cleft chin stubbled. His tall Hessian boots had tracked dirt on the rich carpet.

"Monsieur Monroe," said Ravenel, wearily.

"Sir," said Truly.

The man nodded.

Truly repeated his question. While Fannie and Ursula waited in silent deference, Monroe seemed to just stare at the floor. "I saw the man for just a bit," he said, with a hint of surliness. "Like I told Archer, there was a lot o' visitors here that day."

"We already have a physical description of the fellow," said Truly, "so we can dispense with that too. Now, can anyone here recall the lieutenant-colonel saying anything that might give a clue to his identity?"

Fidgeting, Ursula said that he had spoken only a few words to her, when he made his request about Miss Kibby.

"Well, then—on previous visits, had he been any more talkative?"

Hesitant, Ursula blinked toward the bed.

With a chafing in her voice, Ravenel spoke. "Ursula, use the head you were born with. Tell them about the other time, when the lieutenant-colonel called here in uniform."

"Oh . . . Ja. A fine uniform he vears then, and he brings flowers. But he speaks little."

Truly eyed Fannie. "Miss O'Shea—what do you recollect?"

"I did see him that time, sir," she lilted, "with his bouquet. Briona said nothing about it afterwards—because it meant little to her, I think. She was so pretty and men often took notice of her, but she never crowed about their attentions. Perhaps she did not wish to make the rest of us jealous?"

"And what about the fifteenth of April?"

"I was busy serving drinks. I do not remember seeing Briona leave with the man. Since I am told that he wore gentlemen's clothes this time, I wonder if I would even have recognized him."

Irked, Truly pined for his tobacco. "So . . . You can recall nothing that Miss Kibby might have said about the lieutenant-colonel, or that he said about himself?"

Fannie held her hands out. "Forgive me, sir! Briona was my friend and I would do anything to help! But . . . "

Truly cut in. "A man who visited not once and not twice but at least three times, as his bouquet for Miss Kibby would seem to indicate. To be smitten with her so, he must have glimpsed her on a still earlier visit, don't you think?"

A stillness took hold of the room. Truly traded a glance with Forbes and then regarded the four standing subjects. Looking flustered, Fannie dropped her gaze. Dubray pulled out his pocket watch and glared at it. Expecting Ravenel to break the silence and resume command, Truly turned toward the bed. To his surprise, it was Monroe who spoke.

"A man might come here a few times," he growled, his eyes still hidden. "His visits, they might be months apart. If there's a crowd and if he's dressed different than before, who's to notice him as the same man? 'Less there's something special to mark him? This one was skinny and had pointy hair on his chin, but damned if there was anything else to make you look twice."

Ursula nodded eagerly. "Ja, ja–this is all true."

Folding his arms, Truly at last regarded Dubray. "Doctor, I don't suppose you know anything that could enlighten us?"

"On the day of Mademoiselle Briona's misfortune," said Dubray, in his flowing accent, "I was tending to one of the younger ladies, who had a cough. Therefore–no, monsieur. Medicine and not socializing is my main activity here. And with this in mind, I must object to your disturbing of Madam Ravenel's rest."

"Madam Ravenel has been very gracious," Truly said. "We will be leaving shortly."

Ravenel's tired, melodic voice intervened. "It is quite all right, Antoine. Calm yourself."

At Forbes' reminder, Truly asked about another caller that same afternoon, a planter sort named Jonathan Peavey.

Monroe volunteered that he remembered Peavey sitting alone and leaving after a couple of drinks. "Whenever that little peacock's here, I avoid him. He seems to look down his nose at them what work for a living."

Truly eyed the drooping brim of Monroe's hat, willing for it to rise. "Mister Monroe–we're to understand that he came all the way out here to swill two drinks, speak to nobody and then leave?"

After a pause, Monroe spoke in a shaky rumble. "I come up here to tell you about it, not to explain. Anything else you want?"

"Yes. Do you ever mix with the patrons?"

"I watch 'em. I keep an eye on the crowd."

"Have you ever watched a man named Gideon Van Gilder?"

Another pause. By now, Truly thought, Monroe had surely examined every fiber in the carpet.

"Newspaper man, right?"

"Correct. From New York."

"He only comes here every few months. Big talker, likes to puff about New York. Calls Washington a pigsty."

"Another name for you–Congressman Ezra Underhill."

The hat-brim nodded. "I've talked with him a few times–'bout the war and such. He's not so bad, I reckon."

"I concur with these impressions," Dubray blurted, "but cannot add to them. Now, monsieurs–may I take my leave? I have a case of shingles to attend."

Truly cast him a side-look. "Doctor, how are we supposed to view this ... indifference of yours concerning Miss Kibby?"

Scowling, the physician straightened up but offered no immediate retort.

"Antoine, please," Ravenel called.

"Do you have a more civil question?" Dubray snapped.

"Just this," said Truly. "You share Mister Monroe's impressions of Peavey, Van Gilder and Underhill. In your contact with them, however slight it was, did their words or behavior ever seem to carry a whiff of fear? Fear for their lives?"

Adjusting his spectacles, Dubray managed a neutral tone. "As I say, monsieur, my part here is not primarily social. At one time or another I have exchanged pleasantries with these men, but pleasantries only."

"Thank you for your time, Doctor."

"Merci. Kindly do not keep Madam much longer." Dubray made a brusque exit.

Truly turned to Monroe. "Same question to you, sir." Through his annoyance, Truly felt some deeper agitation as the big man shrugged.

"The ones we get here—they boast, they laugh, they argue politics and such. Nobody comes to bare his soul."

Ravenel gave a light cough. "I too have been aware of these three in the past. The congressman is quite cordial, not especially deep. Van Gilder, aggressive and rather full of air. Peavey? I agree that his last visit was strange, but he always seemed excitable by nature—an example of the rural eccentric, perhaps? The casual habits of men, they are often a mystery. *Je regrette,* monsieurs, but I can add no more." Her words trailed into a yawn.

Forbes asked if anyone had ever seen these three socializing together, or with other identifiable patrons. Again, no real answers.

With maximum effort, Truly smiled. "Madam, you have been most kind. We'd best leave now, before we owe the hack driver a month's salary."

Monroe plodded out of the room, while Fannie and Ursula remained like nervous deer. Ravenel folded her veined hands. In its nest of ashen hair, her wise, weary, gargoyle face seemed to take the agents' measure once more, her chin tilted upward. "Gentlemen, our prayers will be for Briona's soul—and for the success of your investigation."

Truly felt as if he had just been knighted and given a quest, yet denied a sword.

Having shown themselves out, the two men paused on the walkway. "Well," said Truly, "I'd call that about as useful as a toothless barn cat."

"The curse of investigations," said Forbes. "The unnamed suspect who makes barely a dent in people's memories."

"Maybe. But I should've probably been more formal about this and made a day of it—questioned everyone separately. I guess I expected . . . Well, I'm not sure what I expected. But that old gal seemed so much in charge despite her illness, I thought her presence would help us get straight answers from the others. Not that she was much help herself."

"We can always make a return visit, Nate. I'm sure they'd be overjoyed."

"Oh, yes. If we came as customers."

Yet they had confirmed Underhill's patronage of the place, as well as Detective Archer's connection to it. However pious and upright, Archer was no zealot—practical enough, evidently, to form a working arrangement with a highfalutin cathouse. They needed to speak with him.

Still, apart from their La Maison visits, nothing seemed to link any of these men. Least explicable was the lieutenant-colonel's tie to Peavey, a probable anti-Unionist. Truly would have Duke go through the counter-intelligence files for any mention of the latter fellow.

The two agents resumed strolling toward the hack, where Simon Hodge awaited them with stoical ease. "How's your leg?" Truly asked.

"Better," said Forbes. "The prayers of those good-hearted Jezebels working on me, no doubt. . . . So, what did you think of that doctor?"

"About the same as he thought of us. Stuffy bastard."

"And Mister Monroe?"

"For a man with rheumatism, he keeps a fine-looking garden. Wouldn't recommend him for an ambassadorship, though."

Hankering for tobacco, Truly still felt edgy as he got into the carriage. He pictured a busy night at La Maison, with its whole Napoleonic fetish. A crowd of preening oafs, each with a hand stuck in his vest, pining for some spirit-link with old Bonaparte.

Then, as the horses turned, he looked up. In the same second-story window as before, the curtains moved–and between them, he spied a slender, fair-haired young woman in a red dress. She was staring down at them.

16

M. Wakefield Photography Shop
West Third Street

WAKEFIELD STARED AT the framed print of a man with a hand tucked jauntily into his vest. It was one of dozens that he kept on display, testaments to his skill with lighting and texture. He forgot the subject's name and didn't care–just another flabby functionary who he had met at La Maison and offered to immortalize. Another self-styled gent who had perceived Wakefield not as a mere tradesman but as a respectable peer, a man of breeding and elegance. And that was fine. Since the autumn of '61, the pretense had provided Wakefield with his cover. And if a bawdy house could call itself a gentleman's club, a photographer could call himself a "learned professional" or some such thing.

But he had come to despise the fussy dignity of subjects like this one. It underscored the callow, more urgent dignity of the boy-soldiers who stopped here on their breathless way to the front, their uniforms unsmudged. Several of their pale, smooth faces gazed at him now from the walls. He wondered how many remained alive. Before his pity could spill over, an answer came: probably about as many, in proportion, as the boys he had grown up with near Savannah. Late last year, a smuggled letter from his sister had told of their cousin Albert's death at Chickamauga, plus that of two childhood friends from camp fever. And any day now, Sherman's horde would be battering the gates of Atlanta.

The thought of Atlanta spurred him back to his task. On the desk before him lay a single leather glove, a bayonet in a leather scabbard and an upended drawer. The drawer had a grid-patterned piece of paper stuck to its underside—an alphabetic cipher square. In his lap was a slip of foolscap with the ciphered message he had written. He re-checked the symbols, making sure that each was correct: DEFENSES THINNING–ALL WILL BE READY–WILL NOTIFY OF ANY CHANGE–TRIP TO FRONT ON 9TH GAVE NO NEWS. Noting the last item as flatly unnecessary, he crossed it out with his pen. Then it occurred to him why he had put it in. He had wanted to remind them that he was always trying, that he never missed a chance. Back in Richmond, did they still appreciate the man behind the messages? Improbable, he thought, given their grand-scale worries.

Dusk shadows were seeping in, the face-crowded walls dimming. He felt a jabbing pain in his head. Again he stared at that same portrait across the room, focusing like a morbid microscope upon the details—the double chin and the frown of self-regard; one hand gripping a lapel above the watch chain, the other thrust between the vest buttons. The pain in Wakefield's head worsened. Before he realized it, he was across the room and grabbing the picture, smashing it against the desk, stamping the face with his heel and grinding the glass.

In a moment, his breath settled. He slid the drawer back into the desk's bottom slot and lit his kerosene lamp. He got the old pair of lace-up boots from under the desk. Placing the left boot near the lamp, he bent the tongue outward to expose the underside. He pulled the glove onto his writing hand, then picked up the bayonet and unsheathed it.

Hunched over the desk and feeling efficient, he held the bayonet midway along its blade and began cutting into the back of the boot's tongue. His steady hand made him good at most close work. Ink would not have sufficed this time—what if the lad stepped in a creek? He glanced at the cipher by his elbow, matching the symbols as he transcribed them. With satisfaction he signed himself "V. Grayson," then blew the cuttings away. He put the blade down, removed his glove and read the message one last time. Deep inside him a hope ignited like kindling, though he tried to quash it. Much would have to go right before he could succumb to that hope.

He held the bayonet upright on its tip so that it caught the light. Twirling it by its braided brass handle, he admired the craftsmanship as he always had. As a boy he had dug the weapon out of an embankment west of town–French-made, his father told him, and a relic of the Revolution. He sheathed it and returned it to the middle drawer, along with the glove. As he did so, he noticed the edge of a yellow paper near the back. He snatched it out, already chastising himself. Inexcusably he had forgotten to destroy Cathcart's telegram, now ten days old. The text itself doubled his dismay, reminding him of the situation: N.Y. CITY 10 A.M. JUNE 2–GV ALERTS TRIP FAST–TELL THEM BE READY TO RECEIVE–HAVE GV LETTER–I ARRIVE DC TODAY. But Cathcart had arrived, evidently, into the waiting hands of federal agents.

Crumpling the telegram along with the cipher note, he took them out back and fed them to the potbelly stove before returning to his desk. His courier would be here soon. Through the open window he heard the clanging of a blacksmith, the barking of a dog. He thought about the two agents at Cold Harbor, the threat they represented. Again he wondered how the breach had occurred. Cathcart, in his limited yet important assignment, had committed only one indiscretion as far as Wakefield knew–showing up here drunk on the day after New Year's, with his equally drunk cousin. Since that lone incident, Cathcart had proven himself sturdy and dedicated. Now he probably lay in a dank cell at the Old Capitol, just a few blocks south of here. Wakefield sent him thoughts of comfort, gratified to be caring about another's welfare. But within seconds, the feeling gave way to colder reflection.

It was good that he had withheld from Cathcart the why-and-wherefore of his New York duties, and that Cathcart had been sensible enough not to press him about it. Even for a reliable, hand-picked subordinate, one had to avoid shedding too much light, given the possibility of his capture. Still, Cathcart knew Wakefield's identity as well as his address; if not for an apparent Yankee blunder, he would have led them straight here. Close–much too close. Now came the question of whether or not Cathcart's tongue would slip under interrogation. Or worse–whether he would actually break, despite his tough hide. For Cathcart there would be the added torment of confusion, the ignorance of all that Wakefield had never told him. Knowing only one small part of the scheme–his own part–he would lack the fuller sense of purpose that bred fortitude. Plus, the federals had that letter. How much did it jeopardize things? Wakefield would never know its exact contents, unless he somehow wormed it out of Underhill. Meanwhile, he would have to keep his eyes about him, be ready to vanish when necessary–no more lapses.

He got up, walked to the window and viewed the lamp-lit houses along the street. He pictured Savannah. Savannah, Georgia, with its lazy flowered verandas, the family home, his sister's face and the others he knew so well–whichever of them remained. Those were the faces he wanted, not these anonymous ones surrounding him–swollen pretenders, pathetic soldier-boys, this gallery of Yankee ghosts. Then he caught sight of his courier.

Whistling, unmistakable in his pork pie hat, George Otis was headed down the street's near side toward the shop. His stride had the spring of anticipation, and Wakefield felt the usual mix of scorn and gratitude. George, he knew, fancied every mission as a manly version of hide-and-seek. And for most, it seemed, this was what it took–the brainless, youthful zest for daring and secrecy. George turned left and disappeared down the alley. Wakefield hurried to the back door and admitted him.

"Hullo, Mister Wakefield."

"Evening, George." Wakefield secured the door. "How have you been faring?"

George drew a threadbare sleeve across his nose. "All right, sir."

"Things busy at the telegraph office?"

The youth gave a sheepish chuckle. "I slept late, Friday–too much rye, I reckon. The boss gave me an earful."

Wakefield eyed him. "Listen–don't lose that position, whatever you do. A runner's wages might be small, but having you there ensures I'll get any telegram quickly. I value that."

In the semi-darkness, the pimpled face semi-understood. "Yessir."

"Good lad. That said, I'm afraid you won't be getting any sleep tonight."

"I'm good for it, Mister Wakefield."

"That's the spirit!"

Back in the front room, Wakefield turned to see George looking at the shattered portrait on the floor.

"A little accident with that," said Wakefield. He motioned to the desk chair. "Take your shoes off and put those boots on. The message is cut into the tongue of the left one."

Sitting, George removed his cracked shoes and started pulling the boots on.

"Same livery stable as before," said Wakefield. "I've already paid for the horse. Just return it in good condition."

"I sure will. So is it Charles County again?"

"Yes, and the same farmhouse. Bring your shoes along, of course, and hand the boots over when you get there. Are you listening?"

"Yessir." Having pulled the boots on, George remained slumped, staring at them.

"What's the matter?" Wakefield demanded.

Taking his hat off, George looked up with a tense smirk. "I got me a problem."

"Out with it, then."

"A few days back, the provost guard come and talked to my mother– 'bout me and the draft. Lucky thing I weren't home. But it's lookin' like I gotter leave the city or pay a substitute. I don't wanna leave, sir, but where am I gonna get three-hundred dollars?"

Wakefield chewed his bottom lip. "I think I can help. We'll talk when you get back."

George grinned. "Thanks, Mister Wakefield! I don't like to ask."

"I'm glad you did. How do those fit?"

"Near enough. A little tight."

"All right. Up, now."

Getting to his feet, George put his hat back on and paused to look at the walls.

Wakefield was about to hurry him along. Then he realized that he did not want to find himself alone again so quickly. "Does photography interest you?"

"I always like lookin' at these pictures o' yours, sir."

"Let me show you something."

From the top drawer, Wakefield got the picture he had taken at Point Of Rocks some weeks ago, fitted with a brass frame. He held it near the lamp for George to see. The remnant of a pontoon bridge lay stark and half-submerged in the Potomac, with a little wooded peninsula in the background. But it was the portentous roll of the clouds that pleased Wakefield most.

"This was an experiment that turned out nicely," he said. "It was a day of weird light, with fast-moving clouds. The usual emulsion process would've been too slow to capture that sky–it would've left just a hazy white. So I double-printed, exposing one plate for the land part and adding similar clouds from an old negative."

George blinked, nodding. "Right clever." He nodded some more, then looked at the wall portraits. "So how much do these gents pay for a photograph?"

Wakefield laid the photograph on the desk and stared at it, his fingertips touching the ruined bridge. "Depends on the plate size," he said.

Though fairly high-born, Wakefield had resisted some of the harsher biases of his class, the view that its own men were like cut gems and the rest like crude wooden blocks. But looking at George, he saw a wooden block. He imagined driving an axe through it. Then, calming himself, he let the old rationale take hold: "On the same side, he's on the same side." No one knew better than he did how crucial that idea was, or how hideously far one could stretch it. George required no real stretch. George was nothing.

"You'd best get moving," Wakefield said.

With a smile, the South's young homing pigeon left on his adventure. Traveling the Secret Line, the boot would be passed from hand to hand and foot to foot and make Richmond by Tuesday.

Wakefield sat at his desk. In the lamp's flicker he pondered the barren beauty of his photograph—man's work and nature's, in concert with his own. He had been sitting there a good while when the hope began to glow once more, blooming like miracle whiskey and coursing through him. Those visions: the Confederate force moving out, perhaps at this very hour; the gray legion snaking its way north; the gray host descending on the forts of Washington—and waiting there, the Yankee lieutenant-colonel, primed for his colossal act of treason. Of this last element, Wakefield would make certain. The plan was his. If it succeeded, everything would have been worth it—the swallowed years, the loathing and the isolation. Even this madness, like a pecking crow in his brain.

17

West Eleventh Street

TRULY HAD TRIED writing his report for Baker but quickly given up, feeling restless. And despite his after-dinner drowse, despite every excuse for a quiet evening at home, he had taken this stroll through the darkening streets–an aimless stroll, at first, but no longer.

According to Duke, the police detective squad had its office above the Washington Gas-Light Company, along with the Board of Police Commissioners. Truly hoped to find someone working late, someone who could tell him what Detective Archer's usual hours were. Since this afternoon it had become his sharpest desire to meet Archer, this lawman who seemingly tempered principle with practicality.

Nearing the building, he noted two lit upper windows. He found the main entrance locked, then discovered a side door which opened into the hallway. He headed for a central stairwell where a faint light shone down. At the foot of the stairs he heard someone descending and paused. A tired-looking young man in a high collar appeared, carrying a ledger–a departmental clerk, Truly guessed. Truly asked the clerk if he might speak with a police detective.

The young man halted, peering down. "Your affiliation, please?"
"War Department."

The clerk's prematurely baggy eyes narrowed, his lips pressed tight. That legacy of territorial friction–here it was, even in a civic drudge. "Is there anyone up there to speak to?" Truly asked. The clerk huffed a sigh. Irritated, Truly started up the stairs.

"You should know, sir, that Detective Archer came here to work in peace."

Truly halted his ascent. "Archer . . . "

"The acting Chief of Detectives. Chief Clarvoe took ill last month, and Detective Archer temporarily assumed his duties. He is therefore quite busy."

"I'll bear that in mind. Excuse me."

The disgruntled clerk stepped aside as Truly shouldered past him.

Thus far, Truly noted, this case featured a high ratio of surprise. For each strange obstacle, there was a stroke of luck like this one. It was lucky as well, he decided, that he had come alone and not with Forbes. Two federal inquisitors would have looked like intimidation, doubling any resentment on Archer's part. He felt optimistic. Late hours and quiet settings, in his experience, yielded candor more often.

At the dim top landing he found a door with an engraved plaque that read, "Board of Commissioners, District of Columbia Metropolitan Police"–and below this, "DCMP Detective Corps." He removed his hat and knocked, but no one answered. Easing the door open, he peered into an equally dim room with a long table and high-backed chairs. On the far side was another door, ajar, past which he spied part of a desk. Atop the desk, a burning lamp illuminated a white-sleeved elbow.

A deep voice called. "Hello?"

"Detective Archer?"

"Yes?"

Truly crossed the room and stood in the office threshold. Behind the desk, a narrow-shouldered and slightly grayed man with a trim mustache looked up at him. The face was long and stolid, handsome except for a sunkenness around the steady hazel eyes.

"Detective, I hope you'll pardon the intrusion. I'm Major Nathan Truly, with the secret service of the War Department. I want to speak with you about a case." Truly showed him his credentials. "If you're too busy now, could I make an appointment?"

The long, lordly face evinced nothing. The hazel eyes deliberated, one hand toying with a pen above some documents. "Now is acceptable, so long as it's brief." Putting the pen down, Archer motioned to a corner chair. Truly moved it close to the desk and sat.

"The case involves a business establishment of an uncertain kind. La Maison de l'Empereur."

Archer glanced at the wall, then back at Truly. "Nothing uncertain about it, Major. It's a house of sin."

"Beneath the fancy trappings, yes. It has been doing business–unmolested, I'm told–since the mid-Fifties."

Nodding, Archer responded in a measured tone. "I've shut down a few such houses in my time and would gladly do the same to this one. But police resources are strained, so we must weigh and choose–pick our battles, as they say. And La Maison is unusual, given its style and location. It presents no real threat to public order. In fact, the old Frenchwoman who presides there has helped us on several occasions."

"Madam Ravenel. We've met."

"Then you know that she too is unusual. A clever woman, if not a godly one. With her aid, most recently, I arrested a forger at La Maison. We have a standing agreement that she'll alert me to any suspicious characters who turn up there."

"And in return . . . ?"

Archer's face grew subtly tighter, his gaze hardening. "Major–amid prevailing conditions, it is the judgment of the police that an exception be made for this house, whatever its specific trade. If you presume to question us . . . "

"No–no, sir." Truly held a hand up. "I do understand. In time of siege, we have to compromise. My own work demands that too."

The detective's features relaxed a bit. "Is this helpful to you, Major . . . Truford, is it?"

"Truly. Yes, it is helpful–but here's the nub of it. In the course of a government security probe, we've uncovered a certain small group of men associated with the house. I believe that you yourself met with three of these men on the 15th of April. At Brown's Hotel, it was, in the matter of a young lady's death by drowning . . ." Truly caught the slightest ripple along Archer's brow. "–a La Maison girl named Briona Kibby. You met them in the lodgings of Congressman Ezra Underhill, who was one of the three."

Archer remained impassive. "Yes. I'd met the congressman socially a few times."

"The other two men were a younger fellow named Jonathan Peavey and an unidentified lieutenant-colonel. The latter had been with Miss Kibby at the time of her misfortune. If you could tell me what you know about him, and about Peavey too, I'd be much obliged."

Archer sat back a little, looking thoughtful. "Normally, Major, professional standards would bar me from doing so. But, since you're a government man, and since you ask so decorously . . . "

Truly felt the twang in his gut. He had long since learned to beware any confidence bestowed as a gift, especially one wrapped in flattery.

"Until you spoke it just now, I had forgotten Peavey's name," Archer said. "The lieutenant-colonel's name, sorry to say, I cannot recall. But Peavey knew him somehow, and the congressman as well. The two of them came in distress to Underhill, who then summoned me. As an act of professional courtesy, and for the greater good, I agreed to handle the problem with discretion. The harlot was dead, clearly a suicide. I was told that the lieutenant-colonel came from a good family and had an admirable fighting record. He was distraught over the incident and over the prospect of it becoming public, along with his shameful activity. His remorse seemed genuine." Archer's voice had taken on something of an amiable roll. Truly eyed his hands, the fingers interlaced on the stack of documents. The knuckles were white.

Maintaining an easy manner, Truly leaned toward him. "That's just how I understood it. Still, I'm thinking of the tie between these men. It's unlikely enough–a Democratic congressman, a planter whelp and a Union officer–and we suspect that it's illicit too. Before your arrival at Brown's, a discussion was overheard between them . . . "

"You've spoken to Gilchrist." The statement was flat, the tone brittle. Archer's suddenly frigid stare drilled the wall behind Truly's shoulder, and Truly knew that the slippery verbal waltz was ended. "Major–Patrolman Gilchrist is a sick man who should have been retired sooner. His illness has worked strangely on him. It has caused him flights of fancy. I know of no such overheard discussion–and if one did occur, I would disdain to hear it repeated. How this could possibly concern you, I cannot guess." Rising, Archer's voice grew more constricted. "It was a grave lapse on Gilchrist's part to have uttered a word about this, let alone to have eavesdropped on a United States congressman! Were he not dying, were he still on the force, I would take the severest measures . . . !"

"Sir! Detective, I . . . " Mindful of what action might still be taken against Gilchrist, Truly produced a quick lie. "The conversation was overheard by one of the hotel staff who I interrogated–not by any policeman."

Archer said nothing. His gaze drew back from the wall and turned upon Truly, probing like a scalpel. His ears were red, his hands clenched on the desktop. For all Truly's care, he had struck the same nerve that he had struck in Underhill. And he had made a new enemy–Washington's interim Chief of Detectives.

"You imply having only a minor acquaintance with Underhill," Truly said. "But it seems more than that–enough for him to summon you instantly. You–the one policeman best able to handle things, who had regular dealings with La Maison."

"Major Truly," Archer intoned. "I have work to do here."

Truly met his glower. "One last thing. Do you know a horse's ass by the name of Gideon Van Gilder?"

Archer's long face went taut. He replied in a parched whisper. "No. I do not. Get out."

"He's dead, sir–and a bad end it was. He tried to flee, but they tracked him down. So counting yourself, the total of men mixed up in this business is down to four."

In their hollows, the detective's eyes appeared frozen.

Truly patted his hat on. "If you won't tell us about it, one of the others surely will. Think on it, Detective. We'd do everything in our power to protect you. Good night."

Truly got up and left.

Outside, a mist had crawled off the Potomac, muffling the street lamps. Truly headed slowly homeward. From somewhere neither close nor very far came the baying of a dog. Truly halted, gazing into the whitish-blue halo of a street lamp. He recalled what his Uncle Jacob had said many years ago, in a rare moment of sobriety. Old Jake, knowing whereof he spoke, had compared lies to a blood trail and truth to a relentless hound–"Once it get yer scent, it don't give rest." Truly stood there until the howling ceased.

PART III

Portrait Of A Young Squire

The Southern Peopel are rebels to government but they are White and God never intended a nigger to put White People Down.
• SGT. ENOCH T. BAKER, PENNSYLVANIA

Our Union friends Says the[y] are not fighting to free the negroes. We are fighting for the union and free navigation of the Mississippi River. very well let the white fight for what the[y] want and we negroes fight for what we want . . . liberty must take the day nothing shorter.
• ANONYMOUS BLACK SOLDIER, LOUISIANA

A war undertaken and brazenly carried on for the perpetual enslavement of colored men, calls logically and loudly for colored men to suppress it.
• FREDERICK DOUGLASS

The people of the loyal states . . . will not supply men and treasure to prosecute a war in the interest of the black race.
• NEW YORK WORLD, 1864

18

Prince Georges County, Maryland
June 13

A VIEW OF HIS tobacco fields could still make Jonathan Peavey swell with pride. Standing on the rear veranda, he could still picture himself as the planter lord he had always aspired to be. Taking in the leafy, loamy acreage, he could pretend there was no war, no Lincoln, no relentless pull to strip away his birthright. He could imagine that he was headed for a record harvest at top price. He could fantasize that slavery was safe in Maryland and that the laboring backs out there were black ones. Then one of the laborers would stand up to rub his sweaty, aching, white back, and everything was spoiled.

Peavey's eyes narrowed upon the figure, another local rube who he had been forced to hire for pay. And like nausea, it all came back to him: Emancipation, that word too ugly for speech; his best and then his lesser slaves gone, fled by night. Months ago he had dismissed the overseer because there was nothing left to oversee.

Peavey sank into the cushioned chair and stared down the length of his walking stick. Was a birthright too much to ask for? By definition, should it even require one's asking? He looked over the veranda's side and into the woodlot, where another sweaty rube was wielding an axe. Then his gaze shifted to Cato–gnarled, clay-brown, white-bearded Cato, listing to one side. Gathering a few chunks of wood, the slave took them unsteadily to the pile and stacked them, then repeated the process. Reaffirmed as a man of property, if only somewhat, Peavey settled inside. Then Cato dropped one of the pine wedges. He went on a few doddering steps, then made a listing reversal and bent low. As he fumbled for the wedge, two more tumbled from the crook of his arm.

Cato and his black jug of a wife–they were the only ones left. And though Lincoln's repulsive decree had freed only those chattels within the Confederacy, the November ballot would include a state amendment to kill, at last, the institution that Peavey had built his dreams upon. He was crippled with debt. Resorting to paid white labor, he had been unable to maintain a large enough field crew. Planting had stretched too far into the spring, and this would force the harvest well into autumn. Neighboring planters, he knew, were laughing at him over their brandies. Once he would have wept with rage; nowadays he gathered his rage into a roiling ball and set it aside for later. Later would come soon enough. For now, his accounts ledger awaited him in the study, like a box with a coiled snake inside. Slouched, stunned with despair, he let his gaze drift across the fields to the tobacco barns and beyond, to the sparse woods and the muddy Patuxent River.

Then, behind him, he heard the French doors open and the soft, careful voice of Lottie. "Young Master–two gentlemens here to see you."

Closing his eyes, Peavey kept still a moment longer before rising slowly. Then he whirled, flinging the walking stick at the stout, kerchiefed Negress between the doors. She shut them as it struck and cracked a glass panel. He charged the doors and burst into the back hall, where Lottie stood staring at him. Oddly she did not cringe this time. More wary than fearful, her eyes stoked his fury.

"Never!" he shouted. "Never, ever more call me 'Young Master!' It is simply 'Master' now! It has been 'Master' for two and a half years! Do you hear me?" He stalked toward her. "Do you hear?!"

"I do, Master," she said, backing away. "Master it is. Master I will call you."

Halting his advance, he straightened up. He dismissed Lottie with a slicing motion and then proceeded to the parlor. Entering, he stopped short and beheld his two visitors.

"Hello, Young Master." On the settee, Underhill regarded him with a strange, eager expression. "Your face is red. Embarrassment, perhaps?"

In the wing chair sat Archer in his bowler and light jacket, his badge glinting underneath. He did not raise his eyes.

Peavey drew himself to full height. "Why are you here?"

Underhill let out a skewed laugh, almost a giggle. "We enjoy the country air."

Ogling the congressman, Peavey saw that his face was stubbled and his eyes puffy. The tight, lipless smile seemed to mock and seethe equally.

"Gentlemen would stand," Peavey intoned.

"Pardon us," said Underhill. "We heard no trumpets."

"What is the meaning . . . ?!"

"My dear Peavey—you may hear this seated or standing. But do listen. We have come in connection with the one matter that binds us all."

Peavey felt a quiver in his stomach. He looked at Archer, as motionless as a waxwork. "What more could there be?" Peavey demanded.

"Not two months ago," said Underhill, "you happened upon a set of wondrous new facts, or so you called them, which seemed to put a fresh light on our situation. What a day that was—eh, Peavey? With all your grand talk of liberation, our resolve to act in brotherly concert? Except, your facts were not factual."

"But . . . What do you mean?!" Peavey thrust a finger at Archer. "He confirmed it! You confirmed it, Archer!"

The policeman contemplated his shoes. "I did, as well as my eyes and ears could manage. Still, it was you who initiated things. You."

"It wasn't just me!"

"If you're referring to our esteemed lieutenant-colonel," said Underhill, "we met with him before coming here and found him useless. Seems he's been addled ever since that day, mourning his little Irish trollop. An addled mind counts for nothing."

Peavey sneered through his agitation. "You seemed willing enough at the time. It was as much your plan as anyone's."

"And who, young sir, inspired me so? But let us not argue. United we blundered, albeit at your urging, and united we must save our skins. So keep your mouth shut, laddie, and hear some less-than-wondrous new facts. A few days ago, two federal agents caught up with me on a visit to the front. Just how they had become involved with this I don't know. The important thing is that they showed me a letter from Van Gilder, filched from a friend of his but intended for me. In general terms it indicated that you were much, much in error and that Van Gilder had taken flight. Van Gilder begged me to try and make amends."

Peavey's pulse was racing. "Couldn't we track him down? Make him explain?"

Underhill wheezed a laugh. "Alas, my high-born friend, Gideon would find speech difficult–being cut up, as it was described to me, into several pieces."

Momentarily Peavey's breath stopped, his knees trembling.

"I was asked to supply information," said Underhill, "and duly refused. Last night, however, Mister Archer here paid me a call. He said that one of those same agents had just visited and questioned him–and had told him, also, of Van Gilder's sad end."

Peavey eased himself into the rocking chair.

At last Archer looked up, fixing a cold eye on Peavey. "The agent's name is Truly. Should he or anyone approach you, say nothing. Don't try to weave a tale or even to deny their accusations–just say nothing. Above all, don't succumb to threats. If they go so far as to arrest you, the congressman and I will get you released forthwith. It's in our interest as much as yours."

Peavey felt faint. Blinking, he fixed upon a white marble cherub across the room, perched on its pedestal. With its placid blank-eyed stare, the statuette seemed to taunt him, even as Underhill's tone of merriment petered out.

"You fool," muttered the congressman. "You damned stupid ass."

Peavey gaped at him. "What can we do?"

"Yes–what can we do?" Sitting up, Underhill placed a hand on each knee. "Archer and I discussed that on our way here. And considering your particular role in this, we had an idea."

19

Willard's Hotel, Washington

IN THE SMOKE and babble of the great dining hall, Truly found Forbes enduring one of Duke's flutter-handed orations, this one on the subject of ironclad vessel design. Truly sat and explained his lateness; apart from working on his report to Baker, there had been the duty of receiving Reverand Cass, who was taking Sapphira for a carriage ride.

Forbes looked relieved. "Manfred should be along soon. He said he was going to roam about and see the sights."

"Sights? That should be short work. Well, I have a new development to relate, but I'll hold it till he gets here."

"I have news of my own," Duke said, sitting up. "It happens that one of my upstairs neighbors is secretary to a congressional committee. Just a nodding acquaintance, but I approached him about the Underhill matter. I hope you will excuse my posing as someone higher in the organization than I actually am."

"Excuse it?" said Truly. "Heck, I'd say it shows promise."

Duke gave his pie-scallop smile. "Well, once I'd convinced this fellow of my patriotic intent, he took me to Wyman's Oyster House and introduced me to three fellow clerks. None of them knew Horace Ives, who evidently keeps to himself. But it turns out that Ives had a predecessor–Jepson was his name–who one of them had known slightly. What's more, I was told there's an old, unsubstantiated tale about Underhill which stems from the First Battle of Bull Run. An ignominious day, as you'll recall–not just for our forces, but for the civilian spectators."

"Who could forget?" said Truly. "Panic and chaos. Carriages over-turned, picnic dinners left to rot, politicians and society grandees leading the retreat. So our boy Ezra was part of that?"

"It seems he was, but the rest of it's murkier. To begin with, though . . . Few congressmen see fit to hire secretaries—no public funds are allocated for it. Yet Underhill, who's reportedly neither the richest nor the busiest of them, insists on having one. He's said to be a hard taskmaster, the kind who needs someone close by for frequent abuse."

Jepson often griped about Underhill, the clerk said—and it came as no surprise when, shortly after First Bull Run, he was sacked. The details sur-rounding this were queer, however. While in his cups, Jepson told of how he had accompanied Underhill in his carriage to view the battle—and that in the rout that followed, Underhill had committed some dishonorable act. Jepson would not say what it was. He would only leer unpleasantly and state that, if what he witnessed ever came out, "that damned pygmy could not find work as a manure hauler."

Jepson's listeners were skeptical—liquor and recrimination could twist facts, after all. But there was another odd point. Jepson seemed exhila-rated, not bitter over his loss of employment. He made no apparent effort to find a new position, yet did not lack for money. Then, in late '61, Duke's contact heard another strange thing. Jepson had approached a Rhode Island representative, asking where a certain regiment from that state was encamped. He was vague about why, and it was unknown whether he got the information. But shortly after this—the contact placed it in November—Jepson was found dead behind a gambling hell, his skull crushed and his money taken. Those who had known him were shocked but thought it a predictable end. They never heard of an arrest being made. Duke had yet to inquire with the police, but it was doubtful that they had any worthy record of the killing. The department had been in a disorganized state then, having been formed just recently to replace the old Auxiliary Guard.

"My next step will be to find Ives," Duke said, "and try my luck with him. Now, on to the next thing . . . " With a flourish, he drew a leather pouch from under his chair. "Here, slim though it may be, is the dossier on Jonathan Peavey."

Truly smiled. Few clerks had ever boasted such a productive day and a half.

"I found it in a special section," said Duke. "Early in '63, we began trad-ing intelligence with the office of the Baltimore provost marshal. Their detective squad had been quite active in the first year of the war, owing to the turmoil in that city. As a result, they had more information than we on Rebel sympathizers in eastern Maryland."

"Hold on a bit," said Forbes. "Here's Manfred."

Truly turned to see the hunchback wading carefully through the noise and bustle. He carried four slopping mugs of beer, two in each hand. In his black bowler and oversized gray suit, he looked more refined than usual, though diners still eyed him as he passed.

Truly pulled a chair out and called to him. "Decided to chance Willard's beer, did you?"

"Ach! I do not expect it to be so good as in the old country." Smiling, Kirschenbaum set the dripping mugs down and took his seat. "But I am inspired. I have seen now the Capitol Dome with the great statue of Armed Freedom."

"It's impressive, all right," said Truly. "As opposed to what goes on beneath it."

He hastened to introduce Duke, who rose for a mutually eager hand-shake. At Truly's beckoning, a harried black waiter came over. Truly ordered fried oysters, Forbes the shad, the other two the roast duck. Distributing the beer, Kirschenbaum sampled his own and gave a shrug. Forbes, he said, had been keeping him astride of events.

Duke resumed his presentation. From the pouch he took a thin, dog-eared sheaf of paper and looked through it. "Peavey came under scrutiny at the start of the war, when he was briefly jailed. He'd taken some minor part in the anti-Union disturbances."

Truly cocked his head. "A gentleman planter rioting? Alongside the plug-uglies and assorted riffraff?"

"No such direct involvement, Major—just a lot of loud, intemperate statements about the President. Plus he was observed jeering federal troops at the rail depot. Under martial law, that was enough to get him arrested, especially since he came from a prominent slaveholding family."

Thumbing through the pages, Duke stopped to look one over, then delivered a quick synopsis of Peavey's life. He had been born in 1838. His father had founded a Baltimore shipping firm and later a tobacco-growing estate in Prince Georges County. Peavey's older brother Ira, regarded as the family's great hope, was marked to inherit the company but died of typhus. The idea of Jonathan heading the firm was unthinkable, given his abrasiveness and lack of aptitude. In despair the senior Peavey sold the company and retired to his estate, dying soon after his wife's death in 1859. The will gave stewardship of the estate to an uncle of Peavey's, Solon, who had been managing it well for some time. Actual ownership would transfer to Jonathan three years hence, when he turned twenty-four–"in the hope that this period will serve to better develop his mind and character." Solon, meanwhile, would see to Jonathan's "conduct and instruction" and accord him a modest allowance. He would also have full say in the disposition of the house, land and slaves. And even after the three-year period, he could choose to stay on as manager-for-life, with ample compensation. Jonathan could never discharge him.

Truly took a long sip of beer. "And how did our young squire take to all that?"

"Kicking and cursing," Duke said. "By all accounts, relations between uncle and nephew were strained, and the arrangement seemed designed to worsen them. Plus, there was Solon's lukewarm attitude toward slavery. Jonathan, as a youth, had paid an extended visit to some South Carolina kin who lived in grand plantation style. It appears he became enraptured with that life and that it shaped what aspirations he had. But getting back to his contretemps in Baltimore . . . " Duke flipped to an earlier page. "In jail, his secessionist ardor vanished. He reportedly wept at night, to the amusement of the guards, and was released upon taking the loyalty oath."

Forbes smirked. "So much for plantation manhood."

The food arrived and Truly ordered another round of beer.

Putting the papers away, Duke stuffed a napkin into his collar. "Solon Peavey reacted with anger to his nephew's recklessness in Baltimore. He worried that the government's retaliation might not end there, that it might seize the family property. With an eye to that, and to Maryland's political drift, he spoke openly of manumitting the slaves and using free labor. What Jonathan thought of that, with his twenty-fourth birthday looming, we can well imagine." Duke began carving his duck. "That's the bulk of our Peavey knowledge, but the most intriguing part remains."

Truly looked down at his oysters. "Is Solon Peavey dead?"

Chewing, Duke blinked up. "Why, yes."

"An easy guess. Please go on."

Interest in Jonathan Peavey as a security risk seemed to end there, Duke said, but revived a year and a half later. In the fraught days between the Union's defeat at Second Bull Run and the South's bloody reverse at Antietam, the authorities had sought to counter the jump in enemy spy activity. Lists were distributed. Agents of Pinkerton's organization, as well as Baker's and the Baltimore provost marshal, fanned out over eastern Maryland to arrest or monitor as many suspects as possible. It was a Baker man who investigated Peavey—who, as it turned out, was indeed lord of the manor now. And free of his Uncle Solon.

Solon was a vital man despite his years, and liked to take a sailboat out for relaxation. In January of '62, not long before Jonathan's ascendancy, debris from Solon's boat was found near the mouth of the Patuxent, and the body washed up soon after. The family lawyer assumed oversight of the property until Jonathan's birthday. How the boat sank or capsized was anyone's guess—but from Jonathan's standpoint, his uncle had died not a day too soon. Solon had in fact decided to free the slaves and would have signed the papers before the month was out.

Apart from this, the agent's report revealed nothing of significance. In early September, Peavey received a party of pro-secesh gentlemen, former state legislators. They were seeking funds from planters to help agitate against martial law—but in Peavey's case, they came away disappointed. Ownership had apparently given him a more practical turn of mind, and now it was he who feared government confiscation—not to mention imprisonment—should he involve himself in anything subversive.

"Once again—all talk, no action," said Forbes. "A parlor Rebel."

Duke glanced at another page. "He had two other visits in that period. One from a photographer, who came to take his portrait, and the other from a man who went on to some notoriety—Gaston Saint-Felix."

"The gunrunner?" said Truly.

"The same—although at the time, he was just a colorful rogue-about-town, an amusing fixture in pro-Confederate circles. Peavey met him at some social event and enjoyed his seafaring tales. At the estate, they passed the evening in generous quantities of rum."

Forbes sent a questioning look, which Truly answered. "Saint-Felix is a French subject, an adventurer and former slaveship captain. He was captured a few months back while trying to run the blockade. Confined to Fort McHenry, I think." Truly wiped his lips and sat back, his appetite fading. Something was coming together—an ugly geometry of facts, like the pattern on an insect's belly.

Kirschenbaum eyed Truly's plate. "Major, could I maybe try one of your oysters?" Abstracted, Truly dumped his plate's contents onto the German's. The waiter brought their replenished mugs.

"And now to my own news," said Truly. "Octavius—what, if anything, do you know about Police Detective Quentin Archer?"

"A few things. The latest is that he's acting Chief of Detectives, Chief Clarvoe being ill."

"So I have heard."

"If Clarvoe doesn't return soon, it's likely that Archer will succeed him. He has a sterling reputation. He's a widower and a church deacon. That's really all, Major—I've never met him."

"Well, I did. Last night." Truly swigged his beer, then spent ten minutes relating the encounter. "It wasn't just his reaction to Van Gilder's name at the end. Thinking back on it, I'm struck by how he hopped right to La Maison's defense—its immunity to the law, his expedient tie with the place. It seems to me that Archer the Preacher is more Archer the Pragmatist—but there's something more going on. He conceded only what I told him we knew, or what we might have easily found out. Beyond that, everything he said was meant to soften and excuse. He's smart enough. And for all his reputation, I believe he's Strange Bedfellow Number Five."

"Let's say he is, then," said Forbes. "Again it begs the question—what points in common do these men have, aside from the La Maison connection?" Spreading his hand on the table, he drew in his thumb and pinkie. "We know that at least three of them—Van Gilder, Underhill and Peavey—had human obstacles removed from their lives. Violently and mysteriously."

"Right," said Truly. "And all in a period of a few months—late '61, early '62—after which their stars-of-fortune either rose or, having threatened to fall, did not fall. So what about the other two men in the group? Did they have suspicious turns of luck? If we could confirm as much, we'd be close to discovering what this extortive pact is all about."

Duke began to gesticulate, almost knocking his beer over. "I've been thinking too—Van Gilder's letter mentioned payments. In both licit and illicit transactions, payments are made according to a schedule, and Van Gilder's trips to Washington followed a strict quarterly schedule. Might their true purpose have been to pay the keepers?"

"Good thought," said Forbes. "He was due for another such trip at the end of May, but failed to go. That would make sense if Octavius is right about this, and if the rebellion amounted to a collective payment stoppage. It wasn't until the first of June that Van Gilder learned things had gone awry–too late, we may surmise, for him to rush down and pay his regular tribute."

Nodding, Truly rubbed his mustache. "Sometime this week I hope to receive materials from Van Gilder's home and office, courtesy of our Lieutenant Heatherton. If these include a personal business ledger, we might find a pattern of quarterly payment that will match Van Gilder's trips down here. In light of that, though, there's something else to think about." He tapped the table with his finger. "On each of his Washington outings, where did Van Gilder go? La Maison–the one place to which these other men are undeniably linked. So maybe it wasn't randiness that brought him there. Up till now I've thought the place had little more than a circumstantial role. Now I'm thinking that the extortion scheme might in fact be based there."

Downing the last of his beer, Forbes stared at his half-eaten shad. "You think Ravenel and company are at the bottom of it?"

"They're an improbable crew, I admit, especially when you consider the fear and murder involved. An ailing old woman, a snooty doctor and a bad-tempered galoot of a groundskeeper. Still, if they aren't at the bottom of it, I'd wager they know who is."

Forbes looked up. "You know, Nate, I've been mulling over our session with them–that girl Fannie, in particular. For one who had lost a close friend, and under those circumstances, didn't she seem . . . ?"

"A shade too wooden? Yes. Rehearsed, until my impatience got her nervous. But now that I think of it, *all* of their responses were something like Archer's–confirming what we clearly knew or could readily find out, but vague on the rest. A whole danged litany of what they didn't know, hadn't seen or couldn't remember, with plenty of dull excuses thrown in."

Before Truly could stop him, Kirschenbaum hailed the waiter for a third round of beer. Truly tried to recall if he had offered to pay for everyone. Once more he regretted not helping himself to Van Gilder's funds.

"Incidentally," Forbes said, "–we'll soon be getting our long-awaited cell time with Adam Cathcart. I took the liberty of stopping at the departmental telegraph office, and a wire said he'd just boarded a Washington-bound train from Albany, escorted by two District marshals. They'll be depositing him at the Old Capitol."

"Finally!" Truly said. "He'll be here in two or three days, then. Meanwhile, tomorrow morning, you and I should take a ride out to Prince Georges County."

"To call on Jonathan Peavey?"

"Oh, yes. So far we've met a wall of obfuscation, but Peavey sounds like a weak section of that wall. We'll lean on him good and hard—I'm frankly tired of playing delicate with these vermin. We'll give him a lively description of Van Gilder's corpse. We'll threaten prison and property seizure. We'll magnify what we've uncovered and hint that we know more. Whereupon, judging from what we've heard about him, he should crumble like pie crust." Truly accepted his final beer. "We might learn any number of things—not least, how Adam Cathcart fits into the scheme. What's the Confederacy's interest here? That, gentlemen, is the hundred-dollar question." He turned to Duke. "Apart from contacting Horace Ives, see if you can fish up any scuttlebutt on Archer—quietly, of course. The police have no great fondness for our organization—yourself excepted—and I'm afraid I did more damage last night."

Duke burped. "Pardon me. Yes, Major—I'll tread lightly."

Shifting in his seat, Kirschenbaum looked forlorn. "I wish I as well could be of use. More than to merely eat your oysters."

Truly patted his forearm. "You will be, Manfred. That's a promise."

Flushed, Duke offered a toast to Union victory, happily seconded by Kirschenbaum. Forbes looked embarrassed. Truly sighed. "Victory, yes. May God share our every conviction." He clinked mugs with Kirschenbaum, then pulled out his watch.

The afternoon was half flown but the dining hall far from empty. Merchants, politicians and high functionaries sat rumbling, chortling, while the waiters collected what dishes and spittoons they could. Waiters and servants aside, the capital was not known for industriousness. Truly tucked the watch away. "Well, all this means another rewrite of my report. But I will finish the danged thing." Again he sighed. "Meanwhile it's back to the tribulations of fatherhood. Annie . . . er, Anna is going to Grover's Playhouse tonight with Lieutenant Chadwick, and she insists I be there to receive him. Naturally, I'd rather receive a boot to my backside."

Having already drained his mug, Forbes fixed a gloomy gaze upon it.

"So, Major," said Kirschenbaum, "you have a daughter besides?"

The question, as always, made Truly hesitate before answering. "There are two young ladies who call me 'Father.' Anna is the one born of my late wife and me. Sapphira was orphaned when she was small, and we took her in."

"Ah, then—how happy for Miss Sapphira. A fine deed, Major."

"Well . . . It gave fine results. She's a good girl."

Duke suddenly recalled a bit of news. That morning he had run into a former colleague, now a clerk to the Assistant Secretary of War. The man had whispered that Grant was on the move again. Behind their specs, Duke's green eyes betrayed a degree of tipsiness as he leaned in, though he remembered to lower his voice. "The Second Corps is headed toward the James, while the Eighteenth is moving to rejoin the Tenth on the Appomattox. River ferries are standing by, engineers laying pontoons. It looks like another massive flanking maneuver, southward."

"Toward Petersburg," Forbes said.

Truly took a last tepid swig. "Richmond's chief rail hub," he muttered. "Makes sense."

In a few days, the military censors would ease up and the whirlwind of rumor would settle. Truly pictured Sapphira reading about it in the newspaper, Annie hearing about it from her pampered beau. Then there would be new fears not to talk about, horrors-in-progress to busily avoid at supper.

The bill arrived in the waiter's brisk hand. Taking it, Truly looked at it without seeing.

20

North H Street

FOR THE LAST few blocks to the house, neither of them spoke. Albion Cass maneuvered the gig's horse with care, keeping his eyes straight ahead. In Sapphira's mind, their conversation resonated amid the hoof-and-wheel noise–a cyclical echo, round and round. Her reply to his somber, courteous question: a blizzard of caveats, qualifications and regrets, all of which sounded unbearably foolish now. She felt leaden, even with the weight of his hopes lifted from her.

The house came in sight but she felt no relief. "Mister Cass," she spoke. "If any gentleman were to ask the same of me, I would have to answer in the same way. I am only sorry that it is you and not just any gentleman who I've pained so."

Cass eased them to a stop by the front door. Laying the reins in his lap, he looked at her. His lean hickory face projected a strength that would likely carry him well past his fifty-odd years. He spoke softly, without strain. "Miss Sapphira–I would prefer that you spare yourself and simply forgive my imposition. That is all. I am quite gratified to know you as I do." Stepping down, he removed his hat and walked around to her side. He offered his hand but then lowered it as she failed to stir.

Staring between the horse's ears, she felt a sting of fondness for the minister, but hard upon it came the questions that had been deviling her sleep: Would she always feel this way–constricted yet adrift? Unseen yet conspicuous? Fearful of breaking rules, yet eerily close to indifference? Like a demon swarm, these questions seemed to have hatched all at once within her–pounding by night, bumping around blindly by day. "Were things even a bit more just," she said, "the woman before you would reply 'yes' with gratitude. And she would be a woman of worthier spirit."

"Of more settled spirit, perhaps," he said, "but not worthier. Never that."

Wishing that she could stop talking and get out, she kept talking and stayed put. "My life's design is muddled lately, and I am trying to fashion something out of it. Out of the muddle." Like a sneeze, the statement had launched itself before she could stop it. Her face grew hot.

"Consider that the design is less yours to fashion," he said, "and more yours to see." He touched her hand. "In time. With heaven's help."

On the pulpit and sometimes face-to-face, Cass had often sounded ponderous to her. Now he did not. His deep tones cloaked and calmed her as well as any voice could have done. Yet this moment would presently end. He would depart, she would go inside and nothing would change. Tonight in bed, the pounding would resume inside her.

Cass took his hand away. "I suppose your worries over Ben are no help. Just keep praying."

Sighing, she nodded. "The Major disapproves of my going to the Sixth Street Wharf. Still I went there yesterday, after church, and watched the wounded come in. There is no end to it."

Kneading the brim of his hat, Cass looked down at it. Then Sapphira proffered her hand and he took it, helping her into the sunlight.

"There is something more," she said, facing him. "Over time, I've told my stories to audiences of kind strangers. Next month I will do so again, when we go up to Philadelphia. Abolition folk will greet me and attend my every word."

"Naturally they will," he said. "Your story illuminates our mission–that is why I have encouraged you. In you, people see the fruition of every hope since the movement began."

She had to avert her eyes. "Fruition," she thought–could that really be what they saw? She had an urge to run inside. She wanted to go to the piano and pound out a sonata until the strings broke.

"This is the heart of what I am telling you, Mister Cass. I speak, they listen. Women weep and men turn grim, but at the end they smile and applaud. And afterward, some ungenerous thoughts come to me–thoughts which I cannot help. I wonder if they fancy me a character from Mrs. Stowe's novel, a figure of tragic romance. And it's then that I begin to doubt my own story, as if it has all been a shameful masquerade. Or, at least, that I've embroidered the retelling."

Cass squinted at her. "It is the essence that matters, Miss Sapphira. Or so it seems to me. You remember the essential part of it, do you not?"

"In bits and pieces, I do. Like something I might have dreamed. I was only five or six years old, by the Major's guess. My telling of it is based on what Mother Rachel told me, but she was not there to see it. Only the Major and I were there, and he has always been reticent."

"But surely the Major would tell you anew, given that it bothers you so."

Thinking, she placed a finger to her lip. In the same moment, she saw the parlor curtain move and Annie peer out at them. Sapphira looked away. "I did ask him not long ago. He looked startled and then told me such a thin version of it, I couldn't really match it with my own recollections. Then he said that he had work to do. It is as if the memory calls up other memories, things that he would sooner let lie. If so, I don't wish to disturb them."

Cass drew a sleeve across his glistening brow. Poor man, she thought–after such an excursion, to be compelled to stand here in the hot sun, burdened with her rambling. "For some months after my wife's passing," he said, "I spoke little and could barely listen to anyone, even as I tried to tend my congregation. But God did not desert me. He led me slowly out of mourning. I know nothing of what faith the Major may have, only that he has mourned a long while. Still I believe that time will salve his grief. And the moment will come, perhaps soon, when he will hear your wish and give a full account of your first meeting." Cass smiled a little. "A meeting which brought you safely here, to the friends you have."

Sapphira tried to smile back. "Of whom you are surely the best."

Looking down, he put his hat on. "I thank you for your company today." Climbing back into the gig, he noticed the folded piece of paper on the seat. "Your note for Mrs. Sackville," he said, handing it down to her. "I hope it will help."

"Oh–thank you! I will see her tomorrow."

He hesitated before taking up the reins. "She is a capable woman, though not a mild one."

"I would not ask for mildness. I only want to be useful."

"As do we all, Miss Sapphira."

He tipped his hat and they said good-bye. Then he drove off.

Inside, Sapphira placed the note on the hallway stand. As she untied her bonnet, Annie came hurrying downstairs with a quizzical look. Annie's dress was her plainest one, a beige calico, but she could still have turned any male head. On the streets, it often happened. Glimpsing her golden-haired figure in the crowd, marching soldiers would fall out of step. Businessmen would suspend conversation to watch her pass. Market vendors stammered in her presence. Errand boys blushed, while the occasional rough street boy threw a kiss, always from a safe distance.

Her robin's-egg eyes blinked at Sapphira. "At last. I thought you'd be out there till sundown."

"People have conversations sometimes."

"Lieutenant Chadwick will be here in less than an hour. I need you to help me with my corset."

Sapphira hung her bonnet and light shawl. "Was there mail for me?"

"Come on." Annie started back upstairs. "Dennis is punctual. I wish Father was too."

"Did I get a letter from Ben?"

"You can read it later . . . Sapphira!"

But Sapphira was already in the parlor. There on the mantel she found an envelope which bore the looped handwriting she always hoped for. It felt thick in her fingers. She thought of opening it but decided not to–she would read it once Annie was gone. Looking up at Mother Rachel's photograph, she saw that its guardian marigolds had begun to wilt. She made a mental note to replace them. Her gaze hovered on the image of Mother Rachel, the woman who had hummed her to sleep. So this was what it came down to, she thought. In death's wake, survivors gradually settled for the crude solace of pictures, which in time became something more. More, yet never adequate. Though the face in this picture fit no storied idea of beauty, it somehow suggested the beautiful voice that had gone with it. Such a voice–soft as a feather duster, pure as prairie sky.

From upstairs came the thumping of Annie's displeasure. Soon, Lieutenant Dennis Chadwick, the breezy banker's son with the bad arm, good looks and wispy mustache, would appear in full uniform at the front door. Eyes evasive, he would hand Sapphira his cap and announce that he was here for Miss Ah-na. How had his golden-haired belle explained Sapphira to him? What tale had she fashioned for his comfort?

Taking the letter, Sapphira went up to Annie's room and found her standing there in her chemise. Vexation had turned her cheeks a startling pink, as it always did. Pinching the envelope, Sapphira crossed her arms and looked at the bed, where a satin magenta dress lay full-length. She eyed the corset beside the dress and felt a certain queasiness, reminded of a child's ribcage.

"Are you going to help me?!" Annie demanded.

Sapphira stared past her to the gilt-framed mirror, an expensive birthday gift from Chadwick. Seen from the back, tilted, Annie could have been one of those gowned, flaxen-haired dolls that little rich girls carried, trailing after their parents into Willard's or the National.

Sapphira generally avoided fights with Annie. The last one, some months ago, had ended when Annie charged her with failing to appreciate her good fortune. "People always said you looked like Mother," Sapphira murmured. "They still do, don't they?"

The flush left Annie's face, though the glare remained. "Is that so unexpected?"

"Usually I don't see it, but last night I did. I couldn't sleep, so I got up and wandered about. Then I looked in on you–I'm not sure why. There was moonlight on your face, and I tried to recall what it was like to sleep like you, so peacefully. And I saw it–the resemblance. Just for a moment I did."

Annie's hard look had faded, replaced with a vague apprehension. "I am sorry you're not sleeping well. Now, will you help me with this?"

Laying the envelope on the bureau, Sapphira went to get the corset. "Face the mirror, Annie."

21

Peavey Estate

PEAVEY HAD ONCE overheard old Cato talking to a fellow slave, a young male. Hushed but emphatic, Cato claimed to have heard a moaning from the bedchamber of Peavey's long-dead brother Ira. "As the Lord's my witness, that's what I heared! This whole house be fulla sumpin' wicked, like a drunkard fulla rye! Soon, I 'spect Master Solon's drown' spirit be trampin' these halls o-night!" Later that same day, Peavey had flown into a rage over something–a missing glove, maybe, or ashes tracked on the carpet–and brought his walking stick down on Cato's skull, leaving the slave more addled than before. Then he had ordered Ira's room boarded up.

The house always had its share of creaks and less definable noises; combined with the memory of Cato's words, they served to hamper Peavey's sleep. On several recent nights, he had jerked awake and listened for the sound of his uncle's wet trudge in the darkness. But tonight he was not listening for that, or for Ira's death-moans. Drunk but still trembling, propped against the pillows, he did not know what he might hear. Outside, the night was one of warm zephyrs off the Patuxent, rustling the trees and banging a loose shutter somewhere.

His father's hunting musket lay beside him on the bed. He touched its cool barrel. In the lamplight he eyed the door while the tree-rustle filled his ears, the shutter banging like a fist. A creak began in a large rafter and then telegraphed elsewhere, like pain through aging bones. Upon his inheritance, Peavey had ordered the hound kennels relocated nearer the river, where the baying and whining would not disturb him. Now he regretted the move. He should at least have had a dog or two brought into the house tonight, despite his distaste for them.

He reached down beside the bed and brought up the half-empty bottle of sour mash. Taking a swallow, he felt the warmth blossom inside him. He thought of the two successive young women, daughters of local landowners, who had spurned his efforts at courting, citing not just his treatment of slaves but a whole range of conduct. In the latter case he had narrowly avoided a duel with the girl's brother. Though he did not miss either girl's company in the usual sense, he wondered what difference it might have made to have a warm body beside him. But another chug of liquor quelled this reflection. The bottle and the musket were companionship enough. Suddenly the outdoor sounds were wind sounds and nothing more, the creaking a mere noise. The doors to the house were barred. Any intruder skilled enough to get in would receive a musket ball for his trouble and join Cato's ghosts. The force of this resolve sapped the last of Peavey's will to stay awake. His head drooped.

He awoke in discomfort to find that he had rolled on top of the musket. He drew himself upright. On the nightstand, the lamp burned low. Eyes darting in the gloom, he noted that the wind had risen, producing a complex hiss through the trees. Then, with a shiver, he realized how urgent his bladder was. He got out of bed, cursing as he knocked over the sour mash bottle. Grabbing it, he placed it aside and started looking for the chamber pot. Then he remembered that he had smashed it, along with several other things, in his rampage following Archer's and Underhill's visit.

Unmoving, he sat on the side of the bed. Years ago he had heard that the mansions of New York and Philadelphia boasted indoor privies; one of his first commands, therefore, had been to have the house and the master privy connected by an enclosed passageway, with access from the study. He had envisioned finer touches–marble tiles, glazed-wood wainscoting–but the project had gone no further. Now, though spared from having to go outside, he trembled at the prospect of going downstairs. At length he got up and took a candle and holder from a bureau drawer. Lighting the candle's wick from the lamp's, he took up the heavy musket but then hesitated, looking from the door to the window. He listened to the gusting and hissing outside, the wayward shutter, the groan of the house timbers. Setting the candle down, he sat with the weapon across his lap. He could do it out the window, he thought–piss out into the wind and darkness.

Tears boiled in his eyes. Had it really come to this, that he was barred from his own privy? Through the thickness in his head, another thought resounded: he was lord and master of this house, not its prisoner. After another swig of sour mash, he rose boldly if unsteadily to his feet.

He unlatched the door and opened it. With the candleholder in his left hand, he balanced the musket barrel across his forearm and wedged the stock beneath his right armpit. He hooked his finger into the trigger guard. Creeping into the dark hallway, he peered twice in both directions. Then he began to sidle along the wall. Wobbly with alcohol but sweaty with fear, he strained to keep the candle and the weapon steady, stopping twice more to check the shadows behind him. He came upon the fragments of the dashed chamber pot and edged carefully around them. The wallpaper, with its red castle motif, passed within the fluttery light until, at last, he spied a stair post. Tremulously he started down, the stairs creaking beneath his bare soles. The wider darkness of the front hall enveloped him, echoing each step. His shoulders quaked. Halting, he leaned on the banister and listened hard. He heard the wind and his own pulse but nothing more. "Lord and master," he thought, resuming his descent.

At the foot of the stairs he swayed to a stop and shone the candle back and forth, high and low. As its glow swept the floor, he glimpsed a pale object and crouched for a closer look. A pair of blank white eyes met his stare. Flinching, he sucked his breath in and almost dropped the musket, but then he recognized the marble cherub's head. His heart settled somewhat. For an instant he regretted smashing the sculpture, one more familiar thing. Certain that he had ordered the chunks disposed of, he vowed to thrash Cato. He moved on, only to strike his toe on something hard. Tottering, he yelped a curse. The holder nearly slipped from his fingers but he caught it, the candlelight reeling. On the floor in front of him he identified the angel's broken pedestal. He would hurl it at Cato's head.

His toe throbbed but his bladder throbbed worse and drew him on through the darkness, toward the rear of the house. From the walls, portraits of colonial ancestors frowned in judgment. He hurried past them and crept into the study. Shining the candle side to side, he moved around his desk to the passageway door. He leaned the musket against the desk. Though sobering up, he felt his nerve quiver to life as he turned the doorknob and pulled. Relief was at hand. He took up the weapon and proceeded down the narrow passage, mice skittering before him. Along its plank length, the corridor shuddered as the wind mounted once more, whistling between the cracks, fluttering the candle's flame and the hem of his nightshirt. He picked up his step.

Reaching the privy door, he opened it with a quick, clumsy motion. It made a whimpering sound. Inside, he propped the musket in a corner, set the candle on the stand and stepped to the commode. The room's smallness comforted him. Gratefully relieving himself, he tried to let the rest of his tension drain out, along with Archer's scorn, Underhill's contempt, Cato's ghosts and the curse of ties formed in desperation. "Lord and master," he thought. For all that was rightfully his, he had suffered enough.

Finished, he reached for the musket. It was not there. The candlelight flickered on the empty corner. For a still moment he was merely befuddled, as if he had misplaced his walking stick, but then the realization squeezed his heart. With nauseating force it squeezed him and he could not move, could not turn and face the presence behind him. His skin froze. Large, cool fingers gripped the back of his neck and dug deep, pulling him slowly backward. Limp and quivering, his arms seemed to know how useless it was. To the moan of the wind outside, a moan arose in his throat, thinning to a cry as the grip tightened. His legs gave out. He found himself seated on the commode, growing faint with the hand's iron pressure. Abruptly it let go and seized a fistful of his hair, twisting it out from the scalp. Only then did the predator hulk in front of him, blocking what dim vision he had. He felt his hair about to be torn from its roots. His breath came in gasps. Above him the black shape towered, motionless, broad-shouldered in the fluttery light. Then the hand released his hair. The big silent shape moved back slightly, bringing up the musket. Through twitching lips, Peavey let out a higher, thinner cry, cut short as the muzzle entered his mouth. He felt teeth breaking. All he had ever wanted was his birthright.

22

La Maison De l'Empereur
June 14

Shirtless, Wakefield sat on the side of the bed. Sunlight spilled in through the window, refracting as in Bible pictures. Everything looked and smelled pure, enough to make him momentarily forget where he was. Behind him, Delia McGuire stirred, and he looked over his shoulder. She let out a low, peaceful sigh. Her tumble of honey-colored hair obscured all but her lips, which smiled a bit. He rested a hand on her slumbering leg, warm beneath the sheet. Watching her was like watching the sunlight. It was better.

Too soon their respective curses would take hold and pull them apart. The day would begin its descent–from soft light to bright light, bright to harsh and harsh to sullen, and on to nightfall. The two of them would commence that long steep slide, back into gutter business. The very fact which repeatedly separated them seemed to constitute their deepest link: they were both captive to something. Captives, forced to endure that daily downward slide, she for survival's sake and he for the Southern cause. Once he had thought that belief and sacrifice in a transcendent cause exalted the believer. Yet there were times when he felt no more exalted than this homeless, rudderless Irish girl. And there were times when she seemed altogether better than him, stubbornly lovely within her bondage.

But for the moment, he felt joined and equal to her, and the foulness of night felt distant. Even as he cursed this house, he blessed this one small room, this quiet room with soft lemon light spilling in. His hand moved up Delia's leg, along the rise of her hip and the dip of her ribs, to her shoulder. He touched her hair. She rolled gently over, taking his hand in hers. Without opening her eyes, she bestowed her waking smile upon him.

"Hello," she murmured.

"Good morning." He took his gaze away but not his hand. On the chair across from him, their clothes–her folded red dress, his wrinkled white shirt draped over it–seemed in the act of commingling.

"What were you dreaming?" he asked.

She yawned. "I've forgotten already."

He looked as her eyes blinked open, foggy blue.

"You know," she lilted, "I used to be afraid of you."

Rubbing an eye, he yawned. "I suppose I should ask why?"

"Oh . . . There was the way you stood apart. The way you watched people. And you spoke so seldom–like a gentleman when you did, but seldom. I still know but little of you, really." She squeezed his fingers. "You arrived so late last night."

He lay back on the bed as she slid her legs up. He felt the day's first slippage, its first inching toward the precipice. He accepted it. "It's a beautiful morning, my dear."

Her fingers relaxed their grip and he turned toward her. Unsmiling, she eyed the wall.

"A beautiful morning," he repeated. "Why spoil it with questions?"

"I only care that you came," she said, "–not what you were doing before."

"What's the matter, then?"

"Fannie O' Shea is in Madam's favor. She's been gloating about it, smiling at me like the landlord's cat."

"Fannie is a stupid girl."

"Maybe so. But Sunday, when those two men came here, Ursula ordered me to my room and summoned Fannie. Then I heard Ursula whispering to her in the hall, and it was something about Briona–I'm sure of it. Since then, Fannie acts as if she knows something. She hints at it just to torment me."

Caught in the falling sensation, Wakefield shut his eyes. Slide, skid, bump, smash–down and down. He withdrew his hand from Delia's.

"It has been two months, Miles, and no one has told me anything. In April when that Detective Archer came to tell Madam of Briona's death, he never spoke to me, never asked me what I knew. I wailed to Madam about it, but she only slapped me."

"Yes. I remember you saying."

"She said the lieutenant-colonel would be found and punished but to keep my mouth shut. No more questions, she said."

"Listen, Delia . . . "

"Madam had told Briona she was safe from that beast–that he was banned from here. But he walked in freely that day, to drag Briona off and . . ." Her voice clenched and quavered. With a rustle of linen, she sat up and stared at Wakefield. "The other girls talk of Briona drowning herself in the river–and that's when I want to claw their eyes out. Briona still carried a rosary! No matter how frightened or miserable she was, she would never have chosen an excommunicant's grave!"

Wakefield sat up. He beheld her small, peach-soft breasts, the line of her collarbone. They invited his lips again. At the same time he wanted to buy her a white dress, to dress her in white and take her portrait.

"Miles," she said, imploring, "–if you know anything . . . "

"You'd better lower your voice."

She glared at the window. When she spoke again, her tone simmered. "I loved her like a sister–and you said you would help me if you could. But are you with the others? Are you guarding something, just as they are?"

"Is that why you lie with me, Delia? To press your suspicions?"

With a sudden look of hurt, she leaned forward on her hands. "No, Miles."

He reached out and stroked her arm, wishing. He yearned to release it all–what he had done and planned and come to know, the ugly and the momentous. If Delia proved strong enough to hear it–if she could hear it and still hold him close–then something deeper would connect them at last. Something more than captivity, or the refuge of ecstasy, or this damned house. Then he could make promises to her. But since he could tell her nothing, he spoke the one promise he could make without an accompanying lie.

"Delia, listen. I vow to you on my life that the man will pay for what he did to Briona. In ways he never imagined, he will pay–and soon."

Her gaze measured him. Again she took his hand. "You know more than you are willing to say. But that is all right, Miles, as long as the man is punished. Thank you." Kissing his hand, she lay back and covered herself.

Wakefield looked at the clothes-draped chair. Today, once back in the city, he would send another telegram inquiring about the gold shipment. Then he would ride out to see his operative in Rockville, to alert him that his services might soon be needed. It would be best to stay there overnight and avoid the cavalry patrols, but on his way back he could stop here and see Delia.

"I can't come tonight," he told her. "Tomorrow night, though . . . "

From outside he heard the hoofbeats of a single rider, which then ceased out front. He got up and brushed the window curtain aside. Below, the man was hitching his mount to a post.

"Come lie down," Delia said. "Just a little longer. Would you, please?"

Wakefield stepped to one side, peering down as the visitor started up the walkway. It was Archer, his face grim and worn. Wakefield felt a rush of excitement.

Abruptly he shut the feeling out and turned to Delia, who was sitting up again. "How could you be here?" he muttered.

Frowning, she looked away. "Someday soon, I hope to be gone from this place forever. But what else was I to do, once I found myself here?"

He shook his head. "That's not how I meant it. Not at all."

Distantly Wakefield heard the doorbell's jangle, Ursula treading downstairs to answer it.

"I love listening to you," said Delia. "The way you speak."

"If this were Georgia, I'd sound like everybody else."

"No, I don't believe you would."

Wakefield went to lie with his Irish girl a bit longer.

23

Prince Georges County

AT THE MENTION of Peavey's name, the farmer scowled. "After nearly all his niggers run off, two o' my nephews hired on for field hands–but that didn't last long. They had the devil's own time gettin' paid, like the son-of-a-bitch was out to replace black slaves with white!" He spat on the ground. "If you two gents be creditors, here's some advice: Don't haggle with him. Just hang him by his heels, then shake him like a possum in a hurricane!"

They had three miles to go, he said, and pointed the way. From there the muddy road took them along the Patuxent, which glittered through the trees across the meadow. The day was warm and they slowed their horses to a trot. Conversation had been slight for most of the way, but now a small miracle was taking place. In a veritable geyser of self-revelation, Forbes was talking about a Boston girl named Judith.

"You were betrothed?" Truly asked.

"No, but everyone assumed we eventually would be. Poor Judith. She's a fine girl, pretty and sincere. Our families have known each other for a generation. They all wanted it and so did she. I thought I did too."

"And then you were wounded?"

Forbes mulled, squinting toward the river. "My near and dear date the change from then, but to me it seems to have started sooner. In any case, after Antietam I was sent home to convalesce. Of course I got a reception fit for Ivanhoe, and Judith was the most attentive of all. Then Gerald's body arrived home. They wanted me to deliver the eulogy but I wouldn't. I didn't want any glittering pile of words, especially from my own mouth. I wanted to lay my hands on Gerald's stone and say absolutely nothing. My happy brother, the one true rascal among us—now a departed saint. And at the time, it seemed to me they preferred him that way. As a saint, casting light on all their holy convictions. On themselves."

Truly listened intently. This was only the second time that he had ever heard Forbes mention his brother, spared at Antietam only to fall at Fredericksburg.

"Then there was New Year's Eve, '62," Forbes went on. "Emancipation Eve. They had a celebration at Boston Music Hall. I hadn't yet been fitted with a false leg, so I was on crutches. Judith and I sat in the balcony, listened to the hymns and awaited midnight, along with every prominent Abolitionist, both white and colored. In spite of my pall over Gerald, it really was a glorious night. But as I was introduced to this personage or that, the suspicion crept back into me. These strangers . . . They'd look at where my leg should have been and shake my hand—and from the look on their faces, I couldn't help thinking they felt some mutually ennobling tie between us. They approved of me, they approved of themselves. They thought they understood. And it hit me that maybe just once, they should see a man's body explode in front of them. But there was Judith beaming up at me, her maimed champion—and I thought no, how could I ever wish a thing like that on her? I loved her in a distant sort of way, but I saw then that the distance was too great. For all intents, we inhabited different spheres. Do I make sense?"

"More than I've heard in some time." It was fortunate, Truly thought, that nineteen-year-old Annie had never returned Forbes' look of muted longing. Somehow his partner had missed one of the more obvious facts about Annie—how completely she inhabited that sphere of stagy romance and self-gratifying innocence. A well-lit world, wherein brave paladins charged the gates of Hell while their lady beloveds wept and prayed and basked. However unlikely Dennis Chadwick seemed for such a role, he was at least eager to play it—his safe duty with the Veteran Reserves notwithstanding.

They were rounding a bend. On both sides of the muddy track, meadow blended into tobacco field. Up ahead, a two-horse wagon appeared, bumping toward them.

Truly wanted to give Forbes a worthy response—to assure him that in lives and families and nations, wars had a way of ending. Still, he wondered if he could summon the conviction. He watched the wagon's approach. Behind the hunched driver, several bobbing heads with straw hats were visible. As he and Forbes steered their horses out of the way, he looked at the driver and nodded to him. The greeting went unacknowledged. At first, the man's knotted expression appeared to be one of anger. Then, from the shadow of his hat-brim, the eyes emerged and Truly saw fright. He saw it also on the faces of those huddled in back–a half-dozen white youths in rough country garb.

With the wagon past them, the agents looked at each other.

"Not used to strangers?" Forbes said.

"They looked like they had a plague on their heels," said Truly. "Field hands, by the look of them–headed away from the fields, with hours of daylight yet."

Across the whole leafy expanse astride the road, not one toiling or idle worker could be seen. An apple orchard blocked their view to the right, but when it ended they saw a side road running toward an assemblage of sycamores not far from the river. In the trees' shade stood a large gabled house with a red tile roof. Truly's ears caught the raw-throated baying of dogs. Twin masonry pillars guarded the side road entrance, and as Truly and Forbes passed between them, several hounds converged baying and barking from across the fields.

Forbes drew his Colt Navy, inserted a percussion cap and fired into the air. Scattering, the dogs yelped away or snuffled nervously along the tobacco rows. They looked thin and scruffy.

"Slaves gone," said Truly, steadying his horse. "Field hands gone. Dogs worse for wear. Yes, Master Jonathan's fortunes have ebbed some."

They kept on toward the shaded manor. Gradually the dogs recovered their courage and resumed barking. As the pair passed under the sycamore boughs, a white-whiskered old Negro lurched into view and stood squinting at them, listing to one side. He wore a patched shirt and patched baggy jeans, well faded. His half-raised hands feebly clenched and unclenched, as if squeezing cow-teats.

"It just came to me," Truly muttered, "–it's no wonder Peavey favors the St. Charles when he visits Washington."

"How's that?" said Forbes.

"It probably brings fond memories. In its heyday the St. Charles made a point of catering to slaveholders. I'm told that its basement has cells where the property used to be chained up during the master's stay. God knows what they use the cells for now, but you can bet the management didn't cheer Emancipation."

With a hazy gap-toothed smile, the bent old slave watched them come.

"I think I'm going to enjoy meeting Peavey," Forbes said.

"Possum in a hurricane," said Truly.

They came to a weedy oval of grass in front of the house and reined up. The house looked regal despite its withered vines, shuttered windows and blotchy gray stone.

Truly called to the old black man. "Would Mister Peavey be home?"

Smiling, the slave fidgeted. He spoke with a deep rasp, as if through straw in a mason jar. "Ain't seen him, sir. You . . . You gentlemens here to work the fields?"

They dismounted. "The fields?" said Truly. "No—my back's not fit for that, these days. Where might we find the master?"

"Reckon he in there, sir." The gnarled hands kept working, squeezing the invisible teats. "The foreman . . . he go inside lookin' for Master Jonathan and then he run out. He and his boys, sir—they all skeedaddle. And the hounds, they ain't mindin' me a-tall. Can't find nothin' to feed 'em, so they runnin' all about. Young Master, he gonna be cross."

Truly frowned. "Is anybody else here?"

"Lottie, sir—she my wife. She in there."

Forbes hitched their mounts to the veranda. Turning to the slave, he produced a fifty-cent shinplaster from his billfold. "Our horses are thirsty. If you'd water them . . . "

The old man hesitated and then took the bill with a quivery hand, squinting at it until Forbes repeated the request. "Yessir. Mighty fine."

As the slave hobbled away, the agents mounted the veranda steps. Carved above the door's tarnished knocker, a triangular crest featured a winged "P" at its center. Truly knocked. After a fourth unanswered knock, he gave Forbes a glance and turned the knob. He nudged the door open and they stepped inside.

In the gloom they looked toward the staircase, at the foot of which lay a small marble pedestal, chipped and broken. They looked into the parlor. There beside a swaying rocker stood a stout old Negress in an apron and kerchief. Her stare burned with fright or wonder—Truly could not tell which. In her hands she held a roundish white object.

"Hello," Truly said. "You would be Lottie?"

Her curtsy was more like a flinch.

"We . . . " Truly eyed the object clutched in her hands. It was a chunk of statuary—a cherub's head.

"I'll start looking," Forbes muttered. He lumbered off.

Locking eyes with the woman, Truly summoned a gentler tone. "Miss Lottie?"

"Yessir," she said, barely above a whisper.

"Where's the master?"

She blinked at him. Her lips parted but made no sound.

SHUFFLING PAST THE musty rooms and austere portraits, Forbes paid scant attention. He entered a sparse yet spacious kitchen. A few bread-pans full of risen dough sat abandoned by the stove. After parting the curtains for light, he rested against the counter. He would have to start over, look around more thoroughly. Down the length of his poplar leg, however, the throbbing had commenced. He folded his arms and hoped it would pass quickly, but once more he felt disappointed in himself. And even now, with a slavemonger to find and throttle, the memory of his latest bad dream flashed.

In his and Gerald's boyhood bedroom, he had lain listening to a gentle but persistent rapping sound. The sound came from behind the closet door. Pulling off the bedclothes, he discovered with only mild surprise that his leg was back, unscathed. He rose as the rapping continued. He crossed the room, opened the closet and found Gerald there, seated against the wall. Frail and hollow-eyed, his brother smiled up at him, cradling a log-like object. "You lost something," Gerald said. He held up the thing–not a log but an amputated leg, Forbes' own. Looking down at himself, Forbes saw the dripping red stump of his thigh. He started to fall.

Jolted awake at that point, he had kept still a long while, listening to the pre-dawn quiet of the capital. Then he had drawn the blanket aside to look, to accept once more.

But now the memory faded as he thought of Peavey. His gaze drifted out of the kitchen and into the rear hall, where it fixed upon a vertical crack of daylight. He moved toward it and found the back door slightly open, its wooden bar on the floor to one side. One of the bar sockets was damaged, partially pried from the inner frame. Farther to his left, Forbes noted a set of French doors secured with a bolt and chain, one glass panel badly cracked. He stepped through the damaged door and found himself on a small veranda, beyond which several more acres of tobacco sloped away toward a pair of barns and the wooded riverbank. A row of dilapidated slave sheds stood near the field's edge. He looked past the French doors, past a cushioned chair and over the side railing, where a small woodlot opened. Past this, he spied the decrepit old slave drawing water from a well, a few hounds yipping and panting around him. Forbes turned to face the door through which he had passed– the servants' entrance, he figured. At his feet he noticed fresh splinters. Then, midway up the frame, he saw a small but deep notch, newly carved. It was neat and careful work, the product of patience, after which the intruder could easily have stuck his implement inside and jimmied the bar.

Forbes retraced his route through the house. Past the dining room he came to another doorway on his right and peered inside. It was a study. Under the portrait of some other Peavey forefather stood a large desk, bare except for a ledger, a lamp and an inkstand. To the right of the desk, between two bookcases, he beheld a half-open door. The darkness beyond it appeared too deep for closet space. He was sweating. Doors, he thought–damned doors to God-knew-what. Again the image of Gerald and the proffered leg flashed, and he had to shake his head to get rid of it. By the lamp he found a box of matches. He lit the lamp and carried it to the mysterious threshold, where the glow revealed a narrow passageway. About a dozen paces in length, it led to yet another half-open door, this one of cheap unvarnished plank. He ducked into the passage and creaked his way along. Standing before the plank door, he gripped its handle and tried to wish the dream away. Then he stepped through.

The lamplight touched four plank walls and a pitched ceiling. From above, a small window framed a largely shaded part of the outdoors, admitting the faintest degree of sun. Flies buzzed, and outside he heard the hounds barking. A foul odor betrayed the little chamber's function, and his pulse began to settle. Then a sick underlying smell reached his nostrils. Holding the lamp out, he somehow knew that he would not be giving Peavey the possum treatment–and in the next instant, he was staring at a blood-spattered pair of feet. In front of them and at an angle stood the stock of a musket, the barrel running up past the seated figure's blood-soaked nightshirt, past the dead hands that clutched it and ending at what had been a human face. The jaw was gone, the shredded cheek and tongue dangling like seaweed. Gobbets of brain and a white skull fragment clung to the long matted hair. Forbes stumbled back but caught himself as his foot grazed the stock, causing him to glance down and note one more detail: two pale toes jammed into the trigger guard, clumsily substituting for a finger. Keeping its grip on the weapon, the corpse toppled sideways.

24

Central Washington

Dear Mrs. Sackville
I send this note to recommend its worthy bearer,
Miss Sapphira Truly. Of soundest character and dedicated
to the advancement of her race, Miss Truly has done
considerable volunteer work at the "contraband" hospital.
She is deeply appreciative of your service to colored
troops and will prove useful, I believe, in whatever way
you see fit to employ her.

> Your fellow servant in Christ,
> Rev. Albion Cass, Church of the Holy Kingdom

STANDING ON WEST Thirteenth Street, Sapphira refolded the note and looked up. Before her, the mud-colored Church of the Redemption sat squeezed between two drab boarding houses. Its doors were propped open, though the street noise blocked any sound from its dim interior. On both sides of the entrance, benches lay stacked and covered with loose canvas. New England transplants made up most of the congregation. Cass had described even the children as standing quietly during services, accepting not only the lack of seating but the cramped presence of bedridden Negro soldiers. From the pulpit, he said, Ethel Sackville's minister brother had declared this a very mild atonement for individual sins and for those of the world, slavery in particular.

Despite the reported valor of Negro troops at Fort Wagner, Port Hudson and elsewhere, skepticism about their mettle persisted. Still, inevitably, Grant's current offensive had drawn upon their ranks, yielding casualties through illness, accident and a couple of honest battles. These having swamped the two colored hospitals at Alexandria, Mrs. Sackville had forthwith converted her brother's church to accommodate the excess. The widowed New Hampshire matron had lost one son in the Peninsular campaign and another last month in the Wilderness.

Pinching the note, Sapphira gathered her shawl and proceeded to the steps. She thought about Ben's letter. She tried to picture him at her side or somewhere close, silently encouraging. But Ben was in fact some hundred miles due south, facing uncertainties far greater than any this grim little church could hold. Scolding herself, she went up the steps and entered.

In the gloom of the narthex, a yellow cloth banner hung above the inner threshold. She expected it to say, "The Lord is my Shepherd . . . " or something similar—but as her vision adjusted, its jagged black lettering proclaimed, "Do not suppose that I have come to bring peace on earth. I do not come to bring peace, but a sword. Matthew 10:34." Passing beneath the banner, she entered the nave as a stench reached her nose, worse than at the Contraband Hospital. Before her, to both sides, sick and wounded men lay on cots and mattresses, narrowly spaced. Despite the bright day outside, the windows allowed only a dull light augmented by candles. A half-dozen Negro women in black dresses and aprons tended the patients.

Up near the stark altar, one nurse cautiously changed the dressing on a patient's ribs, supervised by a straight-backed white woman whose dress seemed blackest of all. The nurse flinched as the man let out a moan, gripping the sides of his mattress. In a clipped yet earnest voice, the white woman spoke—"Twill be done in a moment, soldier." And then, to the stooped nurse—"Don't stop, Hattie." As the nurse drew another length of roll bandage, Sapphira glimpsed the red, glistening edge of the wound. Mrs. Sackville folded her arms and turned slightly, inspecting. She had a strong jaw and a long nose, her silver hair tied in a bun.

With a will Sapphira inhaled the odor. She watched the nurses bend and bustle—one collecting food bowls, another bathing a supine torso, another ladling water to dry lips. The one with the stack of bowls noticed her and then approached.

"You here to visit, Miss?"

"No, ma'am. I've come to see Mrs. Sackville."

The kindly-faced woman seemed to hesitate before nodding. "I'll tell her."

As the nurse turned away, a nearby patient started coughing. Sapphira watched him shake, wheeze and spit, hanging over the edge of his cot. He appeared younger than she, possibly in his teens. As he rolled onto his back, his large shiny eyes caught sight of her and seemed startled for a second, then shy. He smiled weakly. Sapphira smiled back, then looked up to see Mrs. Sackville advancing upon her. In the widow's expression, something apart from sternness made her twitch inside. It was something that she had seen or imagined on the faces of other female strangers, both white and colored–a nameless suspicion. And as the pale, straight-backed woman drew near, Sapphira saw this suspicion harden into an eerie certitude.

"Yes?" came the clipped voice.

Sapphira gave a late curtsy and offered the note. "If you please, Mrs. Sackville–this is from Reverend Cass."

With raw-looking fingers Mrs. Sackville plucked the note, unfolded it and began reading. Sapphira noticed the stricken boy-soldier gazing at her. She wanted to bring him water, to ask him his name and where his home was. Then she felt something pressed into her palm. Wincing, she saw that it was the note.

Mrs. Sackville's clear blue eyes drilled into her. "Worthy, are you?"

"No, ma'am–it's Truly . . . " To her mortification, Sapphira realized that it was not her name being queried but Cass's adjective. "I'm . . . I beg your pardon, ma'am. What I mean is, the Reverend is too kind. I can only hope that his word will prove accurate." Daring to look up again, she found the clear blue stare no softer.

"Why are you not still at the Contraband Hospital? There are many mothers and children there to tend."

"I've helped there as needed, ma'am. But a new group of Quaker women arrived some days ago to help the staff."

"And the Negro military hospitals in Alexandria–why not there?"

"Simply because I live closer to this place, ma'am, and could be more at your disposal. Also, I heard that your needs are greater."

Mrs. Sackville's jaw tightened. "We do have needs, Miss. There are more men in tents out back. We maintain order and cleanliness only with greatest effort, and provisions from the Sanitary Commission are few. We get the leftovers. Yes, needs we have."

Meeting her inquisitor's look, Sapphira felt suddenly hopeful. She was being tested for nerve, she thought–for humility.

"Still, better that our needful state go on than we enlist the help of fanciful young Negresses. And to be frank . . . " Here the widow paused, though surely not for loss of words.

Gaping at her, Sapphira wondered what being "frank" might mean to such a woman. "I am not fanciful!" she blurted. "I . . . I have a brother at the front!"

"To be frank," Mrs. Sackville continued, "in the presence of men, of the flesh–in the presence of sin, Miss–we prefer that our nurses be plain. Good-day."

With an abrupt turn, she headed back up the aisle. Sapphira watched the crow-black dress move away, halt and then turn to face her again.

"Please thank the good Reverend Cass," said the widow. "But tell him that he is under some misapprehension. What you see here is not the object of our service. Mortal flesh is but a shadow–has Mr. Cass forgotten that? It is God alone we serve."

Distantly Sapphira felt her hand crumple the note. There was no anger yet, nor even shame–only a strange buzzing sensation on her skin. Stooped beside another soldier's cot, the nurse to whom she had spoken sent a furtive glance that said, "Sorry, child, but you see how it is." As she turned to leave, Sapphira heard another coughing fit and spied the drawn-faced boy. With a final hack, he gazed at her and looked sad. She lowered her eyes and did not raise them until she was back out in the sunlight.

She had never asked herself why even on hot days she wore a shawl. Whatever the reason, she was glad for it now, grateful that she could pull it close and not feel completely naked. Only after she had wandered for several blocks did the buzzing sensation quit. And with each corner turned, she felt Mrs. Sackville's eyes in pursuit, clear blue and stabbing after her. Quickening her step, she did not look directly at the people she passed, though their glances stung like nettles. She turned onto a fashionable street and was relieved to find it deserted, its wrought-iron porches enveloped in dreamy heat waves. Washington's more comfortable families had begun their migration to hill resorts and summer homes north of the city, escaping its sultry languor. Feeling dizzy, she leaned against a lamppost. It was hot but she rested her full weight against it, letting the metal burn. Vaguely she wanted it to burn something out of her. Through the street's empty glare, Mrs. Sackville's eyes penetrated once more, seeing into her. "Leave me," Sapphira muttered. Righting herself, she let go of the post and drifted on.

Some distance down Tenth Street she paused in front of Ford's Theatre, with its arched entranceways and splendid new facade. A large glass-protected playbill advertised the season finale, "The Three Guardsmen" by Alexandre Dumas the Elder. Whenever Annie returned from an evening here with Lieutenant Chadwick, she would report her sightings of famous people in the audience, including the Lincolns. Father had also seen a few plays here, whose plots he had described at Sapphira's entreaty. Though she had read most of his Shakespeare collection, her own exposure to the stage was almost nil. When she was about fifteen, in a converted Chicago barn, she had watched a visiting troupe perform scenes from *Uncle Tom's Cabin* and ended up blubbering on someone's shoulder. Some of the more rancorous preachers, she knew, decried plays as insidious things, man-focused and therefore diabolical. Mrs. Sackville was in all likelihood no playgoer. But Sapphira faced a different kind of injunction, less easily ignored. It had nothing to do with her soul, everything to do with her color. But, standing there, she wondered what it might be like to defy law and custom and every other threat–to pass through these doors, to take a high box seat and watch a drama or comedy unfold on the stage below.

Abruptly the buzzing resumed on her skin. With it came the pounding inside, so insistent that it sent her hurrying to the corner of D Street, short of breath. As if to expel one fear with another, she started thinking of Ben. Sixth Street was not far. She could follow it straight down to the dock, where a new boatload of casualties would soon arrive. Stuck in place, she deliberated until all she felt was the heat. She needed to go home. But turning around, she spied something that halted her again–a large black-painted sign. "J.W. MORSE EMBALMING," it said, and in smaller lettering underneath, "Reverence With Scientific Care." It ran the upper length of a one-story whitewashed structure near the corner opposite. Though she noted the Stars 'n' Stripes draped in one window, it was the sign that filled her vision: "EMBALMING." Quietly she spoke the word–so full and final-sounding, like a cannon. She was late to acknowledge the clattering noise coming toward her. In confusion she looked to her right, then stumbled back as a cavalry troop passed at a near-gallop.

She continued walking. At Pennsylvania Avenue she stood motionless again, stunned before the busy spectacle. In the midst of it, on the opposite side, she spotted an elegant white couple strolling arm-in-arm. The lady's pink parasol caught her gaze and held it, a pretty beacon that gradually shrank and then vanished, dissolved in a sea of plainer things. Sapphira thought about the quality of plainness. In the mysterious realm of courting, it was rated a disadvantage. But otherwise, people mentioned it fondly, as they would anything that was familiar, useful and worthy. It occurred to her that the faces she had most loved and trusted were plain ones. On one occasion she had glimpsed the President in a passing barouche and instantly liked his face, as plain as tallow. Concealing nothing, plainness reassured. All else was suspect.

Back in Illinois, a neighbor's servant boy had once told her that she was pretty, and it had filled her with bashful delight. Though she had since grown to mistrust such compliments, it was clear that her face held something other than plainness–enough of it to summon the leers of men, the wariness of women. But if lack of plainness was the cause, why did it not make similar trouble for Annie? Annie, who was not only beautiful but white? Perhaps, Sapphira thought, the combination yielded an even greater advantage than she had guessed, one that allowed Annie to vanquish the judging eyes. A bright shield that dazzled them, deflecting their baser assumptions while calling forth a generous one: Surely God would only have bestowed such loveliness–and such fair skin–upon a virtuous girl.

Several years ago, Father had bought Sapphira a small brass-framed mirror. Mislaying it in the move to Washington, she had been unwilling to announce her act of carelessness, so the gift had gone unreplaced. She now resolved that upon returning home, she would sneak a look into Annie's mirror. Maybe then she could grasp what it was that barred her from usefulness, this absence of visible virtue.

The Avenue bustled–newsboys waving papers, vendors pushing handcarts, hacks and carriages jolting along the cobblestone. A party of men emerged from Willard's, laughing and jostling. Beyond them, the massive Treasury Building blocked her view. The air sweltered. She hated Washington.

25

Peavey Estate

Rocking back and forth, the slave woman named Lottie cradled the cherub's marble head as if, with her lap's warmth, another whole angel might hatch from it. She kept her eyes on a corner of the room.

"Master Solon, he was fine as Peaveys go. When he drown, we knowed pretty well it be trouble for us, with Young Master Jonathan takin' his place. We was all fearin' the day, and here it come to pass. Not a tear Young Master sheds for his uncle–they never got on. No, he was poppin' his buttons–so proud, orderin' us about. Too much o' the cane and the boot from him. And the other colored, they starts to runnin' away, 'specially after word come to us 'bout the Freedom. Me, I would'er gone too, 'cept for my Cato. Cato's head ain't right since Young Master up and hit him with his cane. He weren't fit for leavin', so I weren't leavin'. But Master Jon, he ne'er had the wits for runnin' the place. Spend money on hisself. Take on white men to work the fields but can't pay 'em all, so half of 'em quits. Dogs 'n' horses in a bad way, but he never part with 'em. No, he let 'em starve to death 'fore that."

Between Lottie's puckered hands, the turnip-sized head stared up with eyes of blank white. Watching it rock with her, Truly thought of the few slaves he had met over the years–shack-born, unlettered and steeped in ghost stories, like the poorest of poor whites. Yet Lottie was lucidity itself–speech recovered and thoughts ordered, while others would have wept and raved. Bad luck it was, not having Peavey's live arm to twist, but this house slave made up for some of it.

By her account, Cato had awakened fearful in their shack last night, having heard a noise–Solon Peavey's restless spirit, he insisted. At dawn, as the field hands arrived, Lottie herself had found the servants' door damaged and unbarred, with no sign that Peavey was up and about. After some hours had passed, she could no longer credit the aftereffects of his drinking. Then, passing by the study, she looked in and saw the passageway door ajar. Drawn by a growing presentiment (a presentiment called hope, Truly thought), she braved the passageway to the master privy, whose door she opened just enough to glimpse the feet and the upright musket stock. She then wandered outdoors and informed the field boss, who went to see for himself.

"Master Jonathan sometimes went on trips, didn't he?" Truly asked.

Lottie surprised him with a chuckle. "Oh, yessir! When one like him go off and leave you be awhile, it get your notice! You says a thank-you-Lord when he go and a mercy prayer when he come back. Yessir, he go off for a day or two sometime, to Washington or up to Balt'more. Huntin' for ladies, is what I thinks . . . " Shutting her eyes, she gave a deeper chuckle. "–since none in these parts would have him! Well, sir, I would'er liked him gone more. A few fortnights back–blessed be–he take a trip four whole days."

"A few fortnights ago. The middle of April, you mean?"

"Think so, sir. The tabacky plantin' was gettin' started."

Truly turned to Forbes, looking grave in the wing chair. "That was likely the time of the La Maison incident. If just afterward Peavey went to see Van Gilder in New York and then returned home, he'd have been gone about four days."

Forbes asked if anything unusual had happened of late. Lottie spoke of two gentlemen who had called here yesterday, urging Peavey to sell the place.

"Sell it?" said Truly. "Who were these men?"

"A congress-man and a police, sir."

Truly and Forbes traded a sharp glance.

"Ne'er seen 'em before," said Lottie. "But Young Master, he knowed 'em. They was talkin' here in the parlor and I heared some of it. The police, he don't say much–but the small one, the congress, he tellin' Master Jon to sell, and that make my ears sharp. He say only Master Jon can raise up enough money to . . . He say a word there. Moll . . . molly . . . ?"

"Mollify?" Forbes offered.

"Yessir–that the word. The congress say only Young Master can get up the money and molly-fy somebody or other. And Master Jon gets to yellin', sayin' never, never. And the congress, he say, 'I am a congress-man and he is a police. We be more useful to them.' He say, 'Think of it, Peavey–if any of us get spared, it be us 'fore you.' And Young Master yell at them to leave, so off they goes. Then I needs to hide quick and so do Cato. Master Jon, he in a bad humor to start with, but now he has hisself a fit. Smashin' things–broke this nice angel–and later he's drinkin', cussin' awful at us. Cato and me slips out early, 'fore we get smashed too."

Forbes cleared his throat. "Miss Lottie–Maryland has slavery still, but Washington does not. Washington has plenty of free colored folk. We could arrange to bring you both there, get you help from the Freedman's Aid Society."

Her rocking had nearly ceased. Lifting the cherub's head from her lap, she placed it at her feet and sat back, hands folded. "Right kind o' you, sir. But we got our shack, we got our garden out there. Got bird and rabbit about, and I knows how to snare 'em. Cato and me be stayin' on." Her gaze moved to the ceiling. "This a evil house, for sure. Fulla torment-ful spirits, and now the worst of all. Well, they can board it up. They can burn it down. And it don't matter if Master Jon killed hisself or if someone else done it. The devil come for his mean little soul. Cato and me, we free enough." She resumed rocking. "Free enough," she muttered.

Thanking her, Truly and Forbes withdrew to the hall, where they leaned against opposite stairposts. They could hear the dogs outside. "Quoth the gravedigger," said Truly, "–'The plot thickens.'"

Forbes touched a knuckle to his chin. "Underhill and Archer. If we needed any more confirmation of their linkage, there it is. And for them to come here with such a demand . . . "

"It smells of desperation, sure enough. But this time we have no sight-ing of the murderer, and the killing itself is different. With Van Gilder, the assailant indulged himself in some slow torture. Since then, assuming he's the same bloody fellow, maybe he's learned that we're on his trail, and that his vicious ways helped capture our interest. So with Peavey he's more restrained and businesslike– a forced entry, a patient vigil, a musket blast to the head. But leaving an implication of suicide to confuse the matter."

Not that suicide was so far-fetched, given the dead man's drunk, ruined and terrorized state. But coming on the heels of Van Gilder's death, Peavey's was best viewed as murder. Two killings now, quite different from one another—but each proclaiming, in its way, a rare breed of assassin. Perhaps these "keepers" were in fact blessed with more than one such expert, but that seemed unlikely. "I'll say this," said Truly, "—if it is just one man, he's *mighty* singular. A damned sight more versatile than most."

"Madness with calculation," said Forbes. "Bloodlust with discipline. Savagery with cool intelligence . . ."

"Yep—things that don't commonly go together. From the evidence, we can guess that he kills for logical reasons and glories in the planning—otherwise, he wouldn't be so effective. But along with the killing, maximum terror is what he aims for. For Peavey to be murdered so, he'd have almost certainly been alive, awake and scared out of his weak little skull. Overpowered—and remember, Manfred described Major Spruce as a big, strong-looking fellow. Terror is this man's reward, the thing he feeds on."

Nodding, Forbes gave a low hiss. "So in our circle of five prospective victims, that's two dead. And two who are known to us, yet resistant to our charms. Plus one who's unknown."

"And notably absent from yesterday's visit here," said Truly. "Well, given recent events in Virginia, it's a good wager that the lieutenant-colonel's down there. Heck, maybe he's already had a quick and merciful death, courtesy of the Rebs. Who can say, as yet?"

Outside, the sounds of canine distress went on. In the parlor, the subtle creak of Lottie's rocking ceased again, and Forbes glanced in that direction. "Slaves," he muttered, "—slaves, on our side of the line. In a loyal state."

"In an officially neutral state," Truly corrected. "One with strong Southern ties, at least in these parts. The Ten Commandments may be free of loopholes, but Emancipation sure isn't. For now, be satisfied that Peavey is master no more." He peered into the parlor and saw Lottie standing at the window, looking anxious. "Something the matter, Miss Lottie?"

"Just them dogs, sir. Cato cain't manage 'em."

While Forbes resumed rummaging around the house, Truly went to the kitchen. There he found the neglected pans of bread-dough and called to Lottie. Soon she had a potful of grease frying on the stove, while he had rolled some of the dough into a few dozen sticky balls. To the slave-woman's shock and then delight, he had also broken into Peavey's well-stocked larder and gotten a sausage, which she cut into slices. Together they devoured these as Lottie ladled the dough-balls in and out of the pot. With a still-sizzling basketful, she and Truly proceeded to the front veranda. As they tossed the fried morsels onto the grass, the riotous dogs snapped them up while Cato, bent and squinting, looked on with evident relief.

"There, you curs!" Truly called. "You never had it so good!"

Lottie let out a quavering laugh. Truly handed the basket off to Cato, who commenced tossing the dough-balls as he hobbled away. Lottie joined him, leading the hounds in a yipping, straggling caravan around the side of the house. Chewing a last slice of sausage, Truly watched them move off through the tree shade. He made a mental note to check the stables and see how badly off the horses were.

Just then Forbes clumped onto the veranda, carrying a ledger and a framed photograph. "Found this over the fireplace," he said, holding out the picture. "Here's how he looked with his face on."

Truly took the photograph in his hands. Within its decorative frame, Peavey gripped his walking stick in a haughty pose, his coat buttoned up to the high shirt collar. Truly assessed the pinched face, the upturned chin and long, limp hair. "My, my–he did play the part, didn't he?"

"But Nate–the inscription?"

Across Peavey's riding breeches, the flowing handwritten words read: "To Jonathan Peavey, with greatest admiration, Miles Wakefield–Sept. 1862."

"Ahhh . . . yes," Truly murmured. "'M. Wakefield Photography.' At Cold Harbor."

Forbes nodded. "On the man's trunk label."

Truly lowered the picture. Pondering, he watched the last snuffling hound follow the slave couple out of sight.

26

Bermuda Hundred, Virginia

*W*HERE SOLDIERS WENT, dogs followed, more at home with camp life than the men themselves were. Ben watched one wily cur steal salt pork from an inattentive black soldier, then dodge away in a hail of curses. Several men laughed. "He knows dog scraps when he sees 'em!" one called.

Everyone was dusty and footsore but glad to rejoin the rest of the Twenty-second, glad to be eating their rations in the evening shade. It had been exciting three weeks ago to leave this place of mosquitoes and tedium, but returning here felt unexpectedly good. Back on familiar ground, deep in the fold of an entire colored division, they would no longer be serving as drudges for white troops. Comrades who had been left behind were eager for tales of Cold Harbor, and the men of Ben's company did their best to oblige. In one huddle, Parrish described the aftermath of Grant's assault, and for once he wasn't having to exaggerate. Young fretted about Sable John, who had flown off somewhere. "He be back for his mouse," Reddick assured.

Amid the clink of mess kits, though, a more subdued talk persisted. The returning companies had received no order for bivouac, and others had struck their tents. More conclusively, everyone had glimpsed the pontoon bridge downriver. So much for familiar ground–the march would proceed. Due south, so it appeared–across the shimmering Appomattox, toward the Reb redoubts at Petersburg.

Ben had eaten quickly and now needed a place to sit alone, maybe doze a little. He spotted Tucker eating by himself. Seated with his back to a sapling, Tucker stirred at Ben's approach, but Ben motioned for him not to rise.

"Sergeant, I'm going down the bank a piece, that way. I'll return soon."

Tucker nodded. "All right, sir."

Headed along the bank, Ben came upon Junie and Langstaff. Junie was currying the captain's steed while Langstaff, bareheaded, stared at the bridge through his spyglass. The drummer boy had apparently asked about the horse's name.

"Culloden?" Langstaff said. "'Twas a terrible fight in Scotland o'er a hundred years back, when the bloody redcoats cut the brave heeland clans to ribbons." Lowering the scope, the captain turned around. This was the one subject that ever made him loquacious. "Still, 'tis a glorious name. Sometimes, lad, there's shame in victory, glory in defeat. Brush down there by his withers. Go on, he will not kick ye." Langstaff saw Ben coming and his features took on their customary reserve.

Salutes had been discarded during the march, so Ben didn't bother now. "Anything new, sir?"

Junie stole a glance at them, crouching lower as he brushed the horse. Langstaff paced toward the reeds and Ben followed.

"I just spoke with Colonel Kiddoo," the captain said. "Grant himself came down by steamer today, givin' orders. In three hours or so, with cavalry support, the division will cross the bridge. The whole Eighteenth Corps will follow us o'er before dawn. Ragged though we be, we won't be gettin' much sleep."

A tingle started in Ben's belly. "You mean to say, sir, that colored troops will serve as vanguard?"

"Seems to have fallen that way. The General's decided where to hit next, and this division happens to be closest." Turning the scope in his hands, Langstaff squinted across the river. "Which is also to say, I wish I'd granted ye more shootin' practice, and bayonet too. 'Tis not certain, but we may get our first fight sooner than I thought."

"They'll measure up, Captain."

Langstaff puffed his chest a bit. "If they are to, lad, then their officers must as well."

"Yes, sir. They must." The captain hadn't called him "lad" before. Ben saluted and left him.

Ben passed other seated groups of men, a knot of white officers, some wagons and then a row of latrines. A camp of newly freed slaves, mostly women and children, clung to the edge of a nearby wood. Past a bushy hillock, he came to a ruined farmhouse that he remembered. Farther back, the once-plowed field had become overgrown, and on its far side he could see the charred rail of the slave pen. His men had spent one afternoon burning it, fending off other companies that wanted the sport and the honor. When it had come to chopping down the whipping post, Reddick and one of his platoon drew the lucky straws, but Reddick charitably deferred to Prince, the African. Prince accepted the axe with delight, and the others cheered as he and the other private chopped the post to pieces. That day had been a good one.

Ben found a spot on the bank and sat there, nestling his back against a half-sunken boulder. Down to his left, an apricot sky silhouetted the long, low bridge, with ant-like sentries at its near end. Songbirds lamented sundown. Through the rushes, the river sparkled as if countless jeweled fish had surfaced to catch the last light. Ben had seen places that were more beautiful, especially traveling out west with his father–but no sky, water and birdsong had ever brought a pang so deep. His eyes followed the bridge to the opposite shore, with its dark woods and bluffs.

Tomorrow would expose his worth as an officer. This time, not just his own conduct but that of untried black men would determine pride or shame. A veteran and an officer now–yet the thoughts of an enlisted man still came to him, as they had at Chancellorsville. In that horror and chaos, he had made the soldier's loneliest discovery. Death, he saw at last, was seldom brave, singular and picturesque, more often dumb, random and anonymous. Guns murdered any chance of noble repose. Guns ruled, and their victims knew dignity like stones knew laughter. Honorable survival, maimed or unmaimed, was the sanest thing you could hope for, and most soldiers would in fact survive the war. Ben had thereafter taken this hope into battle, with all other hopes trailing–to find a place in the world, to love a woman, to work happily and make his mark. It had to remain a hope, not a sense of destiny, for your function on Earth might abruptly reveal itself as something quite different. To be chewed up as fodder, spat out as scrap, spent in victory or defeat or a commander's mistake. To be memorialized with a cross among acred crosses, as a name among columned names, from a battle that other battles would soon eclipse. The fullness of this discovery left Ben feeling stupid for days, angry for weeks, and finally just somber. He was, after all, only one of many thousands who had marched off in uniform, amid other uniforms, harboring somehow a wish to go down in legend.

Still, fear was far off for the moment, and this spot felt separate and serene. Ben dozed off trying to recall the name of the last girl he had held, a rented girl in Marble Alley, where he had ventured between passing his board exam and getting his commission. She was small, giddy and unremarkable, but there had been none since her, and he wished he could remember her name.

The snap of a twig woke him to the gloom. Blinking in the direction from which he had come, he saw Tucker's husky shape standing still, head turned toward the burnt slave pen. Ben slid up onto the rock. Tucker saw him and ambled over.

"Anything happening?" Ben asked.

"Not really, sir. They're restless, is all. I told mine to stay put." Tucker sounded atypically dreamy. "Young got his bird back."

"Well, that's good."

The Sergeant halted a few steps from the rock, then gazed at the river. Ben inhaled, taking in the scent of buds, the deeper smell of earth. "We'll go back in a moment. Rest your legs, if you want. You'll be needing them."

Tucker got down beside the rock, propping an elbow on his knee, and neither man spoke for a moment. The bullfrogs sounded like loose banjo strings as the dark water glided by, dappled with moonlight.

"Sir, can you say how soon we'll cross?"

"In less than three hours, I'm told."

"Talk is that we'll meet the enemy tomorrow."

"Not a sure thing. We seem to be aimed at 'em, though."

Tucker nodded, then took a slow breath. "Good," he muttered, and after a pause, "You can count on me."

Ben couldn't quite see his face, still turned to the river. "I know I can." Sensing Tucker's hesitation, he waited.

"They say you were at Chancellorsville, sir. If you'll pardon me, I was glad when I heard that. We hear of white officers who've seen no real action, who applied to command colored just for the promotion."

Ben wanted to tell him about Chancellorsville. About the high spirits that afternoon, camped with few pickets, the woods assuredly too dense for attack. About the flurry of quail, pheasant and then rabbit from the undergrowth–rabbits, rabbits, singly and then in scores, darting crazy patterns through the camp–then a thrashing and bounding of deer, graceful and headlong and slowed in memory, endless in memory, a fandango of critters, a dancing animal tide, and everyone just staring. Card games suspended, men looking at each other, hazy sun through the branches and then the yip-yip of the Rebels, that piercing yell of enemy unseen, upon them everywhere. Stunned faces, the grabbing of rifles, the first shots, the first fallen–flank and rear, rear and flank, they're on us, Christ Almighty they're ON US. Wagons overturned, mules and horses bolting, entire raw units stampeded, Ben and the Wisconsins stumbling, falling, whirling, firing at nothing in the dusk. Load, ram, fire–run. And that yell coming on like wolves, like a hurricane of wolves carrying all before it as night fell, howling in a cataract of shot and cries and ripping branches.

Ben wanted to tell Tucker, to tell someone about it before the moment slipped by on dark water. But why and how would he tell a soldier this on the eve of his first battle? "Yes," he said at length. "I've seen the elephant, as they say. That wasn't the first time for me, only the biggest. I was sick for Gettysburg." It occurred to him there was one thing he could describe for Tucker, what he wished someone had described for him. Something about witless chance, the mad sowing of credit and blame. Once you learned it, heaven's judging eye receded, along with some of the pressure, and all the grim veteran jokes made sense. "Funny thing is, Tucker–in all that mess, the only good thing I did was yell my fool lungs out."

Tucker looked at him.

"The evening when they . . . surprised us, we ended up scattered through the woods. We had a little moonlight but mainly it was dark as an owl's insides. A bunch of us were trying to feel our way to the lines, following the sound of the guns, when there was some movement to one side and then a volley. I went flat into some thorns and they were pouring it into us, and then in a muzzle flash I think I see blue cuffs and start yelling, 'Union! Stop! We're Union!' But I'm not the only one yelling, and they keep it up, so I crawl toward them, calling them every name in the devil's book till I'm hoarse, practically at their feet when somebody gives an order and they quit. I stand up with all these thorns in my hide and somebody has a lantern, and there's my own colonel staring at me, shaking in his boots, and there's two dead and several wounded, the damage pretty well done. And yet the poor man's telling me, 'Thank you, son. Thank you.' And he gets my name and next day I wake up a damned corporal."

Tucker sat motionless. Ben worried that the story had misfired somehow.

"But you kept your head," said Tucker.

"Well, as much as anyone could. My point, though . . . The more details you imagine of how it'll be, the farther off the mark you'll be when it finally happens. Armies impose order and rank because they're meant for battle–the most disordered activity you could imagine. You know how little say you have in that disorder, in what direction it'll take, but once you feel it deep down it takes some of the worry away. You get quick at fixing on the one best thing you can do, no matter the situation. I mean Lord, Tucker, who could've foreseen a night like that, for us or for the johnnies? Do you know, Stonewall Jackson was shot that same night accidentally, by his own men?"

"Yes, sir. I read about it up in Montreal."

Ben's mind pulled back from Chancellorsville. Previously Tucker had mentioned his living in Canada, but nothing particular about it. And this river's peace felt like permission for questions that might otherwise go unasked. "How long were you in Canada, Tucker?"

"Eleven good years, sir." Tucker picked up a pebble, turned it in his fingers. "While still a boy, I was sold to a North Carolina planter who took an interest in me. At his direction, I learned to read and write and figure–all in defiance of state law, mind you. I believe he envisioned me as an especially useful house slave. But it's just as Frederick Douglass said: You have a bad master, you want a good one; you have a good one, you want none. So out of his sight, I also learned how to swim. Then I stowed away on a vessel to Boston and jumped into the harbor. Some Abolition people hid me away and arranged my secret passage to Canada. Once in Montreal I took up my wider education. Later, a Frenchman and I became partners and opened a restaurant."

Ben tried to picture the husky sergeant cutting vegetables. "I take it that army rations were a hard adjustment."

Tucker kept turning the pebble. "I dream about that restaurant. I hope to go back. But when word of Negro recruitment came, I took it as a call. Unfinished business. Couldn't wait it out." With a neat flick of his arm, he sent the pebble into the river. "Once I overheard a pair of new lieutenants, sir, just afore you came to us. They were all smiles, talking about their pay raise. One said that with such benefits from colored enlistment, he could become a hearty Abolitionist."

Ben stared at the black water. Within Tucker's anecdote he grasped a question, not impertinent, not a demand, but in its own way as frank as a courtroom Bible. He could ignore it or answer it. His fingers searched up a pebble and rubbed it. "Igneous," he thought—a nugget of cooled lava from an ancient volcano. He threw it, heard its watery "plop."

"The added pay is fine with me," Ben said. "The shoulder straps are fetching. I thought of these things too. If I said I never did, I'd be a liar."

Tucker said nothing.

"I was at the Applicants' School in Philadelphia before I realized there was something else moving me. You see, I grew up with a colored girl." He felt Tucker's sudden gaze.

"A servant girl, sir?"

Ben sighed. "How do I explain this? It always confuses people. My father was on his way back from the Mexican War when he saw Sapphira at a slave auction in New Orleans. She was five or six by his guess. He's never allowed just what moved him to purchase her. Human mercy, I suppose—though I've known more merciful folks who'd never have done it. Anyhow, that's what he did, and he brought her up to our homestead in northern Missouri. About a year later it hit him that he was a slave owner, so he took out a paper of manumission for her. By then, though, the idea that she should ever leave us was unimaginable. She and I, we grew up calling the same people Mama and Papa, and they saw to her education quietly. It has made for a strange life, and some difficulty—understand, I have uncles and cousins fighting under the Rebel flag. Usually neighbors and kinfolk saw a family servant, for she was always helping around the house, and that's what we let 'em think. Anyhow, I know her face as I know my own. She writes to me from Washington—once a week, at least. To think of her . . . " Ben shrugged. "To connect Sapphira with me here and all of this, it's just queer. But sometimes when I look at the men, I see her too. Real reasons hide from you, my Pa said. When you think you know 'em all, you probably don't."

Ben hadn't imagined saying so much, but in the quiet he felt strangely liberated. Now another man knew about Sapphira, that she was someone real, tethering him to the days before guns, drill and battles.

"Sapphira," the sergeant muttered. "Pretty name."

"Is it? Heck, to me it's just her name. But Saph herself—she's a rare article, I tell you. Her letters are marvels. Sometimes I'd swear she can read my thoughts." Far-off laughter drifted down the bank, and a fiddle started playing. Ben picked out the clatter of loaded wagons and felt the army reabsorbing him. He clapped his knees, got up and stretched. "Time to go back, before they think we've deserted."

Returning, the two of them stepped carefully through the dark and didn't speak. Past the hillock, they saw campfires ahead and fell in stride.

"Well, sir," said Tucker. "I wouldn't have guessed your story."

"Nor I yours, Sergeant. But it's good to know."

Nearing the firelight, they saw Young laughing beside Sable John's T-stand. Facing the hawk like a court musician, a bent private played a jig on his fiddle while the bird-king twitched his head in confusion.

An hour later, the order came to fall in.

27

Central Washington

ALONG NORTH F Street, a sizable crowd and a blaring military band had assembled, celebrating the National Union ticket. Strung between two opposite buildings, a giant torch-lit transparency bore the likenesses of Lincoln and Johnson–"Champions of Liberty, Defenders of the Republic." But the gaslights of the Treasury Building were dimmed, its wide corridors deserted as Truly and Forbes shuffled wearily toward their office. Through the door, they overheard Duke and Kirschenbaum, who had evidently waited up for them. To Duke's eager questions, the hunchback was describing his youthful role in the '48 Revolution.

"So, Manfred–you were right there on the barricades?"

"Ja–but aftervards, they arrest any man who dares speak against royalty. I can no longer work at the military stables and must leave Frankfurt. It is then I first thinks of sailing to the United States . . . "

The two were startled to their feet as Truly and Forbes barged in.

"What did you learn from Peavey?" Duke asked.

"That he takes an eternity on the crapper," said Truly. Before their quizzical looks, he placed his sack on the desk and opened it. "More to the point, the scalawag's dead." He let them gape for a moment before giving a condensed explanation. Then he pulled out the ledger. "Octavius, it seems young Jonathan tried his hand at bookkeeping, with garbled results. See if you can detect a quarterly payment schedule. If the creditor is actually named, that will mean a happy breakthrough for us." He extracted two fistfuls of letters. "To add to your misery, here's some correspondence for you to go over."

Fiddling with his glasses, Duke took the volume and started perusing it.

Truly reached into the sack again and glanced at Kirschenbaum. "Now Manfred, take a good look at this." He withdrew Peavey's portrait.

Taking it, Kirschenbaum stared, then tapped the glass surface with his fingertip. "This is him! The one who visits Van Gilder in April!"

"As we thought. But the inscription—does that mean anything to you?"

The hunchback held the picture out. Stroking his bristly mustache, he murmured the name. "Wakefield . . . Ja, Wakefield!"

"You know him?"

"No, Major. But . . . " Kirschenbaum set the portrait down, his gaze intent. "In Van Gilder's office at the *Comet-American* hangs a photograph of him, mit a signature—the same as this one, Miles Wakefield."

Duke was rubbing his chin. "That name—I think I . . . " He put the ledger aside. Excusing his way to the lower desk drawer, he removed the leather pouch containing Peavey's dossier and took out the sheaf of dog-eared paper. He rustled through it. "Here! From the period of Peavey's surveillance in '62 . . . 'Man with photographic equipment arrives early afternoon September 9th. Dined with subject, stayed the night, took subject's portrait in morning before departure. Man later identified as . . . ' "

"Miles Wakefield," Forbes spoke.

Duke looked up in dismay. "In my summary yesterday . . . the photographer's name didn't seem worth mentioning."

"Nor did it seem so to us," said Truly, "when we told you about our little confab at Cold Harbor."

"Underhill's photographer—that was Wakefield too?!"

"Surely was. What's more, Peavey's house slave confirmed that he was an occasional visitor at the manse. That he'd imbibe with Peavey, flattering him and cussing the Abolitionists." Thinking, Truly drew up straight. "I wonder . . . " He bent down and started rummaging through the drawer that Duke had opened. "Hang it, boys—my powers of recollection used to be a damned sight better."

"What are you hunting for?" asked Forbes.

"You remember my telling of Adam Cathcart's New Year's visit to Washington?"

"Yes–when you had Heatherton tail the fellow. But I thought that came to nothing."

"So it seemed." Truly pulled out the file. "Just an extended drunken romp with his cousin, I thought. They hit a bunch of saloons and then a brothel and then . . . "

Recalling the detail, Forbes arched his eyebrows. "They had a portrait taken."

"Indeed. At a place that I figured was just incidental." Truly's chagrin deepened as he read from Lieutenant Heatherton's conscientious script, dated January 2nd. "'At about four in the afternoon, the subject and his cousin, by now tipsy, called at the M. Wakefield Photographic Shop, 708 West Third Street . . . '" Letting the page float onto the desktop, he sank into his chair. "Very close to which, five months later, Cathcart was nabbed along with Van Gilder's letter." He rubbed his eyes, then drew the brim of his hat down. "I'd wondered if Cathcart had a secret contact in Washington–and all this time, a clue lay right here in our records."

"But it appears that Wakefield could have some extra role," said Forbes, "being associated with at least three of the La Maison group."

"Right. That's mighty hard to see as just happenstance." Through the windowpane, Truly could hear the brassy wail of the band on F Street. He sighed. "I can't help thinking back to Cold Harbor. It seems we did Wakefield a mighty big favor that day. Put him on the alert."

Forbes shook his head, resting against the windowsill.

Keen for distraction, Truly's mind moved on. Last night he had slid his report under Baker's office door–but to his question about it, Duke replied that there had been no response from the director. When Truly asked if he had managed to track down Underhill's secretary, the clerk looked dejected.

"Ives–yes, sir. I found him eating alone at that restaurant, but I'm afraid I failed to win his confidence. He told me to leave him alone and stay out of the congressman's affairs."

"That's all right. You tried. Our next approach will be less tactful, I assure you." Summoning a hearty air, Truly clapped his knees. "Tomorrow, though, our first object should be to snare this man Wakefield for some lively questioning. Bart and Manfred–in the morning we'll meet here and proceed to his shop on West Third. If he's not in, we'll linger and see if he shows up. Failing that, I'd like all of us to meet at my house–three o'clock, let's say–to thrash out what our next move should be." He got to his feet. "Whatever the case, boys, it's time to raise a bit of hell. Because someone's sure raising it on us."

Outside they went their separate ways, Truly taking a detour to avoid the Republican rally. The band had quieted, but as he reached West Fourteenth Street a shrill whistle startled him. Turning, he saw a vertical streak of ruby in the night sky above the President's Park, followed by the rocket's blossom-like burst. To swells of cheering, a succession of brilliant rockets whistled skyward and exploded, illuminating the rooftops. Truly watched, unsettled. His memory was indeed getting worse, he thought. He had neglected to ask Duke for any war news out of Virginia.

28

Truly Residence

SAPPHIRA LAY WATCHING the sparrow-sized angels above her bed. They were not ordinary angels, not fair and cheerful, but had grumpy troll faces. Their bright elastic bodies kept changing color, blue to green to red to white, weaving patterns like warm toffee in the dark. She wondered what they were about, so purposeful in their floating ceremony. Just as baffling were the intermittent popping noises, like gunfire, which threatened to break her trance. Suddenly a louder burst jolted her awake and the angels were gone, their riddle unsolved. With thudding heart she lay there while other bursts rattled the windowpane. Then light flickered through the shutters and she remembered the Republican fireworks. Strange, she thought, that people chose to celebrate with war sounds amid war.

The mock bombardment soon stopped, just as she heard her father enter downstairs. She listened to the rustle of his coat, his quiet steps down the hall, then a pause before he backtracked and entered the parlor. For a minute she heard nothing, aware that he was standing before Mother Rachel's picture. She was glad that she had replaced the lilacs. His steps left the parlor, came up the stairs. She wanted to call him in a whisper but hesitated. Then the door to his room creaked shut and the hush fell once more. Earlier she had looked in on Anna. Queer it was, how she could still gaze fondly upon Anna in sleep. But now, inside her, the pounding resumed.

She drew the covers off, lit a candle and sat at her writing desk by the window. From the envelope she took the creased pages of the letter, along with the sketch of the uniformed colored boy wearing spectacles. After a dozen readings it was not so much a letter as a talisman–Ben's spirit, etched in ink beneath her fingertips. She started reading it again:

Cold Harbor, Vir., June 7

Dear Saph,

It's quieter in camp tonight, most of the men asleep, a few on picket duty. We've been here several days now. The sketch is of Junie, our drummer boy, proud of his new glasses.

I see you've kept up with the newspapers. Do you think Lincoln will make a second term? I would like to believe so, for the surpassing reason that the awful course must be kept as he intends. More unbearable it would be, if the cost thus far turned out for nothing. Still, they say the Copperheads are reaping votes from this bloody campaign, while the Republican hope grows dimmer. There's less talk of it here than of Sherman's progress in Georgia, though there's not much of that either. Guessing what U.S. Grant might do with us next–that's the main topic. The policy on colored troops, however, remains as dull as the policy on pack mules. Only a few of our units have seen action, and my company none at all. So at present I'm out of harm's way, relatively speaking.

Nevertheless, having lately witnessed the worst of anguish, I have again been stirred to ponder. And what I ponder is how little our first fancies and intentions come to matter, how we grow to feel an immeasurably powerful hand writing the play, blotting what our own small hands have written. There is so little certainty to grasp.

Do you remember the day in Missouri when I pressed you into raiding that farmer's grapes with me, and he discovered us? I've forgotten what he yelled at me as he grabbed my collar, but not the names and threats he yelled at you. He didn't have hold of you and you could have run, yet you stood there pleading for me as he swore to sell you off–back where you belonged, he said, where the lash would keep your mischief down. When he cuffed you I must have bitten his leg to the bone, and thank God he was fat and we were fast. If Pa had found out, the licking would have made little difference to me. Seeing the look on you that day in the vineyard, I beheld a scheme of risk and penalty that meant one thing for me and far worse things for you.

I remember too one morning when you were getting Annie dressed, and Aunt Clara was there asking Ma how a family of slight means could keep a colored servant. That was how visitors spoke of you and to you, and it deviled me why our rough-hewn daddy would just hide his face in a book, why a woman as forthright as Ma would just change the subject— why they never did much to correct these invaders. It was of course years before I understood the jagged codes that strangers set, and the cheap stratagems we adopt to wriggle around them. I understand but dislike these codes. You, dear Saph, must hate them.

Ever since then, I have tried on occasion to see from your head and heart, always failing, as I have with others. Yet the very question remains a gift, for it has made the human realm a wider, deeper and more various puzzle. It is thanks to you that sometimes I look at a crowd, or even at ranked soldiers, and see lone faces within the mass, each with a private puzzle that I may sense but never know.

I cannot believe the distance I've come. One day I was a journey-man printer in Wisconsin, and in my spare time combing the lake shore for rock and fossil, envisioning myself as a small-town editor or maybe a learned geologist. Then the war fired me out of a gun, into a life I'd never imagined. Then Ma was gone. Then I was at Applicants' School, struggling with tactical formations and the like. Then I was commanding colored troops. Now I'm here, with my candle burning low. Back in April you wrote of how it felt to see Gen. Burnside's Negroes parading for the President. Here we have met those same troops, and they speak of some in the capital spitting on them as they marched. Like you, I have never been fond of Washington City. Anyhow, we hear of this, and of the Fort Pillow Massacre, and how can we help but spoil for a fight?

Saph, I don't know when or where we'll march next, or if indeed we'll ever be tested. I do know your prayers have followed me and that they always will. In bleakest hour, I've felt them enfold me. Yet I think of certain comrades. In war, you grow to know men you might otherwise have bypassed, giving ear to their stories, however plain, trusting they'll do the same for yours. I knew a private who was working on a patent for an ingenious mechanical saw, another who wanted to catalogue plant life, another who wished to paint landscapes, another who was determined to run for Congress and improve the lot of orphans. One, a writer of humor-ous sketches, planned to write a non-humorous novel that would depict war truthfully. Worthy boys all, boys on whom many prayers were spent. Gone now, as if the soil devoured them. Oblivion instead of deeds. When I think of them now, it feels as if I only dreamed them.

Therefore I tell you, Saph–whether my luck holds or not, and despite the jagged code of strangers, I am forever connected to you in my bones. Most of our experience we can describe for others in some fashion–yet much of your own, I'm certain, dwarfs description as night dwarfs the candle. Knowing only how much I cannot know, I hope that the force of my testament will touch you on nights when you're most alone, and that it will prove comfort enough. Whatever the reckoning.

Ever and always,

Your brother, Ben

Holding the pages in her lap, Sapphira sat there a minute longer. Then she put the letter down, got up, ruffled her nightgown and blew the candle out. Back under the covers, she drifted off with images of faraway Paris–galleries, monuments and boulevards, all from engravings that she had seen.

Night had passed to dawn when she lurched almost completely out of bed, her mind whirling. For a long, chill moment, with gray light filtering in through the shutters, she found herself unable to breathe.

29

Northeast Of Petersburg, Virginia
June 15, 6 A.M.

FIRST THERE WAS only the murk and the damp of dawn, the clink of metal, the tramp of many feet, the low rumble of cavalry hooves, the ranks of bleary-faced men as they neared the turnpike and parallel railroad. Then came the blast. Behind and in front of him, Ben felt a collective flinch. But the troops managed to keep in step, marching another couple of rods before an order halted them. Without the tramping sound, everyone heard the full arc of the next shell—a boom, an oncoming shriek from the right. Its blast ripped the air, neither close nor very far.

Mounted officers conferred while some cavalry rode off to reconnoiter. Sporting his tartan sash, Captain Langstaff trotted by atop Culloden. "Put 'em at ease," he said, and the order was passed. Ben gazed back upon the serpentine column of blue, its shouldered muskets retracting like bristles. No one spoke. Foreboding showed on some faces and eagerness on others, but most were gravely alert, blinking westward. Facing his platoon, Tucker kept a hand on his holster. At the company's rear, Junie managed the double burden of his drum and Sable John's T-stand, with the haughty bird flapping above him.

Another boom. This time Ben saw it, on some high ground about a mile away—the flare and the puff of white, next to a farm house. The shell came whistling and exploded lower, closer. A major's horse reared. Ben turned to the men and looked past them, letting out an audible sigh.

"Can't just eat their breakfast like regular folk." Sabbath Young gave a louder chuckle than the quip deserved. Scanning the Rebel position, Ben saw that it was as good as this terrain afforded, girded by woods on the left and a contiguous thicket in front, wide and dense. It allowed the Confederates an enfilading fire across much of the low ground while presenting a more difficult target for Union artillery. And it commanded the pike, which ran straight toward the woods for some distance before bending south, along with the railroad. There could be no bypass.

Lieutenant Morton, a pale Connecticut seminarian with E Company, wandered over and offered Ben a cigar. Ben accepted it and got out his pocket match case.

"You think we're out of range here?" Morton asked.

"Probably just," said Ben, speaking low. "Of course, they could still be setting their sights."

"Well . . . My men are ready. As ready as they could be."

Ben noted how Morton kept sucking his teeth between cigar-puffs. It made him think uncomfortably of that riddle, of how battle sharpened the senses of one man while dulling another's. Since Chancellorsville he had been reasonably certain that he was the first sort, though he wondered if that could change. Nevertheless, he was responsible for more than himself now—no time for doubts.

He took a long, pleasureful draw on his cigar. In the dew-soaked grass near his foot, he noticed a fist-sized rock with a vein of white quartz—and rather than pick it up, he made himself a promise. Barring death on this or some other field, he would spend as many days as possible collecting rocks and fossils, each a mystic token predating the human race, predating warfare. He would still ply the printer's trade and he would still do pencil sketches of everyday scenes, keeping a foothold in the present. But his best-loved hours would be spent with his rock specimens and showing them to children—"the Rock Man," they would probably call him. And perhaps he would find a woman kind enough to marry a village eccentric.

Between the tracks and the pike, another fireburst littered the air with shrapnel. Morton covered an ear, gazing down the line as a bugle sounded. "There now," he said. The scouting party was straggling back while officers rode out to meet it. Ben spied Langstaff, bulky on his graceful charger. After a few minutes, a mounted private came cantering up the line, looking winded.

Morton called out—"How's it look there, soldier?"

Reining up, the private answered politely but wearily, as if he had repeated the news several times already. "Four-gun battery, sir. Two infantry regiments, maybe three. Breastworks. Small cavalry force."

Morton flicked his cigar ashes onto the grass. "Well, then—we certainly have the numbers."

"And they the ground, sir. Good luck to you."

With a salute, the private rode on.

Morton took a final puff, sucked his teeth and threw his stub away. He patted his holster. "Godspeed, Truly."

"And you, Morton. Thanks for the smoke."

Walking away, Morton twitched as a shell struck beside the pike. Ben leaned over and ground his cigar out. Despite the standstill, some men in G Company began a spirited marching song:

> No more for trader's gold
> Will those we love be sold
> Nor crushed be manhood bold
> In slavery's dreaded fold . . .

The chaplain, an older mulatto, ambled through the ranks while reading aloud from a prayer book. "'From Glory shall His hand reach unto me, and I will enter His gates with Thanksgiving in my heart.'" The more devout of the troops murmured "amen," along with some of the less. Then Langstaff was trotting toward them, Culloden's tail tossing like a pennant. Ben turned to Tucker. The sight of Tucker rooted there like a stout pillar brought a feeling of reassurance. They exchanged a slight nod before Ben ordered the company to attention.

Langstaff drew his horse up beside Ben. "Form right," he intoned.

Ben passed the order, which was being echoed up and down the line. From officer to sergeant to private, it touched off a swirl of feet and haversacks as the entire column faced west. Somewhere a battered-sounding band struck up "We Are Coming, Father Abraham" while a reserve brigade deployed behind the main body. Shouts rang, bull-throated in the cool, moist air, whipping the men into battle formation while the band played with tinny urgency. Ben's company accomplished the move with no more grace than the others, but Langstaff's weathered face betrayed no disapproval. Over near the tracks, mounted, Colonel Kiddoo gazed through field glasses as the Stars 'n' Stripes and the regimental colors came forward. The commanding general rode past with his retinue. High to the left, a shell exploded. Then the band quit playing.

Langstaff raised his bewhiskered chin. "Load arms."

"Load and ram!" As the order flew, muskets slid down and hands fumbled through cartridge boxes. Each man bit off a paper cartridge and poured powder down the barrel, then inserted the ball portion and rammed it home.

"Bayonets," the captain spoke.

"Fix bayonets!"

The long blades flashed up from their leather scabbards, each one perching atop a musket barrel as its socket rang shut. Pulling erect, the troops shouldered their weapons again as Ben drew his sword. The drummers had begun a brisk tattoo. A Union battery opened up, starting a loud dialogue with the enemy guns. Eyes shadowed beneath his hat-brim, Langstaff peered slowly left, then right. Culloden pawed the earth, snorting. Then, backing the horse up a stride, Langstaff puffed his plaid chest and stood in the stirrups.

"You men!" he bellowed. "Ye sable laddies! As a man o' the Scottish hee-lands, I am no stranger t' tyranny! When I see the Rebels, I see the bloody English redcoats! But YOU!! Ye need not see 'em as anything but what they be! Ye'll know what to do! And THEY . . . !!" He thrust his finger toward the enemy. "They'll see ye come streamin', the sons of Ahf-ree-ka back for vengeance!"

"Oh, yessir," somebody whispered.

"What's he sayin'?" whispered another.

With a stern glance, Tucker silenced them as Langstaff thundered on, punctuated by cannons.

"Remember the lash and the auction block! Remember all those borne across the cruel ocean! Remember the dead of Fort Pillow in Tennessee! And ye'll be a credit this day to the United States Colored Infantry! Ye'll be a credit to the whole mighty Union!" His eyes flamed, his face gone red. "This day ye will REDEEM the blood of martyrs with REBEL BLOOD!! AND YE WILL FIGHT LIKE LIONS!!"

In the next startled instant, there occurred something that Ben had experienced a few other times before battle—but here among unblooded black troops and with his duty pressing down on him, it felt blazingly pure. All through the ranks, individual points of tension were fused into one, igniting into something fearsome and unearthly. Cheers broke out—cries for revenge, hollers of Fort Pillow, vows to follow Langstaff and the flag unto death. Men raised their fists, rattled their muskets, jabbed the air with their bayonets as the Celtic chieftain towered before them. Ben looked at Parrish, Reddick, Armstrong, Prince the African–faces taut with loving fury. He glanced at Young, whose eyes were glistening. Only Tucker remained fully at attention, though he fixed Langstaff with a nearly incandescent stare.

Turning, Ben spoke above the clamor. "Sergeant."

"Sir!"

"In case the men need reminding, tell them we do take prisoners."

"I will, sir."

Spreading to the whole regiment, the cheering and shouting drew the notice of Colonel Kiddoo, who lowered his binoculars and turned around in the saddle. Ben let it continue a moment longer before signaling his sergeants to quell the racket. It died as quickly as it had begun, order restored. The drumming had stopped. The flush left Langstaff's face as he dismounted, giving Culloden a pat on the haunch. He drew his sword. At Ben's order, a private led the horse to the rear.

Behind the reserve line, surgeons had set up the field hospital beneath a large tent-fly, next to a phalanx of ambulance and supply wagons. The band members were assembling there–boys and older men in baggy uniforms, forsaking their instruments to serve as stretcher-bearers. Closer by, Sable John's stand had been planted in moist earth, the hawk surveying things like a proud, feathered general while Junie stood to one side, ready with his sticks and drum. Ben called the boy forward. Junie looked like any drummer boy that Ben had seen at such a time–scared and bold equally, tensed to make the most of his small part. Ben told him to hang back and to stop when he reached the thicket. Junie said "yessir" and hurried back to his spot.

The Rebel battery had gone silent. Presently the Union guns did so, having done no visible damage. In the relative quiet, everything in Ben's vision–every man, weapon, sun-gleam and blade of grass–took on a diamond clarity. He stared past Langstaff to the ground ahead. Lush green and studded with shrubs, it sloped gently down for about three quarters of a mile until it reached the tangled, shadowy mass of the thicket, beyond which rose the hill with its waiting enemy. Above, ripening from pink to gold, the few low clouds seemed alive–separate little nations, watchful, maintaining neutrality. Ben's eyes inhaled them.

Having dismounted, Colonel Kiddoo took his place before the regiment. In the same moment, the order to advance rang out, echoing from regiment to regiment and company to company, along the whole line of battle. Langstaff pointed his sword and took up the cry. Ben did the same–"Advance! Advance!"–and the spiked blue monolith hulked forward.

Keeping a few strides behind Langstaff, Ben felt all of F Company in step behind him, tramping to Junie's smart drumbeat. On the right he saw Morton marching stiffly along. He decided it was bad luck to look at Morton. The order came for arms-at-ready and a dense clattering ensued, muskets shifting to a forward angle. At nearly half the distance toward the thicket, the Rebel guns stayed quiet, though the federal force was now well within range.

Behind Ben, a soldier muttered to Prince–"Lions, Prince. He said fight like lions–rowwrrr!"

"Quiet in the ranks," Tucker snapped.

The downward slope grew gentler. At this measured pace, Ben estimated, they would reach the obstructing thicket in three minutes or so. Above that barrier, only the crest of the hill and its farmhouse were now visible, and he spied a cannon with a few tiny figures around it. Over on the Union left, the Fourth and Sixth Regiments proceeded past the bend of the tracks and the pike and into a salient of fir trees. Order remained generally tight. With the steady tramp of feet and the enemy still silent, Ben felt a throbbing in the air around him, in the soil beneath him. The first shell came as an instant of savage release–a flash from the hilltop, a thunderous report, a geyser of earth on the left. Ben heard cries and yells. He saw several men rolling as others poured into the trees and the Rebels let loose, splitting the air.

With no command to quicken the pace, the Twenty-second maintained its parade-like stride. A shell erupted behind the line, another to the right, another ripping through the thicket. Holding his sword level, Ben called over his shoulder–"Steady and forward!" His gaze clung to Langstaff's resolute back. The Fourth in particular was taking it badly, the woody salient rent with cries and explosions. In front of the Twenty-second, the ground shuddered as another shell struck, belching dirt high. E Company's captain dropped his sword and fell, clutching his leg. There were coughs as smoke came drifting, some of the shrubbery having caught fire. Between the blasts, Junie's frantic drum could still be heard–and in one such interval, Ben also heard a razor-thin cry overhead, which he at first mistook for the whistle of shell fragments. Ducking, he jerked his eyes skyward and saw the black speck of a hawk–Sable John, he guessed–gliding toward the enemy lines.

Treetops now blocked any view of the hill. The national color-bearer reached the thicket's edge and turned, waving the flag as the Twenty-second closed the distance and the barrage intensified. Around the dark base of the trees, Ben noted a sparkling and realized that it was swamp ground. Langstaff entered the shade, halted and looked back, his face like raw knuckles. "Wet ground!" he boomed. "Get through as fast as ye can! Assemble on the far side!"

With the shade came the precious illusion of shelter, lasting but seconds before a shell heaved up mud and branches on the right. Ben turned and saw Tucker striding after him. "Wet ground!" he hollered. "Keep them together!" Repeating the order for the other sergeants, he was drowned out by the next crashing impact, close by. He raised his sword, then followed Langstaff into the webwork of branches. His shoes sank, gushing mud as he lost his balance and grabbed hold of a tree trunk. A blacksnake plopped into the water and wriggled away. Glancing back, Ben saw Tucker and his men struggling after him, knee-deep.

A shell sheared off a treetop. Ben lost sight of Langstaff and then heard a splash, followed by a throaty Gaelic curse. Overtaking the captain, Ben found him wet to the waist and elbows, the plaid of his sash smeared with muck. "Move up!" Langstaff bawled, short of breath. But the men could do no better. With rifles awkwardly raised, they slogged and waded and thrashed their way forward. A branch dealt Ben a lash on the cheek as he barreled on. "To the hill!" he shouted. "Come on–to the hill!" An explosion almost directly above him loosed a rain of twigs. Snakes flew. Seizing a tree trunk, Ben spun about and saw a private with a hand to his scalp, eyes cloudy and fingers seeping red. Tucker quickly lifted the man into the crook of a tree and told him to hold on. The others groped past, and in their faces Ben recognized the galvanic effect of first blood. The wounded man called out–"Maggie! Maggie, are these bitin' snakes? Keep the children away!" A few yards to the right, Morton was yelling himself hoarse and Ben remembered not to look at him. Tree limbs cut across his vision. He ducked and lunged, prodding and slashing with his sword until he drew even with Langstaff. Not far ahead, the greater daylight showed through the trees. "Hold 'em a bit," said Langstaff, panting. "Till enough o' the regiment comes up."

Ben's heart hammered, his face stinging where the branch had struck. Yet they had made it through the swamp. Singly and in groups, soldiers burst out of the denser growth, slowing to catch their breath and peer ahead. Langstaff too gazed darkly ahead, his brow caked with mud. Ben realized that the bombardment had lulled. Slogging the last several steps, he reached solid ground, where the foliage parted like curtains. He looked out. His mouth went dry. Ears ringing, he beheld the rising expanse of green—wider, longer, more exposed than he could ever have imagined—and felt a sudden nostalgia for these shadows he had yet to leave. Near the crest he discerned the farmhouse, a Stars 'n' Bars flying from its roof. Next to it stood a section of breastwork lined with johnnies, then the cannon and crew he had seen.

The grassy slope lay bare a logic so simple that it made his head light. The federals were down here and the enemy up there, so the former had to charge up there from down here and shoot projectiles into the living bodies of those up there, while those up there hurled bigger projectiles at the living bodies of those down here. It was logical and it was mad—a logical madness. He turned to see the troops massing along the thicket, hemming it with mud-spattered blue while others emerged from the trees behind them. It occurred to him that at this range the Confederates would be loading canister, the scourge of infantry.

Nearby, Morton stumbled into view, then crouched behind a bush to vomit. It struck Ben that all the bad luck resided not in his fellow officer but on the hill above, cocked and loaded. He in fact wanted to clap Morton on the shoulder, but the thought fled as he turned to Tucker. With Young's help, the sergeant already had his troops in position. Ben nodded to him and he nodded back. Every face bore that peculiar intent look—Prince's most of all, his eyes locked on the hilltop. Musket hammers made the klick-kluck sound as percussion caps were inserted. Along the woods to the left, the Fourth was forming as best it could, trying to close gaps in its line. The national color-bearer stepped from the shade and unfurled the Stars 'n' Stripes, miraculously still clean. Langstaff paced back and forth, glowering.

Without warning, a quick succession of air-blasts struck, shaking the leaves and throttling the fidgety ranks, blinding them with garish flame. Suddenly practical, Ben blinked at the hill and guessed its upward distance—about four hundred yards. He went to make sure that each platoon was ready and then returned to his original spot. A number of officers had moved into the open, including Kiddoo. The colonel waved his cap. Someone else shouted something. Langstaff turned to face the men and Ben called for them to listen up. The captain leveled a finger, jabbing with it. "First quick!" he bellowed. "Then, halfway up–double quick!" He raised his sword. Ben raised his. "Company forward! Charge!"

Shouting the order, Ben followed Langstaff at a loping run, and that blazing clarity of vision took hold again. Like a sudden high wind, a roar issued from the Union multitude as it swarmed into the sunlight, pushing up the base of the hill. It was met by more canister, shrieking metal fusing with human shrieks. With his banner flapping, the color-bearer broke ahead. Ben yelled to his men–"We're going to take those guns!" In the next moment, in the heat of the onrush, he glanced to both sides and went cold. The charge was wildly irregular–the Twenty-second and part of the Fourth bulging forward while the Sixth and most of the Fourth lagged, still emerging from the woods. On the right, the Fifth too was proceeding piecemeal.

The flaming air-blasts continued, as did the maimed cries and the shouts of urging. Through the gathering smoke, Ben could now see two cannons flanking the Rebel breastwork. He moved at a steady jog, barely feeling the ground beneath him. Ahead of him, Langstaff suddenly stopped and turned around, holding his sword aloft. "Remember Fort Pillow!" the captain boomed, just as the air flashed overhead. Lurching, Ben saw Langstaff's chest explode. He saw it again and again as he stood there, deaf in one ear, legs wobbly, steadying himself on his sword-tip, until he focused upon the Scotsman's bloody corpse. Looking back, he saw Tucker, Young and the others getting to their feet, except for two convulsing privates and one who lay still. Tucker appeared stunned. Then Ben heard his own disembodied shout–"Keep going! KEEP GOING!!" Then he was dashing about, here and there before the dazed platoons. "Forward quick! Company forward!" Whirling, Tucker bellowed the command and started shoving his men to action.

The charge continued, still short of the halfway point. Seeing only the green hilltop, Ben forced himself onward as his breath returned and the canister hurtled, bursting like death's pollen. Smoke drifted across his path, and as he passed through it he glimpsed some movement on the right. He looked and saw a spindly Union officer running toward him, gesturing vigorously. At the same time, he saw Morton's company balk, shuffle and then reverse direction. Ben stumbled to a halt as the officer intercepted him. It was Colonel Kiddoo, eyes fierce above his drooping mustache. He shouted something inaudible and Ben saluted, shouting back.

"Lost our captain, sir!"

"What's your name, Lieutenant?!"

"Truly, sir!"

"I brevet you captain! Get them back to the trees and regroup!"

The colonel moved on, waving the rest of the regiment back as more shells shrieked overhead. Ben put a hand to his head and found that he had lost his cap. Then, facing the company, he felt a larger nakedness. "Down to the woods!" he called. "Regroup!" With blank looks they started back down the slope. They passed Langstaff's body and several others. What cohesion remained began to vanish as the men hurried toward the thicket, gathering a few wounded along the way.

Ben had at first tolerated and then enforced military order, despite his natural distaste for it. Often he had pined for the West, where rank and protocol were generally less observed. Now a passion for straight lines and closed ranks ignited him. If the troops reached the thicket as a mob, something not easily restored would be lost. "Platoons fall in!" he cried. "Fall in! Fall in!"

At last the shelling let up.

Minutes later they were reassembled in the shade, waiting, everything steeped in a hush too deep to believe. Blue-clad bodies littered the hillside, the bravest stretcher-bearers venturing out to collect wounded. The color-bearer, gallant and anonymous, was almost the last man off the field. Then Kiddoo reappeared, calling Ben and the other company chiefs together. Noting Morton's pale presence, Ben realized that Morton had been brevetted captain of E Company. Kiddoo delivered stark orders from the general. The attack would be concerted this time, but launched chiefly by the right wing—the Twenty-second and the Fifth—while the even more battered left supplied diversion.

As the group separated, Ben cocked his pistol and inserted a cap. Noting his steady fingers, he realized that Langstaff's annihilation had changed him, stripped him so completely of hope and fear that he wondered how he could ever have felt otherwise. He walked up to Morton.

"Another cigar at the top?"

Morton blinked at him. "I think I could spare one."

"See you up there."

Leaving Morton, Ben found Tucker staring out at the slope, arms folded.

"Tucker—for now, you're lieutenant in all but name."

"As I said, sir—you can count on me."

"Nothing to do but try again."

Tucker swatted a mosquito. "We'll take the hill, sir."

"Yes, we will."

Ben summoned the other sergeants and relayed the instructions. "As you move out, tell them it's for Langstaff," he added. Reddick and Armstrong gave dutiful nods. Parrish actually seemed exhilarated.

Stepping away from them, Ben was surprised to see Junie, half-concealed behind some saplings. With his drum strapped on and pants muddy to the thighs, the boy was using his shirt-tail to wipe his specs. He put them on, then looked worried as he saw Ben approaching. "I'm sorry, sir!" he blurted. "I had to come this far. The whole regiment's here."

Ben placed a hand on his shoulder. "Never mind. But when we go next, don't follow—I mean it this time. Just bang that thing for all it's worth, all right?"

"All right, sir."

From the north came sounds of a cavalry skirmish, beating hooves amid small arms fire. But the stillness stretched on. At the thicket's edge, Young shielded his eyes and gazed upward. Curious, Ben did likewise and saw Sable John against the sky, wheeling like a blown black leaf. For a moment Ben felt as if he had slipped free of his body, rising high and circling hawklike above the fallen, above this green patch of earth. Beyond, in all directions, he imagined an endless bone-littered wasteland. The world was ending, and it had all come down to this green patch of earth— these last two cannibal tribes facing each other, long past redemption, playing out the final prophecy. Ben shut his eyes, just long enough to call himself back down. Kiddoo came striding past, ordering the men to full readiness. Gripping the sword in his left hand and the pistol in his right, Ben stepped into the open. The colonel halted, drew his sword and gazed down-line. Then, catching a signal, he whipped off his cap and waved it. "Twenty-second—charge!"

"Remember Langstaff!" Ben yelled. "For the captain!"

To cries of exultation and Junie's brisk rat-a-tat, the line surged forward. The sun hit with an otherworldly brilliance as the Rebels commenced fire, drowning the cries—and with the tide of legs behind him,

Ben did not feel himself running so much as borne along. Squinting, he barely saw Langstaff's corpse in time to bound over it. Canister flew, bodies fell–three hundred yards to go. The units started fanning out, some troops racing past the colors. Over to Ben's left, half of a G Company platoon went down in a single blast–but the charge swept on, accelerating even as the ground grew steeper. Though he ran hard, the men began to overtake him, and in the tumult he heard Tucker's shout–"Lions, boys! Lions!" They had crossed two hundred merciless yards, with a similar distance still ahead.

Musketry broke from the crest, one bullet whistling past Ben's ear. More troops went down. Up behind their crude breastwork–a rail fence reinforced with timber and hay bales–Confederate infantry loaded and fired at demon speed. Ben clutched his sword and his pistol as an unmistakable fever consumed him–victory fever, the craze to kill. Nearby, a greater blast went off–double canister now. Yelling but unable to hear himself, he kept on, half-blind with the sun and smoke. He stumbled, wiped his eyes and stumbled again before a concussion knocked him sideways. In a shower of dirt-clods he spun, halted and saw Young with part of his head gone, spouting blood. The corporal's big body crumpled. A roar filled Ben's skull as he willed himself onward, spitting dirt. Other soldiers passed him. Not far ahead, the Stars 'n' Stripes wobbled and the color-bearer sank to his knees. Prince came charging out of the smoke, seized the staff one-handed and plunged ahead. One hundred yards to go.

Ben clenched his teeth and summoned a final surge from his legs. A short distance away he glimpsed Tucker still urging his men forward. The Union stampede had lost half its momentum, some of the troops crouching to return fire. The rail fence spat flame and another double blast went off to the rear–but with every second, the battle was shrinking, concentrating. Fifty yards now. Ben slowed to a trudge, his lungs raw. Straight ahead he saw a frenzied Rebel gun crew repositioning their cannon, a big brass Napoleon–rolling it back as their sergeant ranted and cajoled. Ben sprinted a few more yards, then stopped to raise his pistol. He was trying to sight the sergeant when a pain pierced his upper shooting arm. He dropped the pistol, his arm gone limp. With a shudder he absorbed the pain's force, a burning from shoulder to elbow. His vision swayed and he had to look at the ground to keep his balance. Then, a few feet away, he saw Tucker lying in dull-faced agony, the ground beneath him slick with blood.

With his arm going numb, Ben managed to retrieve the pistol and stick it in his holster. His good hand kept a clammy grip on his sword as he staggered on, coughing, his eyes going in and out of focus. A cyclone roar surrounded him. Not far to his right, Prince was waving the flag and bellowing about lions. Men bunched perilously together as they drove forward, onward, blurring in a giant phantasm of light and smoke and heaving shadow. Ben raised his eyes. The sky howled, the sky reeled–and against the reeling blue he spied Sable John, a splinter of night soaring upward, tilting and then diving into the vortex, wings back, down toward the killing storm of men. Ben saw his mother, then his father, then Annie. He saw Sapphira. He saw a lonely wooded shore. He wanted to collect rocks on lonely wooded shores. Then, lowering his gaze, he saw the cannon again.

It was behind the end of the fence nearest the farmhouse, its barrel straight out, its frantic crew loading another shell. The effect at close quarters would be that of a huge sawed-off shotgun. Ben started for it, breathing through his teeth, his useless arm dangling at his side. A soldier bumped past him and he faltered, then caught himself with his sword and kept going. The gunners were ramming the explosive. Picking up speed, he tried to yell. A bullet clipped his thigh. In the din he heard Morton–"They're caving, boys! They're caving!" The ground was starting to level. Suddenly there were colored troops drawing alongside of him, their bayonets extended. "That gun!" he gasped. "Charge . . . !"

Rebel marksmen fell back from the fence and tried to reload. Farther on sat the cannon, deadly patient as its crew scrambled. Ben's arm had lost all sensation. Bounding, lurching like an ape, he kept his eyes on the gun as soldiers raced past him, vaulting the fence. The Rebel infantry scattered. The artillery sergeant shouted a command. Falling against the fence, Ben saw all but one enemy private leap clear of the cannon, its black mouth saying too late, too late, too soon as the lone private yanked the lanyard. Ben did not really hear the blast and just barely saw it–a sheet of flame, then darkness. World ended.

PART IV

Death By A Wide Margin

*The Present, the Immediate, the Actual, has proved
too potent for me. It . . . leaves me sadly content to scatter
a thousand peaceful fantasies upon the hurricane that
is sweeping us all along.*
• NATHANIEL HAWTHORNE, ON HIS
WARTIME WRITER'S BLOCK

*It has come that man has no longer an individual existence,
but is counted in thousands and measured in miles.*
• CLARA BARTON

30

Brown's Hotel
June 15

A WASTED MORNING. UNANSWERED knocks at the door of Wakefield's darkened shop; a restless vigil across the street; Forbes eventually departing to
buy laudanum for his leg pain; Truly leaving with a couple of errands in
mind; Kirschenbaum, a woefully conspicuous sentinel, left behind on the
chance that Wakefield might yet show.

From West Third Street, Truly had proceeded to the War Department
and telegraphed Heatherton once more, asking him to question *Comet-
American* staffers about Wakefield–also, to send the photograph from Van
Gilder's office. Next he went to the Old Capitol, where a sergeant of the
guard informed him that no prisoners had arrived since the previous
morning–no Adam Cathcart yet. Truly's frustration then propelled him
on a search for Congressman Underhill–and after a fruitless trip to the
Capitol Building, he had come here to Brown's.

At the third-floor landing, he encountered a Negro waiter carrying a
tray of dirty dishes.

"I seem to have lost my way," Truly said. "Do you know the room of
Congressman Ezra Underhill?"

The waiter gestured with the tray. "Fourth one down on the right,
sir–sounds like he's practicing a speech."

"Good for him! I'm his elocution teacher–he must be getting ready
for me."

Truly went down the hall to the door, through which he heard the rise and fall of a baritone voice. He smiled at the gold damask wallpaper. In one respect, at least, the passing years had made him more reckless instead of less. When forced to confront a more powerful man–even one who he had already riled–he no longer had to steel himself. Like a merry dervish, he jumped right in.

He listened closely as the voice swung lower, oozing sorrow, curling around each phrase: "In the name of this supposed contract with heaven, the administration has unchained the Negroes and chained itself to an absurdity which galls the most loyal heart . . . " Climbing now, gathering force: "This notion that God-fearing white citizens must now give way to the tide of the darky franchise!" Truly's hand closed on the doorknob. Slowly he turned it. "Further, fellow patriots–how can we continue to call upon their valor and devotion, while building before their appalled vision a future whose black uncertainties . . . "

Truly shoved the door open. With a gasp, Underhill tottered back against his writing desk. He stood there open-mouthed, clutching papers, unkempt in his shirtsleeves. Truly shut the door. "Lord above, I haven't heard such thespian excess since J. Wilkes Booth played *Richard the Third*!"

Underhill's face went from pale to livid. "This is . . . ! How did you . . . ?!"

"It's a hotel, not a fortress. I tried the Capitol first, but no one had seen you. Frightened to go out, are we?"

With a choking sound, the congressman threw his papers. "This is insufferable!"

"Now *that* sounds sincere. When you rise to speak, sir, think of old Nate and you'll get reelected for sure. Is there a spittoon hereabouts?"

Underhill exhaled, rubbed his unshaven cheeks. A grainy weariness entered his voice. "You're mad–and soon to be unemployed. I'm going to write to Stanton, but first I'm going to have you thrown out." He reached for the bell-pull.

"Peavey's dead," said Truly.

Underhill winced. His hand went still, then fell to his side.

Truly took a bite of tobacco. "That shocks you? After Van Gilder, I don't reckon it ought to. You want a chaw?" He offered the plug.

Underhill's coon-eyed stare had an unexpected depth–a look beyond fright, almost calm. Truly sauntered to the open window, sat on the sill. He spat into the street below. "These folks, these murderers, are damned serious. Maybe you didn't fully appreciate that till now. But maybe you can appreciate too what protection the national government can offer."

Underhill looked as if he were only half-listening. He sat in a cushioned wicker chair and gazed into the blackened fireplace.

Having struck the first blow, Truly let loose with another. "We know about your and Archer's visit to Peavey yesterday, and what you were after."

Underhill sat frozen.

"And among Peavey's papers, we found plenty evidence of the connection between you. He wasn't the brightest or the most careful fellow, and the same might be said for Van Gilder. That's why they're dead. But surely, sir, that ampler brain of yours will keep you from suffering the same fate."

Underhill put his hands to his face. "You are speaking to a representative of the United States Congress."

"True. And how long are you going to fancy that as a shield?" Yet the thought distracted Truly. Despite the skill, daring and ferocity of these killers, could they really be so bold as to target a man of high public office, no matter what he had done to cross them? Underhill didn't look up. Truly decided to take the gambit as far as it would go. "But besides that, sir, Detective Archer is talking to us."

Underhill stirred. He lifted his pale, ravaged face and gawked.

Chewing, Truly felt a wave of satisfaction. "You see, Archer knew when to change his survival tactics. Oh, it'll be a blot on his otherwise distinguished record, but show me a man in this town who doesn't have a few."

Underhill's thin lips parted, then moved silently before the words came out. "And what has he told you?"

Truly realized that he had placed himself out on a limb. Taking stock, he switched his tone from breezy to grave. "Thus far, enough to make us certain. He's being interviewed as we speak."

There was a twitch in Underhill's temple, but his stare was suddenly less horrified, more intent. "Then why, pray tell, would you need me? Why, if you have Archer?"

Truly managed a smirk. "Archer knows a lot, but by no means all. We hoped that out of common sense you would supply any missing pieces."

Underhill leered. It was the expression of a desperate but accomplished liar, a veteran bluffer who recognized his own game and knew that his worst fear, for the moment, had passed. He let out a startling giggle. "Were that so, why would you come to me prematurely? Before you even knew what pieces of your fantasy might be missing?"

Truly felt his cheeks start to burn. Why had he not anticipated this in a politician? This shrewdness out of nowhere, sharpened by fear? "The murderers have struck twice, and may do so again at any moment. Frankly, sir, I never thought you'd be so blind to your own interest."

Looking at the fireplace, Underhill said nothing.

Truly spat out the last of his tobacco. "We have the lieutenant-colonel too."

A long pause. "What lieutenant-colonel?"

"Which one do you think, man!?"

"Name him."

"You're in no position to test me, Congressman."

"I believe the reverse is more accurate."

Underhill's abrupt composure rankled Truly even more. The congressman got up, walked to where his papers lay scattered and started gathering them. Truly's gaze wandered to the table beside him. Propped next to an empty claret bottle sat a framed photograph of Underhill. He picked it up. It presented Underhill as dignity incarnate: solemn, impeccably dressed, one hand tucked into his waistcoat. In the upper left corner and in that same flowing hand, an inscription read, "With utmost respect and appreciation, M. Wakefield, July 1862." Truly put the portrait down, then looked up into the muzzle of a cocked pistol.

The barrel quivered as Underhill pointed it at Truly's head. The congressman sneered. "Be gone. If you trouble me again, by God, I'll kill you."

Truly eased off the sill. He tipped his hat, then headed for the door. "You just picked the wrong boat, Ezra. The one bound for the Lake of Fire."

31

Truly Residence

CAUGHT IN A bluff, Truly thought. Checked by an inflated political piss-ant who he had managed to underestimate. Though his reasons had been sound enough, the whole episode seemed so avoidable in hindsight. His mood remained foul until he arrived on his own doorstep and got a surprise. From inside, the sound of the piano made him pause, listening as a dizzy minuet whirled to its finish. Then a pair of hands applauded, followed by Kirschenbaum's voice.

"Most inspired, Miss Sapphira!"

So the hunchback had arrived early. Entering quietly, Truly stood beside the parlor threshold and heard Sapphira's shy but delighted laugh.

"Please, Mister Kirschenbaum. I'm still a novice."

"But your fingers, they have in them the spirit. As a poor man, I have enjoyed few concerts–yet I say, in London or Paris or my own Frankfurt, they would shower you with bouquets."

"Why, thank you! Tell me, though–have you ever been to Paris?"

"Paris? Ja, I stops there on my way to England."

"Honestly?" Her voice became happily urgent. "Do tell me about it!"

Predictable it was, Truly thought, that Kirschenbaum the gifted observer would also prove to be the perfect audience. How long had it been since he had heard Sapphira laugh? Or since a new acquaintance had disarmed her so? Lately he had sensed that she was indulging her morbid side again, keeping vigil at the Sixth Street Wharf. More mysteriously, she hadn't offered him Ben's letter to read, as was their practice, while her remarks about its content were sketchy. At the moment, however, he could imagine her rapt gaze as Kirschenbaum told her of seeing Notre Dame Cathedral and the Arc de Triomphe.

Truly hung his hat and coat beside Kirschenbaum's. "Greetings in there!" he called. Entering the parlor, he saw both of them on their feet, smiling.

"Mister Kirschenbaum has been keeping me company," Sapphira said.

"And here I am to take him away from you," said Truly.

The hunchback held a teacup and a half-eaten roll. "Pardon I am here early, Major. Miss Sapphira entertains me on the piano."

"As she does me, when I beg enough. Well, Bart and Octavius should be here soon. Is Anna about?"

"She went out with some friends," said Sapphira. "To the Center Market, I think."

"Then that introduction will have to wait. Manfred, I'll show you to the study."

Kirschenbaum gave Sapphira a slight bow, then followed Truly down the hall. "A most remarkable girl, Major. I fear I startle her when she answers the door."

"You seemed to have charmed her since."

"It is she who charms. A surprise to me, that your step-daughter should be colored."

Truly thought of all the reactions over the years. Nervous avoidance, ill-concealed bewilderment–even from those he had informed in advance. This was different, and welcome. "I'll tell you about it sometime. Anyhow–I take it our Mister Wakefield never showed?"

"I regret no, Major. But I have learned some little of him."

Kirschenbaum said he had spoken with a neighbor of Wakefield's—a Dresden-born *hausfrau* who was happy to converse in German. She told him that Wakefield's shop was also his living quarters, to which he had moved in late '61. She described him as private but quite pleasant. In recent days, he had kept the shop closed and been mostly absent. The woman had last seen him early Monday, headed off somewhere.

"Somewhere–yes," said Truly. "Out of sight. But not out of reach, let's hope."

In the study, Kirschenbaum perused the bookcases while Truly went to get more chairs. Soon Forbes arrived, his furtive glances checking for signs of Anna's presence–disappointment again. Duke followed minutes later; under his arm he had a copy of *The National Republican,* which he readily surrendered when Sapphira asked to see it. Truly hoped that no news from the Petersburg sector had leaked yet.

With the double window open to the hot, bright day, the four men sat with their tea and coffee. Truly got the most distasteful news out of the way, giving a condensed account of his fiasco with Underhill. Noting Forbes' worried look, he shrugged. "I just thought it urgent to try and crack Underhill before another body turned up. But yes, I know this could make for a distracting ruckus."

"Do you think these people would actually murder a congressman?" Forbes asked.

"Depends on what's at stake, and this we don't know yet."

Duke cleared his throat. Hesitantly he took a note from his vest and offered it. "Major, this was left under our office door. It's from Colonel Baker, concerning your progress report."

From Duke's cautious expression, Truly guessed the tenor of his superior's response. He sighed. "Could you please just sum it up?"

"Certainly, sir. It, um . . . says he read your report with curiosity, but he's none too convinced of the investigation's value. He thinks it might boil down to something quite apart from the organization's concerns–just an odd collection of men who've spent time at the same brothel, and who've been snared by an especially mean blackmailer."

Truly sneered. "The investigation's value? Compared to some of his little quests, this one's more promising than the '49 Gold Rush! Our Great Caesar, Colonel Baker, has in the past ordered men jailed and interrogated for little more than whistling 'Dixie.' Fact is, Lafe's generally less fired up about any case that he's not personally directing." With a huff, Truly slouched. "All right, then–I can fend off his doubts for now. I'll tell him that our entangled congressman is courting the Peace faction, and it might be nice to catch him in a vile scandal."

"Good," said Forbes. "Whatever would shore up our position–preferably before the Democratic leadership demands our little heads on a platter, with the Washington Police singing harmony."

"Indeed. And speaking of the police . . . " Truly turned to Duke. "Have you found anything of interest on Detective Archer?"

"Possibly, Major." Setting his teacup on Truly's desk, Duke began to gesticulate. Two of his more garrulous police friends, he explained, had spoken about the detective on condition of secrecy. Within the department,

Archer was considered ambitious and effective, tight-lipped and mysterious. It was said that he had served as a policeman in Philadelphia, where he managed to vault class lines and marry a woman of fairly comfortable means. They had a daughter. From the wife's side of the family, they inherited a hotel in Bladensburg, Maryland, to which they moved upon Archer's quitting the force. The role of innkeeper seemed ill-suited to a man of his sober temperament, and it was easy to speculate that the venture proved neither happy nor successful. In '61, after only a few years, he sold the hotel and thereby missed the area's subsequent wartime boom. He then moved his wife and daughter to Washington. There he applied for work with the Metropolitan Police and got a waiver for the two-year residency requirement, his qualifications being better than most. He was assigned to the mounted patrol of the Second Precinct.

"Where the Emperor's House is located," Truly observed.

"Correct," said Duke, "–but he wasn't there long. With the department newly formed and the city in turmoil, there were opportunities for an able, dedicated policeman to advance himself. By year's end, he'd been promoted to sergeant of the Ninth Precinct, where he became known as a strict enforcer of the health code, public morals and the good conduct of his men. Shortly before this, though, he suffered a tragedy. His wife Helen seems to have been a sickly and unhappy woman. Rather suddenly, she went mad. Archer placed her in the asylum, where she was found dead sometime in December of that year. A vial of prussic acid was found in her hand, though no one could say how she obtained it."

Truly's twinge of sympathy lasted but seconds before suspicion crept in. "Note the season of her death," he murmured.

Forbes' stare turned inward. "That same period in which Underhill, Van Gilder and Peavey were freed from burdensome individuals. Late '61, early '62."

Duke related how Archer had applied himself with greater zeal and, a year later, been approved for the Detective Corps. This was a natural step—bigger salary, plus a share of monetary rewards. At the same time, his religious zeal became more evident. Occasionally he conducted church services at the city jail, preaching to thieves, brawlers and fallen women. Colleagues took this as a reaction to his wife's sad demise. His daughter Cecelia had meanwhile become a missionary in the Sea Islands, teaching freed slaves.

Truly nodded, ruminating. Secondhand though Duke's information was, it seemed untainted by anyone's malice or presumption. "All right—on to Peavey, then. Have you gotten very far into his ledger?"

"Far enough to observe one or two things. Peavey's bookkeeping grew sloppier as he neared ruin. But throughout the ledger, I found a quarterly payment of two hundred dollars, recorded without notation. The last was made in late February of this year."

Forbes looked up. "That corresponds with Van Gilder's last trip to the capital, when we fancy he made a scheduled payment to the blackmailers."

"Peavey's house slave spoke of his quarterly absences," said Truly. "That would fit too, if each man were required to pay in person. Such a rule would serve as a built-in reminder of their bondage." Not wanting to ignore Kirschenbaum, he looked over at the German. "Any thoughts, Manfred?"

Mulling, Kirschenbaum sipped his tea. "One thing I wonder . . . This stoppage of payments, this plan of defiance—it falls apart. Yet only one man, Van Gilder, tries to escape. If the keepers are here in Washington, the other men are in easy reach for punishment. Yet they do not flee. The one who is most far from them, in New York—he flees. Where is the sense?"

"Good question," said Truly. "Granted, each of them has been desperate to keep his station in life—so it would take a whole lot of fear, a certainty of destruction, to make them skeedaddle like Van Gilder did. From what Peavey's slave told us, it appears that Archer and Underhill have clung to some hope of placating the keepers. Van Gilder had no such hope."

Duke spoke up. "In a fix like that, which would be the most astute response? To run? Or to beg and prostrate—swear to mend one's ways?"

Forbes shrugged. "Maybe Archer and Underhill are right, that their positions will help shield them. And maybe Van Gilder was right, judging himself less valuable and therefore more vulnerable to retribution."

"Or perhaps," said Truly, "he had an extra reason for fear. I'm thinking of his mysterious injuries a year ago. Think of it. It would be only natural to want to throw off these blackmailers—and of the known victims, who would likely have been the first to try? To get arrogant? To imagine the danger as less than it was, and then skip a payment? It would be the one farthest from the threat." The others nodded. "I'd wager that in late May of '63, Van Gilder declined to make his usual trip to Washington. And that he paid for it—not with his life, that time, but with torture.

Torture, with the assurance that his next act of disobedience would be his last."

"So," Forbes murmured, "when all five of them eventually decided to rebel, it follows that he alone saw fit to arrange escape, should the rebellion fail."

"While concealing the true reason for this," Duke added, "–even from his good Confederate friend Cathcart, the very man who arranged the escape plan with Richmond."

"The very man who we haven't questioned yet," Forbes said. "And what about that?"

"Cathcart's still not back from Albany," said Truly, "but I figure he will be sometime tonight. So in the morning, Bart, you and I should call at the Old Capitol. In a way, I'm glad for the blunder that has kept Cathcart out of our reach–because now we'll have a lot more facts and guesswork to throw at him."

Truly had Kirschenbaum repeat what Wakefield's German neighbor had said about him. If they kept stopping by the shop at random times, they might still catch Wakefield. Yet that was unlikely. The man was almost certainly lying very low, or maybe gone altogether.

Fighting dejection, Truly turned to the window. He saw Sapphira on the sunny back porch, munching an apple and reading the newspaper. Here was the one disconcerting thing about meeting at the house–to probe these foul doings, then to turn and see Sapphira.

32

Old Capitol Prison
June 16

THE GUARDS HERE always seemed the dullest in Washington, as well as the firmest on procedure. The sergeant confronting Truly and Forbes examined their papers long enough to bring his reading ability into question. Truly, humming to himself, gave Forbes a wry glance and looked at the building. Nearly fifty years ago, after invading British burned the original Capitol, this three-story brick structure had housed Congress temporarily while the other underwent restoration. Nowadays it housed a far sorrier lot. Sorrier and–thanks to the army ban on prisoner exchange– a good deal more numerous. Captive Rebel troops could not be transferred fast enough to Point Lookout, which was also said to be bursting. Grimy, smelly and lice-infested, the Old Capitol mourned its fate like a gentleman-turned-beggar, and only the great arched triple window above the doorway recalled its grander days. Most of the other windows were boarded up. Sentries tried to keep in the shade as they paced the adjacent First and A Streets.

On the sergeant's bored face, comprehension glimmered at last. He handed back their papers. "I'll fetch the superintendent, sirs. You can wait inside."

Past the heavy door, they entered the stuffy receiving room where several people–friends and relatives of inmates–waited sullenly on two long, opposite benches. Truly and Forbes remained standing as the sergeant kept on through the interior doors. Stationed beside these, a private gave them a vacant stare, leaning on his rifle. Truly looked at the wall. There he beheld an example of Superintendent Wood's mischief: an army recruitment poster, depicting virtuous Union boys in perfect flag-waving formation. "PATRIOTS!" it shrieked, in red block letters. "YOUR NATION CALLS!" It was the sort of star-spangled bombast that Wood himself scorned, but which could only rankle a pro-Southern visitor. On closer inspection, Truly found a scrawled retort–"Calls You To Your Grave, Yankee Scum!"–beneath which Wood's familiar scribble replied, "Dear Sir–Bad humor foretells defeat. P.S. Next time kindly sign your name so we may be better acquainted." Truly's cackle startled all present.

Eyeing the poster, Forbes muttered, "An amusing enough fellow. But let's be careful what we say in front of him."

"I know," said Truly. "Believe me, I know."

For any number of reasons, Truly should have despised William Wood. Forbes did, declaring that he would trust a spirit medium before the Old Capitol's jailer/impresario. To begin with, he was Baker's closest professional confidante. Their joint prisoner interrogations were legendary for their python-like relentlessness. And to the feared Secretary of War Edwin Stanton he seemed a favored pet, shielded from the citizens, administrators and military men whom he routinely outraged. Inside his dingy brick domain, and sometimes outside of it, this army-hating ex-private enjoyed something close to *carte blanche*. No one seemed to know how he had surfaced from an obscure past to his present status–this vague yet broad authority, something that his fat ringful of keys scarcely explained. A model-maker by trade, he had been employed by patent-hungry inventors in the 50's, and this had brought him in contact with big Washington attorneys such as Stanton. The war's outset found him working as a federal secret agent, but within a few months he had received this inexplicable promotion and begun his rise to infamy.

At the Old Capitol, government supplies had a habit of disappearing. Wood's nephew ran the prison commissary, and it was whispered that the two of them were robbing it blind. Though an unswerving Republican and Abolitionist, Wood seemed on good terms with the smugglers and blockade runners who he kept under lock. Even with some of the Rebel troops he appeared friendly, provided they weren't rabid in politics or aristocratic in bearing. With the occasional lady prisoner he was indulgent unto silliness, and most new arrivals were in fact received kindly. To a prisoner brought in on dubious charges, his rights blown away like dandelion seeds, Wood pledged every effort for his comfort and eventual release, then arranged for a detective to pose as the fellow's cellmate. A lapsed Catholic, he reveled openly in non-belief while encouraging Sunday services at the prison. Dubbing him "The Crown Prince of Duplicity" or–invoking the two-faced Roman god–"Janus the Jailer," Truly was nonetheless grateful for Wood's presence on Earth, with its reminder of life's twisted sorcery.

Wood–small, shaggy and muscular in his rumpled clothes–arrived with the sergeant who had fetched him. From his hip dangled the great clinking ring of keys.

"Janus!" Truly greeted him.

"Don't call me that, Truly. Not today." In the furrows of Wood's scavenger face, great worry showed. "One of those damned louts of mine just shot a prisoner." On one of the benches, a crinolined older woman gasped, clutching her bosom. Wood turned to her. "Worry not, Madam. The unfortunate man was no one you would . . . " His deep green eyes deliberated. "Who have you come to see, dear lady?" She blurted a name. "Then rest assured," Wood said, "–the name of the deceased is nothing like . . . " Hesitating, he tapped the sergeant's chest. "Rogers–go find out the man's name, for God's sake." Again the woman gasped as the sergeant hurried off. A male visitor uttered a curse. Wood looked balefully at Truly and Forbes. "So stupid. So unnecessary. These louts they send me . . . "

"Sorry to have come on a bad day," said Truly. "We need to know if Adam Cathcart's been delivered here yet." Struck with a horrible thought, he stiffened. "And more important, whether or not he's the corpse you speak of! William, don't tell me . . . "

Wood looked insulted. "Keep your harness on. Yes, he got here last night. Safe in his cell just now, though a little scuffed."

Truly relaxed. "Scuffed, you say?"

"In Baltimore the marshals made the mistake of removing his leg irons. He tried to jump the train and was subdued. On his arrival here he threw a stool at one of my louts and was similarly subdued. If I didn't know you were itching to question him, I'd have pummeled him senseless myself."

By the left-hand bench, a soft-featured young man in a rust-colored frock coat had risen to his feet. His hostile eyes returned Truly's gaze.

Wood glanced at the stranger. "Oh, yes–the incubus who's been haunting my door, demanding news of the aforesaid prisoner. An even bigger nuisance than you, Truly."

The man's sneer failed to mask his nervousness. Clearing his throat, he wiped his brow with a handkerchief. "James Cathcart," he spoke. "I only wish to know if out of common decency I might be permitted to see my cousin."

Forbes addressed him. "Sir, the charge against him is serious."

"What charge? My family has been told nothing! Is there no cruelty you people are above?!"

Other visitors murmured support. Just then the sergeant returned and whispered the dead prisoner's name to Wood, who announced it to sighs of relief. Nobody's friend or relation.

"Now," said Wood, himself relieved–"you good ladies and gentlemen have waited long enough. Rogers, hurry it up–have you no heart? Have each of them escorted in turn to their loved ones." He looked at James Cathcart–a minor Patent Office official, but one whose prideful air wafted like an overripe fragrance. Wood switched to the voice he reserved for such people. "Tarnation, Nathaniel! What do ye kalky-late we orter do 'bout this here fella? All his fancy sermonizin's got me shakin' in my shoes!"

It seemed likely, Truly was thinking, that James Cathcart's concerns went no farther than his cousin's welfare. And he had shown some grit in coming here. Early in the war, the watchdog Potter Committee had weeded many pro-Southern employees from the federal payroll. Scores of them remained, no doubt–discreetly, and having taken the loyalty oath. But James had much to lose in making himself so visible, his sentiments so publicly clear. And this evident sincerity made Truly think that he might prove useful.

"William," said Truly, "–might we and this gent use your office?"

Wood shrugged.

He led Truly, Forbes and the indignant visitor out of the receiving room, down a corridor and into the stockaded prison yard. Inmates, many of them Reb soldiers in soiled butternut, skulked around while sentries kept watch. Expressions were somber as two guards carried off a body wrapped in a grimy white sheet. Starting up a flight of stairs, Wood shook his head.

Then, from a shaded corner of the yard, a rawhide voice sounded. "There you be, you damned Yankee assassin! Is this how you run your hog-sty here?!"

Wood paused to yell over his shoulder. "Keep a civil tongue, General, or be confined to your cell!"

"Anywhere I cain't see you is all right, damn your eyes!"

Turning, Truly spied the thin, bearded figure leaning on a crutch. No guard moved to silence the wizened Rebel. In his frayed hat and dusty frock, he shook his fist and kept yelling: "Dog! Wretch! Murderer!"

Truly saw the general seventeen years younger, a captain then, cussing his laggard troops across the Eastern Sierra Madre.

"That's the one you told me about?" Forbes asked.

Truly gave half a smile. "Snakebite Dinsmore. Were they all like him, we'd have been better off letting 'em secede."

With Dinsmore's curses still ringing, Wood led them along the catwalk to his musty office, then left to nurse his gloom. With its walls of exposed brick and dirty whitewash, the office could have been mistaken for a cell if not for its one unboarded window. Truly raised the sash, hung his coat and hat on a wall peg and then sat in the rickety desk chair, while Forbes took a stool behind him.

James Cathcart took a chair facing them, looking more anxious. "What now?" he demanded. "Am I to be arrested too?"

"Mister Cathcart," Truly spoke, "–what has your cousin ever said about his activities in New York?"

"Merely that he was writing for the *Comet-American*–which, for you, seems reason enough to lock him up."

"Think, please. Is that all he ever told you?"

"In the name of . . . " He wiped his brow. "He sent me clippings of what he wrote. He described conditions in the city. That's all. The few times that he visited home, most of our conversation involved family news."

"About a year ago, weren't you and your family a mite startled by Adam's sudden departure for New York? And his career change–textiles to journalism?"

James fidgeted. "Well, yes . . . Of course. Still, Adam has strong political feelings, and I admired his acting upon them. We all did."

"What did he say about Gideon Van Gilder?"

James Cathcart made an irritable gesture. "Little. He spoke of Van Gilder's commitment to the Peace Movement, and I gathered they were friends."

"All right. Wakefield, then–what did Adam say about him?"

"Who?"

"During your cousin's New Year's visit, the two of you had a photograph taken at the shop of one Miles Wakefield."

— 213 —

Looking down, James knitted his brow. The memory seemed to stir, but he gazed up with renewed rancor. "Sirs, am I under arrest or not? For the crime of kinship?!"

"No," said Truly. "But a few more plain answers here could win you concessions. Time alone with Adam, gifts for his comfort . . ."

"Concessions?! These things are properly called RIGHTS!!"

"Quite an idealist, aren't you?"

James Cathcart remained tensed for a moment, glaring. Then he gave a ragged sigh. "Yes, we visited the shop. But I wouldn't have recalled the owner's name if you hadn't said it."

"Apart from the taking of the photograph, could you describe the exchange?"

The young man seemed at a loss.

"I know you were both tipsy," Truly said. "Understandable, for that time of year. But you must recall something more."

In James Cathcart's stare, fear mixed with repellence. "I . . . Adam knew the fellow from somewhere. He introduced me. Wakefield was cordial—he didn't charge us—but he also seemed disconcerted. Before we left, he took Adam into a back room and spoke in a low voice. Afterward, Adam was a bit crestfallen. When I asked him about it, he said his friend disapproved of the condition in which we'd come."

"A sermon at New Year's," said Truly. "Of all things! Now, on another matter—Adam's most recent visit was at the end of last month, correct?"

"Yes. I proposed it, since my birthday was coming up. It had been a good while since we'd seen him, so I also persuaded him to stay till mid-week."

"And how did the two of you pass the time?"

The subject squirmed—from indignation, Truly thought, though he detected something more. "In ways that are common enough."

"Details, please."

James scowled. "There were a few drinking establishments, I'll allow, but also visits with friends and kin. And we saw a farce at Grover's."

"Harmless stuff, eh? Just as before?"

"Exactly."

Truly felt a nudge of intuition. "Not leaving anything out?"

"For God's sake, I've answered you!"

"Brothels, for instance?"

The eyes flickered dismay. The face reddened. "What possible bearing could that have on . . . ?!"

"On Adam's fate or yours? None." Truly winked. "So you needn't hold back."

Slouched, James took a moment to reply. "There was one place—more of a gentleman's club, really, out on the Seventh Street Road. La Maison de l'Empereur, it's called."

Truly shot a glance at Forbes. "Been there myself. Please go on."

The young man's tension appeared to ease a bit. "I had been there twice before as the guest of a colleague, so the management knew me. When Adam came down from New York three weeks back, I suggested we go there. It's not the usual sort of place, with foul-mouthed tarts picking your pockets."

Pressed for details, James Cathcart described the active gaming tables, the free-flowing liquor and the circulating girls, the business talk and political gossip. He named a banker, an attorney and a military cartographer with whom Adam and he had shared drinks. What conversation he recalled was trifling, and Truly was about to interrupt when he added, "And the old French woman came around to say hello."

Truly eyed him. "Madam Ravenel—she was up and about?"

"Well, yes—she's old but lively. Amusing too. One of her girls was dancing with a soused fellow, and she cut in to demonstrate a waltz. The whole room applauded her."

Truly watched a cockroach traverse the desktop. "Does anyone else stand out in your memory?"

"Well . . . There was that French doctor who apparently lives at the house. He bored us with an impromptu lecture on phrenology. And that man Monroe sat briefly at our table."

Forbes spoke up. "Monroe, the groundskeeper?"

James Cathcart looked puzzled. "Groundskeeper? Maybe he does do some handy work—but as I've observed it, he's there to play host and maintain security. To supervise the men, as Ravenel supervises the young ladies. He's a polished sort, fit of mind and body—you know, a man of the wide world. Partly because of his lineage, I would guess."

"Lineage?" said Truly.

"Why, he's a grand-nephew of the fifth President! Apparently it's well-known there—a member told us." Having surprised his questioners, James

Cathcart calmed further, recovering some of his lofty air. "So you see, the title of 'groundskeeper' would scarcely befit the man."

"I see," said Truly. Staring down at the desktop, he drummed his fingers. "Come alone here tomorrow and you may have a half-hour visit with your kinsman, no waiting. You may bring him food, letters, books and such. I'll speak to the superintendent. Good day."

Disarmed, James Cathcart hesitated before getting to his feet. He straightened his lapels and started to say "thank you," then squelched the words. To keep any dull-but-dutiful guard from accosting the man, Forbes escorted him out to the street while Truly waited.

Upon returning, Forbes dropped into the now-available chair. "What do you make of it?"

Truly tilted back in Wood's chair. Hearing a tenuous creak, he quickly straightened it. "Ravenel, the invalid grande dame–waltzing with her patrons, holding court like a fairy queen. And Monroe, the world's surliest gardener–and rheumatic to boot–displaying manly charm, vigor and even intellect among the gents, who are no doubt flattered to meet a grand-nephew of President James Monroe."

"Do you believe that last part?"

"Heck, I don't know. I'd wager that George Washington himself has a shady descendent or two."

"Whatever the case," said Forbes, "in Monroe and Ravenel we have a decidedly more talented pair than we imagined. And more deceptive."

"Healthier, too," said Truly, "–that's for darned sure. And more like partners than employer and hireling." He got up from the desk. "It's high time we spoke with Cousin Adam."

A WINDOW, HAPHAZARDLY boarded, projected thin stripes of daylight across the floor and across a small square table, where Adam Cathcart sat hunched. Pale and unshaven, with a tangled mustache, the wiry young man wore a soiled shirt and a tired, sullen expression. There was a yellowing bruise on his cheek. Behind him, by a mattress mottled with grime, a chamber pot added to the cell's reek. A wooden bowl and a food tray lay capsized near the wall, apparently thrown.

Seated across from Cathcart, Truly eyed him in the lamplight. He guessed him to be a particular sort of operative–neither the best nor the worst. The best combined a blithe or an indignant facade with a skill for evasion, frustrating their interrogators to no end. The worst cracked within hours of their capture. Those of Cathcart's apparent ilk—often bright enough but not mentally agile—responded with bitter heroics, a belligerence that guaranteed extra suffering. Seldom cracking, they were the first to sicken and sometimes die in captivity. This noble flaw revealed itself in men of no particular calling or appearance; it was as likely found in a dapper gent as in a burly laborer.

Truly placed the lamp to one side. "How are you?" he asked.

"Go to hell," Cathcart muttered.

"I'd say you're halfway there yourself."

The eyes flicked away.

"You know the charge is spying," Truly said. "Your life's in the balance."

Cathcart swallowed, his eyes burning into Truly's. "Dragged off the street," he croaked. "Shoved and prodded about by idiots. Locked up like an animal—all because I've dared to oppose the government in print!"

Truly held the bloodshot gaze. He could feel the hatred, but also a trace of fright. "Danged if you don't sound just like your friend Van Gilder."

"Mister Cathcart," Forbes spoke. "We know what you're having to endure. I, for one, don't especially enjoy being part of it."

Truly feigned annoyance at the interruption. In Cathcart's distracted look, he saw that Forbes' note of compassion had struck the right nerve. Instantly he moved to exploit it. Though his bluff with Underhill had backfired, this man and these circumstances called for a similar attempt.

"In any case, we're getting answers from another source. Miles Wakefield, namely."

Cathcart's gaze snapped back. In the few seconds it took him to respond, Truly glimpsed all the confirmation he needed—the flicker of alarm, the poignant effort to look bemused. Cathcart resumed his seething. "Even if that name meant a damn thing to me, I wouldn't tell you."

"Why were you bringing that letter to Wakefield?"

Again, a bare moment's hesitation. The upper lip curled. "I don't know the name. Once more, let me wish you a quick slide to hell."

"No matter. Apart from whatever else you've been up to, we know that you were taking stock of military preparedness in New York. We learned that from Wakefield—and he should be able to fill in most of the other blanks. Queer, isn't it? Here's the man you reported to, who you risked yourself for–and he's not nearly as tough a nut."

Cathcart's fingers pressed the table's edge. On his wan face, rage and doubt did battle. "Then why do you need me, Mister? Why, if this Wakefield's already furnishing the lies?"

"Because naturally we want all the details we can get. And because our investigation's entered a new stage–one that involves murder."

Cathcart looked genuinely confused. "Whose murder?"

"Van Gilder's."

The prisoner gaped.

Truly spared no detail as he described Van Gilder's body, watching Cathcart turn paler. The shock was real.

"Now let's review the sequence," Truly said. "You get back from Washington on June 1st; by next morning Van Gilder's burning his way south, using a mapped route that you yourself had given him. Before he can reach the safety of Rebeldom, we find him gutted in his coach. Tell us, what was it that sent him running?"

Some of Cathcart's accusatory glare returned. "You should know! Just a few weeks ago he referred to some government threat against him!"

"Just a story, my friend, to justify his plea for a secret escape plan. Now, what was it you told him that set him running?"

"I told him about my visit!"

"Including your and Cousin James' trip to the fancy cathouse?"

Slouching abruptly, Cathcart let out an odd, flat laugh but didn't speak.

"Do you want the gallows, man?!" Half-rising, Truly leaned toward him. "My view of your friend's corpse is not one that I'll recall fondly! Don't you see that if you fail to cooperate, we'll have every reason to charge you as an accessory?!"

Taking his cue, Forbes placed a hand on Truly's forearm as if to settle him.

Cathcart rubbed an eye, his fingers shaking.

"Mister Cathcart," said Forbes, "your loyalty to your cause is something we can understand and even admire. But surely your friend's assassination is a separate matter. Separate from politics–and from your mission, whatever it might have been. In fact, the killing itself appears to have been highly personal in nature. If you want the killer punished, do not aid him by withholding any related facts. Please."

Cathcart looked at the well-scratched table top. Mumbling at first, he eventually summoned clearer words. "Make of it what you will . . . When I got back from Washington, I went directly from the train station to the *Comet-American*. I had a column due next day and needed some notes from my desk. I also wanted Gideon to know I'd returned. So I went to his office and started telling him about my trip, and just casually mentioned that place where James and I went. I did not understand Gideon's reaction."

"You described seeing Monroe?" Forbes asked. "And Madam Ravenel?"

"I did. It's not every day you meet a President's grand-nephew, or a woman like that old Frenchie. But it was just an anecdote. And Gideon . . . The blood left his face, and he started to tremble. He made me repeat what I'd told him. He grew more agitated. I asked him what the matter was but he wouldn't say. He was in a panic to leave and insisted that I come with him, to his home."

Cathcart's lips looked parched. Forbes unstoppered the canteen and passed it to him. "And when you got there, he wrote the letter and gave it to you."

Taking a big swallow, Cathcart nodded. He handed back the canteen. "He was rushing about, preparing to flee. And writing the letter. Again I demanded to know why my story had upset him so, but he still wouldn't say. I was impatient with him. A man of his position should have greater mettle."

"You must have at least glanced at the letter," Truly said. "What did you think of it?"

Wearily Cathcart shook his head. "It made no sense to me."

"Did you know of his previous contact with Congressman Underhill?" Forbes asked.

"No–and it was strange to read of. Underhill's not exactly our kind of Democrat."

The session lasted another half-hour. Scorning the very question, Cathcart said he knew of no connection between Van Gilder and a Union lieutenant-colonel–what possible sense could that make? He also denied knowing of any ties between the publisher and anyone named Peavey or Archer. On the subject of Van Gilder's quarterly trips to Washington–yes, he had been curious about them and asked to go along, but his friend put him off. After each such trip, Van Gilder had described meetings with congressional Copperheads, but never once mentioned La Maison de l'Empereur. Truly and Forbes dug for other answers, such as why Cathcart had secretly monitored his supposed friend, but once more the prisoner hardened himself against them.

At last Truly arose, picking up the lamp. "The superintendent has approved a visit from your cousin tomorrow," he said flatly. On Cathcart's face, he thought he saw a ripple of emotion. He blocked the impulse to feel pity.

Back outside the prison, the agents leaned side by side against the shading wall.

"Hearing about Ravenel," Truly said, "and her so-called groundskeeper—this, for all the world, seems to be the thing that sent Van Gilder flying. That's what shocked him, maybe for the same reason it shocked us."

"That they were both in the merry best of health," Forbes said. "So we're to conclude that Ravenel and Monroe are the 'keepers'? The very ones he dreaded?"

Truly flipped his hands. "If that's so, it means Van Gilder was tricked just as we were. Led to think that they'd gone feeble, that he and his fellow bondsmen could safely rebel. We can also bet that Peavey was the source of this faulty information—that he passed it along when he went up to New York, mid-April, having been deceived in person at La Maison." Truly's gaze traveled across the street and up the long green rise, to the Capitol Building. "But why all this trickery? What was the point?"

Forbes removed his hat and fanned himself. "Our prime riddle is still thus: Murderous blackmailers on one hand, Confederate spies on the other. Are they actually in league, or just tramping across each others' paths? Cathcart seemed honestly ignorant about most of it."

"True, but here Wakefield—if he really is the chief spy—was just sticking to good practice. Making sure that if Cathcart were caught, he'd have as little as possible to divulge." Truly's stare fixed upon the Capitol Dome, the statue of the sword-wielding goddess on top. "But the question of Rebs and blackmailers—there's the rub, sure enough."

"Coincidence or collaboration?" Forbes said. "For the latter, our suspicion rests on just one fact—that both parties appear concerned with the same small group of men."

"Two facts," Truly corrected. "Van Gilder got his escape route from Cathcart, his lone Rebel connection—yet the killer knew where to intercept him along the way. If Cathcart didn't betray Van Gilder, then someone else in the Rebel network likely did."

Absorbed in thought, Forbes nodded. "Wakefield."

"That's my thinking."

"So our next order of business—a raid on La Maison? Haul them in for tougher questioning?'

"I'm burning to do just that—Archer and the police be damned. But doing it right will take at least a half-dozen men—and Baker's official nod, unfortunately. I'll submit the request by tonight, along with our latest findings. Still, it would help if we could establish a definite tie between Wakefield and La Maison."

Forbes put his hat back on. "That, or find the man himself."

"Well, there I'm not optimistic—he gives every sign of being clever and careful. But there is something we can do right now."

33

West Third Street

IT WAS A modest two-story building, red with white trim. Above the front door hung a small white sign with black lettering–"M. Wakefield Photography Shop." As before, a "Closed" sign stood in the curtained front window. Truly and Forbes slipped into the back alley, where Truly almost tripped over a rumpled figure seated against the fence.

Squinting up, the pimple-faced young man stirred from his slouched posture. On the ground beside him sat an open jug. Rising unsteadily, he jammed a pork-pie hat onto his messy blond head and then grimaced. "Ugh . . . !"

"Good afternoon," said Truly.

The expression turned surly, the puffy eyes darting from Truly to Forbes.

Reaching down, Truly snagged the jug and shoved it into the young drunkard's hands. "Stagger along, now."

The agents elbowed their way past, Forbes giving the youth a light shove in the other direction. Muttering, he wobbled away.

At the back door, Truly used his pen-knife to jimmy the latch while Forbes drew his Colt Navy, just in case. They entered a tiny kitchen with a pantry and a potbelly stove. All was dim and quiet. Forbes latched the door behind them. Truly found some matches and a hand lamp and they proceeded down a hallway, off of which they found a fair-sized storage room.

The lamp illuminated shelves of labeled jars, jugs and bottles—collodion, silver nitrate, potassium iodide—along with frames, paper and other supplies. Below these were stacked dozens of covered wooden boxes, ribbed with thin vertical openings and marked with alphabetical symbols. Taking the lid off one, Forbes drew a glass plate out of its slot.

"Negatives," he said.

"What?" said Truly.

"The used plates."

Truly shrugged. Photography was a hole in his education.

In back, they found the cumbersome travel trunks that Wakefield had brought to Cold Harbor; one contained his folding camera, another the tent-like contraption in which he had prepared his plates.

They exited the room and proceeded to the front of the shop, where they found themselves surrounded. Faces by the dozen stared out of their frames, none smiling at the intrusion. Though posed in conventional sameness, the subjects were varied: a portly dignitary, a hard-bitten sailor, a newlywed couple, a dour Indian chief, a dashing cavalry officer, several infantry privates. A small, neat desk stood left of the front door. Along the wall to the right, two display cases held decorative frames, mats and albums. From the back wall, a stairwell led to the second floor and the agents went up, Forbes still brandishing his Colt.

By the top landing, a door opened into a studio whose walls were painted a soft blue. At the center of it stood a camera with a heavy wooden base and tailboard. It faced a carpeted dais with flanking white-plaster columns and the same plush chair as in the display portraits, plus tall white screens enclosing it on three sides. Gentle sunrays streamed down from a closed skylight connected to a rope and pulley. Positioned around the studio, several mirrors and reflectors spread the light.

On the far side, a door with an oval red-glass window led into a dark and much smaller space. They entered cautiously as chemical odors met them—ether and lavender, plus others that Truly's nose could not identify. "The darkroom," Forbes murmured. "Where pictures are developed." The lamp revealed a leather apron hanging on a hook, a shelf of jarred and bottled substances, a countertop on which disparate objects lay: candles, glass plates, frayed work gloves, a prism, a magnifying glass and a set of metal trays. The agents returned to the hall and finished their sweep, finding only a spartan bedroom with a closet and bureau. Forbes holstered his pistol. Taking the lamp, he offered to poke around in the bedroom while Truly went back downstairs to search the desk.

Truly lit the desk's kerosene lamp and seated himself. By the blotter, he noticed a brass-framed photograph lying face-up. He reached for it. The picture showed a wooded river bend with a sunken pontoon bridge in the middle, carcass-like, and rolling gray clouds above. Its barren beauty seemed to mark Wakefield as something more than a craftsman. It suggested a compromise between his trade–the wall portraits, which made his living–and his finer abilities. Distantly Truly wished that he had come not to ransack the fellow's place but simply to meet him.

The top drawer yielded bills, invoices and stationery. In the middle one he found a ledger and a coin box, along with two unexpected articles: a single well-worn glove and a sheathed bayonet of old manufacture. Examining the weapon, he twirled it between his hands before putting it back. He opened the bottom drawer and was surprised to find it empty. But as he closed it, a faint crinkling sound made him pause, then move it back and forth on its runners. The crinkling persisted. He pulled the drawer completely out and turned it over. Pasted to the underside, a worn piece of paper bore a crisscross diagram, precisely drawn in ink. Each box of the diagram held an alphabetic letter, though no succession of letters produced an identifiable word.

Forbes came clumping downstairs, holding his lamp and a handful of folded pages. "Clothes in the closet," he said. "A bunch of reference books and Walter Scott novels. An empty trunk and gripsack under the bed. And these . . . " He held up the pages. " . . . on a closet shelf, from a sister Caroline in Savannah. I glanced them over. The 'Damn Yankees' theme gets harsher as they go along."

Truly indicated the upturned drawer on the desk.

Setting his lamp down, Forbes bent to scrutinize the lettered diagram. "A cipher square . . . Well, that's pretty conclusive."

"I'll copy it before we leave," Truly said. "If it's not outdated, our cryptographers can make some use of it." Looking at his pocket watch, he sighed. "Let's poke around some more. Before we leave, we'll put everything back as it was."

"You still think he'll return here?" asked Forbes.

"We can only hope he'll chance it, and we can bag him." Tilting back, Truly tried to recall Wakefield's face from Cold Harbor. He wished that he had seen it up close.

34

Brown's Hotel

UNDERHILL, DRUNK AGAIN, looked worse than Wakefield had ever seen him. And for all the congressman's intensity, the two of them had made little progress on his grand speech. Wakefield began to suspect that he had been asked here just to keep a scared man company.

"Ezra, you should lie down for a bit."

Across from him at the writing desk, Underhill gave a mirthless smile, sipped his claret and started rambling again. "When I deliver this address, I want to leave that chamber ringing, you understand? Less than five months to the elections, and this preposterous administration with its weakling President . . . It will fall, Miles. It must fall. And just once I want to pull out all the stops. Tell them where it's all going, what the people think."

"And you are of the people, Ezra. They'll reelect you, speech or no speech. By your widest margin yet, I'd wager."

"Can't afford such cocksureness, Miles. Otherwise, too many might stay home from the polls. In my district, most have stood strong for the Union, if not for this darky-loving Republican cabal that's running it. But since my last visit home, the mail says they're coming to despise the war. No Union man foresaw a season like this. Worse, none foresaw this deluge of free niggers, stealing work from poor honest white men. A greater threat than any military invasion, I say—set loose by our own leaders! Do you know, Miles, that down in occupied Louisiana they're actually talking about letting the darks vote?"

Cradling his own drink, Wakefield hid a yawn. "So you're embracing the Peace faction?"

"Oh, no. Must stay moderate—the speech affirms that. Long as I stay so, they'll have to take me seriously or risk my moving to the other camp. Any day now they'll be repealing the Fugitive Slave Law—just a formality, at this point. But the whole nigger question will come up for discussion again, and that's when I'll take the floor. If I'm forceful enough, the newspapers will take note. Then, having made myself an ideal bridge between the main bloc and the Peace faction, perhaps I'll be asked to address the party convention in Chicago. And then, who knows?"

Perilously close to laughter, Wakefield forced a cough. The dreams that liquor spawned: Party Chairman Underhill, Secretary of State Underhill, a McClellan-Underhill presidential ticket. Wakefield watched the congressman shuffle his papers. "Well, you're a sound strategist. And the speech sounds promising."

Staring at the fireplace, Underhill set his papers down. He placed a hand on Wakefield's forearm. "I thank you for being here, Miles. I value your thoughts above anyone else's. And far above those of my dim secretary."

"Oh, Ives is a good enough fellow."

"But not of our caliber, Miles. Far preferable to have a true friend and equal here."

"As I say, it's a privilege."

Withdrawing the hand, Underhill downed the last of his claret. "I'm stymied on how to finish up. The speech must close in some fitting way. Fitting and memorable."

"It will come to you after a good night's rest. Your nerves have been suffering. And I'm sure that knave Truly's visit was no help." Wakefield sipped his drink. "What could he want from you?"

Underhill massaged his temples. "The War Department has surpassed its usual arrogance, giving free rein to a man like that. To think of him invading my privacy, tormenting me with . . . No, I can't make sense of him. And Ives said a strange man approached him the other day, seeking private information of some sort. I was going to go directly to Stanton, but instead I've sent a written complaint to the party leadership. That will have greater impact. And if there's any justice left, I'll be rid of these bastards!"

Wakefield turned his eyes to the open window. Late afternoon now. He knew he should dig for details, for what Truly had said and demanded. But while Underhill clearly needed to share his rage over the incident, he would evade specific questions–a prime skill of his, even after several drinks. And Wakefield had coddled him enough for one day. He pictured lighting a match and setting Underhill's precious speech on fire, right in his hands.

Just then Wakefield felt his arm seized. Quelling an urge to recoil, he stared at his companion. Underhill, more beggar than congressman, hunched toward him–dark eyes pleading, voice husky with agitation.

"Miles . . . "

"What is it, Ezra?"

"You . . . I must ask you something. In strictest confidence."

Again Wakefield wanted to jerk his arm away. "Let's hear it."

"I've long sensed . . . More than most men, you know something of the world–the truth about it."

"What truth do you mean?"

"About power, Miles. About survival. The real rules that drive us . . . They're hidden rules–merciless, not gentle. You know all that, don't you?"

Wakefield nodded.

Still staring, Underhill let go of the photographer's arm. "What I am about to ask–I beg that you not question me about it."

Wakefield hesitated, picking his words carefully. "Ezra–however I can help restore your peace of mind . . . "

Underhill kneaded his hands together. "In the political realm, a man crosses swords. He makes enemies, some more formidable than others. Such are the facts in my case. Truth be told, I believe that my life is in danger."

"From whom?"

"Miles, please! Just . . . " Underhill rubbed his face. "In your time, you've known all sorts of men, yes? Of both high and low station?"

"I have."

Swallowing, the congressman hunched closer. "Is there not, here in the city, a class of men who fix problems such as mine? For a fee?"

Likewise leaning in, Wakefield lowered his voice. "You are under that much of a threat? One that the law cannot remedy?"

"Yes! Precisely!"

"And you're referring to a class of men who . . . occasionally serve the finer class? Unconstrained by those standards which bind the rest of us?"

"Yes! I must fight fire with fire!" Underhill's eyes darted away. "Could you put me in touch with such a person? Or do you know someone who could?"

Wakefield gazed to the window. He let half a minute pass. "Could you say how large a task it would be?"

"There are two . . . No, three individuals who pose this threat to me. I don't care if the fee is high, just that the hired man be effective. Effective and discreet. Miles, I would be damned grateful!"

Not looking at him, Wakefield got up, walked to the window and surveyed the avenue below. A pretty girl in a summer bonnet crossed the cobblestone. He thought of Delia.

When he next heard Underhill's voice, it was cold and wary. "If you're shocked, I do regret that. And if you can do nothing, it's all well. I'll see to it on my own."

Wakefield saw there was no choice in the matter. As soon as he left here, he would hurry to get things settled. Then he would spend the night with Delia. In her arms, he would push Underhill from his mind.

"Ezra, I believe I can help you."

"Can you? Can you really?!"

"The price will be stiff, of course. I'll find out how much, and where you can meet. Tomorrow night at the earliest. But it can't be here–too public."

"Miles–whoever it is you have in mind . . . He is experienced?"

"Quite, but not known to many. He fits the bill."

"And how is it that you know him?"

"You asked that I not question you, Ezra. Let us observe the reverse as well."

"Oh . . . Certainly."

Wakefield turned from the window. Sitting up, Underhill smiled as if just freed from a dungeon–and for the first and last time, Wakefield felt a trickle of pity for him. "I must leave here presently. But something just occurred to me about your speech."

"What's that?"

Wakefield returned to the desk but did not sit. He laid a hand on Underhill's shoulder. "My friend, history is filled with speeches of defiance and outrage, but you wish to stand out. The people are angry, yes.

But what else are they experiencing, which you may reflect? Watching and listening to you now, it came to me. They feel anguish, Ezra. Anguish and despair."

Nodding thoughtfully, Underhill reached for the claret bottle. Wakefield caught him by the wrist.

"Ezra, give voice to those emotions. Show them your humanity. Make their anguish your own. Tell of how you too have been driven to the brink of despair, to see your country bled so."

Underhill rubbed his chin, then looked up. "But could it be taken for weakness?"

Gazing back, Wakefield sank into his chair. "Privately it takes courage to show one's heart. Publicly it takes still more. Mark my word—common folk know this. They'll respond."

Underhill spread his papers out before him. Fumbling with his pen, he dipped it into the ink vial. "I can see it, Miles. You're right!"

Wakefield sat back, took a breath. "Perhaps something like this—'Gentlemen . . . As I watch sons, brothers and fathers march to death, and as I recall those legions which preceded them . . .'" Underhill started writing. "'. . . and as I behold the poisoning of this republic which I love, my heart nigh bursts. I speak for any man, woman or child who, in darkest hour, has . . .'" Wakefield thought hard. "'. . . has taken stock and wondered how much horror one spirit can possibly ingest. I am only mortal, sirs, and there are moments when I cannot help a certain chill hopelessness.'"

As Underhill scribbled, Wakefield saw his intent red-rimmed eyes go moist.

35

Central Washington
June 17

IN THE SHADE of a poplar, Sapphira set down her basket of fruit and vegetables and rested. She had bought some lemons, less for lemonade than
to brighten the kitchen. Gazing past the fenced perimeter of Lafayette
Square, she saw the stately spire of St. John's Episcopal Church, the elegant homes of high government officials, the wooded grounds of the
President's Park and the Executive Mansion itself. Then she remembered
the last time she had sat here, two long summers ago. It had been with
Mother Rachel, who spoke of the President's little son dying that previous
winter and of Mrs. Lincoln still hiding from public view, inconsolable.
No morbid rumor-mongering–just an obscure mother's pity for a famous
one. Sapphira too had felt sorry, never dreaming that Mother Rachel herself would soon be gone.

Sapphira looked down at the lemons in the basket, their bright purpose
defeated now. She had stayed away from the Sixth Street Wharf, where
the first Petersburg casualties had begun to arrive. She had mailed Ben
a letter of forced cheer and unforced wishes for his safety. But no matter
where she went or how she busied herself, something always nudged her
toward thoughts of mourning–that solemn skein of ritual, part practical
and part religious, meant to channel grief and send the loved one home
in good order. Tears were allowed, certainly, but there was a prescribed
attitude of acceptance, the lack of which showed a lack of proper faith.

She wondered if anyone thought this of poor Mrs. Lincoln. Still, the grief never quite ended. At odd moments it came pressing like a dull sword. She remembered Father spending hours just sitting in his study; Ben home on leave, looking older and harder; Anna shut up in her room.

Taking up her basket, Sapphira rose. The odor from the marsh and the canal was bad today, but the square remained lively. Nearby, an industrious white boy polished an army officer's boots. Box-laden and tray-laden hawkers ambled around, selling soap, trinkets and souvenirs. In the shadow of Andrew Jackson's equestrian statue, children accosted a peddler whose cart held a multicolored boulder of candy; he was chipping off slivers for them, stopping to take their pennies. Sapphira raised her eyes to the statue, the rearing horse. Mother Rachel had remarked that she half-expected beast and rider to leap from their pedestal.

Monuments were supposed to be timeless. Unchanging in the flux of life, they stood for some glory or value that people might otherwise forget. But when the world heaved with death, they became something like pagan idols–dated, disturbingly out of place. Rather than transcend and reassure, they seemed to mock, or to invite mockery. Sapphira thought of the stacked coffins throughout the District, and the bold bronze horse looked silly. She thought of the deathly faces at the wharf, and the bold bronze President looked ridiculous–a harlequin leading a charge to nowhere. Beneath him, the children yelled, squealed and sucked their candy slivers.

Leaving the square, she saw a platoon of Veteran Reserves turn up Connecticut Avenue. Reserve men were those recovering from wounds or illness but, like Anna's Lieutenant Chadwick, fit enough for limited duty– and though Sapphira admired their uniforms of pale blue, their sluggish step inspired no confidence. Neither did the rumpled group of state militia she now saw across the street–men whose age, height and girth varied greatly, but whose swagger recalled the first green days of the war. Thanks to the current bloodletting in Virginia, Washington had fewer troops and fewer quality ones. Garrison and patrol duty had fallen to sorry-looking defenders such as these–but at least the city's forts were strong.

She barely noticed a brougham that clattered by her, until its driver brought it to a stop.

"Miss Sapphira!"

Halting, she stared.

Twisted around to face her, Manfred Kirschenbaum doffed his bowler and smiled.

She went up to him. "Mister Kirschenbaum, how is it you're driving one of these?"

"Is the best way to learn a city. So I lease the horses and carriage and take passengers. They tell me how I should get to their destination but some are less patient, and them I charge more. Do you know something? All hackmen I see here are colored."

"Most in Washington are. But don't you need a license, Mister Kirschenbaum?"

"License? Ach! In New York I do without one." He sidled down, then reached for her basket. "Come, I bring you home."

"Bring me . . . ? Oh." Dismayed, she let him take her basket.

With a flourish he motioned to the carriage seat. "Please. It is a long walk for you."

One of his two bay nags looked at her with indifference. Sapphira lifted her hem and willed herself into the carriage seat, glad for the leather canopy that shaded and partially hid her. As Kirschenbaum placed the basket at her feet, pulled himself up and snapped the reins, she resolved to endure this like an Apostle.

In public, Sapphira always sought to be as inconspicuous as possible, her mind constantly scouting ahead for hazards. Whenever she felt exposed, all the childhood warnings about slave-catchers would rattle up like knives encircling her–the nightmare of a lunging hand and then oblivion. She would hear Father's admonition: "Stick close, missy! If anyone tries for you, just scream like a steam whistle–understand?" And though time had rendered the chill warning obsolete, it echoed even now. Still, the ride shook some of her tension away as it gathered speed. She settled back and a giddiness came over her, unlike anything she had felt in years. Splashing through a mud wallow, they turned down H Street, where the occasional saloon or boarding house broke the sequence of respectable row house dwellings. Sapphira smiled at the hunched back above her. As if sensing the smile, Kirschenbaum glanced over his shoulder and sent one back.

Another hack passed from the opposite direction, its black driver eyeing his misshapen white counterpart and then getting a startled glimpse of Sapphira. Looking up at Kirschenbaum again, she felt a sad twinge. Maybe such daring was not daring at all, she thought, but mere kindness–kindly foreign innocence, nothing more. Or was it? Had that over-the-shoulder grin not held some flash of mischief?

Sapphira was leaning forward out of the shade when a promenading white couple spied her and stopped short. Abruptly she sat back. Pulling her shawl about her, she tried to look straight ahead, but her eyes had a will of their own. Idle youths outside a gaming hall, a scowling groom outside a livery stable–the street was a gauntlet of stares. A sullen heat crept into her. Home was near, but she could not get there soon enough. Windows glared, doorways gaped as Kirschenbaum steered around a horse carcass thick with flies.

Once they had pulled up to the house, Kirschenbaum hopped down and reached in for the basket, but Sapphira did not move.

"Mister Kirschenbaum, why do you think people scorn so easily?"

He didn't answer right away. She wondered if she had only made him feel awkward, but then saw that he was thinking.

"This I used to think on more in my younger times. Strangers see me and often they laugh, or take alarm. Then I comes to see that they are all mad in a way. Mad to be certain, to know what will happen before it happens–what they will see before they see it. In me they see something they did not expect. They are startled–and no one enjoys to be startled, ja? It once troubled me, yet now I laughs at them being such frightened fools."

Sapphira looked down at her basket. "They like what's familiar–of course they do. I like coming home for the same reason. And the music I play, and Mother Rachel's picture. Still, there is much I would leave behind–just as you did, when you crossed the ocean. I dream of that crossing, of Paris, of all beyond that. But ofttimes I wonder if the true thing would measure up."

Kirschenbaum nodded. "Ja, you are wise to wonder this."

"But tell me–do you still feel a stranger?"

Propping his elbows on the carriage, he sighed. "I care less about this, Miss Sapphira. I have friends now. And so long as Manfred is no stranger to himself, he will do well enough." He shrugged. "Europe has the great cities, but it too is a muddle. Princes and kaisers and prime ministers scheming. Burgemeisters counting money, barons kicking servants. Nations crowded together, old and proud, and each by the other is scorned. Scorn they drinks like bad beer, and export it too. Wars there they have had for centuries, and are having now. I should laugh, you know, that I comes to America and find the greatest war of all. Yet here I stays. Wars, they are for land and money and pride. Here too it is for these–but for something finer as well, ja? Let us not forget this. You most of all, Miss Sapphira—do not forget it."

In a window across the street, she saw curtains move and a woman's moon face staring out. "I will cling to the thought," she muttered. She smiled at Kirschenbaum. "I don't know if Father . . . if the major has risen yet. He was up quite late. But would you like to come in for a lemonade?"

To her surprise, he seemed suddenly flustered. "Oh . . . Thank you, but I must be going. I will see the major soon enough, when he has need of me."

She gathered her shawl. "Let us hope that we may both fill some need, eventually."

"Ja, but for now I drives a hack."

As Kirschenbaum helped her from the carriage, she held his knobby fingers more tightly than she needed to. He handed her the basket.

"Thank you so much," she said, curtsying.

He got back into the driver's seat, doffed his hat and headed away.

Inside, she found Anna in her apron and calico dress, feather-dusting the parlor. Sapphira had dusted it yesterday but said nothing of it. However idle or frivolous Anna could be, there was no stopping her when she decided to reclaim the house.

"I got a bargain on lemons," Sapphira said.

Dusting a side table, Anna glanced up. "Who was that little man?"

"A friend of Father's. And mine. He's from the German states."

"His poor back." Anna moved to the mantel. "He certainly seemed familiar toward you. Do you think it's wise to let him drive you around in public?"

Sapphira glared, then looked away. "And when is doing anything in public ever wise?"

"What?"

"Is Father up?"

Lifting one of the vases by Mother Rachel's portrait, Anna dusted where there was no dust. "Yes. He's getting dressed."

Sapphira went to the kitchen and set her basket down. On the table, yesterday's *Evening Star* lay spread out before Anna's chair. Turning to the front page, she saw the banner story: heavy fighting at Petersburg, reinforcements pouring across the James River, the town itself still in Confederate hands. The story cited participating regiments, among them the Twenty-second U.S. Colored.

36

West Third Street

As was his habit, Wakefield had the driver let him off a block from his place. To leave and return on foot was less noticeable, should an idle neighbor be keeping track of him. Thoughts of Delia buoyed his step—the image of her above and below him, her scent on his hands, the delicious ache of holding her. Back in Savannah, no one would have imagined him loving such a girl. Then he realized that no one back there knew him anymore, maybe not even his sister Caroline. It was his first bleak reflection of the day: nobody had a clue to the man he had become. Nobody except Delia—and she knew only one slice of him. Suddenly troubled, he wondered if he could trust Madam Ravenel's word that Delia would be kept for him alone, not forced to lie with any moneyed slobbering cur that wandered in. Then, out of nowhere, the thought of Truly pricked him.

Truly seemed to be making inroads. Where was he getting his information? Was it all from Van Gilder's letter, or from other sources as well? And there was the matter of Cathcart. Wakefield felt glad again for this own foresight, that he had placed strict limits on Cathcart's knowledge. But Cathcart could still jeopardize the whole plan just by giving Wakefield's name. And today marked two weeks' captivity. "Hold on, Adam," Wakefield thought.

But here was his shop. As he got out his key, he heard a pair of feet beating toward him and turned to look. From down the street young George came running, his hat clutched in his hand. Wakefield felt a Southern-born alarm at seeing anyone run for no good reason.

Breathless, George slowed to a trot, grinning as he reached the front of the shop. "Heck, sir–you been gone a good spell!"

"Catch your breath, boy. What is it?"

"Well . . . On Wednesday the provost guard paid my ma another visit, askin' 'bout me and the draft. They weren't no politer. So yesterday I left work early sayin' I had a toothache, and I come here hopin' you had that three hundred for my substitute fee."

Wakefield touched a finger to his forehead. "I've been occupied. I'll get it for you tonight, tomorrow at the latest. But listen, George–are you missing work today also?"

"No, sir. Had to deliver a telegram a couple streets over, so I come by to see if you're in. But hark to this, now. Yesterday I decided to wait for you in the alley, in case you showed, and two men come 'round the side and shove me on my way. But I creep back there and watch 'em break into your place. They was in there a long while, Mister Wakefield–but when they finally come out, it didn't look like they took nothin'. So I can't say what they was up to."

Wakefield stood rigid.

"The older one," George went on, "–he was shorter, a little bowlegged, with a mustache. The other one's tall–walks like he's got a bad leg or a false one. They was talkin' to each other but too low for me to hear. Anyhow, sir–sure am glad to see you."

Wakefield stared past George to the dirt street. Then he reached out and patted his arm. "You've done me a great service."

Beaming, George hooked his thumbs into his baggy pants. "Heck–whatever I can do for you and Robert E. Lee . . . "

"Listen–I have to leave quickly."

George's face fell. "Leave Washington?"

"No, no–just my place here. I can't tell you yet where I'll be, but I'll get word to you. As for your draft money, you'll get it tonight for certain."

Through a gap in the curtains, Wakefield could see several of his display portraits, each an intimate witness to his time here. After two and a half years, he was abandoning this enclosed space where he had yearned, seethed, plotted and almost gone mad. Now he would be truly rootless. He had known that a quick exit might be necessary, but had not expected this pang. Still, there was no choice. Stout-hearted though Cathcart was, he must have cracked or been tricked into naming his contact. And the Yankee agents might return at any moment.

"I'm going to pack some things," said Wakefield. "You must return to the telegraph office, but first would you go find me a hack?"

"Sure, Mister Wakefield."

"Good lad. Very soon I'll be needing you for the most vital mission of all. Be ready."

In the youth's coffee-brown eyes, Wakefield saw a flash of longing for what, when and how. The brash ignorance still repelled him, but this was a face he could trust. Beneath the pimples and the greasy blond cowlick, there was more to value than he had realized.

"I'll be ready," George said, smiling. "I swore off drinkin' rye–for a spell, anyhow."

"I do hope so. Now hurry up."

With a smirk and a nod, George was off to find a hack.

Wakefield unlocked the door and went inside. Upstairs, he stuffed his clothes into his trunk and his books into his gripsack, along with the small bundle of letters from Caroline. He was about to haul the trunk downstairs when he remembered something else. Moving the bed aside, he lifted the three loose floorboards, revealing the space where the Union major's uniform lay folded. He knelt down and lifted it out, along with the gold-braided hat and holstered revolver. On one cuff he noted the dark stains which laundering had failed to remove. His teeth clamped together. Richmond had sent him the uniform in April by secret courier, no questions asked. What would they say, he wondered, if they knew the purpose it had served thus far?

He laid the uniform and revolver in the trunk, then replaced the boards and the bed before hauling everything downstairs. Waiting, he thought dejectedly of his photography equipment–too cumbersome to take just now. Maybe he could come back for it. Wandering to the front room, he set the trunk down. He looked at his desk and saw the sunken bridge photo, the one he was proudest of. He snatched it up. The attack of sentimentality persisted, prompting him to get his sheathed bayonet from the middle drawer. Whatever uses it had been put to, it remained a token of his boyhood. He placed the bayonet and photograph in his trunk. All business again, he remembered the cipher square on the bottom drawer's underside and stripped it off, crumpling and stuffing it into his coat pocket. Then he sat to wait.

He could not blame Cathcart–every man had his breaking point. But with events surging and the plan in motion, he could allow no other close scrapes. From now until the grand hour of reckoning, he would lie low. Truly and his one-legged partner would return here and find their quarry gone. Let them lose the trail, he thought. Let the Yankee hounds quit.

37

Truly Residence

SEEKING SOME MENTAL refuge, Truly had stayed up late re-reading *Gulliver's Travels* and having one too many whiskeys. He rose late, reviving only when Anna passed him two hand-written messages. One, from Duke, said that three boxes had arrived by train from New York, and that their contents included Van Gilder's signed portrait from Miles Wakefield ("With highest regard . . . May, 1862"). The clerk pledged to examine all the contents with care and speed. The other note had accompanied the boxes and was from the intrepid Lieutenant Cyrus Heatherton:

Dear Major,

    Herein find G. Van Gilder financial records and correspondence, plus photograph from his office. Also per your request– questioned some of Comet-American staff and they confirmed M. Wakefield an occasional visitor at paper through '62, though visits petered out the following spring. Was thought to be Washington friend of Van G's who served as informal news source for that city. One editor recalled MW contributing photographs free of charge to the paper for woodcut illustrations.

    Sir, I believe you owe me dinner at Willard's.

              Your servant (God knows),
              C. Heatherton

"Yes, I believe I do," Truly murmured, smiling. At last, one thing had gone right.

Yet his turn of mood did not last. In an unexplained burst of industry, Anna had dusted and polished the downstairs until it looked like a museum, though her calico and feather duster were now replaced by pink tulle and an embroidered fan. Soon—the sooner the better, he thought—Chadwick would be whisking her off to a luncheon for the Sanitary Commission's local planning board. Slouched in his chair and sipping coffee, he made himself listen to her:

"Father, she lacks any sense of propriety! When she receives callers, they end up confused and uncomfortable!"

"Speak softer."

Sapphira was hanging wash out back. Exasperated, Anna lowered her voice.

"Concede this—she was always a bit too obtrusive for her own good. And lately it's worse. It's in her voice, the way she moves, the way she looks at people. How does she expect them to respond? To understand the privileges that you and Mother allowed her?"

Truly sighed. "We did cruelly mislead her, sure enough."

"Cruelly? Father, the two of you were kinder than any . . . "

"To make her think that a few good manners would do, as they did for us. That she didn't need to grovel and scurry, even as we made her pose as a house servant. Danged cruel, all right."

Anna closed her fan and clutched it. "Sarcasm is cruel! Especially when I've held my tongue longer than others might have. Dennis is gracious, but I can tell he's put off by her. Once, last week, she presumed to ask his predictions for the political season—and then to offer hers!"

Fighting to hold his own tongue, Truly took another gulp of coffee. "Annie . . . um, Anna, perhaps it's healthy for young Chadwick to . . . have his frontiers pushed a little."

Anna leaned in. "All I ask is that I not have to dread embarrassment every time Dennis or some other guest comes by! It seems I've spent half my life trying to explain and excuse her! And Father, it's for her benefit as well! Eventually she's bound to offend the wrong person!"

Truly started to say something but his throat closed off. From this angle, he could see more of Rachel in Anna's face. Rachel, who had seen past people's faces, who had understood without words, who had forgiven him for his Mexican adventure—that ballyhooed war of conquest, bearing him off when she needed him most. Rachel—she was there in Anna's fair complexion and delicate chin, most of all in her deep green eyes. And he wondered why, how and when Anna had become such a stunningly silly creature. A better father would have known.

He placed his cup on the side table. "You were only three when I returned from Mexico. Too young for you to remember, I suppose?"

She drew back, perplexed. "It's one of my first memories. Why?"

"There you were, standing beside Ben and your mother, so small and pretty you made my eyes hurt. I scooped you up and that upset you—Mexico hadn't made me any more delicate. Then you hushed and I saw you were looking behind me, at the other little one I'd brought."

Anna looked away.

"Do you recall once telling Saph that I'd brought her because we needed a servant?"

Anna looked at him sharply, her face flushed. "For the love of heaven, Father—at that age, why wouldn't I assume what you let others assume about her? And why would she dredge that up all these years later?"

"She has never dredged it up. I only knew because Ben repeated it to your mother, who repeated it to me. I'm sure she corrected you, but I should have been the one to do it."

"Mother did scold me, if that pleases you. But this has precious little to do with the subject at hand."

"Doesn't it? Then harken, missy. We did mislead her, perhaps, but not entirely. She knows full well why we presented her to people as we did. What's more, she knows that life's a masquerade. I reckon she's just wearying of the mask, as I wish to God you'd weary of yours."

Anna looked confused, then doubly sullen. "And what does that mean?"

"You wish she knew her place. But what's your place, Annie? How high up?"

"May I be excused?"

"I didn't summon you. But try answering the question: where do you see your place?"

Lifting her hem, she turned and padded out.

"Then try this one," he called, "—where in blazes is my spittoon?!"

The doorknocker sounded. He heard her feet reverse direction. "Now you're cursing at me!" she snapped. "At least Dennis is a gentleman!" He heard the swing of the door, her hesitant greeting. "Why . . . Captain—hello."

Briskly Anna showed Forbes into the parlor. Then she hurried upstairs.

Holding his hat, Forbes stood there looking flustered. "Not the man she expected."

"Bart, let me amend myself." Truly got to his feet. "I now believe it's danged fortunate—for you, at least—that Chadwick met her first."

He led Forbes to the study, where he handed him the two messages.

"Well, good," Forbes said. "That should balance out the tidings I bring."

Seated behind his desk, Truly let his head droop. "Fire away."

"On an impulse I went back to Wakefield's shop but—no surprise—it's still dark and shuttered. Then I spied Manfred's German lady. She runs the boarding house next door and has enough English to be understood. When I asked where my old friend Miles might be, she said she'd seen him scarcely an hour before. Leaving in a hack, with baggage."

Truly rested on his elbows. He heard Sapphira come in from the back porch, humming a listless song. "Right through our fingers," he muttered. "Well, hang it. Presumably Baker now has the written request that I left him, about our proposed La Maison raid and our need for men. But I suppose I'll have to pester him, as usual."

From up the hall, the knocker sounded again. Truly went to answer it but Sapphira got there first, admitting Duke, who carried a ledger under his arm. Truly ushered him to the study as Anna appeared on the upstairs landing, visibly vexed that it was not her gallant escort.

Greeting Forbes, Duke lay the thick book on Truly's desk and seated himself. "I haven't gotten to Van Gilder's correspondence," he said. "But his bookkeeping confirms our expectation. Payments simply marked 'expenses'—quarterly, right from the start. At first they're for two hundred dollars, as with Peavey. The entry dates match Peavey's to the week and sometimes to the day—with one exception. A year ago there's a late payment, June instead of May, but this one is for four hundred dollars. And it remains that amount, paid punctually until May of this year. At this point the entry does not recur as it should—which, again, matches Peavey's admittedly sloppier ledger. A few days later, of course, the entire record comes to its end."

"And Van Gilder to his," Forbes said, looking at Truly. "The late payment supports your guess that last year he became a tad cocksure. That he neglected to pay and got himself cut up."

"And got his payments doubled," Truly added, cupping his chin. "All right, now . . . Going by Heatherton's note, I figure that Wakefield slithered into Van Gilder's life just as he did into Peavey's and Underhill's, and in roughly the same time period. The portraits must have been a fine way to snag their vanity, none of these men being especially humble. I fancy Wakefield to be a tolerable good actor, able to tailor himself to each scoundrel's liking. But his connection with Van Gilder . . . It seems to have dissolved a year or so ago, around the time of the Copperhead's injuries. Right after which Adam Cathcart entered the scene."

Forbes took it from there. "If Wakefield's in league with the killers–or keepers, whatever you wish to call them–then these false friendships make sense. By maintaining separate intimacies with each man, he might catch warning signs of defiance–a careless action, an unsuspecting word–and so be able to alert his allies. But Van Gilder lived far from Washington, and was likely the most taxing one to remain in touch with. Perhaps the episode of a year ago took Wakefield by surprise, given that his contact with Van Gilder had fallen off."

Thus, they reasoned, had Cathcart been recruited to the task. Living in New York and actually employed by his subject–his only subject–Cathcart would have had a much easier time of it. To fuel the so-called friendship and to equalize it, he had evidently confided his ties with the Rebel spy network–something that would surely thrill any Copperhead.

"Old Gideon trusted his friend Cathcart," said Forbes. "–and through him, Confederate intelligence. As editor of a pro-South paper, why wouldn't he have? They were the natural ones to ask for help if escape proved necessary. But when that time came . . . "

"They informed their secret partners," said Truly. "–the very people he was running from."

From the front door came another knock. Truly sagged, listening as Sapphira's feet headed up the hall. He heard her open the door and greet the inevitable caller.

"Welcome, Lieutenant!"

The restrained baritone voice replied, "Here for Miss Anna."

"Indeed you are. Please come in and I will fetch her."

Sending Forbes a sour look, Truly stood. "Excuse me. Fatherly protocol."

At the foot of the staircase he encountered Sapphira.

"Father, I forgot to tell you–on my way back from the market I met Mister Kirschenbaum. He drove me home in his carriage and . . . "

"Could you tell me later, Saph? I have to greet Sir Lancelot."

She lowered her voice. "Honestly, Father–it could have been worse."

"Yes, well–he could have been an opium fiend, I suppose. Or from Arkansas."

At the parlor entrance he opened his mouth to greet Chadwick but hesitated when he did not immediately see the lieutenant. He stepped inside. Across the room, Chadwick stood staring out a window at the street, where his family's private coach and coachman waited. His sleeve dangled, his right arm jutting inside a brace. Despite his lengthy hiatus with the Veteran Reserves, he sported the dress uniform of the Volunteer Cavalry: high shiny boots, immaculate white gloves, high-collared jacket with yellow piping, his cap clutched in his good hand. He could have been posing atop a battlement rather than in a family parlor–and for a second Truly was able to grasp, however slightly, the particular allure that Chadwick held for Anna. Of average height, he had a fine profile–nose prominent, chin well-molded–while the sweep of his fair hair and mustache lent a touch of drama. And viewed like this from the side, his gaze had a steadiness that seemed to denote something better than vacancy. Still, who but Chadwick would have his saber strapped on for a social call? A saber, moreover, whose brass-tipped scabbard was at this moment perilously close to the liquor stand.

Again Truly drew his breath to speak but then paused. Should the lieutenant turn suddenly, his weapon would strike the decanter. Flexing his hands, Truly focused on the precious vessel of topaz liquid. He decided to get within reach of the stand before making his presence known. Licking his lips, he took a slow stride onto the carpet. Chadwick kept contemplating the street as Truly crept closer, edging around the piano. Eyes locked on the scabbard's tip, Truly held his breath, briefly motionless before taking a final stealthy stride. In the same instant, Anna's voice came warbling from the hall–"Here I come, Dennis!"–prompting Chadwick to turn on his heel. The scabbard caught the decanter on the neck as Truly lunged, nearly plowing into the table. He seized the vessel in mid-fall and its stopper popped out.

Splashed on the face and sleeves, he knelt there holding the decanter as Chadwick blinked down at him. "Major?"

Truly jammed the stopper back in. "Lieutenant."

"Sir–what . . . ?"

"Father?!" In her star-patterned shawl and bonnet, Anna stood in the parlor threshold, looking at once irked and baffled. "Why are you on your knees?"

"Never too late to pray, child."

Approaching him, she sniffed. "Smelling like a distillery? I think not." In what seemed an impressive act of will, she beamed at Chadwick.

Stepping forward, the lieutenant smiled and offered his good arm. "Miss Anna–the world awaits us!"

Truly got to his feet, placing the decanter on the stand. "Have a pleasant time."

Flicking her fan open, Anna held it like an embroidered little shield as she took Chadwick's arm.

Truly changed his shirt and washed before returning to the study, where Forbes and Duke were talking.

"Major," Duke said, "I was just telling the Captain that Colonel Baker is quite occupied today."

"By an evil spirit? That's no news."

"Actually by a congressional subcommittee. He's testifying about alleged corruption in the Treasury Department."

"Corruption! Now what would our friend Lafe know about that?" Truly sank into his desk chair. "Octavius, I'll go back to the office with you and help sort through Van Gilder's correspondence. If Baker stops by when he's done testifying, I'll press him about my request for La Maison. Still, if he doesn't respond by tomorrow morning, we should raid the place anyhow. Get ourselves an enclosed wagon or two, then strike fast and haul 'em off to the Old Capitol."

"Without the extra men?" Forbes said.

Truly shrugged. "I could beg a favor from the District marshals. Or the Veteran Reserves, even. Heck, I'll think of something."

Duke sat up. "Major–I would like to volunteer!"

Truly felt a headache coming on. He stroked his temples, his hands still smelling of whiskey. "That's appreciated, Octavius." Forbes sent him a frozen look. He tried to picture Duke holding captives at pistol point. Turning, he opened the double window but felt no breeze. "But I'd rather keep you out of harm's way. Understand, to my mind you're worth a whole platoon."

Duke settled. On his face, delight and disappointment did brief battle. "As you wish, sir."

Truly spread his hands on the desktop. "Once more, though, we must pose the central question. What we seem to have here is an alliance between Rebel spies and these other people. And an alliance is by definition a two-way thing, with each party scratching the other's back."

"Therefore," said Duke, "–what's in it for the South? What do they get for their services?"

"Exactly. What's in it for the South? Wakefield and his man Cathcart have labored to hold up their half of the bargain, so what's the other half? Something big, I'd wager."

"Big enough," said Forbes, "for them to spy on and then betray Van Gilder, one of the Confederacy's best friends in the North."

"Right. And with the South's recompense in mind, consider all those government and military gents out at La Maison. Getting regularly soused and serviced, becoming braggarts in each other's company."

Letting the notion filter, Forbes puckered his lips. "That would be bad, all right, especially since this supposed alliance goes back two years or more. Still, it does nothing to explain these recent events."

"It surely doesn't," said Truly.

They were interrupted by a bee. Buzzing through the open window, it began a meandering circuit of the room as Duke cringed. Truly took his smuggled copy of the *Richmond Examiner* and rolled it up. Rising from his seat, he started swiping. "Yessir-ree," he muttered, "–what the devil's in it for the South?"

38

Rockville Pike, District Of Columbia

THE NIGHT WAS moonless, the road only visible by the gig's swaying lantern. Underhill kept the horse at an even pace. Without Wakefield's assurances, he would never have come out here on his own. But despite his anxiousness, he felt like a man reclaiming his destiny, and this drew him on through the darkness. He had encountered no military patrol and was hoping that his luck would keep. To be stopped and questioned would be mortifying.

On both sides, the woods gave way to open space–pasture, maybe, or the grounds of some estate. An awful sense of nakedness gripped him. But when the woods loomed up again, too close, he felt dark shapes ready to lunge. Up ahead, a pair of eyes flickered on the road and he flinched, then saw the shape of a fox dart away. He held his arms tight to his sides, concentrated on his purpose. Suspended from the gig's top, the lantern swayed, its light wavering on the macadam surface.

Wakefield's instructions were precise. Though Underhill kept his eyes wide, he didn't see the signpost for Tennallytown until he was almost alongside it. Slowing the horse, he strained his vision to find the side road and saw it just in time to make the rightward turn. It was overgrown, deeply rutted. He cursed as the lantern bumped his head. Deciding to walk the rest of the way, he pulled to a stop and felt for his pistol. He had brought it in case of robbers, but only the quiet and the darkness concerned him now. Stepping down, he saw a torch's gleam some distance up the road. Wakefield had come through for him.

He unhooked the lantern and looked at his pocket watch–just a few minutes after midnight. He started for the torch. Blossoming apple trees bordered the road, their branches arching, almost meeting over his head. Stumbling, he kept along the center. His steps grew hesitant as he neared the torch. Stuck in the ground, it illuminated a narrow path through the left-hand orchard. Again he wondered why the rendezvous had to be made out here, rather than in the city. Wakefield had dismissed the question, citing the extreme prudence of this man whose name he refused to give. "He'll be there at midnight, Ezra. Make certain that you are too, with the money." To Underhill's consternation, Wakefield had stressed that his role as intermediary ended here–and that it would be folly to involve anyone else.

Underhill swallowed, then ventured down the path. The trees enclosed him. At his back and sides, the shadows pressed in as he held the lantern closer. A branch snapped underfoot and he froze, watching moths flutter in the amber light. From his coat, his shaking hand drew the pistol. He crept forward again. The path opened onto a grassy rise and he raised the lantern. Atop the rise he discerned a grove of white-blossomed catalpa trees, just as Wakefield had described.

His brow was cool with sweat. But his breaths came more evenly as he emerged from the orchard and started up toward the grove. Halfway there he stopped and swung the lantern around, listening hard. Hearing only the crickets, he proceeded through the tall grass and milkweed. He reached catalpas and halted. Petals carpeted the ground, so white that they seemed immune to darkness, like angels' feathers. "Angels' feathers," he thought, feeling dizzy. Usually it took liquor to squeeze out a poetic reflection or two; this time it was just his own thudding pulse. And beneath the thudding, another emotion spread like a bruise–a sad protest, a forlorn sense of affront. Never once had he expected to find himself tramping half-blind through the woods, come to pay a loathsome stranger. Lone acts of desperation were for smaller men, not for him. For years he had labored to distance himself from all that was small and desperate–and yet here he was, alone on this night. The dizziness passed. Determination arose, steadying his legs. He would finish this business as soon as possible, and never again be brought so low.

He cleared his throat. After three attempts, he found his quaking voice. "I have come, sir! Show yourself!" He held his breath to listen, heard nothing, then raised the lantern on the tree trunks. Moths fluttered but the shadows were still. He remembered the pistol in his hand and tucked it away, then took out the wad of greenbacks. With more assurance, he called again—"Five hundred, as agreed!" Still nothing. Suddenly he wondered if the man had left at the stroke of midnight. Could he be so exacting? Would he pass up five hundred dollars so easily?

He heard a slight rustle. "Are you there?!" he demanded, louder. The noise had seemed to come from the grove's opposite side. Though exasperation was making him bolder, he did not intend to cut through the trees. He started clockwise around them, holding the lantern at chest height. "I've no time for this game! Here's your fee, so reveal yourself!"

Rounding the grove, he paused to look down the far side of the rise. In the lantern's glow, he made out a rail fence and a few dark hulks just beyond it—sleeping cattle. He continued cautiously along the trees' white-petaled margin. Grasping the money, he called with hushed aggravation— "Hello! Hello! For Christ's sake, let me see y . . . " He caught his breath, halting just inches from the tree in front of him. It stood out from the grove, and in his distraction he had nearly flattened his nose on it. As he moved to step around, his foot bumped a sizeable object. With a curse he tripped backward but regained his balance. Fumbling with the lantern, he shined it on the spot and saw a small wooden crate, bottom up. Then, at the upper edge of his vision, he perceived something slender and vertical. He tilted the light to see. He beheld a noose.

In his guts, the shuddering began, working down his limbs until the lantern's glow shook with him. The rope dangled from a high branch, its noose expertly tied. He dropped the money. With twitching fingers he reached under his coat for the pistol, but already he felt the large silent presence directly behind him. A hand reached around, closed on his wrist and drew it powerfully back. Another hand gripped his shoulder and squeezed. He dropped the lantern. Feeling breath on the back of his neck, he quaked more violently. The pressure on his shoulder mounted till he thought the bone would break. He cringed, whimpering as a flat, glacial voice entered his ear:

"The letter—Van Gilder's letter . . . Did it give names?"

"No!" he yelped.

"It named none of the others?"

"No!"

Releasing his wrist, the hand thrust under his coat, took the pistol and let it drop.

"Swear to that," the voice muttered. "Swear, and live."

In his rampant heart Underhill clutched the hope like a penny. "I swear," he moaned. Near his feet the lantern lay on its side; around it, little flames licked the grass and fallen petals. He had consorted with devils. And somehow, incredibly, his best friend had betrayed him. Tears blurred his vision. "I swear!" he cried. "I–I would have no reason . . . no reason to lie!"

"No," said the voice. "You would not."

At this, Underhill felt his arms wrenched back. Then he was being lifted forward. In the next instant he was more frantically alive than he had ever been, kicking and thrashing. His hat fell off. His struggle forced a grunt from the killer's chest, and for a moment it even stalled his surge toward the noose, which he could no longer see. There was only the dim firelight, his own flailing shadow on the tree. Lurching one way and then the other, he felt another vicious backward tug; his right arm tore loose in its socket, though his cries were not from pain. Abruptly the killer got his footing back and his power seemed to double. In a deft shift, he kept Underhill's arms pinned with his one and locked the other around his victim's neck. Choking, legs twitching above the crate, Underhill sensed in his foe a relentless, machine-like fury, sapping his own pitiful strength. Then the crushing neck-hold was gone. Panting, jerking his head every which way, he experienced the one true moment of contrition he would ever know. He had consorted with devils. He would pay for eternity.

Maintaining the hold on Underhill's arms, the devil-man seized the noose with his free hand. He worked it around the writhing neck, then tugged the knot down and let go. Underhill gave a howl, cut short as the crate was knocked aside. Swinging, twisting, he kicked at the darkness. His damaged arm hung limp, while with his good one he clutched helplessly at the rope. His throat gurgled. His lungs neared bursting.

Down behind him he heard his killer breathing, while from far off came another sound–the lowing of cattle, he first thought. Then he realized it was the sound of the dead, other damned souls calling to him across the night. And he didn't feel himself being strangled so much as swallowed in darkness. His legs went still and his hand ceased clutching. His eyes bulged. On the ground near the lantern, he saw his hat catching fire, along with a few scattered greenbacks. Surrounding these, the fallen petals blurred and melded–angels' feathers no more but still white as oblivion, white as death itself.

39

Truly Residence
June 18

THE MUFFIN BOY would ordinarily have been more welcome, or at least easier to tolerate. But for Sapphira it had been a bad morning. To start with, Father Nathan had said little at breakfast before hurrying out, just when she thought the two of them might converse in the clear, relaxed, morning way that they used to. And she was beginning to believe, at last, that she hated Anna. Then she nicked a finger while slicing vegetables and had to hunt up some sticking plaster for the cut. Then a pressure started at her temples.

The air overnight had gone from sultry to misty, threatening rain for the first time in weeks. She was taking in the wash when the boy's head poked above the back fence. Despite his smallness, his tousled round head nearly fit the bowler that she had given him.

"There ye be!" he trilled.

She folded a sheet into the basket. "Hello, boy."

With a cloth-covered box strapped around his shoulders, he squeezed backwards through a gap in the fence's corner. Two muffins tumbled out. He picked them up and replaced them in the box.

Sapphira reached for a blouse of Anna's. "Spying over people's fences, are you?"

"That's how I finds 'em, mostly."

Stopping at the well, he slurped water from the dipper. She guessed him to be ten or eleven. Springy, freckled and Irish-pale, he came loping across the small yard. Maybe she could use the company after all, she thought.

"I don't think we'll be needing muffins today."

"No? Awright." Sitting on the porch steps, he set the box aside. "I be hidin'."

"From who? Your mother again?"

"No–a newspaper boy. Took me pennies yesterday, he did. And gave me this." He indicated some scabbing around his ear. "He's bigger 'n' me. But me friends and me, we'll thrash him good next chance we get. But I come to give ye this back, too." He took the bowler off and proffered it. It was dusty, the crown dented. "Me mum said to give it back, 'stead of throw it away."

"Why's this?"

He scratched his rusty curls. "I liked it before, but it gets me in fights. It's how come the newsboy whipped me. Called me Mister Fancy Man, he did–said I was puttin' on airs."

Sapphira plucked another spring clip and dropped it in the smaller basket. "They always find a reason."

"Well, even me friends make fun and try grabbin' it off me."

Her headache was mounting again. "Hang it on the post."

He did so. "Say, are ye the servant here?"

"I live here."

"By y'self?!"

"No, boy. There are others you don't get to see."

"Me name's Rory."

"You may call me Miss Sapphira."

"Miss what?"

She pronounced it again, reaching for a last pair of stockings. "Get those clips for me, would you?"

He hopped down, picked up the little basket of clips and placed it by his muffin box. As he hoisted himself onto the railing, Sapphira noted his grimy shirt. She had an urge to take it from him and wash it.

Rory swung his feet back and forth. "How ye cut your finger?"

"Kitchen knife." She hefted the clothes basket against her hip. "Well, Rory, I must go in now . . . " Mounting the steps, she reached for the bowler on the post. It slipped from her fingers, rolled onto the top step and lay there. She stared down at it, gripped by a chill as Rory went on talking.

"Me mum burnt her arm on our lantern. Right here."

"Your mum should rub balsam on it. You'd best move along, before the muffins go stale."

"Sure you don't want none?"

Sapphira shifted the basket's weight. Her eyes had not left the hat–the battered hat without an owner, without a head. "Come back tomorrow."

"Can I come back if I see that newsboy?"

She was afraid to touch the hat. Before her gaze it had changed into some repellent creature–a dirty, alien, gutter thing that whispered to her. She strained to hear it.

"Hey, y'hear me? Can I come back if . . ."

"Yes," she muttered. "Run along."

She heard him hop down from the railing and take up his box. "Fare-thee-well," he called, fading across the yard.

Suddenly she wished she had let him stay. From the hat's dented crown, thoughts emanated–not as a whisper now, more like a distant bell tolling. Or a distant smell creeping–the odor of wounds, faint but growing stronger. Thoughts tolling of absence, thoughts reeking of ruin and loss. Her head throbbed. The basket was tiring her arm. She bent down and pinched the hat by its brim, then tossed it across the yard.

Indoors, she put the folded clothes away. She checked the racks on which the lace curtains were stretched, but they hadn't dried yet. Using crumpled sheets of yesterday's paper, she wiped the kitchen windows. When she stopped, inexplicably exhausted, she heard a barrel organ out in the street. On most days she would have smiled at the clumsy playful sound, would have gone to see if this one had a trained monkey. This time the music made her queasy. The one sound she wished for was another human voice, even Anna's, but Anna was out. Sitting at the kitchen table, she wondered if she was getting sick. What kind of day was this, skewing her senses, eating at her nerves? Shivering, she rubbed her temples. She tried to pray.

Without exactly deciding what to do, she got up, ventured to the parlor and sat at the piano. Outside, the organ grinder persisted. Through the window she could see him stationed across the street, where some children had dependably gathered and two mothers observed at a distance. The grinder was a placid-faced white man in baggy clothes, patiently turning the crank while his nimble monkey held a tin cup and pennies dropped in. In the misty air, with the squeals and the organ and the small ginger ape presiding, the scene took on a certain strangeness, like her dream of the troll angels. It felt benign at first and then not. A total sham, it seemed, masking something terrible–a pitiless truth. She could sense it gathering force, like a thunderhead. She wanted to hide from it. For a moment, the monkey ceased its twitching movements, and she could have sworn it was looking right at her.

She raised the key cover, flexed her hands to steady them. Shuffling through her sheet music, she chose something difficult–a sonata whose foreign-born majesty might drive the bumbling organ from her ears. She took a breath and started playing. Several stormy chords along, her cut finger began to hurt, but she played harder and harder. Then she hit the wrong key and went still. The note faded but in her brain it kept stabbing–stark, flat, wrong. Laying her head in her forearms she stared deep into the varnished wood as the note stabbed on, louder by far than the noises outside. She raised her eyes. From the mantel, Mother Rachel's clear sad gaze met her own. The next thing she knew, she had thrown on her shawl and was headed out the door. The organ grinder played on as children fussed over the monkey, and no one seemed to notice as she hurried past.

With movement came a sense of escape, quashed in the next instant as dread caught up with her. Her pace quickened. She kept her eyes low, trying not to think. Turning onto Tenth Street, she gathered her skirts, clutched her shawl and broke into a run. Down the misted sidewalk she let her feet fly, heedless of where she was going. A man stepped out of a shop; he saw her in time to hop back, blurting an oath as she sped by. She had forgotten how it felt to run. Giddy, she ran faster until her lungs started burning. Past Ford's Theater now, she slowed to a breathless trudge and went on another block, then stopped to rest against a wall. Her gaze wandered. Across the street she saw the Stars 'n' Stripes draped in a window. Then, looking up, she saw the big sign: "J.W. MORSE EMBALMING–Reverence With Scientific Care."

As the black words swelled in her vision, she eased away from the wall and headed for the corner of Pennsylvania. There she shut her eyes, then opened them. For an instant that was no less vivid for its brevity, she beheld the city burning: shops, hotels and government buildings aflame, the President's House silhouetted in fire and smoke, charred bodies and stampeding throngs across the cobblestone. Washington was the Capital of the Dead.

"There ye be again!"

Her head cleared enough to see Rory bouncing toward her with his muffin box.

"Found me a good corner–but then I seen that newsboy so I had to fly. Burns me, it does–but wait'll I set me friends on him. Say, why're you standin' here?" He peered up at her, his face questioning. "Are ye sick?"

She looked at the busy buildings, the street traffic–everything normal except for the blood drumming in her ears, telling her that the trial was far from over.

"What's the matter?" Rory demanded.

"Must go," she said.

Dodging a wagon and hopping the streetcar tracks, she crossed to the Avenue's dingy side and started south–slowly at first, head down, trying to keep her breathing steady. Time was short and she had a long way to go. But as the minutes devoured themselves, the weakness passed and her legs responded. She fought the urge to run. All that mattered was that she keep moving, threading her way past people whose glances she barely felt. On this boulevard of great and lowly doings, as elsewhere, she had asked God to take her far away or make her into someone different. But not today. Today the shrouding gray light smothered every plea, save one, because life was upon her as never before and because something was horribly, sickeningly wrong and she had to get to the Sixth Street Wharf.

40

Treasury Department

THE MESSAGE, HANDED over by Duke and soon crumpled in Truly's fist, was sharply explicit. Baker would be busy all morning, calling on Secretary Stanton and other worthies, but he definitely wanted to see Truly and Forbes upon his return. Meanwhile they were to take no further step in their investigation. To salvage what they could of these hours, they helped Duke sift through the last of Van Gilder's correspondence, stacking the pages as they were read. Truly went about it quietly, resisting the urge to gripe. Something told him that they would not get to loose their fateful lightening on La Maison.

They had come across nothing from any of Van Gilder's four co-conspirators. This reinforced the thought that the keepers had forbidden such contact between the men, further discouraging any attempt at insurrection. If so, the five of them had either obeyed the rule or, disobeying it, had taken care to destroy what letters they exchanged. Much of the Copperhead's correspondence came from sympathizers both prominent and obscure, some of it treasonous enough to be placed in a separate file. Yet no letter seemed relevant until the agents reached the bottom of the last box. There Truly found a brief one without a postal frank but dated above the salutation–July 30, 1863, several weeks after Van Gilder's maiming. It was a letter of introduction, its bold but graceful handwriting by now familiar. Truly read it aloud:

Dear Gideon,

The bearer of this is Mr. Adam Cathcart, a trusted compatriot. He has read and admired your editorials and is himself a writer of considerable flair and conviction, holding dear those same principles as we. If you could possibly find a position for him on your staff, you would not regret it, as his value exceeds what may be here described.

Cheers to your recent salvos against conscription and this despotic government. I would visit again, but am doing a brisk trade which ties me down. As ever, I hail you as a friend and as a champion of peace.

Your servant,
Miles Wakefield

"There we have it!" Forbes said. "The changing of the guard."

Truly set the document aside. "Well, it could help convince Lafe we're onto something."

Reminded of the director, Truly almost spat. No doubt Congressman Underhill had gone crying to the right people, just as he threatened to do, and thrown up this latest barrier—as if Baker himself had not ruffled his share of fancy feathers, and for less cause. But shockingly, of late, Baker seemed to have entered a more cautious stage.

Having learned rough justice with the San Francisco vigilantes, Baker had returned east in time for the secession crisis, when men of his crafty talents surged in value. He made the right connections, performed the right daring deeds and found himself running his own organization—arresting, investigating, interrogating, trampling everyone in his path. Only in these last few months had the exhilaration of power visibly given way to its nervousness. The progression made sense enough, Truly thought. Accustomed to his high horse but, given his now-numerous enemies, fretful of being knocked off of it—booted back to the dreary days of lynching vagrants and raiding public funds for bread money—Baker had grown careful. He had learned the art of political calculation, weighing every action against its likely result.

Truly pictured what the latter stages might be like: Baker fat and complacent, secure in his position, crushing victims at longer range and with twice the effect, but only half the joy; Baker in retirement, harboring enough lowdown secrets to protect himself, writing his puffed-up memoirs about How I Saved The Republic; in death, buried beneath a statue that looked like him except a good deal handsomer.

Looking into the mist outside, Truly remembered that it was Saturday. Theaters, brothels, restaurants, dance halls and gambling hells were readying for a night of maximum trade, before the piety and remorse of Sunday–while down at the docks, the dead and wounded kept arriving.

"Octavius, you can go home," Truly told Duke. "Nothing's left to do but await our director's smiling face. Go on and spare yourself."

Duke rose and got his coat. He wished them luck and waddled out, nearly colliding with a pretty female Treasury clerk who was carrying a stack of papers. They listened as he sputtered his apologies and hurried off.

"Lord, what are his evenings like?" said Truly.

"No worse than mine, I hope," Forbes said.

With a sigh, Truly stared out the window. A weird day, he thought–and not just because of the mist, somehow.

Just then Duke reappeared in the doorway, looking apprehensive. "Sirs–Colonel Baker is back. He told me to summon you and went directly to his office."

"Hail Caesar," Truly muttered.

IN THE PERILOUS first weeks of the war, when it looked as if Confederate forces might attack Washington and lay siege to the government buildings, tons of supplies had been stored in the Treasury's cavernous basement. Here through successive emergencies they had remained–moldering flour, mildewed leather goods and petrified hardtack, provisioning several lucky generations of rats. Rats skittered across the agents' dimly lit path as they headed for Baker's office, negotiating the labyrinth of crates and barrels.

Some who did not know the secret service director wondered why he would accept the humbling symbolism of a basement office; some who did know him saw a different symbolism and figured that it suited him fine.

In his dank gas-lit chamber he had come to haunt the public imagination, fashioning himself as a burrowed beast of prey. Infamy and prestige were one and the same for Lafayette Baker—and from his basement lair, that prestigious infamy resonated like a snarl.

The pinewood door stood slightly ajar. To Truly's knock, a brusque "Come in" responded and the pair entered. Truly took a chair next to Forbes, facing the desk and the burly man behind it. Noting the set of Baker's jaw, Truly was suddenly glad for the many inept or unlucky agents in the federal secret service—those who made his own record look stellar and thus spared him the worst of Baker's wrath, even when he seemed hell-bent on provoking it. But as the spy chief began speaking, Truly wondered why the voice was so low and deliberate this time.

"Nate—Captain Forbes . . . I'm going to relate all this in order of occurrence. Last evening Mister Stanton received a formal complaint from the Democratic congressional leadership. It claimed that this organization—in the person of you, Nate—had been harassing the bejesus out of Ezra T. Underhill, Honorable Representative from Maryland."

"Colonel," said Truly, "—like you, I follow a case where it happens to take me. And since when have you or Stanton cared a fart about griping Democrats?"

Baker sat back and stroked his long brass-red beard, regarding Truly with a cool, almost light-hearted restraint. "Good try, Nate. Damned, though, if I see how this whorehouse muddle of yours fits into our domain."

Truly held up Wakefield's note. "Then please have a look at this. And hear us out."

"Put that away. And hold your tongue, for once."

Truly eyed the director's garb—black broadcloth today, with a ruffled white shirt, green silk cravat and pricey cuff links. Clothes in this case did not make the man, and neither did the proper speech that he had acquired over time. The rugged frame and cunning gray eyes bespoke the frontier law enforcer. But in Truly's mind, an unwelcome fact poked through: his antagonism toward Baker had less to do with the man's character than with his age—thirty-eight, eight years Truly's junior. Returning the letter to his pocket, Truly felt chastened enough to fall silent.

"Politics is hogwash," Baker declared. "But in this year—an election year like none before—I've made a little discovery. Hogwash can be serious business. A fellow can drown in it. Now come November, such matters as the course of the war and the preservation of the Union will be decided.

Dismiss all that if you want to, Nate, but do it at your own expense. Our Republican masters are quite understandably out to woo as many Democrats as possible, apart from the Copperhead faction. You're aware, aren't you, that the President just picked a War Democrat as his running mate?"

"And a Tennessean to boot," Truly said evenly. "I do read the papers."

"Good for you. The National Union ticket, they're calling it. The point is that the Democrats may flog Lincoln about Emancipation and such, but a majority have stood firm on the prosecution of the war. Now, however, the body count in Virginia's got some of them ready to quit the dance and embrace their party's nominee–McClellan, most likely. Fate's queer, eh? Having spent his command days pretty much prolonging the war, Little Mac's become the darling of the Peace Wing. Say it with me, Nate–'President McClellan.'"

"No, thank you."

"Anyhow, I've just seen some dispatches from Petersburg–and once more, the Army of the Potomac has gone and tripped over itself. The main attack was delayed, then bungled, and now Lee has most of his force dug in. Looks like we're in for the longest summer yet. We may see more draft riots. What with that and gold prices and this bumper crop of widows, the tide's against us, because a lot of voting men will figure that letting the South go isn't quite so disloyal after all. So–in this precarious season, what does our friend Nathan do? He starts badgering one of the very tribe our bosses are courting. A two-termer from Maryland, no less–the state that verily surrounds us and which, you may recall, we've nearly lost a couple of times."

Truly gripped the arms of his chair. "All of which ignores what we've uncovered so far!"

"Ticks on a buffalo, Major." Baker raised a finger. "Ticks on a buffalo, compared to what we're up against. Now if you know what's good for you, you'll sit still while I tell you the rest."

Truly felt Forbes' foot bump his own.

"First thing this morning," said Baker, "I am summoned to the War Department, where Stanton shows me the complaint. Imagine our thoughts when, just as I'm ready to leave, an aide appears with a bit of street news: a farmhand up near Tennallytown found Underhill's body swinging from a tree."

For a few stunned seconds, Truly saw only the chief's upraised finger. Forbes muttered something under his breath. Lips tight, Truly tried to force all expression from his face. "I suppose you'll say I drove him to it? Quite an accomplishment, in just two visits."

Baker lowered the finger. "Fact or appearance–which matters more at a time like this? Underhill wasn't the most respected member of his party, but that won't keep some of them from using this on us. Fortunately for you, he left something that should reduce the outcry." Opening a drawer, Baker took out a sheaf of handwritten pages. "On the chance that he had left some clue to the why and wherefore, I hurried over to Brown's Hotel. I was met there by a police detective who had already gained access."

Truly cut in. "Quentin Archer, by any chance?"

Baker let out an impatient huff. "As a matter of fact, yes. Archer, the acting Chief of Detectives–who even you, in that damned elaborate report of yours, cite as having a good record and reputation."

"None of which would have mattered to you, at one time."

The reference to Baker's former standard of fearlessness struck home. His eyes went from hot to cold. "Even if your evidence, your witnesses and your fancy guesswork were more credible, I'd have to regard Underhill's death as a separate thing–for the following reason, if I may continue . . . " He held up the pages. "This is a speech, apparently undelivered. Underhill dictated most of it to his secretary but wrote the last two pages himself. Archer had transcribed it already for his own report, but he gave me the copy. With all its wailing and gnashing about the times we're in, it serves well enough as a suicide note. It will be shown to a few leading Democrats and then released to the press, and Underhill will go down as a man overcome by grief for his nation. To anyone who cares, I can privately add a couple more details that Archer gave me. First–the tip of his tongue was missing."

In his side-vision, Truly caught a look from Forbes.

"Cut off," Baker said, "apparently with a pen-knife found at the scene. And this we may take as testament to his addled mind. Some mad bit of symbolism, meant to say how he viewed himself . . . " Baker read from one of the pages. "'Verily, it oft seems that in the clamor and sorrow of these days I have been rendered voiceless.'" He lay the page down. "Along with the pen-knife, a near-empty bottle of claret was found at the death site; it's said that the congressman liked his liquor, and doubtless it helped push him past the brink."

"Something pushed him, all right," said Truly, straining for self-control. "But it wasn't madness or liquor or me. Colonel, we're dealing with one devil of a murderer."

For a moment, Baker looked more incredulous than angry. "Are you . . . ? Listen–the man *hanged* himself!"

"And Jon Peavey shot himself, supposedly. And I guess Gideon Van Gilder just carved himself up! Underhill knew both of these men, and Archer too–and a lieutenant-colonel who we've yet to identify. All five are connected with La Maison. There's plenty to suggest that each of them had something to hide and that they were being extorted–Underhill's financial records could give further proof. The letter to him from Van Gilder indicated that they had tried and failed to throw off their blackmailers and were now in danger. Heck–even without the letter, don't you think it's queer that three would die violently in such a short period?!"

Twice during the retort, Baker seemed about to interrupt but did not do so, his disdain turning to sulky hesitation. Truly pressed on. "But lest we forget, Colonel–our main interest here is a Rebel secret agent. Miles Wakefield was tied in some way to all three of the dead men, and we figure he has some kind of long-standing arrangement with the blackmailers. The unusualness of it hints at something weighty–something we'd best uncover."

Truly felt Forbes' hand reach into his coat and extract Wakefield's note, which he had forgotten. Forbes offered it to Baker. "Sir, this confirms the tie between Wakefield and Cathcart, the spy we have in custody."

Baker looked at Forbes as if he had not noticed him until now. He took the letter and pondered it, scratching his beard. "Well . . . " He handed the note back. "Spies are of course another kettle of fish. So, yes–find Wakefield, but be sly about it. Don't stray from the path."

Truly wondered what path Baker could possibly mean. "If 'sly' means 'effective,' we need to raid La Maison. Those people hornswaggled us before, but they won't this time."

Slowly, imperiously, Baker shook his head.

"Colonel . . . !"

"My parley with Detective Archer touched on your own conduct. Whether he's guilty as sin or pure as an angel, he told me something that I–and therefore you–must take seriously. He has drafted a complaint–do you hear the chorus swelling, Nate?–concerning your disregard of his authority. The Superintendent of Police is sure to sign it." Truly opened his mouth but Baker jabbed a finger at him. "Don't bother saying it! Yes, we used to clash a lot with the Washington Police–we were staking out our territory, and they felt we were tramping on theirs. But we've managed to mend fences. Early this year, as you're aware, Superintendent Webb and I agreed to cooperate. The idea is that if we stay out of what the police consider their business, they'll be forthcoming about any suspected profiteers, counterfeiters, bounty jumpers and such–criminals of more concern to us. But the real wonderment? I find I'm wasting less time on territorial skirmishes. I value that, gentlemen. Lord knows I don't mind a good scrap, but my plate's pretty full as it is."

"Colonel–if Wakefield's not a concern of ours, who is?"

"Can you at this point give evidence, not just to me but to Webb, that Wakefield is actually being harbored at La Maison?"

Truly threw his hands up. "Dang it, Lafe! Even if I could, Archer would likely get wind of it and warn them at the house! He's one of the five, I'm telling you. But unlike the others, it seems he's saved his neck for the time being. As long as he uses his position to confound and obstruct us, I reckon his life will be spared."

Again the imperial headshake.

Truly slumped. "The management at La Maison could well be at the center of this whole business, along with Wakefield."

"As I say, then–be sly. You're resourceful enough. Infiltrate the place or put it under surveillance. And until you get something undeniable against Archer, stay out of his way. Understand?"

Truly stayed silent, his face warm.

"We understand," said Forbes.

Regarding Forbes again, Baker remained cool. "Captain–Military Information has been generous to loan us your services once more."

"It's a continuing honor, sir. Colonel Sharpe thinks it vital that our organizations work in concert, whenever it's mutually beneficial."

"Mutually beneficial," Baker echoed. "Yes–in those cases where civil and military considerations are closely joined. But I'm curious, Captain–is this really such an instance?"

Truly's stomach tightened another notch.

Forbes answered mildly. "That's a fair point, Colonel. At first glance, I suppose the military element seems missing. But we must recall that a Union officer is involved–his post and authority yet unknown–and that he's somehow subject to the blackmailers. Blackmailers who we strongly suspect have some pact with the enemy. Ferreting him out may require the knowledge of a fellow army man."

Despite his gloom, Truly felt relief at his partner's acuity. Forbes had stretched the slim justification without breaking it.

Dropping his gaze, Baker nodded. "Very well. I'll be following this more closely. That's all for now, gentlemen."

The two got up. As Truly put his slouch hat on, Baker looked at him.

"Nate, where's that hat I sent you?"

"Dang, I forgot it."

"For God's sake, start wearing it. You look like a beat-up muleskinner in that thing."

At the curb, Truly took out a plug of tobacco and chewed till his jaw ached. The two of them agreed to head for a restaurant near Judiciary Square, though Truly's appetite had all but vanished. Few words passed until they were aboard the horse trolley, seated near some businessmen who were yammering about the gold market.

"Nate," Forbes muttered, "–if we're correct, they've gone and strung up a U.S. congressman."

Spitting over the side, Truly mulled the rotten news from Petersburg. He hoped to hear from Ben today.

"But it just hit me," Forbes went on. "–from a mere blackmail stand-point, it makes no sense. If they wanted to scare their victims into resuming payment, it should have been enough to slaughter one of them and let the others know about it. And if each had a bad secret, no one was apt to contact the authorities. Yet three of the five are dead, including Underhill. Killing him meant an awful lot of risk, though they seem to have gotten away with it. But risk aside, why would they eliminate a steady source of income? Not even try to preserve it by continued terror?"

Chewing, Truly pondered it until the image returned: Underhill swinging from a tree. "Maybe the scheme no longer matters. Maybe there's a larger boon to be gotten elsewhere, for both parties. Still, as you say–why go so far as to start murdering their blackmail subjects? The congressman, especially. And why go about it in such a way? *Luring* them into defiance."

"Entrapping them," Forbes said. "Deliberately creating an excuse to start killing them. When otherwise, they'd have stayed obedient and kept on paying."

Truly shook his head. "It'll vex us, I reckon, until we figure out the Confederate interest in all of this. Which will of course be harder now, thanks to a compromised police official and . . . " He gave his most pained smile. "–the fine public servant we just left. Heck, Archer played him like a danged fiddle, just like Ravenel and her gang played us."

By the Kirkwood Hotel, the trolley stopped for more passengers. Truly and Forbes surrendered their seats to a couple of crinolined ladies. Another well-tailored businessman came aboard and nodded to his fellows, wedging himself onto their bench. Talk of gold resumed as the horses strained and the car eased along. Often interrupting one another, the men spoke in quick turns until the new arrival said, "You hear about that congressman hanging himself?" Faces jerked in his direction. A round of questions and speculations ensued.

Leaning on the hand pole, Truly passed a look to Forbes, then watched the misted street glide slowly by. Absently he recited to himself: "'Vice is a monster of so frightful mien/ As, to be hated, needs but to be seen . . . '"

41

Potomac Waterfront

NEARING THE DOCKS, Sapphira did not realize how thick the fog had become until she turned a corner and almost fell over a man who was being beaten and robbed. His two rough-looking assailants glanced up at her and then put their fists back to work. She skipped around them and kept on. Then she heard a vehicle coming and moved aside. From out of the mist a hearse appeared, and as it rattled by she saw two coffins in back–rosewood, the kind reserved for officers. She paused for a deep, careful breath. From the direction of the wharf she could hear shouts and other crowd noise. The damp, smelly air oppressed her, yet she clutched her shawl more tightly about herself and moved on, head bowed, pressing toward a spectacle that she had often come to witness and thereby callous her heart, but whose looming now threatened to burst it.

The cacophony grew louder as she passed the grimy sheds, workshops and warehouses. Lifting her skirts for a mud puddle, she was startled by a disheveled man who stepped from an alley and bumped her. He stumbled back but remained in her way, smelling of sour whiskey. He squinted at her as she tried to pass. Then, casually decisive, he lurched toward her. In the instant before his hands touched her breast, she let out an implausible cry–high-pitched yet compressed, like a cat set afire–straight into the flushed, puffy face. In the next instant she was hurrying along once more, not sure what had happened but recalling the drunkard's confused bloodshot eyes as she threw herself at him, her hands like claws.

Having turned onto Sixth Street, she could see little at first. A fantastic babble of voices met and then surrounded her in the mist, with shouts and wheels and horse-hooves mixed in. Pulse mounting, she felt as if she had entered a street full of spirits. Then she began to pick out the milling shapes of people. The noise level neared bedlam as she eased into the multitude, which spilled into lots and alleys. People of all ages gazed toward the wharf. First there were the merely curious, craning like carnival goers but not trying to press their way through. Deeper in the throng, grimmer faces appeared–fidgety people, pushing forward–and Sapphira heard a woman crying. For a second her knees went weak, then recovered as several shouting, gesturing men of the provost guard began clearing a path. She cringed against a shed wall as an ambulance broke through, nearly running over a few spectators. A small colored boy with a water jug ran alongside. Sapphira glimpsed the bandaged, upraised stump of an arm, then heard groans as one wheel struck a pothole. Only then did the dream sensation start to crumble. Knowing that she was just one buffeted particle among many, she felt determination prick her like a knifepoint. Whatever awaited her, she would have to be equal to it.

She stood on tip-toe, staring over and around people till she saw the wharf, with the outline of a moored steamer. Alongside the vessel, figures scrambled amid a jumble of ambulance carts, while coffin-laden hearses waited to the left. Stationary torches had been lit to cut the fog. Here and there, the Potomac glittered through. The Christian and Sanitary Commissions had refreshment stands set up by a smoking cookhouse. For six weeks now, day and night, the dead, maimed and dying had been coming in by way of Fredericksburg and Aquia Creek. Many wondered that Grant had any army left.

Calling upon all her craft and surefootedness, Sapphira ducked, squeezed and sidled through the chaos. The guard shoved people aside for another cart, which passed quite close to her, and she forced a look. A half-dozen dirty soldiers lay in back, looking dazed except for one whose whiskered face contorted in pain. Again the crowd surged together. Up ahead, the lone woman's keening took on a savagery of its own, like a violin gone mad–a reckless, tuneless, scraping solo. Sapphira hardened herself against it and worked slowly, circuitously forward. The smell of food wafted fitfully, giving way to the stench of wounds. Covering her nose with her shawl, she watched a teenaged girl totter into an alley and retch. Sapphira kept going. In the clamor she recognized other sounds–cries and groans, the clump of feet on boards. Through a gap she saw two bedraggled litter-bearers loading a man into an ambulance, while another pair scurried up the gangplank. Some who had made it through the provost cordon lined both sides of the plank, before which a haggard officer struggled to direct things. Volunteers carrying jugs hovered around the cart now in use, offering drinks and sprinkling water on wounds.

Nearing the front, Sapphira found herself hemmed in as a swaying motion swept the crowd. She tipped backwards, bumped someone and turned to see an old white woman dressed in black crinoline and a huge feathered hat. The woman's face was like weathered stone, her eyes flat and shiny as a night animal's. Muttering apology, Sapphira looked toward the boat. Arrayed on the foredeck lay the stiff, sheeted forms of those who had died en route. She eyed their protruding hands and feet, heard a moan as the litter-bearers brought out another man. The smells of death, food and smoke warred in her nose. Nausea rippled.

Lifting her gaze, she discerned the bare mast of a schooner over at the Seventh Street dock. She concentrated on it until the sickness passed. Still she felt the press of bodies all around her, with surly voices, and her breathing turned quick and shallow. Avoiding faces, she crossed her arms and gripped herself. Over her shoulder, one man and then another started shouting angrily. She couldn't tell what they were saying; she didn't want to know. Biting her lip, she stared at the corpses on the foredeck. Then an older man in front of her was yelling toward the boat: "Oh, yessir–look at this one! What're you covering there, soldier? Mosquito bites?!"

She looked to the gangplank, where a head-bandaged private stood leaning on a crutch, helped by one of the boat's crew. Both men stared in confusion, hesitant as the jeers flew–"Faker! Coward! Send him back!" Others joined the taunting chorus, including those who lined the plank. Still steadying the soldier, the crewman gave him a probing look. The weary officer in charge beckoned but neither man budged. Sapphira had heard of but never witnessed this sort of thing. Since the Wilderness, it was said, deserters and malingerers had routinely hidden themselves among the honest wounded.

Taking a backward step, the crewman let go of the soldier, who in fact looked ruddier than wounded usually did. The soldier's expression went from hazy to alarmed as the crowd harangued him–"Faker! Coward! Faker!" Someone reached up, grabbed his crutch and jostled it. Wavering, he muttered some protest, just as an empty bottle came hurtling through the air. It missed his head and shattered on the boat's gunwale, where-upon the officer spun around and bellowed—"Damn you, I'll be the judge! I'LL BE THE DAMNED JUDGE!!"

Until now Sapphira had taken little note of the officer, whose shoulder straps marked him as a captain—a distinctly untidy one, with his tunic unbuttoned and pants caked with mud. He was a squat man with a drawn face and matted brown beard. At the moment of his outburst, the hollers and even the weeping of the unseen woman had died—yet he threw his hat down and raved on, fists flailing: "Why, why in Christ's name do you stupid useless bastards come here?! Why in hell do you come down here every single blasted day and stand gawking like it's a damned parade!? You think you have the right?! You think you have any damned say in it?! I will shoot any man who thinks he does! I WILL SHOOT HIM IN THE GODDAMNED HEAD!!"

His eyes flashed, his voice a relentless bray. Spittle clung to his beard. Behind him, the crewman vanished as the private hobbled to the side. The litter-bearers descended the plank with another prostrate form, but all stares remained on the raging captain. "Get your fill of guts, you damned worthless vermin! But the first one that sticks his nose in will get his own blasted trip to the graveyard, you hear me?! DO YOU HEAR?!!" He drew his revolver and waved it. There were gasps in the crowd. Drivers calmed their horses while volunteers momentarily forgot the wounded. The guardsmen themselves looked on anxiously, unmoving. With a tremor, Sapphira pulled her stare a few feet to the left, where the latest blue-clad victim was being lifted into an ambulance. She glimpsed his profile, swathed in dirty dressing. All sound was sucked from her ears; when it returned, she had squirmed to the crowd's forward edge, where she crouched staring toward the wagon.

The captain had quieted, the revolver dangling at his side. For a moment there was only the sound of his spent breathing. Then he holstered his weapon, bent for his hat, wiped his face with his sleeve.

From the ambulance came a long, low moan. Sapphira moved toward it.

"You!" barked a male voice.

Almost to the wagon, Sapphira felt her shoulder gripped. She jerked free for a second, then felt both of her arms seized. Glancing behind her, she saw a stocky guardsman; he looked mystified as she strained against him. Then the captain walked over. She expected a gruff order for her to be dragged off, perhaps to jail, but the captain did not speak right away. As she stopped struggling, her gaze locked with his, and she discovered that rage had borne him to a region of calm. And when she did not look away, there followed a conversation that she knew she would recall only in substance, so plain it was, lost in a swirl of perceptions. She needed to look, she said–needed to be sure. In a quiet, grainy voice he asked what this soldier was to her. Haltingly she tried to tell him, and his strange yet mild attention turned a bit stranger. Still his gaze did not harden or pull back. She felt dizzily removed, wondering if it was a kindred madness in her that permitted this calm exchange–this separate truce, here in the mist with the muttering crowd looking on, in the reek and the groans and the torch flicker, with the guardsman's grip and her body gone numb and the bearers bringing forth another limp casualty.

However long she lived, she would remember this deathly pageant with the captain's eyes at its center, red-rimmed and unutterably tired, unfathomably patient. She would remember all but the exact words that passed between them, that caused his nod to the guardsman, that made the guardsman's hands release her, that sent her stumbling toward the ambulance. More than anything, she would remember the sight of Ben crammed between the other tattered, half-dead forms, one side of his face grotesquely puffed beneath the bandages, the white of one eye blood red and the other one half shut, his bandaged right arm swollen rigid. Her legs wobbled. Her lips shaped his name. It was Ben but not the same, never again the same.

PART V

Vice Is A Monster

Other sins only speak;
murder shrieks out.
• *JOHN WEBSTER (1580?-1625?)*
THE DUCHESS OF MALFI

42

Buford's Gap, Western Virginia
June 21

BEHIND THEM LAY four straight days of fight-and-march, march-and-fight. Ahead of them, through the mountain passes, the enemy wriggled away like a frightened blue snake. It was a moment to curse as well as celebrate. Preferring to do both in private, Jubal Early left his aides and rode on alone.

The ground rose, dipped and grew rockier as he passed through the piedmont shadows, emerging into sunlight atop a knoll. He raised his field glasses and scanned the gap. Only an hour ago, billows of panicked Yankee dust had still been visible–now, nothing. He lowered his glasses and sighed. The pursuit, it seemed, was over. Hunter's force had escaped intact.

The rugged, spreading hues of the Blue Ridge held Early's gaze–rust and green, azure and purple, deeper green. Out here, even regret could somehow feel splendid. Besides, he had fulfilled the first part of Lee's directive: save Lynchburg, remove the threat to the rear. By ceaseless march and rickety rail, his corps had reinforced Breckinridge just in time, bashing the Yankee marauders and hounding them all the way back to the Valley's edge. Now, wide as the mountain vista itself, a decision gaped. He could rejoin Lee at Petersburg, if he thought it best–or he could keep going.

Early was still adjusting to the weight and isolation of his command. With his staff, his manner was more formal and sober. He even cursed less—Jackson would have approved of that. But briefly alone as he was, after days of exertion, he granted himself an outlet that he had heretofore used only in the craze of battle. Glaring at the peaks, he threw his head back and crowed like a rooster. Like the god of roosters he crowed, scaring birds from the trees and making the hollows ring. As the echo faded, he heard pebbles crunch on the slope behind him. He turned in the saddle and saw his second-in-command riding up from a stand of cottonwoods.

John Cabell Breckinridge gave a drowsy smile. "Whatever that was, General, it sure woke me up."

"The bird of victory," Early said. "Rare and coveted."

"Well, you seem to have caged him."

"Maybe—though it's a mite smaller than I wished. How're your ribs today?"

"A good deal better, thank you."

Breckinridge's Cold Harbor injury had aggravated an older wound and he rode with care. Watching him, Early recalled with satisfaction that he now outranked a former Vice President of the United States. In that office and before then, as senator and congressman, Breckinridge had been a bright ascendant star in the political nightscape. Many Kentucky parents had named their sons after him. Despite his relatively moderate views, his distinguished record and oratorical gifts had made him the South's standard-bearer in 1860, when his run for President split the Democrats along regional lines and (cruel irony) cleared the way for Lincoln. His subsequent embrace of the secessionist cause had been tardy—but if any fellow Confederates still held this against him, they were few and silent. The courtly Kentuckian was popular as both a man and a general. Even in a moth-eaten linen duster he looked magnificent on his steed—tall and strong, with striking blue eyes. Around his cupid's-bow mouth a luxurious mustache drooped, the ends like artfully frayed rope.

As Breckinridge drew alongside, Early handed him the field glasses. He took a long look, then handed them back. "Hunter will be having nightmares for a while."

"He shouldn't have escaped," Early grumbled.

Breckinridge eased back in the saddle. "It vexes me too, General. But we've outrun the supply trains, and some of the men haven't had rations since Lynchburg."

"They're tired and hungry, yes. So am I. But if those buttermilk rangers of ours had done what they were supposed to, we'd be eating Yankee bacon right now."

The major general looked quizzical. "Buttermilk rangers?"

"The cavalry. The ones who get to gallop around and woo farm girls while others do the real work. This time they didn't even keep up with the enemy, let alone block his retreat."

Breckinridge nodded. "Their performance fell short, all right. But if Hunter heads back down the Valley, we could still cut him off by way of Rockfish Gap."

Early shook his head. "He has a choice of directions now. Whichever it is, we won't know it 'less our gallant horsemen keep on his tail." He wiped his brow, stared into the distance. "David Hunter–I knew him down in Mexico. I had charge of the Monterrey encampment, where he was paymaster. We got on well enough."

Breckinridge gave a sour smirk. "One thing about this war–you never know who you'll end up fighting."

"Yep. But the fellow's Virginia-born–and if I ever caught him, I swear I'd hoist him up the tallest tree in a lightning storm. Turncoat bastard."

Breckinridge only squinted. Early glanced at him. In his present role the Kentuckian had proven able and cooperative, but Early could not help a flicker of annoyance. He recalled his compatriot's similar non-response back at Lynchburg, when another general had started fulminating about the Yankees. Doubtless Breckinridge had former friends and acquaintances throughout the North. But he sometimes seemed too decorous and above-it-all–and for a fighting man, too soft. Yet his battle record, including his outnumbered victory at New Market some weeks ago, argued differently–and as Early remembered this, his doubt faded.

"So," said Breckinridge, "–is it back to the Valley for us?"

"We will proceed," said Early. "The men will get food and a day's rest, time for the ordnance and supply trains to catch up."

Breckinridge turned his blue-eyed gaze on Early. "But regarding our ultimate intentions, General . . . When you showed me your orders, I believe you hinted at something. Something about an ace up our sleeve?"

Early hesitated, regretting his indiscretion. Secrecy was critical, and Breckinridge already knew far more than tight-lipped old Stonewall would have told him.

For now, the main goal was to unsettle the Union high command, causing it to withdraw forces from Lee's front. It seemed likely that Early could penetrate a good way before the great minds in Washington–famed for political, not military adroitness–were forced to react. But to actually arrive at the gates of Lincoln's city, this little army would have to tramp some two hundred and fifty miles, braving risk upon risk, driving itself to the brink of endurance. Then and only then could Early indulge the distant hope, the absurd hope that so much could rest on a single Union traitor. Until forced to share his secret, he would let it tantalize as he drifted to sleep each night.

Not wanting to insult Breckinridge, he settled on a partial lie. "Lee was equally vague to me–but it has something to do with our spy network. Once details emerge, we'll be contacted and fully informed."

Breckinridge nodded gamely. "Fair enough, General. The immediate challenge should keep us well occupied."

Feeling heady once more, Early gave him a sidelong smile. "Still, the possibility of a strike at Washington should keep us animated. That would be a return visit for you–eh, Genr'l? Unannounced." He cackled. "And with plenty of company!"

Breckinridge failed to smile. "Life does play a trick or two."

Disappointed, Early stroked his scraggly beard. For all the action that Breckinridge had reportedly seen, from Shiloh to the present, he did appear to retain some sentimentality. Time would tell how deep it ran. "I wonder if there's any good whiskey hereabouts," Early said.

Breckinridge brightened. "There's a fine thought!" Riding back down the slope, he grimaced in pain.

Early slowed his horse for him, then gestured toward the south. "That's Botetourt Springs, yonder. Not often that soldiers get to camp at a health resort."

"They'll bless you for that," said Breckinridge. "And for the women's college nearby. I heard some of the young ladies were ladling out brandy juleps along the road."

"Ladies and juleps!" said Early. "What more can a man request, when the fight's done?"

His mind snagged on the subject of ladies. Back home in Rocky Mount lived one who had borne him four children (or was it five?), though he had not seen fit to marry her. He understood Breckinridge to be happily married with children, including a grown son who served on his staff;

his wife often stayed with him in camp. Gordon, one of Early's divisional chiefs, had a whole passel of sons and daughters and a wife who sometimes accompanied him—though not, mercifully, on this campaign. Early could scarcely abide the encumbrance of women. Still, he could not help wondering what married life might have been like. He had wondered it last night when he saw young General Ramseur writing a letter by candlelight, presumably to his new wife.

As he and Breckinridge emerged from a wooded hollow, Early saw a rider coming toward them and was pleased to recognize Henry Kyd Douglas, the spirited young major now serving on Ramseur's staff. The two generals reined their mounts as Douglas cantered up, touching his hat to them.

The major grinned. "Sirs—just happened on some news from the cavalry."

Early scowled. "Good news, or more of the same?"

"Pretty fair, Genr'l. Some troopers overtook an enemy supply train and cut it up. Captured some guns, spiked the ones they couldn't take."

"Fine. We like that. Anything else?"

"Yessir. Hunter's continuing west into the Alleghenies—away from the Valley."

Breckinridge raised his eyebrows.

Rubbing his stiff left shoulder, Early pondered. "Well, there goes any chance of intercepting him. On the other hand . . . Hell, I need a map. Douglas, tell Ramseur that we'll see him at the Springs around five o'clock, along with the other divisional heads."

"Will you be taking a dip with us then, sir?"

Early smirked. "Not me. Reckon I'd kill all the fish."

The major laughed, saluted and rode off.

"It's understandable," said Breckinridge. "If Hunter withdrew the way he came, partisan raiders would dog him all back up the Valley. This way, he's safe from them as well as us."

"True," said Early. "But this line of retreat will take him through some mighty barren country—I've seen it myself. And his provisions must already be low. Which means he can't stop till he reaches the Kanawha—far out of this theater. He could still come charging back at us, but I doubt it. The way he skeedaddled, I'd say he's whipped in spirit as well as fact."

In all likelihood, Hunter would be out of action for at least a couple of weeks. And the Confederates would have a clear shot down the Valley.

"Once we reach Staunton," said Early, "we'll get another day's rest. Do some refitting and reorganizing. Just now, though, I fear we'll have to postpone our whiskey search."

Breckinridge looked almost buoyant. "All right with me, General."

There was much to do and discuss, and their respective staffs were probably wondering where they had disappeared. Yet neither man spurred his horse. A cooling mountain zephyr swept by and they inhaled it.

At Early's command were some 14,000 of the Confederacy's best and toughest men. Over these mythic high slopes that echoed Jackson's memory, the Shenandoah awaited with rich farms and loyal folk. And in all likelihood, no bluebellies until its northern end. The grayback column would march the Valley's verdant length, cross the upper Potomac and plunge southeastward through Maryland, crushing any opposition. Down the dusty roads, through towns and fields already marked with the blood of three years' fighting, Early would lead his men toward the biggest reckoning of all. Yankeedom had hell to pay. And had Breckinridge not been right there at his side, he would have once more tossed his head back and crowed to the blue yonder.

43

Truly Residence

LIKE MOST MEN of his profession, the stout doctor appeared overworked. He had come at the entreaty of a man Truly knew who was on the Medical Bureau, a fellow Missourian who would hereafter be getting a basket of fruit at Christmas. From the physician's brusque manner, Truly guessed that he resented having his string pulled for the sake of one Union boy— one, while thousands more lay on anonymous cots throughout the city, far from the comforts of home. Truly did not care. The hospitals swarmed with infection; only here would Ben have his best chance.

Seated by Truly's desk, the doctor spoke in a gravelly monotone. Truly listened like a sinner learning his first prayer:

"Here there's obviously less chance of gangrene, though he does have the expected degree of infection. Still no sign of tetanus. I tweezed a big splinter from his face, but there must be smaller ones I couldn't find. It's a wonder he didn't lose the eye. A couple of teeth were knocked loose—keep a compress in there except for feedings."

Tardily Truly grabbed a pencil and started scribbling.

"Fever's low-grade," the doctor went on, "so he should have no more delirium tonight. Inflammation's subsiding, but it has a long way to go. Watch the quality of the pus as it drains. Keep up the daily dressing changes and don't neglect the thigh wound, even though it's minor. Same for the eye. Make sure to tell that Negress of yours."

Sapphira, her vigil cut short, had gone upstairs to lie down. "I'll tell her," Truly muttered.

"Use the laudanum sparingly—some pain should help stimulate recovery. Now, about the arm . . . "

Here the doctor became more circumspect. At this point in the war, he explained, some army surgeons smarted from the widely used epithet "sawbones" and were therefore less disposed to amputate. Perhaps this, combined with the relative neatness of Ben's entry/exit wounds, had spared him the saw. The doctor allowed that he himself might have done differently, but no matter—it was too late to second-guess the field surgeon, whose decision would soon prove either fatal or fortunate. Unarguably lucky was the fact that the tumbling minie ball had not taken its usual three or four inches of bone but a wedge of muscle instead, leaving a chipped humerus. Still, the limb seemed wholly paralyzed whenever Ben stirred. Given its bloated state, the cause might be a compressed nerve or a bruised one. Or the nerve might be severed, the arm permanently useless. They would not know for a few days yet.

Putting the pencil down, Truly rubbed his unshaven face.

The doctor lifted the bag onto his lap. In his pouchy eyes, something like cordiality showed. "You can do no more than what I've instructed. And hope. Once he has a major drainage, you'll see a turn for the better."

Truly's throat was dry. "Thank you."

At the door, the doctor accepted two dollars. "Keep the parlor well ventilated," he said, and put his hat on.

Forbes had helped move Ben's bed down to the rearranged parlor. The windows were raised but the drapes and curtains drawn. On and under the bedside stand were those articles for coaxing life back into a body: a bandage roll, a water jug, a bowl and sponge, a tin containing chloride of lime. From the Old Capitol's sick bay, William Wood had donated one bottle of precious laudanum and another of foul bromine disinfectant. Truly sank into the bedside chair, then moved it so he would not have to look directly at his son.

Anna was gone somewhere. Upon first seeing her brother, she had wobbled backward and knocked over the spinning wheel. Her one tremulous attempt at bandaging had succeeded only with Sapphira's irritable guidance.

Except for the clock and Ben's steady breathing, the house was quiet. Truly forced a look at the swathed arm and the bulging, bandaged face against the pillows. A tuft of hair stuck up, like a small boy's cowlick.

Sapphira had placed a compress over the injured eye. Truly listened to the breathing, as intently as he had ever listened to Rachel's at night.

"So this is how it goes," he murmured.

This was how it went, all right—the devil's work, mixing a pinch of truth with a bushel of lies. And powerful lies they were, that could bear off so much smiling youth and return it dead or shattered. Lies that were spawned the way plagues were spawned—unknowingly, with innocent touch. They spread from the dusty, obliging memories of those who had fought the last war, to the ears of any boy who listened. Who could blame a man for his stories, or a boy for listening? From age to age, the message tolled: preserve, protect, defend—and conquer, when God so directs. Not just a message but a stern command: Show your proof, live the adventure, suffer the passage. Far stronger than any time-bound slogan, it echoed within the tales of old soldiers.

These were tales with all the drudgery removed, along with much else that would lose a boy's attention. And as for the tellers, who among them wished to recall heat and thirst, cold and sickness, fatigue duty and forced marches? More than all that, who wished to speak of homeward longings, or terrible officers, or certain comrades-in-arms whom he would sooner have pissed on? Or the sight of friends turned to broken bloody shells? Or that unmistakable scream when flesh encountered flying metal—that shock which should have been no surprise but somehow always was? Or those one-sided acts of war that left a man feeling stained for life?

It felt better to frame it as the newspapers did, as strangers did when they welcomed you home, as songs and pictures and history did thereafter. Better to play up the glory parts—and here was the devil's pinch of truth, for glory there was. What else could you call it when, scouting on a hill, you gazed back down to the valley and saw troop formations with banners high and trumpets blaring? What word but "glorious" fit when, having thought yourself destined to perish under a foreign sky, you came through not just alive but more miraculously alive than you'd ever felt, with your veins singing and a hymn on the breeze? Nuggets of glory, these moments. Humbling, exalting, potent enough to make the whole damned concoction glow.

And when boys heard the stories, that glow was all they saw, drawing them steadily toward everything that it concealed—the whole stinking, slaughtering, endless idiot lie. Truly looked at Ben and saw the corpse of the Mexican boy at Molino. He thought of Ben and himself back in Missouri and later in Chicago, talking on the porch. How many war tales had he polished for easy telling? How many stirring fables from the Land of the Aztecs? He rubbed his eyes. From what felt like a great distance across the room, Rachel's photograph stared at him. He did not return the stare. With his head in his hands, he nodded off.

He awoke as a hand touched his shoulder. The room was darker. Righting himself, he saw Sapphira standing over him.

"Did you sleep?" he asked.

"Some," she said. "Go on, Father."

Fumbling about, he found the piece of paper with his medical notes and gave it to her. Then he went upstairs. For three straight days it had been like this–speaking little and padding past one another, ghosts with separate curses.

Sapphira sat perfectly still, facing Ben. If she stared long enough, she would see only the wounds. Ben would become just a patient and she the clear-minded nurse he needed.

She did not turn around when Anna came in, but the brisk footsteps heralded the change she had dreaded. The steps went upstairs. Ben stirred and gave a low moan yet did not awaken. Yesterday during the dressing change, he had croaked Sapphira's name; today he had murmured it, though his eye remained blank.

Then Anna was at her side. Dressed in dove gray, Anna looked determined if not quite composed. "I'll stay with him."

Sapphira looked at the tuft of hair on Ben's head. She remained still.

"It's my turn, Sapphira. You can go."

"Do you know what to do if the swelling starts up again?"

"Change the dressing."

"You would use the bromine too. And if he yells . . . "

"Listen to me. I visited Dennis's sister in Georgetown–she's with the Sanitary Commission and told me most of what I needed to know. Now, by your leave, I'd like to take care of my brother."

Sapphira shut her eyes. Since the moment that she and Anna first met as children, from their first wary wondering gaze, there had been better things than petty skirmishing between them. Still the pattern had started then, escalating through the years, with Anna keeping a secret bullet in reserve. Now that she had seen fit to use it, the skirmish was done. Defeated, pierced with a word, Sapphira could finally relent. She could quit the field. She was about to get up when Anna touched her shoulder.

"One other thing, Saph–you don't look yourself. It worries me."

Burning inside, Sapphira felt a smile twist onto her face. Anna–the gracious victor.

"You have hollows around your eyes. It's the strain."

Sapphira looked up sharply. "May I use the mirror in your room?"

Taking her hand away, Anna looked puzzled. "Yes."

Upstairs, Sapphira spent a minute looking at her reflection and then went to her own room. For the first time since Mother Rachel's death, she dug out her lace-collared black dress and put it on. She returned to Anna's mirror. Once more she took stock of herself before going back down to the hall. In the parlor's lamplight, Anna sat beside Ben's mounded form.

Sapphira reached for her shawl. "Read those notes there on the stand. If you need more compresses, they're soaking in a bucket in the kitchen."

Again Anna looked confused. "Where are you going?"

"You know, Annie–when you were little, I used to dress you. All the time."

Sapphira left the house.

44

Wyman's Oyster House, New Jersey Avenue

THE THREE OF them arrived outside the grimy-looking restaurant, supper-time noise emanating from its open door. Duke straightened his coat and marched inside. Waiting by the carriage with Kirschenbaum, Forbes re-read yesterday's *Evening Star*.

The top headline concerned an explosion at the Washington Arsenal; it had killed twenty-one of the women and girls working there and left dozens mutilated. At the bottom of the front page, beneath all the war news, Forbes found the story he was looking for. Underhill's death had played just as Baker said it would: overworked congressman's anguish over the nation proves unbearable. Given the *Star*'s appetite for the macabre and the scandalous, its treatment in this case was relatively genteel, though it did mention the noose. It added that some party hack from Underhill's district would be appointed to finish out his term and stand for election.

In peacetime, the shock, buzz and fascination would have lasted for weeks. As it was, the Arsenal disaster, rising gold prices, Grant's stalemate at Petersburg, Sherman's drive into northern Georgia and the ongoing avalanche of casualties would bury this story by week's end. Forbes gave the paper to Kirschenbaum, who tossed it into his carriage.

Then Duke reappeared, his face eager. "He's here, Captain. In back, by himself."

Regarding his companions, Forbes had to suppress a weary sigh. Intimidation was the goal, but fate had furnished him with the least intimidating pair of strong-arms in Washington. "I'll do the talking. Stand on either side of him. Look at him steadily and don't smile."

"Understood," they chimed.

The smells of grease, fish and smoke met Forbes as he led the way in. Clerks and laborers glanced up from their food as he paused, staring toward the back.

"Dark blue vest," Duke muttered.

At a table against the rear wall sat their inconspicuous subject–young but with thinning hair and a small unhappy mouth. Having pushed his half-eaten dish aside, he seemed oblivious to all but the near-empty liquor glass in front of him.

Forbes lumbered up to the table and stood over him. "Horace Ives?"

The pinched face jerked up, gawked at Kirschenbaum and then glared at Duke. "You! I told you not to trouble me!"

Forbes spoke flatly. "If you don't provide some answers, you'll be troubled a good deal worse. You might remember me as well, Ives–from Cold Harbor. We're still curious about your late boss."

"Who you helped drive to despair! What kind of people are you?!"

"Resolute. And out of patience. And are you really fool enough to believe that our little questions drove him to it? Besides–why protect him now? Your time with him couldn't have been too pleasurable."

Looking away, Ives downed the last of his drink. He cleared his throat. "Doesn't make it your business."

"But I assure you it is."

The clerk's eyes had lost their glare. "The police official who called on me said not to discuss it with anyone."

"Detective Archer?" Forbes demanded.

Ives blinked up. "Yes."

"Consider him countermanded. By federal authority."

"Will you gents be ordering?"

Turning, Forbes saw a portly man in a filthy apron. Forbes peered back down at Ives. "Will it be here, or at the Old Capitol?"

Hunching his thin shoulders, Ives looked at the wall. "Here. If it means you'll leave me be."

As Forbes ordered four beers, Duke dragged up extra chairs and the trio sat. Forbes eyed the nervous drudge. "What do you know of the friendship between Underhill and Miles Wakefield?"

Through his resentment, Ives looked surprised at the question and seemed to ponder it. "They grew acquainted shortly after the congressman hired me. How, I could not tell you. Mister Wakefield has a photography establishment, though he's no mere shopkeeper. He's a man of refinement. To me . . . " Ives shrugged. "He has always seemed a fine sort, and to genuinely admire the congressman. Mister Underhill had many acquaintances, of course, but Mister Wakefield appeared to be his only close friend in Washington. For the last election, Mister Wakefield took photographs of the congressman with some of the wounded at Antietam."

Forbes could not help sneering. "In terms of character, didn't it seem a mismatch to you? A fine man, as you describe him, close friends with such a mercenary windbag?"

Ives blinked, then chewed his lip.

"You deny that last description?"

His gaze wandered through the smoky air. "The friendship did seem unlikely in that way. But on the face of it, Mister Wakefield was simply honored to know a congressman so well. He was generous with his ear and his compliments–a man like Underhill never tires of that. And Mister Wakefield made himself useful in several ways. He even helped with speeches." Ives' gaze drew back, hardening once more. "So are you out to torment him besides?"

"He helped with speeches," Forbes echoed. "Including that last undelivered one?"

"Well, yes–why not? They differed in character, maybe, but not in politics."

The aproned man brought the beer in rusty tin cups. Forbes paid him. At first taste Kirschenbaum gagged, then muttered a German expletive.

"We have another dead man to ask about," Forbes said. "Jepson, your predecessor."

Ives' hands slid into his lap. He stared at the tabletop. "Him I did not know."

"But you knew *of* him, didn't you? And the end he met?"

Ives slurped the foam off his beer. "I heard about it."

"Ives, there are strange things afoot here," Forbes said. "Surely you sense that by now. And surely all reasons for keeping silent are cancelled. So unburden yourself. What do you know about Jepson?"

Duke and Kirschenbaum looked dutifully on.

Contemplating his tin cup, Ives suddenly looked twice as weary, twice as lost. "I . . . When I started working for Underhill, I only knew that Jepson had been sacked. It was not hard to imagine why–I'd heard he was debauched. For the same reason, I doubted a vague accusation that was going around, attributed to Jepson. An accusation against Underhill–that he had committed some awful offense, one that would finish him politically if it were ever made public. There was gossip and speculation, of course–talk of bribery, of whoring, even treason–but I disdained to participate. Government clerks are too given to rumor-mongering. Besides, I was glad for my position. And I would have gone on dismissing the charge had Jepson himself not accosted me here one night, at this very table."

Ives took a long swallow of beer. "Sometime in the autumn of '61, I looked up and here's this fellow sneering down at me, obviously in his cups. And he said, 'So you're the poor fool that got my job.' I told him to go away, but he ignored me and demanded I take a verbal message to the congressman. He said, 'Tell him he'd best not welsh on our arrangement. Tell him I'm getting written statements, signed and notarized.' It was all drunken jabber to me and I refused to deliver any such message. I was about to have him thrown out, but he sat down with this leer on his face and said, 'Do you know what sort of man you're working for? Do you know what that son of a bitch did at Bull Run?'"

45

Truly Residence
June 22

"ON THE MORNING of the battle, Underhill, like other dignitaries, drove out to watch the expected Union victory. He brought Jepson along–I suppose to record any patriotic sentiments that occurred to him."

"Bart, you don't need to whisper. I gave Ben some laudanum."

Forbes' voice rose to normal. "When it became a Union rout instead, Underhill panicked and told the coachman to race for the capital. They came upon a group of soldiers blocking the road, some of them wounded, and Jepson saw a Rhode Island regimental flag. The soldiers tried to halt the coach but Underhill yelled for more speed, and they were knocked aside like chickens."

Truly gave a low whistle. "So Jepson must have threatened to make the incident public. Demanded regular blackmail money. He wasn't dismissed from his job, just freed from the need to work."

"But this threat would have worn off eventually," said Duke. "Knowing this, Jepson approached a Rhode Island representative in order to track down the individual soldiers, who would have gladly supplied sworn testimony. Giving him a permanent hold on the congressman."

"But the liquor, it then makes Jepson reckless," said Kirschenbaum.

"Ives told his boss about the restaurant encounter," Forbes went on, "and Underhill was naturally shaken. He denounced Jepson as a liar but swore Ives to secrecy. A month or so later, Ives was shocked to hear of Jepson's murder."

Turning in his desk chair, Truly gazed out the window and shook his head. "To rid himself of an amateur blackmailer, Underhill turned to a bunch of professionals. It's clear why he was so desperate—but damn, he couldn't have known that the cure would be worse than the disease. Same for the other four men, I reckon, when they sold their cheap little souls."

"And on that subject," Forbes said, "Ives had another story. A year ago, a one-page letter arrived for Underhill. It visibly unnerved him and he was quick to destroy it, but Ives swears that he saw flecks of blood on it."

Duke spoke. "We can safely suppose that it was from Van Gilder. He had committed his lone act of defiance, been tortured for it and had his rate doubled. We theorize that the keepers also made him write to Underhill—and to the others, presumably—relating what had happened. An effective warning, should anyone have been considering a similar move."

"And yet," said Kirschenbaum, "this April they all find reason to dare it. Ives tells us that Underhill begins to act excited at this time, just as I see Van Gilder do. Then the congressman meets you and Captain Forbes at Cold Harbor. After this he is in a bad temper and drinking more, afraid to go out. Then, Friday last, he tells Ives to lease him a carriage. Next morning, he hangs from a tree."

"Ives learned of his boss's death only when Archer called on him," said Forbes. "Archer pronounced it a suicide, brought about in part by our so-called harassment. Ives accepted this, though it left a lot unexplained. Archer said that since our conduct would be under investigation, Ives should avoid any discussion of the case."

"Did Ives know of Archer's connection with the congressman?" Truly asked.

"He claimed not to have," said Forbes. "Nor of any with Van Gilder, or Peavey, or an unnamed lieutenant-colonel. It seems Underhill managed to conceal those ties. Oh, and one more thing—I spoke with an old steward at the insane asylum, and he remembered Archer's wife. Said she made rambling accusations against her husband to whoever would listen, though few did. The word 'whoremonger' featured prominently. But people attributed this to her state of mind and felt sympathy for Archer, even though he never visited. Their daughter visited often, right up until Mrs. Archer's apparent suicide."

Taking it in, Truly nodded slowly and leaned on his elbow. "Well . . . You boys've been busy. And it's time that I was, too."

"We understand your distraction," Forbes said.

"Ben's outlook is better," said Truly. "Cautiously better. 'Course, the arm's still a concern. I . . . "

A sharp knock came from out front. Muttering, Truly left the study and went to the door. He opened it and beheld Chadwick in full regalia, his face earnestly solemn.

"Come in, Lieutenant."

"Major–" Striding in, Chadwick doffed his cap and gave an elaborate bow. "My most sincere wishes, sir, for Benjamin's recovery. As a fellow officer and patriot, I salute him!"

"Better not–we'd hate for you to hurt that elbow again. But thank you. I'll fetch Ah-na."

Mounting the stairs, Truly met Anna in hurried descent. She had her canary-yellow dress on and bows in her hair, though her eyes were tired. Truly recalled how wan she had looked this morning when he relieved her, with Ben moaning.

"Is it Dennis?" she asked.

"Yes. Tell me what happened with Saph."

"Isn't she back?"

"No. Where is she?"

"How would I know? She's just being spiteful."

"Spiteful about what?"

"Father, please let me pass."

He stepped aside, then followed her down.

She shot a glance over her shoulder. "You're looking in on Ben, aren't you?"

"Of course I am. Annie, I want a full explanation later on."

"That should come from Sapphira, Father, not me."

She departed with Chadwick. Truly looked in on Ben and found him sleeping soundly, then headed back to the study. A man could only fret so much. When Sapphira returned from wherever she was, he would feel relief and then decide how loudly to yell. Gone all night, he thought–presumably alone, in a city where no white or colored female should ever risk herself. And at a time like this.

Seated at his desk again, he looked at his three companions. "If we can't shut down La Maison and arrest the suspects, we can at least penetrate the place under cover. And for that . . . " He gestured to Kirschenbaum. "You, Manfred, seem the best candidate."

Through his bristly mustache, the hunchback smiled. "At last, I am again to play a part!"

"Well put, since it'll require your acting talent. Besides, some of the La Maison girls hail from the German states and would perhaps be more open with you, for the pleasure of sprackening zei Deutsch. From them you might learn about the lieutenant-colonel, about Wakefield's connection to the place, and about what goes on there besides the usual." Truly's tone turned more serious. "It won't be without danger. You'll need a heavy disguise. However convincing you are, Van Gilder's killer might be present at the house and could recognize you."

Kirschenbaum gave a shrug. "I will be enough disguised."

"You will. But let's keep in mind that these people are danged clever."

"We should pick a busy night," said Duke. "A Friday or Saturday."

"He'll need a letter of reference," Forbes said, "from an established patron."

Truly nodded. "For that, I'm afraid we can't use James Cathcart. His name would alert them, since they must know we're holding his cousin."

"James named a few other patrons for us," said Forbes. "We can pick one to lean on."

"Good. Very good." Leaning back, Truly felt the sun from the window. After five numb days, he once more felt in command of himself. There was purpose beyond Ben.

"Major," said Kirschenbaum, "—may I say, it is a disappointment to not see our Miss Sapphira today. She is well, no?"

Truly's nerves drew tight. "She ought to be home soon. At which time, she will hear a sermon to make Moses weep." He rubbed his hands together. "Now—let's get started on the details."

46

Church Of The Redemption

To DO THIS, to be that. However fierce the yearning, its consummation could be fiercer still.

This dim, cramped church was Sapphira's world now–groaning with duty, frantic with need. The light, slanting thinly down, seemed to come not from outdoors but from far beyond, guiding her among the prostrate forms, from one point of suffering to the next. Having neither eaten nor slept, she wondered if the clamor of battle could feel much different.

Something momentous was happening at Petersburg. Hardly had the first reports arrived when the flood of casualties began–broken colored men, borne within the greater deluge. In beds or on bare floor, around the altar or in tents out back, they had come to heal or die. They signaled the largest-ever use of Negro soldiery in combat. Taken together, they were the fruit of a people's yearning; separately, they just bled. Separately they stared with large liquid eyes, wondering when and how the pain might end.

Tending to one gaunt soldier, Sapphira found his head bandage black with dirt and blood. "Soldier," she muttered to him, "I need to wrap your head again."

Eyes shut, he mumbled something, then grimaced as she went to work on him. She discarded the grimy bandage, took a fresh cloth from her bulging apron pocket and then soaked it in her wash pail. Squinting, wishing for better light, she gently wiped maggots from the deep gash and its loose flap of scalp. At the next bed down, an older nurse was sprinkling water on the raw stump of an arm. The woman glanced over. Sapphira recognized her as the one she had met here several days ago, on her first attempt.

Sapphira's patient let out a moan.

"Lie still," she murmured. She folded another cloth into a compress and wet it, then took out a bandage roll.

"Where is this?" the man croaked.

"Washington City."

"My head . . . "

"Peaceful thoughts. Think of home." As she started to dress the wound, a light shone down on it. She looked up to see the older nurse holding a lantern, her wheat-brown face puffed with fatigue.

"You're the one Miz Sackville turned away."

Sapphira ran a bandage around the man's chin. "I remember you too, Ma'am."

"It's good you didn't quit trying."

From the front of the church, Sapphira could hear the widow's brittle-voiced demand for more linen, more water. "This time she barely looked at me. That's what I counted on."

"I am Mrs. Dalton," said the older nurse.

"Sapphira Truly, Ma'am." As she tied the bandage, the soldier moaned again. "We could do with some sherry."

Mrs. Dalton lowered the lantern. "There's a lot we could do with, Miss. Our surgeon's nearly out of ether. We're having to beg supplies from the Medical Bureau."

In back of the altar, the church's vestry served as an operating room, from which the cries and wails had temporarily ceased. Its door swung open and the Negro surgeon appeared, wiping his hands with a rag. One of the colored army hospitals in Alexandria had lent his services. His face was flaccid, his apron bloody.

Sapphira picked up her pail and spoke in a lower voice. "The smell in here has changed. I'm afraid it's gangrene."

"I know," said Mrs. Dalton. "Those cases we're moving out to the tents as we find 'em. It's just Miz Sackville's preacher brother out there, chanting scripture. He's just marching up and down with his Bible, quoting and chanting . . . "

Mrs. Dalton was off on a listless ramble, but a loud bang cut it short. A nurse had swooned, spilling a wash basin. Mrs. Sackville seized the woman, spun her about and shoved her toward the front doors. "Lord, send me women of mettle!" the widow spat. Her silvery hair-bun had come unraveled. Glaring over her shoulder, she rattled off another series of commands.

Mrs. Dalton sighed. "Were she kinder, could she do near as much?"

Sapphira suddenly felt the dull edge of exhaustion. Leaving Mrs. Dalton, she crossed the narrow aisle and picked out another man at random. This one lay on the floor, his head buttressed with a rolled-up uniform jacket. He was dark, strong-featured, with a sweaty brow and several days' growth of beard. His eyes were dim–but when she softly asked what she could do for him, the clarity of his voice surprised her.

"I'm thirsty, Miss."

Stepping over the other supine bodies, she moved to the beverage vat and dipped a bowl into it, then navigated her way back to the soldier. She knelt, holding the bowl to his lips.

He sipped, then made a face. "What is it?"

"Molasses with water and vinegar," she said. "The sugar will help your strength."

"A bit heavy on the vinegar, but thank you." As he sipped again, his black eyes seemed to clear and focus upon her. Then she tipped the bowl too high, sending a rivulet down his whiskered chin. Wiping it with a damp cloth, she heard some congestion in his breathing.

"Where were you hit, soldier?"

"Left side."

In her mind, she blurted a prayer that it was not a lung wound.

"The ball," he murmured, "–it looped 'round my side to the back. Cracked two ribs on its way. Stuck underneath my . . . "

Another quick silent prayer, this time that it was not his spine.

"The skapel . . . "

"Scapula?'

"Yes. They dug it out."

"Thank God. But pneumonia is still a worry. That and infection." She laid another damp cloth across his brow. Drawing his blanket partway down, she started to examine the dressing.

"Miss Truly?"

It was Mrs. Dalton calling to her. Back across the aisle she stood over another patient, a rangy man too big for the bed on which he lay sprawled. In preparation for a sponge bath, she had begun to remove his shirt but found it stuck to him with clotted blood. Rising to her feet, Sapphira glanced down at her own soldier and felt a second's puzzlement. His gaze was intense, his dry lips parted as if to speak. "I'll return," she said.

Joining Mrs. Dalton, she helped moisten the big man's shirt and gingerly peel it away. He started writhing and nearly fell off the bed. Sapphira used all her strength to settle him and then ease him upright, slinging one thick arm around her shoulders. As Mrs. Dalton began sponging him, he tried to recoil and Sapphira strained against him. In the same moment, she caught sight of the man she had left. He had raised himself on one elbow, staring at her with that strange urgency. She worried that he might be in some new distress, perhaps hemorrhaging.

Mrs. Dalton finished washing the man's back. "Thank you. I can manage from here."

Sapphira eased the soldier down and hurried back to the other one. "Lie down!" she whispered.

He tried to speak but started coughing, his face tight with pain.

Kneeling, she put a hand on his shoulder. "Settle yourself, for God's sake!"

Wheezing, he clutched her forearm. "Sapphira?"

She stared. "You . . . How do you know my name?"

Turning his head, he let loose a jet of spittle.

"Get your breath," she said.

He coughed, squeezing her arm. "I am . . . Sergeant Flavius Tucker."

She muttered the name. In her memory, it sprang to life. "Ben mentioned you in his letters!"

"Is he all right? Do you know?"

"Sergeant, please–lie flat."

"Is he?!"

"He's at home. He's badly hurt." She took hold of Tucker's wrist. "I'll tell him you're alive. Just knowing that will help him. But rest yourself, I beg you."

Tucker swallowed hard. "I need to see him."

"Sergeant, you have two holes in your body!"

"Please, listen to me." The black of his eyes went blacker. "If I stay here, I'll die."

For the first time, Sapphira felt weak all over.

"Miss Truly–do you hear me? If I stay here, I will die."

Gently pressing his shoulders, she urged him down. "Sergeant, I believe you're over the worst of it, but you're still weak. Please . . . " Still his gaze protested so she leaned closer, softening her tone. "You'll receive the best treatment we can give. I'll come back to you as often as I can. I'll . . . " He was not looking at her now, but past her. Turning, she beheld Mrs. Sackville. Pale and straight in her black dress, the widow stood there, hands clenched at her sides. Her eyes were needles, her face a bony hatchet.

Still kneeling, Sapphira tried to sound calm. "Ma'am, the soldier was in some distress."

Mrs. Sackville inched forward. "Take your sin out of here."

Sapphira bolted to her feet. "Miz Sackville, I was calming him! I was . . . "

"I should have known to look at you. To come into this church with your wicked fancies . . . Into this church!" Taking a sudden stride, she flung her open hand at Sapphira's face. Sapphira deflected it with her forearm and backed away. "Be gone!" the widow raged. "Take your foulness away from here!!"

The murky, bustling church seemed to tilt beneath Sapphira's feet, while at its center the pale woman shook her fists, raving and sputtering about sins of the flesh. All other noise took on a dreamlike hollowness. Sapphira kept her hands raised. If Mrs. Sackville tried to strike her again she would deflect the blow, but she would not retreat. Once more the hatchet face came toward her. Then a husky, rumpled, blue-backed figure blocked Sapphira's view. Shaky on his legs, Tucker had risen and donned his dirty jacket. He gave the widow a slight, stiff bow.

"Miz Sackville, I thank you," he said hoarsely. "Miss Truly is blameless. I am the one who must be gone."

With a careful turn, he pulled his cap on. The widow gave some tight-throated retort but Sapphira did not listen. She was staring at the bullet hole in Tucker's jacket—an oblong puncture, the fabric dark with dried blood. Since last night, with numb efficiency, she had tended torn flesh and shattered bone; now the sight of a hole through cloth made her insides quiver. Feeling someone behind her, she looked and saw Mrs. Dalton gazing at her, small and solemn. From her apron Sapphira took out all of her remaining cloths and bandage rolls, handing them over.

"God bless you, Miz Dalton."

"And you, child."

Supporting Tucker on her arm, she left with Mrs. Sackville's damnations ringing after her. The light of day struck—and beneath the wide bright sky, she saw that the world remained after all. People moved, buildings stood and carriage wheels turned as ever. It stunned her there on the church steps, until she had the alarming urge to lean against the man who leaned against her. Despite his condition, he suddenly looked as if he could bear her weight.

"Amazing," she muttered.

Pressing a hand to his chest, he took a slow, even breath. "That woman?"

"No . . . All that time in there, I hardly thought once about Ben."

47

Truly Residence

IT WAS BACK in southern Wisconsin–morning, with frost on the fields. Ben moved among his old regiment. Light as a leaf, he floated past tents and wagons and greeted the men, some of whom he knew to be long dead. None of it felt odd. They were a fantastic, scruffy, polyglot collection: German and Slav and Scandinavian, Irish and Russian and French Canadian–even a few tawny-faced Chippewa, implausible in their Union blue. Together they had driven their officers to drink and earned the sobriquet, "Mob of Babel." How had they ever marched, drilled, fought?

Ben came upon a Negro youth bearing water and called to him by name. The face smiled, and then it was Sabbath Young's face. With a rising sensation, the scene became the hill east of Petersburg, with shelling, rifle fire, falling bodies and the upward rush of feet. In the center of it, Young smiled and then his head blew apart. His body spun, spouting blood. Ben heard Langstaff–"F Company forward! Forward!" Facing the slope, Ben saw Langstaff explode, rise whole, raise his sword and explode again. He saw Tucker face-down on the grass. A sense of his own bodily weight had returned, and he was moving toward the smoke and fire of the crest. Glimpsing the hawk high above him, he felt the bullet pierce his arm. He fell against the rail fence and saw the cannon, and a sheet of flame sent him hurtling, tumbling into black. Then he was in the field hospital, surfacing through the chloroform cloud, rising to pain and the cries all around him. Then, Washington-bound, he lay crammed into the jolting ambulance wagon while the man next to him howled a Welsh mining song, howled it to the stars.

At last he stirred awake. He was lying on his side, staring into the weave of the rug below. Home–a matchless miracle. The sting of his bandaged eye had faded. Still the laudanum had worn off, and he wondered if the throb of his head and arm and the ringing of his ear would ever cease. He wanted Sapphira–where was she?

Slowly, through the ringing, he became aware of an extended murmur that then separated into low voices. They were coming from the hall. He picked out his father's voice and then Sapphira's, unable to hear the words. Then he heard the parlor door open and ease shut. Across the floor, a pair of weathered shoes came toward him. He had an urge to move his head but did not dare. The visitor stood above him, then sat in the chair at his side. Carefully Ben raised his good eye. Over an army forage cap, a pair of brown hands lay folded. Then he stared into the drawn, dark face of Flavius Tucker.

Tucker spoke quietly. "Lieutenant."

Ben looked at the brown hands, then down at the carpet. His ear rang. For what felt like a year or longer, he had been lying within a slow vortex of dreams mixed with raw memory. Here was a most welcome apparition– but it could not be real. How could it be?

Again Tucker spoke, his breathing rough. "My first fight, and look what happens." He held a flap of his jacket open, revealing bandages.

Ben teetered on the edge of belief.

"In the field hospital," Tucker said, "I was lying beside a man from Reddick's platoon. He said we captured a gun, then turned it on the Rebs as they ran. Colonel Kiddoo was all set to promote Prince to corporal on the spot, but then he discovered the language problem." Smiling faintly, the sergeant hunched forward. "We did even better than we hoped."

Ben tried to speak but found his mouth full of something. Probing with a finger, he found the compress and removed it. He felt teeth missing in back.

Tucker was contemplating Ben's arm. "After that, the division kept on toward the main works. They were pinned down by artillery for a few hours. When the charge came, the Twenty-second took the lead. We captured redoubts, rifle pits, more guns. Hardly any prisoners, they retreated so fast. The soldier told me we got a cheer from the cavalry. He swore to it–they lined up and gave us a big hurrah."

The room wobbled. Tucker was alive. Battered–but gloriously, blessedly real. With his good arm Ben made a slow, careful turn as Tucker leaned in, adjusting the pillow. Ben gripped his arm. "Did we . . . take Petersburg?"

Tucker shook his head. "I pieced it together, from what other men said in the hospital. They said the rest of the corps had come up by sundown, but an order came to await reinforcements. By morning it was the Rebs who'd been reinforced. Turns out we could've taken the damned place, if only General Smith had pressed the attack."

Ben relaxed his grip. Tucker coughed, then spat in the chamber pot near his feet.

"I saw you," Ben muttered. "I saw you on the ground."

"Yes. I thought I'd soon be under it."

Ben swallowed. "Sabbath . . . "

Tucker's face turned somber. "He went out fighting. Just like Langstaff. If a man's going to die, let it be at his best moment." He twisted the cap in his hands. "But you . . . One of these days, you'll get to visit Montreal. And you'll eat at my restaurant."

Shutting his eye, Ben tried to picture it. "Might have to do it left-handed."

"You can use your feet, for all I care."

A silence rose between them–peaceful, somehow cushioning the pain. Ben felt no urge to break it, but eventually he did. "How did you find me?"

As if slow to recall, Tucker sat there with his lips parted. He glanced toward the hall. "Sapphira. Sapphira brought me."

———

OUT IN THE hall, Truly stood, paced and stood. Then he realized that he was eavesdropping. Still he hovered by the parlor door, straining to hear. Ben's voice, though barely audible, was a voice engaged with the moment. It came not from some feverish inner dungeon but from the land of the living. Ben had drawn even with his ordeal.

Truly wandered back to the kitchen where the others were seated, each absorbing this intimate turn of events. Forbes' silence was awkward, Duke's vaguely reverent. Sapphira conversed in low but casual tones with Kirschenbaum, seated next to her. Truly watched her. Having heard no hint of explanation from her, he concluded that she had meant to make him worry. Yet his planned tongue-lashing had evaporated. Something about her was different, something more than the funeral dress or the fatigue that veiled her eyes. An odd stillness possessed her. She had slipped farther from his comprehension, and he sensed that no scolding or interrogation could bring her back. He felt inept rather than righteous, sullen rather than stern.

Kirschenbaum made some light-hearted remark, prompting a tired chuckle from Sapphira. Fine, Truly thought–let the little fellow chat her up. Let them enjoy each others' novelty. And if his own role in her life was played out, perhaps he should feel unburdened.

Forbes rose from his seat. "I should be going."

Duke fumbled to do the same. "Yes, Major–we should let you be."

Truly crossed his arms. "Tomorrow we should review the plan, get Manfred rehearsed. I'll write up a list . . . "

He heard the parlor door close. Looking down the hall, he saw the colored sergeant start toward the kitchen, then halt to lean on the newel post. Perhaps as a delayed gesture of civility, Tucker had buttoned his jacket. But he remained a jarring sight–the rough-hewn essence of war, here beneath Truly's roof.

"You should be off your feet," Truly called to him. "Come sit awhile."

Tucker proceeded to the kitchen, where Forbes gestured to the chair he had been sitting in. Tucker dropped into it.

"Sergeant," said Kirschenbaum, "–our complements on the progress of the Negro troops."

For a moment the sergeant appeared tongue-tied, taking in the hunchback's accent or appearance. He gave a light cough. "Thank you, sir. With different orders, that progress would have been better." His eyes moved to Sapphira.

Though she returned the look, her weary poise seemed to vanish, her hands kneading together. "How do you feel, Sergeant?"

"Like a fortunate soul."

Truly cleared his throat. "You know, I believe we've met."

"We did, Major. Cold Harbor, two weeks back. Didn't think I'd have the honor again."

"Ben spoke well of you."

An expression crossed Tucker's dark, stubbled face–sad and distant, but satisfied. He pushed back from the table. "I've imposed enough here. I expect I'll find room and board on the Negro side of town."

"Saph," Truly said, "–give the sergeant directions to Reverend Cass's church. Sergeant, our friend Reverend Cass will gladly find a place for you. And he'll make sure you get medical attention. Tell him we sent you."

"It's the Church of the Holy Kingdom," Sapphira said. "Boundary Street, near Tenth."

Forbes pulled his hat on. "That's a good distance. I'll accompany the sergeant."

Kirschenbaum got to his feet. "And I will take you both in my carriage!"

Looking from one man to the other, Tucker again seemed at a loss. He got to his feet. "Gentlemen, I . . . " His gaze fell on Sapphira. "Miss Truly, I am in your debt. Permanently."

She glanced away.

"The debt's ours," said Truly, "if your visit has helped Ben at all. Please come again."

Clutching his cap, Tucker nodded. "By then I'll be more presentable, sir."

Duke stood fussing with his spectacles, looking shy. "Would it be . . . Um, that is–might I come along too?"

Kirschenbaum cackled. "Ja, we will see how strong are my horses."

As they all trooped out to the street, Truly caught a last, enigmatic glance between Sapphira and the sergeant. Kirschenbaum waved from the driver's seat as the carriage pulled out, bearing one of the more unlikely travel parties the capital had seen.

Truly shut the door, then turned to Sapphira. "Get out of that dress, would you? No one's died."

"Actually, quite a few have."

"Don't toy with words. Go on."

Unfazed, she disappeared up the stairs.

Truly put her out of his mind. Cracking the parlor door open, he peered in and saw Ben peacefully asleep.

48

Southern Shenandoah Valley
June 25

OVER THE LAST ridge, the spires and rooftops of Lexington came in sight. The sunburnt ranks marched along but fell quiet. Word had spread of Yankee barbarism throughout the Valley, and Early's force–Breckinridge's division in particular–included many men from this hill-nestled region. Now friends and kinfolk awaited them, bearing news of what had been lost or endured.

Through his field glasses Early examined the littered parade ground and smoke-blackened towers of the Virginia Military Institute, the sacked buildings of Washington College and the burnt hulk of the ex-governor's house. At the outskirts, townspeople appeared in clusters to greet Rodes' division. Robert Rodes, formerly a VMI instructor, sat stiffer than usual on his black stallion. In the surrounding countryside Early picked out a plundered granary, slaughtered cattle and a ruined smelting furnace. North of town the macadam pike reappeared, ribboning through the Elysian woods and fields toward Staunton. Hours of marching remained on this day.

Raising his own binoculars, Breckinridge paused as a young aide rode up to him.

"Genr'l, my fiancée's staying with kin down there. Would it be all right if I . . . "

"Go ahead, Walsh."

The officer blurted thanks, then spurred his horse down the slope.

Breckinridge scanned the town. "Good people here. Too late to be their champions, I'm afraid."

Early grunted. "We are claiming back the Valley."

"We are. It's just a pity to see civilians take the brunt." Breckinridge lowered his glasses. "We've frustrated the enemy to no end out here. Frustrated men are the meanest."

"Sooner or later, the people suffer," said Early. "Right now ours are suffering most. But when this operation's over, maybe we'll have done something to even things out."

The column continued over the ridge, down the road. Breckinridge excused himself and rode on with his staff. Early's trusted adjutant-general Sandie Pendleton arrived with a message: Hunter's retreating Yanks had at last faded into the barren westward country, too far to come charging back anytime soon. Early could forget about them. Unopposed for now, he could proceed northeastward through other grateful towns, concentrating on the larger plan.

He dispatched an aide to find out the progress of the guns and wagons. Turning in the saddle, he saw John Gordon's division coming up, with Gordon riding tall in front. The regal black-haired Georgian met Early's look but then glanced away. A multiply wounded hero of Antietam, Gordon was as much a warrior as the South had ever spawned. Between him and the equally strong-headed Early, however, relations had never been more than civil, and this march had strained them further.

With his staff close behind, Early rode down the incline toward Lexington, threading among boulder and thicket until he reached the roadside meadow. From there he watched Gordon's men and then Dodson Ramseur's tramp by, noting once more how many of them were barefoot. At length Early himself entered the town. Some of the waiting civilians–ladies, children and older men, for the most part–smiled and hailed him as "Jubilee," but even these ones looked too dazed for celebration. Early held out his hat in acknowledgment. By a fire-gutted house he came upon Ramseur, the 27-year-old "boy general" of North Carolina, whose poise and receding hairline made him seem stolidly older.

"A few of my men have family here, Genr'l," said Ramseur. "I've permitted them to fall out briefly."

"I suppose that's fine," said Early. "For incentive, you might tell them we're expecting shoes at the Staunton depot."

"That will help, sir. We've had too much straggling." Ramseur looked at the charred veranda, its blackened trellises. "The prettier the place, the more there is to spoil."

"And to avenge," said Early.

Ramseur's gaze darkened. "There are rumors flying among the troops, Genr'l."

Privately Early had told all his divisional commanders about the hoped-for destination, while withholding anything more specific. "Let 'em wonder," he told the boy-general. "Let 'em figure it out. Once they do, we'll have ourselves an army of wildcats." He resisted an urge to wink. "Sometimes fact beats rumor, eh?"

Early left Ramseur and led his party down the main street, where the rest of the people had turned out to watch. For a Southern loyalist crowd, let alone a newly liberated one, they were subdued. Still there were scattered whoops and greetings. Here and there, soldiers fell out to embrace wives, scoop up children, huddle with parents. On the steps of a Baptist church, Breckinridge's aide sat with a plump teenaged girl, cradling her hands as she wept and smiled. Early eyed her pale pretty hands, the crack of daylight between their two faces. Passing them, he was disappointed when the girl noticed him, then hopped to her feet with a curtsy. Her beau sprang up with a stiff salute, which Early haphazardly returned. When, he wondered, had couples come to interest him? Then his mind vaulted back nearly three decades, and again he saw himself waist-deep in the swift, swollen stream. Wet to the bone, he had pushed toward the listing, sinking carriage and the face inside it, sure at first glimpse that it would change him, believing things he had never quite believed.

A first lieutenant then and straight out of West Point, he felt certain that it was God within the cold current, summoning just enough force to make him struggle. Drenched in rain and gallantry, he knew it was fate that swirled around him and around the carriage wheels, the hapless driver and the straining horse. Something preordained—a sacred moment, a holy confluence as he slogged toward that lovely imperiled face and all that it meant, a victory that no battlefield could approximate. What a story it would be, he thought—and a fine one it would have been. He recalled too the drumming of his heart, weeks afterward, when the letter arrived from Philadelphia and he broke the seal gently, loath to disturb what her fingers had touched. And inside—a newspaper cutting, the announcement of her betrothal to a man whose family wealth and breeding matched her own. Though it was in fact years before the rheumatism infiltrated Early's back and shoulders, he fancied it as originating on that distant day, with the loss of his Northern beauty. She had changed him, all right.

Presently his mind was working again. He needed to find Breckinridge.

The enemy had torched the houses of VMI professors as well. Viewing their rubble, Early came to the Institute grounds and saw Breckinridge with the assembled cadets. They were at parade rest, taking in the sight of their ruined citadel. The commandant noticed Early and brought the boys to attention. Until a month and a half ago, when Breckinridge called them up to fight at New Market, they had been drilling and studying as usual. This was a homecoming of sorts, dull-eyed before the seared walls and shattered windows, the wrecked ramparts and piles of burnt books. Breckinridge, still mounted, gave Early a blank look as the latter drew alongside.

"We can leave them here," said Early. "Let 'em start putting things back together."

Breckinridge's throat looked hard. "Our peach-fuzz contingent," he muttered. "When I called them up to New Market, no one knew how they'd perform. We just needed every soldier we could get."

Early sympathized but was impatient to move on. "Well, I heard they were a credit."

"Oh, they were. But General, I hope you never have to give an order like that. They charged and took the Union guns. Ten killed."

The staff officers sat hushed on their horses. Pendleton's face had reddened, eyes locked on the uniformed boys. From behind Breckinridge, that general's son and aide-de-camp Cabell looked on—a haunted-looking youth who had inherited his father's deep gaze and distinguished brow.

Early huffed a sigh. "Yep—right commendable. We'd best move along now."

As Early and Breckinridge wheeled their horses, several cadets peered up at the Kentuckian, who noticed them but only managed a nod. Age would clear their eyes. Age would teach them how to absorb loss, but for now the effort clouded every beardless face. Early wished he had the leisure to feel moved.

The two generals rode at a trot along the shambling troop column, past other well-wishers. Now there were calls of "Breck" as well as "Jubilee." Most of the buildings appeared undamaged. Though wanton enough,

Hunter's blue horde had at least been selective. Early spoke of his conversation that morning with the chief quartermaster:

"The enemy didn't have time to destroy much grain and produce. It might even be a record harvest, in which case we can ship food to Lee."

"That's salvation for the horses too," said Breckinridge, "–the ones that haven't starved already."

"Soon as we reach Staunton, we'll set to work trimming and refitting. Rapid movement means traveling light. All second-rate mounts, wagons and caissons we'll leave behind, and General Long will be weeding out the poorest artillery. There'll be strict limits on the amount of commissary per unit. Also, of personal baggage–and I mean officers' too. Pity the man I catch toting a velvet footstool or his sainted grand-dad's portrait."

Looking ahead, Breckinridge kept nodding. "All well advised."

"Apart from that, Genr'l, I mean to give you a worthier command. Echols can take charge of your division, which I'll combine with Gordon's to make a corps. That corps will be yours to lead."

Breckinridge raised his hat to some ladies. "I'm grateful for your trust–especially since Gordon's one fine soldier himself."

Early spoke with restraint. "True, he is. But there's been friction among his regiments–Louisianans, you know–and he doesn't seem to have done much about it. The situation requires better leadership. And if you can handle those mountain men of yours, I reckon you can manage a pack of Delta swamp-rats."

Breckinridge gave a polite smirk. "So be it. Anyhow, these petty squabbles should lessen as we move north."

"If the telegraph's repaired, I'll be wiring Lee a progress report . . . " Early gazed ahead to where the column curled right, passing briefly out of view before it returned to the road. The notes of a brass-and-drum dirge came floating.

"Paying their respects," said Breckinridge.

Though Early scarcely ever felt shame, it flared now like a rash. How could he have forgotten? He and Breckinridge said nothing as the buildings fell away and the slow, downward music grew more distinct–horns muted, drums muffled. Even the horses seemed to sense what lay ahead, their stride somehow heavier, statelier within the husk-footed tramp of the infantry.

By a fieldstone wall the band stood in formation, filling every ear with its sorrowful cadence and melody. Diverging here, the column moved along a rutted path into the cemetery, heads bared and rifles reversed, each company halting upon entry and then proceeding in single file. Farther down, the troops filed out with heads covered, rifles held standard as they fell in and marched back to the road. Some were in tears.

Early, Breckinridge and their parties dismounted, removing their hats. Through the drab procession of mourners, Early saw Ramseur and his party standing motionless amid the white headstones. Kyd Douglas was leafing through the pages of a book; Early assumed it was a prayer book, then glimpsed "Tennyson" on its yellow cover. He recalled that Douglas had been Stonewall's aide-de-camp. Then he spied a small wrought-iron enclosure and the grave within—a mound of sod, a small Confederate flag and nothing more, nothing else to mark the South's most hallowed casualty. The dirge rolled on. Early resented the surrounding headstones; however plain, they seemed a gaudy presumption. None other should be resting here, he thought—none but old Stonewall.

Pendleton stood at Early's side. "Can't you see him?" he muttered. "Half asleep on his horse, giving orders. That look in his eye . . . "

Early nodded. "And sucking on a lemon. Him and those damned lemons . . . " He told himself to be at peace with it, as Jackson on his deathbed had been. Shells and bullets made no distinction; a great man could perish, sure as any lesser one.

The band ceased playing. Early felt the sun's throb on his head. He listened to the shuffling feet of the men, the whisper of their baggy cotton, the smart shift of the rifles. Then, through the hush, Douglas raised his voice—a clear, graceful poet's voice, reciting:

> They are here my own, my own;
> Were it ever so airy a tread,
> My heart would hear them and beat,
> Were it earth in an earthy bed:
> My dust would hear them and beat
> Had I lain for a century dead . . .

It was the way that Douglas faltered slightly on the last line, trying not to. It was this and not the words that did it. Early stared at the tiny flag, the mounded yellowing sod. He stared at the men drifting past: clerks and laborers, tradesmen and homesteaders and college boys—men of city and hamlet, of hill and river and shore. Mother's sons, the fathers of children.

They had answered the call, faced the tyranny, defended the homeland. They had endured the unspeakable and the unforeseeable, with perhaps worse trials to come. Many, like Jackson, would not survive. Yet as they filed past the grave, too many faces appeared dreamy with reverence, stunned as if from the heat. Reverence by itself brought no victories, and it was at last more than Early could stand. To hell with all these somber good manners, he thought–they were not at church. They were at war.

"Listen!" he cried, surprising even himself. "Hear what he's telling you! The Shenandoah has been violated–raped by a filthy Yankee mob!" Though they kept moving, the soldiers looked at him. "This here's an army–an army of men! And Jackson himself would tell you now–enough of mourning! Think of vengeance!"

A soldier yelled, "We'll do more'n think of it, Genr'l!"

Early could feel Breckinridge and the others watching him but did not care. His voice rose to a stabbing falsetto. "Stonewall himself commands it! Vengeance, damn it–not mourning!"

An eruption of vows and curses answered him.

"It'll soon be at hand, boys–the hour of reprisal! I pledge it to you now! I pledge it here, over Jackson's grave!"

Ranting, shaking his fist, Early felt his face grow hot. His voice cracked and then his vision blurred, melding the sun's glare with the green of the hills, the white of the stones and the endless gray line moving steadily north.

49

Truly Residence

THE ITEM WAS buried on page 4, small enough that Truly might easily have missed it. He summed it up for Duke: "Two major rail lines wrecked. A lot of livestock and weaponry captured. Iron works, grain mills and canal boats destroyed . . . Anyhow, a week ago Hunter made it all the way to Lynchburg, where he could have really raised Cain with Lee's supply lines. But it says here he fell back before 'a considerable enemy force.'"

Lowering his own half of the *Evening Star*, Duke looked thoughtful. "Hunter's own force isn't exactly small, as I understand it."

"Right. So I ask–had you heard anything about a major Rebel presence in that area?"

"I recall some intelligence that Breckinridge's command had moved there. It was Breckinridge who stopped our drive up the Valley over a month ago. After that he linked up with Lee's army but was apparently rushed to Lynchburg when Hunter threatened. Still, he's supposed to have only two brigades and a few smaller units."

Truly stroked his chin. "Nothing to justify Hunter's retreat. Unless Breckinridge has been greatly reinforced."

"Without our side detecting it?" Duke frowned. "That would take unusual secrecy on their part, not to mention a lot of luck."

"Well–our wise men had best be looking into it, because there's something else. Hunter must have been keen to get away by the safest route; instead of retracing his steps, he's gone and crossed the Alleghenies, it says here. Deep into West Virginia."

"You think the Rebels are in pursuit?"

"I doubt they'd hound him that far. No, I fancy it's thirst and hunger he's trying to outrun. One of my early assignments took me through that same region–and I tell you, a skinny sparrow would have trouble finding enough forage. Water's scarce too. My point is–if Hunter's that much out of the picture, and if there's a big Rebel detachment out that way, then the Shenandoah's wide open again. The Rebs could make a dash up to Harper's Ferry."

Mulling, Duke gazed at the floor. "And if we were slow to respond . . . "

"As we have been, a time or two? Then I reckon they'd push farther–and we'd have more than just a sideshow on our hands." Leaning back, Truly sighed. He had to chuckle at himself. "Listen to me, eh? Nothing like parlor generalship."

Duke remained serious. "No, Major–it's a good question."

Truly glanced once more at the article, then folded the paper. There was a front-page editorial on the Petersburg situation, which again invoked the spirit of fortitude. The words "slaughter" and "stalemate" appeared nowhere, but could lately be heard in street conversations. Truly looked at his watch–Forbes and Kirschenbaum would be here soon. Nervously he looked around near his feet. "Octavius, what would you say about a girl who'd hide her poor daddy's spittoon?"

Truly's study was his refuge–tonight, from his womenfolk in particular. Between Anna and Sapphira, a chill persisted, even as their healing task with Ben urged harmony. Nevertheless, Ben had moved his arm today. He had done so during another visit from Sergeant Tucker. Now lodging with Reverend Cass, Tucker was still shaky but looked much improved. Plucked so directly from camp life, he was awkward in his pleasantries and seemed to have a like effect on Sapphira, who would acknowledge him and then find some new chore to do.

The hall clock struck eight. Truly got out his old Colt Dragoon with its holster and a cartridge box, then started loading the chambers. Duke was talking about the increased Copperhead activity in the West, but then they heard the carriage outside.

Headed for the front door, Truly stopped to peer into the parlor. Anna gazed up from her knitting. Beside her, Ben lay snoring fitfully. Sapphira had changed the bandages on his face and although the swelling had gone down, the degree of disfigurement remained uncertain. In his half-awake periods he had been muttering things, some decipherable and some not. Anna was doing her best–yet beneath her efforts, Truly sensed a growing agitation.

"I'll shut the door," he told her quietly.

She nodded and resumed knitting.

He shut the door and went to admit his two colleagues. Forbes entered and then turned to face the threshold, gesturing with his hat. "May I present our Trojan Horse–Baron Wolfgang von Lichter of Blumenwald."

Kirschenbaum stepped inside. Leaning on a quartz-headed walking stick, he affected smugness as Truly looked him over. His hair and mustache were expertly grayed, the latter trimmed in a fussy curly style. A monocle magnified one blue eye. For the most dramatic touch, a black opera cape covered his double-breasted frock coat and made his hump less obvious. A high hat, a blue silk cravat and shiny boots completed the ensemble.

Truly grinned. "Your Excellency!"

"'Baron' will suffice," said Kirschenbaum. "Amusing, ja? From Germany I come to escape nobility, and nobility you make of me."

"For one night only. Let's review things in the study and then we'll be off."

Seeing Kirschenbaum's disguise, Duke reacted with conspiratorial delight. Truly repeated the main objectives: information on Wakefield– whatever connection he had with La Maison, as well as his whereabouts; and information on the lieutenant-colonel, perhaps by learning details in the death of Briona Kibby. "You might get Monroe, Ravenel or even Dubray in conversation," he told Kirschenbaum, "but they'll have their public faces on. For what we need to learn, customers should prove more valuable as sources. Of the young ladies, beware of the big-bosomed one named Ursula; she's a lieutenant of sorts, and she took part in that masquerade when Bart and I visited. So did a vixen named Fannie O'Shea, so watch out for her too. As for the other frauleins, chat with a few of them if you can, but keep your guard up. I fear we can't be of much help to you. But we'll be outside with the spyglass, concealed in the woods. Should you fall into serious trouble, wave from a window and we'll come charging."

Truly gave the hunchback some bills from his wallet. From his desk drawer he took out a little derringer, already loaded, which Kirschenbaum tucked under his vest. Last, from the same drawer, Truly took a sealed envelope and handed it over. "Your letter of reference. It's from an occasional patron of the house, a military cartographer–McCall, by name. He was mystified but cooperative, and promised to stay quiet about it."

They had fashioned a thin biography for Baron von Lichter, using a real-life model. Outside of Frankfurt, Kirschenbaum had worked in the stables of such a nobleman, an imperious bachelor who spent more time hunting than managing his estate. "So he is at last useful in the world," Kirschenbaum remarked.

Suddenly eager, Truly rose and strapped his holster on. "Well, gents– let's pay our call."

As they exited the study, Sapphira was lighting a hallway lamp. Kirschenbaum halted and smiled, awaiting her reaction.

"Saph," said Truly, "is that basket of food set to go?"

She did not seem to hear him. Somber-faced, she stared at Kirschenbaum, the lighting stick pinched between her fingers.

He removed his monocle, his smile turning curious. "Miss Sapphira?"

Her stare persisted. "Mister Kirschenbaum . . . "

Duke and Forbes proceeded to the door. Impatient and slightly embarrassed, Truly ducked into the kitchen and took the covered food basket from the counter. Returning to the hall, he heard Sapphira address Kirschenbaum in a toneless voice.

"What is it for?"

"Ach!" Kirschenbaum tweaked his fancified mustache. "You dislike to see Manfred so changed?"

Truly reached for his coat. "Saph, I may be gone all night. Sleep well."

"Goodnight," she murmured, eyeing his pistol.

The hunchback gave her a quick bow, then headed after Truly.

Forbes had leased a four-horse coach–justifying the expense to Baker would be a job in itself. As the others got in, Duke hoisted himself to the driver's box and took the reins.

Gaslights bathed the street. High over Washington, the mottled half-moon suggested a leper's face, half-concealed.

50

East Capitol Street

RETURNING WITH HIS newspaper, Wakefield came up the dark stairs and found his door ajar, its flimsy lock broken. He went still for a moment. Then he leaned to peer inside. In the fluttery light of a hand lamp, a boy was pawing through Wakefield's trunk, stopping to munch a pear from the basket on the nightstand. He looked about ten years old. He took out the sheathed bayonet and examined it. Wakefield lay the paper on the floor. In a crouch, he waited until the boy put the knife aside and resumed his pawing. Then Wakefield barreled in.

The boy had no chance to yell until Wakefield had dragged him out to the stairs. Then he howled, thrashing and kicking. Pinning his arms back, Wakefield hissed into his ear–"I kill burglars, you know. I kill them so they don't steal anymore. Or sometimes, if my mood's better . . . " Launching the boy halfway over the banister, he grabbed him by the legs. "–sometimes I just cripple them." Upside down, still thrashing, the boy choked and hollered. He clutched a post with both hands but Wakefield wrenched him loose. "Say your prayers, you little . . . "

At the foot of the stairs, a candle appeared, illuminating the lined face of Mrs. O'Fallon. She let out a gasp. "Jesus and Mary!"

Breathless, the boy stopped struggling. Wakefield maintained his hold. "Mrs. O'Fallon, my room and my property have been violated."

The landlady clapped a hand over her mouth.

"I'm saying this boy's a thief!" said Wakefield.

"I know, sir. He's my nephew."

Staring down at her wide, rheumy eyes, he heard the boy panting and whimpering. Then he realized that there were no true valuables in his room, his money and pocket watch safely on his person.

Hauling the boy up, he grabbed him by the scruff and shoved him away. The boy stumbled downstairs. Mrs. O'Fallon went to seize him by the ear, but he dodged her and scurried past.

Getting his breath, Wakefield leaned against the banister.

"Forgive us, sir!" the woman yelped.

He did not care to listen. He headed back to his room, stopping to pick up his hat and then the newspaper. As abruptly as the rage had come upon him, it now fled, leaving him empty and bemused. He shed his coat. Gazing at his disordered trunk, he saw the sleeve of his Union major's jacket draped over the side. He got up and stuffed it back in, then saw the bayonet on the floor and tucked that away too, just as Mrs. O'Fallon's round shape filled the doorway.

"Sure it breaks my heart, Mister Wakefield."

He closed the trunk lid. "Spare your heart, Mrs. O'Fallon."

"The boy was bad when he come to me, sir. I've prayed and scolded and prayed."

Finding the pear remnant, Wakefield opened the window and tossed it out. Down in the poorly lit street, another brawl was under way. Several drunken, half-dressed soldiers grappled in the mud while harlots jeered from tenement windows and doorways–drab Irish girls, tribal and raucous. Delia was absolutely not like them, he thought. Delia was vivid and beautiful, quiet and singular. Whatever her legacy, whatever the shame of her predicament, she had it in her to break free. He would help her. And he longed for her tonight, so much that his fingertips hurt. Of the Irish in general, however, he had had quite enough.

"This life," Mrs. O'Fallon moaned, "–it's enough to ruin any lad. So much sin and temptation . . . "

He shut the window. "Indeed there is."

"For myself I ask nothin', but what's to become of him? Jail and gin and an early grave, it'll be! Or to be drafted and blown up on the battlefield, all to free the darkies!"

Wakefield sat on the bed. With her candle Mrs. O'Fallon stood there, wiping her small pug nose with her shawl.

"Come sit down, Mrs. O'Fallon." He motioned to the small wooden chair.

Eyes lowered, she waddled in and sat, holding the candle on her knees. Wakefield looked at her plump hands, the wrinkles in her thread-bare muslin dress. He looked at her veined neck with its tarnished saint medallion, and suddenly he wished that he could take her picture. The handsome, the pretty and the distinguished all sat for portraits–but who would ever take Mrs. O'Fallon's?

"Mrs. O'Fallon," he began, "I first took a room on E Street South, near the Avenue. It had bedbugs, and on the second night a man was stabbed outside my door. I've since heard . . . " He chuckled, prompting a puzzled look from her. "That section, I've since heard, is known as Murder Bay. So I left and found this place here. Thievery is not stabbing, Mrs. O'Fallon, and I've seen only a few bugs. But you understand why I must again look for safer lodging."

She sniffed. "Aye, sir. How could you be wantin' to stay? You're too fine a gentleman."

"And you're a good woman. You do the best you can. And listen, I only wanted to scare the lad–put the fear of God into him."

"Oh, I believe that, sir. Aye, sure–who'd blame you?"

In truth he had wanted to throw the boy, to slap and kick him and break his filthy little fingers. Mrs. O'Fallon's appearance on the scene had been as timely as his own. She was talking again, listing family woes, lamenting her long-vanished husband. Outside, harlots shrieked and jeered as the scuffling continued. The police were nowhere around. The provost guard had already been through, making token arrests, and would most likely not be back tonight.

Mrs. O'Fallon was working up to a full sob. Wakefield dug a fifty-cent shinplaster from his pocket and put it in her hand. She quieted, staring at the bill. "Tell your nephew . . . ," he began. In the pause he tried to think of some stern but kindly admonishment, but could not. Tell him, he thought, that the next man to catch him might just smash his imbecilic skull.

Folding the bill, the landlady sniveled. "God bless you, Mister Wakefield."

"And you also, Mrs. O'Fallon. Now, I think I need to rest."

"I'll be gone then, sir. Aye, I'll be sayin' a prayer for you."

She got up and waddled out, shutting the door behind her. Wakefield stared at the bare floor. In the room below, a man brayed and a woman brayed back, fighting over money.

At La Maison, Delia's arms awaited him. But that was out of the question—the federals could burst in there any day now. The city's poor areas offered the best means to stay hidden, plus cheap rent—and yet this rationale had grown as dim as the street, as frayed as the bedspread. It wasn't just the little dangers. Here, the briefest stay seemed endless, making a man feel lost and buried. Wakefield wondered how many tenants this musty room had seen. How many had strayed here, lain here and battled the bugs? Sat listening to the hard shouts and twisted laughter from outside?

Out in the street, a pistol shot triggered screams and running feet. In the room below, the yelling match escalated. Saturday night, Wakefield thought—night of revelry. At this hour the rooms of La Maison were brightly lit, the gents arriving and the young ladies decked out, actors in the gilded carnal swirl. He could see Delia serving drinks, gliding past the tables as vulpine eyes fixed upon her. His stomach started to burn. He took an apple from the basket and crunched into it, grateful for its sweetness. Then he remembered the newspaper.

Setting the apple down, he placed the hand lamp on the nightstand and started rattling through the paper. He scanned articles, glanced at illustrations and at length found what he was looking for: at Lynchburg in western Virginia, Union troops under Major General David Hunter had recoiled before "a considerable enemy force" and retreated into the mountains.

The plan was happening. Like a giant it was risen, hulking forward. Washington could not feel its first far tremors, but Wakefield could. Tomorrow he would send a coded telegram urging swift delivery of the gold. The gold would seal it on this end. He folded the paper, laid it aside and rubbed his eyes. The night racket no longer bothered him—let them scrap and shoot and scream, he thought. Soon, soon, a roar from the South would drown these lowly little noises.

51

Seventh Street Road

DUKE EASED THEM to a stop, the carriage lamp revealing a pear grove on the left. Through the trees, diagonally, the windows of La Maison burned bright.

The baronial Kirschenbaum sat in the gloom opposite Truly and Forbes. On the way he had alternated between breeziness and solemnity. Now Truly detected a pained smile.

"Major and Captain," said the hunchback, "–I have not for years been to confession. So to you I must unburden something." His hands fiddled with his walking stick. "It is . . . On my journey south mit Van Gilder, I one night took his strongbox key while he sleeps. From the box I took three hundred dollars."

Truly caught an uncertain glance from Forbes. "Manfred–I am dismayed."

Kirschenbaum looked into his lap.

"Dismayed," Truly went on, "that you settled for just three hundred. Also, that I didn't help myself to the rest of it. Also, and most of all, that said rest-of-it ended up in the hands of Colonel Baker. Dismayed, sir! Your penance–that's what you Catholics have, right?–is to say the rosary and spend one night in a high-class harlot's den. In reverse order, that is."

Cackling, Kirschenbaum thumped his stick on the floor. "Ach, Major! I should know that you would have no makings of a priest!"

As the three men climbed out, sounds of merriment came drifting. They had stopped near the orchard's far end, where the mansion grounds began. Over by the head of the walkway, coaches idled and horses stood tied to the hitching racks.

Turning to Kirschenbaum, Truly spoke low. "Bart and I will keep watch from these trees. Keep our angle of view in mind, if you need to signal us. Also remember you're armed, should things go seriously wrong."

Kirschenbaum nodded, impatient beneath his courtesy.

"Good luck," Forbes said. "When it's over, I'll buy the beer at Willard's."

"Not Willard's," said Kirschenbaum. "Thank you, I will find for us a German tavern." Tipping his hat, he bowed, then put his monocle in place.

From his perch Duke whispered, "Have a productive night, Manfred."

Kirschenbaum raised his walking stick, gave the driver's box a playful rap and, in his best imitation of a swagger, started for the house. They watched the caped, stooped figure until it passed the first crowded hitching rack and turned down the brick walkway.

***

APPROACHING THE NOISE and glow of the mansion, Kirschenbaum remained studiously unimpressed. Through the open widows came a dense medley of sounds: laughter and chatter, the clinking of glass, the strum of a harp. Melancholy brushed over him. In New York, lonely times had brought him to a certain shabby brothel where a big Italian woman received him cheerfully, sometimes for less than the usual fee. La Maison was very different and his objective even more so–but for the last few steps, he felt that old bleakness. Standing before the high paneled door, he gathered his will. Tomorrow, whatever tonight's outcome, he would find a priest and confess about the stolen three-hundred. And he would light a candle for the Virgin.

He tugged the bell-pull, stepping back as the door opened and the cacophony spilled out. Before him, in jade-green crinoline, stood a hefty smiling young woman who he guessed to be Ursula.

"Greetings, sir! Do please come in!"

She stood aside and he entered the vestibule, handing her his hat and stick. She offered to take his cape but he declined. Cordially aloof, he presented his letter of reference and she examined it.

"A baron? Such an honor, mein Herr! Willkommen!"

"Danke," he replied, unsmiling.

In her harder-edged German she said that she would pass the letter to Madame de Ravenel, but that it would surely suffice. Any of the young ladies would gladly tend to him and the base fee was ten dollars, payable either to herself or Madame. He took out his wallet and gave her the ten, plus two dollars. Gushing thanks, she led him into the carpeted grand hall. Male voices rumbled from the flanking rooms, spiced with female laughter.

A willowy girl and a well-heeled patron were headed up the staircase. Gazing after them, Kirschenbaum fixed upon the large black drum on the support beam. Truly had mentioned the drum in passing. With its stiff white-eagle emblem it was a strange adornment, wholly unto itself in such a house.

Ursula noticed him staring. "Madame de Ravenel's uncle saved that from the snows of Russia. He vas an officer in the grand army of Napoleon."

Kirschenbaum adjusted his monocle. "An army that my own family helped to defeat. Still, it is . . . a most noble object."

In the sumptuous parlor on the right, a harp solo finished to choppy applause. The musician, a comely redhead, rose and curtsied to her audience of imbibing men and attentive young women. Kirschenbaum noted the portrait of Napoleon above the fireplace. To the right of it he picked out a tall, powerfully built man with a cleft chin and stylish mustache. Dressed in black and leaning by the mantel, the fellow conveyed a watchful authority, looming there amid the color and jabber. Surely this was Monroe.

Clutching his letter and money, Ursula gestured toward the room. "Come, Baron—I vill introduce you to Mister Monroe. He is Madame's associate."

Letting his monocle dangle, Kirschenbaum gazed into the other chamber on his left. It was considerably larger and more crowded. In the cigar billows and the garish light of the Argand lamps, men laughed, drank, ogled and conversed, some of them playing cards while brightly dressed girls worked the tables. Kirschenbaum was used to being conspicuous, but now he wanted to blend in as best and as quickly as he could.

"Later," he said. "For the moment, I would like a brandy cobbler."

With a smile that was more relieved than gracious, Ursula ushered him into the revelry, navigating like a jade-green tugboat around the tables. Then the way grew too narrow for her. She looked flustered, then cross, and signaled one of the serving girls. The girl sidled toward them, holding her silver tray aloft as Kirschenbaum watched her. With her gentle shoulders, large blue eyes and tressed amber hair, she was so pretty that he felt singed. She wore a red satin skirt and red-trimmed Garibaldi blouse but not a trace of mercenary smile, looking sullen as she got to where he and Ursula stood.

Ursula seemed to notice the girl's mood and glared at her, speaking in brittle English. "Mademoiselle Delia, this is Baron von Lichter's first call at La Maison. Seat him with Doctor Dubray and bring him a brandy cobbler."

Eyes down, Delia spoke in a distinct brogue. "Certainly. Come this way, sir."

Kirschenbaum followed her, easing past guests in varied degrees of sobriety, past the well-stocked tavern desk, along a wall lined with paintings and animal heads. She came to a table where two men sat beneath a portrait of Louis XIV. Motioning to Kirschenbaum, she addressed a balding, bespectacled man with a large nose. "Pardon, Doctor," she lilted. "This is Baron . . . " Faltering, she gave Kirschenbaum a glance that was supposed to be apologetic but looked only tired.

Replacing his monocle, he gave a perfunctory bow. "Baron Wolfgang von Lichter of Blumenwald. Good evening, gentlemen."

The doctor rose, bowed. "Doctor Antoine Dubray," he said, fixing Kirschenbaum with a look of interest. He did not bother to introduce his companion, a flush-faced man who sat oblivious before his glass of liquor. With a quick curtsy, Delia went to fetch Kirschenbaum's drink. He settled into a carved high-backed chair across from Dubray.

Smiling at him with crowded teeth, the doctor spoke in his sailing French accent. "From where in the German states do you hail, Baron?"

"Near Frankfurt, Doctor."

"Ah! I attended a series of lectures there once. A fair city, to be sure."

"You are a doctor of medicine, sir?"

"I am. I practiced many years in Marseille before coming to America. The adjustment took effort, yet I consider my position here at La Maison to be ideal. By day it allows time with my books and my research–by night, discourse with men of distinction."

The flush-faced man spat into a brass spittoon beside the table. Tobacco juice trickled down his whiskers. He growled something but the doctor ignored it, addressing Kirschenbaum with polished sincerity. "Alors, Baron–so now you too have come to see the New World."

"I have. The Austrian ambassador is a family friend, and he invites me."

"And what are your impressions thus far?"

"The landscapes are wondrous, Doctor. But New York, Baltimore, Washington–these have a great many lower-class persons, all rude and lazy. Such a burden for so young a nation. Still, it is good to be now among gentlemen."

Sipping a red wine, Dubray nodded. "Vraiment, vraiment. You have the misfortune of visiting in time of war and other chaos. As you observe, the new unwashed have concentrated in the cities–like fly swarms, Baron. It is as I have long said . . . "

The other man belched, staring with watery eyes at the crowd.

Dubray smirked. "As I was describing to this fine fellow, our revolution in France may or may not have been *une necessite historique*. But its principles proved disastrous once, carried to their inevitable excess. Lincoln and his advisers would do well to study it."

At the mention of Lincoln, the other man's face grew redder. He let out another jet of tobacco juice, then a garbled stream of curses.

Glancing at him, Dubray chuckled. "I cannot recall this gentleman's name, but he did say that he once dealt in cotton export. His opinions are therefore less philosophical than my own. But truly, Baron–history begs the question: shall teamsters and shoemakers steer the national destiny? Shall greasy mechanics and–dare I mention?–packs of ignorant Negroes hold high office and shape the laws? Nah! Nature ordains these for labor, oui? They do it well. In France, it took a Napoleon to restore something of the natural order."

"Ja," said Kirschenbaum, "–and to upset it everywhere else."

Dubray looked a bit startled, then smirked at the table top. "Forgive me, Baron–I quite forgot your people's experience with our late emperor. Yet your feelings cannot be too hard. You have come to a house named for him, have you not?" The doctor chuckled, twinkling through his spectacles.

Kirschenbaum granted him a strained smile. "My mistake, sir. I thought this name is for the Emperor Franz Josef of Austria."

Dubray gave a hearty laugh. This was fine, thought Kirschenbaum–with faraway Europe as a subject, he could react with some measure of honesty.

"Order and upset," Dubray went on, "–are these not the habits of great men? Is not the latter the means to the former? Think of Chancellor von

Bismarck. In the foreign news I have read of his admirable work to unite the German peoples."

"Ja—this year, by making war upon the Danes. Bismarck is a Prussian, Doctor. Have you met Prussians ever?"

Dubray shrugged amiably.

"They have a hunger of conquest. Enough to perhaps make a Frenchman worry."

Delia arrived with the brandy cobbler. Kirschenbaum offered her a ten-cent shinplaster but she waved it away. "Madame de Ravenel tells me this drink is free of charge, sir. Your presence honors us." Her voice was as flat as an Irish voice could sound. Kirschenbaum could not help glancing up, appreciating her morose beauty. "I thank you, Miss."

She curtsied and left. Staring after her, the anonymous cotton merchant spoke distinctly for the first time. "I had her," he growled.

The doctor guffawed. "I think not, mon ami. Madame says Miss Delia is only to serve drinks—a lot of them, in your case."

"I had her. Upstairs."

Dubray leered. "Ah, then, what a rogue you are! Madame will have to cut you short down there, like a sausage!"

Sipping his brandy, Kirschenbaum spied Madam de Ravenel across the room. It could have been none but her. In a violet lace-trimmed gown she stood close to the wall, hands to thin hips as she surveyed the doings around her. A large white ribbon adorned her abundant ash-colored hair. Her height was average, her skin an almost tawny shade and her face like nothing Kirschenbaum had ever seen—wrinkled, aquiline, ugly to the point of fascination. Yet even at this distance, her limber smile and bright steady eyes marked her as a force, a mistress in her realm.

Dubray had not yet dropped "greatness" as a topic. Watching Ravenel, Kirschenbaum listened as the doctor grew more expansive and less engaging.

"One measure might be what time and trouble is required to bring a ruler down. See, dear Baron, how many years and armies it took to finally vanquish Bonaparte?"

The cotton dealer was mumbling his way into a stupor. Kirschenbaum saw Monroe stride in from the hallway and look around. "Greatness, doctor?" said Kirschenbaum. "Could it rather be a talent for the annoying of neighbors?"

Dubray's laugh sounded forced this time. "Baron, you are indeed true to your people's blood. Still . . . "

Monroe moved to Ravenel's side. He was over a foot taller than the mistress, bending near as she spoke and gesticulated. His expression was placid and hers animated, but they shared a jaded air of mastery. "Equals," Kirschenbaum thought. Close, well matched–certainly not the decrepit figures of Truly's and Forbes' first visit. With their exchange ended, Monroe ambled toward the rear of the big, busy room.

Dubray's voice had lost its sailing quality and become more of a yammer. "I invite you, sir, to rise above the squabbles of history–which by definition is in the past, n'est-ce pas?–and look down. Tell me that your own people could not do with one such as him! A unifying will!"

Kirschenbaum stared over at Yvette de Ravenel. Standing on tip-toe and craning her lace-collared neck, she had resumed scanning the crowd. Then their eyes met and she smiled–a smile like a yellowed scimitar, curving between the bones of her cheeks. Gathering her skirts, she started briskly in his direction. Kirschenbaum watched the scimitar smile move toward him, then realized that Dubray was awaiting a response.

"So, Doctor, you would offer conquest as a sick nation's cure? This the dead might dispute."

Dubray's tone turned edgier. "Monsieur, would so priceless a thing as national honor have no price?! Would you quibble over it like a . . . like a shopkeeper over his accounts?! And look at what is called the Land of Germans–the fragmentation! Little kingdoms and city-states, little ragged blots on a map!"

Something struck the table top. Thinking it was the doctor's fist, Kirschenbaum gave him a startled glance but saw him looking down at the cotton dealer, whose face lay in a puddle by his capsized glass.

Chuckling, Dubray sipped his wine as a grainy female voice addressed him: "Alors, Docteur–so you have bored another one to death."

Kirschenbaum rose, then bowed to the Frenchwoman. "Madame, I thank you for your most gracious brandy."

"Baron von Lichter." Still smiling, she curtsied. "It is always a pleasure to meet a gentleman of the Continent."

Kirschenbaum looked into her lively black eyes. "Your house, it is a wonder. Very like Europe."

"Ah, then, you feel at home."

"Most certainly. For at the door, a young German lady greets me."

"We have others besides her, Baron. You would care to meet one?"

"Ja, indeed!"

"Then I will introduce you. Please, come."

Kirschenbaum looked down at Dubray and his slumped companion. Smirking, the doctor did not rise. "Enjoy, Baron."

"Danke, Doktor. And you the same."

Gathering his cape about him, he took up his drink and followed Ravenel. Her size allowed her a comparative grace as she waded among the tables, dispensing her blithe comments and imperial smirk. Over by the tavern desk, Delia seemed to be having a hushed yet bitter spat with another server, an auburn-haired girl in an identical Garibaldi blouse. Kirschenbaum's ear caught some brogue-tinged vitriol from Delia's antagonist: "Soon they'll be fed up with you, you lazy little cow! Then you won't be waltzing about like you're better than the rest of us!" Jarred, Kirschenbaum wanted to stop and listen in. But he pressed on after Ravenel, edging past a table where a game of faro was in progress. Monroe stood over it, idly puffing a cigar as cards were plucked from the gaming box.

Back out in the hall, Ursula was stationed on a settee. Hurriedly she got to her feet.

"Allez, Ursula!" said the mistress. "Fetch Wilhelmina."

"Which Wilhelmina, Madame?"

"The smaller one." Ravenel flashed her yellowed smile at Kirschenbaum. "The prettier one."

Ursula rushed into the parlor, from which spinet music now emanated.

"Wilhelmina is a lovely girl," said Ravenel. "Low-born, yet at La Maison we refine them." She added that the transaction would cost five dollars more.

Passing her his drink, he took out his wallet and paid her. "I would like perhaps to take her for a stroll about your grounds. To get out from the noise and have some chat, ja?"

She handed him back his drink. "Mais bien, Baron. Our young ladies are trained for conversation as well."

Ursula reappeared. At her heels was a short, pretty female in a pink gown, her blonde hair in ringlets. Ravenel made a quick introduction. Bobbing a curtsy, Wilhelmina gushed several German platitudes, all so extravagant that Kirschenbaum feared he might laugh.

The doorbell sounded. Ursula went to answer it as Ravenel made a cordial withdrawal. Beaming at Kirschenbaum, Wilhelmina batted her hazel eyes. He took a sip of brandy, then offered his arm. "I would like some night air. Would you?"

"That would be a delight," she chirped, taking his arm. "This way, Baron."

Wilhelmina gave every sign of being simple, her giddiness unfeigned as she guided him down a wainscoted passageway toward the rear of the house. In Kirschenbaum's thirty-four years, very few women had smiled upon him at first meeting and none had seemed dazzled. And here was this one, apparently dazzled, thanks to a false title and a disguise that made him no less homely. Kirschenbaum felt both gloom and amazement, wishing against his will that he could be a true nobleman, just for tonight.

At the end of the passage, giggles and soused laughter came through an open door. Kirschenbaum and his pretty escort stepped onto a spacious, lantern-lit veranda where other pairs sat or stood, some of them kissing in the shadows. The touch of Wilmelmina's hand stirred his blood. But he made himself concentrate, eyes forward as the girl led him down the veranda steps. He inhaled the night. In the window light, most of the rear grounds were dimly visible. To the left Kirschenbaum saw a sizeable garden and a latticed rose arbor; to the far right, a carriage house, a stable and a smokehouse; straight ahead, a stone well and a murky row of sheds farther back, nearer the woods. He and Wilhelmina resumed conversing in German:

"Madame hires free Negroes to tend the garden and groom the horses," she said. "It is strange to see Negroes. I left Bremen only a year ago and much is still strange to me."

"And to me. You may call me Wolfgang, my dear."

She laughed, hugging his arm like a present. "Wolfgang! How queer and wonderful this is. In Bremen I was nothing, and here I am with a true baron!"

"You should not have had to travel so far for your charms to be recognized."

She giggled. "Oh, Wolfgang–few gentlemen here are so nice."

As they meandered onto the grass, one of the shed doors bumped open and a man stumbled out, hitching his pants up. Kirschenbaum pretended to sip his drink and steered Wilhelmina toward the stable. Horses were good for small talk. "I have an eye for horses. On my estate near Frankfurt, I have a herd of two dozen."

"There are just a few here. Oh—we should watch our step." With a nervous titter, she lifted her skirts. "Madame gets upset if we do not stay presentable. Madame slaps."

"Slaps? This is horrid! I will tell her how presentable you are to me, and how delightful."

Beaming, she squeezed his hand as they detoured around a dung pile. The stable loomed ahead of them. From the darkness Kirschenbaum heard a snort, then the toss of an equine head. Wilhelmina pinched her small nose. "God, that smell!"

Pointedly Kirschenbaum inhaled—he had always felt impatient with those who recoiled from horses. "It is nothing, Wilhelmina. Horses smell of life. Like ploughed earth. Like the sea . . . " He halted in mid-step. His monocle dropped.

Still holding her nose, Wilhelmina stumbled, caught herself and looked up at him. "What is the matter, Wolfgang?"

Kirschenbaum stared. Black within the blackness of its stall, the horse would have been invisible if not for the gleam of its eye, the satiny glisten of its neck and especially the white marking above its snout—a chipped diamond shape. Kirschenbaum cleared his throat. "I thought I saw another dung pile in our path. Here, please finish this brandy for me."

"Oh—Madame does not like us to drink while we are entertaining."

"Be kind, my dear. When I drink, I like someone to join me."

Dipping her eye, she gave him a coquettish look. "Well, if it would please you . . . " She accepted the glass and took a tentative sip. "Mm—sweet . . . "

Gently Kirschenbaum detached himself from her and approached the horse. It snorted again. Gazing at the patch of pure white, he reached up and stroked its nose. "Beautiful beast," he muttered. To both sides of him, other horses shuffled in their stalls. He looked back at Wilhelmina. Framed in the dim light, she was allowing herself a more generous swallow of brandy cobbler. "Whose horse is this?" he asked.

She smacked her lips. "That one is Black Marengo. I am not sure whose he is. They never use him for the wagon or the carriage, like the other ones. Doctor Dubray takes him out sometimes. And Mister Monroe. And Mister Wakefield, when he is here."

"Wakefield?" In the pause, Kirschenbaum thought hard for an approach. "Not long ago I met a gentleman by that name. He takes photographs."

"Yes! Our Mister Wakefield is a photographer."

"So he comes here to La Maison?"

"Oh, quite often. He is a friend of Madame's, I think. They say he pays no money. He sleeps here too, sometimes, and idles about with Delia." She tittered. "Some of the girls were jealous when he grew close to Delia, since he is handsome and polite. Then Madame put her to serving drinks, to keep her from all men but Mister Wakefield."

"Delia–yes. I was introduced."

"Poor thing. Mister Wakefield has not been here all week, so we wonder if he has grown tired of her. A few of the girls are cruel–the Princess of Ireland, they call her." Wilhelmina raised the drink to her lips. Then she hugged herself against the cool air. "Wolfgang, I am getting cold. Could we maybe go inside now?" Her voice softened. "To go upstairs, if you like?"

Kirschenbaum stroked Black Marengo's nose. "Of course," he muttered. Staring at the white diamond patch, he remembered the one other time he had seen it–on the dark road near Winchester. His heart thudded. Then he felt Wilhelmina's hand around his wrist.

"Come, Wolfgang. Am I not more interesting than a horse?"

MOONLIGHT BARELY PENETRATED the leaf cover. Duke was gone, having taken the coach to a farm road about a mile back, where he could wait less conspicuously. Behind a pear tree, Truly raised the spyglass and watched a newly arrived carriage disgorge its party of men. "Dang–one of them looks like an Assistant Secretary of State I had dealings with. Well, maybe he just likes to play cards."

Forbes had borrowed Truly's pen-knife. Leaning against another tree, he was whittling a twig to a fine point. "I never thought I'd end up serving my country by keeping watch on a whorehouse."

Truly lowered the glass. "And me, I never thought I'd see an Eastern boy whittling. Careful you don't jab yourself."

Forbes turned the pointed twig in his hand. "They say Grant whittles. It helps him think."

"Then I trust he's whittling a lot these days." Truly took out his pocket watch. Tilting it, he caught some light from the house. "Past eleven now." He trained the scope on an open window. A pair of cigar-puffing gents stood before it, while behind them a girl glided by with a tray. The men moved away and another stepped into view—tall and strong-featured, dressed in sharp-cut black. Truly tried to focus on the face but then it was gone. He felt a dim frustration. "Think I might've just seen Monroe—the healthy and sociable version."

"Let me have a turn with that," said Forbes.

Truly handed over the spyglass. Selecting three trees, he began to pace in a tight triangle. This was the worst sort of duty—tense but tedious, with little or no influence on how things went. Yet there was something more, something indefinable that made his nerves itch.

———◆———

HAVING FINISHED THE drink, Wilhelmina babbled on. She was calling him "liebchen" now. Kirschenbaum sat beside her on the four-poster bed, trying to listen as she fondled his arm and grew maudlin.

"I will return to Bremen. I will! Not to stay, but to find my mother and give her more money than she has ever seen. Then I will ask, 'Would a bad girl do this, Mother? Would a bad girl do this for the one who raised her?'"

The wallpaper had a bouquet-and-parrot motif. Kirschenbaum stared into it, wishing that he could take refuge among the wings and blossoms. Through the near wall came a bumping sound, along with muffled moans. He struggled to block them out. From inside his waistcoat he drew his flask. He removed the stopper, then poured schnapps into the glass on the side table.

Wilhelmina giggled. "Oh, sweetheart—you do not need to make me drunk."

He took a larger swallow than he had intended, then handed her the glass. "Just a few sips, my little flower. To celebrate our meeting."

She stopped giggling long enough to oblige him.

Gathering his thoughts, he put the flask away. "Wilhelmina, there was something else I meant to ask you."

Her hand slipped onto his knee. "What, sweetheart?"

The bumping in the wall grew more rhythmic. He felt her hand. "Now that I think of it—when I met that fellow Wakefield, he did mention a house where he went for solace and entertainment. He did not name it, but this must be the place."

Nodding, she set the glass down. "It must be."

"Well, he mentioned it while describing an event which disturbed him. It disturbed me too, as a listener. Tell me, darling–did an Irish girl who worked here drown not long ago?"

Wilhelmina's drowsy smile faded. "Briona."

"Yes, that was the name!"

"Mister Wakefield would surely know about it from Delia–she was Briona's best friend." Taking her hand from his leg, Wilhelmina fidgeted. "It shocked us all. None of us know for sure how it happened . . . But Wolfgang–Madame ordered us to say nothing about it to anyone."

"Forgive me, please, for bringing up an event so awful. It just makes me worry for you, Wilhelmina. There is simply no telling about these men who come here, whatever their rank or bloodline. Did poor Briona not die while in the company of a lieutenant-colonel? A man called . . . Oh, what did Wakefield say his name was?"

Wilhelmina shrugged. "I only knew him as the lieutenant-colonel, the strange one who liked to gawk at Briona." She took another sip of schnapps, then placed the glass on the floor. Removing her combs, she let her blonde hair spill free and smiled at him. "But my dear sweet Baron– first horses, now this." She snuggled against him. "Do you not enjoy how I look?"

"Of course, my dear." He stared at the petals and parrots on the wall. The bumping from the next room intensified, accompanied by a yelping female voice. Tittering, Wilhelmina reached up, plucked the monocle from his eye and held it to her own. He peered down her smooth white neck to her cleavage. He felt warm all over. In the next room, the noise culminated in a bestial groan. Wilhelmina let the monocle drop, smiling dreamily at him. Life was short, he thought. And here he was, and perhaps Truly had meant for him to mix pleasure with business–a reward for his risk.

He felt her hand sliding up his back. It stopped at his hump, then jerked away. Kirschenbaum stiffened. Without looking at her, he could feel her sitting up straight beside him.

"An accident of birth, my dear."

"Oh . . . I beg your pardon, Wolfgang. I was only surprised."

The heat had left him. He took the drink from the side table and cradled it. "It's all right."

After a moment, she touched his shoulder.

"Dear Wilhelmina," he said, "you have been an oasis for me. But just now I would like to be alone. Time for reflection–about several matters."

Flushed, she looked at the floor. He patted her hand. "Go on, now. I will see you again later."

Averting her gaze, she got to her feet a bit unsteadily. "Yes, Wolfgang–later." She padded out, shutting the door behind her.

Kirschenbaum gazed deep into his glass of schnapps. Like a stone he sank through the clear liquid, straight to the bottom. He heard rustling sounds from other rooms, doors opening and shutting, laughter and voices from downstairs. In his memory they mingled with the sounds of his lost Frankfurt–sounds that reached back to his boyhood: cathedral bells, crying peddlers, the tramp of guardsmen, the taunts of children as he hauled firewood through the streets. But this lasted only a moment. Shaking off the bleakness, he downed his schnapps, took a breath, let his thoughts form. He had to go back downstairs. He had to speak with Delia–in private, if at all possible.

HAVING VIEWED NOTHING of interest on the rear veranda–just the expected socializing–Truly groped his way back through the orchard. Beneath a tree, Forbes sat cradling the spyglass. Out front, by the hitching racks, a trio of black coachmen passed the time in soft conversation. No customers had arrived in the past hour, while several had departed. Less tense now, more tedious. For Truly, it would have been the perfect occasion to tell Forbes the story of his and Rachel's first meeting. He could have told it and managed to stay watchful.

And lately he had been wanting to tell it . . . About riding down to the Indian Territory in the spring of 1840, drawn by the promise of good federal pay; hiring on as a "roving agent"–more like a peace officer, it turned out–charged with settling disputes between the government agent system and the indigenous Kiowa and Comanche and the newly "resettled" tribes and the encroaching white settlers, while keeping out the unlicensed fur trappers and whiskey men; going half-mad after two months of having knives and pistols drawn on him, jamming his Colt into strangers' ribs before even the first word passed; discovering in the course of this how some agents schemed with contractors to swindle the Indians; one such shady merchant, an Englishman named Finnemore, who had short-weighted a band of Cherokee on seed, feed and grain and sold them rancid beef; some of the enraged band calling at his homestead and, finding him absent, snatching his wife and two daughters as surety; Truly negotiating the release of the mother and eldest daughter and promising to return for the youngest, a curiously unperturbed girl who seemed to have taken her father's true measure; Truly tracking down a series of bribed agents, leaving a trail of bloody noses while collecting Finnemore's illicit largesse; the release of the captive girl, named Rachel; their hasty marriage at Fort Gibson and subsequent departure for Missouri, with Finnemore's curses ringing after them.

All of this Truly would have liked to relate, to pass the hour. But just then a two-horse carriage appeared from around La Maison's far side and proceeded down the driveway. In the light of its twin lamps, Truly discerned the eagle crest on its door.

"The house carriage," he muttered. "Hand me the glass, would you?"

The carriage turned onto the main road and headed in the agents' direction, picking up speed as it passed the idle vehicles in front. The concealing tree trunks began to block Truly's view. Then, through a gap, he managed to focus on the silhouette beneath the canopy.

He frowned, lowering the scope. "Dubray. In a hurry, it looks like."

The vehicle rushed by, its clatter fading down the road.

AT A TABLE beneath a portrait of Voltaire, Kirschenbaum sat alone. Through the lively general noise, the spidery notes of the spinet came prickling. Kirschenbaum did not see Dubray anywhere and was glad enough for that. He spied Wilhelmina in a corner, laughing with a dandyish fat man. He watched Delia pass by with a loaded tray–tight-lipped, still cheerlessly separate in the crowd. Having failed thus far to catch her eye, he was again trying to do so when Monroe sauntered past, nodding at customers. There was something ambiguous in his hazy smile, something that could be read as either contempt or cordiality. Then Monroe exited to the grand hall.

"A drink for you, sir?"

Looking up, he saw the auburn-haired serving girl. "Nein . . . " He pulled his mind back to English. "No, thank you."

She curtsied and left him just as Ravenel reappeared, flashing her yellowed teeth. "And was Mademoiselle Wilhelmina to your satisfaction, Baron?" In the lurid light her face seemed to have grown subtly more hideous, her smile more bladelike.

"A most lovely fraulein," he replied. "I would soon like to meet another, but not yet. I enjoy my surroundings."

"Whenever you wish." With a dip of her head, Ravenel left him.

A few tables away, Delia was serving two men. Thinking of her romantic connection to Miles Wakefield, Kirschenbaum decided to hold his name in reserve. Should she prove suspicious at first, a convincing claim of having met and liked Wakefield might win her trust–though he hoped she would not question him too closely.

About to signal her, Kirschenbaum saw one of the men take hold of her wrist. With a lifeless smile she tried to pull away, but the customer tugged her in close. Kirschenbaum got to his feet. Caught in a stooped position, Delia stared at the floor as the grinning man spoke to her, inches from her cheek. Kirschenbaum moved toward them, surprised at how real his indignation was. He stood over the table. The offender's companion looked up dimly but Kirschenbaum ignored him, listening in:

"I fancy you're good for more than liquor, dearie–isn't that true?"

"Please, sir," she intoned.

Kirschenbaum laid a firm hand on the man's coat sleeve. The man flinched, staring up with bunched eyebrows. Pulling her arm free, Delia vanished. Kirschenbaum withdrew his hand but did not move right away, letting his downward stare linger.

"Damn you–get your own," the man growled.

Returning to his table, Kirschenbaum found Delia wiping the one next to it. She glanced at him. "Thank you, Baron. If the gentleman kept on like that, Mister Monroe would have stopped him."

"Miss Delia, I must speak with you. About your poor friend Briona."

She stopped wiping. Squeezing her cloth, she gazed at him as he retook his seat.

He adjusted his monocle. "Please get for me another brandy cobbler. When you serve me, we will pretend only to chat, ja?"

She left and was back in a minute. The drink slopped over as she set it down. Taking a fresh cloth from her apron, she wiped slowly. "Baron, how do you know about Briona?"

For appearances he put on a bland smile but kept his voice low and intent. "Soon I can tell you this, but time is little. The owners here, they wish to hide what happened to your friend?"

"Yes!" she whispered. "And I do not know why, sir!"

"I wish to hear what you know–such as this lieutenant-colonel who took her away."

Heat flickered in her blue eyes. "You are of the law, sir? You will catch him and see him punished?"

"With your aid–ja, Miss Delia. But first, do you know his name?"

"I do not, Baron."

His heart fell. "Miss Briona did not ever speak it?"

"I don't believe she learned it, sir–or if she did, she did not wish to recall, for he frightened her terribly. She had met him but twice before it happened. The first time, he gave her flowers–but the second time, he showed himself for what he was. But listen–I can tell you other things." Delia's whisper intensified. "Baron, please look and tell me if Madame is near."

Kirschenbaum let his eyes wander. "I do not see her."

"And the other girl in red–is she watching us?"

Kirschenbaum had another look. Behind the tavern desk, the auburn-haired one was measuring out glasses of liquor. "No," he said.

"She will be," said Delia. "Fannie's a tattling bitch. But Baron–as soon as I can, I will tell Ursula I feel unwell and must have some air. Then I will meet you by the rose arbor in back."

"I will be there."

"As soon as I can get away . . . " A customer signaled her. Curtsying, she gave Kirschenbaum a last anxious look. "By the arbor, sir."

He summoned the bland smile. "Danke . . . er, thank you."

She left him. Sipping his drink, he gazed at the ornate coffin clock across the room. It was one-thirty.

Around him, the revelry continued. Lamps glowed, the spinet played and cigar smoke drifted. He felt a gnawing impatience, not just for Delia's information but to be up and moving; the chair in which he sat, like most chairs, pained his back. He looked toward the hall. Half in shadow by the staircase stood Monroe–and though it was hard to tell for sure, he seemed to be staring in Kirschenbaum's direction. Tall and broad-shouldered, arms folded–a sleek sentinel in black. Unable to see the man's expression, Kirschenbaum nevertheless sensed the hazy smile. He thought of the derringer beneath his vest. Even as the brandy warmed him, his crooked spine went cold.

SEATED ON THE ground, Truly stared through the trees. In the shadows behind him, Forbes paced slowly back and forth. Another pair of men came stumbling out of La Maison and toward the hitching racks, where the waiting mounts and coaches had thinned. Once more Truly aimed the spyglass at each lighted window. Things inside remained lively enough. A glimpse of Kirschenbaum would have been comforting, but there was no such glimpse. Then, in a first-story window, he sighted a slim woman in a violet dress. He had caught sight of her once before but this time she lingered in the lens: Ravenel, as he had thought. Standing in a knot of jolly patrons, she was holding forth, smiling and gesticulating.

"There's our Madame R.," Truly muttered. "Spry as a faun tonight."

He heard Forbes yawn. "What's the time?"

Pulling out his watch, Truly found a stray beam of moonlight. "Just after two."

He had barely spoken when they heard wheels and hoofbeats from down the road. Truly thought it might be a very late arrival, another gent who had defied the army night patrols for pleasure's sake. Then he remembered Dubray. Rising, he craned his neck toward the oncoming noise. Like twin coals, a pair of carriage lamps appeared through the black woods. The vehicle rattled past the agents and along the mansion grounds, fast enough to startle the remaining horses in front, then took a swaying turn down the driveway. Following it with the spyglass, Truly saw the eagle crest on its door and Dubray hunched in the driver's box, this time with a companion at his side.

"Someone's with him," Truly said, handing the glass to Forbes.

Before reaching the corner of the house, Dubray reined up so hard that his team reared, the carriage lurching. The Frenchman cast his whip aside and jumped down, followed by the passenger; side by side, they strode toward La Maison's entrance. In a bowler and long coat, the other man was slightly taller. Truly seized the glass from Forbes; as he trained it on the figure, a window illuminated the man's long dour face.

"Archer," he whispered, rising to his feet.

Just before the two men reached the front door, it opened wide and Ursula appeared, silhouetted in the harsh yellow light. She stood aside and then ducked in after them, swinging the door shut.

Agitated, Truly lay the spyglass down.

Forbes stood up. "Nate–whatever this is . . . "

"Whatever it is, they're too damned full of purpose. Let's go."

Marching out of the trees, they started quickly across the wide grounds. In his mind Truly saw Kirschenbaum's parting smile, his caped form moving toward the house. His pace quickened. As he drew ahead of the lumbering Forbes, the distance to the house seemed alarmingly greater. "I'm going to run," he blurted, surging toward the lighted portico. In one of the narrow doorside windows, Ursula's round face peered out and then vanished. Truly ran harder.

He reached the portico and vaulted up the steps. Breathless, he tried the door handle but it did not budge. He pounded the paneled wood. Behind him, Forbes came up and leaned breathless against a pillar. With a stab of certainty, Truly knew that seconds mattered. He whipped out his Colt. Using the barrel, he smashed out a panel of the right side-window. He then reached inside with his free hand, cursing as he fumbled for the door chain and then the bolt. Forbes gave the knob a hard twist and they burst inside. In the center of the hall, Ursula confronted them. Bellowing in German, she waved her thick arms, moving one way and then the other to block them. Truly sidestepped her, then ran straight into Dubray.

Still wearing his travel coat, the doctor reeled back and clutched at his spectacles. "How dare you?!" he cried.

Truly brandished the revolver. "Where's Archer?!"

Dubray began to sputter. Ursula, shrieking, grabbed Truly by the shoulder but then Forbes was there, restraining her. Truly struck the muzzle under Dubray's bulbous nose. "Tell me, you bastard!"

With a theatrical groan, the doctor clapped both hands to his chest and rolled his head back. He sank to his knees. "Argh! Mon coeur!"

Shoving Dubray against a newel post, Truly charged into the big gaming room. Women screamed and men scrambled, spilling drinks and tipping chairs over. Oblivious to Truly's weapon, one unsteady patron stepped in the way–"What do you mean, sir, frightening these ladies and . . . ?!" Truly knocked him over a chair and barreled on. Directly in his path, Fannie stood gaping, hugging a pair of long-necked bottles. As Truly reached her, the bottles slipped from her arms and shattered, leaving them both in a spreading puddle of liquor.

He glared into her wide eyes. "Where'd they go?! WHERE?!!"

"Outside!" she yelped. "Behind the house!"

He flew back out to the main hall, where Dubray sat cowering and Forbes still struggled with Ursula. To the left of the staircase, a corridor led toward the rear of the house. Down its length Truly hurtled, while ahead of him he saw an open door with the veranda railing just beyond. Then he heard a woman's screaming–first fitful and then shrill and sustained, coming from outside. Within the cry, one pistol shot and then another rang out. In full stride, Truly felt an electric jolt of anguish that propelled him the rest of the way, through the open door and onto the dim veranda, where he stood motionless. The screams had stopped. In the night stillness, there was only the sound of his breathing, the drumming of blood in his ears. On the ground to his left, a lantern flickered on the arbor's latticework. He leaned over the railing. As he raised his revolver, four people took shape within the lantern's glow.

Nearest the veranda, Ravenel's slight, sharp outline stood facing him; Monroe's tall one loomed behind her. Standing apart from them, his return gaze coldly intent, Archer clutched a revolver at hip level. Half-sprawled behind the policeman, a young woman propped herself up by one arm. Distantly Truly recognized her as one that he had seen through the spyglass–a pretty serving girl dressed in red, her eyes now dazed and her honey-blonde hair askew. Blood smeared her chin.

In an even, bone-dry voice, Ravenel spoke. "You may safely put up your pistol, Major. Detective Archer will do the same."

Archer slipped his weapon into a holster beneath his coat. His face was different from last time–a dungeon face, drawn and spiritless. Truly made no move to put his Colt away.

Forbes lurched onto the veranda and went still, getting his breath.

Truly descended the steps, keeping his revolver on Monroe and Ravenel. He halted a few paces from them. "So glad to see you've regained your health," he murmured. He looked up at Monroe. "Both of you." Monroe's heavy brow shadowed his eyes, though Truly felt them staring. He wanted to get closer, to take the lantern and shine it in the big man's face.

Just then Forbes bustled past, stepped around the pair and picked up the lantern. He gave Archer a probing look, then went to the girl's aid. Truly's attention turned to Ravenel. On her shadowed face he sensed a look of steely amusement. His stomach twisted. "What have you done with him?" he barked.

"You would do well not to menace us," Ravenel replied. "This is a police matter. One of my jeune filles has been . . . "

"I know what kind of matter it is. Answer me."

"Detective Archer has something to tell you, Major."

Truly heard Archer clear his throat. "For various reasons, Truly, we thought you might be lurking about, ready to stick your nose in." The voice was thick and halting. "On our way here, the doctor and I stopped at the Second Precinct station. A party of mounted police will arrive presently, at which time you'll be arrested or obliged to leave–your choice."

Ravenel cut in. "The detective tells me that the police and your Secret Service have lately agreed not to tread in each other's business. Neither Archer's superior nor your own will be pleased at this disruption."

"Tell me where the man is!" Truly snarled.

This time it was Monroe who answered. Slowly pointing a thumb over his shoulder, he spoke in a stark baritone–"Go look." He stepped aside, as did Ravenel. Truly moved past them. Archer backed stiffly out of the way.

The girl was on her feet now, leaning against the arbor. Just beyond her, Forbes stood with his back turned, holding the lantern high. "Nate," he called, barely loud enough.

Moving toward the light, Truly stuck the revolver back under his coat. All thought and emotion contracted, until he felt almost bodiless. Then he stood next to Forbes. At their feet Kirschenbaum lay crumpled, face-down in the grass. His splayed limbs said that he had died running–or crawling, possibly, though his derringer lay beside him. Bending down, Truly saw blood glistening near the top of his head, more of it just below the black-caped rise of his back. Truly stared at the callused hands, fingers bent as if to grasp something. He wanted to touch them, but all he did was hover there.

Like an arid breeze, Ravenel's voice came wafting. "A friend of yours, this so-called baron? How sad that his judgment was not better."

Straightening up, Truly turned around. Forbes too had turned, setting the lantern down. Against the arbor, the girl held a hand to her mouth, eyes clearer now and gazing at Kirschenbaum's body. Archer stood with his hands clenched at his sides. Over by the veranda, the figures of Monroe and Ravenel looked on. Monroe had lit a cigar, its tip like a small molten portal in his head.

Shaking, Truly swallowed before fixing his stare on Archer. "A fine . . . fine little arrangement, Archer. How long do you think it will last?" Truly began edging toward him. "How long, Chief of Detectives?"

Archer's hand inched toward his coat pocket, then fell away as Forbes made an identical move.

Truly stepped closer. "And how will you explain it? Being at the beck and call of a fancy whorehouse?"

Archer's lips twitched. Then he seemed to gather himself, his reply tense but lofty. "I have a reputation, Truly, in case you're not aware. Up to now I've made a special case for this house, but this incident may mean it's time to shut it down. That will be good enough for my superintendent, especially in light of your meddling. We handle things our own way."

"*You* surely do. Starting with your wife."

In the lantern's orange light, Archer's long face smoldered. It was a moment before he spoke again, the words coming from the bottom of his throat. "You can tell whatever damned tales you want–but my reports will include several facts. It will say that this foreigner's manner raised suspicion, and so I was summoned. That shortly before my arrival, Mister Monroe found him assaulting the young lady out here, and the man drew a pistol on him. That I came up from behind and shot him when he resisted arrest. That you then interfered, threatening all present with a revolver. Finally, that the man was apparently sent here under a false identity. Sent here by you, Truly–pursuing a case you've manufactured out of nothing, without regard for police jurisdiction." Archer's teeth showed. "Combine that with your hounding of Underhill, and we'll see who's more credible."

In the silence, Truly heard hoofbeats from the road. Monroe with his burning cigar-tip went up the veranda steps and into the house. Ravenel called to the girl–"Come inside, Mademoiselle Delia." On Truly's right, Forbes stood staring at Archer. The lantern flickered, the hoofbeats neared.

Truly looked at the ground. His shaking had worsened–but when he spoke, his voice came low and steady. "So, Archer–your yellow hide is safe. At least, till they whistle for you again."

"Shut it, Truly."

"Yes, certainly. I'll shut it." He launched himself at Archer's throat.

Within seconds he had kneed the lawman in the groin, elbowed him in the eye and snatched the revolver from under his coat. Flinging the weapon aside, he again hurled himself at Archer while Ravenel shouted in French. He was beating Archer's head against an arbor post when Forbes hauled him off.

A mounted policeman had appeared, holding an oilcloth torch as he cantered toward them. Two on foot burst onto the veranda, pistols drawn. Forbes offered them his official papers. Panting, Truly put his hat back on, then noticed Archer's hat by his foot. He stepped on it. With torch raised, the first policeman carefully dismounted and went to look at Kirschenbaum's body. The other two cast muddled glances at Archer, who stood blinking, rubbing his head.

Holding the mute girl by the arm, Ravenel waved for attention. "A horrible affair!" she cried. "Horrible! But the German brute is dead. I see no reason why lesser charges should be pressed." She turned to Archer. "Do you, Detective?"

Archer steadied himself against the arbor. Cupping a hand to his eye, he croaked, "No. No . . . Lord God, get them out of here."

In a deadening act of will, Truly barely kept himself from lunging at Archer once more.

PART VI

Refuge For The Wren

Remorse is cureless—the disease
Not even God can heal;
For 'tis His institution—
The complement of hell.
  • *EMILY DICKINSON*

52

La Maison De l'Empereur
June 29

IN HIS HASTE Wakefield stumbled on the cellar stairs and almost dropped his lamp. He caught himself on the railing, then saw a candle's flicker below.

"Mister Wakefield—that is you, sir?"

A timorous girl-voice, its accent German. He raised the lamp and saw Wilhelmina staring up at him. Along with the candle, she held a food tray with an empty dish and a ring of keys.

"Come on up," he said.

She rustled up the steps. With a skittish glance, she held the tray out and he took the key-ring. "Mister Wakefield, I do not know why they done this to her. I do not understand."

He squeezed past her, descending into the musty darkness. At the foot of the stairs he raised the lamp to reveal masonry walls with crumbling mortar. For all his time spent at the manse, he had never been down here. He started along a wide dank chamber, past tiers of cobwebbed casks and bottles. Before his advancing glow, a few rats skittered into the deeper shadows; the sight of them fueled his urgency. He came to an archway on his right. Stepping through, he saw stacked trunks and boxes, dusty shelves with canned provisions, jumbled objects such as paintings and candelabras draped in burlap. To get his bearings he began a slow turn but went still almost immediately, shining the lamp in a corner. Coiled there like a serpent lay a length of chain, crowned with something that he could not instantly identify; closer inspection revealed it as a type of neck-shackle that he had heard of but never seen. Intended for the most wayward slaves, it featured long radial spokes that deprived the wearer of sleep. Other such discarded implements lay close by: a rusted branding iron, a lead-weighted cat o' nine-tails, a sharp-tipped goad fashioned from a large animal's leg-bone.

Wakefield recalled Dubray's romantic speculations about the mansion's history–"*Une grande tableaux,* surely, of how life was lived before the natural order's crumbling." Having spent part of his youth on an estate with threescore slaves, Wakefield had seen a few whippings and managed to accept their cruel inevitability, much as he accepted disease in the world. Yet the tools now before him seemed as alien as cannibal cutlery, leaving him repelled and then, more suddenly, appalled that they had distracted him.

Jerking about, he called into the dark. "Delia!" He waited two heartbeats and then called out again, louder. "Delia!!"

"Miles?!"

He hurried in the cry's direction, toward the rear. Past the bulkhead doors on the right, he came upon a long but narrow enclosure with an iron door and a small barred window therein. He jammed the key into the lock, twisted it and threw the door open. On a mattress at the far end of the cell, Delia had raised herself to all fours. Her hair was uncombed, her wan face smudged with soot. She gaped at him. He sprinted the length of the cell. Setting the lamp down, he dropped to his knees and threw his arms around her. She buried her face in his chest.

"Damn them!" he sputtered. "Damn them! If I had known . . . " She was moaning something into his shirt, over and over. After a moment he recognized it as, "Where were you?"–and a spasm of guilt made him squeeze tighter. "Darling, I told you I'd have to stay hidden! How could I have known?"

"Why, Miles? Please tell me why!"

Pushing her upright, he took hold of her limp shoulders. "For God's sake, I've explained that too! It's not yet safe for you to know! It's for your own . . . " He noticed a purplish spot along her jaw. It was not soot. "Who struck you?!"

"Madam did."

His eyes darted one way and then another in the darkness, as if searching for a place to stow his rage. Then, near the edge of the lampglow, he noticed an iron ring imbedded in the wall and a chain dangling from it; from the end of the chain hung a clawlike manacle. Delia had spent the past three nights in a slave pen. He recalled Ravenel's airy comment: "Obedience is the glue at La Maison, and what sort of example is Mademoiselle Delia? She is most fortunate to have you as a protector, Wakefield. Otherwise . . . "

"I'll kill them," he muttered. "When the time comes, I swear on my honor . . . "

Puffy-eyed, Delia gazed at him. "I don't ask for that, Miles." Her voice had lost its quaver. "I would not ask for that. But can you understand . . . how weary I am of those words–'When the time comes?' I don't even know what it means!"

Letting go of her, he pressed a hand to his forehead. "You will! You must believe me!"

"As I must believe you about the lieutenant-colonel? That he'll pay for what he did?"

"Yes, yes! Delia . . . "

"Miles, they shot that little German man right in front of me. He knew about Briona–from you, he said."

Eyeing her, he shook his head. "No–you were lied to. I never met any such man."

Her eyes lingered on him. Then they closed. "He wanted to know more about it. Why, I never learned–but he said we could help each other. They caught us talking out back. Madam told me to scream but I couldn't, so she hit me. I screamed. Then that policeman Archer . . . "

"I know, I know!" He gave a harsh sigh. "They told me about it. Delia, why didn't you heed the warning? You knew they wanted no one meddling in that business."

Hugging herself, she stared past him. "For me it was not meddling–surely you know that. Miles, I don't care if it's dangerous or not–please, please tell me what all of this means!"

"Where you are concerned, I care that it's dangerous! For now, the fewer questions you ask . . . "

"You're with them."

"What?"

Her voice was flat, her gaze empty. "You're with them, dear Miles. But you're afraid of them too."

Wakefield felt cold in his chest. He watched her, huddled like a child on the mattress. If he touched her now it would be to shake her, so he just glared. "I've demanded that you be let upstairs. They have agreed."

"Upstairs," she murmured. "Where Fanny and Ursula can sneer at me."

"You want out of here, do you not?"

"I want out of this house. I want to go far away."

"And you will. But for the present, don't give them any more reason to act against you, understand? They will be watching you."

"'Act against me?' You mean, 'kill me'–don't you? That's what will happen next time?"

He clutched her by the forearm. "No, it won't–because you'll do as I say! Listen–all they'll likely do now is confine you to your room a bit longer. I have books you can read. Once the house reopens, you'll resume your duties just as before. And you'll be all right, so long as you don't act foolishly."

"My duties–yes," she mumbled. "And where will you be?"

"Elsewhere, for at least a few days. It's vital that I stay out of sight. In time, you'll know why–how many times must I say it?"

Amid its agitation, his mind flashed on the week ahead. It had been agreed that a token shutdown of La Maison was imperative. Archer, their shield and servant, could now tell his superiors that he had taken some kind of action. It would do much to quell what public attention the shooting had drawn–and to curtail the threat of federal spying. Wakefield would have preferred an indefinite shutdown. But Ravenel, chafing at the loss of income–and at the crimping of her queenly role–insisted otherwise. Disappointed customers, arriving to find a quiet house, were already being told to return for La Maison's grand Fourth-of-July reopening.

Delia was looking at him, not coldly but solemnly. He went to touch her cheek but she moved to get up. On her feet, she straightened her smudged red vest. "Do you think they would let me bathe?"

He swallowed, picking up the lamp. "I'll see that they do."

Taking her limp hand, he led her out of the chamber and on through the darkness. He had failed her–inevitably, perhaps. In his misery, as they reached the stairs, he imagined turning a revolver on Ravenel, then

Dubray, then Monroe. But with Monroe, the scene did not play as he wished. Instead he saw the weapon disintegrate in his hand and himself standing paralyzed, helpless as the big man's hazy smile moved toward him.

53

Boundary Street

*H*OLDING HIS HAT, Truly stood in the shade of a big willow, close enough to observe if not hear Cass reading his Bible passage. In a city where white, black and mulatto babies routinely turned up dead–in alleys and privies, in fields and woodlots–Reverend Cass bestowed full graveside ritual upon any that came his way. Truly's ears caught the deep, measured roll of his voice. It was somewhat more than Kirschenbaum had been granted. For Kirschenbaum–yesterday, at Mount Olivet Cemetery–there had been a withered old priest muttering Latin, befuddled in the presence of non-Catholic mourners. There had been a cheap headstone and Truly, Duke and Sapphira in mute attendance, watching as diggers lowered the hunchback's coffin into dark earth, far from the spires of Frankfurt.

The afternoon was bright and hot. Behind Cass, two convalescent Negro soldiers waited with their caps off. A half-dozen flock members stood next to the tiny pine casket. Truly thought of the two children that he and Rachel had lost–a stillborn daughter and a fever-struck infant son, bracketing the birth of Anna. Even more than the facts of war, the death of children left him musing on certain words. "Bereavement," for one. "Bereavement"–for Truly, it conjured a black night and a locomotive braking at full speed; a spray of sparks, a clenching of metal and a thousand metal shrieks, all within a single vast shriek as the train hulked, slowed, shuddered to a dead stop.

Cass ended his reading. Clasping his Bible, he stepped back as the two soldiers stepped forward. One lifted the casket while the other got into the fresh grave. Out of the knot of mourners, a young woman moved to the grave's edge and bowed her head–a wisp of a Negress, plain and skinny in her drab calico. He guessed her to be the dead child's mother, but then he noticed the rude little cross that Cass now held; like other such markers in the children's plot, it bore no name. In a moment Truly became aware of a low, lilting hum from the throat of the colored girl, who he now guessed to be the church soloist.

The soldier in the grave reached up to take the casket. Truly thought of his lost babies, then of the soil spilling onto Kirschenbaum's lid. Then he thought of Rachel. It was she who had left him with this affinity for those like Kirschenbaum, who the stars had so visibly failed to bless. They were the ones she had welcomed most naturally, as if acting upon a secret kinship. So nowadays Truly welcomed them, aware that in touching them he somehow hoped to touch Rachel. Had he ever done anything from a pure motive? Probably not. But to touch her in some way–that was his hope even now, watching the stunted pine box lowered from one set of dark hands to another. He was prepared to fail as always, ready for the numbness and maybe to accept it at last. He was not prepared for the singer. He was unready for her to shut her eyes and tilt her hemp-brown face skyward, hands held out from the sides, then to raise her voice and become something not of Earth. From its low warble the sound rose steadily, gathering strength until he could hear the words:

> *Sweet pilgrim where you going?*
> *Sweet pilgrim where you gone?*
> *Gone to Canaan's land*
> *Led by Jesus' hand.*
> *Sweet brother why you going?*
> *Sweet brother why you gone?*
> *To lay my burden down*
> *To wear that starry crown.*

The voice swooped and sailed, reached a plateau and floated there before resuming its climb. Bending farther back, the singer launched her sound to the hot sky. It pierced like thorns. It arced and cut like sorrow, till it was sorrow's own voice. Truly turned his back. Resting against the willow, he gazed over the headstones and wooden crosses to the small roadside church. When the last pure note had faded, he turned to view the scene once more. The soldier pair took up spades and began scooping dirt into the grave. Cass dropped a dirt-clod into it as the mourners dispersed. Truly looked for the singer but did not see her anywhere.

Minutes later he was seated on the plank steps of the church. In a drought-withered garden nearby, a stooped old black woman was picking herbs. From under the brim of her straw hat, she glanced up at him. The glance seemed somehow accusatory. He looked away and saw Cass approaching from the graveyard, stately in his black clawhammer coat. The minister stopped to exchange greetings with the old woman. Then, eyes curious, he continued toward Truly.

"I saw you, Major. I was wondering where you'd gone."

"I just need a word with Sapphira. Whenever she's less busy."

Cass stood before him. "She is doing marvelous well with the wounded."

"I expect so."

With the Widow Sackville's church so hard-pressed, Cass had opened his own to colored wounded, despite its distance from the docks. Sapphira's will had at last found a sure outlet, at least for the immediate days.

Cass inquired how Ben was doing and Truly told him. Wanting no small talk but resigned to it, Truly asked about Sergeant Tucker.

"Improving at a good pace," Cass said. "He's out walking now, getting his strength back." Placing his Bible on the step, Cass eased down beside Truly. "An impressive young man, the sergeant. Reads the newspapers every day. Talks with the other men to keep their spirits up."

The subsequent pause was not exactly awkward, but Truly could not help imagining what the tactful preacher held back: Tucker and Sapphira in close quarters, in daily contact. The stolen nervous looks between them. Glancing at Cass, he thought of the things that supposedly bound men together: faith, blood, race, country, profession. What were these, next to the fact of aging? Those moments of wistful surrender, borne alone? Truly suddenly felt more comfortable.

"I am sorry about your friend," said Cass. "Sapphira told me."

"Thank you. What she could not tell you is that I sent him straight into the lion's den."

Cass looked at him. "Not intentionally, I'm sure. Nor recklessly."

"Recklessly? I wonder if I'm the proper judge of that."

Pondering, Cass looked toward the graveyard, where the pair of convalescents still shoveled. "I know nothing of your work, Major. But I presume it has worth. Worth, and risk as well–they do go together. And I do not mean to wax harmonious over your friend, sir, but I just buried a child. No name for him. Never even got to open his eyes. He was born, he squalled, he breathed the air of risk. It's all 'round us, whether we tempt it or not."

"Surely. And my wife scraped her knee on a buggy wheel and that was that." Truly leaned forward on his elbows. Inside him, something had come loose. "But let me tell you about my work, Reverend. It's played out on a low, dark field–too low for notions of honor, too dark for sight. Each participant must assume that his opponent will strike at any time, ruthlessly; anticipating such, it's vital that he strike first, and more ruthlessly. That's the nature of it. I'm sparing you the details, but it's a filthy game of amateurs. And, no surprise, it draws its share of hoodlums. The baser the man, the more successful he'll likely be, so long as he's smart besides. For God and Country, he gets to sneak, bully and deceive. Even his superiors regard him with contempt, as a necessary evil–but I don't fancy a preacher could endorse such a term, could he?"

Cass gave a mild frown. "'Necessary evil'–a term often applied to war. Which is what I believe you have just described."

For the first time since the night of Kirschenbaum's death, Truly smiled. "Reckon so. A boiled-down version, anyhow."

"Well, what man's exempt from the effects of war? Left to itself, whose soul won't shrivel up in it?"

Truly squinted toward the garden. The old black woman had filled her basket with herbs. Leaning on a gnarled cane, she was drinking from a worn leather canteen.

"You must think of your departed wife quite often," Cass said.

Truly nodded.

"I think of my Nellie still," said Cass. "The cholera took her, along with our son. God's grace never seemed so scattershot. I'll allow there were times I could not pray, other times I fell asleep on my knees. In grief, you either abandon the words or try to choke miracles out of them."

"Your pardon, Reverend, but prayers lost their bang for me some time ago. Long before Rachel died. You know . . . " Truly hesitated, then proceeded to tell Cass what he had told no one since Missouri, where every friend, kinsman and acquaintance had known about it anyway. "Not long after I brought Saph home, it came to me that I was a slave owner, in the strictest legal sense. So I got her a paper of manumission–in spite of which, one Sunday, a new preacher decided to blast me from the pulpit. For being a slaver, as he supposed I was. Saph was right there with us, too, distressed and confused as any child would be. We walked out. Rachel went and found herself another church, but I never bothered."

"Ah," said Cass. "So a single man, a single injustice poisoned the well for you."

Truly shrugged. "Well, who's to say I wouldn't have quit regardless, for some other reason? But after that, the House of God was just a house to me. Some scriptural passages have left their teethmarks, mind you. 'Wide is the gate and broad is the road that leads to destruction,' et cetera–I always thought there was something to that one, for all my apostasy."

"Well, now–there's a telling selection!" Picking up his Bible, Cass rose stiffly. "I will send Miss Sapphira out." He went up the steps, then paused by the double doors. "Major, you're one apostate I wouldn't mind seeing here again. Shall I hope for that?"

Truly spoke over his shoulder. "Stranger things have happened, I figure."

Cass went inside. Getting up, Truly faced the doors like a courtroom defendant.

At length Sapphira emerged, dressed in black, her hair tied back in an attempt at plainness. She paused on the top step. "Father . . . ?" Squinting past him, she saw the old woman, now seated with her cane and basket beneath a little magnolia. "Mother Sadie," Sapphira greeted her, curtsying. Fanning herself with her hat, the woman nodded. "Good day, my daughter," she rasped. Sapphira shielded her eyes, staring down at Truly.

"I have to go away for a few days," he said.

She eyed the Colt that dangled from his holster belt, next to the handcuffs.

He took his hat off. "Listen, though. Yesterday, when we were burying Manfred . . . You kept giving me this danged *look*."

Placing a hand on the step rail, she sighed. "Surely you won't deny me that, when you deny me answers."

"Saph–a few hundred times I've asked myself just how I failed, if I could have seen ahead but didn't. I believe I'll be asking that the rest of my life."

"You think I blame you? That I'd blame you worse if I knew more? I know you would have done next to anything to prevent it. Still . . . "

"Saph, please–"

"I knew him only a short while, but he was a friend to me. Now he's dead. Why?"

"I don't know. How, yes—but not why."

Her eyes burned down at him. "Will you be able to find out?"

As far as he could tell, she was in fact not blaming him. Yet she would, if left her without the barest understanding. Sitting on the bottom step, he patted the space beside him. She settled there. Through the sparse woods, he could see the two soldier/diggers resting beneath the big willow. He locked his gaze upon them and started talking.

"We've been conducting an investigation. Bart and I believe it to be important, although Colonel Baker quite clearly does not. Given this lack of support, it's also dangerous—that part I reckon you've grasped. Several persons are involved, including the man who shot Manfred."

Leaning close, Sapphira pressed her hand onto his.

"But his position protects him," Truly went on. "What's more, Bart has been called back to the Bureau of Military Information. Our case has lost its official sanction, and they need him in Virginia—that's why he wasn't at the burial. I did get a note from him, though, promising to rejoin me if it's humanly possible."

Sapphira's hand slid away. "And where does that leave things?"

"For now, in the ash heap. This disaster of ours was the last straw for Baker." More like a ton of straws, Truly thought.

His assault upon Archer had been the focus of Baker's wrath. The hard-won accord between the police and the secret service was near ruin. Only Archer's astounding broad-mindedness, so it went, had spared Truly a five-hundred dollar fine and up to two years in prison. Further, Superintendent Webb could yet release Archer's account to the newspapers: how the detective saved a girl from a lascivious foreign imposter, only to be set upon by a half-deranged federal agent. If the police could not win respect by a gentleman's agreement, they might well seek it in the court of public opinion. Baker, once so heedless of such threats, was eminently heedful of this one. Enough to shelve the case and banish Truly, who at any rate had failed to connect La Maison with Wakefield, this phantom Rebel spy.

"What has Colonel Baker done?" Sapphira demanded.

"He's contrived to humble me—and to get me out of town. Down in Port Tobacco there's a postmaster suspected of smuggling for the Rebs. I intend to make quick work of him. I'll play fellow believer and bag him if he's guilty, then return to Washington. At which time, I'm supposed to give a full report and take on some other earth-shaking task. I can tell you, though, that I'm going to be a regular tortoise in getting back to Baker's door. That's what happens at my age–a fellow slows down. But between said homecoming and said appearance before the illustrious Colonel, I'm going to take up where I left off." Taking Sapphira gently by the elbow, he turned his stare upon her. "I'm not yet sure how I'll go about it–but nothing will stop me, understand? Nothing. Because it's Manfred I'll be thinking of."

Her look of absorption had turned grave. "I understand," she muttered.

"Good. Now . . . " Rising, he helped her up. "An unlucky postmaster awaits me." He swept his hat on. "Keep up your good work."

"I'll pray for you."

"That wouldn't hurt." Turning away, he stopped to look at her once more. "My regards to Sergeant Tucker."

She blinked, as if pulled from a trance. "I'll tell him."

Behind the church, Truly's rented horse stood grazing. Climbing into the saddle, he saw Kirschenbaum on the ground behind La Maison. Archer, as part of his charade, had ordered the place shut down; Truly guessed that it would soon reopen, once the threat of official scrutiny had passed. Business as usual–on the surface, at least. Meanwhile, Truly would go to Port Tobacco and do what he had to do, then return to Washington and set to work in earnest. Like controlled fear in battle, controlled hate would keep him sharp, guiding and sustaining him.

Trotting out to the dusty road, he saw Mother Sadie fanning herself beneath the magnolia. The shade and her dark hue blended to conceal her face, and he was grateful. He did not want to see her eyes again. Touching his hat to her, he thought he saw her nod in reply.

54

Northern Shenandoah Valley
July 2

ALONG WINCHESTER'S MAIN street, the cheering dancing crowd pressed closer, leaving just enough room for the column of tattered graybacks. A large Stars 'n' Bars flew from a church belfry while scores of small battle flags, retrieved from hiding places, waved aloft in jubilant hands. Girls threw garlands, dogs wagged and barked and small boys marched alongside. Here and there, someone would grab a soldier's hand and thrust food into it.

John Breckinridge rode with care, reining his horse to keep from trampling any well-wisher. At the margins of his vision, the little banners flapped like red leaves in the wind. An old woman seized his hand and kissed it. A radiant young woman pushed forward to give him a bouquet. To cries of his name, he responded with a nod or a wave of his hat. Breckinridge had long ago acknowledged his own quiet vanity and resolved not to fret about it, so long as he practiced certain virtues. He was therefore glad that he had thought to trim his mustache and don a clean outfit of blue Kentucky jeans.

Somewhere back down the dusty pike, a regimental band found its breath and struck up "Dixie." The cheering swelled anew. Breckinridge peered over his shoulder and spied Cabell—different from his other children, the one who seemed to oscillate between devotion and resentment. Happy now, a proven soldier and valued staff member, hailing strangers as he cantered along. Emotion caught Breckinridge by the throat. In these rarest of moments, it all felt worthwhile–the strain, the tedium and even the horror. The lowliest private became an exalted knight in rags, ready to march another thousand miles and fight a hundred battles.

Passing the general store, he tossed his bouquet to an enraptured little girl. At last he reached the far side of town, where the crowd thinned and fell away. Like a dream, the delirium faded. He spurred his horse along the shuffling troop column. Up ahead, through the shimmer of heat waves, Gordon's men were spreading into the roadside meadows for bivouac.

The Valley was all but retaken, its precious granary secure once more. They had encountered not a single Yankee soldier since Buford's Gap. But while today's march had been mercifully straightforward, tomorrow's would not be. Northward lay the West Virginia panhandle, with the Union strongholds of Martinsburg and Harper's Ferry.

Breckinridge found Gordon in a leafy glade. Seated on a cracker box, the Georgian was shaking a pebble from his boot.

"Yes–take care of those feet," said Breckinridge.

Gordon pulled the boot back on. "It's the men's feet that worry me, Genr'l. All we get are promises about shoes."

Breckinridge dismounted. "The enemy's said to have huge stores at Martinsburg. Maybe shoes among them."

Grumbling, Gordon rose. He signaled a staff sergeant to water Breckinridge's horse.

"Quite a reception back there," said Breckinridge. "This was Jackson's favorite town, did you know?"

"I can see why. Cheers help the spirit, if not the feet."

Glancing at Gordon's face, Breckinridge saw the concave spot where he had been shot at Antietam. It marked him as the centurion he was, along with the fierce eyes and erect bearing. The two of them sat side by side on the cracker box. Hats on their knees, they watched the grimy little tents poke up across the fields' green breadth. "Well, John," said Breckinridge, "–other than that, how be you?"

Gordon opened his mouth but hesitated. Amid the shifting, impersonal details of a campaign, so simple a question could take anyone off-guard. "Ah, well–things just feel queer, is all. It struck me that it's a year exactly since Gettysburg."

Breckinridge looked off. "By God. So it is."

"A whole year since . . . all of that. It's foolish but I can't help thinking about it. And there are other things–small things, I'll allow. A chaplain complained to me about those Indians attached to the cavalry."

"The Cherokee scouts? I'm told they're very good."

"Maybe so. But this fellow said some of them have scalps hanging from their saddles."

Whenever Breckinridge heard any bad utterance concerning Indians, protests mounted on his tongue. As a young lawyer in Iowa Territory, he had hunted buffalo with the Sauk and the Fox. He had learned to revere their ways, though he could only pity the degradation of some. "Well . . . Maybe it's true and maybe not. I'll look into it."

"And speaking of the cavalry, here's a strange one," said Gordon. "Some of McCausland's men were reconnoitering up Back Creek Road, just west of here, and they found a fancy carriage in a thicket. They pulled it out, figuring we could use it to haul feed or something–but when they looked inside, it was all smeared with dried blood. Blood and gore everywhere, McCausland told me."

Breckinridge made a face at the ground. "Huh! Who can imagine?"

"Didn't help McCausland's mood. The way Early treats him, his humor's bad enough."

"Old Jube does seem to have a bias concerning horsemen."

"As I have concerning Old Jube, unfortunately. Sorry to strain propriety here, Breck, but I figured you knew as much."

Breckinridge nodded. "I heard it went sour between the two of you at the Wilderness."

"Sour?" Gordon made a spitting noise. "You could say that, all right! He was my divisional commander and we were both under Ewell. I discovered the enemy's right flank was exposed and quickly reported it. Early refused to believe me and convinced Ewell not to attack. When that man's of a certain mind, Christ himself could not get a hearing!"

The sergeant returned with Breckinridge's horse and hitched it to a tree.

Though Breckinridge expressed disdain for gossip, he sometimes listened, and now he found himself pondering another tidbit about Early. He had heard it over a campfire at Cold Harbor. The tale went that as a recent West Point graduate, Early had one day come upon a carriage sinking in a flooded stream. Inside was a beautiful debutante from Philadelphia, who he promptly rescued and was deeply smitten with. But his desire suffered a hard death when she sent him a newspaper cutting, the announcement of her engagement to another man.

Over the past week, Breckinridge had observed his commander at odd moments–poring over maps, piping out orders, berating the scouts. It felt bizarre to know anything so private about such a man. With his unsparing eye, hunched shoulders and wolf-gray whiskers, Early did not seem to fit the story, even considering the effect of years. Then again, who could ever tell what a man's face and manner concealed?

After a quiet spell, Breckinridge spoke again. "Listen, John–I know he has a petty streak. I also know that you could lead this corps every bit as well as I can, if not better."

Gordon gave an embarrassed flip of his hand. "No, Breck–you were the worthiest choice. On my honor, I'm more than content with that."

Breckinridge ignored the modesty duel. "He can be unreasonable, I'm certain. But so can any number of able chiefs. And you have to concede his record of ability–even at the Wilderness, as I understand it. Jackson saw something in him and now Lee does."

Gordon gazed across the meadow. A cloud bank passed overhead, shadowing the tents and the swarm of gray-backed figures. "You won't catch me questioning Genr'l Lee's decision."

In the shade nearby, some officers of Gordon's staff were sharing cigars, glancing over at the two generals. Breckinridge hoped that he had not been speaking too loudly. He asked Gordon about his wife and children. Gordon replied and then asked the same. Just then one of Early's aides came riding up, saying that Early wanted to see Breckinridge at the mayor's house.

With the aide, Breckinridge rode back into Winchester, where Rodes' men were now passing through the tumult. The aide led the way to the mayor's home; leading citizens were gathered there to welcome Early and his subordinate commanders. The mayor, a wall-eyed little man, was jovial as he ushered Breckinridge to the parlor. There at a card table sat Early, hunched over a map and scribbling notes, a spittoon by his booted foot. On a stand beside him sat a bottle of whiskey with two empty glasses. The drapes were drawn but the wall lamps burned bright. Early's eyes sparkled as he looked up, chewing vigorously, his grizzled beard stained with tobacco juice. For that instant, he could have passed for the town lunatic.

"I cleared the room for us," he said. He spat, then motioned to the bottle. "Have a swallow, will you?"

"Mighty fine, Genr'l." Pulling up an elbow chair, Breckinridge tossed his hat aside and sat by Early. He poured himself a whiskey.

"The taste of the hills," Early said. "And something else–folks say it's your old blue-bellied friend Sigel commanding at Martinsburg."

Breckinridge sipped, smiled. "That's fair news. The way we were able to lick him at New Market, I'd say he's every bit as skittish as Hunter."

"Skittish Yankees and Shenandoah liquor–things do seem to be going our way. As for Harper's Ferry, the garrison's reportedly small, with a General Weber in charge. Another Dutchman–one of like temperament, we hope." Spitting out his chaw, Early missed the spittoon. Breckinridge pictured the mayor's descendants pointing out the hallowed carpet stain for visitors. "I got a dispatch from Lee," Early went on. "He says not to invade Maryland till all's in readiness. In my estimate, though, we'll be good and ready as soon as we take Martinsburg and the Ferry, provided we capture enough of the enemy stores."

Early tucked his pen and notes away. He downed the rest of his drink and poured another. "I've sent cavalry to wreck the rail bridges west of here–let's hope they manage it. Later we'll hit the Chesapeake & Ohio Canal. That way, Hunter's force won't be able to race after us once our backs are turned. To the east, for now, Mosby and other partisan ranger groups will keep us covered. Because tomorrow we move against Martinsburg."

With his index Early traced one line after another on the map. Above the town, he explained, cavalry would seal off the enemy's main escape route across the Potomac, while his own corps would block the route to Harper's Ferry. Breckinridge's would move straight toward Martinsburg, driving Yankee advance units before it. It was a plan worthy of Jackson– one that, if fully successful, would trap Sigel's estimated 10,000-man force. Eyeing Early's weathered brow, Breckinridge admired the brain within. Then he looked at the brown-stained whiskers. Against his will, the tale of the Philadelphia damsel intruded once more.

"With that accomplished," said Early, "straightaway we'll move on the Ferry–give 'em a Fourth of July they won't forget, eh? Then . . . " He stopped, noticing Breckinridge's gaze. "A question, Genr'l?"

Among his political gifts, Breckinridge retained that of the quick recovery. "No questions, Genr'l. I'll press the attack as hard as possible."

"Good, then." Early settled back with his whiskey glass. "We'll do Lee a service, all right. The faster and closer we get to Washington, the sooner Grant will be forced to draw troops from Petersburg. But that's only if he wakes up in time–and if he doesn't, heaven help the Yankee government. God-a-mighty, Breckinridge, we'll have ourselves one royal fandango!"

Breckinridge stared toward a window, a crack of sunlight between the drapes. He put on his most casual tone. "About that, Genr'l–should Providence take us so far, could an army this size possibly hold the city? For more than a day or two, I mean?"

"Hold it? No." Early took a belt from his glass, then wiped his mouth. "But treat yourself to these visions: the United States Treasury sacked, the Navy Yard torched, the warehouses burned or emptied, the federal arsenal blown to bits, the government buildings . . . " He chortled. "Abe Lincoln and his cabinet carted off to Richmond! Anyhow–general havoc wreaked upon them, as they've wreaked it upon us. And the world will sit up straight, Breckinridge. Yankee pride will take its worst beating yet. Enough, just maybe, to make them elect a Peace President and grant the Confederacy its due, at long last."

Breckinridge made himself nod. "At long last."

As sunlight burned red-gold between the drapes, Breckinridge pictured the spires of Washington. He saw them burning. In that haughty, disordered city he had endured trials and tasted pleasures. Studying the arts and the pitfalls of power, he had upheld Southern honor as the crisis mounted toward war. He had made friends, lost friends, grown older and left something of himself behind–some residue of spirit, still there. He felt a tightness in his jaw.

Then he blinked the flaming vision away. Pledged to the South and scarred by his pledge, he was a soldier now. Whatever he could honorably do to end the nightmare, he would do, or die trying. The North had caused him no end of sorrows. With a firm smile to Early, he tossed back the last of his whiskey.

55

Grounds Of Executive Mansion
July 4

JUST PAST THE long iron fence, passers-by paused to stare. For Flavius
Tucker as much as these gawkers, the day's spectacle was unprecedented.

Washington's established black community had turned out to make
the Fourth of July its own, thronging the wooded grounds between the
War Department and the Executive Mansion. Through the gates, carriages with gaily caparisoned horses were still arriving. Couples in their
best finery–sporting canes and parasols, high hats and flowered bonnets–
strolled arm-in-arm along the gravel walkways. Sunday school groups ate
picnic lunches on spread blankets. Children frolicked and chased each
other. Around the speaker's platform, groups of people conversed on
light or weighty subjects and drank lemonade. Throughout the crowd, a
sprinkling of white faces lent the most singular touch of all.

What was happening in the country? Where would it take people?
Here such questions arose from wonder, not dread, and Tucker felt as if
he had washed up on a magical island. Elsewhere in the city, celebrations
were strangely muted, though today marked even more than the nation's
birth. It was a year and a day since the gory triumph of Gettysburg, a year
precisely since Vicksburg's fall. But festooned with limp flags, Washington
as a whole seemed distracted–addled in the heat, hazy with summer
dust. Meanwhile, at Petersburg, Atlanta and a thousand other places,
the war lumbered on–victory still denied, the end as distant as ever. In

the newspapers, like an endless Biblical scroll, the black-bordered lists of Union dead kept unfurling.

Only in this sun-swept park could true celebration be found. Tucker remembered the words of the song– "No more for trader's gold/Will those we love be sold/ Nor crushed be manhood bold . . . " That was one hope, but here gaped a related one: that Emancipation would yield many more scenes like this.

Cass had introduced him to several people. Noting his patched and laundered uniform, black women curtsied and black men pumped his hand. They praised him, talked politics, commented on the progress of the war. But repeatedly his attention strayed across the wide, peopled lawn to the shade trees. There black children gathered flowers and sailed on swings, laughing and squealing; and there watching over them was the most beautiful and perhaps the most embattled woman he had ever met.

It was the first time that he had seen Sapphira happy. Resplendent in a white dress, she had her hair tied up in a blue bow. Tucker was glad that she had not spied him yet. For now he wanted to watch her as she pushed a little girl on a swing, helped a little boy who had fallen, shared a laugh with an older female attendant. Without shudder he could recall the moment of the minie ball's impact, then the sight of her above him in the church hospital. "Alive," he muttered. He felt buoyant, drunk on sunlight, happy in a way that threatened to leave him voiceless. But the feeling lasted only seconds. There were conversations at hand. Entangled again, he saw the staid Cass before him and felt a rueful unease. The minister's fondness for Sapphira was plain enough, however subdued. Beside Cass stood a white Abolitionist preacher with bushy sideburns and a benign smile. Tucker had already forgotten his name.

"And you came back to volunteer," the man said. "Most commend-able! Sergeant, I cannot tell you how it feels to see our work's fruition."

Along with the comment, there was something in the man's demeanor that nettled Tucker. A kind of pleasureful self-regard, as from an inventor admiring his own invention. Tucker gulped his lemonade.

"Strange, about Canada," said the white preacher. "It has provided haven for escaped slaves, but now too for Rebel spies and agitators."

Fending off boredom, Tucker responded with a rush of words. "Well, sir, that only reflects their British rulers. From the start, British sympathies have been pretty well split. But I do think England and also France will stay neutral, simply because it's their safest path."

From the man's expression, Tucker could not tell if he was impressed with the comment or taken aback. "Yes, well–one would hope they would have moral qualms besides, to keep them from ever backing the South."

"We would wish so, sir. But governments take practicality as their guide, as people generally do. They consider moral qualms too costly. I therefore think that our goal should be to make their absence costlier, by somehow joining it to the practical. Look at the Emancipation itself. Only when it fit Union war aims did Lincoln proclaim it, and even then it didn't touch those slaves in the neutral border states and occupied areas. At any rate, it's only when a great ideal becomes practical that it gets let out of its cage, to be stroked and petted awhile. It's only then that leaders pull out those grand gospel phrases." Catching himself, Tucker saw how the preacher's smile had faded. "Of course, from all of this I except good men like yourself, who've stood for what's right all along."

The man's features relaxed a bit, though his pleasureful air was gone. He swabbed his brow with a handkerchief. "Lincoln was lamentably slow with his decree."

Cass had seemed content to just listen, but to Tucker's relief he now joined in. "But that tardiness does not necessarily mirror the man's heart. Cold practicality may rule as you say, Sergeant, with so many self-interested parties involved. But cannot strong, true sentiments lie beneath it, waiting for release? And cannot new ones take root over time? This war has worked changes on all of us and will doubtless work more, not least upon the President." Turning to his white acquaintance, Cass gave one of his half-smiles. He gestured to the activities around them. "And lest we forget–he and Mrs. Lincoln did grant us use of these grounds."

The man gave a forced chuckle. "Oh, I'll give them that. Especially since next summer, they may not be here to dispense such kindness. Whatever my reservations about the President, I shudder to think who his replacement might be. And what it could mean for our cause."

"I'll echo you there, sir," said Tucker. "Congress has adjourned, but I read that the Copperhead faction is meeting somewhere, sharpening their knives for autumn. Some editorials sound as if Lincoln's whipped already."

The man nodded grimly. Then, switching tone, he remarked on the success of the day's event. Admission fees would help finance the construction of a permanent school for freedmen's children. "The next stage in the uplifting of your race–most auspicious!" Half-listening, Tucker peered toward the trees. With a little girl in her lap, Sapphira rocked gently on one of the swings.

The white minister looked at his pocket watch, remarking that he was due to speak shortly. He left to look over his notes.

Alone with Cass again, Tucker sighed. "Pardon my getting windy there."

"If you did, Sergeant, I'd say it bodes well for your continuing recovery."

Out of reflex, Tucker touched the patch on his jacket. He was in fact breathing and feeling better. Soon, once sufficiently recovered, he would report to the Bureau of Colored Troops. Again he looked toward the swings but did not see Sapphira.

"Truth be told," Cass said, "just now I was thinking you'd do well as a public speaker."

Though flattered, Tucker shook his head. "I'm no orator, Reverend."

"Neither was our Miss Sapphira, but you ought to hear her nowadays."

Tucker looked at his cup and jiggled it, swirling the lemonade. "In Montreal some years ago, there was a newspaper article about my restaurant, and it mentioned my humble beginnings. An Abolitionist chapter in Vermont read the story and wrote to me. In time I was persuaded to cross the border and address one of their meetings. I was reluctant–the idea of an audience scared me near as much as any slave-catcher did. But some part of me wanted to do it. I'd subscribed to *The Liberator* and read the writings of Frederick Douglass and had developed a few notions of my own. So off I went and got a warm reception–I was preaching to the converted, after all. But afterward the chapter president took me aside and said, 'Stick to the plantation horrors–leave the philosophy to us.' He also advised me to toss in some 'slave dialect,' as it was more affecting . . . " Tucker spied Sapphira. Wandering through the crowd, she was headed in his and Cass's general direction. Her white dress flowed. "A better man might not have been so vexed," he went on. "But right then I decided my first speech would be my last. To such an audience, anyhow."

Cass nodded. "Well, you're doing enough already. As a soldier."

Like fingertips along his limbs, Tucker felt Sapphira's approach. "If I haven't said it lately, Mister Cass–thank you. For opening your home to me, and for everything else."

A woman with a tray came by and they gave her their cups.

"I am glad for the means to help," said Cass. "Well–time for me to give Reverend Ames his introduction." The half-smile appeared. "And here comes Miss Sapphira. Why don't you get her a lemonade?"

In a tongue-tied instant, as the minister strode away, Tucker grasped the true extent of Cass's generosity. He turned and saw Sapphira gliding toward him. She smiled, though their gazes failed to meet.

"Hello, Sergeant."

He doffed his cap. "Miss Sapphira, could I get you some refreshment? You did the same for me, as I recall."

"True, I did. But thank you, I'm not thirsty at the moment."

She surveyed the goings-on and Tucker did likewise. Through a gap in the trees he saw the White House gardens in bloom, a few small outbuildings and then the mansion itself. "I wonder if the Lincolns will pay us a visit," he said.

"That would be a crowning touch," said Sapphira. "But I'm told they often stay at their cottage near the Soldier's Home, to escape the heat."

"No matter–it's a fine start for the school. And once it's built, you'll have a teaching position if you want it."

To his dismay, her lovely face turned pensive. "That could be."

Together among the wounded at Cass's church, they had sometimes conversed with ease, though never for long. But with no immediate task to occupy her, Sapphira seemed blurred and abstracted. Tucker's own mood suddenly fell. He wondered if his feelings were as visible to her as they apparently were to Cass, and if they worried her. Still, he recalled those moments when their eyes had not only met but lingered, each time as one or the other was leaving.

"Do you feel well today?" she asked.

"The walks have helped. Soon I'll be my old self, I reckon."

She cast a blank look to the crowd. "And then you'll be returning to your regiment."

He tried to gauge the regret in her voice. "Yes."

Still looking away, she gave a slight nod. "Ben has described you as a model soldier."

Cass had mounted the speaker's platform. In his oaken voice, he began the introduction.

"A model soldier?" said Tucker. "My lieutenant is generous, but I can't agree. I don't feel born to the uniform. I have no trouble remembering the pleasures of life before rifles and drill. I'd rather be back in Montreal, at my restaurant."

"Well, now that I think of it," said Sapphira, "Ben's no model himself. He'd sooner be drawing pictures or collecting rocks."

As Cass quit the platform, the smiling Reverend Ames stepped up. Sapphira clapped a little, Tucker less.

"My friends!" the preacher boomed. "On this most wondrous occasion—the celebration of liberty's march, of cherished hopes abounding—I cannot but think of God's infinite grace . . . "

Tucker gazed idly toward the Avenue, along the iron fence with its white onlookers. Outside the open gate he spied a group of colored men staring in, dressed in rags and straw hats. He looked back at Sapphira, his eyes catching on the smooth line of her neck. "Mister Cass . . . tells me you're a first-rate speaker yourself."

She glanced at him. "Only compared to what I was." Her response seemed to end there. Then, with a stoniness that startled him, she went on. "My fate was pure mercy compared to others'—compared to your own, Sergeant. Yet in two weeks I'll go up to Philadelphia and speak to an Abolition group there—and as always, I will describe for them how an orphaned slave child was plucked from the clutches of evil. I'll receive their applause and solicitation. Then, I assure you, I will feel like running and not walking out the door. I don't expect this makes sense—but I tell you, I dread this engagement as much as I did my first, though for different reasons."

As Tucker beheld her, the minister's speech became a senseless yammering in his ears. "You can compare your fate with mine or any other," he spoke. "I'd wager that little has come to you easily."

She looked at the ground.

"Miss Sapphira, would you like to go to the fireworks with me tonight?"

Her smile flickered up. "I would like to very much. But Anna's going there herself with Lieutenant Chadwick. She's looking after Ben right now, and tonight will be my turn."

Hiding his disappointment, Tucker nodded. "Well . . . He'll be in the best of hands."

Ames was offering more hosannas to freedom. "So it is with brave hope—nay, with brave certainty—that we advance our mission, though the land runs red, toward a completion which will glorify our Holy Master!"

Tucker turned his head, staring toward the ragged black men by the gate. In his side-vision he saw Sapphira look at him and then follow his gaze.

"New arrivals from Virginia," he said.

It had been a good while, he reflected, since he had last been forced to think about it. Sapphira seemed to read his thoughts.

"And just a few days ago, they could be bought and sold," she muttered.

"Yes," he said. "Owned and stored and used, like a horse or a hammer. Say whatever you might–when you step back and truly behold it, it's just so peculiar."

Ames' speech rolled on. From the sidewalk, the men stared like apparitions, dark beings conjured in the heat.

"Would you excuse me?" Sapphira said.

"Certainly."

Brooding, Tucker watched her disappear into the crowd.

Ames' oration was winding down. Tucker saw Cass with a group of convalescent privates from the church. He supposed that he should go and mingle with them. He headed toward them but halted halfway there, catching sight of Sapphira. Moving through the crowd, she was carrying a tray of lemonades toward the straw-hatted freedmen. He watched them stir and gape as she neared, an emissary from the dream before them.

<hr />

THROUGH THE BARS of the fence, Truly observed the celebration for a good while before he noticed the motley black men doing the same. They stood a few yards to his left, seven or eight of them. Their baggy pants were streaked with grime, their shirts little more than shredded cotton. He looked at them, then back at the festivities–the decorous families of barbers and hackmen, stonemasons and domestic servants. It struck him that despite peasant revolts and wars of independence, it somehow always came down to high hats and straw hats. Once the last cannon of this war had sounded, much would be changed forever–but not this. Not the fact of high hats and straw hats, of bare feet and polished shoes, rough cotton and smooth silk. On this day celebrating freedom, America's newest bastard sons were free indeed–free to stand idle at the curb and spellbound at the gate, invisible to the closed, sunny kingdom within.

With an expression of waking, one of the refugees removed his hat and nudged the man beside him, who followed suit. Truly looked where they were gazing and saw Sapphira, coming toward them with a tray full of drinks. He raised a hand and took a breath to call but stopped himself. He eyed her careful step, the tray in her careful hands. She gave a muted smile as she reached the men, her white dress mingling with their rags of dyed butternut. Taking their drinks, some grinned while others kept their eyes down. Truly strained to hear. She called them "gentlemen," wished them well, gave them directions to the Freedman's Aid Society. In eager chorus they said, "Thank you Miss" and guzzled their lemonade.

Truly's eyes followed her back across the lawn. Rachel would have done the same, he thought. Rachel would have seen them too, from the distance. And as the blustery speech ended to a wash of applause, he wondered what cheers would ever sound for an auction-block child, grown to this gift of sightfulness. His gaze drifted to the shade trees, where Negro children swung on swings and chased each other. Loving their clumsy grace, he thought of the hardscrabble years when Ben, Anna and Sapphira were small. There were any number of images, but what came to him now was less an image than a mere impression. An impression of performing some sitting task, mending harness or sharpening a blade, while Ben stood quietly at his side. A small, watchful presence and then a soft weight against him–thoughtless, still intent, resting as on a fence post. Had he told Ben to stop leaning on him? He hoped not. He hoped that he had gone on with the task, letting himself be trusted without thought, like a fence post.

"So this is Independence Day. Incredible."

The male voice came from behind. Hoping that it was not addressing him, Truly concentrated on the swings, lazy pendulums in the distance.

"Next they'll be inside the place," said another man, "dancing on the furniture with their pickaninnies."

"Block the gates, I say. Pen 'em in, along with the lunatic who's responsible."

Truly turned around and viewed the pair, topcoated gents with neat beards. But his attention was immediately diverted. In a passing barouche he recognized the amiable young face of Sam Finch, a War Department telegrapher. The carriage turned in toward the gate. Truly looked away, but Finch had glimpsed him.

"Major Truly!"

Truly sighed. He had risked such an encounter by wandering here. "Hello there, Sam."

Finch's colored driver had stopped the carriage in mid-turn. Truly headed for it, shoving between the two churlish commentators. They huffed in his wake. Finch was seated amid cumbersome gear of some sort–a tripod, covered boxes and a large travel trunk.

"What mischief are you up to?" Truly asked.

Finch patted a boxlike object on the seat beside him. "Making group photographs." Truly noticed the object's cylindrical snout and realized it was a camera, wrapped in black cloth. "I've done this for years as a hobby," Finch said, "and my uncle asked the favor–he's with Freedman's Aid. And what brings you, Major?"

"Idle curiosity. Plus I know a few of the folks here."

"Well, then–do hop in."

"I don't have a ticket."

"No matter." Finch grinned. "You can be my assistant."

Looking toward the spectacle, Truly shrugged. "Well, it's high time I found honest work."

Finch moved over, placing the camera at his feet. Truly wedged in beside him and they headed down the driveway.

"So how's life for you brass-pounders over there?" Truly asked.

"Frantic, generally. The President still stops by on occasion–we enjoy his yarns and he seems to enjoy our company. How about yourself, Major?"

"Been out of town on assignment. And by the way–you haven't seen me."

"Ducking Colonel Baker, are you?"

"I have bodacious reasons for it, believe me."

"Fear not, then."

Finch had the driver halt beneath a lone tree, where they began to carefully unload. Shedding his coat and rolling his sleeves up, Finch opened his big trunk. Out of it he erected a canvas-draped structure on collapsible legs. Recalling Wakefield's identical contraption at Cold Harbor, Truly asked what it was. "Portable dark-tent," Finch said. "With this, a photographer can prepare and develop his plates in the field." Taking the lid off one box, Finch started removing trays, dishes and labeled jugs. "I'm doing just one exposure per group, no more. Major Eckert said he couldn't spare me for long."

"Are things flaring up again at Petersburg?"

"Not there. We're getting reports of . . . "

"Father!"

Truly looked up and saw Sapphira hurrying toward him. Sending her a drowsy smirk, he excused himself and ambled out to meet her. Even before her arm slipped around his and they strolled toward the crowd, he felt looks and stares multiplying–some startled and questioning, others hostile, not all of them from beyond the fence. Her arm began to slide away but he caught it, holding it briefly to his side before letting go.

"Well, this is a happy shock," she said. "It's as if you dropped out of the sky."

"No such sorcery, child–my friend smuggled me in. You look right pretty, I must say."

She smiled at her feet. "Thank you. And how . . . " Looking up, she lowered her voice. "How did you fare in Port Tobacco?"

"Quite well, actually. I . . . " He caught himself. Sapphira was relishing her scrap of inside information–and in the rich brown of her eyes, he saw greed for more. This had to stop. "It went fine," he said.

He had posed as a Rebel courier needing to get to Richmond. The trusting postmaster had agreed to ferry him across and Truly had netted him, along with a boatload of quinine and illicit mail. Rather than place his prisoner at the Old Capitol (apprising William Wood of his return to Washington would have amounted to telling Baker) he had traveled to Annapolis and jailed the man there.

He and Sapphira paused just short of the crowd. He asked about Ben's progress and she told him. Truly noticed Tucker not far away, pushing a small boy on a swing. Then Cass appeared out of the multitude, greeting Truly with a handshake and a cup of lemonade. Truly gratefully accepted the drink. Cass left to confer with Finch, who had set the camera on its tripod and was busy with preparations. The camera's presence sent a stir through the crowd as buttons were buttoned, hats and bonnets straightened and children assembled in tidy ranks.

Tucker eventually walked up, his jacket slung over his shoulder. He was winded, coughing as he shook Truly's hand.

"You exerted yourself too soon," Sapphira scolded him.

"Young 'uns do that to you regardless," Truly said.

As the sergeant wheezed, Sapphira's hand made a tentative move toward him but then dropped, just brushing his elbow.

Cass reappeared. "Our group's first. Major, why don't you join us?"

"My homely heathen mug, stuck in this pretty sea of piety? No thank you, Reverend."

"Please," said Sapphira. "It's a special day."

Truly sighed.

Sapphira helped Tucker get his jacket on. As the four of them neared the still-forming group, Truly slowed his step, falling in with Cass so that Sapphira and Tucker were first to reach the back row. There they all took their places, side by side. Colored ladies fanned themselves, hushing fidgety children in front. In the near distance, Finch emerged from his little dark-tent and proceeded to the camera, carrying a photographic plate-holder which he then loaded into a slot in the camera's side. Unscrewing the lens cover, he paused to squint at his subjects. Then he burrowed under the black hood behind the viewfinder, one hand adjusting a little knob. Repeatedly he poked his head up, taking stock of the elegant assembly before ducking back under the hood.

Truly peered sidelong at Sapphira's smooth profile, then beyond it at Tucker's rugged one. Sapphira made some comment about how good the children were being. Tucker coughed, nodding agreement. The sun beat down.

Finally Finch hunched beneath the hood one more time while covering the lens with his hat. "Hold still, everyone!" Fans and children went motionless. Finch pulled the thin black panel from the camera's side, then took his hat away. After a few seconds' exposure, he again covered the lens and slid the panel back in. "Thank you!" he called.

In a burst of relieved chatter, the group broke up as another one started gathering.

"There," said Sapphira. "Painless."

"Compared to a branding iron," said Truly, his mind already moving on. From his coat pocket he took the scrap of paper that Duke had given him. He eyed the penciled street address.

"Another errand, Father?"

And there she was, peering over his elbow. Amazed and annoyed, he tucked the paper away. "Oh yes, child–I'm off to give Jeff Davis a good slap."

Her expression bordered on petulant as he took his leave.

From the concession stand Truly fetched a cup of lemonade for Finch, who looked a bit wilted. Thanking him, the telegrapher gulped the drink.

"I must resign as your assistant," Truly said. "The day's getting on."

"That's all right," said Finch. "There's no shortage of help here."

"Quickly, though—what was it you were saying about the wire reports? I haven't seen a newspaper since Friday."

"No? Well—first off, there's been raiding in the northern Shenandoah. Burnt bridges, torn tracks, some lines cut. And Sigel's evacuated Martinsburg."

Truly stared. "What?"

"He withdrew his whole force across the Potomac. Now he's holed up on Maryland Heights, convinced that he's facing superior numbers. But you know poor Sigel's reputation. Matter of fact, there's talk of replacing him." Setting his cup on the grass, Finch got a new glass plate from his boxful and turned to his dark-tent. "Stanton's skeptical and so is General Halleck. They seem to think it's just a cavalry raid, or some frisky partisans. Excuse me, Major."

Finch's upper half vanished within the canvas folds. Truly waited, thinking. Under the little tent, fluid dripped from a vertical pipe into a bucket. At length Finch emerged, wiping his hands with a rag.

"But Sam," said Truly, "—at Lynchburg two weeks ago, General Hunter also thought he was outnumbered. Enough for him to beat it into West Virginia and leave the Valley open."

The next group was almost ready. "That's so," said Finch. "But Hunter's no Hannibal either."

"But what if he was right? And what if Sigel's right? If we've somehow failed to detect a major Rebel detachment out there, with little to oppose it . . . "

"Not a pleasant prospect, I'll allow."

Fitting his hat on, Truly looked at the trim phalanx of colored people, all waiting in their Sunday best. "I'll be off, then. Happy Fourth."

Finch did not hear him, having ducked back into his enclosure.

Truly started away but then halted in mid-stride, looking back. Cradling a plateholder, Finch backed out of the tent.

"Sam—what about Harper's Ferry?"

"Harper's? . . . Oh, yes—that's the latest." Finch moved toward his camera. "About two hours ago, their telegraph went dead."

56

Treasury Building

NEGLECTING TO KNOCK, Forbes startled Duke nearly out of his chair.

"Captain!" Duke exclaimed, gripping the desk.

Forbes shut the door. "Your pardon, Octavius."

Gladdened, Duke gathered the papers he had dropped. "Sir, what brings you back?"

"I'm looking for . . . " Atop the cabinet Forbes spied a food basket, its contents half-eaten. "Not to be rude, but are you done with that?"

Duke fetched the basket and presented it. "Finish it off, sir."

"Thank you." Forbes had scarcely eaten anything today. Without a trace of Beacon Hill decorum, he dropped into the desk-side chair and started devouring a slab of corncake.

Seated beside him, Duke turned glum. "Haven't been eating much, myself. Not since Manfred."

Forbes tried to recall what it was like, to have so little experience of violent death. Still, the thought of Kirschenbaum halved his appetite, and he finished the corncake in silence. Duke adjusted his specs, then gave Forbes one of his sudden attentive smiles. Brushing crumbs from his lap, Forbes realized that Duke had never before seen him in uniform. Earlier, at the Truly home, lovely Anna had registered no such effect; she had simply stated that as far as she knew, her father was still in Port Tobacco. Anna, Anna . . .

Forbes cleared his throat. "Well, Octavius, I was hoping you'd be here. Would you know when Truly might return to Washington?"

"Why–he already has, Captain."

Forbes sat up.

"As a matter of fact, he gave me an even bigger scare–poked his head in the window, maybe two hours ago. Just before leaving the city, he'd asked me to find out Quentin Archer's home address, so I'd gotten it from a police contact. I gave it to the major and he left."

Forbes frowned. "Archer's address . . . ?"

"He didn't say why. He asked if I thought it likely that Archer would be home today, and I told him no. Given the unruliness of the holiday, the police should be out in force, including the Detective Corps."

Taking his hat off, Forbes thumbed the brim. "I suspect our friend's indulging in some more calculated risk." Duke's myopic hazel eyes turned reflective. Looking at him, Forbes was surprised to feel a weary gratitude. Gentle souls were hard to come by.

Forbes' departure for the front had come so swiftly upon Kirschenbaum's murder, it was as if the killing itself had catapulted him back to that world of guns, filth and protocol. Assigned to interrogations, he had lost himself in that decidedly un-Christian duty–probing Rebel deserters, tricking and browbeating Rebel prisoners. Over three relentless days he had worked upon those dirty, half-crushed men with twangy accents–foiling evasion, angling past defiance, targeting fatigue, naivete and stupidity. Then, on the third day–a breakthrough. A troubling one.

"Well, you asked why I'm back," he said. "First of all–do you remember the recent battle at Lynchburg, after which General Hunter retreated west?"

"Certainly," said Duke. "The major and I have discussed it. There was word that Breckinridge had two brigades or so at Lynchburg, not enough to explain Hunter's turnabout."

"Right. All the same, we'd heard nothing more to indicate Rebel reinforcements in that area. Nothing, that is, until a few days after the fight."

Forbes explained how a Petersburg prisoner revealed the departure of Jubal Early's corps, about a week previous. The Information Bureau's failure to detect such a movement seemed unlikely, until Colonel Sharpe realized that Early might have benefited from coincidence. Just before Early pulled out, Lee would certainly have tightened his pickets–to keep enemy scouts at a distance, and deserters out of enemy hands. It was a standard precaution. In fact, whenever Lee had done this in the past, it alerted the Bureau that he was up to something big. But in this instance, at the same time, Grant had tightened his own pickets to conceal his march against Petersburg. The opposing armies would therefore have been blind to each other's movement.

"We do have a liaison officer with Hunter's force," Forbes said. "But with all the partisan activity in the Shenandoah, he's been unable to get a message through. So we were left with the word of a single prisoner—and even then, who could say if Early hadn't since rejoined Lee's army? We had to get corroboration, plus some fresher intelligence.

"When I returned to the front last week, there was a new influx of prisoners from the Petersburg lines; I had an operative pose as one of them and then report their small talk. He heard one mention a brother who was with the famous Stonewall Brigade—part of Early's corps, the Second. The fellow wondered aloud how his brother was faring, that brigade having gone west in mid-June. This spurred me to question a newer captive, a talkative boy who we'd placed in solitary to make him chattier. His regiment had been positioned near the Second, and with minimal trickery I got what seemed to be confirmation—not just of Early's departure, but of his continued absence. Now come these reports of havoc in the northern Shenandoah. Martinsburg and maybe even Harper's Ferry have been abandoned, their commanders both claiming a major enemy presence in the area."

"Then the deception's ended!" said Duke. "Surely we're moving to meet the threat?"

Forbes shook his head. "You'd have to know the federal army. Received wisdom is hard enough to overthrow in civilian life, but in the military it's harder still. This information of ours contradicts the official view, and the official view is that the people of the North are safe and sound. To think otherwise is to admit poor planning, poor vigilance and worse danger. And that Lee's fooled us yet again, in grand style. What's more, the fears of our generals out that way—Hunter, Sigel, Weber—are easily discounted. They're thought to be of questionable nerve.

"Grant said he'd welcome further news on the subject—but given the stalemate at Petersburg, he'll take no major step until stronger evidence comes along. Still, Colonel Sharpe decided to go a bit farther, lest anyone call him derelict later on. On occasion he has sent a Bureau officer up here to meet with the Secretary of War and the Chief of Staff, to give them a broad view of current intelligence. This time I got that duty, with instructions to mention Jubal Early. I also brought along three hand-picked scouts to send into western Maryland."

Forbes described his morning meeting with Stanton and Halleck. On the subject of Early, Stanton had reacted as if to a joke he considered crude. Believing like Grant that it was a minor cavalry raid, he had asked the governors of Pennsylvania and New York to call up their militias—but that was all. Halleck, for his part, had seemed confused and irritable.

On Duke's pudgy face, real worry showed. "Isn't anything being done?"

Forbes took a plum from the basket. "Halleck's sending a detachment of Washington troops to reinforce Sigel—a mistake, to my mind, since that will strip the city's defenses even more. Fortunately, he's also agreed to a separate reconnaissance mission. Tomorrow some Illinois cavalry will move toward Point of Rocks, northwestward, and two of my scouts will accompany them. The other scout's going with Sigel's relief force." Chewing, he spat the plum pit out the window. "If our fears are correct, then Washington's as vulnerable as a babe. Baltimore, too. I'll be taking stock of things in both cities, along with whatever the scouts wire back to me." Forbes shifted his leg, then glanced at the shelf clock. "Point of fact, I'm headed to Baltimore this evening. Do you know if the trains are running?"

Subdued, Duke took a moment to answer. "I'm not sure."

"Well, I'll find out. So what about you, then? How've you been occupying yourself?"

Duke indicated a pile of fat, discolored envelopes on the desk. When he had gone digging for Jonathan Peavey's file, he said, he realized he had fallen behind on organization. So he was putting the files in order. Forbes nodded absently. The mention of Peavey had jarred him, calling to mind all the other corpses.

Truly would not give up—that was certain—and perhaps he could somehow untangle these questions on his own. More likely, though, the tangle would remain. More likely the questions would persist like phantom pains, gnawing at both of them for the rest of their lives. On Forbes' way back to the front, he had written and re-written his report about La Maison, which Colonel Sharpe had then read with disquieted interest. Yet the essential mission of the Military Information Bureau lay on a higher, more anonymous plane—in the discernment of enemy troop movements, not of sordid little doings on the home front.

"When you see the major next," said Forbes, "please tell him I'm staying at Markham's boarding house. My official duties come first, of course, but I'll help him if I can."

"I'll tell him, Captain."

Forbes tugged his hat on. "Keep up the good work."

"Thank you, sir. But, you know . . . " Duke sighed. "I have to question what all this paper-shuffling's worth. Sometimes, Captain, I long to know the war as you've known it. The real fight. Out there, a man can see and feel what his sweat's buying, and there's the chance to test his courage." He managed a philosophical smirk. "Still . . . I guess we each have our place."

For Forbes it was as if a warm bubble had popped, leaving him cold and queasy. He contemplated the clerk's name–Octavius Duke; majestic as a coat-of-arms, it seemed ludicrous attached to such a fellow. Duke was like too many deskbound little men. Gorged on martial reveries, they lamented war in the specific while worshipping it in the abstract. Forbes wished that every one of them could be locked in a room with Matthew Brady's battlefield photographs, all those portraits of the dead. Yet that would not be enough. Only the actual experience could cure them, and this they would never have–because they had to be kept at their desks.

Forbes got to his feet. "I'll be off, then."

"Good luck to you, sir."

Turning, Forbes glimpsed the pile of fat envelopes. Then he froze, staring at them. "Octavius–about Peavey's file . . . "

"Yes, Captain?"

"For that brief period of surveillance in '62, it recorded visitors to his estate, including Wakefield. But there was also . . . some Frenchman?"

"Gaston Saint-Felix, you mean. The slave trader turned blockade runner, currently imprisoned."

"Where, again?"

Duke peered up in puzzlement. "Baltimore, sir. At Fort McHenry."

Forbes blinked, lost in thought. Abruptly, he leaned down and clapped Duke on the shoulder. "Octavius, you're a good man!" Then he exited, leaving the clerk to wonder.

57

North Washington

LOCATED NEAR THE corner of North M and West Eighth, Archer's was one of several small, respectable dwellings in this tract. They were probably among the first built here, before the wartime surge of development. Now dingy tenements overshadowed them like a ruffian gang. Children played and squabbled in the dusty street, some of them clutching little Union flags or streamers. A haggard woman dumped a slop bucket in the gutter. Archer would likely move elsewhere, Truly thought, should his Chief of Detectives title become permanent.

Truly passed once to make sure of the address. The house was of the two-story saltbox type, brown with green shutters. Like its next-door neighbors, its rear bordered a wood lot where some boys were playing war. Using sticks for rifles, they yelled, crouched and fired from behind the stacked timber. With watchful neighbors in mind, Truly moved to defuse suspicion. He knocked on the door of the right-hand house. No one was in, so he went to the left-hand one, where he was answered by a wizened old man.

"Pardon me, sir," said Truly. "Could you tell me if this is N Street? N as in Nicholas?"

"M Street," the codger replied. "M, as in Mistaken."

"Oh! So if I cut through the wood lot here, I'd be on the right street?"

"You've sorted it out, young fellow."

"Thank you. Happy Fourth."

Having established himself as more lost than sinister, Truly cut around the house, then over to the rear of Archer's. There, near the lot's edge, a conveniently placed privy hid him from the boys, who in any case sounded too engrossed in battle–"Pow! Got you, Willy!"–"You didn't!"–"Did! Right in the head!"

Unsurprisingly in this heat, a window by the back door had been left open. With a final check to all sides, Truly moved to the window and hunkered there, hands cupped to his mouth. "Hello!" he called, ready to bolt. "Archer!" There was no sound. He tried the door and it was locked. Returning to the window, he raised the sash higher and hoisted himself through.

He rolled onto the floor and, rising, found himself in the kitchen. It felt good, violating the privacy of Kirschenbaum's murderer–and if he found what he wanted, that would feel better still. At the same time, he had to steel himself. Often, in this line of work, he had rifled through other men's possessions. A fellow's wash stand, tooth powder and feather pillows bespoke a frail humanity, whatever his crime–but on this occasion, such reminders would be unwelcome. Whatever Truly saw or touched here, he would cling to the image of Archer with his pistol, of Archer sneering, of Kirschenbaum's crumpled form.

The parlor's decor was spare, featuring walnut furniture, a fine carpet and a print of the Crucifixion. On a stand lay a heavy old Bible open to First Corinthians. The dining room proved even more austere, its table unadorned. Above the fireplace was a clock, a rural landscape and a pair of candles. No sentimental objects, none of the bric-a-brac clutter seen in so many homes, including Truly's. And no photographs. Even the wallpaper with its styled brown medallions looked faded and somber. This stark aspect should perhaps have been no surprise, given the fate of Archer's wife–but a daughter had lived here too, and there was no obvious trace of her.

In Archer's shadowy bedroom Truly found a single bed, a chest of drawers and a closet full of plain-colored clothes. He wondered what man would voluntarily awake to so barren a chamber, day after day. Entering another room, he found it empty except for a bed frame, its floor dusty. He went back downstairs and discovered a cramped study off the dining room. A scrolled mahogany desk with a wing chair faced a large, tacked-up chart of the District. To the left, a window looked out on the wood lot.

He moved to sit at the desk and start rummaging, but it was then he saw what he had come for.

In its pewter frame, Archer's portrait sat atop a bookcase. He was posed at an angle, wearing the badge and double-breasted frock coat of a police sergeant. His straight hat and dour lawman's gaze sealed the look, which befit the graceful inscription beneath it: "To Quentin Archer, servant of God and soldier of Law, with highest esteem, Miles Wakefield, March '62." Truly lay the photograph on the blotter and sat, marveling at the emotional logic of it. Mere flattery would probably have been wasted on Archer, himself a skilled practitioner of lip service. But Wakefield catered to more than vanity. Picking out a cherished dream that each man had of himself, Wakefield had then affirmed it, not just in words but with a permanent image. This more than anything had let him play the fawning friend, even to one as lone and grim as Archer.

By the unlit lamp in front of him, Truly suddenly noticed another photograph, this one in a varnished wooden frame. It was not of Archer's daughter or late wife but a row of young policemen, strong and erect on the steps of a stone building. With some scrutiny, Truly identified a younger Archer near the middle, sporting a full black mustache. "First Precinct, Philadelphia 1850," was lettered in one corner.

The volumes in the bookcase were mostly legal and religious. Looking out the window, Truly saw the boys still at war, two of them pretending to bayonet a third who writhed on the ground. In the desk Truly found a few police reports and some minor official correspondence, but nothing personal until he checked the last drawer. There he found a green volume that proved to be a scrapbook, half-filled with newspaper articles dating back to Philadelphia. He perused the most recent articles, all of them small: in January, Archer's arrest of a high-living forger "at a gentlemen's club known as the Emperor's House"; in March, two items on his breakup of the Center Market thieves' ring; in April, his award of a merit citation; in May, the illness of Detective Chief Clarvoe and Archer's temporary appointment.

Closing the scrapbook, Truly started to put it back. Then he noticed a magazine in the drawer. Its yellow cover featured a plump, cherry-lipped woman in a gossamer skirt, her breasts barely concealed by dark cascading hair. Above her reclining form, fancy letters proclaimed, "SINS OF THE ANCIENTS." Truly began leafing through it. The crude illustrations depicted one tumultuous carnal scene after another: Egyptian overseers whipping nubile maidens, Roman centurions raping fur-clad Gallic women, a Mongol chieftain being orally serviced by one of his harem. Captions provided explicit if ungrammatical commentary, all in a tone of revilement. Eyeing an Inca woman in the grip of a conquistador, Truly considered penning "Hello Archer" across her wide buttocks, then thought better of it. Mildly feverish, he placed the magazine back beneath the scrapbook and closed the drawer. He could dawdle no longer.

He picked up the portrait and left the study. As he passed the fireplace, he glimpsed something–a fragment of white among the ashes–and halted. Crouching at the hearth, he spied it behind a charred log and plucked it out. It was the remnant of an envelope, apparently tossed in when the fire was low. Despite smudging, most of the return address was visible: Miss Cecelia Archer, care of the American Missionary Association, at some plantation on St. Simon's Island, Georgia. Archer's daughter, the teacher of freedmen–the faithful one, who had visited her mother at the asylum while her father stayed away. Truly returned the seared wafer to the ashes.

With the grace of a crab, he climbed out the window, then pulled the sash down to its original level before striding away. In the wood lot, to his puzzlement, he came upon the boys' discarded stick-guns. He emerged onto N Street and turned left. It was a good distance back to the omnibus stop. The lurid magazine articles dogged his mind, and to banish them he thought of the photograph in his hand. He wondered how soon Archer the Preacher would notice it gone. If he achieved some break in the case, if he could kindle any sort of official interest, the portrait would help establish Archer's link to Wakefield. But for now, his act of burglary meant little in the way of real progress. What could he do next?

The question hit him squarely: What next? In his few days at Port Tobacco, he had been absorbed with making an arrest and getting back to Washington. Now he realized how lost he was–long on will, short on ideas. He missed Forbes and he cursed Baker. Discouragement slowed his walk. Then, from his rubble of thought, an idea rose to hearten him just enough. In La Maison's eight-year history, many girls and women had lived and worked there and then moved on. Ravenel herself had mentioned sending each one off with best wishes and a little pocket money. Many had no doubt continued their trade elsewhere, perhaps in some of the 450 other known brothels in the District. Limiting his search to the upscale places, Truly might track down a graduate of the Emperor's House and learn something important from her, maybe even the lieutenant-colonel's name. As he envisioned this quest from one flesh parlor to the next, the magazine images stirred anew. He resumed walking, trying to drive them out. Abruptly a smell did it for him—the smell of smoke.

Gazing down to the corner of West Tenth, he saw a tenement burning as a sizeable crowd looked on. Black smoke billowed from the second story windows. Drawing near, he spied the wood lot boys in the crowd, hopping and jostling to get a view. Maybe a fire company would appear, sober or not, before the entire block burned down. Holding the photograph to his side, Truly edged his way along the crowd, passing through the cries and coughs until he reached the intersection and turned south. As he did, a ranting male voice grew distinct within the clamor, drawing looks away from the blaze and toward the street. Some faces were dull and others amused as the rant blistered along, vying with the flames and smoke: "Lo, ye nest of vipers! Ye wretches of Babylon!"

Alone in the middle of the street, a wild-eyed man shook his fists at the multitude. Truly wondered if he was a resident of the doomed building, come unhinged. But his clothes were those of a vagrant—a patched and ill-fitting Quaker coat, soiled baggy pants and a plug hat that looked stomped-upon. The bones of his craggy face stood out as he flailed and thundered: "Know ye not that the path of gold and mean pleasures leads to eternal fire?! See thy fate and tremble! Hear the rumbling of great Jehovah's wrath as the hour draws nigh! LOWLY FOOLS!!" Truly had halted in his tracks, all but forgetting the crowd and the conflagration. He had heard his share of hellfire preachers but never one like this gutter apparition, this raging sawmill of a voice.

"Woeful city! Altar of wickedness! Ye shall end as Egypt, buried in her shame!" A rock sailed past the raving man, who did not seem to notice. Then a second rock struck his forehead, knocking his hat off. As the man staggered back, Truly edged toward him but then froze.

"Shut it!" one youth hollered.

"Back to the asylum!" yelled another.

To a burst of yells and screams, Truly jerked around and saw a fiery timber crash to the street. It struck no one, but other smoking debris rained down as the people drew back. Bloody-browed, the street-corner Jeremiah spread his arms wide and glared straight up. "Hasten!" he roared. "Hasten, O Time of Reckoning! Then behold the mighty city laid waste!"

Truly became aware of a clanging from down the street. He saw a cloud of yellow dust. Then he saw the horse-drawn engine jouncing toward the scene, its crew clinging to the sides. The vagabond did not turn to look. With a sweaty grimace, he inhaled, pointed skyward and erupted yet again. "It has all built up to something, I tell you! Something which can only be REDEEMED BY FIRE!!"

More people stopped watching the flames to watch the madman and the oncoming engine. The rapid engine, the raving man, the red engine not slowing, the filthy man, the engine headed straight toward him. More heads turned to watch. Truly could make out the star-spangled bunting on the engine's body. Some twenty feet separated him from the lunatic, now waving his arms as he heralded God's retribution, the devil's horsemen coming to trample proud sinners—"Hark, the horsemen!"

Truly's palms were moist, one hand tight on the photograph. The engine's frantic bell began to drown out the tirade. A firefighter yelled. In a flash Truly realized what the crowd was waiting for, what he himself was waiting for. He sprang, hurtling toward the shabby figure.

Clangor and hoofbeats filled his ears as he barreled into the man and lunged after him. Rolling as he hit the dirt, he heard the engine storm past, trailing curses. He coughed on the dust. Squinting, he saw the engine take the corner in a wide, lurching arc, losing two firefighters off the back. Onlookers scurried as the driver leaned back hard on the reins. The horse team reared to a stop. The two fallen crewmembers got up and retrieved their leather helmets. The others jumped down as one, most of them grabbing buckets and unreeling the canvas hose while two brandished knives, shoving and kicking the crowd back. Flames danced along the tenement roof, smoke belching from every window.

Truly started to rise but pain shot from his left knee. "Blazes!" he snarled, gripping the joint. Carefully he straightened up. He bent for his hat, dusted it off. Several feet away he saw the man's battered plug hat and Archer's portrait just beyond it, lying face down. He hobbled over, picked up the portrait and found the glass protector cracked. Almost as an afterthought he glanced over his shoulder.

Jehovah's prophet stood glaring at him. Beneath wisps of silvering hair, blood mottled his brow and his stubbled cheek. Heat seemed to radiate from the crags of his face, with its off-center nose and crooked teeth. "The hour is nigh," he growled.

"Happy damned Fourth," said Truly. Limping off, he wished that he could move faster.

But a new disquiet crept over him, picking at his spine. And he remembered the day of Antietam. Miles to the rear, atop a ridge, he had listened as man-made thunder engulfed the sky. With McClellan's army smashing into Lee's, he had imagined a huge black portal on the horizon and soldiers pouring through, rank upon rank. Spilling into the void. At first it had felt like a monotonous dream, nothing more. Then came the sensation–that picking at his spine, something like the dread of battle and yet worse. A dread devoid of hope. Safe behind the lines, he felt not only small but coldly, utterly separate. The guns were God, pummeling him to vapor. They roared extinction.

Behind him, against the chaotic noise of the fire, he could still hear the zealot raving–"Soon the Judgment! It shall cause thy tower to fall! It shall make of thee a pyre of flame!"

58

Seventh Street Road
July 5

WAKEFIELD'S POISE HAD helped make him the spy he was. Yet he felt nervous, not relieved. Nervous despite his disguise–the growth of beard, the laborer's clothes, the tattered hat pulled low. Anxious despite his having left the city, passing into open sky and flat rural green.

The wagon rocked beneath him. Again he looked back at the crate. There it was, roped and nailed. On the lone strength of his word, the impoverished Confederacy had scraped together a quarter-million Yankee dollars in gold, then sent it by dim circuitous channels to sit in this wagon. Wakefield tried to grasp the idea that so much fate, so much of the South's hope and trust, could reside in one pinewood box. Staring between the two horses, he felt the gold's weight on his shoulders.

But soon he would be with Delia. Soon he would ease the strain of their last meeting. He would make up for that–resume protecting her from the gargoyle masters of La Maison, reassure her that he would not have to vanish again. And their bodies would mesh as before. He flipped the reins, felt the sun, listened to the wheels. For both Delia and himself, the days of bondage could now, perhaps, be counted on one hand.

He reached La Maison, its front still decked with Fourth-of-July banners and bunting. At the hitching rack, a few mounts awaited their owners. A colored hireling with a sack was picking up ribbons, streamers and dead firecrackers. By the front door, the broken side-window remained boarded. Wakefield glanced up at Delia's lace-curtained window. He steered the horses down the driveway and pulled up by the cellar bulkhead. On foot he continued around to the back. Two more colored hirelings were hoeing the garden while another pair cleaned the stable. Above the rear veranda hung a large red-striped banner–"God Bless Generals Grant & Sherman," it declared. On the steps underneath sat Wilhelmina and another German girl, sunning themselves.

At his approach, the second girl called out in surprise, "Mister Wakefield–that is you?!"

He smirked, tipping his hat. "I'm sampling the rough look."

The girl smiled in confusion. Wilhelmina looked away. Behind them, the door opened and Monroe stepped out, smoking a cigar. Quickly the girls budged apart for him as he descended the steps. He was dressed in a work shirt, suspenders and high Hessian boots. Though hatless, he seemed even taller than usual, his shoulders broader, a smile playing at the corners of his mouth. Wakefield's stomach tightened.

"Well, Wakefield–what have you brought us?"

"A marble statue."

"Lovely. Can't get enough of those."

Falling in stride with Monroe, Wakefield retraced his steps.

"May we assume it's the full amount?" Monroe queried.

"We may. It took four dock workers to load it."

At the wagon, puffing his cigar, Monroe eyed the crate as Wakefield stood behind him. From a point just above Monroe's left temple, an old and particularly ugly scar extended well into the scalp before vanishing under thick black hair. Wakefield had noticed it before but never asked its origin. Tossing his cigar, Monroe strode toward the tool shed. Waiting, Wakefield examined his dirty, blistered hands–he would have to wash them before touching Delia.

Monroe returned with a jimmy-bar. He lowered the wagon's tailboard and climbed up. "Got something for these ropes? I seem to be missing my pen-knife." Reaching over the side, Wakefield opened his trunk, took out the bayonet and handed it up. He felt a chill as Monroe unsheathed it and held it up, smiling–"Ah, yes!" Monroe deftly cut the ropes around the crate. Setting the blade down, he picked up the jimmy and methodically began to pry the lid open.

Restless, Wakefield shuffled his feet. "It came on a freighter from Halifax."

Monroe grunted as he yanked a nail out, his figure momentarily blocking the sun.

Wakefield sighed, trying to calm himself. It was not like him to blather. Still, he felt something akin to awe. Most men would have been ripping the crate apart; Monroe proceeded as if it contained, in fact, nothing more than a marble statue. Wakefield attempted the same nonchalance. "So you did it up big for the Fourth?"

Monroe set the jimmy down. "Yes–our grand reopening. Took in a lot of money." Shoving the lid off, his hands rustled down through the packing straw. "But . . . " He pulled up a gold ingot and grinned at it, showing strong teeth. " . . . not near as much as this!"

"Two-hundred and fifty thousand," Wakefield murmured, as much to himself as Monroe.

"Fitting," said Monroe, "given the service you require."

"Which you must now see through," said Wakefield. "The South is hard-pressed, and you can take this as a measure of . . . "

Monroe lobbed the ingot at him. Startled, Wakefield caught it.

"Buy yourself a shave," Monroe said, chuckling. Standing to full height, he gave a majestic yawn. "I'll get those darkies to unload this."

Wakefield turned the slim-yet-heavy gold bar in his fingers–what centuries of men had killed and died for, he thought. He had always felt indifferent toward it. But surely he merited compensation, something extra for all he had done. Still, by definition, true sacrifice sought nothing in return.

Climbing into the wagon, he peered down into the crate. In their nest of straw, the gleaming ingots lay like ranks of gold teeth. He replaced the bar among its identical fellows and then turned to Monroe. Up close like this, he had often been surprised to find himself just two inches shorter. He managed a steady look into the cold gray eyes. "As you say–if you and the lady push it to a successful conclusion, you'll deserve every ounce of this."

Monroe's grin bordered on a sneer. "As I say. It just puts me in a generous mood."

Dropping his gaze, Wakefield bent to get the bayonet. He sheathed it and stuck it back in the trunk, which he buckled shut. "I'll be talking with you and Madam later." He stepped down, hefting his trunk and gripsack after him. Monroe hopped down and ambled away, whistling.

Returning to the rear of the house, Wakefield saw that Wilhelmina and the other girl were gone. His impatience had cooled. With a brush of anxiety, he recalled Delia's bruised, benumbed face, the flatness of her voice. He set his baggage down by the veranda and went to the well. He splashed his hands, wiped them on his clothes. Only then did desire return, spurring him up the steps and into the house.

He passed the kitchen, then stopped as the door to the storeroom opened, almost bumping him. Fannie O'Shea emerged. Lugging a basketful of vegetables, she elbowed the door shut and then gasped as she noticed him. One of her eyes was bruised purple. Looking scared, she gave a half-curtsy and hurried off. So, thought Wakefield–Ravenel, for whatever reason, had at last turned on her little pet. The girl had needed a good slap. Still, her fearful look had unsettled him. He proceeded past the storeroom and the cellar door and then up the winding back stairs. From the second floor he heard Ursula's angry, booming voice. He found her berating a colored maid. Seeing him, the hefty woman went silent and waved the maid away. Her round face composed itself but he detected foreboding in it, with a trace of malice.

"Mister Wakefield, sir—Madam vaits for you in the study."

He stared at her. Then, in a surge of alarm, he rushed past her to Delia's room and banged on the door. He shouted her name twice before throwing the door open. She was not there. "Where is she?!" he yelled. Looking back down the hall, he saw that Ursula had disappeared. He raced down the main staircase and into the parlor, where he found the door of the adjoining study wide open. Hands clenched, he stalked toward it. "What have you done with her?!" he shouted.

The dry, languorous voice of Madam Ravenel answered. "Settle yourself, Wakefield."

He entered the study. Hands folded, Ravenel sat behind the ornate walnut desk—and fleetingly, her hideous elegance stilled his rage. She wore a maroon Zouave jacket with gold braid, her hair twirled and gathered high in a gold net. Her sloe eyes stared. On an ordinary face, the expression would have been bland; on hers, it conveyed something primordial, the patience of a ceremonial mask. Wakefield felt his own face burning. "Where is she?" he croaked.

"But what has happened to you, mon ami? You look like a mudsill."

Advancing to the desk, he eyed her thin, furrowed neck and imagined snapping it. Then he caught a slight movement in his side-vision. Glancing into a corner, he saw Dubray seated there, nervously sipping tea.

Ravenel stared up. "Wakefield, you must sit. And you must listen."

"I'll sit when I wish! Tell me!"

She sighed. "You requested," she began, "–no, you rather demanded–a softening of Mademoiselle Delia's punishment. Out of regard for you, I ignored my misgivings and agreed to this. Delia was confined to her room for a few days. Then, with the house opening its doors again, she was given a strong warning and returned to her duties–merely serving drinks and the like, as you also demanded. I instructed Mademoiselle Fannie to watch her. Yet last night, Delia took advantage of the festivities and slipped away unnoticed. Vanished in the night, Wakefield."

Reaching behind him, he pulled up a chair and sank into it. His gaze wandered among the paintings and bookcases, then came to rest on the fireplace mantel. He saw the leonine photograph of Monroe. He remembered Monroe barging into the shop that day, idly requesting a portrait free of charge. No visitor could have been less welcome.

"So," said Ravenel, "your little wren is flown. And we are left to ponder the implications. Where she might go, what she might do . . . "

Staring out the window, Wakefield saw the four Negro laborers hefting the crate from the wagon. Monroe stood supervising, a riding crop clutched in his hand. Wakefield felt a raw barrenness within. "I brought the gold," he muttered.

"So I have observed," said Ravenel. "Well done. But see how you change the subject, having pressed it so loudly?"

He glared at her. "I told her nothing! I hinted nothing!"

"This I believe–but think of why we had to discipline her to begin with. We discovered her having a private chat with the little baron, just before we disposed of him. Who knows what passed between them? You see, Wakefield–whether or not you were discreet with the girl, she is still a danger. She could identify . . . "

"I know!" he snapped. "I . . . " Whipping his hat off, he forced his mind to focus. "Listen–if you didn't think we're now safe from the federal men, would you have reopened for business? Would you have advised me to come here for sanctuary? Archer assured you that the investigation's been foiled. Truly came within a hair of being prosecuted, for God's sake!"

"I assure you he did not. Would we have desired such a course? A public forum, shedding light on us?" Ravenel laced her knobby fingers together. "However, Major Truly and his associate do appear quite stubborn."

Wakefield tried to match her stare. "They are only two men. Two men who now have no lawful authority behind them."

"Wakefield, have lawful considerations ever stopped *us?*"

He flushed. "We . . . You are of a special caliber, Madam."

"I thank you for the compliment. Let us hope it does not describe our foes as well." Ravenel settled back. "As for Mademoiselle Delia, it is in fact too late to worry. She is out of our grasp."

Hearing a sniff, Wakefield looked over at Dubray. The doctor had set his tea aside and was fussing with a handkerchief. "Sentiment, Wakefield, is the greatest threat. It has brought down empires." He honked his nose. "If not for your own sentiment, Delia's offense might have been more effectively dealt with."

In the blur of an instant, Wakefield was out of his chair and throttling Dubray by the lapels, twisting them, his throat contorted in curses. Dubray yelped and struggled, trying the wrench Wakefield's fists away. Keeping his hold, Wakefield dug a knee into the doctor's solar plexus, barely aware of Ravenel's raspy shouts behind him. Then he felt her talon-like grip on his forearm. He stopped shaking Dubray but did not release him. With his spectacles atilt, the doctor blinked up, his homely face a deep red. Wakefield breathed through his teeth.

"Wakefield," Ravenel muttered, practically in his ear, "–are we allies or not?" He let go. Ravenel let go. Like a thornbush oozing honey, she addressed Dubray. "Antoine, we should perhaps be more delicate with our friend. Especially on so sensitive a topic."

Jittery, Dubray straightened his specs. Wakefield picked his hat up, righted his chair and sat. His eruption had left a stony composure. Again Ravenel faced him from her desk–and in the silence, he recognized his own hatred for the obstacle it was. Yet it was hard not to mind Ravenel's glinting gaze, searching him for other weaknesses. He stared past her. In the corner, Dubray crossed his legs and looked morose. Wakefield cleared his throat. "If we're apportioning blame, Madam, let us start with the business about Van Gilder. Had he been dispatched by other means–*normal* means–would the Yankees have been half so keen to pursue it? A corpse is one thing, but . . . " Hearing a soft thump, he stiffened and looked over his shoulder. Monroe stood there, shutting the door behind him. He held a small varnished-wood box.

"I see I'm fashionably late," he said.

"And with dirty boots," said Ravenel. "Tsk-tsk."

"I'll get Ursula to lick them." Monroe chortled–a deep, static sound, like a muffled drum. Ambling to the desk, he set his box down and proffered a key to Ravenel. "The bulkhead doors are chained and pad-locked. Add this to your ring." She took the key. Pulling up a lyre-back chair, Monroe placed it beside Wakefield and plunked down. "So I'm called upon to defend my methods," he said airily. "Well–hear me, then."

He pressed his fingertips together, a delicate motion which never failed to make Wakefield edgier. "With the disguise and all, I reasoned that I'd be able to halt the coach and gain access. In letting the coachman live, I reasoned that he would proceed to Strasburg and there serve as witness, once Van Gilder was found in his altered condition. To outraged townfolk, he would describe a Union officer entering and exiting the carriage. The result: Van Gilder duly punished and silenced, and a fictitious Union major implicated. Effectively confusing the whole issue. Should I have guessed that the coachman, this deformed little German, was a government spy? Or that other federal men would be sniffing about? This escaped you, too, my friend. And give me my due–when the hunchback reappeared in disguise, I found him out."

Wakefield sent an involuntary glance to Ravenel. On his last visit here, she had recounted the death of the bogus baron, whose description left him troubled. It had nibbled at him until he recalled one of Cathcart's letters, in which the agent mentioned Van Gilder's servant–"a simple-minded German hunchback." It appeared now that the dead man had been no simpleton but a skilled Union operative–and that he had been concurrently spying on Van Gilder. That explained, in part, the surprise federal menace of the past month. Wakefield wondered if Ravenel had somehow guessed this failure of intelligence and was waiting to use it on him. Her very stillness seemed to mock him.

"Monroe," said Wakefield, "–for your alertness, I have nothing but praise. But back to the matter of Van Gilder. Underneath all the fancy reasoning, weren't you just . . . " He was staring at the wooden box on the desk. " . . . indulging yourself?"

"You wound me, Wakefield. Discipline is my hallmark and forbearance my guiding light. But when there's room for a little sport, why begrudge me?"

Without looking, Wakefield felt the icy smirk. He hid a shudder, recalling Monroe's placid description of what he had done to the Copperhead. "Sport," he muttered.

Dubray snorted a laugh. "Ah, Monroe–what a surgeon you would have made!"

"Besides," said Monroe, "the man had defied us once before and I'd let him live, albeit with a scratch or two. But he failed to take me seriously enough, and that was a personal affront. Weasels must be skinned. Dubray's drug made it an interesting experiment, too." He chuckled. "I did conclude, however, that I like it better when they struggle."

To Wakefield's relief, Ravenel broke in. "Enough, then—let us dwell in the present. Wakefield, you will very soon be calling on our lieutenant-colonel?"

"Tomorrow, yes. For now, I'll be riding out to Rockville to see an operative. I'll send him northwest to make contact with General Early, who I figure is fording the Potomac as we speak. So far, the Yankees seem insensible to the threat. I've detected no military response around the city or in the newspapers."

"Magnifique!" chirped Ravenel. Reclining, she gave her yellowed, bladelike smile. "The days are few, Wakefield. Think of how your countrymen will remember you. Once this is accomplished, the South may at last receive foreign recognition—perhaps from my native land?"

"I can only hope, Madam." He needed no one to tell him the possibilities, least of all this harpy. But the South's desperation was a more prominent thought. On his way to the docks this morning, he had seen an oversized Stars 'n' Stripes flying above the Navy Building and asked a guard about it. The guard told him that the feared Confederate raider *Alabama* had been sunk off Cherbourg, France, two weeks ago, and that word of it had just reached the capital. The hope of French recognition, or that of any European power, now seemed fainter than ever.

Wakefield noticed Ravenel glaring at him, though the awful smile remained. "Unless," she said, "—unless, of course, the Union agents return to disrupt our lives. This would sorely test our optimism."

So she was not through making him squirm. He eyed Monroe's box. "Yes, well . . . We'll be prepared for that contingency."

"About Major Truly," said Monroe. "I have a personal request."

"What could that be?" said Wakefield.

"Suppose he does return to devil us. Should you encounter him before I do, it is my wish that he not be killed."

Wakefield shot him a look. "That he not be killed?"

"Yes. That he be taken prisoner." Monroe's eyes and voice had never presented such a contrast—mild voice, granite eyes.

"Monroe, I . . . If Truly were to crop up again, we could scarcely let him live."

"Take him prisoner." Monroe folded his brawny arms. "That is my request."

Wakefield hesitated, then shrugged. "All right."

"Good." Unfolding his arms, Monroe grinned. "Now, concerning the operation itself–I'll need to borrow that uniform again. Since you saw fit to take it back from me."

"I did so because I was concerned–understandably, I think–over what extra purpose you might put it to. More *sport*."

Monroe blinked at him. "And do you have such scruples in this case?"

"No, because you will definitely need the disguise. I'll give it to you."

"And that marvelous bayonet of yours–that, too." Monroe held his hand out and flexed it. "Since the day I spied it in your shop, I've frankly coveted the thing. Just feels good to grip."

"All right. If you must."

"As for the lieutenant-colonel . . . When you see him, there's something you should bring. Other than our greetings." Monroe nodded at the box.

Glancing at it, Wakefield felt a quiver in his gut.

"Just some added persuasion," Monroe said. "Go on–take a peek."

Ravenel and Dubray looked on curiously. From the window, early afternoon light gave the box a skin-like sheen. Wakefield leaned forward, flicked the latch and raised the lid. Inside were a trio of small glass jars, each with a white label and tin cover. Standing, he took one out and held it to the light. The label obscured its contents but he saw clear fluid inside. He read the label's crabbed lettering: "Gideon Van Gilder." He turned the jar in his palm. A bobbing eyeball stared back at him. The jar dropped from his hand, struck the desk and went rolling.

"Careful," Monroe said.

Snatching up the other two jars, Wakefield stared at them. One labeled "Jonathan Peavey" held several chipped teeth at the bottom, while above them floated a glob of grayish matter. The other, labeled "Ezra Underhill," contained a wedge of purplish matter–half a human tongue, it looked like. Wakefield hurled Peavey's jar and was about to hurl Underhill's when it was grabbed from his hand. Standing before him, Monroe held the jar away, his head cocked in a look of challenge.

"I want him scared!" Wakefield bellowed. "I do *not* want him driven over the edge!!"

"Please sit," said Ravenel. "Oh–look at my carpet!"

The thrown jar had struck a bookcase beside Dubray. Still cringing, the physician blinked at the scattered teeth and glass fragments near his feet, the patch of carpet stained dark. Monroe's expression was unchanged.

"I told you!" Wakefield sputtered. "A man who's mad with fear is worse than useless!"

"Gentlemen–please sit," said Ravenel.

"First I'll repeat something that I did not think needed repeating!" Wakefield paused to breathe, his glower taking in both Monroe and Ravenel. "Too much terror can have the opposite effect. If he thinks he's facing an arbitrary force–one that acts on bloody whimsy, no more–he will feel hopelessly trapped. Believing that he has nothing to lose, he may well try something desperate. That's why I pressed for the course we've taken–so that we'd appear dead serious but reasonable. Do these . . . " Quelling another shudder, he pointed at Van Gilder's jar on the floor. "Do these *trophies* of yours make us appear sane?! As if we might spare him as promised, should he obey?!"

Ravenel had her eyes closed. Delicately she massaged her temples. "Fascinating insights, Wakefield. You have made your point."

Monroe bent down and picked up the Van Gilder jar. He placed it in the box, along with Underhill's. "Dubray–gather those teeth for me, would you? And that bit of brain?"

Dubray got down on his knees and started picking through the broken glass.

Wakefield locked eyes with Monroe. Before the cool granite gaze, he wavered between wonder and revulsion. "So far, we've conveyed some sense of principle. Harsh principle, but principle nonetheless. Please help to maintain it. We lured the man into blundering, along with the others. So when we offer him pardon in return for what we want, he must trust the offer. In the midst of his fear, he must see one clear hope for survival–to do as we require."

Monroe closed the lid on the box and latched it. "It's your project, Wakefield." He picked up the box. "Now, with all of your kind permissions, I think I'll go lie down." With a nod, he strode out of the room.

Dubray stood with the teeth and the glob of brain cupped in his hands. Wakefield sneered at him. "I wish to talk to Madam alone." He opened the door for Dubray, who shuffled out. Wakefield shut the door and retook his seat. Ravenel gave him that look of weary patience.

"Who is Monroe?" he demanded.

"Whatever do you mean?"

"Is it true he's the grand-nephew of President Monroe? Is that even his real name?"

"Why would you care about such a thing?"

"I'm curious, is all."

"Is it implausible that one of such blood might be found here?" She gestured to the walls. Two portraits showed haughty-faced men in rich garb. "My grandfather was governor of Guadeloupe, my uncle a marshal of Napoleon's. You see, I too have traveled rough seas and ended up where I never thought I would. But what does it matter? Am I not remarkable in my own right? Is not Monroe?"

"He's mad," said Wakefield. "Do you care to address that?"

"Some would call it genius. I can assure you, Wakefield—you shall never meet another who fits his purpose so well, with so perfect a blend of passion and intellect."

"Passion?! Oh, that's just a shade too delicate. He's mad—and apt to jeopardize us again."

"I disagree. If any man has control of himself, it is our Monroe. And it does pain me that you doubt him, after all he has accomplished for us both."

"That request of his concerning Truly—what's the meaning there?"

Ravenel sighed. "Monroe has shown a certain fascination with Major Truly. Why, I do not know—do you think he tells me everything? But you tire me, Wakefield. So little time left, and here you sit fretting about the wrong things. Amusing, too, that you would question Monroe's judgment, when your own failed so obviously in the matter of Delia."

Wakefield stared at her neck. When he resumed listening, her tone was instructive, almost conciliatory.

"We each have our lonely appetites to satisfy. Monroe's are singular, I grant you, but should we apply to him an ordinary measure? I think not. What is this notion of sanity? An invention of dull, weak men, I say—a shield for their dullness and weakness. You have seen Monroe successfully mingling with our patrons. If there is madness in him, it is controlled and selective. It is the madness of the artist. Civility is his talent but savagery his art, and does not savagery have a certain magnificence? He plans the moment of its release–and in those fearful moments, his mind is as clear and hard as a gem. No, Wakefield, he is not addled. Quite the contrary, he knows exactly what he is doing."

Wakefield let her words echo, not quite sure what he was hearing. Taking up his hat, he rose. "I should leave now. I'll take Black Marengo, if that's all right."

"Of course, mon ami. All for the cause."

He crossed the carpet and halted at the door. He looked back at her.

"Something else?" she asked.

"Madam, what is it that binds you to the cause? Now that you have your gold, I mean."

"Do I hear an insinuation?"

"A question. A final one. You realize, don't you, that the Confederacy could not tolerate a betrayal of its trust?"

"Enough. Enough of this." Sitting back, she ran a finger along her jaw. "You have helped us, we have helped you–and now comes the culmination of our partnership. For a common aim, we act from separate reasons. You believe that gold alone is what moves us? Speaking only for myself, gold is marvelous. But I have another reason–less tangible, but as real as riches. You may rest easy, Wakefield. As long as you stay here, you need not hire a food taster nor sleep with your pistol."

"Thank you. But what is that other reason?"

She spread her small talon hands, then laid them flat. "Nostalgia, I believe the word is. A longing for days past." The smile sliced her face. "Go on now, Wakefield."

Out in Black Marengo's stall, Wakefield found one of the colored laborers grooming and sweet-talking the horse. Something made him blurt a compliment to the youth for the job he was doing. The youth gave a flustered smile and proceeded to saddle the horse. Stroking its satiny black neck, Wakefield looked toward the mansion; its gabled hulk etched the bleakness within him. In this stately snakepit, his one light of refuge had gone out. Delia was gone. Like a glass shard, the thought of her cut into him. Still, how could he blame her? How could he not but admire her daring, as well as her loyalty to a dead friend? No longer would she be trapped among ghouls.

Mounting up, he tossed the youth a coin.

Then he was riding toward Rockville. Soon, he thought–soon the hated alliance would end. Never more would he have to ape friendship with men he detested—watching them, flattering them, listening to their bilge. When his mission was achieved and the South swept to victory, he would be free. Then, through the smoking rubble of Washington, he would search for Delia.

59

Truly Residence

SHELLING PEAS IN the kitchen, Sapphira was thinking about Flavius Tucker when she heard the parlor door bang shut. She looked up and glimpsed Anna hurrying for the stairs.

"Anna? . . . Anna!"

Sapphira caught up with her on the middle landing and blocked the way. Despite her remote expression, Anna was pale and trembling. "What is it?" Sapphira demanded.

"You can have him," Anna muttered.

She went to shove past but Sapphira held her arm, eyeing her. "You were doing well with him. What's the matter?"

Anna twisted her arm loose. "Maybe you're meant for these things, but I'm not. That's all. You're the last one I have to answer to."

Sapphira leaned closer. "Then how would you answer to Mother?"

"Let me by!"

"You didn't have to kick me out of the way, Annie, but you did."

"Move!"

"Go back to him, Annie."

Anna flushed pink, her voice a clenched sputter. "I'm sick of having to step around you! And don't dare tell me what to do!" Again she tried to barge upstairs and again Sapphira caught her. Recoiling, she lashed out, but her hand missed Sapphira's face.

Sapphira's stiff palm caught her full on the cheek, knocking her backwards. In the next instant, Sapphira had her pinned against the wall, straining as she shrieked and wriggled and then went limp. Her cries turned to sobs, her streaming eyes clamped shut. Released, she sank onto the step, sob-choked and hugging her calico knees.

Sapphira's ears rang as if it was she who had been struck. Slowly she sat down next to Anna. "What happened?" she muttered.

Gasping and sniffling, Anna bowed her head. "He was telling me . . . He saw his captain blown up." Sapphira's hand hesitated, then came to rest on Anna's warm back. "One second his captain was a whole man," Anna continued, "and in the next he exploded. Parts of him . . . Why would he tell me that?! As if I'd wish to hear such things!"

Drawing a breath, Sapphira gazed at the empty hall below, the sunlight cutting in. Absently she stroked Anna's back, watching the dust motes circulate.

Slowly Anna sank against her. "Why did he never write me a letter like the one you got?"

"You read it?"

"You left it on your dresser."

Sapphira sighed. "He still sees you as a little . . . picker of daisies. But you're not that anymore, are you?"

"No. I'm not."

"Show it, then. Show yourself. Tell me you'll try."

Anna rubbed her cheek, ran a hand through her golden hair. "I'll try."

"And Anna—you never asked for me, and I never asked for you. But if I wasn't here, it's fair certain what my lot would be: bought and sold and whipped and ignorant. Would you have preferred that?"

"No." Anna's arm tightened around her waist.

In the parlor, minutes later, Sapphira found Ben sitting up and buttressed by pillows, his arm nestled in its sling. The facial swelling was gone, as were the bandages. Viewed sidelong, the scabbed abrasions looked like lumpy Indian war paint. She wanted him to look up. Held in her gaze, he might understand how she really saw him—in a glow of resurrection.

"I didn't know you were here," he said, his voice dry.

"Reverend Cass suggested I take a day off. I trained two new volunteers last week." She sat in the bedside chair. "Look at me."

"Could you bring me a mirror? I'm curious."

"Later, if you want. Look at me."

Moving his head slightly, he stared past her.

"Tell me about Petersburg," she said. "Leave nothing out."

"Never mind, Saph."

"You'll tell Annie but you won't tell me?"

"She's a ridiculous girl. Seen too many plays, read too many ladies' magazines. If it was Judgment Day, she'd be griping about the theater cancellations."

Sapphira might have chuckled aloud. But her palm tingled, recalling its collision with Anna's cheek. "I have images in my head, pictures of how fine life could be. Maybe they're foolish, but time will tell."

"Yes. It will."

"You carried such pictures. You prized them, but the guns blew them away. And now you want to blow Annie's away."

"To kingdom come. Don't you?"

"Oh, I've wanted to. Even without seeing what you've seen, I've wanted to, with meanest vengeance. But that isn't my task or yours. Events are doing the work. When you came back to us half-dead, Annie didn't run away. She fought to care for you. And she's learning. Underneath, she knows she can't escape the harder things. I catch it in her face sometimes."

He had closed his eyes. At length, he carefully cleared his throat. "Well–I suppose it's enough that she has to look at me."

Sapphira stared at his face, the weepy scars. She touched his chin with her fingertips.

His eyes flickered open. Drawing up his good hand, he lay it on her wrist. "So it's not ended for me," he muttered. "I keep thinking that."

"Please believe it," she said. As her gaze consumed him, he did not look away. She touched his greasy hair, as gently as she would have touched a newborn. "How's your pain?"

"Down to a dull roar. I'm trying to ease off the laudanum."

"Tonight I'll apply new bandages." Withdrawing her hand, she sat back. "Or perhaps Annie should do it."

"Tell her to, then. Tell her I'll keep my wicked mouth shut this time."

"And you seem well enough to be moved. She and I can haul your bed back upstairs."

"Don't tell Chadwick. What would he say about his little blossom exerting herself?"

Sapphira smirked. "I'd ask Father to help, but he had a limp this morning. Said he got it shoving someone out of a fire engine's path."

Ben squinted. "Things sure do happen to Pa."

The doorknocker sounded. Going to answer it, Sapphira suddenly realized how much she hoped it was Tucker. She opened the door. Octavius Duke stood there clutching his hat. Behind him stood a young white woman, beautiful despite her pallor and disheveled honey-blonde hair. There were mud splatters on her red dress, smudges on her red-trimmed blouse. Duke blurted a greeting and asked for the major.

"I'm afraid he is out," said Sapphira, gazing at the pale young woman. "Could I be of assistance?"

"This is Miss . . . " Faltering, Duke looked apologetically at his companion.

"Delia McGuire," she spoke with a lilt. Fatigue veiled her blue eyes. "I need to speak to Major Truly."

"And to lie down," said Sapphira. "Come in, please."

Duke stepped aside for Delia and hovered after her.

Sapphira took her by the arm. Leading her toward the stairs, she saw her eyelids flutter. "Lord, Miss—you're dead on your feet!"

"I need to speak with him," the girl murmured.

"You shall. For now, you need to sleep."

"Tell him it's about his friend. The little German man."

Halting, Sapphira gaped at her.

Delia appeared startled out of her haze. "You're hurting me."

Sapphira realized that she was squeezing Delia's wrist. She relaxed her grip. "The little German man?"

"Yes—at La Maison de l'Empereur. The one they killed."

SEATED BY THE guestroom bed, Truly waited as Delia McGuire finished her soup. Questions massed in his brain. But he wanted to let her nerves settle and to let himself absorb this turn of luck, after the day's frustrations. From Marble Alley to the Northern Liberties, he had limped from one pricey bordello to another—the Wolf's Den, the Haystack, the Ironclad, the Blue Goose, Sal Austin's, Julia Deane's, Madam Russell's Bake Oven—presenting himself to officious madams and then querying their harlots. None claimed to have ever worked at La Maison or to know anyone who had. But now, beneath his own roof, this Irish girl graced his vision. He took her tray, set it down by his chair, watched her devour an apple. Though sleepy, her eyes had an almost feral desperation.

She glanced at him, then stared at the bedspread. "Major, I feel so badly about him. About your friend, the baron."

Kirschenbaum's fake title struck him as almost funny. "That's done. I'm just glad you managed to get here."

She handed him the apple core and he placed it in the empty soup bowl.

"Madam Ravenel chose last night to reopen the place," she said. "There were banners and fireworks. It was busy and noisy enough for me to slip away from Fannie."

"That would be Fannie O'Shea?"

"Aye, sir. Madam's watchdog."

"When we visited the house, we questioned her along with the others. She sounded hollow to me, especially when we asked about Briona Kibby, her supposed best friend."

Delia's wan, pretty face went hard. "Fannie is a lying bitch! Excuse me, Major, but *I* was Briona's best friend. *I* came over on the boat with her. But just before you visited that day, I was ordered to my room. Somehow they were ready for you."

"I know. And just now I realize that I glimpsed you then, looking down from your window."

"Aye. I was keen to know who you and the other gentleman were."

Truly leaned forward. "If you're up to it, could you start at the beginning? About Briona and also about Manf . . . I mean, the baron."

Delia settled back against the pillow and lay there, hands folded, her gaze on the ceiling. "Briona and I worked as laundresses in Cork. We dreamed of crossing to America." Truly had not reckoned on her starting this far back. But lulled by her tuneful voice, he did not rush her.

Despite their differing backgrounds, Delia told him, she and Briona had been fast friends from the start. Briona, an unlettered product of Ireland's west, had lost most of her people in the famine and barely survived herself. Delia, by contrast, had a father who worked for a London-based shipping firm; her mother, a Polish refugee of minor nobility, boasted a degree of schooling unusual for her sex. The family's ruin had commenced with the father's disappearance at sea, after which relatives proved unhelpful. Consumption soon claimed the mother. Reduced to laboring over a washtub, Delia at last met Briona, and the two inspired each other with New World fantasies. Over three years of toil, they scraped together enough money for the Atlantic crossing. Arriving malnourished and near penniless on the Baltimore docks, they were approached by Madam Ravenel. "She acted kindly," said Delia. "But once she'd taken us to La Maison, we had some notion of what it meant. And there was much else we never foresaw."

One night, she said, a man with a pointy beard showed up. He did not appear to be there for the usual reasons. He had some business with Madam and seemed in a hurry to get it done with. An odd man—anxious, gloomy. "On his way out, he caught sight of Briona. She was my own age but looked younger, almost like a child. Some men are drawn to such an appearance, but this one was spellbound. Later Briona told me how polite he was when he approached her, but how persistent too. It amused her, more than anything. But he returned a few nights later, with a bouquet—and in the uniform of a lieutenant-colonel, all decked out to impress her."

Truly had been fighting not to interrupt. "What was the lieutenant-colonel's name? Did Briona ever tell you?" His heart fell as Delia shook her head.

"To me, at first, he was just a funny man who had eyes for her. Then, when he took advantage of her—that was on his next visit—I asked her his name. But if he had told her, she'd forgotten it in her fright."

Truly gave a dejected nod. "His first visit would have been when, Miss Delia? Late February, by any chance?"

"Twas, I believe."

That figured, he thought. At the time that the lieutenant-colonel first set eyes on Briona, a quarterly payment would have been due, requiring his call at the house. His next call, purely to charm her, must have been when the hackman Simon Hodge saw him entering. "Tell me about that third visit. He took advantage of her, you say?"

"He did, devil take him. Briona came to me trembling. He had called, in uniform again, and gotten permission to take her for a carriage ride. She said he drove her out along the forts guarding the city. He was boasting to her, saying he commanded them."

Truly leaned in. "He claimed to command the forts of Washington?!"

"All or some, Major. Briona said he called them 'his' forts."

Unlikely, Truly thought. The rank of lieutenant-colonel, though high, did not suggest so lofty an assignment. And when a man puffed himself up for a woman, there was no telling how he might lie or exaggerate. Still, this would bear looking into.

"Briona did not care what it was that he commanded," Delia said. "For even as he fussed and fawned over her, she said there was a dreadful hunger about him. Then he began to say foul, twisted things. Then he pulled the carriage into a glade and started pawing her, pulling at her dress. Once he had forced himself upon her, he took her back to the house. Briona said that he appeared nearly as shaken as she, that he kept begging her pardon. Her pardon, Major!" Delia paused, gazing at the wall. "I'm not sure what use this may be–but she also said that when he stepped from the carriage, he swooned and had to catch himself. And he had not been drinking."

"Good," said Truly. "Any detail is useful." And this one, he thought, echoed something that Officer Gilchrist had described–the anonymous man's apparent dizzy spell at Brown's.

"Once she told me all of this," Delia went on, "we went to Madam and pleaded that she bar this dirty wretch from La Maison. She gave us no answer, but the visits did stop. It was some weeks before he came again."

"The fifteenth of April," Truly said. "Surely a terrible day for you."

"Terrible and strange. It was a Saturday, so we were busy. I was serving drinks when Briona ran up to me in terror. Madam had just told her that the lieutenant-colonel would soon arrive. If he wished to take her out in his carriage, she was to go along and treat him nicely. Madam threatened punishment if she did not obey. I wanted to hide her, but Ursula dragged her off to get ready. Soon the lieutenant-colonel appeared, in fine civilian clothes this time. First he went up to Madam's chamber. After that he left with Briona on his arm, and she gave me a last fearful glance. She was helpless and so was I."

"Miss Delia–didn't another man arrive just then? A young, long-haired gentry sort?"

She sighed, thinking. "Aye, Major, I know who you mean." She described such a visitor, prideful and unpleasant–a match for Jonathan Peavey. He went upstairs as if by appointment, she said, just as the lieutenant-colonel had. But soon he hurried back down and left the house.

Delia returned to the subject of her late friend. Come early evening, she said, her fears for Briona were horribly surpassed. From some of the other girls, she learned that Detective Archer had arrived, asking about a La Maison girl who had drowned in the Eastern Branch some hours ago. Delia tore upstairs and burst into Ravenel's chamber, where she found the proprietress with Monroe, Dubray and Archer.

"It wasn't till afterwards, when the shock wore off a little, that I truly recalled the sight of them in that room. It baffles me still. Though Madam had seemed as healthy as ever that morning, here she was in bed as if ill. Dubray had his doctor's bag open. And Monroe, he was acting very different–pacing at the foot of her bed and cursing her, saying he'd had enough of her bossing him. Also he was moving stiffly, as if his joints had all at once gone bad. And Archer just stood there watching them. When I rushed in, they barely seemed to notice me till I started raving. Then Ursula came and forced me to my room. Archer left without seeing me–me, who could have told him more than anyone. Nor, I later heard, had he questioned any of the other girls. He had simply declared Briona's death a suicide. And Madam and Monroe? Later that night they were their usual selves again–close in conversation, not sick at all.

"I didn't eat for two days. Then Madam summoned me. She said she regretted what had happened, but the lieutenant-colonel would be dealt with. I was not to discuss these events with anyone. I begged her to tell me more–which earned me a slap, of course." For the first time, Delia's gaze was more mystified than bitter. "Major, what were they up to? Do you know at all?"

There was much, Truly realized, that he would likely have to withhold from this valiant girl. He might even have to lie to her. But if he could afford to answer her frankly on a given point, he would do so. "It was a well-planned charade, staged for the lieutenant-colonel and then for Jonathan Peavey–Peavey was the prideful young gent–and finally for Archer. We're not certain why. But those three men were connected to each other and to La Maison, through some murky dealings. And as you may have guessed, Captain Forbes and I were similarly hornswaggled when we paid our call." Before other questions could form on Delia's lips, Truly pressed ahead with his own. "Was Detective Archer familiar to you before then?"

She nodded. "He came around often enough, so that we knew him by sight."

"He has admitted as much," said Truly. "Only he claims it has all been official in nature, that he and Ravenel have an understanding. It wouldn't be the first such arrangement in the annals of law enforcement. Still I was surprised to hear of it, given Archer's pious reputation."

Delia's expression turned caustic. "Pious, you say? Well . . . I can tell you that he does indeed come on police matters. But it's said that something else draws him–the thing that draws most men. And it's whispered

. . . " She glanced away. "His lust is of a particular sort, they say. Ursula is the one who sees to him."

Truly pictured Ursula–pasty, broad-shouldered and buxom in her green taffeta–then thought of the magazine that he had found in Archer's desk.

"Major, you wanted me to tell what happened to the baron?"

Truly looked at his knees. "Manfred Kirschenbaum was his real name, and he had no title. To get into the house, he required a false identity." He looked up at Delia. In a way, she connected him to Kirschenbaum. Speaking his friend's true name brought a certain comfort, a hint of how absolution might feel. "In any case, yes–I need to hear about that too."

Delia drew the blankets up. She proceeded to tell how she had shown Kirschenbaum to Dubray's table, how he had later approached her and how they had met by the arbor out back. Despite Truly's correction, Kirschenbaum had become fixed in her mind as "the baron."

"I told the baron most of what I've told you, about Briona and the lieutenant-colonel. Suddenly Monroe appeared–he'd stolen up on us. He grabbed the baron, snatched a pistol away from under his cloak. Then Madam was there. I pleaded with her and Monroe. I said we had just been chatting, but they seemed to know better. The baron protested. Then Archer came out of the house and he was holding his revolver. Monroe told your friend that he would let him make a run for it. Madam had me by the arm. She told me to scream and when I couldn't, she slapped me so hard my brains rattled. So scream I did.

"Just before Monroe shoved him forward, the baron made the sign of the cross. Then he ran. Archer shot him down. Monroe placed the pistol beside his body–and the next thing I knew, you and your other friend were there. I was dizzy and my mouth was bleeding. I understood nothing of what was happening or being said. But when you threw yourself at Archer, I just wanted you to keep hitting him, thrashing him. Then the other policemen arrived, and it was finished. As punishment I was shut up in the cellar. Madam made me sign Archer's report, which was a pack of lies."

Delia had turned her face away. Truly watched the motion of her breathing beneath the covers. She could be no older than Anna, it occurred to him. "Delia, did you learn anything afterwards? As to how Manfred was found out?"

She hesitated before answering. "I did–though like so much else, it makes precious little sense. While I was locked away, a German girl named Wilhelmina was assigned to bring me food. She's kinder than most, and was troubled by what had happened. She confided that she had spent time with the baron that evening. He had gotten her tipsy, but all he wanted to do was stroll about and talk and ask questions. He dismissed her when she accidentally offended him–she touched his back and was startled to find he had a hump. After that, she started babbling to some of the girls about this queer nobleman, this German hunchback who seemed less interested in her than in horses. Monroe overheard this. He pulled her aside and made her tell everything about the baron. Monroe had a special interest in your friend's hump–also, in his curiosity about Black Marengo, the stallion they keep out back. Then, when she said that the baron had asked about Briona, that seemed to seal something in Monroe's mind. He went to speak with Dubray, and Dubray left in the coach."

Truly's stream of thought had divided, one branch following Delia's story, the other swirling about the tall, silhouetted image of Monroe–Monroe puffing calmly on his cigar, staring back at him.

Delia went on. "But for me, the oddest thing Wilhelmina said was how the baron had heard of Briona's death. He said he had heard of it from Miles."

In a tremor of excitement, Truly's mind became one again. "Who, now?"

"Miles Wakefield, the one good man in my life." Delia gave a hopeful look. "Do you know of him?"

So much for absolution, he thought. It was time to lie, time to mislead. "Can't say I do. Although, Manfred could have mentioned him to me and I forgot. Age and memory, you know."

"Miles is a Southerner," said Delia. "From Georgia. But you need not hold that against him. He is a photographer and loves his trade. For me, his visits made life in that cursed house almost bearable. He was my only solace after Briona died." She brushed some hair from her face. "I've been angry with him, though. I believe he knows more about what happened but hasn't told me. Like Madam, he has promised that the lieutenant-colonel will pay for his crime but also resisted my every question. He insists it's dangerous to even ask about it, but refuses to say why. So, fancy my shock that he had spoken freely about Briona to a stranger."

At last–confirmation of Wakefield's link with La Maison. Delia's was the most innocent of betrayals. And now, like a snake, Truly had to exploit it. "Perhaps we could meet with Mister Wakefield–persuade him to help us with what he knows."

Slowly Delia shook her head. "In that regard, Major, he is like a wall. And lately he has kept away from the house. I could not say where he is, though he does have a shop in the city."

Truly suppressed a sigh. So the hide and seek would continue, he thought. Though a prize in other respects, the ill-used Delia would be of no use in snaring her beau. Her ignorance of Wakefield's activities seemed genuine, another tribute to his discretion.

Her voice lilted on. "The last time I saw Miles, he had me released from the cellar. He said he'd gotten Madam to let me out. Miles dislikes the old hag but seems to have influence with her, for some reason. Once again he would not tell me anything–nothing about Briona's death, or your friend's. He denied ever meeting the baron, but I fear I don't believe him." Delia's tone turned bleaker. "That's partly why I have come to you, Major. Because however much I care for Miles, I cannot trust a man who keeps so much secret. At first I believed that he visited the house only to see me–but he is somehow tied to those people, Madam and Monroe and Dubray. On that last visit, he would only say he had to stay out of sight for the time being, that he was up to something risky and important. It would be achieved very soon, and then we could be together. But I'd had my fill of such talk. When the chance came to escape, I took it. I hid in the woods all night, and this morning I hailed a teamster and rode in with him. I recalled Archer addressing you by name after he killed the baron, and Madam referring to the Secret Service. So once in the city, I asked an officer of the provost guard where the Secret Service was. He escorted me to the Treasury Building, where I found Mister Duke."

Truly was seeing Monroe again, this time in a Union major's garb: awaiting Van Gilder's coach in the shadows along Back Creek Road–the Copperhead's escape route known to him, the location carefully selected. Waiting as the night nurtured his lust, the patient lust of a true-born killer. Thus, three weeks later, did a chatty tipsy harlot cost Kirschenbaum his life, stirring Monroe's memory of a misshapen coachman. Still, Delia's story revealed just how well Kirschenbaum had done in his final doomed hours, smoking out much of the needed information. Through a fresh prickling of sadness, Truly felt proud of him.

Looking at Delia, he smiled a bit. "I'm thankful for us both that you proved resourceful. I've been searching in vain for any female who formerly worked at La Maison, who could tell me some of what we needed."

"There was but tiny chance of that, Major. When Madam grants anyone permission to leave, she hands over that girl's savings plus a small bonus–but with a warning to leave the District and not return. It is not known why, but there are awful stories of those who failed to obey and were found out."

Truly nodded. "They leave little to chance, I reckon. Such a rule, backed with such tales, would serve to thwart a prying stranger like myself."

"I wish I could help you more," said Delia. "I was there fewer than six months, though it seemed like an age. Most of the girls kept me at arm's length. They were jealous, I think, because of Miles. We met shortly after I came there, and he arranged that I not have to consort with other men, though I earned the going rate." She rubbed her forehead. "My savings . . . "

"Do not worry," Truly said. "I'll see to it that you're compensated. And lest we forget, you do have your life." And much else, he thought. If Wakefield actually loved this fair fugitive, whatever her trials and origins, Truly had further cause to admire him. Just then he noticed her gaze upon him, neither hard nor sharp but pressing steadily.

"Major, I have spoken truthfully. And I've told as much as I can. Don't think me ungrateful, but I must ask–what is your interest in all of this?"

He should have expected the question, from one so direct. Meeting her insistent blue eyes, he chose his words with care. "My organization is sworn to root out treason. This officer we seek, this nameless man responsible for Briona's death, is quite possibly involved in something treasonous."

Delia looked at the ceiling. "So Briona is just . . . a detail?"

"She is not central."

Her silence pained him.

"But mark my words," he said. "If we catch him . . . *when* we catch him, I will take that much more pleasure in it. It will be a mighty pleasure to crush the man who took your friend, as I hope to crush the one who took mine." He eyed her uncertainly. "Your trust is in short supply, I know. But can you trust me this far?"

To his relief, she gave him a drowsy smile. "Aye, Major."

"Now, I know you need more sleep . . . " Rising, he felt the sprain in his leg and leaned against the chair. Almost instantly the pain passed, only to uncover a different kind in his brain. A raw friction, as if his thoughts were stuck in place. There was something he had missed, some shadowy equation that resisted focus. Like the noise of a lone cricket, it chafed at him. "One last thing, Delia. Those stories you mentioned, about females who left La Maison but failed to leave the District . . . "

"Yes?"

"I don't suppose Monroe figured into that?"

Pulling her legs up, she rolled onto her side. "Every girl at La Maison fears Madam, and that pig Dubray too. But Monroe? If I yell in my sleep tonight, you'll know he's entered my dreams. Never mind the stories about him–it's something in his eye and his voice, in the way he moves. He frightens men as well. He frightens everyone except Madam. To her he is the grandest gift, a prize beast–smart and tame enough to move in any crowd, yet still a beast."

As Truly listened, the chafing in his head became a steady throb. Far down in his memory something was stirring, crawling toward the light.

"Do you know anything private about him?" he asked.

Delia's hand touched her throat as she lay there, blinking. "If you catch him with his hat off, there's a bad scar along his scalp. I once heard a drunken patron ask him about it, and Monroe said it was a war wound. A wound from Mexico."

In a wash of cold, Truly recalled staring at Monroe in Ravenel's bed-chamber–the big sullen man, eyes hidden beneath his hat brim. He had wanted Monroe to look up–a sudden, inexplicable wish, forgotten until now.

Reaching down, he drew Delia's blanket up to her shoulder. "Sleep well. You're safe."

"Thank you," she murmured.

Truly shut the bedroom door. The cold sensation clung to him, even as the image of heat waves shimmered up–a veil through which the deserts and mountain vistas of Mexico appeared. He could taste the dust.

Minutes later he was in his own room, on his knees before the open cedar chest. He knew what he had to find. Still he made himself search slowly, deliberately, resisting his agitation–and as he picked through the tokens of his past, a state of dreaminess cocooned him. Near the top, smelling of mildew, lay several copies of his published memoir. He took one out, stroked its green binding and turned to the title page: *Sojourns of a Frontier Scout* by Nathaniel Tecumseh Truly, Chicago 1858. It had caused no great stir, though subsequent lecture fees had enabled him to quit Pinkerton's agency–amicably enough, that first time. But after trying his hand at other writing, the war's onset had found him restless and uncertain, vulnerable when Pinkerton's telegraphed plea arrived from Washington: MOMENTOUS TIMES–GOOD MEN NEEDED–AMPLE PAY–PLEASE COME EAST. What if he had declined? Would the war tides have left him relatively untouched, sitting on his stoop outside Chicago? With Rachel still at his side?

He closed the book. Like so much else, it was laughably dated now. He stacked the volumes on the floor, then took out a folder of mail from long-ago readers. Without bothering to sample them, he recalled some choice ones. An Iowa army chaplain, lambasting his portrait of plains Indian life: "As an emissary of Christian civilization, you have failed utterly and shamefully to present these beings as what they are–savage of mind, immoral of habit, ghastly of ritual–all in the name of your supposed 'truthful detachment.'" A New York professor of classics, citing an opposite failure: "Snared in a web of homey detail, random anecdote and novel exploit, you never ascend to that loftier plane from which the reader may appreciate the essential nobility of these tawny Children of God's Earth, nor the simple, shining purity of their ways."

Truly went deeper into the musty chest, steadily backward in time. There were journals and family documents, some of Anna's baby clothes, Sapphira's paper of manumission, a crude wooden duck that Ben had whittled for him. There was the county sheriff's badge that he had worn for three years, following his return from Mexico. He paused to unfold a yellowing 1850 copy of the *Missouri Republican*. A banner headline announced the death of President Zachary Taylor, whose idealized, black-bordered image appeared beneath it. Another front-page story reported the ongoing Congressional deadlock over slavery, its proposed spread into the newly conquered territories of the West. Turning to an inside page, he located a colorful but far smaller story, its facts well stretched, of how Macon County Sheriff Nathan Truly had tracked, surprised and jailed three robbers encamped along the Chariton River. Reprinted and further embellished in the *National Police Gazette*, the tale had caught Pinkerton's eye in Chicago and prompted a letter from him, describing his nascent detective agency and offering Truly an interview, plus travel reimbursement.

"Fate," Truly murmured, "thy name is Allan Pinkerton."

"I remember that."

Jarred from his reverie, Truly looked over his shoulder. Ben stood stocking-footed in the open doorway, his arm in its sling and a fresh bandage masking half his face.

"My sheriff daddy, bringing in the bad men. That puffed me up for a year or so."

Laying the paper aside, Truly picked up the whittled duck. "You remember this too?"

Ben took the hand-sized bird and examined it. "Not what you'd call a prodigy, was I?"

Truly sat back against the chest. "You were a good boy."

Though still a mess–his hair snarled, his wrinkled shirt reeking of sweat–Ben was at last becoming whole underneath. He handed back the duck. "I get to sleep in my own room tonight. Saph got poor Octavius to help drag my bed upstairs."

"Well, he's always eager to help."

"Say, who's the Irish girl? And what's this Maison de Emperor? Sounds like somewhere in France."

It was disconcerting to hear Ben speak the name, inexpertly or not. Truly gave an impatient sigh. "It's a high-toned bawdy house, and I wish to hell it was in France."

"Where, then? Marble Alley?"

"No, way out on the Seventh Street Road, just north of Piney Branch . . ." Putting the wooden bird aside, Truly eyed his son. "And why in tarnation would the address matter to you?"

"Oh, I just thought I'd heard of all the fancy places."

"Just heard of 'em, eh? Well–before we drop the subject, here's some advice: Even if you end up a general, don't think of setting foot there."

"No call to worry, on either count. I wouldn't have asked, except the girl was in such a state and going on about it. And Saph seemed pretty worked up herself."

Truly felt the agitation creeping back in. These names, this knowledge–none of it had any place in this house, except in his own head.

"Well, I'll let you get back to reminiscing," Ben said, making an awkward turn. "As I always say, Pa–things sure do happen to you."

"Look who's talking. Shut the door, would you?"

As Truly watched Ben shuffle out, a rush of gladness briefly swept his worry aside, bringing to mind some other startling good news: Forbes, according to Duke, was back in Washington. Come morning, Truly would try to catch the Bostonian at his usual boarding house.

He resumed his search of the chest. He withdrew a beaten pair of boots, squeezed their soft leather and placed them on the floor. Peering farther down, he saw the folded, faded blue uniform. His heart sped up as he reached in with both hands. He was about to lay the uniform with the other mementos when he hesitated, then pressed his face into the weathered cloth. Closing his eyes, he inhaled. He inhaled the dust and sun of 1847, letting it swirl through his head. It smelled of adventure. It reeked of shame.

He heard the shouts of men, the crackle of musketry, the booming of howitzers, the braying of pack mules. He saw looming mountains, glittering lakes, deep-cut valleys full of orchards, songbirds flitting above the chaparral; the cooled black lava of the Pedregal, a fireless hell; Mount Popocatepetl, a snow-crowned god against the sky; Mexican lancers crossing a ridge, fading like a mirage; the distant glint of artillery. He saw tents and hovels, cathedrals and haciendas; ruined pyramids stained with ancient blood; fresh blood staining the walls of Molino and Chapultepec. He saw the tattered American column as it snaked through the great plaza, past gentry and peasantry who stared and stirred and clutched rosaries, murmuring the prayer of the vanquished: "Merced, Maria. Madre di Dios, Madre di Dios . . . "

He placed the uniform beside the boots and took out a wooden box. He removed the lid. Inside was his commendation from the Battle of Churubusco, signed by General Winfield Scott himself, and underneath that a string-tied packet of letters. He sat up cross-legged with the packet and pulled its string, which broke. The letters spilled into his lap. He would have lingered over each one, especially Rachel's, but felt an urgency keener than dread or sentiment. Rustling through the bone-dry little pages, he glanced at dates and random phrases, casting letters aside until he found one of his dated August 3rd of that year, written somewhere near Puebla.

Even as he read the first line, the truth erupted–a deep detonation, a heaving in his brain. Recognition, disbelief and then certainty. The chill came surging back, though the letter seemed to burn in his hand. "My dearest Rachel," it read. "For short periods we have been cut off from the

coast by guerilla activity, but I trust this will get to you in its own time."
Images reeled, vivid as a saber's flash—stark fragments that cut and sliced
and then fused into a scene. At its center was a pair of eyes staring back at
him, hard and gray and almost devoid of expression—staring as an endless
wail filled his ears, shrill and horrible. He read on:

"I now see that there are places and persons truly forsaken by God,
evils afoot in the world that, once glimpsed, make a man ache for the
refuge of what he loves best. How can I explain myself to you, who would
never have chosen to hear such? But my mind's burden is heavy. And I feel
forced to tell of how yesterday, I met the devil's own begotten son."

60

Fort McHenry, Baltimore

FORBES HAD OFTEN wondered what it might be like to confront an actual profiteer of the slave trade. In part he was merely curious, but it was more than that. From boyhood he had carried an image of the slaver, this anonymous symbol of all that the moneyed yet God-fearing Forbes clan had ever loathed. He pictured a man of brutish physique, with tight lips, clenched hands, dirty fingernails and a matted black beard. The face reflected low cunning, the kind of nerve unchecked by scruple–a scavenger's intelligence, or that of some lesser predator. Yet the small, cruel eyes would flicker panic, a growing fright before the weight of God's judgment, soon to fall. Greed fattened in the counting house, pride puffed at the helm of an evil ship–these would shrivel before the clear accusing eye of Bartholomew Forbes, would wither as a legion chorus of victims swelled from the shadows, damning the wicked man's soul to eternal fire.

Now, at last, Forbes beheld his slaver, and all the mental preparation had proven worthless. Gaston Saint-Felix, if not for his stubble and his grimy shirt, could have been mistaken for a French attorney or even a diplomat. Resting his back against the cell wall, he sat in the gloom and regarded Forbes with what looked for all the world like good-humored patience. Four months' confinement had not faded his tan or dulled his gaze. His folded, muscular hands looked capable, while his grayed temples and high, delicately lined brow lent a thoughtful impression. His mouth, creased at the sides, seemed to verge on a smile.

The fort's amiable commandant had supplied the known details of this prisoner's infamy. Saint-Felix came from Marseille. While still a young man, he had skippered a slave vessel between West Africa and the Caribbean, until the French anti-slaving squadron began to choke the trade along its section of African coastline. He then offered his services to an American syndicate based in New Orleans. After several lucrative voyages, his employers discovered that he had been making stops in Cuba, selling off a portion of his human cargo and pocketing the receipts. Returning to France–with a shrug, one imagined–he vanished for some time before surfacing in Washington in the war's second year. He became a vaguely sinister gadabout in pro-Confederate circles and then vanished once more, making his way South. Armed with references, he raised enough capital to buy the clipper *D'Artagnan* and start running small arms for cotton. For a year or more he repeatedly foiled the Union blockade and prospered on the European cotton market. It ended in March when he, his crew and his vessel with its load of Enfields were captured off Cape Hatteras. Forbes was less pleased to think of Saint-Felix's possible execution than of his languishing here, never to touch his distant, bloated bank account. Still there were those cordial ocean-blue eyes, eyes that expressed no plea for human mercy or heavenly grace.

The commandant had also provided Forbes with a comfortable cane-seated chair. Shifting in it, he tried to concentrate.

Saint-Felix spoke. "Am I correct that you have not brought me an official pardon?"

"You are," said Forbes.

"Or to prepare me for the gallows?"

"No. There'll be a trial first."

"No matter. It is good to have a visitor. I have had very few."

"It's hardly a social call."

"All the more intriguing, then."

There was also the factor of Saint-Felix's voice. Forbes had heard these rhythms once before, though not in this fluent English. As a youth, at the mansion of a family friend, he had eavesdropped on a pair of colored female servants from the Lesser Antilles. He had no clue what their conversation was about–the laundry, perhaps. Yet he grew strangely warm as he listened to their French patois–leavened, so he imagined, by the phantom-soft tones of Africa. Night sounds that burbled like a lullaby, undulated like reeds in a brook. It was this same liquid melody that Forbes heard now, in baritone, from the throat of an unrepentant slaver. He felt a little sick.

"I'm here to ask about a brief acquaintance of yours, from nearly two years ago," Forbes said. "Jonathan Peavey–you remember him?"

The ocean-blue eyes seemed to deliberate.

"A young tobacco grower in Prince Georges County," said Forbes. "You were once an overnight guest at his house."

"Ah! Yes . . . Two years, you say? Mon Dieu, it seems a lifetime." Saint-Felix drew a casual foot up onto his mattress. "An odd request, if I may say. There are more interesting experiences I could describe, and more interesting men."

"I'm certain. But it's Peavey I would like to discuss."

"Tell me, Captain–is that a false leg you have?"

"Yes. Let's stick to Peavey, shall we?"

"A token of the battlefield, no doubt. *Alors*, sir–we all pay for our choices, do we not? In my case, by forfeiting choice itself."

That voice–mellifluous, maddening. Forbes wished he could block out the tone and still hear the words. In dismay he saw how little Saint-Felix resembled the tense, weary, simpler men he was used to interrogating, let alone the slaver of his imagination. "Listen, Saint-Felix. You have nothing to lose and I have nothing to give. I didn't come here with coercion in mind."

"A gentlemen's chat, then? That does me great honor, Captain."

Forbes' lips tightened. "As I was saying–in that period, you were known to a certain part of Washington society. You met many members of the planter class, including Peavey."

Saint-Felix nodded. "I partook of the gaiety, yes."

"How was it that you were invited to Peavey's estate?"

"I rather invited myself."

"I know you were looking to purchase a fast vessel. That was why you called upon him, I presume?"

On the handsome, aging face, a smile appeared. "If you have met the fellow yourself, I ask this: Can you think of any reason besides money to call upon him?"

"Frankly, no." The two of them traded chuckles. It might be advantageous, Forbes thought, to imply a deeper knowledge of Peavey than he actually had. "You had yourselves a pretty rum-soaked night, didn't you?"

"I confess I have had many of those."

"Not unusual, for a man of the sea. But can you tell me what you talked about? Beyond the prospect of running arms to the South, I mean."

Saint-Felix peered at him. "You claim you have nothing to give, Captain. That is shockingly modest, coming from an officer of the illustrious Union Army." He made a loose-handed gesture. "And despite your casual approach, you have bothered to come and see me–me, of all your government's many prisoners. Your pardon, sir, if I express bafflement."

"You're not baffled. Deluded, maybe." Forbes heard the edge in his own voice.

"Understand that I am first and last a man of commerce," said Saint-Felix. "Haggling is a most difficult habit to break."

In the dank air, Forbes felt a weight shift invisibly against him. Venom rose, bitter in his mouth. He had long recognized this as his worst, most self-defeating trait. Yet staring at Saint-Felix, he found himself imagining implements of torture: thumbscrews, hot pokers, the rack. "A man of commerce? Then I would think you'd be less prone to fantasy."

"Fantasy? Au contraire. Whatever my position, I must consider this very real interest of yours. And what real answers I may supply."

Forbes folded his arms. "And what do you fancy yourself haggling for?"

Saint-Felix shrugged. "A reduction."

"A reduction?"

"Of the charges against me."

Forbes gaped. From deep in his chest, laughter broke. Like a forgotten prisoner it broke free, booming, throttling him until he rose from the chair and leaned against it. Saint-Felix blinked at him; it was sublime to grin back. "Thank you!" Forbes exclaimed. "Merci! We share at least one attitude." He adjusted his hat. "In running the blockade, you risked capture; in coming here, I risked a waste of time. I won't bemoan the outcome, anymore than you do. Enjoy the rest of your stay."

"A change of prisons, then," said Saint-Felix. "Someplace more agreeable."

Forbes' laughter sprung anew. "Let me aid your perspective. Rather than here, you could be up at Governor's Island or in a naval prison, sharing lice with some syphilitic Jack Tar!" He gestured to the small open window. "And would you even have this wondrous harbor view?"

Saint-Felix looked fleetingly irritable, then composed. "A cigar, then."

Forbes eyed him.

"A cigar," Saint-Felix said. "And a bottle of rum."

Forbes stepped to the window. Inhaling the sea brine, he scanned the grassy humps of shore batteries, the windless blue of the Patapsco River. A listless sentry paced along a rampart. From out there, fifty years ago, British ships had bombarded McHenry in vain. The guns quieted, the smoke lifted and the banner yet waved. In the dawn's redundant "early" light, it waved, and Francis Scott Key scribbled his anthem. A people's anthem, a hymn to democracy, strung with notes too steep for the common voice.

Turning, Forbes rubbed his chin. "That's more appropriate. Still, there's nothing to stop you from spinning falsehoods, is there?"

Saint-Felix sighed. "True, Captain. But that would be petty mischief, nothing more. I prefer . . . " A chuckle pumped out of him. "I prefer things on a grander scale."

Yes, Forbes thought. To one like Saint-Felix, lying for lying's sake would seem the province of mere scoundrels, unworthy of him. Forbes moved to the barred door window and called for the guard. The man's face appeared, his eyes garrison-dull.

"Soldier, ask General Morris if he might send a cigar and a bottle of rum to this cell."

The eyes blinked. "Sir."

The guard left and Forbes sat. Saint-Felix stretched, grinning. "You see? We each had a thing to gain, after all."

"Two things, in your case."

"Actually, I have a third one in mind."

Tensing, Forbes glowered. "I thought our little contract was settled."

"Calm yourself. You are a cultivated man, I can tell, and your company pleases me. There is so little here to stimulate the mind. Vacant guards, jabbering fellow prisoners, occasionally one of your execrable newspapers."

"And this third thing you'd like?"

"A novel, sir. If at all possible, the latest work by Dumas. I do enjoy him."

Forbes studied him. "I doubt they have a copy lying about."

"When our visit is over, ask the general to obtain the book and send it to me."

"Dumas the Elder or the Younger?"

Saint-Felix feigned indignation. "Dumas *père*, of course!"

"Consider it done."

"Magnifique!"

Again, the easy grin. Trying to ignore it, Forbes watched a spider scale the chipped wall.

He had spent the night in a smelly waterfront hotel, disturbed by fireworks as the City of the Rocket's Red Glare hailed the Fourth. But the sun had risen on excitement of a different nature. With Baltimore's pro-Confederate majority suppressed since the first months of the war–its elected officials jailed here at McHenry and substituted with federal men– resentment turned to fist-like anticipation as rumors filtered in from the Harper's Ferry region: rebel horsemen, fanning eastward into Maryland. Pro-Union optimists such as the hotel desk clerk believed as Grant and the War Department did: not a major invasion but a cavalry raid, albeit one of unusual daring. Among the patriot minority, however, alarm was more evident–in the rattle of newspapers, in the flutter of conversations, most of all in the clumsy, hurried drilling of militia units. At this hour Forbes should have been on the train back to Washington, drafting a telegram to Colonel Sharpe. Instead he was here, trading small items for information of uncertain value–here with this genial slavemaker, a man who wore his depravity like silk.

Neither of them spoke again until they heard the jingle of the guard's keys. Saint-Felix looked up brightly as Forbes opened the door. The guard held up a small basket. "Sir, General Morris figured your request was for the prisoner. He thought he would see to your pleasure as well." Upright in the basket, a bottle of rum kept company with two cigars, two small glasses and a box of matches.

"Such kindness!" Saint-Felix exclaimed. "Then I will not have to indulge alone."

"Thank the general," Forbes mumbled, taking the basket. The guard locked the door. Forbes set the basket down by Saint-Felix's mattress and retook his seat. "So–as to your conversations with Peavey. What did they cover?"

With ceremonial flourish, Saint-Felix bit off the end of one cigar, then lit it before proffering the other. Forbes kept his arms crossed. Smirking, Saint-Felix lay the cigar and matches on the floor and settled back. He took a long draw. "What did we discuss? Northern wickedness, Southern virtue, the recent success of Confederate arms. He spoke with a passion that I encouraged, hoping to turn it to my advantage. Soon, however, I suspected that Peavey's chief talent lay in raving, not in action. When I mentioned my quest for an arms-running vessel, he steered to other sub-jects. He boasted of his slaves, his house, his tobacco crop, his statuary." Saint-Felix puffed, chortled. "Maryland is a neutral state, yet still a Union one. And he loved the role of *grand seigneur*–who would not? The more he spoke, the more I saw that he would do nothing to jeopardize himself or his property." Setting his cigar down by his feet, he picked up the bottle of rum.

"What else?" Forbes demanded.

Saint-Felix struggled with the bottle's stopper. "Perhaps it would help if . . . " The stopper gave, dribbling rum onto his thigh. Unbothered, he poured a glassful. " . . . if I knew what sort of thing you are seeking."

"Your impression of Peavey fits mine," said Forbes. "A sniveler, a par-lor rebel. It struck me that he might be thrilled to find himself . . . " Forbes gave a cold smile. " . . . with a true man of action. That your tales of manly adventure might not only excite him, but stir his envy. And that he might, especially under the spell of liquor, make some amusing attempt to match these tales with some of his own. Fanciful lies or well-embellished facts."

"Ha!" Saint-Felix chuckled. "High marks to you! Yes, my stories did seem to affect him. I should possibly have been a novelist, do you think? Another Dumas?" He had filled both glasses. Raising one, he held it out to Forbes. "Come, we shall toast an end to war."

Forbes sat motionless.

"Captain–in the name of civility . . . " Saint-Felix stretched closer with the glass. "I detest drinking alone."

"I'll make sure you get the novel," said Forbes. "So what did Peavey come out with?"

With a sigh, Saint-Felix placed the spurned glass by Forbes' chair, next to the spurned cigar. He retrieved his own cigar and re-lit it. "As a matter of fact, Peavey told me something quite striking. Enough so that I lost all desire for his aid and partnership. So that when I departed the next day, I did not look back, and was thankful that my overtures had come to nothing."

"Let's hear it."

Sipping from his glass, Saint-Felix contemplated Forbes' boots.

Forbes hunched forward. "Saint-Felix . . . "

"How can I go on? How, when you have clouded my head with melan-choly? If you were one who simply abstained from drink, you would have said so by now. I can only conclude that you regard me in the harshest light."

"Whatever would make you think so?"

"I am a well-bred son of Marseille."

"And we had a damned bargain!"

Saint-Felix puffed his cigar, its coal glowing red. Peering up, he exhaled a cloud. "But there is so much in life that we never bargain for. A lost leg. A lost ship. Prison . . ."

The voice oozed, floated, coiled like tendrils. Forbes watched the smoke above Saint-Felix's head, winding like a ragged blue shroud. He looked down and saw the glass of rum, set between his chair and a crack in the stone floor. Out of the crack, a black beetle emerged. It scuttled over the cigar, bumped against the glass and navigated around it. Reaching down, Forbes had a sliding sensation, till he thought he might topple sideways. He picked up the glass. Without a glance at Saint-Felix, he raised the rum to his lips, paused, then took a sip. Momentarily it numbed the inside of his mouth. Then he saw his family. There in the winding cigar fumes, they stood watching him–his tall father, stern and sad; his small, elegant mother, stunned and sad; his three sisters, troubled and mystified; Gerald, separate in the mistier background, inscrutable. And all the while, the rum burned, tasting of chains and murder.

"To war's end!" Saint-Felix proclaimed. He took a smart swallow. His eyes squeezed shut and then opened, attentive once more.

Forbes held the glass on his knee. "Go on," he muttered.

Saint-Felix coughed, then wiped his lips. "Peavey was saying that extraordinary men such as we had to run a gauntlet of knaves; bold steps were required to secure our destinies. His conspiratorial air grew tiresome at this point, but I made myself listen. He said that with certain parties in Washington, he had formed a powerful alliance of some sort."

"Did he name anyone?"

"Two persons," said Saint-Felix. "One called Monroe, supposedly a grand-nephew of Monroe the American President–Peavey made a special point of that. But it was the other name that seized my attention. Back in my wicked and beloved Marseille, they still speak of Yvette de Ravenel. In a port renowned for its brothels, Ravenel ran three of the very best, featuring beauties from all over the Mediterranean. Men of high rank and title called there to spend their francs, as did I on a few expensive occasions. I never met the woman herself, but you can imagine my surprise when Peavey mentioned her." Looking reflective, Saint-Felix sipped his rum. "There were, of course, stories about her. Before she began to lose her looks, she was a highly successful courtesan in Paris. She was said to come from Guadeloupe, where she learned the so-called black arts as a girl. Marseille is known for its intrigue, and Ravenel maneuvered through it like a grand eel. Artful blackmail was a specialty of hers. Artful murder, too, though never as a first resort. A physician named Dubray was a partner of sorts, rumored to be an expert in the field of poisons."

Forbes looked down at his glass. "If she was so entrenched there, why did she come to America?"

"Why? Even Napoleon overplayed his hand, Captain, and Ravenel overplayed hers. As with Napoleon, the price was exile. There was a gentleman, a count, who was a frequent customer at one of her houses. Ravenel's ladies catered to all bents of passion, and this count's was particularly colorful. Strenuous, too, for on his final visit his heart gave out. Using the circumstances of his death, Ravenel tried to blackmail his family, who had extensive property. To avoid scandal, they would almost certainly have paid a large sum. But Ravenel had something else in mind–a choice tract of land which the family had owned for generations. She would not relent, and it proved too much for their honor. They declared secret war, pulling every lever available to them. And Ravenel was thwarted. Her police protection was withdrawn, her houses shut down. She realized her blunder and that it was too late to negotiate–that her very life was in danger so long as she remained in France, let alone Marseille. Abruptly she disappeared, along with Dubray. All of this I heard on one of my last trips home, though no one knew what had become of her." Saint-Felix downed the last of his drink and poured another. "Some months after Ravenel's disappearance, the count's widow, their son, their daughter-in-law and two guests were found dead. A bottle of cognac in their cellar had been laced with poison."

Forbes raised his glass. He took another fiery sip.

"In Peavey's telling," Saint-Felix went on, "he was one of several men in league with Ravenel–her, and this associate Monroe. Peavey presented it as a fair union of equals, but you can see why this provoked silent mirth on my part. And why my interest in his friendship ended then and there– shoomp! Like a guillotine." With his cigar hand, Saint-Felix made a chopping motion. "While I have never been noted for caution, I wished to avoid even an indirect connection with the lady. Yvette de Ravenel is a collector of men. She plays to their weaknesses and they dance to her tune. I can imagine her longing for the good old days in Marseille, when she called the tune for so many. She would be well aged now. But if Dubray is still with her, and if her partner Monroe is of similar stripe, I would wager that she has done well enough." He grinned. "Fools like Peavey are plentiful everywhere, are they not?"

"Indeed they are," Forbes said absently. He realized that he had drained his glass.

With a look of serenity, Saint-Felix went on. "Peavey referred to Ravenel's current establishment, La Maison de l'Empereur. He offered me an introduction, so that I might enter this circle and gain my own ends. I declined as graciously as possible. In the morning, as I prepared to leave, I found Peavey suffering the aftereffects of our night and also the horror of his indiscretion. He begged me to tell no one what he had revealed. I assured him I would honor his wish, having no reason not to." Saint-Felix smiled. "Until now."

"Did he describe any others in the group?" Forbes asked. "A Union officer, for instance?"

Saint-Felix cocked a skeptical eye. "No. And what an unlikely association that would be. Here, let me refill your glass."

Forbes stared at the Frenchman's hands–one holding the bottle, the other his fuming cigar. Weathered hands, the nails not especially dirty.

"Captain?"

"No, thank you." Forbes turned his eyes to the window. The sun lanced in, harsher than before. Squinting, he saw Gerald's face staring at him. He placed the glass on the floor, next to his booted wooden foot. The ghost-pains had started. "I'll be leaving now."

"Must you, really?"

Rising, Forbes crushed the glass beneath his heel.

Saint-Felix blinked at the fragments. "Remember Dumas."

"I will." Forbes moved to the door. About to knock for the guard, he suddenly recalled something that he had heard at Harvard, from a visiting French journalist. He looked back at Saint-Felix. "I've read Dumas too, in translation. I enjoyed *The Black Tulip.*"

Saint-Felix looked pleased. "*Le Comte de Monte Cristo* is my own favorite."

"Dumas has Negro blood, did you know?"

Saint-Felix gave a blank look, then shrugged. "I did not, sir. Interesting."

"Isn't it? His paternal grandmother was a Negress from Santo Domingo. He's a quadroon."

Ogling, Saint-Felix drew on his cigar. "That charming accent of yours, Captain—may I ask where it is from?"

"Boston," said Forbes.

"Ah!" The Frenchman nodded at the floor. "The New World's Abolitionist capital. I thought so."

Forbes suddenly felt better, despite the growing throb in his leg.

"Such a contrast we are," Saint-Felix said. "We could learn much from each other."

"How odd that you would think so."

"Do not be so certain, Captain. I could for instance take you across the waves . . . " Saint-Felix stubbed out his cigar on the floor. " . . . across the waves to the Great Bulge of Africa. To the coastal kingdoms where black kings of black subjects eagerly sell black captives by the shipload. All this despite the efforts of pious individuals like yourself." He propped his elbows on his knees, hands dangling. "More than that, I could take you to the singular little nation of Liberia—founded, as you may know, by American Abolitionists and colonized by former slaves. Former slaves who may be witnessed beating, whipping and otherwise abusing the native tribespeople. Tribespeople who nonetheless continue to prosper as tribes—engaged, as they have long been, in the coastal slave trade. Sending shiploads of dark bodies ever westward." Around Saint-Felix's head, smoke lingered like swamp mist. His smile cut through, while the pain in Forbes' leg cut deeper.

"That's supposed to alter me on the subject?" Forbes said stiffly.

"No, no, my dear Captain. And on second thought, you are quite correct—we have little to teach each other. I believe that, despite war or any other experience, you will go on imagining things as you always have. A world of demons and angels, all so easily recognized. Rather like a novel." Eyes twinkling, Saint-Felix looked up. "I envy you a bit. In the world that I see, such grandeur is rather lacking. Plainer ideas drive men to do this or that. Storybooks are for me an escape, but what must they be for you? A glorious confirmation. Yes, I do envy this."

Forbes knocked for the guard. "You're no demon, Saint-Felix. Just a damned bore."

"*Tien!*" the Frenchman exclaimed. "No one has ever accused me of that. But let us not part on such a note. Listen—what sort of fix is young Peavey in? You have made me curious."

The guard's face appeared through the barred window. "Sir?"

Forbes looked over his shoulder. "Peavey's dead."

"Oh?" Saint-Felix sat there, freshly alert. He reached for his rum. "Do tell me how!"

"I'm through here," Forbes told the guard.

"Captain? Captain!" In Saint-Felix's voice, a shade of indignation. "Really, sir, would it hurt so to give an answer?"

Away from the guardhouse, Forbes beheld the stockaded parade ground; sentries idled while low-security prisoners strolled about, most of them deserters or other Union army violators. He limped up onto a rampart and stood there. The river glittered, as did the Chesapeake beyond, where the British fleet had bobbed with cannons thundering. His thoughts were like boiling mud. Turning, he gazed across the harbor to the buildings of Baltimore.

On April 19, 1861, a week after Fort Sumter was fired upon, a mob of pro-Southern Baltimoreans had clashed with Massachusetts troops on their way to defend Washington. In Boston, news of the deaths and injuries brought war clamor to a howling peak. Forbes was as angry as anyone. Soon to enlist along with Gerald, their male cousins, their boyhood friends and Harvard classmates, he felt an extra charge of resolve. Yet there was, as well, something akin to sorrow. His main thought was that on the anniversary of Lexington and Concord, of the revolution that ultimately cast off royalist tyranny, citizens of one original colony had attacked the troops of another. Some people mentioned the date but not the feeling, this sense of fine things spoiled. Forbes realized then how steeped he was in all the patriot legends, all the fables of young nationhood—the simplest, bravest, warmest images of the Republic. Nowadays, when he dared reflect, he wondered if this would be his most enduring grievance—not a dead brother, dead friends or a lost leg but his original grievance, the destruction of these cherished images. Yes—always the schoolboy. The mocking slaver was right.

Then he remembered how he had awakened this morning, tossing and flailing in the smelly hotel room. And he remembered the dream. In the thick of his old regiment, amid shot and shell, he was charging across a field toward a line of trees. At first he was bounding along, breaking into the lead. Then he faltered and the other men swept past him. Hobbling to a stop, he looked down, and through his torn trouser leg he saw his wooden limb, a limb not of crafted poplar but some cheaper wood, crude and scarred. Someone was calling his name through the din. He looked and saw Gerald not far ahead, waving a sword. Then he heard what his brother was shouting: "Don't mind it, Bart! Don't mind it!" But Forbes dropped his pistol. Somehow balancing on his good leg, he seized the wooden one and pulled it off. Instantly, bees started pouring from his stump–bees, bees in dense billows, like cannon smoke. Their drone enveloped him, drowning out the battle. Flailing, he teetered and began to fall as they swarmed out of him, darkening his vision, stinging him to the bone.

61

Truly Residence

IT WAS WELL after dark when Truly finally came downstairs. In the parlor he found Sapphira curled asleep on the settee, a book of verse in her lap. He extinguished the lamp and sat in his armchair, gazing at her recumbent form. He did not want to wake her. He wanted just to sit with her, here in the tick-tock quiet with faint lamplight coming in from the hall and Rachel's portrait looking on. But within a minute, Sapphira stirred.

"You'd best go to bed," he said softly.

Yawning, she worked herself upright. "Are you staying up again?"

"I just need to think some." But he had already done more thinking than he wanted. Brushing hair from her face, Sapphira set her book aside. Truly suddenly wanted her to stay.

The hall clock ticked out a long moment. "Was Miss McGuire any help to you?" she asked, her voice still sleepy.

"Quite a bit. Still a lot of obstacles, though. We'll see."

"This La Maison de l'Empereur—does whoever killed Mister Kirschenbaum live there?"

A clammy unease came over him. Leave it to Sapphira to remember the house's name, let alone pronounce it perfectly—she of those Parisian fancies. "The owners were party to the deed," he said. "The actual killer's connected to them."

"I won't ask you anything more," she said. "I wish to, but I won't."

Framed in the gloom, her face was a featureless dark oval, but she was definitely looking at him. Looking at him and doing what she had always done–shaping his responses, eliciting the unpredictable. Sooner or later, he thought, a man discovered how comically little he knew–how much was left to blind chance. It had been blind chance that took him wandering through the streets of New Orleans one day, down to a marketplace rumbling with bidders and spectators, where a black child stood frozen on the auction block. Forcing his mind to stillness, he pressed the child's image on the shadowed young woman before him.

"I'm thinking," he said, " . . . about all the things you've wanted to know."

"I told you, I'll stop now."

"I mean since far back." Shifting in his chair, he felt the sudden weight of her attention. After a few seconds' hesitation, he began. "I've never really told you about Mexico. My reasons for going . . . They seemed strong enough at the time. I was never a wizard at farming–and when the war came, my experience as a scout made me valuable. It meant a year of steady pay. And it would get me out in the far yonder once more– this time, as part of the biggest historical fandango the frontier had seen. 'Course, it was also the biggest land theft since Ghengis Khan set his eyes on central Asia. A boon for slavers, too, since they were itching to expand their territory. But to me, that was all something for the Eastern high-hats to thrash out.

"So off I went, like a fool. I was just an army hireling, really, but they gave me sergeant's stripes so I could help lead reconnaissance. I met a lot of young officers who went on to become the generals of today, for North or South. Once, I found myself taking orders from a certain topnotch captain named Robert E. Lee." Longing to digress, Truly resisted the urge. "I got my excitement, sure enough, and some of it I would never have chosen–things we did to the Mex, things they did to us. Describing it would serve no purpose, except in one particular case."

Sapphira's silhouette leaned slightly forward, the hall light glistening on her hair.

"After the victory at Cerro Gordo," he went on, "the army spent a few months at a city called Puebla, awaiting reinforcement. Then word came of a division under Franklin Pierce that was marching inland from Veracruz. It had been stalled by guerilla attacks and other problems. My scout unit was part of a brigade sent to escort this division the rest of the way, and we had little trouble getting to it. But then we learned of one straggling regiment farther back, in the foothills. I joined some cavalry sent to fetch this regiment, which we found at a pretty little town sur-rounded by citrus groves. We distributed water, commandeered wagons for the sick and made ready to move out. Just then, the guerillas attacked. Not many of them—we repelled them within minutes—but this coot of a volunteer colonel ordered a full deployment. These were scared, tired recruits, mostly from New England, unused to the terrain and climate. An hour later, we were still thrashing the brush for scattered platoons. The civilians kept their heads low; they must have wondered how on earth we were succeeding as conquerors.

"I was prodding some men out of a lime orchard when I noticed a hacienda a short way off. I rode toward it, thinking more troops might be holed up there, and it was then I caught this high-pitched wailing. As I gal-loped into the courtyard, I saw a tall soldier standing over a Mex woman. The woman lay there shrieking at the sky. Her dress was torn. The soldier was hitching his trousers up. I sprang off my horse and moved toward him, but I became aware of another noise beneath the woman's scream-ing. Then I saw past the soldier. There was a little girl of six or seven lying against a white masonry wall. The wall had a blood-spatter—he'd thrown her against it. And the sound coming out of her . . . It was nothing you'd ever expect from a child, no matter how hurt. A kind of loud, hoarse gur-gling. And I looked at the soldier and he looked at me, the strangest look. He had these clear gray eyes—no alarm in them, nor even resentment. Mild annoyance, maybe, as if I'd interrupted his dinner or his card game. I think I cocked my head, just like a dog when it's curious. I stared at him like you'd stare at a mythic creature. And the woman shrieked, wailed . . . wailed. The soldier's rifle stood against the wall, out of reach. I had my Colt and my Bowie knife—and as I drew them, he flew at me.

"He had his size, plus the speed of a rattlesnake. He had me down in seconds. I kicked and bit and held onto my weapons, but finally I had to throw the revolver aside. I gouged his eye and rolled out from under him. As I jumped to my feet, I saw the child staring over at me. Her upper lip was split, a tooth broken. I've never been able to forget that sight, that small dying face and her eyes on me, going dimmer. And in that instant I had a horrible thought—that she didn't know I was someone else. That in her dimming sight I was the one, I was the monster. Then, in my side-vision, I saw the soldier lunge for my Colt. I rammed him as he got to it, then I tore his scalp with my knife. Up till then he'd barely made a sound—it was amazing how calm he seemed. But now he roared. He roared as the blood blinded him, and I kicked him to his knees. I kicked like a stung mule, wanting his noise to drown out the woman's and the child's. When I stopped to get my wind, he managed to wipe the blood from his eyes. His eyes were different now, nothing casual in them. He was frightened. That's how I wanted him to die."

Truly's voice trailed off, his gaze fixed upon the wall behind Sapphira's head.

"You killed him?" she murmured.

"I would have," he said, swallowing. "Sure, I would have done him like an Apache. But right then my captain rode up with some horsemen. They took in the sight. I kept my eyes on the soldier and kept saying get a surgeon, get a surgeon, though the child was past hope. Finally the captain told me to put my knife away. He ordered his men to seize the soldier and they did, getting in some kicks of their own. He would pay for this with his foul worthless life, the captain told me, but army process would be observed. And it was time to move on. The mother flailed in the dirt, not letting us near her—and what could we do, really? We told some townspeople; they would see to the mother and child as best they could. As for our prisoner—on the march back to Puebla, he broke his guard's neck and escaped. When I heard of it, I went on a cussing rant. The captain was angry too, and embarrassed. He said the man might yet be caught. But the man was never caught. What with the embarrassment of his escape and the slim chances of getting him back—and with the war still going, after all—the army seemed disposed to forget about him. And would you believe . . . In all of that, I never learned his name. Reckon it hadn't occurred to me that he had one—a name, like any man.

"Anyhow, we marched on to the final battles. Mexico City fell. I spent a lot of time wandering the plazas, riding through the great valley. I had some broken Spanish from my younger days—so in those first few weeks, I'd describe the soldier to any beggar or tradesman or campesino or Catholic priest I met up with, telling them what he'd done. None of them could help me. There was little to do but cultivate a belief in hell. There was little to do, period. I was longing for home, as most of the troops were. General Scott did his best to maintain discipline, but there was still some plundering around the city. One morning, at the outskirts, I came upon a church that had been sacked. To the more God-fearing troops, these churches were a papist abomination; to the rest, they were just strange and foreign and thus a fair object for their discontent. Lucky participants came away with things made of gold or silver. Me, I was just bored and curious when I walked in. I looked over the broken saints, the ruined altar and what was left of the stained glass. And behind the altar, I found something the looters had missed. It was wrapped in a seared purple cloth—a chalice, gold with precious stones in it. I looked at it for a spell, thinking of Rachel and our raggedy little homestead. Then I left with it.

"So there it is—your old Papa Nathan went to Mexico and looted a church. Theft is simple when a man feels soiled already, right down to his bones. Soiled by the whole business of invading and occupying. But on some nights I'd take the chalice from its hiding place and gaze at it, and the child's face would gaze back. That broken little face . . . It would not leave me. Not until three months later, when another face replaced it. In New Orleans."

Around the oval shadow where Sapphira's face was, Truly saw everything: the crowd, the stout auctioneer, the chained figures.

"When I came drifting into the marketplace, I had Missouri on my mind—home, with Rachel and Ben and Anna. Soon I'd be staring out on the same land from the same cabin, measuring the kind of man I'd become. Then I realized what the spectacle before me was. Some dandies up front were doing most of the bidding. And I saw you. The auctioneer nudged you forward with his baton, up onto the block. You were four or five and dressed in sackcloth, about knee high to a pony. And the fellow called out, 'Gentlemen—some quick business. Though her mother be dead, the child is of hardy stock. The farsighted master will see in this pickaninny a useful house servant or field worker, whichever he choose—one who with proper care and discipline will render years of faithful service.' He spoke of your childbearing years when you'd produce more valuable property, more future labor. 'Satisfying yield for but a small investment'—that was his phrase.

"The bidding started at seventy-five. At first there were no takers and I just watched you, working my way toward the front. The auctioneer stressed that you had no sores or diseases. Then somebody raised his hand; next thing I knew, I'd raised mine. I think the first bidder was miffed to find himself competing with a scruffy specimen like me, because he kept it up. And I kept raising my hand. It was . . . There was something in your face, something about you that shut my mind down. Then it was done, and I had you for two hundred twenty-five. Not that the exact price mattered.

When I pulled the chalice out of my sack, the trader gaped at me and then grabbed it, probably thinking he'd never meet a bigger loon.

"On the boat up the Mississippi, we got plenty of looks from the other passengers. We watched the water and the other boats and the cattle along the bank. You had a few words mastered–'eat,' 'drink,' 'sleep' and such–but that was it, far as I could tell. I figured I'd find you a home with some free colored family. A few days later we came down the road toward the homestead, and I was carrying you along with my gear. You were asleep. I didn't know or care what I'd tell Rachel–I was too worn out. But I knew you wouldn't be going to live elsewhere. They'd call me a damned Abolitionist or a damned slaver, but they could all go sit on a rusty nail. See, they say redemption's never cheap–the poor pray for it and the rich dream of buying it–but that day, it felt like I'd gotten mine for a pittance. I'd gotten you, at least, and that was enough. And you were spared the plantation. Other things, I wished I could have spared you. I know I should have told you all of this long ago–I was afraid it would come out sounding like just another yarn, I reckon. But understand this–when I first saw you, I reached for you like a falling man reaches for anything that'll hold. I'm no churchgoer, but I've had one miracle: sundown on the fields and you on my shoulder, coming down the road to the old place."

Sapphira was looking down. Across the room, a breeze nudged the curtains. He heard her exhale slowly. "What was it that you saw in me? In my face?"

"Something they would have had to beat out of you."

She remained still a while longer. Then she got up. Moving past him, she proceeded to the dark fireplace. She stood there gazing at Rachel's portrait on the mantel, the vases with fresh wildflowers.

Truly's throat pulled tight. "But the world hasn't changed near enough. Someday, too soon for me, you'll take yourself and your fondest desires out there. And you'll pay for daring to have them. Tenfold, you'll pay–and there won't be a damned thing I can do about it."

"Father, how much dread would you have me feel?"

"Enough–no more, no less. Fear can be a good friend."

"Yes–and a tiring companion. As when it compels one to play house servant before strangers."

"Now hold there!" He twitched as if stuck with a hot poker. "Hold there, missy! As soon as you were able to comprehend, we told you why!

We explained the difference between how we saw you and how others would have to see you! We explained the hazards! All those . . . those rock-boweled Abolition prophets up North might call it a sinful compromise, but who among 'em ever had to protect a child from all that?!"

"Father–Father, you only gave words to what I knew already. It's not you I'm chafing at, or your reasons." She leaned against the piano. "It pleases me to maintain this house. Someone had to, with Mother gone. Yet I appear to myself, at times, as the very thing that guests and strangers see. Consider, please, that a pose may come to feel as true as the poser's own skin. And that once she realizes this, she knows it will have to end."

Rubbing his forehead, Truly said nothing. His insides felt blistered.

"What awakened this in you?" she asked. "What has happened?"

He wanted to stop talking but it was too late. An old barrier had given way. From the shadows, like chill black water, he felt the deluge of all that he had ever feared and fought, swirling with all he had ever loved. "The man I fought that day at the hacienda," he said, "the soldier who did that crime and escaped–he's here in Washington."

"Sweet Lord," she whispered.

"I didn't realize it until today, when Miss McGuire told me a few things. It's him, all right. Monroe is the name he goes by, but I believe it's false."

"And this is the one who killed Mister Kirschenbaum?"

"He was involved. In that, and much else. He's in league with others who find his nature useful. I have to stop them–and him, as I failed to stop him once before. Somehow I have to."

Sapphira gazed at the fireplace. "Well, then . . . It's you I'll be dreading for, not myself." There was numb resignation in her voice, along with a kind of wonder. Truly stared at the empty settee. In a moment, he heard her start to leave and looked up. She paused in the parlor doorway. "The cattle," she muttered, "–I remember them. On the riverbank."

He smiled a little.

"And the chalice . . . That, too." She turned fully toward him. "I saw you pass it to someone, this glittery thing. I was sorry because I wanted to hold it." In the hall's dim lamplight, she went motionless again, as if straining to hear a distant voice. "It had sapphires, didn't it? All around the middle."

Truly nodded. "Rubies too, child. But as a name, I didn't care for 'Ruby' quite as much."

Her hands reached to the sides, touching the threshold. Fleetingly the shadows of the room felt like shelter again, nothing cold or alien. "Thank you, Father."

"Good night, Saph."

Then she was gone.

The clock sounded a long series of chimes—eleven, perhaps twelve. Steeped in quiet, Truly's thoughts gradually became diffuse. He was starting to doze when a breeze touched his ear and he looked to the open window, the night outside. He got up, went over to the window and gripped the sash. As he pushed it down, something moved in the outer darkness. He leaped back.

"Nate!" a voice whispered.

Truly peered through the curtains. He saw the glint of an insignia and then the military hat, then Forbes' face beneath it.

"I was working up the nerve to knock," Forbes whispered.

Truly let out a ragged breath. He hurried out to the front door, admitted Forbes and clapped him on the back. "Good thing I wasn't armed."

"True." Forbes took his hat off. "And we have problems enough."

"What is it? Octavius said you went to Baltimore."

"Yes—where at this hour they have refugees pouring in from the western counties." Forbes had circles under his eyes. "Just before I got the return train, I questioned some new arrivals. They spoke of Reb cavalry along the Potomac and widespread raiding. Meanwhile, our only force out there has abandoned Harper's Ferry and Martinsburg and now it's burrowed in on Maryland Heights. That's all we know, since the telegraph's been cut."

Looking down, Truly scratched the back of his neck. His thoughts had been moving in a private direction; now the war reared up, hurtling them into reverse.

"So here's the nub of it," Forbes said. "—could a few marauding horsemen cause a scare this big? The War Department seems to think so."

"I know it," said Truly, scowling. "Seated firmly on its giant lazy ass, as usual!" He lowered his voice. "Octavius told me some of what you've learned. About Jubal Early."

"Right. Early—with an entire corps. Now, if he swings toward the capital, it will be imperative that Grant send reinforcements."

Truly nodded. "And if he's late doing that . . . Heck—isn't anyone else paying attention?"

"Only your friend Wallace."

"Lew Wallace? What's he doing?"

"The best he can. As chief of the Middle Department, he's based in Baltimore, but I didn't get to confer with him. He'd already left for Monocacy Junction, planning to scrape up stray infantry units–acting without orders, mind you, so he's probably risking court-martial. But as I understand it, he's bent on feeling out enemy strength and meeting any thrust toward Washington or Baltimore."

In early spring, a minor case had landed Truly in a meeting with Wallace, that deceptively gloomy-looking general from Indiana. The two of them had stayed up much of the night discussing Greco-Roman history. And it was perhaps the man's acute sense of history that explained his present initiative, a quality that his superiors so damnably lacked. "Well, good for him," Truly muttered. "Still, if Early has a force that large, he'll kick Wallace aside like an old bucket."

"Most assuredly," Forbes said. "I've sent a wire to Sharpe at City Point, and tomorrow I hope to hear from the scouts I dispatched. Maybe we can rouse Grant to action. Nate–I'm thinking of all this, and of Wakefield and La Maison. And . . . Well, I've more to tell you."

"Believe me, so do I. Come sit down."

Some three hours later, Forbes lay snoring on the parlor sofa while Truly sat in the dark of his study. Chewing, lamenting his lost spittoon, Truly turned his chair and spat through the open double window. The revelations echoed–his own about Monroe, Forbes' about Ravenel. If nothing else, these confirmed what had been born of that pairing. By themselves, this man and this woman would have been lethal rarities; together they were unique, a sum hideously greater than its parts. In each murder and machination, Truly perceived the cold broad scythe of their intelligence. He thought of Wakefield–precise, ruthless and resourceful, yet by all accounts a man of warm blood. Truly reflected once more that only something of huge potential, of vast mutual benefit, could have forged and sustained such an alliance. And in the quiet, the thought of the nameless lieutenant-colonel kept jabbing.

He got up and started pacing but then blundered into a bookcase. He cursed softly. Spreading his arms, he leaned against the window frame and spat his chaw into the darkness. He let his mind range northwestward, up the Potomac and into the far hills. He could feel it out there–Early's Rebel behemoth. He could feel it as it slept, soon to rise. Soon, squinting to the red dawn, it would sniff the breeze and hulk to life, its scarred gray hide spiked with banners and bayonets. On gun wheels and wagon wheels, on massed hooves and legion feet, it would stir the dust and trample the grass, taking to the roads again. Onward, nearer, with terrible resolve.

PART VII

A Shield Of Tin

The widow-maker soon must cave—Hurrah! Hurrah!
We'll plant him in some nigger's grave—Hurrah! Hurrah!
     • ANTI-LINCOLN SONG LYRICS 1864, SUNG TO THE TUNE
        OF 'WHEN JOHNNY COMES MARCHING HOME'

I see no bright spot anywhere, only humiliation and disaster.
     • GEORGE TEMPLETON STRONG,
     NORTHERN DIARIST, 1864

62

Near Sharpsburg, Maryland
July 6

*H*ERE, WHERE ARTILLERY had ripped the earth and sky, where barns and haystacks had burned, where battle lines had surged, withered and disintegrated, trailing bodies through the bullet-lashed corn and along the wooden fences–here, where slaughter had reigned, all was peaceful. The day was warm and clear, the corn high and the barns rebuilt. To the west, a Confederate encampment ringed the fair Unionist town of Sharpsburg, its citizens pondering their fate before another invasion. To the east, between steep wooded banks, Antietam Creek looped its way to the Potomac. Early's musings today were unusual, and he wished that the others had not wandered off so soon. He wanted to ask aloud if human struggle ever amounted to much. Once the smoke cleared and the last cry faded, what really remained except headstones and fever dreams?

He raised his field glasses. Across the undulating green of the landscape, by the Hagerstown Pike, he spied the tiny white church with no steeple. The church had marked the battle's axis. From behind it, through those same trees, Early had led his brigade to "relieve" Hood's division, though the latter was mincemeat by then. He recalled the gun roar, drowning the Rebel yell and the Yankee war-whoop; men charging, heads bowed to the tempest, falling like locusts in a fire. September 17th, 1862–nothing before or since had matched it. Not Gettysburg, not the Wilderness or Spotsylvania.

On a stone bridge over the creek, two boys sat with fishing poles, feet dangling. Scanning along the Boonsboro Pike, Early picked out the solitary figure of Gordon, dismounted now, lost in thoughts of his own. Early lowered the binoculars. Against all his usual feelings toward Gordon, a sense of brotherly connection took hold. On that endless roaring day, the Georgian had defended a stretch of sunken road known thereafter as Bloody Lane. Through one Northern assault after another, the position held fast until Gordon was carried from the field, five times wounded. His men fought on, only to die in rows and mounds amid a final onslaught. Yet their stand had exhausted the enemy and unsettled McClellan, who then failed to exploit the breach.

Early dismounted to stretch his legs. Doing so, he saw Kyd Douglas riding slowly toward him up the gentle slope.

Halting by Early's horse, the major gave an absent smile and hopped down. "I was just remembering, Genr'l–late that day I found Jackson eating a peach, sitting there with his dead all 'round him. You know what he said?"

"'God has been good to us,'" Early quoted. "I heard it from someone."

"Well, I was thinking too–for all that, God *was* good to us. Wasn't He?"

Shy of this Almighty reference, Early looked away. He ran a hand through his beard. "Suppose so, if it was Him working on McClellan. I didn't truly see it till it was all over, but McClellan could have finished us here. If he'd thrown his reserves in . . . "

"Or even if he'd renewed the attack next morning," said Douglas. "But no, he just sat there and let us limp back across the river."

"Yes, well . . . There's no substitute for nerve."

God was as good an explanation as any. It had been good enough for Jackson.

Rubbing his sore hips, Early assumed a hearty air. "Your father was right hospitable. In your next letter to him, pass along my respects."

Douglas gave an appreciative nod. Though brief, their visit to the nearby home of his widowed father had been pleasant. "He was honored to have you. Since the day I joined up for the South, he's taken a heap of abuse from Yankee neighbors."

"It must be an extra trial, coming from a border state," said Early.

The major's eyes turned distant. "I was speaking of that with General Breckinridge. It's worse for him. Seems he's related to half of Kentucky, folks on both sides of the war. Including Mary Lincoln, did you know? 'Cousin Mary,' he calls her."

Early grunted. "Do tell! Well, we might be calling on Cousin Mary pretty soon. *And* her husband."

Douglas removed his hat and wiped his brow, then pointed. "There he is now."

In the distance, Early picked out the mounted, majestic figure of Breckinridge in his dark blue coat, trotting along the road toward Gordon. Gordon remounted as Breckinridge drew up, and the two began speaking. Early sighed wearily. Logistical matters had begun to crowd his head once more. First, though, there was an issue that he could postpone no longer. "I need a word with him, Douglas. You'd best be getting back to Ramseur's camp."

The major departed. Early mounted up and descended into the rolling terrain, losing sight of the two generals. When the pike reappeared, there was only Breckinridge riding toward town. Early veered to intercept him. Seeing him, the Kentuckian reined up.

"Gordon was asking about the shoes again," said Breckinridge.

Early drew alongside. "They should arrive tomorrow."

"Good. Back at the ford, it was hell for the barefoot ones–all those sharp rocks."

Early was tired of the shoe predicament. "They're going without a lot of things. Forage and supplies are scarce, but we're doing our best. It's more vital than ever to maintain order." From Breckinridge's pained look, it was clear he had guessed where this was leading. Early continued briskly. "It hardly needs saying: we can't permit a repeat of Martinsburg."

Breckinridge gave a stoic nod. "No. We cannot."

"Your men's gladness was understandable. Marching up to the depot and seeing all those Fourth-of-July victuals the enemy left–it must have seemed like paradise."

"After days of eating parched corn, yes. Still . . . "

The enemy retreat had been too swift. From Martinsburg, from Harper's Ferry, across the river to the safety of Maryland Heights–all before a major attack could be pressed. Yankee skittishness had foiled rather than aided Early's trap. Yet it had proven a boon for Breckinridge's corps at Martinsburg, where rail cars and warehouses groaned with abandoned delicacies. The resultant orgy of eating, drinking and plunder did not bode well for discipline.

"I'm issuing a general order," Early said. "Any more marauding and such will be summarily punished."

"I'll see that it's enforced," said Breckinridge.

The discomfort passed. Once more Early was glad to have Breckinridge at his side. Whatever the glittering titles of his past, he could still listen manfully to criticism.

Early pulled the stopper from his canteen. "That's not to say we can't exact retribution. I've sent McCausland up to Hagerstown . . . " He took a swig and offered the canteen to Breckinridge, who took it. "It's a fair-sized place. He has orders to return with two-hundred thousand dollars, cash or gold or both. If the citizens don't raise it, the town burns." As Breckinridge gave back the canteen, Early checked for signs of chivalric disapproval. There was a slight aversion of the eyes, nothing more. "Our primary goal remains one of diversion," Early said. "Washington has sent no fresh troops our way, so we can conclude that they underestimate our size. But now we want to frighten the bejesus out of them. Our cavalry's ranging as wide as possible, along with the partisans of Mosby and Gilmoor, striking in small groups wherever they can. In Yankee minds, we'll go from a minor raiding party to twice our actual strength."

Breckinridge smirked. "Not that we don't pose a real threat as we are."

"Yep–quite a raiding party. And at this moment, we represent the northernmost reach of the Confederacy." He squinted down the pike, then across a wheat field to the creek. Through its curtain of trees, the creek sparkled. "I tell you, we had the devil's own day here."

"So I'm told," said Breckinridge.

Early fiddled with the reins. Against the sky, a long chain of crows straggled eastward. "The way the ground is, you couldn't see it all from a given spot. You could damn well hear it, though. At dusk we were collecting our casualties and I looked out on the field–up there around the church. It was squirming. I knew it was wounded men out there, dying men, but the whole field was like some crawling, moaning thing. Just acres of . . . " He glanced at Breckinridge. Previously assigned to the western theater, Breckinridge had not been here two years ago but had, no doubt, seen his share of crawling fields. These somber reflections should end now, Early decided. "Is Gordon set to make his demonstration against the Heights?"

"He's moving within the hour," said Breckinridge.

Against all of Early's fighting instincts, he would order no assault against the dug-in foe. Time and speed were paramount. "While Gordon executes his feint, the cavalry will probe the mountain passes north of here. Then we'll push the whole force through, toward Frederick. We'll be gone before they know it."

"Frederick . . . ," Breckinridge murmured. "Pretty close to Washington."

"Forty miles or so," said Early. Further instructions from Lee would soon arrive, as would further word about the traitorous Yankee officer. In a high-flown mood, Early lifted his gaze to the blue distance. The crows were bobbing black flecks. "Not far at all," he said.

63

East Washington

IN THE IDLE coach, Truly sat opposite Delia McGuire. Rest had brought some color to her face. Anna and Sapphira had donated a trunk full of clothes, books and other comforts, plus the stuffed food basket which sat on the floor. In a powder blue dress and bonnet, Delia fluttered a fan and looked out the window, still tense.

"The Old Capitol is a place of safety," he told her. "In part, because it's a prison."

The fan went still. Delia's eyes grew large.

"But you will by no means be a prisoner, understand? It's run by a fellow named Wood–a sugar-tongued coyote, if there ever was, but kindly enough. In his care you'll be secure and fairly comfortable, for the time being."

Her face settled. "It couldn't be worse than what I've come from, Major."

"Good girl. I wish it was a castle, but it's the best we can do here in Washington. And we will be visiting you."

She sighed, fanning herself. "Aye, then. But what is it we're waiting for?"

Truly tapped his hat against his knees. "Well, here's the awkward part. Wood is a friend of sorts–but he's a better one of my boss Colonel Baker, in whose eyes I'm a leper just now. I'm not even supposed to be in the city. I'd therefore like to keep my presence a secret so I can work freely. So I've asked my partner Captain Forbes to take you inside, introduce you and explain the situation in general terms. Forbes had business at the War Department, but he's to meet us here afterward. Please remember, though–do not mention my name to Mister Wood."

Delia nodded. "I'll remember."

Truly felt a bite of frustration. Here in the very shadow of the Old Capitol, he prickled with thoughts of a certain inmate. Silently he cursed Baker, lamenting the need to lie low.

"What's that big dome up there?" Delia asked. "With the statue on top?"

"It's the present Capitol Building, where Congress meets. The statue is Armed Freedom." Truly palmed his watch and glanced at it. "The dome was being constructed at the war's outset. They considered suspending work but decided to keep going. So there it is."

Peering out, Delia said nothing.

There were immigrants of the effusive sort, Truly thought–people full of clumsy comments and exclamations. And there were those like Delia– more muted in their hope, braced against the alien panorama.

Sitting back, she fussed with her shawl. "You've already done me great favors, Major. But there is one more I'd like to ask."

"Ask away."

"Should you meet up with Miles, for any reason, tell him . . . Please tell him that I'm sorry, but he must understand. And that I do long to see him again."

Truly looked down at his hat. "If we do meet, I'll tell him that."

"Thank you." She looked distracted. "What is that noise?"

Truly heard it–a fife and drum, along with shouts and other racket. Curious, he stepped out of the coach and gazed down South A Street, where stray geese and pigs scattered before a quirky parade. A strutting sergeant of the provost guard led the way. Shuffling after him came a man flanked by slovenly guards. The fellow's torso appeared perfectly rectangular until the dust parted, revealing a placard that read, "Pickpocket and Thief." Two more soldiers followed–a small fifer and a large, lumbering drummer, playing a decidedly inept rendition of "The Rogue's March." Several jeering boys brought up the rear.

"Serves 'im right, by God," spoke the burly black coachman.

Backing up, Truly watched the procession pass by. The prisoner, in handcuffs, was a bucktoothed young man with a goatee. He stumbled and one of the guards steadied him, just as a thrown pebble caught him on the rump. The harsh tune persisted, fitful as the ill-matched pair of musicians tried to keep in step. Truly coughed on the dust. As the last boy bounded past, he saw Forbes across the street and strode over to him.

Forbes wheezed into his fist. "Pathetic!"

"I know. My ears hurt."

"Not the noise–that sorry-looking escort of his."

"Washington's down to the dregs now, for troops. So what did you find out?"

Forbes patted the dust from his uniform. "Grant's had a mild change of heart. He's decided to send a division of the Sixth Corps, plus three thousand dismounted cavalry."

Truly's shoulders drooped. "That's all, eh?"

"Afraid so. And they're headed for Baltimore, not here. They've embarked from City Point and should land tomorrow, then race to join Wallace on the Monocacy."

"Well . . . That'll help the odds a little, I reckon."

Forbes squinted at the street. "Pilots and bargemen have been coming down the Potomac all morning, scared out of their wits. They report Rebel crossings at every ford north of Muddy Branch. One of my scouts wired in, too, saying he's heard of a large enemy presence just beyond Catoctin Pass–and that Sharpsburg has been occupied."

Truly eyed a pebble by his foot. Stepping on it, he rolled it beneath his heel. "I don't suppose this has thrown the Department into action?"

Forbes gave a bitter laugh. "Barely a stir. Stanton has assured the President that the threat's overblown."

Truly kicked the pebble aside.

A barouche carrying a pair of gaily-dressed couples rattled by, trailing laughter and dust. Muttering, Truly pictured that grim, box-like building across town where Chief-of-Staff Halleck reigned over paper stacks, where Secretary Stanton ruled like a cold Norse god. He pictured them fussing and scribbling, disdaining these distant alarms from lesser mortals. The pair of them mirrored Washington itself.

Annually, since the war began, Southern forces had moved north, spreading alarm from every hill and steeple. Each time, it had culminated in a great bloodletting–Bull Run, Antietam, Gettysburg–after which the Confederates were obliged to withdraw, leaving the Union capital unharmed and uncaptured. Smaller, briefer scares had punctuated these major ones, further inuring Washington's populace to fear and rumor, till a certain pride took root. A nonchalance, feeding the city's other haughty notions of itself.

Forbes glanced over at the waiting coach. "You're really going to stick her in that hole?"

"No–you are. It's the best solution, if we're to keep her close at hand. Besides, females have stayed there before."

"Female spies, Nate. Lady Rebs, who perhaps deserved it."

"Wood will tend to her."

"That's my main fear."

"Come on, I'll introduce you." They started across. In a low voice, Truly added, "Don't mention Wakefield. She seems fond of him, to say the least, and ignorant of his doings."

As they climbed into the coach, Truly told the driver to pull up at the prison entrance. Forbes had seen Delia but once, and briefly, on the night of Kirschenbaum's murder. Clearly charmed, he exchanged pleasantries with her as they rounded the corner.

The coach halted and Delia peered out, looking apprehensive. Truly patted her hand. "A guest," he said. "Not a prisoner." Instantly he felt foolish, realizing how slight a distinction this might prove. Still, Delia worked up a smile.

"Visit soon, Major."

"As soon as possible, Miss McGuire."

Taking the food basket, Forbes helped her get out.

Truly slouched low. Once more he longed to pass freely through the prison doors, to seek out the one other man who knew what he knew, and who perhaps knew more. He heard Forbes address a guard, asking to see Wood. The guard's reply was interrupted by a higher, heartier male voice–"Captain Forbes! How pleasant to see you, sir!" After a pause came Forbes' flat response: "Lieutenant Chadwick."

Truly sat up. Outside the coach, Chadwick prattled about his latest assignment. "A dull task, to be sure, but someone has to keep watch on the rabble here. Captain, I declare I've never seen a worse lot of mopers and grumblers. I tell them it's a darned sight better than they deserve. 'Should've considered it before you fired on Sumter!'–that's what I tell them."

Forbes managed to introduce Delia, explaining that she was here for safekeeping, as part of an intelligence matter. Chadwick expressed some fancy solicitude and invited the pair inside. At Forbes' direction, the guards removed Delia's trunk from the boot. Truly listened as they all bustled into the building. For the next few minutes, he deliberated. Then he got out of the coach.

Two Veteran Reserve guards stood by the big double doors. "Excuse me . . . " Truly showed them his papers. "I'd like to speak with Lieutenant Chadwick, as soon as he's free." One of the guards ducked inside. Truly told the coachman that the wait would be longer than expected, then handed him a fifty-cent bill.

Soon, in his light-blue uniform, Chadwick came strutting out. He beamed at Truly. "Major! Another fine surprise!"

Grinning, Truly pumped his good arm. "I was dozing in the coach, but then I thought I heard your voice. How are you mending?"

Chadwick drew himself up straight. "I have the pleasure to say I'll be examined next week, and that I expect to be returned to field duty." He was in fact wearing no brace. Lifting the arm, he straightened it carefully. "You see?"

Staring at the limb, Truly wondered if it could possibly be true. "Dear me. Well, Chadwick, we'll all miss having you around. Still, General Grant needs you."

Chadwick turned solemn. "The separation from Miss Anna will be painful. But to be kept so long from the front . . . Well, sir, that's been painful, too."

"I'm sure. Listen–I'm here on secondary business. I know the super-intendent's busy at the moment, and I'd hate to disturb him. So I was hoping that you could help me."

"Name your wish, Major."

For the first time ever, Truly felt glad for Chadwick's presence on earth. "There's a prisoner I'd very much like to interview. If you can direct me to him . . . "

———————◆———————

THE SICK BAY was a long, dim chamber, foul-smelling despite its open windows. Ogling Truly, the sour-faced steward jerked a thumb toward the far end. "Last one down." The man's lip curled. "Soon as the son-of-a-bitch is better, he's getting transferred to that officers' camp in Ohio. And we won't be missing him, either."

Truly moved down the row of cots, most of them laden with pale, dozing men. Coming to the last one, he beheld the lank form of Brigadier-General Gustavus Adolphus Dinsmore, CSA. The grayed Virginian lay without bedclothes, his tunic unbuttoned, one bare foot resting on the crutch by his cot. With his hands cradling his head against the pillow and his eyes shut, he appeared more leisurely than sick. Yet the rutted, bewhiskered face bore a hint of scowl.

Staring, Truly pictured the face as it had once been; he suddenly wished for a mirror so he could view his own. Then the hard lips parted, emitting a twangy voice. "Who the devil is it?"

"Nate Truly."

One heavy-lidded eye flickered open. It examined Truly for a few seconds, then closed again. "Don't mean spit to me."

"Truly, formerly Sergeant. I was one of your scouts in Mexico."

On the lined countenance, there was no change.

"Did you hear me, General?"

Dinsmore drew a long, dry breath. "Yes, damn your eyes. I'm lame, not deef."

Truly found a stool. He placed it by the cot and sat. "How are you feeling, sir?"

The lips twitched. "Here in this pig-palace? Just marvelous, thank you. The rancid stew, the half-boiled beans–they do a body good. And this leg? Well, I'm sure some Yankee sawbones will be taking care of it, real soon. Yes, damn you, I'm neck-deep in bliss."

"Could I bring anything for your comfort?"

"Yes. A loaded pistol, to shoot that varmint Wood in the ass with. Then you."

Truly reached into his pocket. "How about some tobacco?"

"Keep your damned Yankee tobacco."

"It's not Yankee. Look."

The dark eyes opened. They looked at the proffered plug and then, narrowing, at Truly.

"Plug, not short-cut," said Truly. "I get it over in Alexandria."

The gaze lingered. Dinsmore slid his hands down, folding them across his narrow chest. "I saw you here, 'bout three weeks back. Huddled with your varmint jailer friend. Says I to myself, 'Yon wretch was a scout of mine down in Mexico.'"

"One of your better ones."

"That so? Well . . . " Dinsmore yawned. "You knew which way the sun traveled, I reckon." Gripping the sides of the cot, he strained to rise. Truly reached to help him, only to be cuffed on the wrist. With a grimace, the general drew upright. "So—come to reminisce with your old captain, have you? Put our trifles aside?"

"Not exac . . . "

"Well, you can go jump on a cactus, Yankee skunk! 'Cause a Yankee skunk's what y'are, Dixie tobacco or no!" He snatched the plug from Truly's hand, then bit the end off.

Truly watched him chew. "You're as sweet as ever, Snakebite."

"Go to hell." Turning his head, the general spat.

From the other end of the chamber, the steward piped up. "Not on the floor!"

Dinsmore brought up his crutch and shook it. "Come on back here!" he yelled. "Come on, and I'll teach you respect for the Confederacy!"

"Shut it, you crazy fool!"

"I'll stick this where you sit, Nancy-boy!"

"I hope they take both your legs, God damn you!"

Dinsmore's cheek worked, growing fuller. "Think I could squirt him from here?"

"General, listen . . . I came to talk about that time with the Mex woman. And the child."

Dinsmore stopped chewing, then slowly resumed. Truly waited. After a moment, the Confederate spat out this chaw. "What, praytell . . . " His voice fell to a low rumble. "What would call that up? After . . . what—seventeen years?"

"The soldier," Truly said. "The one who did it—I've found him."

The general's gaze grew sharp, then gradually dull. Easing back onto the pillow, he smacked his lips. "Well . . . Fancy that."

"I've found him but I can't get at him," said Truly. "Not just yet."

Dinsmore lay still, his eyes on the ceiling timbers. "Time to time, I've thought about it. I've seen it in my mind."

"So have I. All too often."

Dinsmore scratched his cheek. "I should've let you finish him, of course. Hell, I should've pitched in—cut 'em to pieces then and there. But I was shook, I'll allow—me, who'd cut down any number of Mex with his saber. An officer must keep steady. He gets shook, he grabs onto proce-dure, due process, the rules."

"I understand. Whatever the case, he killed his guard and got free. I tried to track him down later, you know, after we occupied the capital."

"I did too. I went to his colonel, then on down to his fellow privates. A few seemed like they'd been in awe of him but most had kept their dis-tance, for some reason they couldn't name. Talking 'bout him, even his sergeant seemed a mite disturbed. He was a Northerner, they said–strong, educated, high-and-mighty acting. There was speculation 'bout why he'd joined the army, that he might be on the run from something."

"General–I never learned his name. Do you recall it?"

Dinsmore stroked his beard. "His Christian name . . . It was some Roman emperor, I think."

"Claudius? Tiberius? Vespasian?"

"No, no . . . Hell, it'll come to me. Anyhow, I tried to figure where a man like that might run to. You remember that battalion of traitors who fought us? Army deserters?"

During the hard and perilous campaign, American deserters–fam-ine Irish, for the most part, and of faint loyalty–had cast their lot with Mexican President/General Santa Anna. As befit Santa Anna's appeal to their shared Catholicism, he had named this turncoat legion after Saint Patrick. "The San Patricios," said Truly. "Yes–I wondered too if he'd joined up with them. 'Cept, we captured most of them at Churubusco, when we stormed that fortified convent. I managed to get a look at each prisoner before they were hanged."

"Well, I questioned a few of them," said Dinsmore. "And I got a description of such a man–big and dark, with a scarred head. They said he joined them just before Churubusco and then vanished–killed in the battle, maybe, or else a deserter. Desertion becomes a habit."

Truly's gaze fell. "So it did plague you. But anytime I mentioned it, you turned away."

Dinsmore glared up, stained teeth showing through his whiskers. "Because I was disgusted, damn your eyes! Every bit as disgusted as you! The bloody bastard got away, and there wasn't any magic lariat to yank him back! Yes, I should've put about five more guards on him–but could I have known how smart he was, or how dangerous?! Once he was gone, what the devil was there to say 'bout it?!" Raising the tobacco to his mouth, he started nibbling. "I've sired nine young 'uns, Truly. Six that lived, four of 'em daughters. Comprendo?"

Truly stared into a corner. In one of the cots, a man groaned.

"Trajan."

Truly blinked at Dinsmore. "What?"

"Trajan. That was his first name."

Truly leaned in. "Trajan what?"

Dinsmore nibbled on the plug.

"Monroe is what he goes by now," said Truly.

Gazing off, the general shook his head. "Nope . . . No, it was one syllable."

"Do you see the first letter?"

"No . . . Damn it, I never thought I'd have to speak it again. I never wanted to." Tiredly he rubbed his brow. "Can't think of it. Leave me be."

The steward gave water to the groaning man, holding the ladle at arm's length. He sent Truly a sneer. Thinking of Forbes, Truly rose from the stool. "All right, General. If I get the chance, I'll come again."

"Not if I'm lucky."

"And I'll bring some decent food."

"Throw in some bourbon."

"All right. Vaya con Dios."

"Vaya con Diablos, damn your Yankee eyes."

Pensive, Truly headed back along the row of cots. By an open supply cabinet, the steward took a deep, furtive sniff from a jar.

"Heath!"

Turning around, Truly saw Dinsmore propped on one elbow.

"Trajan God-damned *Heath*," said the general.

Truly muttered the name. Sniffing the jar, the steward scowled over his shoulder.

"You say you can't get at him?" said Dinsmore.

"Not yet," said Truly.

"Well, listen–when you're able to, remind him of what he did."

"I will, Snakebite."

"And Truly . . . " Leaning out, the Confederate leveled the tobacco plug at him. "Don't just shoot him, you hear me? Take a sword, hold it good and long over a flame. Then run him straight through his foul, twisted, murdering yellow belly!" The general slumped back onto the cot. "That, damn your eyes, is an order."

Crossing the prison yard, Truly tried to be inconspicuous. He kept a nervous eye on the second-story catwalk and Wood's office door, slipping among the guards and inmates. In the midst of them he spied Chadwick and waved thanks. The lieutenant gave a smile and a salute, then resumed berating a prisoner.

Truly found Forbes leaning against the coach, arms crossed.

"So much for lying low," Forbes said. "What were you up to?"

"Jawing with old Snakebite. Chadwick smuggled me in."

"Ah, yes–it was delightful to stumble onto him."

"How'd it go with Wood?"

Forbes let his arms fall to his sides. "When he got a look at Miss McGuire, his eyes went big and he promised her the best cell in the place, despite overcrowding. He said he wouldn't put her with the female inmates in Carroll Annex; those slatterns might abuse her out of jealousy, whereas the men are apt to be chivalrous. It occurs to me that this will place her near Wood's office, so I fancy he'll be a mighty faithful visitor. Nate, what have we done to that poor girl?"

"Arranged for her to be treated like a queen, it sounds like."

"At what cost?"

"Only your sense of gallantry, it seems. If you're challenged about it at the Pearly Gates, put the blame on me."

The coachman peered down at them. "Where to now, sirs?"

"Seventeenth Street," said Truly. "Army Headquarters."

They got in and the coach pulled away. Truly told Forbes what he had learned. "Heath's his real name–Trajan Heath." Forbes looked to the window. Amid the coach's bumping, Truly thought he heard him sigh. "What is it?"

Forbes shrugged. "You've learned something about Monroe, just as I learned a thing or two about Ravenel. Somewhat enlightening, but . . . " He looked Truly full in the face. "Do these things really help us one bit? No. And this is the stage we've come to. Without sufficient backing from on high, our own powers seem darn near played out. We're only two men."

"Point taken," said Truly. "But now we're going to hunt up General Augur. As commander of the District defenses, he might be able to identify our lieutenant-colonel, if the man really is involved with fortifications."

"And if not? Where will that leave us?" Before Truly could answer, Forbes hunched forward. "Nate, there's something else you ought to consider."

"What?"

"Taking your chances and going to Baker." Truly opened his mouth but Forbes' look hushed him—a pinching about the eyes, frustration fighting deference. "Please—I know the idea's repellent to you, but the military situation's changing hourly. Add to that the new things we've uncovered, and you just might get him to budge. Given the emergency—and this certainly looks like one—he might decide to disregard the police after all and let you raid La Maison. Swoop down, make the arrests and maybe even snare Wakefield—wouldn't that be sweet?"

Truly opened his mouth but said nothing. Forbes—blast his precocious wisdom—was right: this was no time to let personal vanity call the tune. He pictured himself before Baker's iron gaze, pleading. Could he stomach it? And would the spy chief just order him out of Washington again to chase smugglers? If that happened, he would resign for sure.

"Time's shrinking," said Forbes. "We must be careful how we use it."

Fiddling with his hat, Truly nodded. "There I can't argue. But if first we manage to get a clear identification of the lieutenant-colonel—name, post, regiment—Baker would be a lot more apt to listen. And to budge."

"All right," said Forbes. "Lord knows, you know him best."

"Regrettably so."

The coach took a corner. Looking out, Truly saw a group of militiamen outside a feed store. One lifted a muddy pig by its hind legs, chortling as it squealed and wriggled. The others guffawed, passing a jug around. Against the storefront, their muskets leaned idle.

64

Near Sharpsburg, Maryland

DOWNSTREAM, SEVERAL CANAL boats were burning. Flames illuminated the trees and danced on the water, roiling with the sparkle of sundown. Breckinridge gazed along the canal's towpath to where the soldiers stood, some still holding torches as they observed their handiwork. In their whoops and postures, the mood was plain: torch fever, barbarian fever, steadily rising. It was a force that had to be managed, channeled like this waterway. Maybe that had been Early's main intent in sending the cavalry to Hagerstown. Maybe the town's ransom mattered less than the chance for controlled mayhem, an outlet for these mounting passions. Still, it was hard to condone such a thing and fancy one's cause as sacred. Breckinridge tensed with distaste. By now, if the town had failed to cough up its treasure, it was burning like these luckless boats.

As the shadows deepened around him, he listened to the soldiers' hoots and laughter, watched the smoke billow into the fading blue dusk. An hour ago, he had found Cabell in the company of some motley Alabamans, all getting drunk on corn liquor. Mixed shame and defiance had showed in Cabell's face before he saluted his father and wandered off. Apart from that, Breckinridge missed his wife. It was eight days since her last letter had caught up with him, that one containing a pinch of rose petals. And her frail health worried him, as always. He hoped that she was at least comfortable in Richmond.

The great conflict had sent destinies hurtling, his own more than most. Now, hurtling back toward Washington, there were moments when he felt less like a general or statesman than a piece of driftwood, borne on an angry gray wave. Back to the city of his finest, headiest years, where ambition and sentiment had slowly strangled one another. He could never look upon those years as he had wished to, not through all the smoke and death and battle flash. In those times, he had harbored the preposterous hope of becoming a national savior, one who would preserve not only the Union but Dixie's honor–who would forge a compromise, lasting and bloodless. In the dignity of public utterance and the glow of warm parlors, he had walked the line between friendship and conviction, never dreaming what it would all come to.

In the U.S. Senate, through the war's first summer, he had opposed all military measures while assuring Northern friends and acquaintances of his loyalty. But with the declaration of martial law in Kentucky, and with his arrest imminent, he had at last defected to the secession banner. This sealed his reputation in the North: two-faced, they called him–a beguiling Southern snake. The most bombastic of judgments, surely, yet he acknowledged its crumb of bitter truth. Like many who were polished, sentimental and a bit too fond of admiration, Breckinridge could not bear the pain of complete, face-to-face candor. Not with the Union ladies he charmed, nor the Union men whose sherry and conversation he enjoyed. Warfare, by contrast, had proven a bizarre kind of refuge from such pain. In that swarming netherworld, even an erstwhile Vice-President might find some sense of manly communion. Communion, clear purpose and the constant struggle for order, trampling all petty concerns.

At times he had loved the arena of Washington. But to have bared his divided heart amid the hysteria, to the contempt of individual eyes and tongues–that would have required greater bravery than the battlefield. Nowadays, in his absence, former friends presumably hated him. Soon they would hate him more. He thought of his grand house on I Street, now reportedly a soldiers' hospital. He thought of Cousin Mary in the Executive Mansion, trapped in the storm's eye. Mary Todd Lincoln–vivacious, vulnerable and full of frantic airs–joined to the man whose ascent had triggered the calamity, whose election Breckinridge himself had grimly confirmed before the Senate. What would become of her if the Confederate host descended upon her city, his former city? He watched a flaming boat drift stern-first toward the opposite bank. Then, soul-weary, he walked back to his waiting horse.

Riding out of the trees, Breckinridge smelled wood smoke and saw campfires ahead. He began to feel better. As he skirted the camp's edge, men looked up from their roasted ears of corn and stood to greet him. He nodded, touching his hat-brim, then steered toward the apple orchard where Early's tent and field desk were set up.

He found Early in a thunderous mood, stalking and fuming around the tent. Breckinridge gave his horse to an orderly who looked relieved to see him. Before he could ask what the matter was, Early pounded the flimsy desk-top and turned to face him.

"Those buttermilk rangers of ours have done themselves proud again!" Early huffed, glowering. "Imboden barely scratched that rail line I sent him to tear up!"

"Does he have anything like an excuse?" asked Breckinridge.

"Oh, yes! He fell sick, supposedly, and discipline crumbled—with the result that they did no more damage than their gallivanting permitted!"

Breckinridge frowned. "Then Hunter could still come back on us from the west."

"Yes, damn it! He could combine with that force up on the Heights and begin pursuit. Now all we can do is hope he stays timid." Early chewed his bottom lip. "Then there's the matter of McCausland."

"Didn't he get the rans . . . the levy?"

"He got one, all right, but not what I instructed. Two-hundred thousand, I said, and what does he return with? Twenty! Seems he misheard me and dropped a zero!"

Breckinridge had to fight a smile. It wasn't poor McCausland's blunder so much as the sound of Early's voice. A shrill rasp, it suggested a cane-waving old man who had found goats in his turnip patch.

Early stormed on. "Hagerstown needn't have feared a thing—oh, no! Not at the hands of our mighty horsemen!" He cuffed the air. Then, taking a breath, he started to calm down. "Well . . . When we get to Frederick, we'll try again. The town's prosperous enough."

"Demand two million," said Breckinridge. "Maybe then you'll get the right figure."

The joke elicited a grumble. Folding his arms, Early leaned back against the desk. "A courier arrived about an hour ago. Lee's son Robert, no less."

"Do tell!" Breckinridge stepped closer. "An extra-important dispatch, then?"

Early's voice fell. "It concerns the prisoner-of-war camp at Point Lookout, below Baltimore. Fifteen, maybe twenty thousand of our boys are held there, and a plan's been hatched to free them. In a week or less, some attempt will be made–by gunboat, I imagine–to cut the shore-line telegraph and distract the garrison. It's up to us to get some small part of our force there and liberate the prisoners." He paused, looking at Breckinridge. "Challenges aplenty, eh? But I suppose we can meet this one too. Soon as we reach Frederick, I'll send some cavalry toward Baltimore to wreck communications, after which they'll hurry south to Point Lookout. Obviously we'll need someone solid to lead this, for a change. Bradley Johnson, I'm thinking."

Apart from this news, Breckinridge was glad to hear Early's rancor fading. "Good, General. If nothing else, that will spread the alarm even further."

"The plan doesn't stop there," said Early. "Once the prisoners are freed, the healthier of them will be sorted into companies and marched to join us. If we manage to arm some of them, at least, we'll pose an even larger threat. To meet it, Grant would have to send greater reinforce-ments–three full corps, maybe. It's worth trying, I figure. We'll see."

In the gloom, Breckinridge moved to the desk and leaned there, next to Early. "General, it's time for me to ask again. You said there was some-thing else afoot, involving Washington and our civilian spy network. Did Lee's message include anything about that?"

"No. But someone's due to contact us about it. I've issued an order to the pickets: should they encounter anyone claiming to have confidential intelligence, he must be taken to me without delay."

"You expect this will come to anything?"

"I expect nothing, at this point. It's some dim little gambit they're about, underneath this big one of ours. Lee himself allowed that it was chancy. Still . . . " Early shrugged. "If and when we're contacted, you'll be notified straightaway."

At the sound of hearty laughter, Breckinridge turned to stare through the neatly spaced apple trees. Nearby, silhouetted by a campfire, members of Early's staff sat talking and eating.

"Young Lee's over there, if you'd like to meet him," Early said, repair-ing to his tent.

Breckinridge strode toward the fire, where the men were eating roast pig on a spit. Noticing Breckinridge, a short one in rough civilian garb put his plate down and stood up.

"About time we had a Lee in camp," Breckinridge called.

Robert E. Lee, Jr. touched his cap and stepped forward. "Genr'l, sir—an honor to finally meet you." The firelight revealed an ascetic young face, nose prominent and mouth finely shaped, in contrast to the rugged little frame.

Breckinridge did not know the lad's current rank—only that, in keeping with the father's views on character formation, he had begun as a private. Shaking Young Lee's hand, he had a sad, fleeting thought of Cabell. Why did Cabell never look this happy or at ease?

"So you're our Philipides," said Breckinridge.

"On this occasion—yes, sir," said Robert, Jr. "I wish I could go the whole way with you, but I'm headed back tomorrow."

The others made room for Breckinridge at the fire. Sitting at the end of a log, he declined a plate but accepted a cup of chicory coffee. Soon someone was telling a funny tale about capturing a Yankee colonel in his underwear. Breckinridge chuckled. It was full darkness now, the fire winking off eyes and wedding rings and brass buttons, etching shadow-lines on each face. Breckinridge's tired eyes strayed back to Early's tent, its open flaps emitting lamplight. A short distance beyond, from the black barrier of the woods, a few dim shapes appeared and drew closer. The lead figure held a lantern, in whose glow the others grew more distinct: two rifle-toting privates, guarding a scruffy civilian with a horse in tow. Other than Breckinridge, only Early's adjutant Pendleton seemed to notice the little party; slipping away, Pendleton headed through the trees to intercept it.

Breckinridge missed the climax of the colonel-in-underwear story. Once the laughter had petered out, a squat major on his left spoke of Frederick, some twenty miles distant. "That's where that old Yankee hen insulted Stonewall, remember? Waved the stripey flag at him while we were marching through." No one claimed to have witnessed the incident, though all knew the cursed ballad it had inspired, now cherished throughout the North. Grumbling remarks ensued about the town and what punishment, in Jackson's name, might be exacted this time. "Torch fever," thought Breckinridge—yes, even in the upper ranks. He took a hot swallow of coffee. Then someone recalled that Frederick was the hometown of Bradley Johnson, the Maryland cavalry chief, and talk of retribution ceased.

Distracted, Breckinridge again gazed toward Early's tent. The guards had left while the remaining soldier, a sergeant, held both the lantern and the horse's reins. Hat in hand, the civilian was speaking to Pendleton. Then Pendleton ducked into the tent, only to quickly reemerge and motion the visitor inside.

The fireside talk had shifted to Petersburg. Asked about events there, Young Lee spoke of the colored troops who had spearheaded the first Union assault. "Beauregaud's boys put up a stiff fight, but a few of them allowed they were surprised. The Negroes attacked in good order, they said, and captured some field pieces. Must have been quite a sight." In the leaden pause which followed, Robert looked suddenly uncomfortable. The fire crackled. Then the squat major licked his fingers, grunting, "Well . . . You can train a dog to fight. And a horse to march."

The conversation moved on. Restless, Breckinridge put his cup down and excused himself, giving Robert a pat on the shoulder. Headed back to Early's tent, he encountered Pendleton.

"Sandie, was that fellow a scout?"

"A courier, Genr'l. From Rockville, sent by someone called V. Grayson."

Breckinridge nodded and kept on. Ahead, he saw the civilian emerge from the tent and take his horse from the waiting sergeant. The two men headed off. In a moment, Early came out in his shirtsleeves and stood rubbing his lower back. Breckinridge slowed his step as he approached, not wanting Early to feel pestered. But it was Early who spoke first.

"That was it."

Breckinridge reached his side. "Our Washington contact?"

Early nodded. He did not face Breckinridge but spoke to the darkness, his words hushed and rapid. "The whole thing centers on a Yankee lieutenant-colonel who's posted to the capital defenses. By persons allied to our cause, this man may be coerced into helping us."

Caught between dueling emotions–shock with excitement, dismay with morbid intrigue–Breckinridge listened hard.

"As we close in," Early said, "this officer will take command of a particular fort on the District's northern perimeter. He will be under the close eye of our friends, to ensure that he goes through with it, and they'll also be following our progress. Once we're within ten miles or so, under cover of night, a party of picked men will be sent ahead to the fort. They will send a signal, upon which the garrison will be quickly withdrawn; just as quickly, our party will occupy the place. That will give us our toe-hold. Upon confirmation, our main column will rush forward to secure the point and pour through the breach. Cannon fire will be directed at the flanking forts."

With a straw-like rustling, Early scratched his beard. His tone grew keener.

"If, in this whole operation, we only succeed in taking pressure off of Lee, that will be enough. But to actually break through the city's fortifications . . . I tell you, until now it seemed little more than a pleasant notion. But this contact of ours, this V. Grayson, has been keeping Richmond abreast of troop strength in Washington. It's drastically low–the troops of poor quality, the best guns sent to Petersburg. They'll still put up a fight, of course, and the forts themselves are reportedly strong. Still, while I'd give the Point Lookout scheme maybe a one-in-ten chance, this other business is looking better. It could be the last ingredient we need."

Breckinridge drew a slow breath. "An enemy traitor," he said, almost whispering.

From the far side of the orchard, the staff officers' laughter and story-telling could still be heard. Early turned his head in their direction, the thrown firelight tingeing his nose and whiskers. "I don't know what to think of it, either. I look at everything we've been through–the fighting, the marching, the killed and wounded. The times when victory felt close, then as far as the moon. Doesn't feel quite right–does it, Breck? After all of that, to prevail not by guts and steel but by trickery, by the act of one coward."

Breckinridge was less startled to hear Early call him "Breck" than to hear these reflections, so like his own. Somewhere in Early's gnarled being, he too kept a blood-born sense of honor, quite distinct from the standards of war.

"But spies and tricks and treason," Early went on, "–they do play a part, bigger than we'd care to think. I'd wager they always have. And the Yanks have sure as hell used them on us, whenever possible. We're duty-bound to act on this–on any advantage, especially when it means fewer losses. These raggedy boys of ours have suffered enough, don't you think?"

Breckinridge nodded, then remembered that Early could barely see him. "Too true," he muttered. He let his gaze drift. Through the woods, across the whole dark landscape, campfires flickered by the thousand.

Like earthbound stars hailing their high brethren, or living souls hailing the dead.

"I'm no praying man," said Early. "That was Jackson's chief regret about me, I think. But tonight I thank God for this command. And for not making me some worm of a Yankee turncoat, waiting to do the deed."

"Amen to that," said Breckinridge. Inhaling the sweet smell of the apple blossoms, he realized that his inner tussle had subsided. In its wake was a simple, somber clarity, though the morbid intrigue remained. Who was this lieutenant-colonel? He had known his share of career army officers before the war, as well as Northern politicos who had since volunteered. Could this sorry man have been among them? "Were you told this officer's name?" he asked.

"Monks," Early said. "Orlando Monks. It's good to know, in case he ends up in our custody."

Staring off at the campfires, Breckinridge repeated the name silently. He'd never heard it.

65

Tennallytown, District Of Columbia

ON RECENT NIGHTS, Lieutenant-Colonel Orlando Monks had barred the
doors and secured the windows of his cottage. He had slept with a burning lamp and a loaded revolver by his bed, under which he kept bullets,
firing caps, matches and a tin of coal oil, along with his sword. Still, nothing could ward off the nightmares. When sleep overtook him, he would
see himself being dismembered, often with the torch-lit face of Monroe
staring down, as big as a wagon wheel. Other times, he would dream about
Ball's Bluff.

Since that battle, far greater disasters had befallen the Union. No one
mentioned it anymore. Yet for Monks, the 21st of October, 1861, marked
the resounding verdict on what he was and would always be. Before that
day, he had been able to cultivate some hope for himself.

He was the last of four sons, part of a prosperous Ohio clan whose
male portion included lawyers, engineers, professional soldiers and a
noted Abolitionist preacher. One of his grandfathers had fought with
distinction in the War of 1812, while the other had served two terms in
Congress. While still a youth, Monks worked in his father's construction
firm and evinced a plodding sort of competence, if not resourcefulness.
His quiet but anxious nature made him the butt of teasing and crippled
his few efforts with females, whom he preferred to spy upon.

His family regarded him with mild annoyance–an attitude which
turned to horror when, at age seventeen, he revealed an unsuspected side
of his nature. His father found him in the woods with an eleven-year-old

neighbor girl, known to be feeble-minded, who he had enticed away from her poor family's hovel. She and Orlando were engaged in act so base that his father had to mentally deny it, convincing himself that he had witnessed some more recognizable sin—simple fondling, maybe, or indecent display. Condemnations rent the air. In the heavy days that followed, young Monks shed tears of fright and remorse. He offered no excuses, no elaborate lies. His silence owed partly to a lack of imagination but also to one of his subtle virtues: a private, mournful honesty about the urges he felt, minus any real strength to resist them. Nevertheless, fear proved deterrent enough for some time afterward.

The incident was suppressed and vague stories were circulated about the neighbor girl's "wildness," until her family had to leave the area. But with the honor of the Monks name still at risk, it was decided that only the rigors of military tradition could shake Orlando from his wickedness. Letters were written, pressures applied, and he found himself at West Point. There, other cadets paid him scant attention, thinking him odd. Yet his obedience and fastidiousness combined to carry him along, despite average grades. Earning few demerits, he graduated at the middle of his class and was commissioned to the tiny Corps of Engineers. Postings followed in the South and along the Eastern seaboard, involving fortification and logistical work. In these he displayed that same plodding competence and in time was promoted to captain.

Confirmed in their wisdom, kinfolk expressed relief that Monks had found a manly niche in the world. On one visit home, he was even presented with his paternal grandfather's sword from 1812. It seemed that rather than an embarrassment, he might end up an object of family pride—a general, in due course. None of them knew that while stationed in South Carolina he had gone ominously astray—that his attentions to the thirteen-year-old daughter of local gentry had raised ire, threatened scandal and caused his transfer to the New York harbor defenses. Since no written record was ever made of it, the episode survived only in the gossip of fellow officers. Yet it left Monks badly scared again. And while he had begun to frequent New York's myriad brothels, always requesting girls who were half his age, he resolved to be discreet. He had grown fond of military life, though it had won him no close friendships. He liked the privileges of rank, the emphasis on order, the authority it gave him over other men.

Monks was thirty-two at the war's outbreak. Even in the staid Corps of Engineers, men spoke of the impending chance for glory. The contagion acted more slowly on Monks–but act it did, and then he too was full of reveries. All along, despite his uniform, he had thought of himself as the boy who had been caught with the neighbor girl–as a lowly creature, snared in a crossfire of contempt. Often he worried that people could see into him. Now it seemed that he might reveal himself as something better, far more than he or anyone had ever suspected. That was what happened in war, ofttimes. Besides, no less a man than General George B. McClellan had started as an army engineer–a fact that, for Monks, took on near mystical significance.

Assigned to logistical duties along the Potomac, Monks applied himself with more than the usual diligence. For once he felt truly needed, anticipating his first encounter with battle. What hero might emerge under fire? What better man, from his gloomy reflection in the mirror? At Ball's Bluff, his chance arrived.

Monks had heard other men describe the defining moments in their lives–in the Mexican War, or some other circumstance of danger. Their voices and their eyes would grow distant, as if they were remembering a palace they had once entered, or their first-ever sight of the ocean. Instead of "defining" them, the event had seemingly stripped them of all definitions, all sense of limit. Totally awake for that moment, each felt as if he could do anything. Afterward, limits settled back into place. Yet a glow lingered, along with a sense that a man might rise out of himself and meet any crisis.

Ball's Bluff defined Monks as a coward. Thereafter, nothing else about him seemed to matter as much. He went in small and came out smaller, with some part of him permanently stunned. Considering the terror and tumult, his memory of that day should have been more vivid. But most of it remained a queasy blur: splashing water, whipping branches, crackling muskets; the cries of trapped men, growing fainter as he rowed to safety on the Maryland side. Only a few fragments remained sharp. One was his discovery of the waterlogged boat, miraculously hidden in the reeds. Another was the glaring, bandaged face of Captain Yale as he sputtered through pain, making some indecipherable vow. Ten nights afterward, Monks entered into the pact that saved his career and sealed his damnation. His problem was quelled and his bondage begun, along with that of four other strange men. Within a few weeks, he was reassigned to the capital defenses.

Except for a flurry of bridge construction during the Chancellorsville campaign, he had remained in Washington ever since. This suited him quite well, as he hoped never again to be caught in hostile fire. Two of his brothers were now officers in the volunteer army, marching with Grant out west. In letters, his family wondered why he was stuck in the capital, laboring in obscurity while others saw action and gained commendations. In his replies, he emphasized the scope and importance of his work. Still, he too wondered about his status and the reason behind it. The question chewed at him. While Yale's allegations had never reached the official record, perhaps they had reached someone's ears and been repeated. Monks checked anxiously for signs of this. In the demeanor of some colleagues, he did detect an extra degree of chill. But in time it became moot, as those familiar with him were transferred and replaced. And Chief Engineer General John Barnard, his gruffly officious superior, seemed pleased enough with his performance.

It became evident, in fact, that Barnard truly valued Monks' dull talents. While more dynamic subordinates worked on design problems, Monks performed duties that were less desirable but just as necessary– surveying, supervising civilian laborers, staking out rifle pits. His eventual promotion to major was no bureaucratic accident. Few had as much experience with the District fort system. And with fellow engineers constantly being called to the front, it seemed likely that he would take on a larger share of the oversight.

Long before his new epaulets, however, Monks had at last acquired a friend in Washington. Miles Wakefield, loaded down with photography equipment, had hailed him on the road one day and asked directions. In the exchange that followed, Wakefield complimented him on the fine military figure he presented, then offered to take his portrait free of charge. Monks was bemused at first. In his barren adult life, he could recall no man or woman who had seemed actively interested in him as a friend. But he enjoyed Wakefield's companionship whenever time allowed. Over dinner they discussed war and politics. Their views and perceptions matched well and Wakefield was a good listener, full of Southern courtesies and Northern sympathies. To Monks' baffled pleasure, the photographer seemed to admire him. Upon his elevation in rank, Wakefield presented him with a bottle of bourbon and took him to dine at Willard's. When

Monks' eldest brother died of typhoid at Vicksburg, Wakefield offered his condolences. Once, with too much drink in him, Monks suddenly confided his taste for very young females. Fear gripped him as soon as the words were out, but Wakefield betrayed neither shock nor judgment. It gave Monks the nerve to suggest a brothel foray; though his companion demurred, the two of them appeared to have reached a deeper intimacy. Yet even with Wakefield, Monks never came close to revealing his worst secret.

Every three months, with two hundred dollars in hand, he called nervously at La Maison de l'Empereur. The money pained him less than the reminder of his shackles, his ignominy, his earthly bane. But given his regular army pay, money was indeed a problem, and it forced him to work a progressive lie upon his family: he was aiding displaced Negroes, he wrote, and needed help in the noble endeavor. In the Monks clan there was enough Abolitionist sentiment to produce a response, and contributions arrived fairly often. He never questioned the importance of timely payments. Yet in June of '63, he was horrified to receive a blood-dappled letter from New York. In the letter, apparently coerced, Gideon Van Gilder confessed that he had tried to welsh on the arrangement and was lucky to be still alive, albeit with doubled payments and the scars of physical torture. The palsied script warned Monks against any similar foolishness.

Late that same year, at Fort Lincoln, Monks fell from some scaffolding and suffered a bad concussion. Wakefield visited faithfully during his convalescence. Returning to duty, Monks experienced frequent dizzy spells. And he had something else to brood upon. It was expected that Grant would soon arrive from the west and take command; a spring campaign would surely follow, the most massive so far. Just as surely, it would pull guns and officers from the capital defenses, whose construction was by now far advanced. Engineers too would be needed at the front, more than ever. Tremulously Monks wondered if he would once more be ordered into hellfire. In that event, he would have to obey. Within him, in fact, there glimmered a miniscule hope of redemption—a hope that he might measure up this time, despite the terror. He began a shaky letter to Madam Ravenel, explaining that he might have to make future payments through the army mail and not in person, as she had insisted.

He need not have worried. General Barnard, himself soon to join Grant's field staff, handed Monks a physician's voucher and assigned him to the Veteran Reserve Corps. The voucher cited the effects of Monks' head injury. Beyond that, however, his connection to the Reserves would be incidental. His new duties were solitary and specialized, for the most part, with no direct command of troops. He simply had to make unscheduled inspections of the forts and batteries and evaluate their readiness. Whenever he found a serious lag in upkeep, he could make recommendations and order certain tasks performed. The northern perimeter was a special concern, he was told, since it boasted few natural barriers against attack. For convenience, a cottage was provided for him at the village of Tennallytown, near Fort Reno. And to give him commensurate authority, he was brevetted lieutenant-colonel.

Monks thanked Barnard and asked no questions. He knew that officers with far worse conditions–amputees, malaria sufferers–had been sent to the front. Yet he had been bumped up to lieutenant-colonel and given a leisurely assignment, one that seemed tailor-made. Moreover, he had been spared another direct confrontation with war. For this he gladly gave up his tiny dream of atonement. As for his shame, he no longer felt its full weight. A numbness had sunk into him. In the safety of a new routine, it would sink deeper and let him go on functioning, perhaps until the war's end.

Soon afterward, he met Briona Kibby.

In retrospect, Briona's death was not the calamity that it had seemed, but a premonition of calamity–a cosmic reminder that he, of all men, should avoid tempting fate. For on that same day, Jonathan Peavey had proposed a group defiance of La Maison–and Monks, in his near insensible state, had agreed to go along. Now, just as he had been warned, his bondage had become a death sentence. He did not think of the other four men, and so did not blame them. Thinking only of himself, he blamed himself alone–the squalid boy who had done wrong and been caught.

By day he made rounds from fort to fort, an automaton on horseback, absently noting how the garrisons had dwindled. With the exception of a few experienced battery crews, only VRC troops and state militia now manned the strongholds. Behind their salutes, he thought he detected a puzzled mockery, a questioning of who he was and why he was there. Back in Tennallytown, he caught similar looks from villagers. He counted only three or four as acquaintances, though he had been here for four months. Their eyes and greetings showed a tentative respect for his uniform, but also that smirking puzzlement. Monks would have liked to think himself mysterious, but knew that he held no such allure. Despite Wakefield's generous compliments, he now realized that his person fell far short of splendor. He was an anomaly, nothing more–a lean-faced, gangly man with a high forehead, thinning brown hair, dazed light-blue eyes and a weak chin. After the Briona disaster he had shaved his imperial, partly as penance but also to prevent identification by any unknown witness. Still he felt naked. Inside him lay the foul compost of his defeats, and strangers could smell it. He wondered if his neighbors had noted his lit window in the wee hours, or heard his moans.

By night, in his spartan cottage, lethargy became near-paralysis. Trapped between dread and despair, his brain hatched no desperate plan for salvation. He stared at the window, the prowling darkness outside. Seated at his desk, he touched the handle of his revolver and sat still, then at length began writing his latest report. He pressed hard on the nib of his pen, almost breaking it. But in a while he felt lulled, cocooned in the particulars of the fort system. In his mind, the war had receded to a faint rumble, as irrelevant as a storm on the sea. He had heard of the hasty Union withdrawal from the northern Shenandoah. He was vaguely aware of rumors–increased guerilla activity upriver, some enemy movement out of the Valley. These bulletins entered his head like vapor, then dissipated as he lost himself in writing–page upon page of detail. Stopping to rub his eyes, he read and re-read the cramped, blotted script, often crumpling a page to start over.

Sometimes a sound would startle him–voices from the street, the clop of horse-hooves. Heart thudding, he touched his revolver, realizing at the same time that no bullets or lamplight could save him. Monroe was coming. Monroe would choose the right means, the right moment, and it was useless to run–Van Gilder had tried that. Silent as a shadow, Monroe would come for him. Under the covers, awaiting sleep, Monks often pleaded aloud with the Almighty. He pleaded for divine witness to his suffering, the fires of his remorse. He was already in hell, he protested. The Almighty did not answer, and so answered him: he would pay a still greater price. He would pay, and not just for violating the pact. Briona, Ball's Bluff, Captain Yale, the feeble-minded neighbor girl–for these and all his sins, for all the craven evil inside him, his life was forfeit. This was not hell, but hell's waiting room.

IT HAD BEEN weeks since he had seen or heard from Wakefield. Though he made no move to seek him out, he wondered why his friend had dropped from sight. And each time he wondered, his already seared nerves began to throb.

He returned from his rounds in late afternoon and found a note under his door. He recognized the flowing script as Wakefield's: "Orlando— urgently need to see you. Meet me at Mooreland's Tavern for supper. If you do not get this in time, I will visit later in the evening. Regards, Miles." Monks held the note a long while before crumpling it. Like a cold mist, the realization spread through him—the most deadening so far. Once inside, he did not bar the door. He did not draw his revolver and search the four rooms, as had become his habit. He hung his coat and hat and sank into his desk chair. Eyes on the floor, he watched the rectangles of sunlight stretch and redden, shadows spreading from every corner. At the moment of sundown, a gleam drew his eye to a side table. He saw the framed, glass-protected portrait with Wakefield's inscription—"To Captain Orlando Monks, with loftiest regard, June 1862."

Monks lit a lamp. Then he went to the table and picked up the portrait. Against the light-gray studio backdrop stood his uniformed image, a cape slung across the narrow shoulders. He had wanted to look distinguished, but the effect was merely stiff. For a few disembodied seconds, he was able to assess the gaze as if it belonged to someone else. The dark-circled eyes looked haunted, making him wonder how they looked now.

Dropping the portrait into his wastebasket, he heard the glass crack. He placed his chair at the room's center and sat again, hands folded, facing the door. He waited, unmoving as the house grew darker. At last he heard a horse outside, a rider reining up. Boots crunched along his path. The knock came. Tight-throated, he did not answer until a second series of raps.

"It's open," he called.

The door creaked open. Wakefield stepped in, eyeing him. "Hello, Orlando."

"Hello."

Taking his hat off, Wakefield shut the door. "Been a while, eh?" The tone was carefully casual. Monks only blinked as Wakefield studied him. "You know—the last few times I visited, you worried me. Shaving your beard and all. You seemed out of sorts and wouldn't explain."

Monks neither responded nor looked away. Very seldom had he been able to look a man so steadily in the eye.

When Wakefield spoke next, his tone had cooled. "Can you explain now, Orlando?"

"You know," Monks croaked.

Wakefield's stare lingered, then fell. He hung his coat by the door, then took a chair and placed it back-first in front of Monks. As he did so, something caught his eye. He went to the desk and peered down at the wastebasket. Bending, he fished out the cracked portrait and looked at it, then dropped it back in. He took his seat, arms resting on the chair back. "So . . . What clued you in?"

At first, Monks could not stop looking at him. He felt as if he were passing through a thicket of thorns. Swallowing, he stared past Wakefield's shoulder. "Back in April . . . the day Briona died, I found myself at Underhill's." He glanced at Wakefield, checking his reaction to Underhill's name. Monks had never before mentioned him. With a deepening chill in his eyes, Wakefield nodded. "I was in a bad state," Monks went on. "The others were talking. I knew what it was about, but I wasn't listening. Once, when I looked up, I saw a portrait of Underhill on the table beside me. It was inscribed by you, just as mine was. So it seemed that you knew Underhill too, and I thought it strange you'd never mentioned knowing a congressman. But I was in no condition to think much, or to remark on the picture. I don't believe Peavey or Archer noticed it. And I forgot about it, until three weeks ago. I came home and found a note from Underhill, telling me Archer's address and to be there first thing in the morning. There was some grave matter at hand.

"Come morning, I met Archer and Underhill there. They told me we'd been fooled. They said Van Gilder had somehow found this out, then been murdered while trying to escape south. Everything had come apart, we needed to decide what to do. But I couldn't speak. And as I sat listening to them, I saw Archer's portrait on a bookcase–also signed by you. Then the two of them grew impatient with my silence, so they dismissed me and went to call on Peavey. Riding home, I thought about a lot of things, including you. Such a coincidence, that you should know three of our number–us, who had nothing but La Maison in common. I wondered if you'd had Peavey's acquaintance as well, and Van Gilder's. What could it mean? Shortly after that, I saw a newspaper story about Underhill's death. Since then, I've been waiting for . . . " Monks realized how he was talking to Wakefield–openly, earnestly, as if nothing had changed. His chest hurt. "Still . . . I didn't see the truth about you until today, when I read your

note. The sight of your handwriting–it made me think of those other portraits I'd seen. And of how you've always been interested in my doings, in
whatever was on my mind–out of kindliness, I thought. But now it's clear
to me. You're with them–you always have been. Watching me, watching all
of us, for them. Pretending friendship."

Chin raised, Wakefield let his hands dangle over the chair back. He
stuck out his bottom lip. "Well, Orlando–you're a shade more perceptive
than I thought."

Monks took in the face before him, its casual disdain. So familiar, so
unfamiliar. The face that had looked at him with seeming fondness, listened to him with seeming patience. Over these two years, had he ever
suspected anything about his lone friend? He was not sure. But even if
he had, how could he have wanted to pursue such doubts? Looking at
the photographer's long, tapered hands, he recalled parting pats on the
back, accompanied by a kind word. Inside, he lurched toward hatred but
fell short, frozen in a sense of awe. His head began to reel. He gripped
the sides of his chair. Through his dizziness, he managed to fix upon
one thought: he was at their mercy, and so at Wakefield's. What did his
betrayer want?

"Fine, then," said Wakefield. "I won't have to explain as much. But I
do have one more question, which is this: what the devil happened with
Briona? Tell me about it."

The floor tilted one way, then the other. Monks held onto his seat. "I
didn't kill her."

"Liar."

"I didn't! I . . . I . . . " Monks blinked hard, trying not to stammer. "Ever
since that afternoon, I've wished that I never saw her in the first place. But
I did. It happened in late February, when I came to make a payment. She
drew me like a spell. Soon after that, I returned and brought her flowers.
On my next visit, I got permission from Ravenel to take her for a carriage
ride."

"I heard," said Wakefield. "And you took advantage, didn't you?"

Monks stared at his hanging pale-blue coat by the door. His head had
stabilized. "I drove her back and left. Next day, Ravenel sent a message
saying I was banned from La Maison, except for payment calls. I had to
reconcile myself."

Some weeks passed, Monks said, before he got another message from
Ravenel. It said that Briona had forgiven his actions. A probational visit

would be allowed–by appointment, Saturday afternoon, and for the usual fee. With a promise of good conduct, he could take Briona for another ride. He had not pleaded for this second chance but did not question it. He was only glad. When the day came, he went there in his best suit and was directed to Ravenel's bedchamber. She was under the covers and Monroe was stalking around, both of them seeming mysteriously unwell. Dubray was there too, with his medical bag. Ravenel started to admonish Monks but Monroe kept interrupting, cursing and ranting at her. "I was shocked but didn't try to figure it," Monks said. "I was anxious to see Briona. And soon she was brought to me. Such a little jewel she was . . . " He faltered, biting his lip.

"Go on," Wakefield muttered.

Monks drew a shallow breath. "She seemed nervous, though–frightened of me. I was confused and disappointed by this, but I treated her gently. Just a little ride out to the Eastern Branch, I told her–nothing more." As they left the house, he was surprised to meet Peavey on his way in, and they exchanged stiff greetings. Then he was off with Briona–but on the way, she started whimpering. Why this, he wondered, if she had forgiven him?

"I grew agitated," he said, dry-mouthed. "When we got to the Branch, I picked a secluded spot and tried to take her in my arms–just to comfort her, understand? But she screamed and slapped me away. Then she jumped from the carriage and I ran after her. I knew I was wicked, but I didn't want to be. For her I would have tried to be good, as I'd never done. But then she went into the water. I followed as far as the reeds, but I had to stop. I can't swim. She tried to . . . " Grief and hopelessness surged as one, wringing him. Wheezing through his teeth, he began to blubber. "The dress must have weighed her down. I watched . . . I watched her thrash, till I could bear it no more. The dizziness came, so I just sat there. Then it was quiet. I've never felt so ill, so horrible. All of a sudden Peavey was there beside me, yelling, pulling me to my feet . . . "

Through tears, Monks stared at Wakefield. He had hoped that the honest story would soften Wakefield's look; confessors were supposed to grant some measure of absolution. But the sneer and the chill remained, more pitiless than ever. Monks wiped his nose on his sleeve. "After that, I couldn't think straight. Nothing about that day makes sense. We met at Underhill's, then Archer left us to visit the house. When he returned, he said that Briona was now officially a suicide. But it seemed he'd mainly gone to confirm what Peavey and I had witnessed–the state that Monroe and Ravenel were in . . . " A renewed wave of bewilderment swept over him. "It was a trick. A trap for all of us. Why?"

Wakefield's sneer vanished, his face and voice turning mild again. "Let's simply say that they were testing you. And all of you failed."

"I'll pay them double!" Monks blurted. "From here on, tell them it will be four hundred dollars per quarter! I can get it . . . "

Slowly Wakefield shook his head. "That won't do it, Lieutenant-Colonel. The money no longer matters." He hunched forward. "There is one thing and one thing only that you can do–that you *must* do to save yourself. Do it and you will not only live, but will be free of La Maison forever. No more payments, no further association."

In the quiet, Monks gaped, absorbing the words. His ears burned. "Tell me . . . "

Wakefield's hands slid down to his thighs. "You are aware, are you not, that a Confederate force has entered Maryland?"

The leap of subjects almost left Monks dizzy again. He squinted, remembering that a war was still being fought.

"Orlando?"

Monks nodded.

"That force is a goodly one. And it's headed for Washington."

Monks' heart turned over.

"With nearly all of Grant's army in Virginia, opposition will be weak," said Wakefield, all business now. Getting up, he went to the desk and indicated the wall map that faced it, showing the District defenses. "The main columns will come down the Rockville and Seventh Street Roads. The action will therefore be centered on Forts Reno and Stevens, guarding those roads. With defense units spread so thin, there'll be much alarm and confusion; District command will be scrambling. They will of course concentrate on these key forts and a few others, but not on the majority." Suddenly, more clearly than ever, Monks was struck by the smooth Southern cadence of Wakefield's voice, the liquid Georgia vowels. Wakefield's index traced the city's northern defense perimeter; it settled on a black dot beside Rock Creek. "Fort DeRussy, midway between Reno and Stevens, should be a significant weak point. The terrain's irregular there, and Rock Creek virtually dry; its ravine should allow a small Confederate party to approach unseen, especially by night."

"You're a Rebel," Monks muttered.

Wakefield looked at him. "As I say, Orlando–you're a damned sight more perceptive than I thought. Now listen up." Stepping back, he crossed his arms. "Starting tomorrow, you are to make daily appearances at DeRussy. I'm sure you've been there on inspection, but the garrisons change frequently. We want DeRussy's current one to be familiar with your face and authority. Right now it's manned by a militia company–Ohioans, like yourself. Chat them up, especially their captain. Be sure to announce that home-state connection–it will make them more at ease with you. Other than this, lie low. Submit no reports; visit no other forts or batteries; do nothing to remind superiors of your existence.

"Once the Southern troops are a day's march off, one of us will come for you. You'll be safely ensconced at La Maison until the proper hour, when you leave for DeRussy. Monroe will accompany you." From his guts, Monks experienced a larger swell of panic. His shoulders began to shake. "He'll be at your side," said Wakefield, "disguised as a Union major. To make sure you see it through."

The shaking worsened. "See what through?" Monks asked hoarsely.

Peering down at him, Wakefield placed his hands on his hips. "The garrison will know you well enough by then. And you'll be the highest-ranking officer on the scene–regular army, too, unlike them. Whatever their previous orders, they'll look to you for direction. Meanwhile, a Confederate advance party will make their way down the Rock Creek ravine. Their signal will be two waving torches by the creek ford; upon sighting it, you will order DeRussy abandoned."

Monks sat rigid, his lips twitching. "You . . . You want me to hand the fort over?!"

"Essentially, yes."

"And the city . . . The city . . . "

"Washington's perimeter will be breached, Stevens and Reno out-flanked. And the city will fall. Without this action of yours, it might still fall before reinforcements can arrive–but that's questionable. The plan I've just described will eliminate any chance of my countrymen being delayed at the gates."

Monks beheld the map, the dense grid-lines representing the nation's capital.

Wakefield continued. "Should you encounter any insubordination, quash it fast. Use your authority. Monroe will aid you in this, as well. To reassure the men, you can say there's a stronger defensive line being formed south of the fort—also, that your orders come directly from the commanding general. They'll believe you."

With a moan, Monks raised his trembling hands. "Miles . . . I can't."

Wakefield took a slow step toward him. "Orlando, is there some doubt as to the position you're in? If so, let me remind you about Van Gilder's fate. And Underhill's. And it should be no surprise that Peavey is dead too. Need I describe what their last moments were like? Archer is alive. He had the sense to take the offer we gave him—to render his services as a lawman, in return for his life." Wakefield leaned down, just inches from Monks' face. Too late, beneath the icy insistence, Monks saw a touch of what he had longed to see—a softening, a ripple of regret. "Listen," said Wakefield. "I would not have wished to carry it out this way. But do exactly as I say, and you will live. You'll live, free of Monroe and Ravenel. And me."

Monks blinked up at him. He wanted to clutch him by the lapels, to wring them, to implore. Yet he could barely speak. "Benedict Arnold," he quavered. "A traitor. Like Arnold in the Revolution."

"No," Wakefield said firmly. "Arnold cast his lot with the losing side, didn't he? But the South will prevail. Besides—in the aftermath, it should be near impossible to sort out who ordered what. Still, if you wish, you can find your way into the protective hands of Jubal Early—whose troops will be all around, I assure you."

"Let Monroe be the one!" Monks sputtered. "Let him pose as a lieutenant-colonel! I could lend him my uniform! Or you—you could do it! For Christ's sake . . . !"

Stony again, Wakefield stood his full height. "Think, damn you—what is your value to us? The fact that you're a professional soldier is what. You know details, terminology, military procedure. Should anyone question your authority or identity, they will find that both are quite real, not an act that must be maintained and improvised. Your experience will show. Green troops will accept and obey you. No, Lieutenant-Colonel—you're our man. You cannot hide, and there is only one path to salvation. All others lead to death, of a sort you can scarcely imagine."

Abruptly Monks lurched to his feet. Stepping back, Wakefield looked alert but unperturbed, his hands ready to grapple. Monks turned and tottered out of the room, into the tiny kitchen, up to the back door. He threw the crossbar aside, then stumbled out into the night. Sinking into the tall grass, he vomited. When he seemed finished, he arose on rubbery legs, head swimming. Wakefield stood at his side, framed in the window light.

"You'll be all right, Orlando. Now, please repeat the plan I've told you. Step by step."

"Miles . . . "

"Do it."

With terse corrections from Wakefield, Monks haltingly repeated the steps, his trajectory to high treason. When he had listed them all, he heard Wakefield sigh.

"Very good. Remember, also, to follow events in the next few days. Check the newspapers. Keep an ear open for reports of Early's progress."

Monks listened to the cicadas–a dense, pulsating rattle, louder and louder. All at once he felt himself surrounded by demons. Demons in the dark, hell-things crawling toward him through the grass. Wakefield's voice had lost its intensity but was somehow more horrible, worse than the swelling rattle of the insects. "Don't try to escape, or to make the slightest move against us. You know better, I trust–but if you dare try, you won't succeed. The story of Ball's Bluff and Captain Yale will be released to the papers and to your superiors–with some alteration, of course, to conceal our own involvement. The same for your role in Briona's death. Plus, a letter will be sent to your family in Ohio. But with all that, we will hunt you down before the authorities can, as we hunted down the others. So just follow the plan. Follow it, and be free at last."

Monks gagged, spat, cackled. "Free!" he rasped.

"I'll leave you now. I've a paper for you to sign, in case I run into a night patrol."

Back inside, Monks lent his skewed signature to Wakefield's note, vouching for his Unionist loyalty. Handing it over, he gave Wakefield a last, wondering look. The Rebel agent looked as if he might say something more, but he did not. He reached for his hat and walked out.

Monks barred the doors and sat. Through the ringing of his ears, Wakefield's voice echoed until a final truth sunk in, like fangs: he had been damned from the beginning. If he slept at all tonight, he knew he would awake bawling and writhing once more. But for now he felt almost peaceful. Never again would he have to ponder what sort of man he might have been, under different circumstances. He got up and walked to his bedroom. From under his bed he got his sword and unsheathed it, staring at the engraved symbols near the hilt: MONKS 1812. He sat on the bed. He held the cool, sharp blade to his throat. Then, holding it out, he turned it around and placed the point to his stomach. He pressed just enough for it to hurt. Another man, he knew, would have closed his eyes and thrust the steel home–or, more painlessly, held his pistol to his head and pulled the trigger. But for Monks it was mere pantomime. Given the condition of his soul, he knew he had to survive this. He slid the sword back into its scabbard.

———

WAKEFIELD WOULD HAVE galloped away, but the fingernail moon cast too meager a light. Keeping Black Marengo to a trot, he tried not to think about Monks. But it was no use. The lieutenant-colonel's face had been that of a drowned man, a corpse staring up from the deep-sea bottom.

For two and a half years, Wakefield had played friend to five men, each of whom had strained his acting talent to the limit. Like all fools, they had tended to believe whatever made them feel important and comfortable. The tendency had been a curious one in Archer and Underhill, who showed some degree of calculating intelligence; Monks, like Peavey and Van Gilder, had never seemed to possess such cleverness. Still, on his own, the wretch had finally done what the others had not–grasped the sham friendship for what it was. The ability had been there all along, and yet Monks–starved for companionship and admiration–had declined to use it until now. Wakefield felt something beyond pity or repugnance, much like what he had once felt for the tale of Judas Iscariot. A smothering gloom. Trotting down the dark road, he yearned to put as much distance as he could between himself and the accursed federal officer.

All was quiet except for the crickets and the cicadas, the crunch of Black Marengo's hooves. No sign of patrols. Wakefield had traveled these roads on countless occasions, taking stock of forts along the way–dreaming, speculating, formulating the plan. The air flowed warm over his face and hands. Like a falling star, Delia crossed his mind–where was she tonight?–and then faded. He stared northward into the darkness.

As a boy, at the estate of his uncle, he and his cousin Albert had played war–Americans versus British, usually, and his spoiled cousin always demanded the American role for himself. There was less dispute when they played battling knights, using sticks as swords, whacking and swiping till they both collapsed in exhausted laughter. Wakefield's doting uncle eventually presented them with matching tin shields forged at the estate smithy, and these soon became warped and dented in the chivalric contest.

Months ago, upon news of Albert's death at Chickamauga, the first image in Wakefield's head had been not of his cousin's smooth boy-face, but of two battered little shields.

He was riding straighter in the saddle. As if blessed with night-vision, he saw the Yankee forts in detail: bare parapets, untended guns, empty rifle-pits and lonely, pacing sentinels—a giant shield, altogether, but one made of tin. The capital's mighty illusion. "Early, don't be late," he muttered, "Early, don't be late, don't be late"—repeating the words like a children's rhyme, till they joined the rhythm of his heart.

66

Arlington Heights, Virginia
July 7

MAJOR-GENERAL CHRISTOPHER AUGUR, District Commander, was a hard man to track down. But it seemed they had finally done so.

On the shaded side of the Lee mansion, a dozen or so horses in finest livery stood grazing. Four guards were posted at the magnificent front portico. Smoking a cigar, a dapper young captain leaned against one of the massive Doric pillars. Forbes went to speak with him while Truly disposed of their mounts, paying a colored groom to water them. Returning to the mansion steps, he met Forbes.

"Eureka," Forbes said, without enthusiasm.

"Super," said Truly. "Did you get who else is here?"

"Brigadier-General Barnard, for one. He's Grant's chief engineer, evidently here on short notice; until this spring, he was in charge of Washington's fortification project. Also, a Colonel Alexander, who took over the project from Barnard. And Brigadier-General Bacon, commanding the District militia. And Colonel Wisewell, the military governor—don't ask me what the title means, but the Veteran Reserves come under him."

Truly fanned himself with his hat. "The tangled roots of authority."

"More tangled than that," said Forbes. "According to this fellow here, General McCook's been called up to command the fort perimeter. And two other generals are on their way, duties yet unspecified. It seems that Augur's just one player in the band."

"Hm. Let's hope they don't all play solo. Heck–if privates were so easy to get, we'd have nothing to worry about."

Still, Truly thought, the oversupply of generals was more encouraging than not–a sign, at last, that the War Department had been jolted from its torpor. In any case, the developing situation had spurred Augur to assess the capital's defensive readiness. Truly and Forbes had dogged his frenetic movements since yesterday: from Georgetown to the Marine Barracks, to the Arsenal, to the cavalry depot at Geisborough Point. At Geisborough, the head teamster had directed them to the Lee place, site of this hasty conference. The presence of these other military worthies was a bonus, as they might prove helpful if Augur did not.

The young captain went inside. Forbes mounted the colonnade and went to its far side, where he rested in the shade of a pillar. Truly took a stroll among the oak and pine, stopping to take in the vista. Back across the Potomac and the Long Bridge lay Washington, a good deal more majestic from this height. He picked out the Capitol Dome, the President's Park, the still-unfinished shaft of the Washington Monument, the exotic red towers of the Smithsonian, all those churches–spires like gleaming spears, monuments like protective gods. The city looked proud and lazy, not vulnerable.

Turning back toward the great white house, Truly admired it anew. Here in the war's first week, Robert E. Lee had decided to refuse command of the Union forces and follow his native state. The results of that decision were visible enough; all across the hilly acreage, the new Soldier's Cemetery seemed to have erupted whole from the soil. Here and there, pairs of sweaty black diggers worked among the graves. The estate had been seized after Lee's departure and put to varied use, such as lodging for the Engineer Corps, but its formal confiscation was only recent. For the exquisite reason that Lee had not shown up to pay his taxes, the government's fist had closed upon his property. Seldom had the cool abstractions of law served so bitter a purpose. Now, as fast as shovels could dig, the cemetery grew–plot upon plot, rank upon rank of white markers, advancing on the manor itself.

Truly found Forbes still resting against the pillar, his hat over his eyes.

"Say what you want about Lee," said Truly. "To give up this place, he must be a man of conviction."

Forbes squinted, adjusting his brim. "There are worse trades."

Glancing at his partner's leg, Truly felt like a jackass. He sidled away and sat on the top step. The search had afforded him and Forbes time for idle talk, maybe too much of it. But some worthwhile speculations had emerged–among them . . .

Back in April, when Monroe and Ravenel were supposedly coming apart, why had Archer not shut La Maison down in a flash, as he could have? He could even have fabricated some excuse to shoot the pair, and Dubray for good measure, before they could retaliate. But he had refrained–and Truly now believed that they had some extra hold on the detective, to defend against such a double-cross. Something, perhaps, that involved his precious reputation. Truly thought of what he had found in Archer's desk. He thought of Delia McGuire's veiled reference to the man, that his lust was "of a particular sort." Maybe, by a prearranged method, they were poised to expose him, should he dare strike. But if that were so, would he not have risked such exposure by withholding his blackmail payment, along with the four other men? The question led back to Archer's special value as an investment.

According to Duke, the blackmail rate–two hundred dollars per quarter, eight hundred per year–was what a police detective made annually. And in late '61, when the scheme commenced, Archer had been just a regular roundsman. He could not have borne the financial burden even now, with the cash rewards that detectives sometimes got. It seemed likely, therefore, that he had been exempted from the payments–that his debt took the form of services rendered. And render them he had, providing ever-stronger protection as he rose through the ranks. His fellows-in-bondage need not have known about this separate arrangement–and in April, when they conspired to stop paying, they included him without a thought. With no payment to hold back, he would have let them take all the risk while pretending to share it, waiting to see which way the cat jumped.

Just then the mansion's main door swung open and they got to their feet. The captain stepped out and signaled the two colored grooms, who started gathering the horses.

"Looks like the confab's breaking up," said Truly.

"New question, Nate," Forbes said. "We suppose that all of this murder and calculation centers ultimately on one man–the lieutenant-colonel. Like the others, he's been under La Maison's thumb for two or three years–so if they want him to commit some treasonous act . . . "

Truly finished the thought. "Then why didn't they simply lean on him?"

"Yes! Why bother with that elaborate ruse, et cetera, when he's already in their power? Why even involve the other four?"

The grooms each led a pair of horses around to the front; one stayed with the animals while the other went back for the remaining ones.

Truly eyed the paneled door, the guards at parade rest, the captain looking on. "I've wondered plenty about that myself—that, and the whole bargain between Wakefield and La Maison. If we've guessed right, this current scheme of theirs dwarfs any that might have come before. Its promise for the Southern cause is downright monumental. And since no mere swap of favors could seal it, I figure that Monroe and Ravenel have been amply paid—more than enough to let them retire from the blackmail business. With their decision to scuttle that business, only two of their victims would retain real value: Archer, their official watchdog—and the lieutenant-colonel, around whom the new scheme revolves. The remaining three had to be killed off. This made examples of them for the first two, but it was also for safety's sake—to prevent any busybodies like us from interrogating them. They knew of the lieutenant-colonel and his connection to La Maison. And they knew what Monroe and Ravenel were capable of."

"All right," said Forbes. "But it still doesn't explain the plan's intricacy. You once asked the question yourself: Why go about it this way? Fool their victims and trigger the whole thing?"

Truly shrugged. "Maybe only Wakefield could answer that—because I believe it's he who fathered the plan. Its object is Confederate victory, after all, and who else would have been moved to concoct it? He would have insisted on having a direct hand in it, to better ensure that Richmond gets its money's worth. Think of how the five men were duped into rebellion; then, consider what we know of Wakefield. We know he's thorough. Also, he has insight into human nature—enough for him to have successfully masqueraded as each victim's friend."

"I'm not sure I understand you," Forbes said.

"All I'm saying is this: If there's no plain reason for how he's orchestrated things, then there must be a subtle one—as subtle as the man himself. And I'd wager it makes good sense."

Again the door swung wide. As the guards snapped to attention, a staff lieutenant emerged and held the door. The military chiefs filed out in full regalia, a passel of aides following them. At the steps, the captain approached the lead commander and addressed him, gesturing to the two agents. The general looked in their direction and the entire party halted, a mob of pressed blue, shiny leather and glinting brass.

With his stony brow and flaring reddish whiskers, Augur would have appeared stern on a good day. But strain intensified the look.

Striding up to him, Truly removed his hat and introduced himself and Forbes. "We're here on an urgent matter, sir."

"And I'm leaving on one," said Augur, pulling his hat on. "Make this quick, please."

Truly had not expected a patient audience. Speaking rapidly, he felt the collective stare of Augur's retinue. "General, we have strong reason to believe there's an officer assigned to the defenses, a lieutenant-colonel, who is prepared to commit treason."

A dent appeared between Augur's eyes. He blinked hard. At his elbow, a stocky gray-bearded general glanced at him and then at Truly, looking grave but lost. On his hat, the Engineers' castle insignia pegged him as General Barnard.

"We have not learned his name," said Truly, "but we thought you could help us."

Augur gripped his sword hilt. "You know the potential crime, but not the culprit?"

Until this instant, Truly had been unaware of his own chewed nerves. "Given the state of affairs, General, I'm sure you don't have time for a full explanation. We need only describe what we do know of him . . . "

"Excuse me," came a brusque voice. From behind Augur, a fat grim-faced colonel stepped up, tugging his hat on. Noting the castle insignia, Truly recalled the colonel's name as Alexander. "General, it's three o'clock already," said the officer. "I really must get out to Fort Stevens and survey things."

"Go on, Colonel. I'll be back from Falls Church come evening."

Alexander flashed a salute to Augur and then one to Barnard before hulking down the steps and mounting up.

Truly resolved to drive the subject home before another senior officer could take flight. He met Augur's glare. "I was saying, sir—we know this much about the man. First, he's been known to sport an imperial." Truly cupped a hand beneath his chin. "Also, he suffers dizzy spells." He turned his gaze on Barnard and the other two chiefs. Barnard seemed confused somehow, his deep-set eyes wavering. Behind him stood the stout General

Bacon, his moon face intent with interest. Truly knew the militia commandant to be a successful grocer; despite the fancy uniform, with its red cuffs
and yellow piping, he still looked like one. By elimination, Truly identified
the gloomy, black-whiskered officer to Bacon's left as Colonel Wisewell.
"He's described as dark-haired, tall and thin," Truly went on. "As late as
April, he held some post in the fort system."

"April?" Augur huffed. "Do you realize how much has changed since
then?"

"Plenty, sir, I'm sure. But can you . . . ?"

"Do you at least know what branch he's with?"

Truly's innards had started to burn. "No, General."

Augur let out a sound that was half-groan, half-sigh. Running a hand
through his whiskers, he looked like a dyspeptic lynx. "Major . . . Even
if this officer has not been sent to the front, as so many have, it's hardly
certain that I would know him. I still have a fair number of subordinates,
and they're scattered throughout the District. Lieutenant-colonels among
them, of course–we have a couple of them right here." He motioned to
his staff. Gazing at the befuddled group, Truly began eyeing each face.
"But your description does not fit them," said Augur, his voice a blunt
instrument. "Nor does it fit any others I can think of. In my nine months
in this command, I've seen but a handful on a regular basis. Furthermore,
faces have come and gone from week to week. I couldn't even give you a
reliable roster, just now. And who's to say the fellow still holds that rank?
The army has seen a wave of promotions, lately."

Stunned by the cranky barrage, Truly felt grateful as Forbes stepped
up to intervene.

"Then with your permission, we'll put it to every man here." Facing
the group, Forbes raised his voice. "Sirs, you have all heard the description. Do you know of any officer who matches it, even in part?" Bacon
and Wisewell turned to look at the fidgety aides. There were mutters and
grumbles. To one side, the young captain looked embarrassed. "Please
search your memories," said Forbes. "I should add that this man may
already have something questionable in his background. Something you
may have heard about in private conversation . . . "

Truly avoided Augur's face but noticed Barnard's, now more irritable
than confused. Pointedly the grayed engineer took out a pocket watch
and glowered at it.

Augur's hand made a cutting gesture. "That's enough, then. Good day to you." He hurried down the steps. As his entourage bustled after him, Truly felt their sullen glances.

With the groom holding his horse, Augur mounted it. Truly came down the steps and looked up at him. "You would agree, General, that our suspicions are alarming?"

Looming above, Augur grasped the reins and peered down. "At the moment, Major, there are far more definite things to keep me occupied. I regret that we could not assist you." His tone might have been a tardy effort at civility, yet it sounded patronizing. Behind him, Barnard, Bacon and Wisewell mounted up while the aides scrambled atop their own horses. "If you dig up some less sketchy information, do let me know," Augur said. "Until then, best of luck."

Truly stepped back as the general wheeled his horse. "Same to you, sir—tenfold. Because you'll sure as hell need it." His words were lost amid the flurry of hooves. With Augur leading, the cavalcade rode out, its dust powdering the leaves and headstones. Truly stood watching the riders disappear, then turned to see Forbes at his side.

"Well, wasn't that worthwhile?" Truly muttered.

"We had to try, Nate."

The guards were looking at them. The busy grooms had brought their horses around.

"I have to stop by the Department," Forbes said. "To see what's come in on the wires."

Truly nodded. Walking to the horses, he slapped his hat against his thigh.

Heat shimmered on the road as they descended toward the river. Truly's mood worsened by the minute. He had a major's commission, he thought. Like Baker's colonelcy, it was little more than a prestige item, a gratuity that came with his senior detective's rank. Still, it was high time that he got himself a uniform. He thought of how Augur and his brass-button toadies had looked at him, as if he were begging alms. Not as they had looked at Forbes—Forbes in his captain's garb, wooden leg and all.

"Did you see Barnard?" Truly grumbled. "If he's that addled, they ought to cashier him."

"Supposedly he's an excellent engineer," Forbes said. "Maybe he was just preoccupied."

As they rounded a shady bend, the river and then the span of the Long Bridge came in sight. So did a lone rider, slowly ascending through the heat waves.

"And Augur's staff!" Truly groused. "Have you ever seen a duller pack of schoolboys?! Gawking at us like cattle!"

Forbes sighed. "It's an unfortunate truth: no officer likes to hear of a brother officer gone to treason. It strikes at all they hold sacred."

"They'll be struck a damned sight worse, if we don't find this bastard."

"Yes, Nate. I'm as convinced as you are."

Truly decided that he had fumed enough. Recalling what Forbes had urged yesterday, he appreciated his partner for not repeating it. Yet the question dangled: was it time to try their luck with Baker? Flies buzzed, birds twittered and the horses clopped along. Truly made himself stop thinking. Idly he watched the rider's approach. They had closed to a distance of about four rods when the man waved.

Forbes glanced over. "You know this one?"

A checkered coat was draped over the man's saddle. Straining his eyes, Truly picked out the red suspenders, green knickerbockers and domed hat. But it was the medallion-sized ears that sparked recognition.

"Hey there, Truly!" came the clarion voice.

"Hello, Noonan," Truly called back.

As they met and halted, Noonan's narrow freckled face wore a lazy grin. "Caught any Reb spies lately?"

"Printed any military secrets lately?"

"If I tried to, I'm sure your able censors would thwart me."

"We can only hope." Truly had no yearning for small talk, particularly with one so prone to it. But he felt too listless to escape. "Captain Forbes, may I present Mister Israel Noonan of the esteemed *Washington Evening Star*."

"A journalist?" Forbes intoned.

"Worse. A dandified one." Reaching out, Truly plucked one of Noonan's suspenders like a harp string. "It's a wonder he's survived the front, being such a fine target. For both sides."

Noonan looked stoical. "Truly, you just need to quit envying me. Anyhow, I'm trailing the elusive General Augur. He's supposed to be holding some soiree at the Lee place."

"And a bodacious affair it was," said Truly. "Except, the champagne ran out and he moved on."

Noonan drooped. "Damn. I would've ridden faster–too hot for this nag of mine, though."

"Don't feel badly. We barely rated an audience, ourselves."

The reporter scratched a big ear. From his saddlebag, he produced a pencil and notebook. "Be a friend, Major, and tell me what senior officers attended."

"I knew I should have kept riding." Truly rattled the names off while Noonan jotted them down. Hearing General Bacon's, the reporter paused. "The District militia? Lord, they must be desperate."

"Make your own inference. Now–Forbes and I have pressing business."

Noonan put his implements away. "Well, I might as well head back with you."

"Suit yourself."

As a trio they rode on. Noonan lagged slightly, though his breezy questions kept up.

"So, Truly, what brought you gentlemen out this way?"

"So, Noonan, why aren't you off covering Petersburg?"

"I was. But the army seems to have launched a secondary war–on those of my profession. One day they quite literally got out the tar and feathers, so I skedaddled."

"Shocking."

"Besides, there's plenty to cover here. Which leads me to ask . . . "

"Save your breath, man."

"Not as a journalist. Just as a loyal citizen of this nation's capital."

"I'll take that to mean 'off the record.'"

"Can you assure me, perhaps, that what appears to be happening is in fact not happening? Because I'd dearly love to think so. That Lee has not pulled off a master stroke–against a city whose defensive readiness has sunk, of late, from dubious to abysmal."

Truly glanced over his shoulder. "Don't you read your own paper? The latest editorial says that Washington's safe. All rumors to the contrary are alarmist and defeatist."

"Ah, yes–my ever-optimistic employers. Yesterday I turned in a story based on eyewitness accounts from some river pilots. My editor threw it back at me and demanded more substantiation. Boatmen are full of tall tales, he said."

Truly had to chuckle. "Sounds familiar–eh, Bart?"

"Quite," said Forbes.

The road began to level, widening as it swung down toward the river. At last Noonan drew his horse alongside Truly's. "Harken. A year and a half ago, an army commission recommended that we maintain a garrison strength of thirty-four thousand men–well-trained, infantry and artillery both. Now, I've spent the past three days riding about the District, taking stock of things in my amateur way. You ought to see my notes. I've observed hundred-day state militia falling over one another, trying to practice-fire a cannon. I've seen Veteran Reservists who can't march without coughing or stumbling. These, gentlemen, are the warriors to whom the defense of the capital has largely fallen. There may be other, better troops available beyond the city, but I've made an estimate for those immediately at hand. Care to guess my total?"

Truly gestured to Forbes. "The captain's been looking into that himself."

"I figure about ten thousand," Forbes said.

His thunder effectively stolen, Noonan cleared his throat. "Yes. Even fewer, possibly. If you'll pardon my saying so, Halleck was an ass to waste that relief force on Harper's Ferry."

"Oh, we'll pardon you that," said Truly.

"God knows if it's even made it there safely," Noonan said. "The point is, we sure could have used those men now. As for the cavalry probe he sent out–we don't know how that's faring, either. I can tell you that Baltimore's pretty well choked with refugees–we'll be getting ours soon enough–and that the pro-secesh there are in high spirits. Much of loyal Maryland's in a panic, but not Washington. No, here we're too sophisticated. We've heard the cry of 'wolf' too often. Trouble is, this time there's really a wolf out there–a damned big one."

They were silent as they rounded a stand of pine. The Potomac glittered before them. Along the bank, a row of buildings appeared and then the bridge, guarded by a run-down fort with the Alexandria rail line running through it. Noonan said he was thirsty. Reining up, each got out his canteen and took a long guzzle.

Noonan wiped his chin and regarded Truly. Beneath his hat brim, the reporter's freckle-rimmed eyes were impatient. "The wolf has a name," he said. "Jubal Anderson Early, they're saying. Now, do you think Lee would send a lieutenant-general on a minor errand? Send a corps commander deep into Union territory, just to burn a few bridges and scare some farmers?"

Truly stoppered his canteen. "That would be a first-rate question for your bosses. And mine."

"I've tried asking it, but that infernal department of yours has drawn the curtains and barred the doors! All they'll say is that General Hunter will save the situation, that he'll come storming out of the west and hit these 'raiders' from behind. Except, Hunter has not been heard from in days. So now it's you I'm asking. What do you say?"

Truly stared off, rubbing his rough chin. Across the water, the Washington docks bustled. Upchannel, between the Aqueduct Bridge and Analostan Island, a motley fleet of boats and barges lay at anchor. These crafts had been arriving hourly, steaming downriver or pushing down the canal, collecting there like frightened amphibians. They brought news to which few would listen. "I say . . . " Truly hesitated. "I would say, God help me, that I'd trust your findings over anything the War Department might tell you, or that your editors might print. It appears that a scratch force under General Wallace will be making a stand on the Monocacy. A few thousand reinforcements from Grant should reach him as early as tomorrow. Once engaged, Wallace will be able to feel out Early's strength. All we can do, meanwhile, is pray that we *are* being alarmists, that panic and rumor have magnified the menace."

Noonan's smile had returned, with a touch of despair. He shook his head. "Tarnation, it seems I am ahead of you on this one! Not that I take any comfort in it."

Forbes removed his hat. Wiping his brow, he ogled the reporter. "Enlighten us, please."

Noonan squinted at the river. "I got a letter this morning, posted from Frederick. It was from a man I know, a Jew peddler. Since he gets around, sometimes out to the Shenandoah, I've used him as an occasional source and found him reliable."

"What did he tell you?" Truly asked.

"Some days ago he was out along the Valley Pike, near Winchester, watching Rebel troops enter the town. Hard-looking veterans, he said, and Winchester gave them a welcome fit for Jesus. My friend hid in some trees with his wagon, to avoid getting plundered." Staring at Truly, Noonan cradled his canteen. "He was there a good while. By his reckoning, the column was about seven miles long."

67

Truly Residence

As Truly entered, Anna came downstairs and reached for her bonnet. "I want to stop by the Old Capitol, in case Dennis has a free moment. Who knows? He may be at the front next week."

Truly hung his hat but then paused, ogling her. "You're going there by yourself?"

"Civil custom is a luxury in these times, Father. There are worse things to bear."

From anyone else, this casual concession to "the times" would have sounded mundane. From Anna, who had always seemed to prize the war's most theatrical aspects while resenting the rest, it was near miraculous.

She tied her bonnet. "Ben's asleep, finally. I have stew cooking. Sapphira can add to it, if she gets home before I do."

"Where is she?"

"Off with Sergeant Tucker–she told you about it. There's a singing recital at the Contraband Hospital." Anna took up her parasol. "Father, have you heard anything about Rebel raiders in the countryside? There was talk of it at the Center Market."

Truly wanted a drink. "There's some enemy activity in the western part of the state. They're keeping an eye on it."

"Well, I'm glad we're here and not out there."

"My regards to the lieutenant."

"See you, Father."

He held the door as she made her blithe exit.

Truly poured a tall whiskey and got out his tobacco. Hunting for something to spit in, he glared at the spot where Anna had stood, then went to the cellar. There he found a spider-webbed clay pot. He set it by his chair, flopped down and started chewing.

Now he confronted his last and foulest option: to appear before Baker and present his case anew. He spat, missed the pot and forced himself to think.

He would have to bring along the report that he had haphazardly written, with some obfuscation, on his mission to Port Tobacco. But he would also bring Archer's portrait, linking the policeman to a confirmed Southern spy. In exposing a corrupt and perhaps traitorous lawman, and by derailing the scheme in which he figured, the Secret Service could redeem itself and chasten the police–Truly would stress this. He would outline Delia's revelations and those of Saint-Felix, although Baker might sneer at them ("A mick harlot, you say? And a frog arms runner?!"). In that case, Truly would harp on the lieutenant-colonel. The mere idea of treason amid military threat, as Forbes argued, might scare Baker into giving assent. With three or four agents, they could at last raid La Maison. Even if the arrests did not include Wakefield, the subsequent interrogations might reveal his whereabouts. He pictured Monroe strapped to a chair, helpless. He thought of old Dinsmore's "order" involving the flame-heated sword.

By the time Truly was done chewing and on his second whiskey, it had all started to seem palatable. Belatedly he thought of the bowler Baker had sent him. The muffin boy had returned it, according to Sapphira, but where was it now? Then the doorknocker sounded. Answering it with glass in hand, Truly expected Forbes but found Duke instead. The clerk stood clutching his hat, his face troubled.

"Octavius. Come in."

"Thank you, Major. I . . . I just ran into Captain Forbes."

Truly motioned to the setee. "A drink for you?"

"Oh–no, thank you, sir. I'm . . . " Duke sat down, fussing with his hat and specs. "The captain told me to say he won't be coming by. It struck him that he should be drafting another detailed telegram for Colonel Sharpe, given the changing military situation."

In his day-to-day absorption, Truly had forgotten how much else Forbes had to do. He nodded. "I'm sure he could use a rest from me, anyway."

"The Department's in quite a tizzy," Duke said. "Two of the captain's scouts–the ones with the cavalry expedition–wired in from Frederick. There's been a hard skirmish west of the town, at Catoctin Pass. Our horsemen drove the enemy back at first, then ran up against superior numbers and had to withdraw. The expedition's now cooperating with General Wallace, trying to hold Frederick."

Truly sipped his whiskey. Between Early's juggernaut and Washington, Wallace stood alone, no doubt envisioning himself as a modern-day Cincinnatus. Truly wished him well. Then he noticed Duke still squirming. "Something else to tell me?"

"Yes, sir." In Duke's abject pause, Truly somehow guessed the message. "Colonel Baker summoned me to his office. He said he'd been informed of your return to Washington, and had guessed that you were working on the La Maison case. He demanded confirmation of this. I'll allow I was quite shaken–you know how his presence affects me–but I think I pretended ignorance passably well. But . . . "

Leaning on his elbow, Truly stared past Duke to the window. "So I'm sacked, then?"

"No, sir. No, he knows your value. I have his letter here." Duke started to take the folded paper from his pocket.

"Just tell me the nub of it," said Truly.

Duke gave a sigh. "It's suspension without pay. For the rest of the month."

Truly sagged. In his thickening whiskey cocoon, he remained blank for a long moment. "I suppose Wood glimpsed me," he said at last. "Yesterday at the Old Capitol."

Duke shook his head. "I asked a couple of fellow clerks about it, in confidence. They said it was the jailer in Annapolis. When you handed over your prisoner from Port Tobacco, you said you'd be retrieving him in a few days. But cell space became tight after the Fourth of July, when there were arrests for drunkenness. So the jailer contacted Colonel Baker, demanding to know when you'd fulfill your word."

"Oh." The first emotions leaked in, curiously familiar. There was pain of a sort, and a baffling sense of relief. Then it hit Truly that two years ago, he had experienced roughly the same thing with Pinkerton. Quite an employment history he was forging. "Well, I did play with chance on this one."

Duke hunched toward him. Truly was startled to see that he had tossed his hat aside, his pale hands balled into fists. "Major, I had never spoken back to that man! But I had to tell him that whatever you'd done, you'd done out of sound beliefs! I wanted to remind him of your evidence, your key points. But . . . " Duke's face had reddened. Truly conjured the scene: Duke stammering, Baker ballooning with rage. Unclenching his hands, the clerk let out a ragged breath. "The colonel threw his letter at me and said to deliver it, or else I'd be out on the street."

Downing his drink, Truly rose. He clapped Duke on the shoulder. "Can't reason with a boulder, my friend. But I appreciate your trying."

"Major, I think I will have a drink. A small one."

As Truly went to the side table, he found himself adding up the months he had worked under Lafayette Baker–nineteen of them. A tricky dance it had been, requiring those same gifts that the work itself did: instinct, foresight, calculation. A feel for when to sidle or retreat or collide head-on. Though exhausting at times, it had kept his wits sharp and his spirit anchored. He missed it already. He felt hollowed-out, wishing for anger to rise and fill him. Having poured too big a drink, he handed it to Duke, who thanked him and glumly stared at it. Truly paced to the mantel and leaned there. "I'm thinking . . . Maybe I could camp out in the woods by La Maison–watch the place, see if Wakefield shows." Even as he said it, he realized the impracticality of such a plan. Results would be far from certain. And by himself, stripped of authority, any riskier moves would be risky indeed. "Or I could ride out to the forts, question soldiers about the lieutenant-colonel."

Duke gave one of his rare skeptical looks. "There are about sixty forts, sir. Strung out along thirty-seven miles."

Foundering, Truly looked down at the hearth. "Well, if I limited myself to the northern perimeter . . . " But with only a sketchy description and no name, this would still take a lot of time and effort, which might be better spent on some other plan. What? Could he really be this helpless? From the corner of his vision, Rachel's portrait looked on.

"He called me a gnat," Duke mumbled.

Slowly Truly returned to his chair and sank into it. "He mistakes a lot of us for insects, Octavius. Maybe because his brain's so infested with them."

That won a chuckle from the clerk.

"And what's more, if I ran this infernal organization . . . " How many times had he spoken that phrase? He would have to stop. "If I ran it, I'd give you a position that no gnat could fill. You would oversee the consolidation and cross-checking of intelligence from every quarter. You'd be present at every meeting. And getting five times your current salary."

Duke's boyish smile twitched to life. "Honestly, Major?"

"No lie. And you know what else?"

And so Truly might have gone on–hollow-sounding, descending into babble, pathetic to his own ears–had Sapphira and Tucker not arrived just then.

"Hello, Father–and Mister Duke." Sapphira entered the parlor while Tucker remained in the hall.

Duke put his drink down and rose to greet her. Looking up, Truly did not speak right away. Sapphira had changed. Despite having worked most of the day, she showed no sign of fatigue; on the contrary–even in her black nursing dress, she appeared vibrant. There was an ease to her smile, a glide to her step and something else, more elusive. "So it begins," Truly thought. Melancholy dulled his happiness for her. Rising to beckon Tucker in, he felt emptier still.

Sapphira was extolling the singers they had heard, a family sextet from Boston. Tucker looked stronger and steadier. He held his cap in one hand and something rectangular in the other, wrapped in velvet.

Sapphira turned to him. "Let's show them what we brought."

Removing the cloth, Tucker handed the wood-framed object to Truly. It was the group photograph from the Fourth-of-July picnic. In rich sepia tones, the phalanx of Negro children and adults gazed out. Truly picked out Reverend Cass and then his own solitary white face in the back row. To the left of him, Tucker and Sapphira stood stiff as candles. He passed the photograph to Duke. "Fine memento. How'd you come by it?"

"Your friend Mister Finch's uncle came to the performance," said Sapphira. "He knew some folks from our church would be there, so he brought a few prints from his nephew. Very kind of him. Is that stew cooking?"

Nodding absently, Truly eyed the picture in Duke's hands.

"Father, I was wondering if the sergeant and Mister Duke could dine with us?"

"Of course. Prints, you say? Copies?"

"Why, yes."

"They can make copies of a photograph?"

Regarding him, she chuckled. "Yes. You didn't know that?"

Truly's hands flew up. "No, dang it! I know all the words to *The Blue-Tailed Fly*, but in some other areas I'm a plain dunce! Just tell me, how are these copies made?"

Startled, she blinked at him. "That I do not know."

Truly looked to Tucker, who shrugged. "There's some method of passing the glass-plate image onto specially treated paper. That's the extent of my knowledge, Major."

Catching up with the conversation, Duke placed the picture on the piano top. "That's right. I'm no authority, but I've done some reading on the subject." Gesticulating, he explained that the exposed glass plate–the original, or negative–could be developed in a chemical solution and presented as a finished photograph. The old Daguerrotypes were limited to that process, he said. But some years ago, a Frenchman had developed a process whereby the image could be printed–several times, if need be, and with no loss of detail. The negative and the treated paper were pressed together in a printing frame, then exposed to sunlight for a short period. So the image was passed from one to the other.

Wishing for a clearer head, Truly regretted his second whiskey.

"Father, why the curiosity?" Sapphira demanded. "Are you just interes . . . ?" She broke off, having sighted the pot-turned-spittoon. Barely masking her disgust, she picked up the receptacle and left the parlor.

Tucker's chestnut-brown face had turned serious. "Pardon the change of subject, Major, but we heard some talk at the hospital. About an enemy thrust into Maryland–a raid, maybe even an invasion. Can you say if there's any truth to it?"

Truly drew a finger across his mustache. "I'm afraid it's more than a rumor, Sergeant. Mister Duke and I were just discussing the whole business."

Still enjoying his informational role, Duke jumped in and sketched the situation for Tucker–the impending Union stand on the Monocacy, the tardy but growing belief that between fifteen and thirty thousand Rebel troops had crossed the Potomac. Truly picked up the group photograph and stared at it.

When Duke's briefing ended, it was a moment before the sergeant spoke. "Well . . . If it comes to that, I'll be fit enough to fight."

Truly put the picture down. Excitement took full hold of him, burning through the whiskey haze. He cleared his throat. "I'm sorry that Ben's asleep, Sergeant. Have a seat, though, and please pardon Mister Duke and me. We have to go to my study."

"Thank you, Major."

With the wondering clerk at his heels, Truly strode toward the study. Abruptly Sapphira stepped from the kitchen and into his path. He lurched to a stop and Duke blundered into him.

"Dang it, Saph!"

"Your pardon." She did not move. Having donned her apron, she held the stove bellows like a weapon. "The fire was nearly out," she murmured. "I threw some onions into the stew. I hope someone has looked in on Ben in the past hour. Before heaven, I promise I'll make Annie tell where she hid your spittoon."

"That I would appreciate. Now . . . "

"Father, you're staying for supper, aren't you? Not rushing out somewhere?"

"I . . . "

"For then it will be just myself, the sergeant and eventually Annie. Please think on that."

"Set places for us, my dear. Now, please . . . "

She stepped aside. With Duke in tow, Truly rushed to his study.

Opening the bottom drawer, he took out Archer's portrait and laid it on the desktop. Duke shut the door and stood watching. Truly got out his penknife. Bending over the policeman's photograph, he examined the crack in the glass protector, next to Wakefield's dedication. Carefully he worked the knife tip into one of the radial cracks, then pried out a small, triangular shard. With his fingertip he poked the portrait's surface where the fragment had been. It was paper.

"A print," he said, peering up at Duke.

"Yes, Major. That's why it required a protector."

"When a photographer makes a print, if I understand you, he may then keep the glass original. The negative."

"That's right. Often they keep them on file, in case the customer wants another . . . " As his voice trailed off, a stunned look crossed Duke's face. "Yes . . . Wakefield took pictures of the other men."

"To help win their friendship," said Truly. "And why not the lieutenant-colonel too?" He drew his wallet and plucked out a bill. "Supper will be a while yet. Go lease us a horse and wagon, will you?"

Duke snatched the money. "Yes, sir!"

"Let's hope Wakefield hasn't been back to clear out his shop—but I'm guessing that wise caution has kept him away. Once our errand's done, we'll get hold of Sam Finch. His expertise is needed. Then . . . " Through his soles, Truly imagined he felt the martial tramp of the invader—stronger now, like a great distant heartbeat. "Then we'll get down to work. Maybe we can identify our traitor, at long last. Heck, we have to." He twirled the penknife in his fingers. "Before Jubal Early swoops in like a howling gray angel."

PART VIII

Comes The Gray Angel

*I have been defeated; the enemy are
not pursuing me, from which I infer
they are marching on Washington.*
• MESSAGE TO WAR DEPARTMENT
FROM MAJ. GEN. LEW WALLACE,
JULY 10, 1864

68

Monocacy River, Maryland
July 9

FROM THE TOWN of Frederick, Early's party rode southeastward along the Washington Pike. Ahead of them, the artillery duel grew louder, resounding over the lush summer farmland. One river bend and then another appeared, intermittently brilliant beneath the high sun, while drifting white smoke marked the battle front. Early turned off the macadam surface, entered a pasture and slowed to a halt, digging for his field glasses. The others reined up around him.

"That's a mighty strong position," Sandie Pendleton observed.

At first, Early did not entirely grasp it as he peered at the enemy center. Ramseur's men had swept through Frederick a few hours ago and were now pushing across wheatfields along the railroad spur. Before them, offering desultory fire, Yankee skirmishers fell back toward the sluggish Monocacy. On the river's near bank, a tight bluecoat formation guarded a railroad bridge where the spur and the main B & O line merged, continuing eastward. A stone's throw to the right, a similar formation shielded a covered bridge that served the pike. A fortified blockhouse stood between the bridges, anchoring the whole position like a spike-head while, on the far bank, other Yankee elements waited to frustrate any crossing.

From the north, a clatter of small arms told him that Rodes had deployed, pressing the enemy right wing astride the Baltimore Pike. But the main assault would have to be against the left, to secure the route to

Washington. Scanning that way, Early saw that the Union commander had anticipated well, placing the bulk of his infantry along hilly ground east of the river.

Early handed Pendleton the glasses. "Your eyes are younger. Tell me if you see any sign of reserves back there."

The adjutant general gazed for half a minute. "None, Genr'l. Not in large numbers. I'd estimate their total strength at seven, maybe eight thousand."

"That sounds right to me." Taking the glasses back, Early gestured south. "If we can get a division or more across, then extend our right and mount a strong attack, they'll have to change fronts in order to face it. At which point we can exploit any confusion and roll 'em up."

Two other staff officers had dismounted and gotten out the map, each holding a side of it. One traced the Monocacy with his finger. "Don't see any fords or bridges that way, sir. None that's close enough, according to this."

"There must be one, damn it! We need scouts. Anyone know if McCausland's back yet?"

"Barring any real troubles, he ought to be," said Pendleton.

Early scowled. Too often, with McCausland, "ought to be" fell shy of "is." The cavalryman's assignment had been simple enough: cut telegraph wires, rip up more of the B & O and then return as fast as possible. "We'll have to do our own scouting, then. Let's get at it."

The party rode on, turning down a divergent road. The road and tracks ran parallel to the river until, separately, they bridged a curling creek. On the creek's near side, Breckinridge's corps lay in wait. Early signaled a halt. On a grassy rise across the river, a Yankee battery let loose and frightened the horses. Early nearly dropped the glasses as he steadied his mount, wondering if they were out of range.

"Genr'l—look yonder!" Pendleton pointed.

From the west, along the creek's far side, Early saw a cloud of dust and then flapping guidons, followed by a large body of horsemen: McCausland's battalion. They crossed the road and then the tracks, headed straight for the Monocacy. Through the glasses, Early watched as three lead riders–tawny men in buckskin, probably Cherokee scouts–reached the creek's point of confluence and dismounted, then waded into the mud-brown river. The water came up only to their waists. Holding their carbines high, two of the scouts kept on while the remaining one motioned for the rest to follow. Rider after rider dismounted, plunged in and started wading toward the opposite bank.

"God-a-mighty!" cried Early. "He's gone and done something right!" Checking the Yankee gun, he saw its crew manhandling it to a new position while some infantry moved up, lying on their stomachs or crouching. Again Early peered downriver. McCausland was holding back about a third of his brigade to tend the riderless horses. The rest of his men continued to pour across, vanishing into foliage along the Monocacy's east bank. Not far beyond it, they began to reappear in a gently sloping cornfield. With sabers, carbines and pistols drawn, the wet troopers were forming a battle line. Near their right, an enemy shell sent up a spout of earth.

"Foot charge," Early muttered.

Another shell struck in front of McCausland's line, but with no sign of faltering it started through the corn. Onward it pushed, quick and then double-quick, headed for the battery atop the grassy rise. An enemy fusillade crackled. Several gray-clad bodies fell but the rest surged on, their order commendable as a shell sailed over their heads and exploded uselessly. Thinking of McCausland, Early granted himself some credit. Since Lynchburg he had made his disapproval of the cavalry chief well known, thereby holding him to a stern standard. Surely it had helped drive McCausland to this startling deed of valor, rash though it was. And at least a suitable ford had been located. Early passed the glasses to Pendleton. From his saddlebag he took a pencil, a book and a piece of writing paper. The book was a signed gift from Jackson, a collection of religious essays which Early had never even glanced at; its cover provided a writing surface.

"Pendleton—Gordon's division is closest down there, correct?"

"Yes, Genr'l . . . My God, they're going to take the battery!"

Early looked up. Even without the glasses, he could see that the Yankee gun crew had fled. The supporting infantry began to waver, their volleys degenerating to random pops as McCausland's men broke out of the cornfield, closing the last fifty yards. The bluecoats retreated. The gray troopers swarmed over the rise, a few stopping to turn the gun on the enemy.

"Bully for them!" cried one officer.

Pendleton shook his head. "They can't hold it. Without support, they'll be driven back."

Even as the adjutant said this, a solid line of blue materialized along a ridge farther on. The retreating Yankees halted, rallying as the new line swept down from the ridge. Before the counterattack, the Confederates finally stalled, spitting fire as they lurched back toward the captured gun. The gun's would-be crew gave up trying to fire it and rejoined the fight.

"McCausland will get his support," Early declared. He finished writing his dispatch and handed it to a lieutenant. "To Gordon—fast. And ask Breckinridge to join us, if he's ready."

The lieutenant galloped down the road.

Early jotted a second note, this one ordering up a couple of General Long's batteries. A second junior staffer took it and rode off. Now there was little to do but wait and watch. Dismounting, Early unbuttoned his tunic, and most of the others followed suit. Pendleton stayed mounted, gazing across the river as McCausland's men fought on, disputing every blade of grass. With its flanks threatened and men dropping, the battalion fell back to the rise in fair order.

Down by the creek, dust stirred as Gordon's division lumbered forth, leaving gear strewn and tents unstruck. Within minutes, platoons and whole companies were splashing across the ford, rifles held aloft, men wading waist-deep to the east bank and pawing their way up.

"Gordon always gets 'em moving," said Pendleton.

Early gave his adjutant a glance. On the noble, long-chinned face, a smile had surfaced—an admiring smile for Gordon. Everyone seemed to admire the fierce son of Georgia. Raising the glasses, Early grunted—"That's only what's expected of him." Down by the ford, the red-shirted Gordon was easy to spot atop his black charger, urging his men across. He did look fine.

Tending the horses on the west bank, McCausland's remaining men could only watch while, on the other side, their hard-pressed comrades fought to buffer Gordon's movement. Nevertheless the infantry too drew fire as it fanned out and deployed in echelon. By the railroad, one of Long's Napoleons unlimbered and commenced shelling, while another was rolled with some difficulty across the ford.

Swift and efficient though the crossing had been, time slowed as Gordon's still-forming division began sidling to the right. The sun grew hotter. Early paced, stroking his beard and chewing his tobacco. Looking at his pocket watch—one o'clock already—he wondered how things were progressing back in Frederick. There, under the eyes of a Confederate officers' delegation, town fathers were scrambling to raise two hundred-thousand dollars from the citizenry. Early hoped the effort would succeed.

Torching the town would cause more delay, given that so many of its homes were of brick. And a wagon full of Yankee gold would please Richmond.

At the rail junction back upriver, the cannonade and rifle clash had intensified. Scanning that way, Pendleton rose in his stirrups. "Genr'l, they've fired the bridge. The blockhouse too."

Early seized the glasses and observed twin columns of black smoke rolling skyward, flames leaping from the blockhouse and the covered bridge. Under steady fire, Ramseur's men moved in. The federal center had withdrawn across the Monocacy, though it still held the iron railroad bridge. "Fine," said Early. "Billy Yank is good and nervous."

He swung his gaze back to Gordon's division, still maneuvering slowly to the south, its extreme right having vanished beyond some woods. The Union line had moved forward in that sector, thinning as it strained to meet the threat. Mounted officers cantered back and forth, gesticulating. Sweeping the higher ground, Early realized the full difficulty of the command he had given. A network of wooden rail fences traversed the sloping fields; studding the fields were stacks of harvested grain, like orderly brown hillocks. When the Yankees inevitably pulled back, these would obstruct attack while supplying good defensive cover.

The two couriers returned, soon followed by Breckinridge and his staff. The Kentuckian announced that his other divisional chief, John Echols, was preparing to lend any needed support. He had no sooner said this when an eruption of shell and musketry heralded Gordon's assault. Mounting for a better view, Early saw a thin curtain of skirmishers appear from the trees. Massed infantry followed–so dense, for an instant, that it looked like a surge of gray lava. Fire flashed from the Union line. The oncoming brigades slowed but did not pause, pouring out and expanding in a great wave–rifles bristling, blades gleaming, flags like ship-masts in the smoke. The roar of guns stoked the general thunder, a pummeling monotony that devoured the minutes.

Two hours later, with the entire Union left collapsing, Early rode with Breckinridge and the others toward the rail junction. They had drawn alongside the tracks when Early dug his spurs in and broke ahead. In the smoke and flash from across the river, he caught jarred glimpses of the enemy in reeling retreat. His back felt nothing. Like a dream of youth, his whole body sang and he heard himself cackle. "Go it!" he yelled. "Go it, Gordon!" The breeze having shifted, black smoke traveled down from the blockhouse and the covered bridge and began to obscure his vision. The din of war enveloped him: the cataract of rifles, the whistle of minie-balls, the yells and screams, the shell shriek and cannon thunder. And through and above it all, floating, that Rebel cry–shrill as falcons, ice to the spine, the sound of one nightmare engulfing another. Tossing his head back, Early crowed.

He emerged coughing from the smoke. Slowing his horse, he saw federals flying back across the eastward rail line, Confederates scrambling over the last fences in pursuit. Up at the junction, Yankee artillery had gone silent. Early stopped and got out his binoculars. He watched Ramseur's men pour across the river shallows and the iron bridge, the enemy center crumbling. Early's staff clustered around him, all nods and smiles. At the head of Ramseur's skirmish line he spied a familiar tan horse, its rider waving his hat in celebration. Kyd Douglas had evidently joined the final assault, spurning his duties as Frederick's provost marshal. Three thoughts struck Early at once: he could court-martial Douglas; he would not court-martial him; he would have liked having a son like him– brave, capable, insufficiently solemn.

"Lord above, Gordon's a wonderment!" someone exclaimed.

Pulled from his reverie, Early cleared his throat and turned to Pendleton. "Head back to Frederick. Find out about the levy. If they're still stalling, prepare to fire the town."

"I don't think they'll need convincing now," said Pendleton, heading off.

Soon afterward, Early was riding among Gordon's sweaty, powder-blackened infantry as they gathered prisoners. Some stopped to jeer Echols' men as they streamed tardily past. To the north, stuttering rifle fire persisted. Corpses littered the fields and hillsides and dangled from fences, with carrion birds circling above. Along the riverbank, commandeered boats ferried wounded to the Frederick side, where they were loaded into ambulance wagons.

Early's staff had dispersed for the moment. In the middle distance, Gordon sat atop his charger, looking more grim than triumphant. Breckinridge rode up to him, hand extended in congratulation. Closer by, Early recognized one of Gordon's aides, a gangly major who was supervising the collection of dead. At Early's approach, the major gave a dazed salute.

"What can you tell me about your losses?" Early demanded.

The major looked side to side. "I'd reckon about a third of the division, sir."

Early gazed down the row of outstretched bodies, some already bloating in the heat–limbs stiff and clothes disheveled, some with eyes wide to the afternoon sun, mouths open as if they had died in conversation. Even the bearded ones looked no older than twenty.

"Make sure to collect weapons and cartridges," said Early. "Shoes, too."

Squinting up, the major seemed to sway a bit. "Yessir, Genr'l."

Early watched a cartload of captured flags and rifles roll by. Hanging over the side, a white-and-blue guidon caught his eye. "Hold up there!" he called, and the teamster yanked the reins. Leaning down from his horse, Early grabbed the little flag by its swallowtail and examined it. It displayed the Greek Cross. Waving the teamster on, he watched a line of guarded prisoners stumble by, some of them daring an upward glance at their conqueror. He eyed the badges on their caps–again, the Greek Cross. A set of hoofbeats distracted him, and he turned to see Breckinridge cantering up.

"Where's Gordon?" Early asked.

"Gone back to town," said Breckinridge. "To personally check on medical supplies. His brother's badly wounded and so's his senior brigadier."

"I see." Early pointed to the prisoners filing past. "Look at those insignias."

Breckinridge looked, narrowing his eyes. "The Sixth Corps!"

"A division of it, anyhow," said Early. "Last seen at Petersburg."

The Kentuckian smiled. "Then Grant's pulling troops from the main front."

Yes, Early thought–and that was good for Lee. Yet it conflicted with what had become Early's most fearsome hope, his blazing vision of what lay ahead. "If Grant sees the full threat we pose, he'll be sending the rest of the Sixth. More, possibly. I'd wager they'll be in Washington mighty soon, if not already. And we can't afford a bloody repulse."

Breckinridge mulled it over. "Once we're there, we can determine enemy strength. If it's too much, we can withdraw–but we won't know till then. We've just over thirty miles left to go. This fight cost us a day's march, but the race may still be won."

However quiet and cryptic Breckinridge had been on the subject of Washington, he seemed game about it now. Boldness was catching. "Very good, then," said Early, heartened. "And lest we forget, a hidden advantage awaits us." In his side-vision, soldiers dragged more battered corpses into line. He turned his gaze to the pike, following it till it vanished in the low distant hills. "At dawn, your troops will lead the column out. Drive them hard, Breck. By tomorrow night, we need to be on Washington's doorstep."

"Then we shall be," said Breckinridge.

They spent a minute discussing Bradley Johnson's expedition. Johnson's eight hundred horsemen had left at sunup, aiming for the Baltimore vicinity and thence down the cape to Point Lookout, where thousands of Southern captives needed liberating. On their way, the troopers would spread more panic and destruction.

Pendleton arrived at a gallop, announcing that Frederick would not have to burn; its leading citizens had agreed to scrounge up the two hundred-thousand in bank loans. Apart from that, the town's supply depot abounded with clothes, blankets, foodstuffs, medicine and horse livery. Best of all, someone's cellar had yielded a cache of that rarest delicacy, ice cream, packed in ice and woodchips. "If we head back now, we can get ourselves a heap of it!" cried Pendleton.

Breckinridge chuckled. "A good day for the South, all-round."

Early grunted agreement. Riding off, he cast another glance toward Washington. The way was open. Everything now depended upon speed–speed and, quite possibly, a single Yankee traitor.

69

Truly Residence

IN HIS LEATHER apron, Truly stepped through the open bulkhead doors into strong sunlight. He squinted about his small back yard. In each hand he held a loaded printing frame. Along the shadeless areas of the porch and fence, other rectangular wooden frames stood side by side, each containing a glass photographic plate. Truly walked to the privy and propped the two new frames against the sunward side.

He rued the fierce urgency of this project. With fresh facts and terminology teeming in his head, he would have enjoyed a less demanding pace–time to really marvel at the whole phenomenon, the elegant magic of light, shadow and chemicals. But in his cellar, box upon box of Wakefield's plates awaited scrutiny; of these, dozens would require printing. Truly had to make full use of daylight, of which there was maybe two and a half hours left.

Heading back to the cellar, he stopped to check his pocket watch. Then, hearing Sapphira's voice, he looked up. She had returned a short while ago from the church hospital, her shift having started at dawn. Still in her black nursing dress, she ushered Forbes through the open porch doorway and peered down. The tired look said she was resigned to perplexity, at least for now. As she vanished inside, Forbes gazed around the yard.

"What news?" Truly asked.

"Grant is sending the rest of the Sixth Corps," Forbes said. "Two divisions under General Wright. They left City Point this morning and should get here day after tomorrow. Also, the entire Nineteenth is being sent, though its arrival time's uncertain. It was returning by sea from New Orleans when the order came."

Truly wiped his brow. "So we can't expect reinforcements before Monday. And with Early as far as the Monocacy . . . Dang, this is going to be close!"

"Barring a miracle, yes. Meanwhile there's no word on Wallace's fate, not even from my scouts who are with him." Forbes leaned over the railing. "Now, then—what's your idea here?"

"Let me demonstrate," said Truly. Waving Forbes off the porch, he led him down to the cool, cramped cellar. "Despite the ventilation, there are certain odors to put up with."

On a stool at one of the two work benches, Duke sat scrutinizing another negative by lamplight. He paused to smile up at Forbes. "Greetings, Captain!" Stooped beneath the low ceiling, Forbes muttered hello and took his hat off. He stared at the stacked wooden boxes all around him.

"Bart, do you know much about photography?" Truly asked.

"Not really."

"Well—at this point, I know enough to appreciate how little I still know. And I'm only delving into the printing aspect. But I also appreciate something more about Wakefield—namely, that it's no coincidence he's both a spy and a portrait photographer."

"Why do you say?"

"Because at their best, the two seem to draw upon the same mix of talents. There's the scientist's sense of detail and procedure, plus the artist's knack for reading humanity. But for a man like Wakefield, photography could also be a balm to the soul. A spy lives in isolation, but picture-taking might connect him with the wider world—the human ken. For me, though, it's just a bodacious discovery—the exact crossroads where science and mysticism walk up and say 'howdy.' You take a glass plate coated with collodion—that's gun-cotton dissolved in ether and alcohol—and chemically sensitize it, then expose it for just a few seconds. And the image that results will outlast any tombstone."

Noting Forbes' pensive look, Truly decided to stop rhapsodizing.

"So when I learned about photographic printing, I thought of all the boxed-up glass plates in Wakefield's shop. Photographers customarily save these, the negatives, so that customers can order extra prints later on. For that reason, or just out of habit, Wakefield must have done the same for his La Maison subjects. I hoped for this and now I know it, because this morning I discovered Archer's negative in one of the first boxes."

Truly gestured to the open boxes, each with thin vertical side-slots and the plates packed neatly inside. "I'm betting that somewhere among these is a negative of the lieutenant-colonel. The plates are boxed alphabetically, as you see, each box marked with its letter. Usually the customer's name appears scratched into the plate's upper left-hand corner.

"Anyhow, lacking any real guideline, we're proceeding from the A's on down—so I dearly hope the fellow's name isn't Zimmerman. Octavius and I have been examining each one. It's hard on the eyes, especially with the dark and light portions reversed. But when we think we see a wiry man in an officer's uniform, that plate is set aside for printing. Octavius has already taken some prints to the Old Capitol for Miss McGuire to look at, including a few from Wakefield's display walls. Thus far we've come up empty, but sooner or later she'll identify our man's picture, which I hope will bear a name besides. Then we can go after the bastard."

Forbes rested his weight against a sawhorse. "You think there'll be time enough?"

"At the rate we're going . . . " Truly shrugged. "Heck, who can say? The day's been perfect for development—hot and cloudless—and it'll likely be the same tomorrow. But there are a heap of soldier portraits, as you'd expect, with a healthy percentage of officers."

In his downward gaze, the Bostonian seemed caught between hope and skepticism. "One thing I've always wondered—the negatives, as you say, show dark and light in reverse . . . "

"By definition, yes," said Truly. "Dark areas, so-called, are those that absorb light, while so-called light areas reflect it. It's this variability in absorption and reflection that creates the image in the first place. It's what makes photography possible."

"All right, then—but how is the shading put right in the finished picture?"

Truly felt the novice's delight in knowing correct answers. "One way is to chemically whiten the lighter parts of the negative and then darken its back side, using black varnish or some other means. This makes the image appear positive—in other words, as the human eye sees it. The Ambrotype process, it's called—Rachel's portrait upstairs is an example. Of course, it renders the plate one-of-a-kind, unsuitable for printing. And there's a loss of detail, whereas we want to preserve as much as possible for Delia's eyes."

In his didactic exuberance, Truly abruptly realized how much he sounded like Duke. This cost him his train of thought, whereupon Duke jumped in. "But the printing process accomplishes the same thing, Captain, only better. In the image's transference from glass to paper, dark and light are reversed yet again, owing to that absorption/reflection factor. And the resolution's much finer than with the Ambrotype." The clerk held up a sheet of printing paper. "These come pre-treated with albumen–egg-white mixed with ammonium chloride, that is. We spent the morning sensitizing a ream of them, floating them in silver nitrate. Once we pick out a negative, we compress it with a sensitized sheet inside a printing frame, which is then placed outdoors. The frame absorbs sunlight through its window until a positive copy is produced. We have a storage nook set up as little darkroom–candle-lit only–for developing, fixing and washing the finished prints."

Twitching his eyebrows, Forbes gave a thin smile. "Gentlemen, I am duly impressed. How'd you learn all of this overnight?"

"Sam Finch was our main fount of knowledge," said Truly.

"Finch, the Department telegrapher? I see a lot of him over there."

"They keep him busy, all right, but he managed to scribble some notes for us. I also found a photography shop on South B. The owner's a talkative sort, and he fleshed out Sam's instructions for me. Of course, in my ongoing tumble toward pauperhood, I felt obliged to pay for something." He went to the opposite work bench and reached under it. Taking up the small framed portrait, he lobbed it to Forbes. "Apart from my less-than-lovely puss, what you're looking at there is an example of yet another process. Tintype, it's called. Instead of glass, it uses a black enameled tin-plate. It's the most direct way of producing a positive, but it's also pretty crude. Too crude for Wakefield, who I can say is a real craftsman. And his portraits are the rare eight-by-ten size."

Forbes ogled the little picture. "Not exactly your cheerful self."

"Yes, well–I was feeling a bit pressured, for some reason. Speaking of which . . . "

Truly took up the two latest negatives that Duke had put aside and set these into the two available printing frames, along with sensitized sheets of albumen paper. He shut the frames, then secured them with their wooden brackets. Toting them out to the yard, he left Duke anxiously querying

Forbes about the military situation. Truly positioned the two frames along part of the fence. Realizing that at least four others were past ready, he hastened to collect them.

"Hullo there, Pa."

With his armload of frames, Truly turned to see Ben standing on the porch. Ben's arm was in its sling but his face was unbandaged, the injured side scabbed over. "Ben–how be you?"

"Well enough. Bored. Been lying down. Say, what are you doing out here?"

"Developing photographs."

"Honest? What for?"

"Mainly to identify a traitor before he hands Washington over to the Rebs and loses the war for us. Otherwise, it's just for amusement."

Ben's good eye narrowed, matching his fast-healing one. "Dang. And I thought you were only cleaning out the cellar."

"You'd best go back inside, Ben. This heat can't be good for you."

"Well . . . Keep to it. Hate to think I got blown up for nothing."

Truly watched him go inside. Then, checking the sun's progress, he noted the encroaching shadow of the house. Sundown would suspend printing until tomorrow, and he would be limited to the duller task of examining Wakefield's negatives.

Back down in the cellar, Duke was expounding to Forbes about the wildly varying estimates of Early's strength. Truly proceeded to the blanketed storage nook. From an eye-level shelf, a candle shed faint light. He set the four frames on the makeshift plank counter and opened the first one, then extracted the plate. Slowly he peeled the print away. He pulled on a pair of thick work gloves, the fingers already frayed by chemicals. Then he bathed the print in a tray of "hypo" fixative, washing away the excess salt crystals. Shaking off the last drops of solution, he held it up near the candle and scrutinized the seated figure. Between the image and his straining eyes, hope quivered. Yet even as he took up his magnifying glass, he recognized the subject's dark uniform as that of a sailor, and a foreign one at that; on the mariner's thigh, a cap bearing Cyrillic letters identified him as Russian. Wrong man, wrong service, wrong damned continent.

He moved on to the other prints. The next two showed bearded officers who looked respectively too young and too old. But the last one pictured a gaunt soldier–a major, his epaulettes said–who sported an imperial on his chin and seemed the right age. Truly's spirit lifted. He yanked his gloves off, snatched up the print and swept the blanket aside.

"We have a contender," he announced.

Duke hopped to one side of him while Forbes moved to the other. Staring, Forbes shook his head. "Sorry. This one's cavalry–see the insignia?" He tapped a finger on the officer's hat. "So he couldn't be directly involved with the forts. Besides, our man has dizzy spells. Wouldn't have lasted at a full gallop."

Truly frowned at the still-wet portrait. Puffing his cheeks, he tossed it onto Duke's bench. "Octavius, would you go fetch the two by the privy? They must be ready."

"Yes, sir, Major." Duke headed up the steps.

Forbes stood there with a remote expression. "Nice and cool down here," he said.

"Could I get you a drink of something?"

"Thank you. I'll take a swig from your well on my way out." Crossing his arms, Forbes gazed idly along the cluttered shelves. "Lord knows, I'd like to just stay here and watch. But I have to go see if any new wires messages have come in. I'll stop by when I can–maybe help out, if you need me to."

"That's good of you, but I think Octavius is all I need."

"I'm afraid you might be losing him."

Truly gave Forbes a sharp look. "How's that?"

"There's talk . . . " Forbes sighed. "With the shortage of men, they might be organizing the departmental clerks for defense."

"For . . . ? Aw, hang it!" Truly sank onto the sawhorse. "So that's what he meant! When he got here this morning, he said, 'Before this is over, you might even see *me* toting a rifle.' I didn't give it a second thought."

"He just said the same thing to me. I'm trying hard not to envision it."

Truly rubbed the back of his neck. "Maybe I could convince him to stay on with me."

"Unlikely, Nate. If such an order comes down, there'll be no exceptions made." Forbes patted his hat on. "Besides–however loyal our friend is, I doubt he'd let anything ruin his one chance at martial glory."

Truly thought of Duke's enthusiasm for battlefield tales–not just those of Forbes, but even Truly's musty yarns from Mexico. "No–he wouldn't."

"Carry on, Major Nate." Favoring his real leg, Forbes lumbered up the steps.

Truly sat still. From the work bench, his cheap tintype portrait stared back, insufficiently cheerful. He heard Forbes and Duke exchange good-byes, then the sound of Duke stumbling back down the steps.

"Careful!" Truly called.

As the clerk appeared carrying the new frames, his specs atilt, Truly eyed his small, pale hands and tried to imagine a rifle in them. He could not. Beneath his leather apron, he felt the pocket watch, a ticking little tyrant against his side.

70

Tennallytown, District Of Columbia

TRAJAN HEATH–A.K.A. MONROE, a.k.a. Major Henry Spruce–knew how and when to strike. And he knew when to be patient. Steeped in years of practice, his patience had become a glacial force. He could actually enjoy waiting, and therefore did not mind his present vigil at the edge of these woods, watching the village rooftops turn brilliant in the evening light. With the day's heat receding, he planned, savored and anticipated. At the same time, he let his mind roam. Gradually he stopped feeling like Monroe–La Maison's enforcer, Yvette Ravenel's ally, the official charmer of bores and martinets. He stopped feeling like Major Spruce, despite his false beard and uniform. He became Heath again.

Around Heath's boyhood locale in central Pennsylvania, stories endured about his landowning father. These tales featured the senior Heath's strength, enterprise, brutality and occasional madness. More than one household servant had supposedly died at his hands. Neighbors, employees and even relatives had feared him, and were relieved when he died in a suspicious hunting accident. That occurred when his son Trajan was five years old. But young Heath's frail, haunted mother soon remarried, and her new husband was a wholly different sort of man–a prosperous Quaker who took a dutiful interest in his stepson, and who grieved terribly when his wife died in childbirth, along with the baby who would have been Heath's half-brother.

Heath, large and strong for his age, appeared promising for the most part–clever and observant, if not exactly studious. Yet he could be willful in small matters and tended to bully other children. Each such episode earned him a lengthy scriptural admonition. But in his thirteenth year, Heath noticed a change in the adults around him, including his stepfather—a cast of foreboding in their eyes whenever they turned his way; a hesitation in their voices, even when they were being stern. Troubled and confused, he wondered if they had detected the deepest truth about him, though he could not imagine how; he had a precocious talent for secrecy. But in time he understood those hints of dread, realizing that he was not only growing up, but more and more resembling his late father. He took a strange new pleasure in this. Yet no one could have reasonably guessed what was incubating beneath his handsome young surface; to do so, they would have had to follow him on one of his lone walks into the forest. They would have had to spy on him as he tended one of his homemade traps, carefully extracting some small, live animal and then, with his hunting knife, slowly disemboweling it.

The defining event of his adult life took place when he was twenty-four. On a serene late-autumn day, he visited an elderly Quaker couple who lived at the edge of his family's property. The couple, Henry and Abigail Spruce, were cousins of his stepfather and had been allowed to settle there. Ignorant of Heath's background or indifferent to it, they treated him with a direct and natural kindness that he had never known. Bemused, he found himself visiting often—doing chores for them, bringing a fowl or rabbit for their dinner. He would sit at their table, saying little while Abigail cooked and Henry commented on crops, weather and local events. Heath at that time was managing the land for his aging, dispirited stepfather—a probational arrangement, given the reputation he had forged by then. Though he was still regarded as clever, his whoring, fighting and general meanness had shamed both his family and the Quaker precepts by which they had tried to raise him. Warnings about God's judgment had long since given way to the worldly threat of disinheritance. But the threat seemed to be working at last. With no time left for devilry, he showed steadiness and competence in his work, and prophecies about his future took on a guarded optimism. It was hoped that some good, brave, solid woman would marry him and complete the gentling process.

On that afternoon, with his goodbyes said, he left the Spruces' cabin and walked back to his waiting horse. With one foot in the stirrup, he froze, gazing across the piney acres to the rugged Alleghenies, the yellowing western sky. On the horizon he saw a shining paradise, a garden realm where people of all ages sang, laughed and cavorted, dwelling in harmony. At the same time, he felt a churning and then a clawing inside, as if his chest were a sackful of wildcats. His muscles hardened against it, even as the Edenic spectacle absorbed him. He felt the warmth, heard the harps and laughter, smelled the fragrant trees. Then, from the margins of his sight, shadows crept in to encompass the golden scene; melding, they closed upon the vision until it was gone, smothered in black.

Heath stared at the side of his horse. The churning and clawing subsided and he felt strangely hollow. A static whistle-sound arose, high-pitched, like dry wind through his skull. With it came a sensation akin to loneliness–that, and the solemn pride that comes with facing one's destiny, whatever the price. And he knew he could never live or be as they wanted. Not for him, the distant gardens. Born to darkness, he would remain forever separate.

He had long observed people when they were not observing him, while demon whispers filled his head. They had been right to think him dreadful, he now decided, but stupid to think him changeable. In their dreary, prayerful, tepid sameness, they had still mistaken him for some version of themselves–one who might be coaxed, pulled, prodded into the fold. He resented their assumption, this sweet phantasm they had conjured and then imposed upon him. This warm-hearted falsehood, gleaming most purely in the smiles of Henry and Abigail. And the whistle-sound began to change, falling in pitch and yet intensifying, until he recognized it: the whispering–the demon tribe, calling him home. No half-measure would do.

Taking his foot from the stirrup and an axe from the woodpile, he returned to the cabin. He burst in on the old couple and as they gaped at him, destiny gaped as well: burning red, infinite black–an unspeakable majesty. A night realm, where blood flowed like lava. Then, in a five-minute blaze of annihilation, he cut himself free. Deaf to the shrieks and pleading and final muttered prayers, he heard only the clamor in his brain–hell's hosannas, exalting him. Exalting darkness. He could not have refused it, any more than a prince could refuse a crown.

Back at his own cabin, Heath bathed, ate dinner and slept soundly. His flight, the next morning, came almost as an afterthought. He never knew how long it took for the horror to be discovered; before any "wanted" posters appeared, he was gone with the volunteer infantry to Mexico, not even bothering to use an alias. But the war failed to fully accommodate his nature. In another formative event, a brush with death and military justice, he killed a soldier assigned to guard him and escaped. He briefly joined the San Patricio turncoats before deserting again and making his way north to Texas.

The Gold Rush of '49 brought Heath to California. Along the American and Sacramento Rivers, he jumped claims, murdered several prospectors and ended up leading a vigilante group. Altogether, his size, strength, education and agile mind proved a sweeping advantage, drawing other men into his orbit. Practicing the use of this advantage, he learned to calculate, to curb his recklessness. He did not curb it enough, however. In the boomtowns and mining camps, other gang leaders feared him as a potential overlord and moved to topple him. To avoid dangling like one of his own lynch victims, Heath fled once more, this time to the Deep South.

In Mississippi, Heath established himself as a "breaker" of willful slaves. Planters overlooked his Yankee accent and were soon paying him top fees. Still, he grew restless. News of adventurer William Walker's military expedition sent him down to Nicaragua, where he bought cheap land and helped fight the native loyalists. He quickly gained influence in the community of American filibusters and aspiring planters; like them, he envisioned Nicaragua as America's southernmost state, where a bold man might carve out his own slave fiefdom. Among the local peasantry, Heath became an object of particular fear and hatred, especially when young women began vanishing near his property.

Then the neighboring republics declared war. Cholera decimated the American invaders, who suffered a series of defeats, and the pro-slavery government collapsed. Heath survived all of this but lost his land and his savings. When the rebels finally burned his house, he took refuge with a fellow adventurer who he then murdered and robbed. He sailed back to the United States and drifted up the Eastern seaboard. Though never one to dwell on misfortune, he allowed himself a period of aimlessness, time to formulate new schemes. In Washington, one night, a whoring binge took him to La Maison de l'Empereur, where he met Yvette de Ravenel.

By then, having learned the sublime pleasure of premeditation, Heath regarded his earlier, more impulsive crimes as a careless waste. He had also worked on his social graces. Whether in rough or genteel company, his manner was amiable and his presence striking. Selectively he had begun introducing himself as "Monroe" or sometimes "Madison," claiming blood ties to the late Presidents so-named. This, along with his tales of Mexico, California and Nicaragua, seldom failed to spark fascination and solicitude. No one could have known that he had, up to this point, murdered thirty men, half as many women and three children. Of his rapes and other assaults, he had not kept track.

Sometimes, out of nowhere, the memory of Henry and Abigail arose— blood on the floor, blood on the walls, the twenty-odd pieces in which he had left them. And the poignant, barren feeling would take hold, tinged with satisfaction. More frequently, however, he recalled a courtyard in Mexico. He did so usually while looking into a mirror, touching the jagged scar along his scalp's left side. In a life of mortal scrapes, often with considerable odds against him, he had experienced true terror only once. Raw, blinding terror—he had felt it in that courtyard, facing not a mob of enemies but a single opponent: a small, silent man who clutched a Bowie knife, lunging and charging with crazed determination. On his knees in the dust, Heath heard the demon chorus, rising not to exalt but to devour him. Tasting his own blood, he glimpsed the black infinity, gaping not in welcome but to swallow him forever.

That, too, he had survived. But it remained his one truly disturbing memory, a weight of gloom whenever he contemplated the scar. He never dreamed that destiny would again bring him face to face with that unique antagonist. Yet on the momentous twelfth of June last, at La Maison, it had done so. Playing the "groundskeeper" Monroe, he had trudged into Ravenel's bedchamber, peered from under his hat-brim and beheld fate's handiwork. In that first lurching moment, he could not believe it. Then, like a slow tidal wave, a sense of wonder rolled through him; quelling it took the greatest effort as the federal man's voice questioned him. Growling in reply, Heath chanced another look. From the windows, soft sunlight became the glare of Mexican skies; as if spawned from that mystical light, the man stood there—bantam, bowlegged, suitably aged. It was him. Not another bad dream but the living, breathing man. Most sublime of all, he did not seem to recognize Heath.

Since then, by day and night, Heath had treasured the mental image of his foe. Repeatedly his brain closed upon it, like a fist upon burning gems. He relished the burning. Very soon, he and Truly would face each other once more, though it would unfold quite differently. Terror would flow in the opposite direction this time. And the hour was near—he felt it in his hands, in his teeth. But for this, as for all such things, he could pleasurably wait.

———◆———

IT WAS SUNDOWN, the moon a pallid actor in the wings. On the nearby houses, windowpanes turned a rosy-gold. Monks' white cottage sat apart, just beyond a copse of willows. Heath had spied the bay horse in its stall, indicating the lieutenant-colonel's presence. Still, for Heath's purpose, the dark of night was best–darkness, his faithful consort.

Tethered to a tree, Black Marengo snorted. Heath took an apple from his pocket and fed it to the horse. Then, amid the crunching sounds, Heath heard a rustling somewhere behind him. He looked down a shadowy bridle path through the woods. A farm boy about ten years old came into view, idly thrashing the shrubbery with a stick. He did not notice Heath until he entered the clearing, whereupon he halted and gazed up.

"Hullo there," Heath said.

"Hullo, sir . . . You seen a spotted pig hereabouts?"

"No, I have not."

"Our sow, Carlotta–she done run off. Ma says I have to find 'er."

Heath stroked the horse. "Well, I'm sure she's about. It's getting dark, though, so maybe you should head on home."

"That sure is a right fine horse."

Heath said nothing.

The boy seemed to be admiring his height. "You a general, sir?"

"I'm a major."

"Oh." Looking down, the boy jabbed the ground with his stick. "They say the Rebs is comin'. Is that so, sir?"

"It might be."

"If they do, I'm fixin' to throw rocks at 'em."

"That's the spirit! Now, I think you should . . . "

"My pa's in the army, you know. Down in Virginia."

"Is he? Then I reckon your mother needs you at home."

"But I ain't found Carlotta yet." The boy looked up. "Can I pat your horse, sir?"

The tree shadows had lengthened; across the boy's wrinkled white shirt, one lay slanted like a black sash. Heath cast a look toward the village. "Yes. Come and pat him."

Smiling, the boy dropped his stick and approached Black Marengo. The horse snuffled as he stroked its side. In the animal's shadow, the boy's form was dim except for a tuft of blond hair, touched by the fading sun. "You know, there's another army fella who lives over that way."

Heath eyed the blond cowlick. "Is there?"

"Yessir. Officer fella, like you. 'Cept, he's a little queer—never talks to nobody. My friends and me, we call 'im Goat Face, on account of he sorter looks like a goat."

"Oh, now—that's no way to speak of a United States officer." Heath stepped behind the boy. In the gloom, against Black Marengo's side, the boy's hand was a floating patch of white.

"You out here scoutin' for Rebs, Major?"

"That's right. But I haven't seen any."

The boy stood on tip-toe, reaching up to stroke the horse's mane. "If they come, we can lick 'em—can't we?"

"Of course we can." Heath's hand slipped under his tunic.

"I hope they come. I wanna see 'em get licked."

"You just might."

Turning around, the boy smiled up. "Mister Lincoln's got a summer place out this way, did you know?" He fell silent, looking where Heath's hand had gone. A warm breeze blew.

Looming, Heath stared down, then turned his eyes away. Through a stark webwork of branches, he saw the red dusk. His hand slid from under his tunic, then down into his pocket. He took out the last apple, gave it to the boy and patted him on the head. "Here, feed it to him."

Eagerly the boy stepped in front of the horse and proffered the apple. The horse took it whole. "Yike! He nearly got my finger!"

Heath paced to the other side of the clearing. He sighed with relief. He was not a base animal, a mere mass of instinct. Though his passion ran deeper than most men's, he was no slave to it. He could choose when to act upon it, knowing that his essential power lay in restraint. Without turning, he spoke to the boy. "I hope your sow comes home. Leave me be, now."

"I could help you look for Rebs, Major."

"Go on, boy."

After a pause, he heard the boy rustle away from him, back up the path.

In the welcome quiet, Heath waited another half-hour, pacing around as night fell and the crickets grew loud. Lamps lit the houses of Tennallytown. In a rear window of Monks' place, a lone muted light shone.

Heath untied Black Marengo and led the horse out of the woods, into the wide meadow. The moon gave some light as he crossed, moving toward the copse of willows. Reaching it, he tied the horse again. Then he started for the cottage. Emerging from the tall grass, he saw that even the one lighted window had its curtains drawn. He slowed his stride, treading more lightly. Around him, the billowing cicada noise engulfed the crickets'. From its stall, Monks' horse let out a snort.

For a moment Heath stood listening at the rear door, then pressed it gently. It was barred, as he had expected–but like many such rustic doors, it allowed an inch or so of play. He drew out Wakefield's bayonet. As quietly as possible, he pushed it into the crack at about waist level, then worked it upward till it touched the crossbar. Monks' horse gave a low whinny. For the next minute, Heath remained still. Then he relaxed his pressure on the door. Wedged in, the blade could still be moved vertically. He used it to slowly lift the crossbar, which he then grasped by its near end while pushing the door open. He slid the bayonet into his belt and squeezed through, maintaining his one-handed grip. In its slot, the bar's other end creaked protest, but then he was inside. He eased the door shut behind him, replacing the bar.

Crouched, he exhaled with no sound, his eyes adjusting to the kitchen's gloom. He caught a rough, spasmodic noise that he presently identified as snoring. Smiling, he straightened up. Both the snoring and the faint lamplight came from the other side of the house. He entered the main room, beyond which a door stood ajar; just past it, in the low-burning light, he saw a hand hanging off the side of a bed. He moved toward it. He stepped into the little bedroom.

Monks lay there with his face upturned, the bedclothes kicked off. He had made a perfunctory effort to undress, leaving one sock on, his pants and shirt unbuttoned. On the nightstand, a half-consumed bottle of rye stood beside the lamp. On the floor beneath his hanging hand, an old sword lay alongside its scabbard. His snore was fitful, throaty, with a moaning undercurrent. Moving to the foot of the bed, Heath saw a service revolver dangling from Monks' other hand. He leaned down, detached the revolver from limp fingers, then stuck it into his belt with the bayonet.

Moving to the nightstand, Heath carefully picked up the lamp and raised it, casting its glow on Monks' lank rumpled form. Sweat glistened on the sleeper's high brow. In his open mouth, a strand of spittle vibrated with each rye-soured breath. Abruptly he stopped snoring. The skin of his face went taut as his head began rocking, side to side against the pillow. "I'm sorry!" he moaned. "I'm . . . No! I'm sorry!"

Raising the lamp higher, Heath smiled. Monks' eyelids twitched, blinked, blinked harder, then opened wide. With a shriek he flailed to life, shielding himself with one arm while the other groped down beside the bed. In the next instant, his flailing ceased. He cringed against the headboard, eyes bulging, his breath coming in gasps.

Heath stood motionless. "Have you followed instructions? To the letter?"

"Y-Yes!" Monks yelped. "I . . . Yes!"

Heath lowered the lamp. "I trust you have–I've been watching you these past few days." He ran his fingers along his belt till they touched the bayonet handle. From behind the quaking upraised arm, Monks gaped at him. "It is time!" Heath said, in his brightest tone. "You will come with me to La Maison. There you'll stay till the Confederate force closes in– tomorrow night, most likely. At that point, you will go to Fort DeRussy and assume command. And I'll be with you, Orlando." Leaning over the bed, he gazed into the bony, wide-eyed face. "Right there at your side."

When he had stretched the moment long enough, Heath moved back to the nightstand. He smirked as Monks jerked around to face him. Even without the beard, Monks' face did resemble that of a goat–a very pale goat, just now. Heath set the lamp down. With his boot heel, he shoved the sword away from the bed. Then he went to the bedroom window, brushed the curtain aside and looked out on the moonlit meadow. He thought of the oncoming Confederate host. He thought of the crate full of gold. He thought of Truly and sighed, his fingertips pressing down on the sill. In all his dreams of bloody triumph, he had never envisioned this–such a grand culmination, as if every dark star had converged to favor him.

"Get ready," he muttered, as much to himself as to the man behind him. Turning from the window, he saw Monks standing on the other side of the bed–still gaping, trembling from head to foot. Heath looked him over, then cracked a grin. "Why, Lieutenant-Colonel . . . I do believe you've pissed yourself!"

71

Around Washington
July 10

FROM GEORGETOWN TO the Eastern Branch, from Boundary Street to Buzzard Point, throughout the capital, church bells tolled the alarm. They tolled for the usual Sunday reasons, but above all they tolled alarm, clanging and resounding through the still streets. Awakening to news of the Monocacy defeat, loyal inhabitants understood that rumor had erupted into fact– that for all the threats their city had survived, its hour of greatest peril had come. And bells which were meant to call minds heavenward called them instead to the city's northern fringe, where raw under-strength garrisons held the earth-banked forts and listened for the enemy.

"Let us be vigilant," the President urged, "but keep cool." Responding, Washington's Unionists sneered at the hysteria in Baltimore, which now seemed the less likely Rebel objective. In the mounting heat, children played, couples promenaded, thieves prowled and police made rounds. Half-empty omnibuses crawled along Pennsylvania Avenue while hack-men sat nodding in their carriages. On hospital wards, nurses bustled while soldier patients slept or read newspapers. In billiard parlors, the usual men ignored both the crisis and the day's sanctity, though their laughter was more subdued.

Many more people went to church. Before fan-waving congregations, ministers of discreet Southern bias turned indiscreet, delivering thinly veiled sermons on the evil of men–and governments–that tried to upset the natural order and thereby stirred heaven's wrath. Abolitionist ministers, for their part, invoked Job, Daniel and the early Christian martyrs to describe how God tested the righteous. In the streets, Veteran Reserve companies stopped to catch their wind before stumbling on; state militia hurried one way while teamsters led horse trains in another. With studied composure, citizens paused to watch. The city was vulnerable–this they knew. Still, faith endured that their military protectors had a grip on the situation and were acting with speed and competence. Help would arrive in time.

In the telegraph room of the War Department, receivers and transmitters rattled like brass teeth. Operators sat scribbling and sending while the supervising major read the letter-sized sheets of yellow carbon, each decoded phrase adding shape to the crisis. Chief of Staff Halleck paced back and forth, rubbing his desk-worn elbows. In his office, Secretary of War Stanton had already suffered an asthmatic attack and now he had a nosebleed; taking the arm of an assistant, he tottered to his couch and lay down.

Things were more chaotic across the street at Army Headquarters. Amid a swirl of staff officers, General Augur met with the newly arrived General McCook, who would command the northern works. Other generals had helpfully materialized, including a personal favorite of Grant's; protocol required that each be assigned some portion of the defense. To McCook, Augur explained that only two Ohio militia regiments held the line between Rock Creek and Bladensburg; the intervening rifle pits were largely empty. Three thousand dismounted cavalry had come in from Baltimore, having landed too late to help Wallace on the Monocacy; they received a grateful welcome, until all but five hundred of them proved to be sick with dysentery.

Civilians knew nothing about sick troops or unfilled rifle pits–nothing about worried generals, shaken officials or the true level of depletion. In most quarters, an air of cool vigilance prevailed, barely distinguishable from the normal summer lethargy. Then, in early afternoon, outposts reported dust-billows along roads to the north and west.

⎯⎯⎯◆⎯⎯⎯

OUTSIDE THE CHURCH of the Holy Kingdom, Albion Cass saw some of his parishioners off. Tucker had already left on his walk, taking Sapphira with him. Though not fully recovered from his wound, the sergeant had mentioned wanting to offer his services for the city's defense.

Cass reentered the church, where about half the congregation quietly remained. Slowly he walked up the aisle, past the cleared area where the more seriously wounded men lay on straw mattresses, tended by two volunteer nurses. With the weight of eyes upon him, he wished that Tucker had stayed awhile–the sturdiest convalescent, a scarred black warrior in uniform, whose mere presence might have checked these people's fright. In front of the pulpit, Cass turned to face them. They were recent folk, mostly–chain-marked contrabands, unlettered, still in sackcloth, free now. His truest people, though he had learned few of their names. In the sweltering hush their faces looked at him, some pleading and others impassive, all of them waiting for something more. A promise of some kind, stronger than hymns or homilies. He could not give it to them. In his sermon, he had tried and failed.

At the end of one bench, an old man rocked and prayed softly, his eyes squeezed shut; behind him sat Mother Sadie, the herb woman, her lips silently moving. Nearer the front, three small bedraggled children stared up while their stone-faced mother cradled a newborn. Flies buzzed. Cass drew himself erect. "Friends," he began, "–we must . . . " But the words would not come. He began to feel as he had during the river floods of his youth, when the rain spurned all prayer–when the levees broke and people scrambled for the high ground, and there was nothing to do but stand mesmerized as the endless muddy water rushed by. The enemy was coming, yes. But what truly mattered was this thing he could not speak–a promise that God would keep it all from happening, when He had let so much else happen. What mattered were these dark faces, trapping him between love and shame, pity and anger–these creased brows and smooth young cheeks, swirling like debris through his brain, till it felt as if he too might be borne off in the current. Then he saw the choir soloist.

In a dim corner at the back, she stood wraith-like in her drab gray dress, her large eyes watching him but watching him differently–intent, yet without fear. He had thought she had left with the other singers. Returning the stare, he tried to remember her name. And he began to speak: "Tell me, please–what good is faith, if we only proclaim it in safety? What use, if we abandon it on the eve of its testing?" With the slightest nod, the singer closed her eyes. Cass let his voice climb. "When the cock crowed thrice, Peter saw that he had left his faith behind. Abandoned it to lighten his load as he ran in fear–fear of that crucifying rabble. But the cock did crow, and he knew he had abandoned his one most precious thing. And he wept bitter tears. Friends, shall we weep bitter tears?"

A few people stirred, muttering an "Amen" or a "No, Lord." Cass's gaze swept the benches, then came to rest on a little copper-colored girl. The tears on her face told what had seeped into her: terror-tales–burnings, whippings, lynchings, the Rebels coming to bear her off. "If we could understand God's ways," Cass went on, his voice clear and sharp, "faith would be a useless thing. But we are small. We are small and we are blind. Shall we doubt His wisdom–us mortal folk, so small and blind?!" Amid fervid mutterings, he focused on the child, letting her bright wet gaze envelop him. And the words wrenched themselves free. "It shall not happen. He will not let it happen."

AT THE CHURCH of the Redemption, Mildred Sackville caught Nurse Dalton huddled with a younger nurse, whispering.

"You are not here for idle chatter!" she hissed at them.

The younger one meekly withdrew, but Nurse Dalton responded in a low voice. "Miz Sackville . . . " The widow glared at her. "If they take the city, what are we to do with these men? They could be made prisoners, or worse."

"If the city falls . . . !" The widow held up a bandage roll; shaking it, she spoke in a bristling murmur. "Should it fall, it will be proof of our unworthiness before God!" Redness rimmed her vision. As the colored nurse stared back at her, she felt another headache coming on. "You will speak of this no more!" Shoving the bandage roll into her apron, she turned away.

She moved down the aisle, through the groans and the effluvium, past beds and cots filled with limp, dark bodies. Nurses glanced up but kept working. The throbbing in her head suddenly dissipated, leaving a lightness. Anxious to get out of sight, she slipped behind the plain pine-board altar and balanced herself against the wall. She ached for sleep. But lately, when she slept at all, she had dreamed of her two sons killed in battle. Side by side in their schoolboy clothes, they peered down from a high cliff; each time she tried to climb toward them, her arms weakened and she slid back down.

On careful feet she moved past the small vestry to the open rear door, where the daylight momentarily stunned her. Squinting, she beheld the blue sky above the building tops and felt God hulking somewhere beyond, grave-minded as He assessed the squalid world with its wretched little beings. Everything was filth. Filth clung to her hands, to her face, to the skin of her body. Biting her cracked lips, she felt her heart flutter. Then, lowering her gaze, she saw the two rows of mud-streaked tents—hopeless cases on the left, walking wounded on the right. She thought of her brother's sermon that morning—an odd, rambling creation, full of gauzy parallels between the Dixie slaveholders and the bloody Aztecs and the hideous pharaohs of Egypt. Just then, staring down the muddy lane between the tent-rows, she spied her brother. With his Bible in his lap and his hat over his eyes, he was seated on the bench along the plank fence in back. A few bandaged black soldiers sat at either end of the bench, giving him room.

Unmindful of the mud, she moved down the lane toward the reposing figure. Standing soldiers hobbled out of her path. Watching her come, the seated ones struggled to their feet and edged away. The widow stood before her brother. Chin to his chest, he was slouched against the fence, hands folded across the leather-bound Bible. Carefully she took the book from him. As she gazed upon his sallow, flabby form, a kind of wonder took hold, growing until it dwarfed her body's ache. An edge of the light-headedness returned, and for just a moment she envied his weakness. "Caleb," she spoke. Stirring slightly, he emitted a snort but did not wake up. Only then did her mind flash white. The Bible caught him hard on the ear and knocked him sideways.

OUTSIDE CITY HALL, a dirty man in a patched Quaker coat harangued a crowd. Waving his arms, impervious to the heat, he condemned Washington as a pit of blighted souls. The crowd filled half of Judiciary Square, having gathered to await news from the forts or a reassuring statement from the mayor. Instead they were treated to this ember-eyed vagabond, this specter who raged about Jehovah's vengeance and Satan's impending victory. "Hark—the horsemen! Harken, ye woeful city!" Some spectators smirked while others watched in befuddlement. Yet all listened, until at length the police came and dragged the man off to the asylum.

AT THE OLD Capitol Prison, William Wood gazed at his loveliest responsibility, her face half-concealed by the flowers he had brought. Moving the vase, he reached across the small walnut table that he had stolen for her, adorned with the lace tablecloth that he had also stolen for her. He clasped her hand. As she smiled, he dropped his gaze. "Do pardon me. To one in my position, a kindly smile seems miraculous."

"But Mister Wood," said Delia, "–it's you who've been so kind!"

He squeezed her fingers lightly. "Dear Delia, to receive you otherwise would have been criminal. Bad enough that you must stay here, of all places, among traitors and ruffians."

Holding him in her sea-blue gaze, she leaned forward. "If you could know my former state, Mister Wood, then you would understand my gratitude."

He sighed. "That, Delia, is a true comfort–and a rarity in my life. Heaven knows . . . " He nearly gagged on the expression. A nominal Catholic, he had long since embraced the creed of skepticism. "Heaven knows, my dear, that I would sooner be fighting at the front. But when this post was urged upon me, I took it as my own thankless cross to bear. Still, I never foresaw the stone-heartedness I've encountered here–the sheer meanness of these fools, scoundrels and popinjays, all of them charged to my safekeeping. Every day I try to make the best of our shared predicament, to balance firmness with humanity–and they appreciate none of it. Ah, what a jest! Let them lambaste me as a tyrant, but the jailer too is jailed. Chained in the cell of his duty." He felt Delia's other hand on his. With a hopeful thrill, he gave her his shyest smile. "But what sort of man am I, inflicting my private woes upon you? You–my Irish blossom!"

"I will tell you what sort of man you are, Mister Wood. To me you are the answer to a prayer. My generous protector. A kindred soul. It is as if . . . "

He was distantly aware of some disturbance outside; ignoring it, he let Delia's eyes and lilt caress him. "Yes, my dear?"

"It is as if . . . Mister Wood, what is happening out there?"

She was looking to the open cell door. Wood heard the raucous singing. With a frown he released Delia's hand, got up and went out to the catwalk. In the sunny yard below, some two dozen assembled prisoners were offering a lusty rendition of *The Bonny Blue Flag*. General Dinsmore, predictably enough, led them—propped on his crutch, waving his hat in time to the Rebel anthem:

> *Then here's to our Confed'racy; strong we are and brave.*
> *Like patriots of old we'll fight, our heritage to save.*

Around the singing phalanx, Veteran Reserve guards stood in a state of alert indecision, their rifles cocked. The song ended in a tumultuous Rebel yell, with raised fists and waving hats.

Dinsmore caught sight of Wood. "Ha!" he cried, pointing up. "How do you like that, you scurvy hound!? That's one tune you'll be hearin' when old Jube gets here! Damn your eyes, we'll make you sing a few bars of it, just afore we hoist you!"

From Dinsmore's compatriots came cheers, jeers and cackles. For weeks now, Wood had been meaning to send Dinsmore to that officers' camp in Ohio. Clearing his throat, he placed his hands on the railing and called down. "If and when old Jube gets here, Dinsmore, I reckon he'll make a fine addition to your choir. Matter of fact, I'll make him your cellmate."

"Dream as you like! Once he shows, we'll see how big a jester you be, damn your . . . !" The Confederate straightened. Keeping his crutch steady, he removed his hat with a flourish and gave a deep bow. A few other prisoners did likewise.

After a moment, Wood noticed Delia at his elbow.

"What are they about, Mister Wood?"

"A serenade, my sweet. To lighten the tedium. Only, I fear their next selection might be unsuitable for feminine ears—so please go back inside. I'd hate it if these rascals offended you."

Bemused, Delia reentered the cell, just as Chadwick came clambering up the stairs to Wood's side. "Sir, they're mocking us!"

"Thank you, Lieutenant. You cut to the very soul of the matter."

"It could turn into a riot, sir! What should we do?!"

Staring at Chadwick, red-faced and sputtering, Wood felt his first real concern for the capital's safety. Another troop detail—civilian volunteers, maybe—would soon relieve the lieutenant and his men, who would proceed to the northern defenses.

Touching the wad of keys on his belt, Wood's fingers absently tapped out a rhythm. "All right, then. For now, they'll get no more visitors—that's

likely how they heard about the invasion. As for the entertainment here
. . . " Again the yard erupted into song–*Dixie*, this time–and Wood had to
shout over it. "Tell your men to back off and shoulder arms! Heck, tell 'em
to smile! When this ditty's over, move in with a couple of your fitter men
and drag old Gus to his cell! Repeat the process in threes and fours, and
for God's sake don't mind what they yell at you! All of them will be under
lockup until further notice!"

Chadwick looked a bit calmer. "Sir!" he said, saluting.

Wood looked down at Dinsmore, his gray hobgoblin. "I'll be down
shortly, Lieutenant."

Chadwick whirled off.

"Lieutenant!"

From the head of the stairs, Chadwick looked back.

"When the song's done, you might clap. They're not so bad."

Back in the cell, Wood found Delia perusing one of the illustrated
ladies' magazines that had come with her. "Well," he said, "we must allow
for occasional high spirits." They smiled at each other. Retaking his seat,
he took her hand again. "You were saying, my dear?"

Thinking, she looked to the side and then beamed at him. "Aye! I was
saying, it is as if I crossed the ocean to find . . . a lost uncle. My perfect lost
uncle!"

Wood held the smile, his face beginning to hurt. Outside, the hearty
chorus of the prisoners continued:

> *In Dixie Land I'll take my stand*
> *To live and die in Dixie . . .*

BY TWO O'CLOCK, word had spread that the dust-billows were not those of
Early's men but of refugees. Some of these had already arrived; now they
came in a deluge, bearing tales of a mighty Confederate host. Their loaded
wagons soon jammed the main roads. So did herds of lowing cattle, their
owners determined that they not end up as rustled Southern beef. Near
Fort Slocum, one herd spilled off the road where an Ohio militia company was drilling, creating a spectacle that looked like a battle, a stampede
and a mass bullfight combined.

In the city, hoarding ensued as people mobbed the marketplaces and prices surged, doubling and then tripling. At the rail depot on New Jersey Avenue, the train was late amid rumors of raiding up the line. Gangs of pro-secesh ruffians prowled the dingy streets of the waterfront, chasing down colored men and beating them senseless. On certain residential streets, other Rebel sympathizers made merry–toasting Jeff Davis, cheering Jube Early and Bobby Lee. The lifting of their long prudent silence made their tongues bold, taunting passers-by with predictions of Confederate triumph, of hangman's nooses for Lincoln and his cabinet. One such reveler went too far when he displayed a homemade Stars 'n' Bars on his veranda, touching off a brawl that left a dozen men hurt and several others jailed.

From the towns and countryside, the flow of fugitive wagons continued. By other routes, wealthy men rushed home from hill resorts or the seashore; quietly they began arranging to empty bank accounts and ship valuables to safety. Unbeknownst to the Lincolns, a vessel was ordered to stand by for their escape. Alert composure remained the rule through most of the city–but by the time news came of a cavalry skirmish on the Rockville Road, there was havoc in the alleys, bedlam in the squares, panic in the black shantytowns.

Orders flew as the city wrung out the last of its manpower. In vacant lots, federal clerks shouldered antiquated muskets and started drilling. Along with some sailors and marines, mechanics and carpenters mobilized at the Navy Yard and trooped out; quartermaster employees soon joined them, as did colored laborers toting picks, shovels and axes. At the military hospitals, able-enough convalescents accepted firearms and tottered out into the sunlight. Scouts, meanwhile, had reported Early's main column marching hard upon Gaithersburg just north of Rockville, some fifteen miles away.

SAPPHIRA HAD THE day off from nursing. Deciding to stock up on provisions, she and Anna counted out the money from the pantry jar and divided it. Sapphira would go to the Center Market, Anna to the one at North K Street; if one place proved too drained of goods, the other might not. Ben was resting again. Against their protests, he had taken a walk and returned groggy from the heat.

Just before Sapphira left, she went down to the cellar, where Truly labored alone over the photographs. He seemed piqued at the interruption and only nodded when she explained what she and Anna were doing; feeling piqued herself, she left him to his strange fixation. Yet even amid the city's tumult, she had a fixation of her own: Flavius Tucker. He had gone off to help fight the Rebels. With a basket swinging from her arm, she headed for the Center Market, thinking of the walk that she and Tucker had taken after church. She thought of his face as he looked at her, the touch of his hand in the cottonwood shade. His halting recital of what he wished to do with his life. And her response—a barrage of emotion, expressed only in the palest, most inadequate of words.

SEVERAL BLOCKS AWAY, Wakefield gripped the wagon seat as George Otis steered them onto West Third. Even this sleepy neighborhood had come alive, its denizens dashing about or chattering in small groups. Wakefield tried to absorb it. Great events were in motion; the signs of growing chaos excited him. They also unsettled him, for at this late hour he had remembered his shop. His shop, on this street which could burn as well as any, in this city now threatened by Early's swarm. Originally just a means to an end, photography had sustained him, perhaps even more than he realized. His heavy studio camera would have to stay, as would most of his supplies. But it would take only minutes to retrieve his folding camera, his dark-tent, his best pictures and a few chemicals, all suddenly precious.

At an intersection, he and George let a company of civilian defenders troop by. An ornate flag identified them as the local Union League, middle-aged men armed with old swords and sidearms; with bold step, they tried to make up in bravado what they lacked in everything else.

George smirked. "Right now, sir, I wish I'd gone and 'listed for the South. To be out there with ol' Jube, ready to knock these sorry sons-a-bitches into the Potomac . . . "

"Keep your voice down," Wakefield muttered. "Besides, you are with the South—just not in uniform. And worth more to Early, too."

The League men passed and George snapped the reins. "So where to after this, Mister Wakefield?"

"A place out on the Seventh Street Road, name of La Maison de l'Empereur."

George looked quizzical. "Is that French?"

"Yes. It's where I've been hiding out. We'll have to take mostly back-roads to get there, since the main ones are jammed."

"What sorter place is it?"

"Well, they call it a gentlemen's club." George considered the remark. As a leer came to his pimpled face, Wakefield had to chuckle. "Rein yourself, boy. The last thing you need is distraction."

The leer became an anxious smile. "But when it's all over? As a reward, sorter?"

"When it's over . . . " Wakefield shrugged. "I don't see why not. Anyhow, the people who run the place are . . . They're allies of ours."

George verged on giddiness. "So what'll we be doing? What's my part?"

"Remember those Yankee agents who rousted you and then entered my shop? They're why I had to disappear. It's unlikely they'll bother us again, but we can't let our guard down. My part will be to confirm the success of our operation, for myself and Richmond. This is best done from La Maison, since it's close to the fortified perimeter. I have two loaded pistols under my coat. All you need do is keep watch and be ready, just in case."

George grinned. "Mighty fine, Mister Wakefield!"

They had only another block to go. As the wagon bumped along, Wakefield made a humbling admission to himself. In the improbable event of a Yankee raid on La Maison, it would be good to have George there. But the youth would fill a more immediate purpose: human company. Simple company–a coarse buffer between Wakefield and the smoother, colder beings beneath that roof. On this last, most critical night, it was supposed to have been Delia at Wakefield's side. Yet he would not dwell on the sick disparity. If he had to endure one more night among those creatures, he would take whatever benign companionship he could.

Up ahead, he saw the hanging wooden sign with his stenciled name. George pulled up by the shop and the two of them hopped down. Getting his key out, Wakefield unlocked the front door and led George inside.

"What do we need to take?" George asked.

Wakefield did not answer but stood motionless, trying to grasp what was wrong. Then his eyes lit on a bare patch of wall. One of the display portraits was gone. After a moment of mental struggle, he recalled the portrait's subject: an army officer. Here and there, other photographs were missing, all of them with officer subjects. Wakefield ran to the kitchen and lit a hand-lamp, then hurried to the storage room. There he took in the sight–an eruption of open space, where the stacked wooden boxes should have been.

"Mister Wakefield?" came George's voice from behind.

Wakefield raised the lamp and stared at the shelves. Silver nitrate, hypo solution, printing frames, albumen paper, development trays–gone. "Damn it to hell," he muttered.

"Sir, what's the matter?!" George pleaded.

Wakefield licked his dry lips. "Change of plan," he said. Reaching under his coat, he took out a pistol and handed it to George.

72

Truly Residence

TRULY HELD THE print in his gloved hands; still dripping with solution, it presented a spindly man in an army captain's uniform. The tilt of his cap revealed thinning hair and a prominent forehead; combined with his unfocused gaze, the latter feature suggested puzzlement rather than brains. His cape, more like a wrinkled tablecloth around his shoulders, fell short of any romantic effect. His beard–a neat, dark imperial–lent the face its lone touch of distinction.

Since yesterday, Duke had spirited maybe two-dozen prints to the Old Capitol, where Delia examined each before shaking her head. Of the present batch, this one held the most promise. The plate came from one of the "M" boxes but, unlike most, had no name scratched into its upper-left corner. Truly was about to call Duke to his side when he remembered that the clerk had left an hour ago. Leaving the portrait to dry, Truly pulled the gloves off and leaned back against the work bench. He was out of coffee. His fascination with the photographic process had dimmed. But out in the yard, several more prints would soon be ready. About two hours of adequate sunlight remained, and that would leave a score of selected plates unprocessed, the last several boxes unexamined. From the open bulkhead came sounds of the city's commotion–running feet, marching feet, hooves and wheels, bursts of shouted conversation.

Rousing himself, Truly lifted another box onto the bench. He noted that, unlike the others, this one bore no letter. He slid onto the stool and proceeded to remove the negatives one by one, holding each plate up to the light of the kerosene lamp before setting it aside. His eyes and brain had adjusted to the black/white reversal, enabling him to work faster. Most plates–those of women, children, families, non-officers and male civilians–he could discard at a glance. Whenever he came upon what looked like an officer's image, he would scrutinize it with the magnifying glass and then either discard it or keep it for printing. One boxful, on average, yielded four or five possibilities.

The present box was yielding a run of non-possibilities, though not the usual kind. These were not even portraits but outdoor scenes, most of them pastoral. Truly lingered briefly over one, showing hills in the distance and horses grazing by a lake. He recalled Wakefield's photograph of the sunken bridge, the rolling clouds above. Once more Truly reflected on the elusive Southerner and the vital purpose that photography must have served for him–linking his tense, cramped, solitary life with the rest of humanity. But these peaceful vistas implied escape, not only from that life but from all human activity.

Truly thought of the one time he had seen Wakefield, a month ago at Cold Harbor. A tallish fellow in his mid-thirties, he recalled, with a trimmed sandy mustache. There had been no way of guessing, back then, what he encountered in the man: not just an antagonist, but an extraordinary one. Again Truly hoped that when all of this was over, when the need for hard-eyed enmity had passed, he would have the luxury of talking casually with Wakefield, even if it was just about photography.

He lay the scenic negative with the other rejects and went through several more. This box seemed designated for pictures unrelated to Wakefield's paid work, and Truly thought of abandoning it. Then, in the lamplight, he beheld a plate image so different that he could not immediately tell what it was. He discerned two figures–a kneeling or crouching one and, behind it, a bulkier standing one in some dynamic pose. Then he picked out a wall lamp, a bedstead and other interior details. With the magnifying glass he peered at the standing figure; he made out the folds of a dress and then, moving upward, a set of bare enormous breasts. Around the woman's head and knees, a blur indicated that she had not been still for the camera. A look at the other subject–male and definitely kneeling, head bowed, revealed that he too was stripped to the waist.

Truly set the negative down, rubbed his eyes and stared at the cryptic figures. Between fatigue and bemusement, he barely noted the creaking on the bulkhead steps. He guessed that Saph or Anna had returned early.

"Back so soon?" he called. Then he realized that the descending tread was too heavy. Turning around, he saw Forbes standing there, his army tunic unbuttoned to the day's heat.

"I'm on my way back from the mayor's house," Forbes said. "I'm the lucky one they picked to go soothe him and give a candid account of the situation."

Truly gave a flat chuckle. "Candidness pretty well defeats soothing."

"Too true." Taking his hat off, Forbes sank onto the other stool. "Speaking of civilians, I don't see Octavius here. May I assume the worst?"

"You may. Just as you warned, he's off to play soldier with the clerks' battalion. Eagerest damned patriot I ever saw."

"I suppose I'll be on the front line myself, soon enough. Probably be more useful there anyway." Forbes slouched, looking thoroughly dispirited. "Wallace lost a good part of his force yesterday and he's falling back on Baltimore. Early, of course, is barreling straight toward us. Our cavalry's engaged with his near Rockville."

Truly whistled through his teeth. "Rockville . . . Well, at least the heat's in our favor. There must be some straggling in his ranks."

"Right. But even if just his lead elements get here by morning, who will they be facing? The most motley, ill-trained defense force ever assembled! Octavius and company. We can only pray that the rest of the Sixth Corps arrives as soon as possible." Forbes eyed the boxes of negatives, the stacked plates. "But that too could become a moot point, couldn't it?"

"If our traitor acts tonight—yes. The Rebs will be within quick striking distance."

"For the moment, I doubt I'll be missed at the War Department," Forbes said. "Could I maybe run your latest pictures over to Delia?"

"That I would sure appreciate." Truly reached for the scrolled-up print of the army captain and found that it had dried enough. Aligning it with a square of cardboard, he began fitting it into the last available picture frame.

"Another item," said Forbes. "Early has reportedly sent a large cavalry detachment toward Baltimore. Also, some vague intelligence has come in from Southern sources, concerning a plan to liberate the prisoner-of-war camp at Point Lookout. This cavalry sideshow may be part of that plan, so Lookout's been ordered evacuated."

"Hm . . . No shortage of trouble." Taking up his gripsack, Truly put the framed print inside. Then he gathered the others that were ready for viewing–six of them–and put them in too. "The last one's nameless. On the others, I've marked the names in pencil."

Forbes had gotten to his feet–but as Truly held the sack out, he did not reach for it. His eyes seemed lost in the lamp flame, its dance on the cellar wall–and on his 26-year-old visage, for an instant, Truly saw time creeping. Its fine prophetic marks, its shadow-like progress, molding the features into a gaunt mask. The eventual last version of Bartholomew Forbes.

"One of my scouts is dead," said Forbes. "Killed on the Monocacy. His partner wired in this morning." Absently he tapped his hat against his false leg. "He was a tailor from Michigan. A good scout, one of the best. Same age my brother Gerald was. I got a dispatch from him on Friday–and now all I can think is that while I was reading it, there was still a living man out there. Those little black symbols off the telegraph–they were his pulse, his voice, his brain at work." Forbes gave the slightest shrug. "But how could it still feel like this? After everything, why does it feel so damned strange? Strange and sad, like I've just seen a star go out?"

On the wall, the lamplight danced its lithe arabesque. "Because," said Truly, "–when it's someone bright and young and healthy enough, you can't help thinking it was only a cursed slip of chance. Never mind all the talk about destiny and God's will and such. 'Less you're drenched head-to-foot in religion, it seems like something that needn't have happened. A stupid accident, when a heart would have otherwise kept beating and a pair of lungs breathing, a brain working just fine. And yes, it's tarnal strange to think about. Sad, too." He held out the sack of photographs. Forbes took it. "I'll follow you out," said Truly. "I need to collect the next batch."

Outside, Forbes shouldered the sack and lumbered toward the street, where his horse stood tied to a gas-lamp. The dust had not yet settled from the passing of the last defense unit. At fences and doorsteps, neighbor women conversed in anxious pairs and trios, some with children at their skirts.

Hurrying, Truly gathered all the printing frames from around the yard and took them to the cellar. He removed the plates and peeled off the prints, then started loading each frame with a new plate and a sensitized sheet of albumen paper. With five frames loaded and one still empty, his gaze fell on the plate which bore the two mysterious figures. The image in no way resembled what he sought, but an eerie curiosity had seized him. Knowing that it was frivolous, he fitted the plate and an albumen sheet into the last frame. Then he toted all six frames outside and propped them along a section of east-side fence, where the sun now beat strongest.

Next he took the just-developed prints to his makeshift darkroom, where he began fixing and washing them. This step remained pleasurable. Every time a picture emerged dripping from the hypo tray, he felt pride in his and Wakefield's handiwork–there was, indeed, a bizarre sense of collaboration–plus the renewed hope that this face was the one. From the glistening rectangle of paper, salt crystals melted away to reveal some other officer. But Truly's concentration soon faltered. He felt the hope leaking out of him, replaced by a too-familiar leadenness. Then he recalled his and Forbes' musings on death–something he could well have done without, because now he wanted to talk about Rachel. And he wished that Forbes could have stayed.

He wanted to tell about Rachel finding the injured Mormon fellow, thrown from his horse near their Missouri homestead. How she fashioned a litter and dragged him to the cabin, where she nursed him. How she sent little Ben on a seven-mile hike (Truly himself being away in St. Louis) to notify the man's family. How she received his kin but insisted on keeping him three days more, so he would be well enough to travel. How she remained blithely ignorant on the subject of Mormons, whom she should have despised as everyone else did.

For this and similar acts of misplaced charity, the Trulys' sodbusting neighbors came to view Rachel as queer–or "innocent," as the kinder ones said. And it was well that they did. Even on the frontier, where gumption and know-how were valued in both sexes, no female attribute could charm and reassure–and mitigate–like a lily-pure innocence of spirit. Still it was a remarkable judgment, given that Rachel had seen and experienced more of the world than her judges had. Further, there was that bothersome way she had of making innocence look knowing and queerness like a virtue. She was not a saint–Truly had to remind himself of that. When harried, she could become sarcastic. When weary, she could become morose and secretive. And there were her Byzantine feelings toward Annie, who too much resembled Rachel's beautiful, drama-prone sister. No, Rachel had not been a saint–except compared to him, possibly.

What other stories would he have told about her? Only the last one, perhaps. About returning from the Antietam campaign to find her bedridden, her knee scraped on a buggy wheel. Of hearing that the infection had spread too far. Of the day itself: October 2, 1862–sitting there enveloped in her fever, her breaths inhaling him little by little. Of discovering what it was to love every microscopic particle of someone's face, even as it grew dimmer, slipping into an oblivion he could not quite believe. Of the final implosion of hope. Of the endless, inward, useless cry of "no" and then the realization, sweeping through him like a prairie fire till there was only desert left, a vast arid sorrow of the bones.

He found that he had left the darkroom and was seated on his stool, his gloves off. Watching the lamp flicker, he thought of phrases that people sometimes dared to use: "after the war" and "when it's all over" and even "when things are put right again." Younger ones spoke of that future day as they might of love and marriage or fame and riches–anything radiantly imagined–while older ones spoke of it as a return to fond havens, a reawakening, as if the headstones would vanish and the dead rise whole. It was crucial that people could dream so. Only dreams of this sort could ignite their hope–and only hope's signal fire could draw them through a night strewn with rubble, gibbering with ghosts. Truly wondered what his own sustaining dream might be, his own flickering mirage. But then he noticed the unmarked box of negatives in front of him. Mechanically he reached into it and started where he had left off.

To his surprise, the next plate proved to be another version of the preceding one, with the woman blurrier and the kneeling man–pale and sinewy, with a hint of mustache–bent lower. The woman bore two odd new details: a square-ish object in her one visible hand and a drooping tendril-like thing that seemed to grow from her hip. The opaque sequence continued through the next three plates, each with some variation in the pair's posture. Next, to his further surprise, came a regular portrait negative. Why had it been segregated, here with these anomalous images?

Tilting the plate toward the lamp, Truly discerned a large, well-tailored male civilian. He was about to place it back in the box when he paused for a harder look. This one too had no identifying name in the corner. He raised the magnifying glass, concentrating on the face. For a few seconds, the transposed light and darkness confounded his tired brain. Then the back of his neck froze, and he realized that he beheld the lion-proud image of Trajan Heath.

73

Archer Residence

THE PASTOR'S SERMON, this morning, had compared slavery and rebellion to a seductive harlot, and the metaphor had lodged in Quentin Archer's mind. It had nagged as he shook hands outside the church, pulsated as he shed his deacon's robe and walked home, did not stop until he entered his study. On the desk where he had left it, he saw Cecelia's letter. Sitting, he stared at the letter and wondered why he had not burned it in the fireplace; he had been quick to burn the others, sometimes without reading them. But he had read this one, and it was different.

For a few hours, he did nothing of consequence. Several times he left his desk but soon returned and sat, listening as the neighborhood's Sunday quiet turned to bustle and chatter. He considered taking the horse cars to his office and doing paperwork, but made no move to do so. Noting how the sunlight through the pane had mellowed–late afternoon now, he guessed–he felt a bemusement laced with dread. He looked at the old Daguerreotype from Philadelphia: himself and the other young policemen, all strong and dutiful. Then he glanced at the bare top of his bookcase. Yesterday he had noticed his portrait's absence and wondered what had happened to it, how long it had been gone. Little about his life made sense anymore. But that letter . . .

It had arrived on Friday. Despite the St. Simon's address, the handwriting–not Cecelia's but a careful, loopier script–had intrigued him enough to make him break the seal and start reading. Now he picked it up and again forced his eyes upon it, like a penitent upon live coals:

Pike's Bluff Plantation
St. Simon's Island, Ga.
June 30, 1864

Dear Father,

Having contracted one of the maladies of this clime, I am dictating to my dear friend Rose, who I hope will not be too affected by what she hears. I cannot say if I shall be gone when you read these words. But with death's shadow close by I must plead with you once more, for the sake of your immortal soul.

I cannot regret my coming here to work with the freedmen. Among them and my fellow teachers I have at last come to know communion, common purpose and true Christian love. Does this matter to you even slightly, Father? But I will not go on about myself. It is your own chance for redemption that matters here. So for a moment, please forget my past recriminations, just as I must forget your cold silence, and hear me anew.

In the days before you had Mother dragged off to the asylum, I confess I believed your version of things–that she had lost her senses, that her accusations against you were part of some awful delusion. Only later, on my visits to her, did I come to grasp the truth. Away from your influence, I saw it in her face and heard it in her voice and felt it in the details of what she said. She was indeed at her wit's end–for such unsparing frankness, she had to be so. But outer torment and not inner demons had driven her there. Real and not imaginary betrayal.

She told me of the unspeakable malady you had given her. She spoke of following you about the city, undetected, to dens of sin where you would act not as a police officer nor as a Godfearing man, but as a slave of the flesh. And she told me of the materials she had found in your desk. To my own shock and sorrow, I too found them when I secretly looked. I had thought you to be an honest man whose wife had gone mad. Now I realized that you were the cause, not the sharer of her suffering.

After that I am sure you noticed the change in my manner, though I could not bring myself to face you with what I knew. Had I done so, might I too have been sent to the asylum? In my grief following Mother's death, I only wanted to put as much distance as possible between us. This I did, and in that distance have found the words to express my horror. The horror that you, my father–a supposed adherent to God's Law and upholder of man's–have sinned so long and terribly.

But I no longer speak from rage or woe. It is rather out of urgency that I implore you to repent. To kneel before our God, admit your deeds and face this blight upon your soul. Remember that Damnation holds far worse things than any rack or prison cell. Repent, as I myself now must. If this be the end for me, my prayer for you will surely echo with all the rest.

Your daughter,
Cecelia

Archer put the letter down. From the street outside he heard the racket of passing wagons. He felt as if he might be dead already, eavesdropping on the busy world of the living. With a shudder and then no feeling at all, he wondered if Cecelia were still part of that world.

In the summer of '61, she had been a nervous, unsmiling girl of eighteen. In that same war-filled summer, he and Helen had sold the Bladensburg hotel and moved the few miles to the capital, whose newly constituted police force he promptly joined. Suddenly invigorated, he embraced the calling that he had forsaken years before in Philadelphia. He resolved to rise within the embattled young department, where his experience and dedication were quickly recognized. He realized how much he had missed the job, how he prized being known as an effective lawman. Moreover, he prized being known as a good and pious citizen–it helped him think of himself as one. Yet even before the resumption of his police career, he had made a few secret forays to the District's better brothels, including La Maison. Now, his work exposed him almost daily to the flesh trade, which he was sworn to suppress. And amid his professional rejuvenation, he felt himself caught in the undertow of morbid lust. He worried that his wife might somehow detect it in him; Helen was perceptive enough and high-strung besides, and he loathed domestic upset. And this worry brought him to her bed one night, for the first time in years–an act meant to divert her suspicion, but which ended up exposing him.

Hardly a month after his taking the oath and badge, Helen made her discovery. Her distraught charges threatened everything–his reborn ambitions, which were after all so modest and respectable compared to some. And with a ruthlessness he had never suspected in himself, he forced her into the madhouse. Yet it became clear that this would not be enough. His betrayal had unhinged not just her mind but her tongue. In his one tense interview with the asylum's director, a session full of veiled language, he pretended shock over Helen's physical problem and her ravings about how she had contracted it. It would not do to simply turn the charge upon his innocent wife, to accuse her of promiscuity attendant to madness. While every conventional bias favored his word over hers–stable husband and lawman versus madwoman–whispers of the whole unseemly business would surely leak out and damage him. Plus, one way or another, her relatives would soon hear of her ordeal and maybe try to win her release. And already he had seen the change in Cecelia–her icy glances each time she returned from visiting Helen.

What words might Cecelia have written, if any, had she known the fuller truth? That he had killed her mother in a more direct and literal sense, by way of an unholy bargain?

The pact had been sealed on the last night of October 1861, in an upstairs room at La Maison. In Archer's recollection the scene glowed unaccountably red, its details dagger-sharp: Ravenel's face, hideously majestic by candlelight; Dubray, an eager observer in a corner chair; Monroe, casual but attentive in another corner; around the table, the drawn anxious faces of Monks, Peavey, Underhill and Van Gilder–vaguely repellent men who Archer knew only as fellow patrons; each of them speaking his request in turn, in the presence of all; Monks stammering beneath Ravenel's gaze, which then moved to Archer; Archer speaking his own terrible request, his throat tightening as the words came out; Monroe's patient listening smile and then his nod; the movement of Ravenel's long dry lips, laying the terms down–explicit instructions, assurances, warnings.

Shortly afterward, Archer found himself free of Helen and her heedless raving. Free too of Cecelia, who had left for the Sea Islands. Among sympathetic superiors, colleagues and fellow churchgoers, the dignified mantle of Widower settled over him, all the thicker for the pitiful circumstances.

The deed had been carried out with a stealth and a cleverness that Archer could not have enlisted elsewhere. In return, he had pledged to use all his influence to protect La Maison, for as long as the enterprise existed. He was just an ordinary roundsman at the time, but his stated zeal for promotion satisfied Ravenel, who regarded him as an investment. In view of this, plus the fact of his more limited means, she exempted him from the ten-year schedule of quarterly payments–a purely practical move but one which she kept secret from the four other men, to preserve an image of strictness. He even received gratis medical treatment from

Dubray, who stemmed his whoring malady with chloride of lime. Archer felt less thankful for the healing powder than he did for its sting; clenched within the pain, he could imagine himself engaged in some private act of atonement.

On the cold face of it, he had done well in the bargain. Yet he could not long pretend that this was so—that he had traded the curse of Helen for a lighter curse, or even an equal one. In his police work, an adherence to fact and logic made him generally effective, even as he built a wall of pretense around his private life. But fact and logic always threatened to breach that wall. There was the fact that La Maison held more than his mere life in its fist, and the logic that required him to submit. The alternative was total disgrace, along with violent death. Never could he have foreseen how the tendrils of that night would burrow into him, sapping his already diseased spirit, till it seemed his righteous facade might crack and crumble as he walked down the street. Often, lying awake in bed, he felt a pressure growing in the shadows; he felt it pinning his limbs, taking him by the neck. Often too he gazed at his revolver, hanging in its holster by the study door. He did so now, till his insides began to throb, but then he let his gaze fall to Cecelia's letter. Its looping lines blurred and blended. Again he thought of burning it, then realized that it would feel too much like burning Cecelia.

Then he recalled another letter—Van Gilder's blood-flecked testament of warning and supplication, which he had read at this desk a year ago. The warning, in Archer's case, had been unnecessary. He in fact took a twisted satisfaction in knowing that Van Gilder, and presumably the others, were finally as stripped of illusion as he. Still, on a fateful Friday this past April, they and he had lapsed into illusion. Summoned by Underhill to Brown's Hotel, he had heard Peavey's excited report and then sped to La Maison, under the pretext of investigating the Irish whore's death. What he saw there seemed to confirm Peavey's account: Ravenel seriously ill; Monroe afflicted with rheumatism, possibly in mental decline; loud rancor between the two of them. The prospect of freedom seemed to gape at last.

Now, for all Archer knew, he was the lone member of the circle yet unbutchered. Baffled over what had happened and why, he was more than ever a pawn, a stooge and an official liar for La Maison. At its bidding, he had even committed a murder of his own. Once more his eyes drifted across the room to the revolver. There was perhaps only one form of self-reclamation left to him, one way to break the bonds of the Emperor's House. Were he to choose that way, he would at least be facing hell of his own accord instead of being sent there. Then he pictured himself in church, standing paralyzed as the whole congregation turned to stare at him. Then he remembered the morning's sermon, the harlot image, and his veins began to simmer.

Sweeping the letter off the desk, he opened the bottom drawer, removed his scrapbook and tossed it aside, then took out the yellow magazine. He looked at the gossamer-skirted woman on the cover–her black hair long, her face wanton, her pale breast exposed. With quickening pulse, he turned to the scene of the Egyptian slave girls; naked and huddled, they cringed beneath the whips. A faint sting spread across his back and shoulders.

The carnal spell broke as a knock sounded from the front door. For a bizarre moment, he felt certain that the police had come for him. He shut the magazine away and went out to the hall as the knocking continued, growing insistent. He opened the door slowly. On the steps stood Wakefield. Behind him, in a wagon seat, a pimple-faced youth in a pork-pie hat looked down.

"Quentin," said Wakefield, "I need you to come with me."

Archer blinked, unmoving. It was weeks since he had last seen Wakefield. More confusing was the photographer's manner, devoid of the usual deference.

"Pardon the short notice, but please go get your sidearm. We need to stop Truly."

Jolted, Archer opened the door wider. He looked up at the youth, then stared into Wakefield's face. "What . . . What do you know about Truly?"

"Enough, including your tangle with him. Hence my thought that you would enjoy this little errand. It's me who he's devilling now, you see. It would help to have another man along, especially a policeman, and I'm hoping you know where he lives."

His mind spinning, Archer gripped the threshold and leaned forward. "Miles," he muttered. Wakefield's expression remained closed yet maddeningly direct. Out of his muddled alarm, Archer felt a surge of wrath. "What do you mean by this?! Coming to my home and demanding that I tag after you?! And how do you know about my affairs?!"

Wakefield dropped his gaze. Placing his hands on his hips, he drew a sigh. "Well . . . A bewildered man is a less willing man, I suppose." He looked over his shoulder. "Wait here, George." Impatiently he motioned Archer aside and then entered, shutting the door. He left his hat on. "To cut to the heart of it, Quentin–Ravenel and Monroe would very much like it if you accompanied me."

Taking a backward step, Archer eyed Wakefield as if seeing him for the first time. He thought of the actual first time–one Sunday in early '62 as church let out, soon after his promotion to sergeant. Introducing himself, the photographer had shaken Archer's hand and congratulated him for his recent publicized capture of a horse thief. The two of them lamented the capital's ballooning crime rate.

"You're in it with them," Archer croaked.

"It makes sense, if you think about it," said Wakefield.

Archer's hands squeezed tight at his sides. "You . . . ! It was you who took those . . . "

"The pictures? That was Ravenel's idea. Not long after the bargain was struck and the service rendered, she decided to get further assurances from you. Some extra thing to prevent your going astray."

Archer's tongue felt thick. It was a moment before he could speak again. "I've held up my end of it. I've protected them."

"True enough. However, you did conceal the fact that you'd met with the others, in violation of the rule. That you'd willingly participated in the plan." Archer felt the blood drain from his face. He drew a breath to speak, but Wakefield's caustic eye stopped him. "Don't bother denying it. I used to tip the servants at Brown's Hotel, and they'd keep me apprised of Underhill's visitors." Wakefield drew up a chair and sat. Brisk and precise, he went on like an attorney splitting some legal hair. "Of course, they'd contacted you on the false assumption that you paid quarterly tribute, just as they did. And naturally you did nothing to correct them. Should the payment stoppage come to grief, you figured it would be their heads and not yours . . . "

On he went in his clipped tone. He knew everything. "When Van Gilder's fate became known, you kept your head and continued to play along with the others. Then you went tattling to Monroe and Ravenel. Useless information, really–and altered, as to how you'd learned it. But they were happy that you'd come back to them. And in truth, Quentin, they are quite satisfied with all you've done since then."

Archer heard the words clearly but they seemed to come from another room, crowded back by his own thoughts. He was thinking back to when

Wakefield asked to take his portrait–"So I can shamelessly boast of knowing you, sir." Thereafter Wakefield had become one of his friendliest acquaintances. Until Archer became a deacon and had to stand by the altar, the two of them had often sat together in church. It was Wakefield who later suggested the innovation of photographing known criminals and keeping their pictures on file; presenting the idea as his own to the superintendent, Archer had gained credit for bold thinking. On Wakefield's occasional visits to Archer's house, they had reflected on the travails of bachelorhood and widowerhood. Once, somehow, they got onto the subject of prostitutes–poor wastrel girls, more and more visible throughout the city, so in need of guidance and uplifting. At the time, Archer thought he heard a certain edge in Wakefield's voice; he wondered if the man shared his violently split reaction to the descendents of Jezebel and lived with the same secret pain. Isolated in that pain, Archer experienced a welcome, unexpected sense of affinity.

There was no affinity now–just the nausea, the pressure in his throat. "Why did they do it?" he blurted. "Why did they . . . " He swallowed hard. "Why did they trick us like that?"

"Quentin, I've spent precious minutes enlightening you. I will not spend one more." Wakefield rose from the chair. "Right now, you must perform another service–perhaps the last we'll ever require of you."

As their gazes locked once more, Archer fluctuated between hope, hatred and chill fright. Outside, more commotion swelled from the street.

"Do you have Truly's address?" Wakefield demanded.

Archer nodded.

"Fetch it, please. And your revolver."

Almost in a trance, Archer returned to his study. He rummaged in the middle desk drawer until he found a slip of paper. Two weeks ago, he had obtained Truly's address from the War Department. He had needed it for inclusion in his letter of complaint–a small formal detail, but one which he took care to jot down and save: Nathaniel Truly, 762 North H Street.

Glaring at the name, he recalled the sneer on Truly's face, the words of hate, the sudden blows to his body. He had hurt for days afterward. Yet it was the echo of those choked, taunting words that made his jaw clench. He put the slip in his vest pocket. Buckling on his holster, he felt less like a stooge, a penitent or a soul adrift and more like a stone-hewn killer.

74

Old Capitol Prison

Reaching the top step, Forbes paused for breath and put the sack down. Below, in the afternoon shadows of the prison yard, a new guard detail took up positions. They were District militia this time–poorly drilled, their movements clumsy. A few of them shouldered old flintlocks and some wore incomplete uniforms, a mismatch of fancy frocks and hats with work clothes. Chadwick's Veteran Reserve men assembled in the sunny part, preparing to march out.

All prisoners were apparently under lock, though some remained audible from their cells. "Fare-thee-well!" called one. "Remember–when you shoot, the bullet comes out the skinny end!" "Chadwick!" yelled another. "If ye hurry, ye can catch the last boat out before ol' Jube gits here!" Facing his little column, Chadwick cut a dignified figure until he swatted a fly on his cheek, prompting another yell–"Don't thrash yourself, son! Leave that to Early!" Laughter rang. Forbes thought he saw a few of Chadwick's men fighting smiles. Scowling, the lieutenant put his hands behind his back.

"Well, Captain–at least I'm rid of that particular oaf."

A few paces along the catwalk, William Wood leaned against the railing. Forbes, to his own surprise, suddenly verged on sympathy for Chadwick. Taking up the sack, he lumbered toward the superintendent.

"And what's more," said Wood, "at least it's you this time and not that fussy little clerk."

To his greater surprise, Forbes felt thoroughly indignant on Duke's behalf. "Mister Wood, that fussy little clerk is off helping to defend the city."

"Honestly? Shoulder to shoulder with the likes of Chadwick?" Wood rolled his green eyes skyward. "Poor George Washington! What must he be thinking up there?"

"At any rate, I've brought . . ."

"More photographs? Oh, joy." Ignoring the proffered sack, Wood regarded Forbes curiously. "I'm moved to ask–is every Bostonian born without a shred of humor?"

Forbes cleared his throat. "Kindly save your questions for the prisoners."

"One more, Forbes. Are you aware that I hold the rank of colonel?"

Forbes eyed the jailer, small and shaggy in his threadbare green vest, the loaded key ring dangling from his belt. "I am now, Mister Wood."

"A colonel," said Wood, "like my scurvy friend Lafe Baker. But it's just for show, isn't it? A paper title, something to flatter us."

Below, Chadwick yapped an order. His men more or less snapped to.

"Not that I was never a real soldier myself," Wood went on. "As a poor private I served in New Mexico Territory, where from time to time I was ordered strung up by the thumbs for one petty infraction or another." Raising his callused thumbs, he appraised them glumly. "You know, I believe that's why I have such pity for these prisoners of mine, scum though they may be. I feel their pain."

Forbes watched Chadwick pivot on his heels and bark, "Forward–march!" To hoots and catcalls, the formation began trooping out. Forbes sighed. "So, then, Mister Wood–should I henceforth address you as Colonel?"

The mocking peasant smile crossed his face. "Inflict that silliness on a paladin like yourself?! Demand salutes and such trash? Heavens no, Forbes. It wouldn't feel right. But listen here . . . Just moments ago, little Miss McGuire had an interesting recollection. One that might have bearing on your case."

Forbes cocked his head. "And what's that?"

"I'll have her repeat it for you."

Wood gestured behind him, just as Delia appeared in a cell doorway. She wore a lavender dress with a lace collar–one of Anna's, it seemed to Forbes. He doffed his hat.

"My dear," Wood said, "would you please tell the captain what you asked me?"

She looked puzzled.

"About the uniforms," he added.

"Oh . . . I simply asked why the guards–those ones that just marched out–why they wore pale blue instead of dark blue."

"It's the blue of the Veteran Reserves," Forbes said. "Semi-invalid troops, on light duty."

"That's what Mister Wood told me."

"Yes," said Wood. "To which you responded . . . ?"

Delia's eyes turned fretful. "Captain, I swear I scarcely recalled it until I came here and noticed those guards."

"Whatever it is, Miss McGuire, don't worry. Tell me."

"The second time I saw the lieutenant-colonel at the house–when he came in uniform, that is–his frock was of that same pale blue." Seeing Forbes' expression, her own turned gloomy. "I'm sorry! How was I to know it mattered?"

"Of course, of course–it's all right." Slowly, Forbes twisted the neck of the sack.

"The captain has brought more photographs," Wood said. "Let's give you a look-see."

Ushered by Wood, Forbes followed Delia into the cell, where she sat at a lace-covered table adorned with flowers and some illustrated magazines. Wood moved these while Forbes dug into the sack, removing the seven photographs and stacking them in front of Delia. Solemnly she picked up the top portrait and gazed at it. No reaction.

Turning away, Forbes looked around the relatively spacious cell. Its two unboarded windows granted the light and air which other residents were denied. Besides the table and chairs, the cell boasted other furnishings–a cedar chest, a full-length mirror, a feather bed with a varnished frame and embroidered linen.

Wood smirked at him. "From the home of an arrested secesh. I've taken good care of her, you must admit."

"Well, her safety's the main thing. These La Maison people are worth fretting over."

"No doubt. So, Captain–your unnamed suspect is with the Veteran Reserve Corps."

"It would seem. He might since have been returned to full duty, but I'm thinking about his reported dizzy spells. If they're chronic, they could still qualify him as semi-invalid. And even if they don't, the VRC's an unofficial refuse heap for less-than-impressive officers." Forbes could see Delia in the mirror. Still looking downcast, she pondered the third portrait in the stack before putting it aside. Forbes felt a jab of discouragement.

"Truly's still at it, isn't he?"

Forbes blinked at Wood, who grinned like a weathered imp.

"Isn't he?" Wood repeated.

Bushwhacked, Forbes felt as if the secret had been plucked directly from his brain.

Wood cackled. "The dog! I knew it!"

"Mister Wood . . . Colonel Wood . . . "

"Would that goose of a clerk have brought those damned photographs here of his own initiative? Would a busy officer like you have done so, without Truly's impetus? Your loyalty is commendable, Captain."

"It isn't just that!" Thinking of Delia, Forbes pulled his voice lower. "It isn't just personal loyalty! Ask yourself, sir–are higher-ups consistently wise and smart? Is your friend Baker? I don't mind pleading with you. Please do nothing to hurt this investigation–or Major Truly."

Wood's grin vanished. Stiffening, he stepped back and glowered. "Damn you, sir–give me credit! Right from the start I've done nothing but provide help! *Discreet* help, I might add!"

Forbes had never been able to tell how much of Wood's manner was real and how much crafty burlesque. But faced with this outburst, he could only beat a fast retreat. "Yes, yes–I beg your pardon. I just . . . "

A gasp from Delia interrupted him. Blue eyes agape, she was half-turned in her chair and holding up the last portrait. "This!" she cried. "This one! That's the bloody man!"

Forbes lurched over to her and snatched the portrait, staring at it. A thin, caped, bearded officer met his stare.

Wood stepped to Forbes' elbow. "Sorry-looking fellow," he commented.

"A captain," Forbes said. "Probably taken two years ago, like the other La Maison portraits–time enough for a couple of promotions. Hang it, though–this is the one without a name!" Holding the portrait closer, he tried to make out the insignia on the captain's hat. "Do you have a magnifying glass?"

"In my office," said Wood.

"Good. Miss McGuire, are you absolutely . . . ?" Glancing down at her, Forbes saw no need to complete the question. On her beautiful, blanched face, horror mingled with triumph.

Wood touched her on the arm. "Thank you, my dear. We must leave you for the moment."

"Aye," she murmured. "Just find him, please. Find that murdering coward."

Minutes later, hunched over Wood's desk, Forbes trained the small magnifying glass on the portrait. On the captain's hat, he discerned a badge with a castle tower insignia. "Engineer Corps," he mumbled.

"Let me see." Taking the glass, Wood gave the portrait a measured look. "Surely is."

Brooding, Forbes stared into the scarred wood of the desktop. "How can that be?"

"What do you mean?"

"Three days ago, Truly and I described an officer like this one to General Augur and other top brass. The group included Colonel Wisewell, who commands the Veteran Reserves, and General Barnard, who until recently was the District's chief engineer. We got no response from them—and in Barnard's case, I now find that extra baffling. Because as I understand it, the District engineering staff has always been small. You would therefore think he'd remember any subordinate officer—any one, at least, who'd been assigned here for a fair length of time."

Putting the glass away, Wood tilted back in his chair. "That's a teaser, all right. But you now have a confirmed picture of the culprit, thanks to our little shamrock."

Forbes pinched his bottom lip. "An engineer."

"Yes," said Wood. "That branch most intimate with the capital defenses. Now, please hasten to digest the fact—because if your suspicions are correct, well . . . " The jailer smiled sourly. "All I can say is I hope you catch him quick. Because I'd just as soon keep my neck the way it is—unstretched." He picked up the portrait and thrust it at Forbes, who clutched it with both startled hands. "More generally, though, I'd prefer that the Rebs not get to seize the City of Washington and burn it down. Good luck, son."

"Thank you, Mister Wood."

With the picture tucked under his arm, Forbes left, hurrying along the catwalk and down the stairs. First he would gallop back to Truly and announce that all of his cellar puttering had paid off. Then, amid the capital's chaos, the two of them would again have to find Augur, Wisewell or Barnard, or whoever else might look at the portrait and speak a name, along with some guess about where the traitorous officer was posted.

The unseen prisoners remained frisky, raising three loud cheers for the South. As the third one died away and Forbes rushed out of the yard, a voice called after him: "Yessir, Yankee boy—you'd *better* run!"

75

Truly Residence

STARING, TRULY LAY the wet print down. It showed Archer half-naked on his knees, eyes shut in a grimace. Above him, though her face remained a blur, the bare-breasted female was almost certainly Ursula. In her right hand she held a whip. In her left, she held what appeared to be a book.

Truly pulled his gloves off and slumped onto the stool. Focusing on Archer's twisted face, he felt a dull, thick repugnance, like smoke in his belly. He was staring not at a man so much as a state of damnation made flesh. Finally averting his eyes, he slid the picture behind a stack of glass plates.

A warm vagrant breeze came down from the open bulkhead, brushing his neck and fluttering the low flame of the lamp. With the day's heat-laden descent toward evening, the cellar had grown darker, the neighborhood quieter. He supposed that the clamor had concentrated elsewhere— in the squares, around the government buildings, along the main roads north and west. Barring good news from Forbes, he would resume his work at sunup—unless it dawned overcast, or if it became plain that he had simply lost the race. Should he be so thwarted, there would be nothing left to do but get a rifle and join in the defense.

Yawning, he laid his head on his forearms. "Come on, Bart," he murmured. "Dig those spurs in."

He began to doze. Rising out of himself, he drifted about the house, room to room. Then he found himself standing in the middle of Archer's silent house. Anxious, he scrambled through an open window and landed outside, where he came upon Van Gilder's coach. He opened the gilt-trimmed door. Smelling blood, he peered inside and saw Kirschenbaum sitting there in his nobleman's black cape, apparently unharmed. He was eating a plate of fried oysters. "Anything to report?" Truly asked him. The hunchback kept eating. "Manfred?" Truly pressed, growing agitated. "Manfred!" Then he heard a sharp noise from behind.

Starting awake, Truly quickly remembered where he was. He relaxed, sinking back onto his forearms. But from behind him came the noise again–a creak, someone on the bulkhead steps. He turned his head slightly. "Bart?" he called. No one answered. Then the descending creaks resumed, and through his haze Truly realized that it was more than one set of feet. Confused, he sat up, rubbed his eyes and turned fully around. In the gloom at the foot of the steps, Archer faced him. Truly went still. On Archer's face, the hint of a grimace conjured the photograph, and Truly wondered if he might still be dreaming. Then he saw the clutched revolver, its glint decidedly real.

"Raise your hands," Archer muttered, starting toward him.

Slipping off the stool, Truly waited as Archer closed in.

"Up!" the detective barked. Holding the revolver at his hip, he reached out to grab Truly's collar.

Leaning back, Truly raised his right hand while his left gripped a stool leg. His sudden lurch sideways proved quick enough. He swung the stool upward and struck the pistol, which fired. Splinters flew. Recovering his balance, Truly dropped the stool and lunged at his enemy, grabbing his pistol hand and seizing him by the face. Archer stumbled backward, snarling through Truly's dug-in fingers. Over the larger man's shoulder, just then, Truly glimpsed another man looking on–Wakefield. The distraction cost him dearly. He caught a punch to the ear, followed by a shove that sent him tripping back over the stool. As his spine hit the work bench, the pain paralyzed him, then dulled as a terrific blow to the head knocked him senseless. Crumpling, he heard a cascade of shattering glass on the floor. Blackness swallowed him.

He might have stayed mercifully unconscious if not for a kick to the ribs and then a shout: "Stop! Stop, you fool–that's enough!" Distantly his ribs ached as he rolled over. He felt the cool earthen floor, glass fragments beneath him. In his slit-eyed vision he saw the flickering lamp on its side, its glass shell broken. He saw the glitter of smashed photographic plates.

He saw three pairs of trousered legs. Through the thunder in his skull he looked up and beheld a dim figure directly over him, peering down and holding a cocked revolver. The face came into focus–young, blemished, impudent, eyes hooded by dirty-blond hair. He had seen it somewhere before.

Archer was talking in a clenched voice. Carefully shifting his gaze, Truly saw him with Wakefield, who held a restraining hand to the policeman's chest; in his other hand Wakefield held a pistol, though down and away. "I'll say how things are done," he intoned.

"Why not be rid of him, here and now?" snapped Archer.

Wakefield took his hand away. "Because Monroe wants him alive. Is that sufficient?"

76

Central Washington

FORBES ALTERNATELY RACED and trotted his mare along Pennsylvania Avenue. He meant to cut north toward H, but carts, coaches and pedestrians jammed the side streets. Ahead, the teeming stalls of the Center Market came in view, its crowd bulging across the broad cobblestone. He slowed and then swung his horse to the far right, crossing the omnibus tracks and maneuvering around the throng. Then it struck him that he should make a quick stop at the War Department. He was pointed in that direction, and it would be wise to leave some word concerning his absence.

The busy Avenue merged with Fifteenth Street, beyond which he saw the President's Park and then the massive Treasury Building. Something glinted on the rooftop and he shielded his eyes. By some ungodly effort, a big howitzer had been placed up there and buttressed with sandbags. The sight made his stomach contract. In this and all of the city's defense preparations, the worst fears now held sway. Forbes envisioned the Rebels storming the Treasury, sacking the War and Navy Departments, burning the Executive Mansion. He pictured the Lincolns fleeing as the Madisons had fled fifty years ago, just ahead of the torch-bearing British. Deep in the wood of his leg, he felt a twinge and then a series of twinges, working upward.

He crossed the street and swung left, past the Treasury's south portico. A graveled curve of road took him behind the President's white mansion, where gardens bloomed and fat trees spread their shade. Dismounting, he led his horse along. The leg pain began to subside. Then he emerged onto Seventeenth—and in a storage yard between War and Navy, a new spectacle greeted him. Federal clerks of all heights and body shapes stood in formation, shouldering rifles of varied design. Their captain, an older clerk with an antique saber, stood facing them while a morose-looking Army lieutenant paced up and down the ranks, barely pretending to inspect. At the edge of the yard, on horseback, a portly senior officer looked on. Forbes studied the faces as he passed. Beneath their civilian headwear, they were no different from those of any raw recruits—some bored and others excited, some befuddled and others gravely earnest.

He was about to hurry on when he glanced at the mounted officer and halted. Slouched in the saddle, the portly man presided with an expression of carefully controlled disgust. It was Colonel Alexander, the District's current chief engineer—the one who had bustled off so importantly at the Lee place, not deigning to listen. Forbes had felt distressed at the time; now he felt offended. From his saddle bag, he pulled out the portrait and marched toward Alexander.

"Sir." Alexander looked down. Planting himself beside the colonel's horse, Forbes met the lofty, distracted gaze and saluted. "Captain Bart Forbes, Bureau of Military Information. You saw me three days ago at the Lee Mansion." Before Alexander could react, he held up the portrait. "This man is a lieutenant-colonel and an engineer. We believe he is about to commit an act of high treason which could seal the capital's fate. Please identify him if you can, sir."

Alexander's pouchy eyes narrowed, fully attentive now. He reached down and took the portrait. Stepping back, Forbes willed his mind blank as Alexander examined the photograph. On the colonel's jowly face, puzzlement fused with recognition. His lips moved. Before he realized it, Forbes had hopped forward and grabbed the strap of Alexander's stirrup. "Sir??"

Alexander eyed Forbes and then the hand on the strap. "Monks," he said. "Orlando Monks." He tried to hand the portrait back but Forbes made no move to take it.

With "Orlando Monks" resounding in his head, Forbes fought to mask any glimmer of gratitude. "Colonel—you did not stay to hear us out, as General Barnard did. But when we gave our description, Barnard said nothing. He of all men must have known this Lieutenant-Colonel Monks. Can you tell me why he did not open his mouth? Why he didn't tell us a damned thing?"

"My guess, Captain, is that he in fact did not hear you. General Barnard is near deaf as a post." Leaning down, Alexander poked the portrait at Forbes' chest and Forbes took it, letting go of the strap. In his cool baritone, the colonel went on: "Some engineers, like artillerymen, spend a lot of time around cannons. General Barnard has heard more than his share. He does read lips–but to make him understand what you're saying, you must face him and shape every word. At the Lee place, he was likely too preoccupied to interrupt you and mention his handicap."

Forbes held the photograph to his hip. "Then what about Colonel Wisewell, sir? He commands the Veteran Reserve Corps, to which Monks has supposedly been assigned."

"Yes–but Wisewell wouldn't necessarily know him at all. Monks is . . . " Breaking off, Alexander sighed, turned his head and gave a brusque hand-signal. The lieutenant ordered the clerks at ease. Forbes made room as Alexander slid his bulk down off the horse. Dismounted, the chief engineer was somehow more imposing. His nutmeg-brown eyes were clear and steady, conveying a native skepticism which Forbes had seemingly overcome, at least for the moment.

"High treason, you say?"

"Yes, sir. As a result of blackmail, we think. May I ask–based on what you know of Monks, does it make any sense to you?"

The colonel pondered. "Most of what I know about him comes from Barnard. I never really . . . Well, let me tell you. Do you recall the disaster at Ball's Bluff?"

Forbes nearly flinched at the reference. "All too well, sir. I lost two friends there."

Among the litany of Union debacles–Bull Run, Fredericksburg, Chancellorsville, names which fell like great leaden dominoes–Ball's Bluff scarcely echoed these days. Coming on the heels of First Bull Run, however, it had stirred rage and dismay at the time. Forbes had heard about it from survivors–how a federal detachment crossed the Potomac in boats and scaled the high bluff, whereupon an undetected Rebel force struck from the woods. As the bluecoats streamed back down the bluff, the enemy let loose a merciless fire from above, turning the rout into a horror of capsized boats and bobbing corpses. Many Massachusetts boys numbered among the nine hundred drowned, fallen and captured. The dead included the colonel in command, who was also a U.S. senator and close friend of Lincoln's.

"Monks was there," said Alexander. "He was a captain then, detailed to the operation along with another engineer captain. Both of them got out alive, although the other man . . . " The colonel paused, thinking. "Yale—that was his name. Captain Yale returned wounded in the arm and in the jaw, barely able to speak. I have to stress that from here on it's pure rumor—but word circulated that Yale was enraged at Monks, that he'd seen him turn coward under fire and jeopardize other men. As soon as he was able, he would see Monks hauled before a tribunal.

"Both of them had been with the vanguard at Ball's. Monks led a squad of civilian laborers who were supposed to clear the way whenever the woods got too dense. Yale was with the Topographical Corps, a separate organization back then, and had come to correct the outdated maps for that area. When the shooting started, Yale took part—and it was then that he allegedly saw Monks bolt like a rabbit, leaving his laborers behind. In the general rout, Yale sustained his wounds but made it to the riverbank, where he hid in the reeds and bandaged himself. Then he saw Monks paddling away in a boat—by himself, mind you, when there were too few boats to start. Soon after, some other survivors found Yale and got him across. Those are the sordid details, Captain—all second and third-hand. Had they been proven, they would naturally have sent Monks to hell."

"Would have," said Forbes. "Except that Yale died, didn't he?"

The colonel ogled him. "And how did you know that?"

"Just a guess, sir."

"A rather good guess. Yale seemed to be on the mend, at first—but he went suddenly, about two weeks later. So Monks dodged an enquiry. There was grumbling, of course, and speculation. Monks came from a moneyed Republican family in Ohio, which couldn't have hurt. By contrast, you may remember what happened to General Stone, who had directed the river crossing. His Democrat leanings were no secret."

Forbes nodded. "I recall that too, sir."

In the aftermath of Ball's Bluff, public wrath and political expedience had demanded culprits to punish; any vaporous charge of disloyalty would do. So Congress formed the Joint Committee on the Conduct of the War, a supposedly non-partisan panel whose makeup nonetheless reflected the Republicans' lopsided majority. General Stone's crucifixion was its first order of business, after which he went to prison.

"Among fellow engineers," Alexander continued, "Monks remained in bad odor—he's a queer man, in any case. But he was also a fair engineer, of a sort. He excelled in a range of dull but important tasks. In the construction of the fort system, he showed if anything an excessive attention to detail. That's half of why Barnard held onto him, even as he let more talented officers go for front-line duty. But the other half involved what Barnard sensed about him.

"In a crisis, as you can see, it's not unusual that an engineer must drop what he's doing and join the fight. The thought of Monks in another such situation, in charge of men—that worried Barnard. Maybe the rumors played into it, but the general detected a skittishness in him that did not bode well. Just before Chancellorsville, he did send Monks into the field on a bridge-building operation; the man was disgracefully jumpy, fretting over how close the enemy might be.

"When Barnard got his appointment to Grant's staff and I succeeded him here, we had a lengthy briefing session, during which he raised the subject of Monks and confided most of what I'm telling you. He knew the demands of the spring campaign would pull most of the Corps' experienced officers into Virginia. He had therefore settled the Monks issue once and for all—by transferring him to the Veteran Reserves. Conveniently, Monks had injured his head in a fall and was suffering dizzy spells, though these didn't really hinder his work; that made the solution more plausible. Yet he would continue to serve as an engineer—as an inspector of fortifications, to be exact—and his lieutenant-colonel's brevet gave him wider authority. That way he could initiate maintenance projects and the like, with VRC troops at his disposal. He was required to send me written reports from time to time—although, in effect, he would be serving under Wisewell too. An unusual arrangement, ambiguous—but one which preserved his value *and* kept him off the battlefield."

Stroking his chin, Forbes nodded. "And which kept him obscure."

"Obscure?" Alexander huffed. "Captain, I met the man two or three times, early on—but since then, aside from having to read a few of his overblown reports, I've scarcely had occasion to *think* of him. In a crowded room, he would make no more than a vague impression. A case in point: given the emergency, and being ridiculously short of staff, I've called in every available engineer from the coastal forts—but Monks? Monks, who's practically in my own back yard? I confess that until you handed me that picture, he had completely slipped my mind. And you can be pretty sure he has slipped Wisewell's."

Forbes thought of Monks' boast to Briona Kibby–that he "commanded" the forts. An exaggeration, yes, but not a lie exactly. "Colonel, do you know where he might be found?"

"I believe he lives in Tennallytown, close to the defense perimeter. But if he is up to something . . . " Again Alexander paused to eye Forbes, as if reviewing his first impressions.

"Yes, sir," said Forbes. "I doubt we'd find him there now. But other than that?"

"Other than that, good luck. The District's a boiling cauldron and it will be hard to hunt down a specific officer, let alone an obscure one. Listen, what form do you expect this treason to take?"

"The most obvious thing Monks could do is take command at some segment of the line, or at a particular fort, and then surrender it by pre-arrangement."

The colonel's jowls twitched.

"In the present chaos," Forbes said, "he could take charge at some vulnerable point, without the awareness of District Command. To the troops, whether they're VRC or state militia, it will seem natural if a Reserves lieutenant-colonel appears and starts giving orders."

Alexander glared at the ground. "Logically, then, you should focus your search along the northern perimeter–the direction of Early's approach. Get help in this, if you can. At each fort, you can ask if Monks is present or nearby, along the intervening rifle pits. I would suggest, however, that if this whole business is true . . . " Rising, the pouchy nutmeg eyes measured Forbes yet again. "Captain, I missed your name."

"Forbes, sir–and I'm either right or a raving fool. If it's the latter, you can have my dripping head when all of this is done. But yes, I'm asking you to trust my information."

With an air of decision, Alexander turned to his horse. From the saddlebag he took a large, well-folded sheet of paper and gave it to Forbes. "A map of the capital defenses. I have other copies."

Forbes slipped the map into his tunic. "I'm very obliged, Colonel."

"I was saying, you'd be likelier to find Monks at one of the forts, not commanding a segment in between. The forts may be miserably manned but the guns are top-of-the-line, with an overlapping sweep of the terrain. In Early's shoes, I'd want a fort. It would ensure a wide breach that his army could pour through, safe from flanking artillery." Scratching an ear, the colonel looked over his shoulder. "All right, Forbes–I have to march these gentlemen out."

"One last thing, sir. If and when I catch up with Monks, I'll need a signed order stripping him of his duties and placing him in my custody. You have the authority."

Alexander gave a frayed sigh. From his saddlebag he produced a black pen case, a small sheet of paper and a traveler's ink vial. He used the portrait as a writing surface. Scribbling, the colonel twice interrupted himself, once to ask Forbes' first name and again to signal his lieutenant. The lieutenant signaled the senior clerk, who ordered his men to attention and then to form a marching column, four abreast. They accomplished this with a maximum of bumping and shuffling. The colonel passed the finished document to Forbes, along with the portrait.

Forbes blew on the paper. "Thank you, sir. I'll let you know . . . "

"Yes–please do." The colonel hoisted himself back onto his horse.

With a pained smirk, Alexander led his column of scribe-warriors out of the yard and up Seventeenth, past the War Department, past Army Headquarters across the way. Forbes went to his waiting mare, tucked the portrait away and read the colonel's order:

> Bvt. Lnt.-Col. Orlando Monks, Engineer Corps, currently attached to the Veteran Reserve Corps, is hereby relieved of all duties and placed in the custody of Cap. Bartholomew Forbes, Bureau of Military Information, to be held for questioning. — Col. B.S. Alexander, Chief Engineer, District of Columbia.

Forbes' brain was buzzing. With the ink dry, he folded the paper and put it with the map in his pocket. He reached for his reins–but as the rear of the column turned up the street, he caught sight of a waving hand. Below the heads of taller clerks, he spied Duke beaming at him, still waving, carrying a musket of Mexican War vintage. Duke was completely out of step.

Minutes later, in the bustle and clicking of the telegraph room, Forbes found the superintendent. No, the rangy Major Eckert told him–the names of specific fort commanders were not yet available. Everything remained in flux. Militia, VRC and various ragtag units were either on the march or stretched wire-thin along the perimeter, struggling to close gaps. General McCook, in charge of the outer defenses, had left to organize a reserve

camp along Piney Branch; not until sunup would he know the full disposition of his forces, or have any clue about Early's. Regardless, the world's
most fortified city would fall–harder than twenty Jerichos–if Grant's two
relief divisions failed to arrive in time. (Or, Forbes added mentally, if he
and Truly failed to find Monks tonight.) Yellow flimsies–letter-sized telegraphic copy-sheets–littered the room as Sam Finch tried to gather and
organize them, his boyish face drawn with fatigue.

Forbes rushed back outside, mounted up and took another gravel
path, crossing in front of the Mansion. Over in Lafayette Square, he
saw other civilian companies assembling, their makeshift officers strutting about while gangs of children gazed on. The mellower sunlight heralded evening, drawing shadow from each tree, statue and portico–but
to Forbes, it was still the blaze of noon. Happening upon Alexander had
been a wondrous bit of luck and he felt ready to burst, thinking of Truly
and all there was to tell him. But as with everything thus far, they would
have to do this the hard way.

77

North H Street

SINFUL PRICES, DEPLETED bins, ill-tempered merchants, the rude tussle of the crowd . . . Lugging her basket, Sapphira tried to forget what she had just endured at the Center Market. She began counting her homeward steps, losing track and starting over, numbing her brain on purpose. Still, a memory came swirling up–an Illinois memory, of the day she met the neighbor's servant boy. She remembered his gaze, gently nervous as they spoke. She remembered his skin, a burnished mahogany that seemed to glow from underneath; it had triggered a startled awareness of her own color, which she had somehow forgotten. But a larger feeling had come over her–a giddy, fumbling sense of intrigue. An expectancy, nameless and somehow delicious. Then Father had appeared. As the boy dashed back across the field, she stood there with a hand cupped to her mouth, staring at the man whose house she lived in and whose name she bore. His bulging tobacco cheek went still. But his look, as she recalled it, showed more wonder than consternation. Then he told her to go feed the chickens.

And now Flavius Tucker's image took hold. It felt as if he had always been there inside her, ready to rise, to enfold her heart and daunt it at the same time. She wondered how he looked in civilian clothes. She tried to picture him as a boy, as a youth in the slave fields, as an industrious young man in far Montreal. In her head his voice resonated, full of solemn enquiry. What was he asking of her?

But there was her house—blessed relief. Neighbors were either eating supper or gone elsewhere, partaking of the crisis. Down the long, quiet street, she saw a wagon disappearing, trailing dust.

Inside, the rooms were silent, Anna not back yet. Sapphira placed the basket on the kitchen table and assessed its contents: speckled fruit, stunted vegetables, a small pheasant badly plucked. She hoped that Anna was faring better at the North K Market. Then she padded upstairs and looked in on Ben. Snoring softly, he lay half-dressed on the bed, the scabbed side of his face against the pillow, his bad arm angled against another pillow. On his writing desk she noticed a pen, an ink bottle and an unfinished sketch. The sketch was a street scene, its lines crude and tentative. He had been practicing the use of his left hand. In the wastebasket, several crumpled attempts lay like spent carnations.

She got a bucket and went out to the well. The yard looked barren and she realized that Father's printing frames were gone. Drawing water, she glanced at the open bulkhead doors and thought of going down to announce her return. Then she thought better of it, recalling his response to her last interruption. She was inside washing vegetables when the knocker sounded.

Wiping her hands on her apron, she opened the door and saw Tucker there, holding his cap. "Sergeant—come in!" In her surprise, she felt glad and then tremulous.

Entering, Tucker looked somber, distracted, his forehead glossy with sweat.

"Ben's asleep," she said. "Annie's out and Father is . . . he's occupied."

Tucker fiddled with his cap. "It's you I've come to see," he said.

She showed him to the parlor. Sitting at one end of the settee, she motioned to the other and he sat, not looking at her. She gazed at his dark profile. "What happened?"

He coughed lightly, then settled back. "The Bureau of Colored Troops was closed so I went to Lafayette Square, where some irregular units were forming. A militia captain waved me toward a squad of colored laborers. They had a spare shovel. I took it and watched some cavalry ride past, some militia marching out with rifles. And I looked at the men around me with their picks and shovels, waiting there in the sun. I put the shovel down and walked away. The captain hollered at me but I kept walking. I suppose I'm lucky he didn't shoot me . . . "

A fit of coughing seized him. Sapphira patted his back, then took a drinking glass out to the well. Filling the glass, she felt a spot of dull pressure in her chest. Back in the parlor, Tucker had stopped coughing but gratefully accepted the water. He guzzled with his eyes shut.

In her nursing manner she stood over him and began to feel less anxious. "It's just as well. You're not fully recovered. Digging in the hot sun—that would have been . . . "

His eyes lifted, their soft weight silencing her. Exhaling, he wiped the corner of his mouth. "I want to fight, Sapphira. That's why I left what I had and crossed the border. I've done my share of digging. For reasons that I deem worthy, I came to wear a uniform and fight—and if I cannot, I'd sooner be back in Montreal, where there are no slavemen. And no Abolition men, God bless them—no pale orators to preach to me about my radiant future. Because I have considered my future—and pardon me, I have considered yours. I've thought of Reverend Cass and the people in his congregation. And the laborers. And the refugees on the street, carrying little ones. And the men of my regiment. Even if this war is won, I see little to call radiant."

The awful and familiar sense of nakedness swept over her, as strong as ever. Standing over Tucker no longer felt right, so she sat beside him. "But it must be won," she muttered.

Hunched, Tucker rolled the empty glass between his palms. "Yes, it must. Still, they give you a shovel instead of a rifle, spare coins instead of pay, talk instead of listening—talk instead of anything. Always ready to tell you about yourself. And I'd wager that a hundred years from now, they'll still be doing it, going on about what's best for us. Playing master—out of habit, I reckon."

Her eyes caught on his sergeant stripes, grimy white against dark blue. She wanted him to put his arms around her or leave. "Please stay for supper," she murmured.

"Thank you, I'd best not."

"What are you going to do?"

When he did not answer right away, she looked at his face. He was smiling at her, faintly, but then the smile fell away. "I was hoping that Major Truly had a spare shooting iron, one in good condition that he'd be willing to lend."

"I . . . I believe he does, somewhere."

"I'd be obliged. If there are any colored troops at the northern defenses, I mean to join them. If not, I'll join any unit that will have me. If none will have me, I'll do what I can."

Sapphira felt the pressure point in her chest. Against her will she pictured Tucker perched in a lone tree, taking aim at an oncoming wave of graybacks. She eased a breath out. "Flavius . . ." His gaze remained steady, drawing her as she struggled for words. Abruptly she stood up. "Father's in the cellar. I'll go ask him."

As much for refuge as to honor Tucker's request, she hurried to the hall and opened the cellar door. "Father," she called, starting down the steps. Between creaks, she listened for a grunt of reply. "Father," she repeated, louder. She halted in mid-step.

On the earthen floor below, a rectangle of ocher sunlight stretched from the bulkhead. In a corner of it, something glittered. Sapphira stared hard, then discerned what looked to be glass fragments. Her pulse rose. Drumming like a command, it filled her ears, repeating itself until she obeyed and took the last few downward steps. She came upon a stool lying on its side; standing over it, she noticed splintering under the seat rim. Beyond it, by one of the work benches, she saw a pile of broken glass—shattered photographic plates. Shards crunched underfoot as she neared the bench, gaping. Where the sunlight shaded into gloom, she nearly stepped on an oil lamp. It lay there broken, its wick dead, the floor seared black around it. Squatting, she touched the cracked glass cover with her fingertips; warmth lingered, like someone's fading breath. Her gaze traveled along the floor's surface, then went still at the sight of dark droplets—a chain of them, snaking out of the shadows and into the light.

Around her, the stacked boxes and dingy brick walls seemed to pulsate. She remained crouched, even as she heard feet descending from the yard. Against all that her eyes and guts were telling her, hope flared to life as an elongated shadow and then a pair of dusty boots appeared. Their owner, a tall man in uniform, came stooping through the threshold. "Nate!" he called. "Nate, I've . . . " It was Captain Forbes. Framed in the ocher brightness, he stood there squinting at the stool, at the floor, at the broken lamp by her knees. His face went slack. Motionless, Sapphira stared up, waiting for his eyes to meet hers.

She had always wanted answers. Seldom had she gotten any. Now, in the silence, that desire gathered force by the second, turning to blind ferocity.

78

Near Rockville, Maryland

OVER THE HEADBOARD, scar-like, the words had been singed into the rich paisley wallpaper: YANKEE HORE 1 DOLER. Breckinridge shot a reflexive glance over his shoulder, as if the lady of the house–long since fled with her family–might materialize and catch him here like a hapless schoolboy. He had come up here to be alone, perhaps to lie down after the brutal day's march, but now he could not. For while he understood hatred–even the devouring sort, as pure and patient as fire–its handiwork always left him dispirited. Stepping around scattered clothes and bureau drawers, he left the bedroom and went back down the carpeted staircase.

The house reportedly belonged to a top railroad official and staunch Unionist. It was the tasteful sort of residence where Breckinridge, as a peacetime statesman, might have found himself an honored guest. Regardless of the owner's political stripe, he would have felt in his element here, conversing and making merry among those of his class. He did not want to think about it. By the time this place had been seized as quarters for the general staff, soldiers of the vanguard had tramped through it and amused themselves in varied ways.

Breckinridge avoided the parlor, where his aides sat talking or dozing. In the dining room he found upended chairs, a pile of smashed china, a toppled cabinet, slashed brocade curtains, gouges in the mahogany table. Moving down the inner hallway, he passed a study where a desk and bookcases lay overturned, books and papers strewn everywhere. Then he nearly tripped over a hobby horse. He looked down at the painted wooden horse and pictured a small boy riding it. He thought of children in general, but the images inevitably became those of his own children. A father's duty, so it went, required him to take a hickory stick and curb their Original Sin. But when you looked at them, especially in that pearl-perfect age of first speech and first steps, sin was the last thing they brought to mind.

Moving on, he found a ransacked pantry and then a kitchen with more smashed plates on the floor. Gruff talk and laughter came drifting through a shattered window. Stepping onto the rear veranda, he surprised a half-dozen grubby soldiers lounging there, rifles propped against the railing. They had a liquor jug but were drinking from a silver tea service. Bleary-eyed, they lurched to their feet.

A stocky, bewhiskered sergeant cleared his throat. "Uh–Genr'l Breckinridge, sir!"

Standing his full height, Breckinridge regarded the sergeant and then the other men.

"Join us for tea, sir?" a private ventured. The others gave tentative chuckles.

Breckinridge glared at the sergeant. "Put the cups down."

Rapidly sobering, they obeyed.

"What's your regiment?"

The sergeant straightened up. "Forty-fifth Virginia, sir."

"Wharton's Brigade."

"That's right, Genr'l."

Beneath coatings of dust and stubble, they all looked familiar. In each cowed expression, Breckinridge sensed a concealed smirk, ready to rise as soon as he turned away. These were the raucous boys, the leering plebian boys that a nation sent to do its dirtiest jobs. They were indispensable. For them, in time of extremity, no specific command was needed or even advisable. Leaders had only to let the leash slip and then avert their eyes. The North had these boys aplenty; so did the South. Brained with the cudgel of ignorance, set loose upon the lawless borders of history, they could be counted on for more than smashed windows or stolen teacups. But in this campaign, it was not their hour yet–not quite.

"Maybe General Wharton failed to tell you," Breckinridge intoned. "We've come to shame the enemy, not ourselves."

Looking down, the sergeant managed a one-shoulder shrug. "Beg your pardon, sir, but . . . It were a hard march today. None of us straggled–so the boys 'n' me just thought . . . "

"I'm not talking about the liquor, Sergeant! After a day like today, every man in this army deserves a nip–though I'd stick to water, if I were you. I'm talking about in there." Breckinridge poked a thumb over his shoulder. "Or are you all just innocent lambs?"

A couple of men shuffled their feet. The sergeant's hands came up in a weak gesture. "Sir, there were a lot o' soldiers in and out o' here and . . . Well, I guess we done a little mess-makin'. But if you don't mind me sayin', Genr'l–it's a far holler from what the Yanks done to our people in the Valley."

"So we're to take them as our model? It seems you've forgotten General Early's rule about plunder and such–and the penalty for those who violate it."

The sergeant drooped.

"But, sir!" spoke one of the privates.

Breckinridge studied him. He was younger, slighter than the others. And in the angry pleading of his eyes, Breckinridge sensed another difference–something that might once have been gentleness.

"Genr'l," the youth blurted. "I have kin back in Strasburg. They didn't have a tenth o' what these ones do, but Hunter's men burned their house! Their house and their fields! They took all their animals! You . . . You don't know what it's like, sir!"

The sergeant looked up in alarm. "Henning! Now, Henning, that's enough!"

Breckinridge made a patting gesture to the sergeant. "It's all right. Soldier, I . . . " Before the flushed, prematurely hard face, he thought of Cabell. He wanted to place a hand on the youth's shoulder, to shake it or squeeze it hard. Upon him he felt the other men's eyes, apprehensive yet somehow challenging. "Soldier, I lost my house to the Yankees, and I saw what they did in the Valley. But we can't let them drag us down. We can't start acting like dogs, like land pirates, warring on women and children. Let the Yankees lose their honor, not us."

Private Henning looked sullenly at his feet.

"Besides," said Breckinridge, "where we're going–where we'll be tomorrow, boys–there'll be no shortage of military targets. Anything you need and don't have . . . " He felt a sudden bulge in his throat, like a heated stone. He swallowed with effort. "Once we're in the city, you can help yourselves to the depots and then burn what's left. The government buildings, too. It'll be the greatest blow the South has struck so far. You'll get back at them for the Valley, all right–several times over." From their dusty exhaustion, the soldiers stirred. One smiled, another nodded. "For now, though, I want you to go back in there and clean things up. Put the silver back, and anything else you took. Sergeant–see that it's done. Be an example."

The sergeant touched his cap. "Yessir."

"And you . . . " Breckinridge pointed at Henning. "Up in the master bedroom there's a rude slogan burnt into the wall. Peel it off or paint it over–just make it gone."

Still red-faced, the youth gave a deliberate salute. "Yessir, Genr'l."

Ordering one soldier to gather the tea service, the sergeant led the others inside.

Breckinridge went down the veranda steps. Staring across the grassy grounds, he watched the infantry trudge along the road toward Rockville. From around a wooded bend they appeared singly or in clusters, bedraggled silhouettes within the yellow dust. The temperature today had cracked the mid-nineties, breaking unit cohesion and dragging the column out for miles. No amount of urging could spur the men, some of whom had fallen prostrate by the road. In front, outnumbered Union horsemen had fought McCausland's troopers while others had struck at the rear and captured stragglers.

Having passed from ripe orange to coral red, the sun burned through the trees beyond the road. As Breckinridge squinted, the trees became an image of Washington–Washington ablaze. He blinked away, then noticed a dead Union cavalryman by a bush. It was always worse to see a lone corpse, he thought, rather than a whole field of them. In a field of slain men, you could avoid fixing on a particular one–the eyes, the bloating.

Wandering across the grounds, he saw a group of staff officers by a well, guzzling from their canteens. He circled wide, pretending not to notice them. Nearing a persimmon grove, he caught some movement within the lengthening tree shadows. He halted and saw that it was Early's dun-colored horse, grazing. Closer by, he spied a pair of booted legs outstretched.

Early's voice piped up. "Over here, General." Breckinridge ambled into the shade, where Early lay with his head resting against his saddle. His folded hands lay on his stomach, his black-plumed hat on his chest. "Stretch yourself out, why don't you?"

Hesitating, Breckinridge glanced toward the shambling figures along the road.

"General's prerogative," Early drawled. Reaching to the side, he picked up a saddle blanket and tossed it at Breckinridge's feet.

Breckinridge dropped his hat on the grass, then folded the blanket and placed it against a tree root on Early's left. Reclining, he let his listlessness take full hold. The heat remained thick, though a faint breeze heralded evening. Overhead, orange berries and bell-shaped white blossoms coated the branches. From the road's direction, the shuffle of weary feet turned flat in his ears and seemed to recede. He forgot about the grizzled commander at his side. Fingers interlaced, he started dozing, but Early's voice pricked him back to awareness.

"So–we're almost there."

Breckinridge kept his eyes shut. "Maybe ten miles from the outer defenses."

"And how do you like it so far?"

Breckinridge let out a long, drowsy sigh. "If you're familiar with my career, General, you know that I spent several years in Washington."

"Of course. Occupying the second-highest seat in the land, among others."

"I am as determined as you are to bring the Northern government low. But those were among my fondest years–and returning as a blood enemy . . . It's hard to believe, is all."

In the subsequent pause, Breckinridge wondered what Early's reaction might be. Yet there was a certain relief at having expressed himself.

"Pardon the question," said Early. "But is it true that Mary Lincoln's kin to you?"

Breckinridge blinked up at the white-blossom canopy. He sensed what Early was driving at and felt no resentment, though ordinarily he might have. Here was his chance to address the whole matter in plain language. "She's a cousin," he replied, "of indeterminate distance. As are Lincoln's Postmaster-General Montgomery Blair and his brother Frank, who's a major-general for the North. And I should mention my minister uncle Robert, who has helped lead the movement to colonize free Negroes in Liberia. In Baltimore last month, he addressed the convention that renominated Lincoln. My life has its share of knots and riddles. To preserve both the South and the Union, I ran for President–honor compelled me. But they say I ended up clearing the way for Lincoln. And you're also aware, I'm sure, that I was a latecomer to the Confederate cause. To the North I appeared a lowdown schemer and to the South, a man of questionable ardor. And to both, no doubt, I seemed in many ways a typical politician."

"As I understand it," said Early, "any question of your ardor has long since been settled."

"I trust it has. Thank you for saying so. But I don't regret hanging on in the Senate as I did, trying to prevent the slaughter. When you're trapped between war and dishonor, it's like being roasted on a spit. Eventually all your hope gets burned away."

Adjusting his position, Early rested his back against the saddle. "You know, I argued against secession."

Breckinridge frowned with interest. "If I ever heard that, I must have forgotten."

Early nodded. "As a county prosecutor, I was sent to the Richmond convention as a delegate. I opposed the fire-eating faction, long and hard. People forget that until Sumter happened, Virginia's secession was in no way a sure thing. God-a-mighty, though, I can still hear those snooty peacocks from the Tidewater region–thundering for war, positively lusting for it, terrified that the Yankee Satan would swoop down and take their precious slaves away. Not that they would be doing the fighting–oh, Lord forbid! No, that part would fall to plainer men, men without slaves or plantations. At the time, I'd seen little of war. Straight out of West Point, I went to Florida and tangled with the Seminoles. In Mexico, my unit arrived too late for the fighting, so I served as military governor at Buena Vista. Still, it was enough to give me an idea of war's meaning–a clearer one than those prissy gasbags at the convention had."

"I thought I had a clear idea," said Breckinridge. "Who could have imagined, though?"

"Yes. And who would've imagined us here today, doing this? But we are, Breck. Once a man's path is decided, he can't look back."

"True enough."

"You can't look back. You fired your bridges back in '61, as I did mine."

"Right."

"Be thankful that you were equal to it. And lest we forget–the Yankees richly deserve it, and not just for the Valley. I remember when they bombarded Fredericksburg before the battle there. No thought of civilians. A nobler being like Lee might refrain from hating them, but I don't. In the aggregate, they're lesser men. I wish them hell, and hell is what we'll give them."

Slowly Breckinridge sat up. Over the road, with its dust-billows and laggard infantry, the sun cast a fiery halo. He looked at the grand peach-colored house–its gables and chimneys, its shadowed corners, the pitch of its black tile roof. A castle of civility. At an upstairs dormer window, a soldier stood looking out–homeward, perhaps. Noting the narrow face and shoulders, Breckinridge recognized him as Private Henning. And he concluded yet again that Early was right. In a time of razor absolutes, no soldier–no general, certainly–could indulge a misplaced sentiment. Nor could he dwell upon complexity. It amounted to lowering his shield, asking to be cut down. "General," he said, "it is a privilege to be part of this."

The commander eased himself upright. "In our dotage, we'll reminisce about it. Long after we're dust, people will speak of it." He scratched his head, pulled his hat on. "Has McCausland secured Rockville?"

"He has. The head of the column, if it can still be called that, will bivouac thereabouts. Not a minute too soon, as far as the men are concerned." Breckinridge tugged his hat on and stood. "The sky says we're in for another scorcher tomorrow–there'll be lots more straggling, I'm afraid. And the Union cavalry will keep flailing at us."

"We'll move well before daybreak, then, in tight formation." Moving to rise, Early grimaced, and Breckinridge offered a hand. With a grunt of thanks, he took it and stood rubbing his shoulder. "McCausland will continue down the Rockville Road, taking along some light artillery. He'll demonstrate against Fort Reno, near Tennallytown, and exploit any weak spot there. As for the main force, we'll march it southeastward to Silver Spring . . . "

Breckinridge felt a punch of dismay. At the crossroads of Silver Spring stood the summer home of cousin Monty and that of his father, Francis Preston Blair, Maryland's foremost Unionist and kingmaker. In the house of the elder Blair, whose hospitality matched his guile, Breckinridge had hoisted many a glass. Amid the good-humored chiding and political banter, he had weighed the monstrous question of what to do if war came: stay on, or go South? Now he could only marvel at the Almighty's wry poetic genius. He hoped that the arrival of the Confederate host would find all Blairs wisely absent.

"We'll turn down the Seventh Street Road," Early was saying, "and launch our main attack against Fort Stevens, which anchors the northern defense line. Today I got hold of a Washington paper, but it gave no clue about the city's possible reinforcement. That chafes at me. If the balance of Grant's Sixth Corps arrives before we do . . . Well, as you said—it's a race."

"And the alternate plan?" said Breckinridge. "The one involving Fort DeRussy?"

In Early's sudden glance, Breckinridge caught something furtive yet easily read. Early did not wish to let on how this sordid, secret gambit tantalized him. "DeRussy is just west of Stevens," he said, "on Rock Creek. Speaking of which, I trust my special instructions have been carried out?"

"They have indeed," said Breckinridge. "Back at Gaithersburg, a chosen regiment is resting up. So is McCausland's volunteer party, which includes a few of Long's artillerists. The volunteers number forty—adequate for the mission, I think, but few enough to permit a stealthy approach. They've been provided with the best mounts."

"Very good," said Early.

Just then Breckinridge noticed John Brown Gordon on his black charger, coming slowly down the side of the road. In his dusty red shirt and black slouch hat, he looked tired but rode tall, eyes slitted against the dust. His horse kept a plodding pace, its head dipping low with each stride. Trudging troops looked up, touching their caps as the Georgian rode past them; he nodded and spoke, no doubt telling them it would not be much farther. Breckinridge was glad that Gordon had not seen him lying down.

Early spoke. "As soon as you get your corps bivouacked, summon both the volunteer party and the supporting regiment."

"I'll have a courier standing by," said Breckinridge, turning back to his commander.

Watching his horse graze, Early stood half in the shade, half in the reddening sunlight. "You know—before we're done here, we just might turn this whole damned war on its head."

79

Central Washington

"*W*AIT, WAIT—YOU SAY you saw a wagon pulling away?"

"Down the street—yes. Captain, where have they taken him?"

"Did you see who was in it?"

"I wasn't close enough. Please, who do you think it was?"

Forbes' voice was taut and urgent, Sapphira's parched and flat. Behind Forbes, amid the stacked wooden boxes, Tucker stared down at the trail of blood drops. Sapphira's head felt constricted as if by strong hands, holding in the chaos. Before the stunned, groping look on Forbes' face, she struggled not to shout.

"Is he at La Maison de l'Empereur?"

"I . . . I don't . . ."

"I heard the name from Miss McGuire. I know you've been investigating some dangerous people there. They killed Mister Kirschenbaum. Is that where they've taken Father? Will you answer me?"

"Sapphira, I . . . Yes, yes—in all likelihood. But listen . . ."

"Captain, if that's where he is, that's where we must go."

"For God's sake!" Forbes whipped his hat off. He glared at the floor.

An old soul, she thought—an old soul in a damaged young vessel. In Forbes, she had long sensed an injury which perhaps predated the war. Along with admiring him, she had pitied him without knowing fully why. He always seemed trapped in his stiff nobility, in his brooding knight's armor—and now that armor had cracked, revealing a turbulence as severe as her own. Seeing this would ordinarily have brought dismay, but she was beyond dismay. A sick throb filled her as it seemed to fill the dim cellar spaces, leaving no room for middling emotion. Deciding that she could stand maybe ten seconds' more of the captain's paralysis, she waited. Tucker had stepped to the side, lips parted as he looked from Forbes to Sapphira.

Gazing past her, Forbes drew a long breath before speaking. "The case we've been pursuing involves high treason. It also involves the Rebel army that's closing in on the city. Nate . . . The major was reproducing photographs, trying to find a portrait of who we're looking for–an army officer, who we believe is prepared to cause a fatal breach of our defenses." Tucker murmured an oath. "Now the major has been taken. They wanted to prevent us from identifying this officer, their pawn–but they're too late. With one of the major's prints, I have just learned who our traitor is. But *we'll* be too late if we don't find the man tonight. It can't wait."

Sapphira felt her eyes bulging. "Captain . . . "

"It can't wait, Sapphira." His eyes strayed into a corner.

She took a quick stride toward him but then froze, her fingers spread as if to seize, to tear. In the shadowy quiet she eyed the captain's pallid profile.

"I am sorry," he muttered.

Her hands fell to her sides. Already her mind had let go of the anguished man before her and was turning blindly inward.

Tucker had moved to one of the two work benches. With his foot he moved the broken lantern aside. "Is there a candle down here?" she heard him ask. "I'm thinking he might have left something, some clue to help us."

Floating to the blanketed storage nook, she felt a brush of gratitude for Tucker; his practical impulse showed that he, at least, had set bewilderment aside. She took the candleholder from the shelf and brought it to him. Having found a matchbox, he lit the stunted candle and raised it. She watched as he began searching among the articles on the bench–the containers, the picture frames, what remained of the glass plate stack.

"I am sorry," Forbes repeated. Eyes lowered, he stood clutching his hat. "There is one hopeful thing. Apparently they haven't done as they did with their other victims. I mean, had they simply wished to kill the major on the spot . . . " Sapphira felt a rise of nausea. " . . . they would have done so. But it appears they subdued him and took him prisoner. Whatever their reason, it may well keep him alive until I've done what I must do. Then . . . " He looked at her, his gaze simmering. "Then, on my honor, I will speed to that cursed place and free him! I swear to you!"

At that instant Sapphira found her own resolve, grasping it in her depths like a sharp stone. An inexplicable calm arose. It let her look gently upon Forbes, who was both stronger and blinder than she had thought. "Do as you must, then," she said. "And I'll do likewise."

Her response took a moment to register; as it did, Forbes looked perplexed and then alarmed. Averting her eyes, she saw Tucker turn from the bench. The sergeant appeared newly bewildered, staring at a paper print in his hand. Stepping to his elbow, she looked at the scroll-edged photograph and beheld the strangest scene she had ever viewed: a white man and woman, both naked to the waist–the man kneeling while behind him loomed the large woman, one hand wielding a whip and the other clasping a thick book. In the light from Tucker's candle, Sapphira eyed the man's grimacing face. A ghastly fascination came over her, cut short as Tucker passed the picture to Forbes. With narrowed eyes, the captain examined it. He muttered to himself and then placed the picture on the bench, face-down. "Sergeant, I need your help."

Tucker's glance at Sapphira was too quick to read. "You have it, sir."

"I know you're not quite recovered," Forbes said. "Can you ride?"

"Short of a flying gallop–yes, sir."

"Good, then." The captain gave Sapphira a firm look. The photograph seemed to have jolted him out of his misery, back into the teeth of the moment. "Sapphira–with the sergeant's aid, I will make quicker work of this. You must . . . "

"Be patient?" she interrupted.

Fidgeting, he looked toward the glare of the bulkhead passageway. "A hard task, yes–maybe the hardest. But it's the only sane thing to do."

"You're a fine man, Captain." Staring into his face, she wanted him to see that she meant every toneless word. "Father has said so, more than once. But you don't understand."

His jaw tightened. "Whatever you're contemplating, don't act on it. Do not act foolishly!"

"What you are telling me is to not act at all. To wait and pray while Father is held by murderers–including that devil Monroe."

Stymied, Forbes started to speak but went silent, his lips pressed tight.

Slowly Sapphira shook her head. "You expect far too little of me–and in another way, too much. You are right to place your soldier's duty first.

You have my blessing, Captain, if that matters at all. But I don't require yours."

"That's enough!" he yelled, his face flushing.

Startled, she came perilously close to laughter as Forbes sputtered something and then broke off. Once more he seemed to recover himself, though his red face still glowered. He spoke hoarsely: "Do you think for a second that he would want you anywhere near this whole business? You, by yourself!? Keep your senses, for heaven's sake! Do not make it any worse!"

Again a light-headed laugh nearly escaped her. "Worse, Captain?"

Tucker had set the candle down, his gaze shifting between the floor and Sapphira's face.

"Sergeant," said Tucker, "–meet me at Howard's Livery Stable on Tenth Street, next to Ford's Theater. I'll have a horse ready for you."

"All right, Captain. I'll leave presently."

Forbes lumbered to the bulkhead steps, glass crunching beneath his soles. In the reddening light he paused but did not look back. "Sapphira, I am begging you."

"God protect you," she spoke.

He put his hat on and lurched up the steps, out of sight.

In the steeping shadows, the candle silhouetted Tucker's broad-shouldered bulk. He was studying her. "I'm begging you, too," he murmured. "Please stay clear of this."

"You'd best hurry. He needs you."

"I want to come back to you. Not just tomorrow, but when the war is over."

The constriction returned–hands around her brain, squeezing. "I am not prepared for that wish. Something's missing from me. It may always be."

"Sapphira–if you were but half of what you are, my wish would be the same." His husky form drew up straight. "I want to be a worthy man for you."

The brave term echoed–"A worthy man." Throughout history, she supposed, men had spoken such words with the same ardor, in the same posture. Yet she felt that if she reached out and pushed Tucker, he would topple like a clay statue. She pictured the hospitals, the cemeteries, the boatloads of wounded. She thought of Ben, of Tucker himself in the church hospital. How could men speak of women's frailty while forgetting their own? That terrible frailty?

She shut her eyes. "Flavius," she muttered. With a start, she felt him take hold of her arms.

"Please," he said. "Stay here. For my sake, as much as yours."

Her voice came in a knotted hush. "I have been hindered long enough. And too much has been lost already." Slipping her arms free, she opened her eyes wide and gazed into the dark of Tucker's face, inches away. *"Too much has been lost already."*

Expecting another plea, she waited to deflect it, but Tucker just looked at her a moment longer. Then he turned away. He crunched across the glass to the bulkhead. Glancing over his shoulder, he adjusted his cap and said nothing. He ascended the steps. Wanting to call after him, she found herself unable to speak. Then he was gone, up into the red sunlight. On the red-tinged section of floor, the glass shards glittered like diamonds. She craved whatever sorcery would cancel all thought, would let her believe that Father was upstairs in his study, that she was standing here amid strewn diamonds. Then she saw the dark blood drops. Like beads from a broken necklace, they trailed through the bits of glitter toward the steps.

Moving to the work bench, Sapphira picked up the photograph and turned it over, holding it close to the candle. She forced herself to stare–at the kneeling man with his grimace, the looming woman with her book, her whip and her breasts. Her pulse resounded in the stillness. Putting the picture down, she blew the candle out.

A minute later she was up in Ben's room, leaning over him. "Ben?" she whispered, touching his good arm.

His eyelids fluttered.

"Ben, are you thirsty?"

"Nope."

"Listen–that place that Delia came from, La Maison de l'Empereur?"

He gave a shallow yawn. "Yes?"

"Did Father mention to you where it was?"

Shifting position, he showed the scabbed side of his face. "Seventh Street Road, I think he said. A good way out." His bloodshot eye opened a bit, peering up at her. "Why?"

"I'll tell you later. Sleep some more."

She left him and went down to the study, where she lit the desk lamp. She found the revolver in a bottom drawer, along with a box of cartridges and one of percussion caps. "A modified Colt Dragoon," her father had called it–his best friend since his days as Macon County sheriff. She took it by its smooth wooden stock and sat in the desk chair. Trying to recall the loading procedure, she gingerly eared back the hammer until it caught. She stared into the weapon's empty cylinder, then pointed it at the floor. Her fingers quivered as she took a paper-hulled cartridge from its box and tried to insert it. She was pressing it with her thumb when she caught the sound of Anna's voice outside–a voice of breathless good spirits, thanking someone. Sapphira heard the front door open.

"Thank you so much!" Anna warbled.

An older male voice replied heartily. "It's nothing, Miss. No true-blooded man can bear the sight of a pretty young lass in distress."

"Oh, just set them down there. No, there on the stand–fine! Sir, please let me pay you."

"Now, no true-blooded man takes money for helping a lovely girl in distress."

"Really, you're too good."

Slouching, Sapphira rested the revolver on her knee. She listened as Anna's true-blooded rescuer made his exit, voicing the hope that the two of them would meet again at the market. As the door shut, Sapphira broke out laughing. Loud, rude, ringing laughter–it throttled her until the pistol dropped from her hand. Anna appeared in the study doorway. Startled, she stood there in her white bonnet and olive taffeta dress, a satin reticule dangling from her shoulder.

Sapphira let the last of her laughter dribble out. "Poor man. He'll be going to the market a lot, won't he?"

Anna glared. "Are you mad?!"

Blinking tears away, Sapphira reached toward the floor. "Craning his poor neck, searching for Miss Annie."

"It is hardly a joke!" Anna blurted. "It was horrible! I managed to get a full basket but was nearly trampled in the process! Listen, though–it's late, and why haven't you at least started cooking? Why aren't the lamps lit? What's the matter with . . . ?" She went mute as Sapphira sat up, cradling the revolver.

"Annie, do you recall how to load one of these?"

Anna's eyes had widened. "What are you . . . ?"

"I'll tell you, but come look at this."

Gawking, Anna approached the desk. "That's Father's."

"You've seen Lieutenant Chadwick load his sidearm, haven't you? What comes next?"

Anna stared at the weapon. "I think . . . the loading lever. Under the barrel–that rod there."

Sapphira noted the rod along the barrel's underside. Still aiming at the floor, she pinched the tip of the rod and pulled it downward. Between hammer and cylinder, a blackened little plunger appeared and rammed the cartridge home. "Yes–that's it. And the cap must go onto that nipple there, behind the charge." She began loading the five other chambers.

"What is this?" Anna muttered. "You're that worried about the Rebels?"

With slow precision, Sapphira inserted another cartridge. "As worried as anyone."

"Where's Father? In the cellar still?"

Sapphira released the hammer, eased it shut and placed the revolver on the desk. "Father's been abducted."

Anna's mouth fell open. Blanching, she backed away until a bookcase halted her. "What?"

Sapphira rooted in the drawer and found the worn leather holster. Laying it by the pistol, she got up. She stepped over and placed her hands on Anna's shoulders, gazing into her stunned green eyes. "Explanations must wait–I scarcely know them myself. Right now I need any money you have left. And a sash–I need a sash. Are you with me, Annie?"

With shaking fingers, Anna touched the base of her throat. She nodded.

Sapphira hurried upstairs. In her room she shed her apron and calico dress, donning her black hospital dress with the wide front pocket. She returned to the study and took a fistful of percussion caps, pouring them like copper seeds into her pocket and then adding several cartridges. Anna padded in with the money and a yellow silk sash. Taking these, Sapphira stuffed the wrinkled bills in with the ammunition. She folded the sash to the width of a man's belt and then wound it about her waist, pulling one end through the holster's belt-loop.

"Ben's all right, but look in on him later," she told Anna. She slid the pistol into its holster; the weight made the sash droop and she cinched it tighter, tying it with a knot. "If Captain Forbes and Sergeant Tucker make an appearance, tell them I've gone to the Emperor's House." Still speechless, Anna followed her to the front hall. Sapphira reached for her shawl but hesitated, then took down her brown wool capuchin and threw it on; she left the hood down but pulled the cape in close, hiding the revolver.

Anna stared at her, eyes gleaming. "Saph?" she quavered.

Sapphira opened the door. Balking on the threshold, she turned and gave Anna a quick embrace. Then she was off.

Through the gas-lit twilight, past block after block of shops, row houses and humbler dwellings, Sapphira felt the rhythmic bump of the pistol beneath her cape. Her brisk stride served her well, and within fifteen minutes she had reached Sixth and Pennsylvania. On opposite corners, the National Hotel and Brown's faced each other like rival grand potentates.

The intersection was unusually quiet, with only three weary hackmen waiting outside the hotels. She approached one of the two in front of the National, asking him if he knew of the Emperor's House on the Seventh Street Road. His steep gaze conveyed offense as the question registered. No, he said coldly–he knew of no such house. The second hackman was polite, though his eyes avoided her; apologizing, he said that he preferred a closer destination for his day's last fare.

The sting of the first man's look had disconcerted her. She paused to arrange her thoughts, then crossed to the lone driver outside of Brown's. Looking up at him, she tried to summon a casual confidence.

"Pardon me, sir–I need a ride to a house out on the Seventh Street Road."

Stirring from his hunched posture, the driver nudged his hat back. He was a rawboned, furrow-faced man with skin the color of weathered brick, his turkey neck too thin for his collar. In the gas-glow, his sentinel eyes assessed her. She was about to repeat herself when he softly responded. "Well, Miss . . . When you says 'out,' how far to do you mean?"

"A good distance, sir, but I'll pay double." Careful to keep the pistol hidden, she dug into her skirt and took out the wrinkled wad of bills.

He glanced at the money but remained inert, the reins limp across his knees. "There's a lot o' scared folks comin' down that road, so I hear. And them Rebels close behind. I don't know if I could get you there–nor near there, even."

With a surge of determination, she placed her foot on the step plate. "However close you can get will do." Climbing in, she settled onto the threadbare seat. The man straightened his back, flipped the reins, clucked his tongue to the horse.

As the carriage jounced across the cobblestone, she let her body jounce with it. An unreasoning sense of relief swept over her. Then she remembered fully what she was doing and who for. Straining to wipe her mind blank, she reached under her cape and touched the revolver, its casing as smooth and cool as a serpent.

80

Near Rockville, Maryland

*F*LEETINGLY, THE LOW red sun transformed the landscape into a place where time meant nothing, where a man's spirit could roam at ease. A weird, dreamy realm of long shadows and brassy luster. John Breckinridge allowed himself a moment of weakness, contemplating how he once might have been President of the United States. Few had ever appeared so destined for that pinnacle. Still, destiny could be opaque.

From the outset of the 1860 campaign, he had known that he would fall far short; the chief backers of his candidacy guaranteed as much. They were Deep South fire-eaters, for the most part–planter lords who, unlike Breckinridge himself, trumpeted slavery and the pursuit of happiness in the same breath. Their interests shaped the platform on which he ran, canceling whatever appeal he might have had for moderate Northern voters. In Northern eyes, that slaveholder's platform eclipsed both his distinguished record in Congress and his border-state lineage, which might have made him a credible champion of compromise.

The Republicans had dared not campaign in seething Dixie, where tar and feathers awaited anyone who came to boost Lincoln. And too few Southerners could have stood to vote for Stephen "Little Giant" Douglas, the Northern Democratic candidate, nor even for the slaveholding moderate John Bell, on the Constitutional Unionist ticket. Without the fourth choice of Breckinridge–the Pericles of states' rights, whose reputation outshone all others in the region–they would have taken up arms before the first ballot was cast.

The nomination had in fact appalled him, stunned him with the knowledge of what it meant: split party, split nation, Lincoln, the abyss. In darker moments, he wondered if the fire-eaters had tricked him, exploited him to achieve their longed-for goal of disunion. Whatever the case, it had always seemed that his inner split mirrored the country's–and that like the country, he would at length be forced to choose. (Lincoln's reckless "House Divided" speech now echoed like prophecy.) Inherited from his revered father and grandfather, this fracture pained Breckinridge in any number of ways, above all by making him feel a hypocrite. Participating in slavery, declaring it constitutional; detesting slavery, privately favoring gradualism; dreading the consequences, contributing to the consequences, seeing no way out. A hard business to explain, even to oneself. Perhaps hypocrisy was the lot of all reflective men. Yet in the South's hour of need, someone had to seize the standard and defy Northern usurpation. Caught between dueling principles, he had chosen what he perceived as the higher one–as he believed the sainted Founding Fathers would have chosen. Breckinridge was nothing if not a man of principle.

The bigger riddle was how the whale of politics had come to swallow him, principles and all. On the stump, he defended the slave code with a grossly magnified passion. Harnessing the power of hysteria, he outwardly credited slave-revolt stories in certain Democrat newspapers, all of them strangely wanting in detail and first-hand citation. Nimble as a dancer, he distanced himself from the Buchanan administration, with its legacy of fumbling impotence. (No great feat, really–vain old Buchanan had consistently ignored the counsel of his young vice-president.)

All great events appeared as destiny once they came to pass. For this and other reasons, Breckinridge rejected the Northern Democrats' cry of "spoiler," their charge that he had handed it all to the Republicans. What he could not deny was that in the fray, he had ceded too much of himself. A measure of integrity–blood-precious, irretrievable. Never mind his subsequent efforts to preserve the Union peacefully. For seventy-two electoral votes, he had let himself become just another symbol of mad-dog partisanship. He hoped that posterity would chisel him some kinder epitaph–but if it failed to do so, his ghost would not rise in protest.

Breckinridge pulled himself back from the red horizon, from the rubble of his past, back to the reassuring confines of time and place. He gazed into the gloom. Near the woods over to his left, two nodding sentries tended a herd of captured livestock. At several points across the field, campfires enshrined groups of men eating pig or rabbit. Hundreds more slept where they had dropped in the tall grass, others on gum blankets seized from the Martinsburg stores. Beneath the phosphorescent winking of the fireflies, their sprawled forms called up other body-strewn fields–Shiloh, Stones River, Chickamauga. A pale hunchback moon had risen but the day's heat lingered, like the earth's own slumbering breath. Breckinridge felt the trance returning, the pull of all that was lost and damned and cherished–all those final reckonings. Resisting it, he made himself turn on his heel and stride back toward the house.

Staff officers sat or stood on the veranda and front steps, some of them eating from china plates and bowls, faces haggard in the soft window light. With a vigorous cheekful of tobacco, Early paced by the road, pausing to spit, peer northward and glance at his watch. Breckinridge spied McCausland standing alone by the veranda. He seemed to be watching Early. Among his men, the cavalry chief had earned the name "Tiger John"–and with his Roman nose and small deep eyes, he usually did look fierce or at least resolute. Not tonight, however.

Struggling to satisfy every gruff order from Early, McCausland had met repeated embarrassment, repeated scowls from a commander who scorned his men as "buttermilk rangers." His failure to cut off Hunter's retreat had stung, surely, as had his mistakenly small levy on the people of Hagerstown. His performance yesterday on the Monocacy and today in front of Rockville should have redeemed him–but as far as Breckinridge knew, Early had spoken no word of praise or credit. Tonight McCausland's careworn face suggested nothing of the tiger and everything of the spurned child, the one who strove hardest for approval.

Kyd Douglas and Sandie Pendleton were seated together on the steps, the latter with a large scrolled map across his knees. The two rose to greet Breckinridge, who then sat between them, and Pendleton unrolled the map. A newly drawn masterpiece from the chief topographer, Major Hotchkiss, it showed the District of Columbia and adjacent areas, with fortifications marked in black. "For the volunteer party," said Pendleton, his glance conveying quiet excitement. Word of a secret operation against Washington had swept the upper ranks.

Nodding, Breckinridge shifted his eyes to Early's lamp-lit figure. Early had gone still by the road, staring into the darkness as if he had heard something. McCausland bustled over to him and assumed the same pose.

Within a moment, most of the officers had gathered at roadside, waiting as the intricate rumble of hooves grew louder.

Finding himself beside McCausland, Breckinridge decided to speak. "Well, this'll surely be a feather in your hat."

The brigadier gave him a distracted look. "Reckon it will. So long as my boys succeed."

"They will, if yesterday was any indication. That was one fine performance at the river."

McCausland's eyes flickered gratitude. "Thank you for that, Genr'l. We lost a few, but . . . " The words trailed off, his attention drawn back to the dark road.

Hoofbeats filled the night as an orange glow appeared and quickly grew, shuddering on the trees where the road curved. Upraised torches followed, silhouetting a jumble of mounted men, which proceeded to order itself into a column. As the officers moved back, an aide of Early's stepped forward with a lantern and waved it. One torchbearer led the little column, with three more riding along each flank. Breckinridge again felt mesmerized, watching them come. And for an instant, fire and shadow fused the riders into a single apparition—a burning, rippling, glinting beast of prophecy, inevitable as plague.

One horseman spurred past the lead torchbearer, then slowed and drew erect. The others slowed as well, bunching together on their shiny huffing animals. With a distinct sense of drama, the first man reined up and swung down from his saddle. He was a lanky, strong-jawed captain with black hair past his collar, handsome despite a scar along his cheek.

Facing Early and McCausland, he snapped a salute. "Sirs—Captain Martin Guillespie reporting."

Tobacco juice stained Early's grizzled beard. His eyes betrayed no anti-cavalry bias as they assessed the young captain, who in no way looked like a "buttermilk ranger." "Guillespie—where are you from?"

"Culpeper, Genr'l."

"Ah! For ready and willing men, we can always count on old Virginia, eh?"

Breckinridge traded a smirk with Douglas. Early seldom missed the chance to extol his native state, often at the expense of the dozen others represented on the Stars 'n' Bars. In command circles, this chauvinism had stirred resentment among non-Virginians; in the Army of the Valley, most accepted it with a shrug, as they had the quirks of old Stonewall.

But it amused Breckinridge doubly this time, as he spied at least two dark Cherokee faces in the party.

"It is my privilege, Genr'l," said Guillespie. "I'm to inform you, sir, that the Twenty-third Virginia Infantry is on the march behind us, and will arrive as soon as possible."

Spitting out his chaw, Early motioned toward the veranda. "Tell 'em to gather 'round. Over here, in the light."

Guillespie ordered his volunteers to dismount and congregate. They did so with a clatter of sabers and carbines, their expressions keen as staffers made way for them. Breckinridge found a place by the step railing. Above him, the dashing captain leaned in while Pendleton held the map's top edge and Early its bottom. Early found their present location, then traced a line toward the District boundary.

"Continue through Rockville till you're just west of Rock Creek. At that point, leave the road and follow the creek south and east. Follow it across the Brookville Road and into the District, where it bisects the enemy works." He cut a glance to Guillespie. "Use utmost stealth. Watch out for pickets and videttes, and of course put out your torches. You'll have some moonlight to go by. Owing to the drought in this area, the creek bed will be dry or nearly so; you can use it for extra concealment as you come in close. Your objective . . . " The men pressed in closer. By the quivery strand of Rock Creek, Early's index tapped one of the tiny black rectangles that indicated a fort. "Fort DeRussy. As you can see, it stands midway between the two key forts in that sector–Stevens to the east, guarding the Seventh Street Road, and Reno to the west, guarding the Rockville. Those are the two main routes into Washington. Now, by way of a ruse, secret operatives have arranged that you may take DeRussy unopposed."

In a flurry of shuffling and whispers, volunteers looked at one another. Guillespie jerked a hand up for silence. Early's knobby finger moved a bit. "When you reach this ford–here, where the creek intersects Milkhouse Road–you'll be a stone's throw east of DeRussy. You will send a man forward with two torches, which he will wave in tandem. Upon this signal, the garrison will evacuate, and you will occupy the fort with all haste. You will then send back three messengers by divergent routes. Along the Brookville Road they will find the Twenty-third Virginia in position, poised to rush forward and secure DeRussy. With this done, the regiment's colonel will send a message to me, upon receipt of which I will alter our main plan of attack. General Rodes' division will be redirected, straight into the breach."

Early let go of the map, letting it scroll up into Pendleton's hands. Clearing his throat, the commander straightened his back and scanned the intent faces around him. Torchlight gleamed in his eyes, fluttered on his beard and brow. "For the moment–for the precious moment, gentlemen–the enemy appears weak. Today we encountered only small cavalry units. Before our threat, I'd wager he's also overextended and in disarray. We reason that given this situation, plus the confusion of nighttime, your seizure of DeRussy will go unchallenged for a couple of crucial hours, by which time the Yankees will have lost the chance to retake it. If they make the attempt any sooner, the artillerists among you will direct the defense. If the two neighboring forts fire upon you, return fire. Hold fast until the Twenty-third arrives. You will represent our toehold . . . " Raising a fist, Early held it at chest level. His voice fell to a throaty monotone, almost a growl. "Our toehold–in ultimate victory. If you succeed, you will have the everlasting gratitude of the Confederacy. From the Chesapeake to the Rio Grande, to wherever else our flag proclaims us, future Southern generations will celebrate you." His gleaming gaze fell upon Guillespie, whose gaze gleamed back. "You–the heroes who gave us the Yankee capital!"

No one moved or spoke, and there was only the sound of horses fidgeting. Breckinridge noticed Guillespie's hand squeezing his saber handle. On the scarred side of his face, the veranda latticework made a crisscross shadow, like black war paint.

Taking the map from Pendleton, Early thrust it at the captain. "You have roughly ten miles to cover. Go now–and Godspeed."

Guillespie took the map. "Sir!" Saluting, he yelled for his men to mount up.

They scrambled back to their saddles. As Guillespie steadied his mount, McCausland strode over to him and the two shook hands. Guillespie whirled his hat high, bawling the order to move out. The aides waved or held hats aloft until the last rider had galloped past–shadowy centaurs, trailing flame into the darkness. The pounding of their hooves receded. Their torches shrank to burning pinpoints. Staffers exchanged wide-awake looks as they resumed conversation, several of them gathering about McCausland. On the veranda, Early stood pondering his watch.

In the gloom by the steps, Breckinridge noticed Cabell standing where he himself had stood. Instead of his usual sullenness, Cabell bore a look of quiet absorption, still gazing southward. It was a relief to see him sober. Breckinridge walked over and his son muttered hello. Reaching under his open tunic, Breckinridge took out a roll of cheroots that Gordon had thoughtfully bestowed on him. He gave one to Cabell and took one himself, then fired them with a match. Smoking, the two of them ambled down the road.

"So, Father–do you think . . . ?" Cabell left the pointless question unfinished.

"It's not what you could call a gamble," said Breckinridge. "Because if there's any chance of success, we're compelled to try. Duty-bound. Everything Early said back there . . . " He puffed his cheroot. "All of that is true."

By the meadow, they found Kyd Douglas standing alone. Breckinridge offered him a cheroot and lit it for him. Side by side the three of them gazed upon the slumbering troops, the fireflies like a jeweled net over the field. They listened to the dense friction of the crickets, the bristling swell of the cicadas.

Douglas sighed, expelling smoke. "It's one of those times," he murmured. "Big things in motion. Out of sight, mostly–out of our influence. And a fellow knows that once it's over, everything will be different–different in ways only a seer could predict. And he goes still inside and thinks, 'Remember this, remember it well.'"

In Breckinridge's nostrils, tobacco smoke mingled with the smell of earth. He felt a furtive glance from Cabell, with the weight of other, older questions. It wearied him. Yet within his fatigue, there arose a feeling like embers in the blood, like fireflies coursing through him. "Yes," he said. "All the reckonings."

Perhaps it was false, this sense of cosmic judgment. Perhaps there was but one true judgment–the Final one, of scriptural fame. And maybe everyone misunderstood even that, believing it came at the literal end when in fact it was always happening. Night and day, around the clock, perceivable only in sharp fragments.

Breckinridge peered up at the moon–a hunched monarch, rising to rule the night. "Remember this," he thought.

81

North Washington

TUCKER HAD RIDDEN a horse exactly twice in his life, at a friend's farm near Montreal. His inexperience alone would have made it hard to keep up with Forbes, but the rapidly falling night made him even more cautious, afraid that his roan gelding would stumble as they passed beyond the light of houses. And there was the pain of his wound. As he trailed Forbes' mounted shape along West Tenth Street, his still-tender ribs and scapula flared up, worsening until he listed in the saddle. All the while, Sapphira's image flashed like dry lightening: her face, starkly beautiful, haunted in the candle's glow; her eyes of polished stone, staring; her lips, telling him to abandon his most fervent hope.

He had been foolish to speak as he had. Given her state, what could he have expected but a crippled response? Perhaps she simply did not want him after all. But in her hushed evasion, she had implied something worse–that she would, indeed, ignore his and Forbes' pleading. That she had declared her own war.

Some ten yards ahead, Forbes rose out of his hunch, glanced back and began slowing his sorrel mare. The street had become a rutted country road, running due north past woods and open fields. Westward, the ascendant gibbous moon defined a Negro shantytown, a tight collection of hovels with sparse firelight. In the surrounding flat terrain, more scattered and numerous fires illuminated the refugee encampments, their huddled wagons. Tucker gained quickly on Forbes, following him past an intersecting road. Hurting, he drew even and was startled to see Forbes in a slumped posture, his face averted.

Tucker gathered his breath. "Sir, what is it?"

Forbes squeezed his pommel and leaned on it. "Infernal leg . . . I need to get down."

They each pulled to a stop. Tucker dismounted and helped Forbes down, whereupon the captain began to pace in slow deliberate circles. Tucker tethered the horses to a crabapple tree and rested carefully against the trunk, hoping that his own ache would subside before long. Stretching their necks, the horses rustled for apples. Out on the road, Forbes trudged around and around. At length he ceased his circling, balanced on his false leg as if to test it and then started haltingly toward the tree. Tucker watched him come, reflecting that "heavy" described more than Forbes' gait. It was a general quality. To a large degree, Forbes reminded him of the other Bostonians he had met as an escaped young slave.

Tucker's Boston interlude remained one of his strongest memories, alive with danger and dizzy triumph. It was the smell of the wharves, the cry of the gulls, the dim light of the attic where he was given refuge. With his plunge from the ship into the cold harbor water, the world had burst unbelievably wide, leaving him both scared and proud. In those few unreal days before he left for Canada, members of the Vigilance Committee brought him food and other comforts. He was grateful to them, these heavy godly white people, but something about them unsettled him. It was an air of taut certainty when they spoke, a burning clarity when they looked at him–as if it was not a boy they saw, but some glittering artifact they had salvaged. Somehow, despite their kind words and solicitude, they invoked the very faces that he had risked everything to flee–masters and overseers, so sure of their earthly roles and of Tucker's own.

In that one respect, at least, Forbes differed from his Puritan brethren–and hence, God knew, from the planter lords of Dixie. His look and speech conveyed confidence, of a sort, but none of that blazing certainty in which those others seemed to revel. Quite the opposite–when duty did not immediately engage him, he appeared lost, fogbound, as if trying to remember something. It was an unexpected frailty to find in any white man. And it freed Tucker to like him, in a tentative way, though he could never envy him.

Holding his side, Tucker realized that the throbbing had begun to lessen.

Forbes placed a hand on his mare and leaned against her, draped in darkness. He let out a sharp sigh. "Well–we're quite a pair."

Tucker coughed, wincing. "Pardon the question, Captain–how is it your leg still bothers you?"

Forbes gave a sickly chuckle. "What I have are ghost-pains–and I scarcely understand them myself. You see, the limb may be gone but the nerve-ends don't know it. From time to time they consort with the brain, which transmits pain as if the leg were still there."

Amazed and repelled, Tucker tried to grasp the idea. "I understand it happened at Antietam, sir. Sapphira told me. That's a proud enough badge for any man."

Forbes stopped leaning on the horse and began stroking its back. "Actually, it didn't happen in the main engagement. The day before, my regiment was with Hooker's corps on the right. We crossed the creek near Keedysville and blundered into enemy pickets. Their artillery kicked up. The next thing I knew, I'd joined the Brotherhood of the Stump." On the mare's back, his strokes became slow and even. "I was taken to a barn set up as a field hospital. That first night, there were just a few other wounded. I was under morphine but the guns still woke me at dawn. By mid-morning the barn was full and they moved me outside. By noon the surrounding acre was covered with wounded and by mid-afternoon they covered the surrounding five. There were pyramids of amputated limbs outside the barn. Twice, the roar of the fighting died down and then erupted farther south. Come evening, it all turned quiet except for the wails and moaning. I was evacuated to Frederick, and that's where I heard my company had been decimated, my regiment half destroyed."

The captain's words came in a murmured rush. Tucker sensed him riding out the last of his pain, distracting himself. In the crickety stillness, the horses crunched at crabapples. Tucker found himself wondering about the Twenty-Second, the men of Company F. How were they doing, mired in the Petersburg siege? How many more had gone to the hospital or the grave?

"Regarding Sapphira," Forbes said. "I trust she will hesitate–that she'll regain her senses."

"Sir, I don't believe she'll hesitate," said Tucker.

Forbes' hand went still on the mare's shoulder, then slid off. In his compressed murmur, he went on. "I swear I can't imagine why Major Truly confided those things to her—it was damned indiscreet. Whatever she believes, though . . . if our mission here was not absolutely vital and time not so short—heaven help me, I would be breaking down doors to free him. And shooting whoever needed to be shot."

"I'm convinced of that, Captain, and I believe Sapphira is too. But can you tell me—who is Monroe? Why did she call him a devil?"

Forbes told Tucker about the House of the Emperor—about Ravenel, Dubray and the killer known as Monroe, whose true name was Heath. "But for now, Sergeant, another man will have to absorb our attention." Forbes dug into his saddlebag. "Here, light a match." He handed the little box to Tucker, who took out a match and struck it. Forbes held up a photograph. In the sulphurous glow, Tucker took in the long, bearded, sunken-eyed face of a Union army officer. "Orlando Monks—a captain at the time, now a lieutenant-colonel. An engineer attached to the Veteran Reserves. I have a warrant to bring him in." The captain explained why as Tucker felt his pulse climb. "If Early can exploit the breach before Grant's reinforcements arrive," said Forbes, "he will take the capital."

Tucker's match sputtered and he shook it out, quickly lighting another. Forbes put the portrait away, then took out a map and unfolded it. Worn and well-creased, it revealed the fat diamond shape of the District. Forbes ran his index along the diamond's northern edge, forming an inverted V: "We'll limit our search to this ten-mile section. The forts therein number thirteen, with supporting batteries and rifle pits in between. They're placed at half-mile intervals, as you see here. I'll start from the western end, on the Potomac; you start from the eastern, on the Old Bladensburg Road. Rock Creek divides our area more or less in half. We'll work toward each other—toward the creek, that is—asking at each fort if Lieutenant-Colonel Monks is present or nearby. If anyone questions you, say you're from General McCook's headquarters and have been sent to confirm who's in command where along the front. Understood?"

"Understood," said Tucker. "But sir, what am I to . . . " The match singed his fingertips; cursing softly, he threw it down and lit another. "What if I do locate Monks? What then?"

"Ride on and find me. Stop at other forts to see if I'm there—but if I'm not, we'll rendezvous soon enough. Then we'll proceed to Monks' fort and arrest him. On the other hand, if I find him first, I'll arrest him and leave word for you. Regardless, we'll keep on toward each other till one of us locates him."

Leaning in with the match, Tucker scrutinized his projected route of search. Barring an early, lucky discovery of Monks, it would take him to Forts Saratoga, Bunker Hill, Slemmer, Totten and Slocum and then across Piney Branch, to Fort Stevens by the Seventh Street Road and from there to . . . But Forbes began folding the map.

"I've memorized my route," Forbes said, "so you can take the map and matches. This is as good a place as any for us to split up. At the next crossroads, go right. That will take you east to Boundary Street and beyond."

Tucker put the articles in his saddlebag. He and Forbes led their animals back to the road, then mounted up in clumsy unison. They did not speak again. As they reached the next crossroads, Tucker swung right. Several trots along, he threw a final glance over his shoulder, but Forbes had vanished into the warm darkness.

With the moon brighter and the stars fully out, the way was more visible, and Tucker no longer feared stumbling as he rode. The ache in his ribs and back was nearly gone. Urging his horse to a pace just under a gallop, he thought of Monks' portrait and felt a charge go through him. A few hours ago, he had stood holding a shovel at Lafayette Square. Now another duty had befallen him, more critical than he could ever have foreseen—and he feared that if he rode any slower, he would sink under its weight. Hunching forward, he slapped the reins. Then, as his horse surged, it occurred to him that he was a colored man alone and weaponless.

82

Two Miles North

IN THE LANTERN's shaky light, the farm road began to widen. Not far ahead, campfires illuminated its shrub-bounded left edge, along which a line of vehicles sat. Sapphira hoped that this detour would prove worthwhile. Above her, the driver's back remained straight as a post.

As they neared a covered wagon, Sapphira saw two white oxen still yoked to it. A man sat nodding against a rear wheel while three blanketed children lay beneath the tailboard. As the hack crept by, a bonneted woman peered up from tending the fire, whose flickering etched lines in her weary face. There followed a series of similar vignettes—another crackling fire, another roadside wagon or carriage with its drooping team of animals, the drawn staring faces of dusty white folk. Sapphira stole glances at them, wishing she could race by.

Taking his hat off, the driver leaned sideways to avoid a tree branch, then straightened up and replaced the hat. A moment passed before Sapphira realized that he had turned his high-collared neck and was looking at her. "All o' them flyin' from the Rebels," he said. "And here's you, Miss, movin' right towards 'em."

Her gaze fell to the darkness of her lap. Just now she did not want another soul to think her crazed or foolish. "The Rebels aren't as far as the fortifications, sir. Surely they'll be delayed there." When she looked up again, he had turned his eyes back to the road. "I did not wish to come out here," she added, "but someone close to me is in bad trouble."

"That's all your affair, Miss. I'm-a just seein' if your eyes is both open."

She hugged her knees, rocking. She wondered how close the Confederates were. For all she knew, they had in fact reached the defenses or even broken through.

Above the noise of the hack, she began to make out other, less definable sounds. She raised herself to look. Up ahead, where the grass and shrubbery grew sparse, an undulating glow revealed the junction with Washington's main artery, the Seventh Street Road. On the road she discerned a stream of close-packed vehicles creeping southward.

"Hate to say, Miss," spoke the driver, " but I reckon this is where I turn 'round."

Still the hack jounced along as the noises grew more distinct, mixing and clashing: the clatter of wheels, the crunch of hooves, the squeak of springs and rawhide, the occasional voice or baby's squall. As the farm road joined the crowded main one, it splayed into a clearing, and there the driver made a half-turn before pulling to a stop. Sapphira beheld the southbound exodus: carts, wagons, surreys, buckboards and rockaways, generally two abreast and heaped with belongings. Their dangled lanterns caught the sheen of horse flanks, the strain of fugitive faces.

Trying to absorb it all, Sapphira did not immediately notice that the driver had gotten down and opened the hack's door. He offered his gloved hand and she took it. Under her cloak, the pistol bumped her thigh as she stepped down. She reached into her dress pocket, feeling among caps and cartridges until she found the bills.

The driver took his money with a nod. On his furrowed brick-brown face, the indifference had cracked just a little. "Miss, how far you got left to go?"

"I don't truly know," she said. "Listen, sir–back on the Avenue, I did not say my exact destination. I know nothing about it and have never been there, but I must find it. It's called La Maison de l'Empereur, or the Emperor's House. Do you know it?"

His brow-lines deepened. He fixed his hat, then glanced uncertainly at the road. "'Nuther mile 'n' a half, you crosses a little crik and the house come soon after, this side of the road. Long yeller mansion, set back a bit." Abruptly his full gaze settled upon her, intent, as if trying to divine her once and for all. He frowned. "That be a wicked place!" he blurted. "Wicked! And you goin' there all alone?!"

"Thank you, sir. Very much."

Pulling her hood up, she started off. A shallow roadside ditch separated her from the horse-drawn multitude, whose cacophony enveloped her. She kept her eyes low at first, then raised them to behold the endless, jumbled caravan–lantern after muted lantern in the dark slow current, the dust-cloud overhead like a ghostly miles-long serpent, trailing northward.

She stumbled over a fallen branch but caught herself, then continued at an even stride. On her left, woods hemmed her in for a while but then started thinning out. By the road some distance ahead, lighted houses began to appear. Just then she was startled to see a low shape moving along the ditch, coming toward her. Halting, she watched as the shape resolved itself into a spotted dog. It snuffled to within a few yards and then recoiled with a growl and a whine, sniffing the air. The mongrel's eyes glinted as it scuttled around her–two points of luminous green, frantic with the knowledge of night, chaos and long odds.

Sapphira kept on and soon passed the first ramshackle house, where an old couple sat watching on the porch. Presently she came to another home. At the fence stood a silent family of six, none of whom seemed to notice her passing. Once more she made herself look at the bustling road. She let the noises fill her, felt the rhythmic tap of the pistol against her thigh. From beneath a fringed canopy, one dim face glanced down at her, but the rest gazed numbly ahead.

The woods had fully receded when she saw a cottage some twenty feet back from the road. The light from the open door silhouetted a small, bent observer holding a candle, its flicker revealing the face of an old black woman. Passing by, Sapphira gave an absent nod of greeting, then slowed as the frail sentinel gazed at her.

"Missy, is that you?!"

Recognition brought Sapphira to a standstill. It was Mother Sadie, the herb woman, who she had greeted at church only this morning.

The old woman came tottering up, one hand clutching a frayed shawl to her breast. She spoke in a dry hush. "Missy, what're you doin' out this way? Rebels comin'–don't you know?"

Sapphira wanted to move on but could only fidget. Reaching out, her hand enclosed the veined little fist that clutched the shawl. "I'll be all right, Mother Sadie."

From the shadowed folds of her face, the woman's eyes glistened up, disbelieving. "With all them gray soldiers plaguin' the land? No, missy– you best stay here with Sadie. I make us some mint tea. Come sunup, we go down the road to the church and take us sanc'chary." Letting go of the shawl, she grasped Sapphira's fingers. "Come on, chile."

Sapphira stared at the lamp-lit cottage doorway. "Sanctuary"–like a warm strong hand, those syllables enfolded her. Weakening, she suddenly pictured the auction block in New Orleans. She could see the crowd but not herself, and she wondered how she had looked on that day. And how had her birth mother looked? Her birth father? She wondered what her true date of birth was, her precise age. Given the good fortune of her life, these answerless questions had always seemed unworthy. Nowadays she seldom experienced them as questions, more often as a mysterious sting shooting through her, like sparks from an anvil.

Sapphira looked down at the candle flame, then at Mother Sadie's small hand. Bending, she kissed the knobby knuckles and slipped her own hand free. "Bless you, ma'am–I cannot stop here."

As she hurried away, the herb woman's cries pursued her, shrill above the road noise: "Missy, come on back here! Where you goin'?! Missy, WHERE YOU GOIN'?!"

Once the cries had dissolved behind her, she looked up and saw that a rolling grassy field now bordered the road, pale-bright beneath the moon. She pulled her hood down. She looked at the procession on her right–the sullen monotony of wheels and horses, of faces and lanterns and baggage, the silvery dust swirling high. Slowing, she began to breathe more evenly. For a moment all noise seemed to fade, and she realized that she no longer had to look. Separate from the spectacle–alone, on foot and moving in the opposite direction–she was somehow still part of it. Small and anonymous, she was part of it, for the night had made small, anonymous beings of everyone. Strangers on the fear-borne tide.

Wanting a better view of what lay ahead, she veered into the field. Dimly she made out a bridge that spanned a creek and forced traffic into a bottleneck, the vehicles creeping singly across. Soon she came to the creek and found it all but dry, a bed of smooth rocks and muddy rivulets. She lifted her skirts, stepping carefully from rock to rock. From the bridge, she heard two men in a loud dispute over whose turn it was.

With a final giant step, she made the opposite bank and trudged her way up. The ground crested and she resumed her steady gait, letting her arms swing free. The warm air was like petals on her skin, her cloak's hem whispering over the grass. Stars jeweled and dusted the night–and suddenly, at the farthest corner of her mind, she saw herself. Not her physical being, but something which she knew to be her essence. The slightest pinpoint of fire, like one of those fainter stars that were visible only from the eye's margin.

Again she became aware of the pistol at her side and wanted to hold it, to see how it felt now. Without stopping, she brushed her cloak back and drew the weapon. Its weight and balance felt perfect, as if it had been molded for her hand alone. Yet her hand felt oddly distant–and abruptly, so did the rest of her, as if she were gliding a few feet above herself. But this sensation too proved fleeting. Back in her body, she envisioned the Rebel swarm just a few miles away. Agents of wrath–thousands of them, like a gale descending. But her fear was gone, absorbed into the firmament. Her purpose had returned. Drumming in her heart, it was back, urging her toward deliverance or obliteration–she did not care which.

She thought of her imperiled father–but his image faded as the night gaped, taking her into its depths. There were the star-billows and the high hunched moon and the pistol in her hand–the teeming road with its spectral dust and lanterns and the Colt Dragoon in her hand–the marauding Rebels unseen and the smooth metal weapon tight in her hand. She was muttering with each breath–a prayer, she supposed, or just gibberish. But it was neither. Tilting her face to the moonglow, she pressed on, tireless, scarcely believing the words tumbling out of her:

"Lay on. Lay on, Johnny Reb. Shake the earth, fire the cannon, rattle the chains, storm the walls, humble the spires, shame the buildings and trample the last drop of pride from this cursed city. Give us a reckoning."

PART IX

Lucifer's Drum

Charge once more, then, and be dumb!
Tell the victors, when they come,
When the forts of folly fall,
Find thy body by the wall!
• Matthew Arnold,
The Last Word

83

La Maison De l'Empereur
10 P.M.

THE GOWN SMELLED of decades-old perfume, of vanished youth, of Marseille. Standing before the gilded full-length mirror, Yvette de Ravenel regarded herself while the colored maid arranged the marabou feathers around her shoulders and neck. As usual she avoided looking at her own face, concentrating instead on the ruby necklace, the silver filigree earrings and especially the black satin gown, its breast and sleeves adorned with red fleur-de-lis. She had last worn it some thirty years ago, at a public *fete* celebrating the King's birthday. Arriving on the arm of a dissolute marquis, she had relished the looks of lust, fear and consternation that she provoked, each one signifying her hard-won notoriety. During the evening, however, a rash young heiress snubbed her and made her feel like the girl that she had once been: Yvette Vachon, the scorned waif from Guadeloupe, daughter of a prostitute and a disgraced naval officer. Three weeks afterward, the heiress was found disemboweled in the bed of her drug-addled lover; the unfortunate man recalled nothing about the night before and went swiftly to the guillotine.

Even without taking her beginnings into account, Ravenel had done spectacularly well for herself. With salons and bordellos as her battlefield, she had grown into that rarity, a female Napoleon. In the hall of her main establishment in Marseille, a painting of the late Emperor on his rearing white horse Marengo greeted visitors. But it hung there for a more private reason, as a reminder of those qualities that had taken her this far: wits, ruthlessness and a diamond-hard will.

She ran her fingertips down her flowing ash-colored hair. Wishful, she chanced a direct look into the mirror, but the gown and jewelry had altered nothing about her face, an angular ruin. Though she was in her mid-sixties and had endured much in life, nothing quite explained how her face had turned so fully against her.

With her feathers arranged, Ravenel turned and left the bedchamber, the maid padding after her. In the hall, she paused at the sound of girlish group laughter. She had thought it best to keep her dozen girls drunk on champagne and confined to the upstairs sitting room. With no customers around and Monroe absent, the chance of escape attempts had risen.

"Go see to them," she told the maid, who curtsied and hurried away.

Ravenel proceeded in the other direction, down the lamp-lit hall. Entering the south pavilion, she opened a pair of French doors and stepped onto the balcony. Out there along the Seventh Street Road, the sluggish flow of vehicles continued toward the sham safety of Washington. The sight transfixed her. Again the past swirled up.

Like her youth and allure, Marseille was no more than a perfumed dream, its fire and glitter fading with the years. The painting of Napoleon on Marengo was gone too, stolen or misplaced in her hasty decampment for the New World. All of this pained her but she tried not to dwell upon it. America had furnished enough pliant, desperate little beings to fit her purposes, letting her achieve an approximation of what she had lost. Moreover, this night promised a crowning satisfaction–triumph, on a scale that no other time and place could have offered. Tonight she would preside over a country's debacle.

Without the fortune in gold, she would not have committed herself to the plan. The gold guaranteed that she would come out ahead. It swelled her power and multiplied what options she might enjoy in the years remaining. Resolved to maintain La Maison in an even more lavish style, she had many other decisions to make. But whatever new scheme she embarked upon, Monroe would figure into it–Monroe, her *bete magnifique.* So would her simpering lieutenant Dubray, her one living link to the old days.

Though she had told Monroe to do his utmost at Fort DeRussy, the ultimate success or failure of Southern arms meant little to her. She had fulfilled her part of the bargain, and if General Early's assault merely prolonged the war instead of finishing it, so much the better. In that case, the South might go on paying for her rarefied services. Meanwhile, through the doors of La Maison, the nightly parade of puppets would continue.

Yet even the gold felt secondary. At this hour, what mattered most were the endless cargoes of fright along the road. Abruptly she cautioned herself, resisting the rise of exultation in her breast. "Too soon," she thought. Behind her, from down the hall, she heard Ursula bawling orders at the maid. In a moment, the big-boned German appeared at her side.

"Madame—Mister Wakefield asks vat you vish for now to do vith Major Truly."

With a new jolt of pleasure, Ravenel remembered the unexpected prize that Wakefield had brought. "Tell Wakefield I will be down presently."

"And also, Madame—Mister Archer says he requires of me."

"See to him, then. But make quick work of it."

"Ja, Madame." Ursula left.

Amid swirls of moonlit dust, the horse-drawn exodus shuddered on. Placing her hands on the balustrade, Ravenel at last gave in to jubilation. She was indeed an empress, a conquering admiral at the helm. Who would have thought that at this late stage, her destiny and that of a nation would so gloriously intersect? That she would transcend the petty business or whores, murder and blackmail to ignite conflagration? That Yvette Vachon de Ravenel, born to contempt and privation, would become the bloody hand of history?

ACROSS FROM WAKEFIELD and the young ruffian named George, Truly sat listing in a plush chair. He was still wearing the blood-flecked leather apron. The throbbing had begun to diminish in his back and ribs, though not in his head. As the clock struck the hour, he shut his eyes and stuck a finger in his ear.

On the jarring, roundabout trip to La Maison, he had assessed his situation and found no way out of it. A few times he had thought of jumping from the wagon, but physical pain and Archer's vigilant revolver had stopped him. For the moment, he could only recall certain episodes from his past and squeeze a desperate faith out of them—those times when he had confronted apparent doom and yet managed to escape. But as his eyes darted to the parlor entrance and the front hall beyond, a chalky taste rose in his mouth. And the cold-steel words reverberated—"Monroe wants him alive."

Archer had disappeared somewhere. Slouched at one end of the lace-cushioned sofa, Wakefield rested his pistol on the sofa's arm. In the Argand lamp's unsparing glow, fatigue lined his face. The Confederate had seemed to grow more morose on the way here, frustrated as the refugee traffic forced one detour after another. At the sofa's other end, George held his pistol stiffly on his knee. He appeared uncomfortable yet fascinated with his surroundings. From some echoey region of the house, giddy female laughter spilled down and made the youth stir, his blemished face expectant.

The laughter trickled away and Truly heard someone descending the staircase. With a shudder he hoped that it was just Ursula again, but the steps were too slow; he braced himself as they reached the hall, drawing nearer. A man's shadow cut into the parlor. Then Dubray stood there, dressed in a pea-green clawhammer coat. His specs gleamed as he grinned over at Truly.

"*Tiens,* Major—you seem a good deal more subdued this time."

Truly looked away.

Dubray ogled the near side of Truly's head, the hair sticky with blood. An arch solicitude entered his voice. "A little accident? You should let me examine that."

"I suspect your cures would finish me off, Dubray."

"Ah, but suspicion is part of your trade, n'est pas?" He wagged his finger. "You are wrong to doubt my skill. Back in Marseille . . . "

"Back in Marseille, I'm sure you did your share of mischief. Touch me and you'll lose that pretty face of yours."

The doctor chortled. "From one in your position, such threats sound a trifle hollow."

"So, Wakefield—this is the company you keep?"

George cocked his weapon. "I'd bite my tongue if I was you, Yankee."

Wakefield gave his henchman a weary look, then turned it on Dubray. "Silence is golden. Make yourself scarce, would you?"

Dubray's smile dimmed, edging on a sneer. "You forget, Wakefield, that you are still a guest here. I am a resident."

Slowly the Confederate stood up, the pistol dangling from his hand. He leveled a stare at Dubray, who began to step backward but then

straightened up, gripping his lapels. "Yet . . . I am gracious enough to
honor your request. I do have a request of my own, however." He smirked
down at Truly. "Much of my research requires human subjects. Therefore,
I ask that the major be turned over to me in due course–once Monroe is
finished with him. Whatever his condition . . . "

"Get out," said Wakefield.

With a sniff, Dubray strode out of the parlor. Truly drew a silent breath,
trying to quell the nausea creeping into him. Shifting position, he eyed
Wakefield, who had retaken his seat.

"Cowards can be dangerous," said Truly. "When they retaliate, they're
sneaky about it."

Wakefield peered at him, then gave an absent nod.

"By any chance, Wakefield, do you know what your man Monroe wants
with me?"

"No."

"Well, I have some idea. Seventeen years ago . . . "

"I don't care, Truly."

"Seventeen years ago, down in Mexico . . . "

"I think Mister Wakefield wants you to shut up," George intoned.

Wakefield's gaze sharpened. "Listen–I have what you'd call a marriage
of convenience with these people, Monroe included. I don't have to like
them. As a representative of the Northern government, you've no doubt
seen similar arrangements–maybe participated in a few?"

"Sure. Lafe Baker and I, for one jolly example. But this gang here–I'd
say they're in a class by themselves, wouldn't you?"

Wakefield sat up, placing the pistol across his knee. "And you're asking whether I've searched my soul over that, are you? Well, Major . . . " His
cheeks grew red, his voice almost guttural. "Thank you ever so much for
your concern–but perhaps one of us can afford such a high-minded consideration, while the other cannot. And let me tell you–few things sound
quite as ludicrous as high-minded talk from a Yankee!"

George appeared lost, glancing from one man to the other. In
Wakefield's intent brown eyes, Truly sensed not just rage but a rage to
be understood. Then he wondered if the impression was merely wishful,
born of his own clammy fear.

"Mister Wakefield," came a husky female voice.

Looking up, Truly saw Ursula dressed in burgundy crinoline, filling
the parlor entrance.

"Madame says she vill come down shortly."

Slouched again, Wakefield nodded at his knees. Ursula sent Truly a look of disdain, then turned and left. Another burst of distant feminine laughter came floating down, pulling George to attention. Truly eyed Wakefield's cradled pistol; it was pointed away from him. He considered lunging for the weapon, but Wakefield's hand tightened on it.

The Southerner spoke in a quiet drawl. "Can you tell me how Delia is?"

Truly blinked at the pistol. "Who?"

"I'm asking how she is, not where. I assume she's out of my reach."

"All right, then–she is well. She asks you to understand that she could take no more of this place. She prays to see you again."

Wakefield contemplated the angels and flowers in the carpet weave. "Thank you."

Quiet fell, except for the clock's ticking. George had his pistol aimed at Truly's stomach. From his frame above the fireplace, Napoleon maintained his imperial stare. Truly, his head throbbing, stared into the folds of his blood-dappled apron. He could only hope that the last batch of prints had included the correct one, and that Forbes was taking action. Still, he told himself, it would be best not to think of that. Best to concentrate on the moment–to wait and watch, trusting his luck. Was there any greater optimist than a man condemned?

84

North District Perimeter
10:15 P.M.

RIDING WEST ON the Bladensburg Road, Tucker saw the Seventh Street cross-roads straight ahead, with an endless procession of southbound vehicles. Wheels and hooves raised a curtain of dust to the moonlight, through which he saw higher ground and then the beveled walls of Fort Stevens. He slowed as he neared the congested thoroughfare and then turned to ride alongside it, opposite the traffic's flow. In the murky lantern light, a succession of drawn white faces looked down at him, but he paid no attention.

Tucker's gelding huffed and snorted. This strenuous and as-yet fruit-less search had improved his horsemanship threefold, he judged, though he realized the slightness of such a claim. Aware that he had reached the search area's midpoint, he wondered if Forbes had found and appre-hended the traitor Monks. Then again, had the captain's information been sound to begin with? Tucker could only hope so.

He had passed Stevens before a gap in the caravan allowed him to cut across and start backtracking. Behind a little vale, the fort stood with its staked walls and platformed cannon. Torches lit the ramparts at intervals, with sentries pacing. Along its front lay piles of felled timber and, closer in, a long rifle pit with capped heads peering north. Tucker came to a high arched gateway by the road, torch-lit and topped with the Stars 'n'

Stripes. Staring at its timber doors, he steeled himself. His reception at the seven preceding forts had ranged from bland to bemused to scornful. What would it be this time?

"Who goes?!"

On the wall by the stone arch, two soldiers stood clutching their rifles. Tucker straightened up as he entered the firelight, the sentries staring down at him. They lowered their weapons. As with most of the troops that Tucker had encountered tonight, their uniforms marked them as hundred-day state militia. One was fair-haired and spindly while the other was dark and thickset, with a drooping mustache.

"Can you tell me," Tucker called, "if a Lieutenant-Colonel Orlando Monks is in command here, or somewhere close by?"

The one with the mustache glanced at his partner, who looked dumbstruck.

"Monks," Tucker said. "Lieutenant-Colonel."

The spindly one shrugged. "I don't . . . Hans, do you know who's commandin'?"

The other replied in a German accent. "Na, I don't know nuttin'." Leaning back, he looked over his shoulder. "Sergeant! Who, sir, is command of us? You know this?"

"Who's asking?" came a peevish voice.

The German pointed down. "This one."

A dim figure appeared, leaning over the parapet. Tucker's side had begun to ache once more. "Sergeant, I've been sent from General McCook's headquarters to . . . "

"Well, look at this! We're scraping the bottom of the barrel, sure enough."

Tucker's nerves flared, the ache spreading as he stared up. Above him, the sergeant was just a stout form carved from shadow, his face invisible.

"So what is it, buck?"

Tucker forced his voice to a stentorian level. "I've been sent to find out if Lieutenant-Colonel Orlando Monks is in charge here, or anyplace nearby."

The shadow-form snickered. "So, how's it feel to be all decked out like a real soldier?"

Tucker heard a shuffling. On either side of the capped silhouette, others poked up.

"Hey, boys–feature this," called the sergeant.

"Do you know the name?" Tucker barked.

"You wouldn't be getting short with me, would you?"

Tucker's gaze swept the palisade–the watchful shapes, the sergeant's stout figure, the archway with the limp flag. "Short?" he said. "No, Sergeant–not at all. If you please, though, do you know of a Lieutenant-Colonel Monks?"

The sergeant made a spitting noise. "Can't say I do, laddie-boy."

"Anyone else up there–do you know the name?"

After a pause, there were two or three mumbles of "no."

"If I say there's no damned Monks here, then there ain't," growled the sergeant. "Now–you'd best be off. I fancy McCook's waiting to get his boots shined."

Someone chuckled.

Tucker had thought himself inured to it by now–but his gut was suddenly a furnace. He imagined reaching up the sloped height of the wall, his arm stretching like a cable and his hand an iron claw, to take the man's face. Without a word, Tucker turned his horse–and as he rounded the fort's rear corner, a rifle shot startled him almost out of the saddle. The gelding broke into a gallop. He held tight as the ground began to dip, aware of hard laughter from above. Then the ground grew even, letting him bring the horse to a gradual stop.

Catching his breath, he looked up at the stars and then all around. In the gloom he saw the fort's outbuildings: officers' quarters, a privy, a row of barracks. He had entered a hollow in back of Stevens, whose torch-studded outline loomed on his right. The horse snorted as if in indignation. Like rage made flesh, Tucker now felt the pain of his wound–a fiery coal in his side, trying to burn its way out. As the pain passed, he flexed his leather-sore hands and thought of the sergeant, that stout silhouette peering down. How often had he encountered this same tormenter, the guise and voice scarcely differing each time?

With a blind man's caution, he guided his horse out of the hollow and emerged into moonlight. A rougher, narrower road took him away from the fort, past woods, grain fields and flowering trees. A black finger of cloud crossed the moon. Perhaps he would find Monks at the next stop–or better, find him already in Forbes' custody. Once they had jailed the traitor, they could rush to Major Truly's aid. And to Sapphira's aid as well? Riding faster, he gritted his teeth against the ache. Having consulted his map several times already, he knew that he was on Milkhouse Ford Road. A short distance ahead, it would ford Rock Creek and take him to the next federal bastion, Fort DeRussy.

85

La Maison De l'Empereur
10:15 P.M.

STANDING IN THE parlor entrance, Ravenel gave Truly a ceremonious nod. In her black gown and white costume feathers, she looked like a mythical being–part woman, part vulture. At her side she clasped a silver derringer. "I would like a moment alone with the major."

Wakefield uncrossed his legs. Holding his pistol steady, he looked mystified and then annoyed. "That might not be wise."

"Go have a drink, Wakefield. I am armed, and this young man of yours . . . " She glanced at George, who had not stopped gazing at her. Taken off guard, he blurted his name. "Monsieur George," she said. "You may stand outside the parlor."

George got up. With a sigh, Wakefield did the same and the two exited past Ravenel. She crossed the room and eased into a fanback wicker chair near the hearth. In all of her feathered, bejeweled majesty, she sat cradling the derringer, gazing up at Napoleon's portrait. Truly eyed her little silver weapon, then sent a furtive glance to the hall. He saw George's shadow.

Ravenel smiled, presenting a barricade of yellowed teeth. "And is it not a relief, Major, when all masks are put aside? When intelligent people may converse frankly?"

"Oh, yes. A privilege, for certain."

"*Vraiment!* For too brief a moment, we may abandon thoughts of gain or loss. Therefore, Major, I tell you–any man who stirs such special regard in Mister Monroe stirs the same in me."

Truly's eyes moved to the clock. He wished that it could tell more than the time.

"It will be a while yet before he returns," she said. "Would you like a drink?"

"No, thank you."

"But you do know Monroe from somewhere else?"

"We have met before."

"Ah, the strangeness of fate! Do tell me about it."

"Haven't you asked him?"

"Monroe and I have shared much, Major, but this one secret he stubbornly withholds. Hence my fascination. But then, I have always found him fascinating. Do you not find him so?"

"Sure. A boil is fascinating in a way, before you lance it."

Pursing her long lips, she studied him. "I cannot convince myself that you of all people would settle for such an image. So base, so simple."

"I can think of others, Madam."

Resting her elbows on the wicker arms, she leaned forward. "I would much rather hear how you made Monroe's acquaintance. When and where? Come, now–we have time."

"Monroe is not his true name."

The skin of her sharp face seemed to tighten, the dark eyes twinkling. "I suspected not! Well, then–what is his true name?"

Beneath his lingering pain, Truly felt a twist of satisfaction. He had something that she wanted. And if he was not destined to survive this night, he could at least use his exclusive molehill of knowledge to draw something out of her. "Tell me, Madam–how did *your* path cross with his?"

"See there–you too are curious! Delightful!" She settled back comfortably. "It was here, one busy night in the year of '58. When I received him, he presented a letter of reference. It said that he was the grand-nephew of the late President Monroe, and that he had recently returned from the failed American adventure in Nicaragua. This interested me, of course, but mostly I was struck by his presence–smooth and cordial and yet altogether manly, with something else that was less definable. Later I was conversing with patrons when a servant informed me of a disturbance upstairs.

A scream had been heard from one of the bedrooms and my enforcer, a brutish yet obedient man from Marseille, had gone to investigate.

"I found Monroe in the room, straightening his clothes. On the floor was poor Marcel, strangled with a piece of wire. Huddled in a corner was one of my jeune filles–naked and somewhat bruised, quite terrified. Understand, Major, that I had seen much of violence before–and though I was in the presence of a uniquely dangerous individual, my reaction was more of wonder. I sensed that his storm was over–that I had little to fear, so long as I did not try to obstruct him. On an impulse, I asked him to describe what had just occurred, and he obliged me." Ravenel fondled the derringer, her voice drifting into reflection. "What most interested me was his calm. And his words to me–so refined and intelligent, despite the subject at hand. He had taken what he wanted and no more. He had released the beast within himself and then commanded it back into its cage. Doubtless he recognized that I too was unusual. So I closed the door, inquired about his present circumstances and then made my proposal, with certain conditions. Obviously I needed a replacement for Marcel. Monroe accepted, and that night the body was quietly disposed of.

"Soon it became clear that Monroe would be wasted as a mere factotum. In him I beheld an equal–truthfully, the only one that I had ever deemed so. His talents qualified him as my partner, and since then he has shared equally in the profits." She dipped a mocking eye at Truly. "So you see, your tawdry estimate of him falls far, far short. An ordinary man may be but a blemish upon the Earth–but Monroe? In the study and practice of terror, he is a high priest."

As Ravenel's purring narrative wound to its end, Truly saw the courtyard in Mexico and the blood-spattered wall. He waited a moment before speaking. "He is good at killing, I'll grant you–so long as the advantage is all his. Let's look at his list of known victims, Madam. For Underhill he murdered a drunkard. For Van Gilder, a frail old publisher and that stooge attorney. Then there was Peavey's aging uncle and Archer's defenseless wife. I never learned who he killed for the lieutenant-colonel, but I fancy it was someone just as challenging. Speaking of that, what's the lieutenant-colonel's name?"

Ogling him, Ravenel gave a more muted smile. "So now you dismiss Monroe as . . . what? A common bully?!" She chuckled, shaking her ashen locks. "Such an obstinate man you are, Major. Need I explain that wolves kill sheep? Think of the nerve, the skill, the planning in each of those cases. How the authorities were left duped or baffled."

"So he's smart too. You both are. A mighty small point, but I'll grant it."

"As for your request for our lieutenant-colonel's name–honoring it would do no harm, at this stage. However, I have not yet heard Monroe's true name."

"It's Trajan Heath."

Touching her angular chin, she blinked. "Trajan Heath," she muttered. "Hm . . . Merci. Still, I believe that I will always think and speak of him as Monroe. Just Monroe."

"Suit yourself. And the lieutenant-colonel?"

"Monks, Major. Orlando Monks." She contemplated the carpet. "I tell you, it is remarkable. In times of peace–if any time may be so-called– enough pliant little men have appeared at my door. But in times of upheaval? Then they come swarming."

Truly nodded. "And it's no chore picking out the desperate ones, is it? The ones who might need your other services? After a drink or two and a bit of prodding, they let it slip–a curse, a gripe, a yelp of distress."

Her dreamy expression fell away and she looked pleased with him. "And sometimes it is just the look on their faces. Yes, that is indeed how we went about it–with five subjects, carefully selected. For the additional income and other advantages that I sought, five was a sufficient number. One must always be thinking ahead, buttressing oneself against misfortune. Little did I dream, however, that one of those whimpering five would prove far more valuable–the key to a much greater design."

"Monks, you mean."

"Monks, yes. And how did you say you met Monroe?"

"I didn't say. As you observed, Madam, we have the time. Please go on."

She sliced a smile at him. "Very well, Major. You merit a few answers. And I confess that after all this secrecy, it is enjoyable to find an appreciative ear."

She spoke of a clandestine meeting on All Hallows eve, 1861, at which each of the five men was made to speak his wish aloud. In exposing their baseness to one another, she reasoned, they confirmed it to themselves as well, and thus entered the pact in a more submissive spirit. Four of them were to make their first quarterly payment of $200–hefty enough, though within the means of each—in a month's time. Archer was privately exempted from payment, in recognition of his future value as a policeman. La Maison, for its part, would render its services with expert care, in a way that implicated no one.

Payments were to continue every three months for the next ten years, at which time the debt would terminate—except for Archer's non-monetary debt, which would continue indefinitely. And payments were to be made in person—a rule which assured discreet delivery, but which also gave the men a regular and palpable reminder of their bondage. Anyone who defaulted would face terrible consequences, as would anyone who revealed the pact to an outsider. There was, of course, no danger that any of them would ever go to the authorities, since that would reveal his own complicity. But as an added measure, they were forbidden to meet or communicate with one another; by thus isolating them, Ravenel sought to prevent any plan for united insurrection.

"But threats only go so far," she said. "How were we in fact to monitor our subjects? Monroe could not do it, though he served as an effective source of fear. His duties here kept him busy—and aside from that, he was known to the men. We wished to keep a frequent yet hidden eye upon them."

"And that's where Wakefield came in," said Truly.

"Yes, Major. In Washington, among those who ply this ancient trade of ours, one finds much sympathy for the Southern cause. Reaching into that community, I contacted the Confederate intelligence network and asked if we might strike a bargain. And to my great good fortune, the representative they sent was Wakefield—one of the few who could have filled this role in any satisfying fashion. Despite some of those frailties that afflict men in general, he had the cleverness and the subtlety that I required."

Full of zest and candor, Ravenel went on to confirm more of what Truly and Forbes had theorized. With contrived encounters and well-timed visits, Wakefield had gained each of the five's friendship and confidence, all the while looking for signs of indiscretion vis-a-vis La Maison. In return, select girls at the house obtained intelligence from high-placed federal clientele—secrets that Ravenel carefully screened before passing them along. Boastful officers, lovesick functionaries, besotted politicians—with these at its disposal, La Maison had played no small part in the capital's plague of intelligence leaks; at least twice, Ravenel claimed, the house had contributed directly to a Union military defeat. Moreover, Wakefield found collateral value in Monks and Underhill. In friendly conversation with one or the other, he gathered occasional tidbits on military plans and congressional infighting, respectively.

But over time, Wakefield spread himself too thin among the five, and the first real trouble caught him unawares. He should have foreseen that it would come from his least convenient subject, Van Gilder. Living farthest from Washington, Van Gilder was the one most likely to forget the warnings and fancy himself untouchable. Wakefield might have observed the symptoms had he not curtailed his visits to New York. But when June of '63 arrived, the proud Copperhead failed to appear with his two-hundred dollars.

Monroe favored the maximum punishment but Ravenel decided to keep the delinquent publisher alive, if not unhurt. She wanted to preserve the income. In a surprise visit from Monroe, Van Gilder suffered a nightlong session of terror, torture and then forced transcription. Within days, each of his fellows-in-bondage received a blood-flecked letter confessing his mistake and warning them against any similar action. The effect on each of them was as profound as if Van Gilder had been executed. As a final touch, his quarterly amount was doubled to four-hundred.

This episode made one thing plain: Wakefield needed help, another agent who could stay in New York and watch Van Gilder exclusively. For this, Wakefield produced Adam Cathcart. Cathcart met with Van Gilder, showed him his letter of introduction and, to really excite the Copperhead's interest, confided that he was a spy for Richmond. Shaken since his ordeal and still mending, Van Gilder welcomed the comfort of a new admirer and fellow partisan, an actual Southern spy. So commenced another sham friendship. Reporting by mail and wire to Wakefield, Cathcart was soon monitoring his subject's travels, visitors, correspondence and general behavior. Given the relative slightness of his assignment, Cathcart had time to perform unrelated tasks, such as gauging the level of anti-war sentiment in New York and funneling prepared subversive literature to the *Comet-American*.

The whole *quid pro quo* arrangement worked well until the early spring of this year. Then, abruptly, the stream of intelligence from La Maison patrons slowed to a trickle. Grant had taken command of all federal armies; in preparation for his great campaign, he had moved with vigor to seal off leaks. It was then that Wakefield had his grand and timely inspiration, a plan that made the original scheme dispensable.

"Thus, here we sit," lilted Ravenel, "on a momentous eve. Tomorrow, one world shall die in flame so that another may rise."

Truly found himself staring up at Napoleon, probing the ruler's obsidian eyes. "Leaving you well paid, no doubt."

"But of course, Major."

"Listen, though. If you had this fellow Monks in your control already, why this fancy procedure that involved the other four? Why didn't you simply threaten Monks into doing what you wanted?"

"*Mon Dieu*–all of this talk from me, and none from yourself! Tell me how you met Monroe."

"It was in Mexico, during the war down there."

"Interesting, but I asked how."

"Later, maybe. Why did you proceed as you did? Why that whole big ruse to entrap them, when you could have just focused on Monks and let the others be?"

She gave an airy sigh. "Have you no theory as to why? No guess?"

"I'm tired of guessing, Madam."

Again she raised her chin, tapping it with a finger until a smile appeared, more whimsical than before. "Perhaps a picture would help. A demonstration." Rising from the chair, she leveled the derringer. "Come, Major. I will show you."

Truly got up, feeling his bruises. Ravenel called George in and told him to accompany them upstairs. With the two muzzles at his back, Truly shambled out to the hall and past the ornamental shields, to the staircase. There, just below the mounted black drum, a large Stars 'n' Bars hung from the support beam.

"Ah," he said, "–announcing your heartfelt loyalty, eh?"

"Eventually it will be displayed over the front door," said Ravenel, "though it is too soon for that so now. But we have another flag over the back, should General Early's men approach from the woods. Given the habits of victorious troops, it is only prudent."

George spoke up. "Washington'll be seein' a lot of that flag, Yankee."

As Truly reached the foot of the stairs, Ravenel's voice halted him. "Just a moment, if you please." Looking over his shoulder, Truly ignored George's mannered ruffian glare and saw that Ravenel had backtracked. Over by the vestibule, she reached into a tall wicker basket and drew out a walking stick. "I used to ascend like a butterfly, but now? Oh, the woes of aging!" She tapped her way back toward the staircase. "Up we go." Trudging upstairs, Truly raised his eyes to the Confederate banner and then to the drum, that black anomaly. He eyed its white eagle symbol, the hooked beak and jagged wings.

"My uncle saved that in the retreat from Moscow," spoke Ravenel. "He was a marshal of the Empire."

"How proud for you, Madam." Truly passed the middle landing, where Marshal Ney's bust stood guard. "And how danged remarkable. The grand-nephew of a President and the niece of a Napoleonic bigwig, under one roof!" He heard the footfalls behind him, the bump of Ravenel's walking stick. He felt her eyes in his back. A little farther up, he realized that the footfalls had ceased. He halted and turned, seeing George a few steps below. Cocking his weapon, the youth stole a puzzled glance back at Ravenel, who remained on the landing. She leaned on her stick and met Truly's gaze. In her eyes, he grasped something eerily intimate. And he knew that his station had risen, from worthy plaything to object of hate. Down at Ravenel's side, the derringer glinted.

"I keep it for more than pride's sake," she said, her tone still airy. It took Truly a moment to realize that she was still talking about the drum. "There is a poetry about it, a savage bit of truth–savage, like anything pure. I care something for the truth, Major. When I look upon the drum, I think of how I have profited from this war. Then I think how strange it is that war yields so much talk of God. For their God men take up arms, and to their God they pray for victory. You have heard much of this too, I am certain."

"Too much, now that you mention it."

Her gaze left him and meandered up the staircase, losing itself in the high rafters. "And in reference to the opposing side, they speak of His antagonist, the Dark Emperor. They see two deities pitted against each other. But I see it differently–not as a contest of deities but as a joint enterprise, a partnership. In wartime, men of all flags may believe that they are answering heaven's trumpet and nothing else. Yet beneath those stirring notes, all the while, there is the beating of Lucifer's drum. Their minds may be too dim to name it, nor even to note its effect–but in their veins they feel it. And off they go, into the whirlwind, convinced it is God alone who summons them." Her eyes drew back and fixed upon him, bright and steady. "So, Major–how does my theology strike you?"

He shrugged. "I've heard worse."

"I was once a great beauty. Do you believe that?"

George was looking at her, uncomprehending. Truly wondered if this was the moment to lunge.

"Cast that silly thought from your head," she murmured. "Look at me and answer."

With his imagination, he tried to soften the crone features as he studied her. From her buzzard-like form, he tried to conjure an exquisite youthful one. "Yes. I believe it."

Slowly, her long lips made a smirk. "How gallant of you to say so." She raised the derringer. "Let us proceed."

At the top landing, she directed him to the left. From some room in the other direction, he heard a smatter of giggles and one girl's slurred, sobbing lament–"I vant to go home!" As Truly passed a series of closed doors, his ears caught another sound ahead of him, a repetitive snapping noise. It became a louder, sharper *thwack* as he neared the room of its source, which came up on his right. Amid the sound, he heard a grunted male command: "Read it! READ IT!!"

"You may stop there," came Ravenel's voice. "Monsieur George, open that next door. Then take that lamp from the wall."

Pointing his pistol, George sidled past Truly. He opened the specified door, then took the burning socket lamp from the wall beside it. From the preceding door, the razor-sharp *thwack* issued, along with the snarling voice: "Find it, goddamn you! Down the page!" George looked distracted as he motioned Truly into the dark room. Truly entered and the pair followed him, George placing the lamp on a dresser. They were in a small bedchamber. In the lamp's glow, Truly beheld his reflection in a full-length mirror–his cheek caked with blood, like the apron. From behind the nearest wall, the noise persisted, joined now by a husky, halting female voice, its words too muffled to hear.

Truly undid the apron straps and slipped the collar over his head.

"Yes–do shed that unsightly thing!" chirped Ravenel. "Then step over here." Having opened a closet, she gestured to it with the derringer.

With the leather apron bunched in his hand, Truly took two steps and stared into the empty closet.

"The panel in back," said Ravenel. "Slide it over."

The small white panel was set at chest level, on grooved runners. Stooping, Truly gripped the knob as another *thwack* issued from next door–and in that instant, he somehow knew what he would see. The panel slid aside to reveal a well-lit room and Ursula stripped to the waist, her breasts white and huge as she flailed the whip, landing it on Archer's naked back. On all fours, Archer bared his teeth and squeezed his eyes shut. Among the policeman's bleeding lash-marks, Truly noticed a pale crosshatch of healed ones.

Ursula paused with the whip. Flushed, she squinted at a thick open volume which she held against her forearm. Through the breathless murk of her accent, she declaimed: "'Nor thieves–nor the greedy–nor drunk-ards–nor revilers–nor . . . '"

"Wrong passage!" Archer shouted. "Wrong passage, you cow! 'Know ye not that he which is!'"

Sneering at the text, she flexed her whip arm before droning on: "'Know ye not that he vich is joined to a harlot . . . '" Already her hips were in motion, the whip arcing. "' . . . is one body?!'" The lash brought a half-stifled cry from Archer, whose blood dotted Ursula's white belly. Swiveling back again, she kept reading: "'For two, saith he, shall be one flesh. But he that is joined to the Lord is one spirit. Flee fornication!'" The whip snaked out and struck.

"Bitch!" cried Archer. "Oh, you whore!"

Truly looked away. With a satisfied expression, Ravenel leaned on her stick while George stood dumbfounded.

"A tormented soul, as they say," said Ravenel. "I have heard that he has delivered many a strong sermon to *les femmes de la ville* at the city jail. In your experience, Major, have you not noticed how an outward rage toward the flesh may conceal an equally fierce craving?"

George crouched, gaping past Truly.

"This is how Wakefield got the photographs," Truly muttered.

Ravenel nodded. "In Archer's case we needed as much assurance as possible, else he might turn his official powers against us. Had he made any such move, prints would have been released to his superiors, to his church, to the more scandalous newspapers. And I must say that Archer has served us well."

With huffing emphasis, Ursula was repeating the scriptural passage. Another lash, another sputtered curse. Truly did not look. Instead, with the barest turn of his head, he peered back at George. Still gawking, the youth had inched past Ravenel to the closet threshold. He blocked most of the lamplight but Truly could still see the pistol pointed at the floor, dangling carelessly from two fingers.

"Fine, Madam. But if there's some grand illustration here, I've missed it."

"You asked why we carried out things as we did."

"Yes. Why did you?"

"I credit myself with some insight into the mortal mind, but here I must credit Wakefield. The idea was his–and when he explained it, I had to concede its worth. You see, Major . . . How did you meet Monroe?"

"Go on, please."

"Obstinate man–here it is, then. In our lives, we each adopt a code of sorts, without which we are lost . . . "

Half-listening to her, he tried to ignore the ongoing sounds of Archer's penitence. With one eye he watched George's crouched form and dangling weapon, just a few feet behind him. His hand squeezed the wadded apron. Stooping a bit lower, he braced his foot against the wall.

"A system of reward and punishment," Ravenel was saying. "Just now, evidently, Archer believes himself in need of the latter. The code differs from one individual to the next, but the important thing is that it remain intact . . . "

Staring into the plaster, Truly relaxed his grip on the apron and let some of it unfurl.

"Yet if the rules are preserved, and a subject violates them, he will accept the consequences. In his heart, he will understand it as his due. He will submit, so long as he feels assured of survival. Lieutenant-Colonel Monks, therefore, was led to transgress . . . "

Truly sprang shoulder-first, backwards, flinging the apron into George's face. An elbow to the jaw sent the youth stumbling back as Truly lurched after him, groping madly for the pistol. He seized the weapon by its muzzle end and jerked it free–but at the same instant, in his side-vision, Ravenel hopped nimbly out of the way and whirled to face him. He had not been quick enough–she had a clear shot. But what he felt next was a hard, precise blow to the forearm, knocking the pistol from his hand. Recoiling, he lost his balance as a second blow glanced off his shoulder. Then he lay against the closet door, clutching his forearm as Ravenel peered down at him. Pointing the derringer, she held the walking stick at an upward angle, sword-like. Around her shoulders, her downy white feathers were askew, but her face betrayed neither anger nor alarm. George appeared beside her. Red-faced, he gripped his recovered pistol.

Truly's teeth were clenched, his arm throbbing.

George swung his foot back for a kick but Ravenel's stick sliced in front of him. Faltering, he blinked at her.

"Do not blame him for your own carelessness," she said. Her look of amused curiosity returned. "And we do not want him too damaged. Mister Monroe would be disappointed, I sense."

Trying to shut the words out, Truly flexed his arm. Despite the pain, he decided it was only a deep bruise. "That was right agile of you, Madam."

Ravenel spun a neat pirouette. "These legs have danced many a waltz, Major!" She waved the stick. "I brought this as a modest alternative to shooting you, should you prove less than cooperative." Again she aimed the derringer. "Be assured, though—a repeat attempt will cost you a hand. Possibly a foot." His eyes locked upon the stick—the quartz head, the lacquered shaft. Ravenel noticed him looking, then glanced at it herself. "Ah, yes—a memento of your little German friend. The imposter."

Before Truly's stare, the quartz gleamed like ice—and as he glared up at Ravenel, a molten hatred surged. "The world's full of imposters," he croaked.

In her eyes, the amusement flickered out.

"You want to hear about my first howdy-do with Trajan Heath? All right. It was just after he'd murdered a small Mexican girl and raped her mother. We had ourselves a little tussle, and you know what? In a fair fight, he's not much." Truly's lips drew back. "Lord, didn't he howl, though! Down on his knees, he howled—for his worthless stinking life. And if my captain hadn't stopped me, Madam, you'd have never met your ever-so-wondrous equal."

Gradually Ravenel's yellowed smile arose, a bit tentative this time. "Such a poor tale, Major. Quite unworthy of you."

Truly drew a tight breath. "You would say that, wouldn't you? So I reckon it's useless to mention the big ol' gash I left on his head. That was my memento to him. I just wish to Christ I'd kept carving . . . " He yelled as the stick jabbed into his stomach. Buckling in pain, he heard another whip-crack from the next room.

"At last, Truly," said Ravenel, flat-voiced, "you have wearied me."

SAPPHIRA HAD TRIED the cellar bulkhead but found it secured. Since then, she had done nothing except haunt the shadows. From the sheds to the smokehouse to the stable to the carriage house, she skulked, pausing repeatedly to stare at the mansion. Her thoughts too traveled back and forth, wearing her nerves down. How to get inside? How to avoid detection? Was he really in there? Was it too late? Taking action, at this point, required a precise and practical knowledge that seemed beyond her. Leaning against a corner of the smokehouse, she tried to hold still. She gazed across the grounds, past the well, the garden and the latticed arbor. Draped above the veranda, a large Confederate battle flag proclaimed the stuff of her nightmares. It was more than a banner, there to welcome the forces of slavery. It was a sentinel beast whose star-eyes glared back at her, announcing a more potent threat within.

The veranda windows were lit and so were several on the second floor. At the near end, a pair of them had their sashes up and curtains partly drawn. Out of these, girlish laughter continued to trickle down. Sapphira considered looking for something to stand on, so she could start hunting for an unsecured first-floor window. Touching the pistol beneath her cape, she was working up the nerve when a veranda door swung open. Down the steps came a colored woman in a maid's white bonnet and apron, a pail in each hand. She proceeded toward the well.

Gliding through the dark, Sapphira passed behind the sheds and then crept in a semi-circle, skirting the woods. Then, in a straight line, she proceeded to the arbor and slipped inside it. She peered through the latticework. The maid was a short, thirtyish mulatta, listless as she hauled up the well bucket; her return steps would take her past the arbor. Crouched, Sapphira waited amid the sweet scent of the roses, still unsure of what to do. A stray breeze riffled the vines. It seemed a long time before the maid had filled both pails and started back to the house, slopping water as she went. Sapphira stepped from the shadows.

With a gasp, the maid dropped the pails. Sapphira rushed up to her, grabbing her shoulder and jamming a hand over her mouth. "Hush!" she whispered, but the woman began pushing away. With a burst of strength, Sapphira seized her around the waist, keeping her mouth covered as she dragged her out of the veranda's light. "I won't hurt you!" Sapphira hissed. "Hush, or they'll hear!" On an impulse, she added, "You know what they're like!" The maid went still.

In the moonlight Sapphira gazed into the woman's large wet eyes, then let the hand slip from her mouth. She felt her trembling. "I'm sorry," Sapphira murmured. "But there's something . . . " She eyed the woman's dusky cheek; it looked swollen. "Someone hit you?" The maid swallowed, then nodded. Glancing at the house, Sapphira listened; all she heard was more girl-laughter, mingled with wagon noise from the road out front. She pointed toward the big flag above the veranda. "You know what that means?" she whispered. Still mute, the woman looked. "The Rebel army is coming. The slavemen's army, coming to take Washington." Still gazing at the flag, the maid began fiddling with her apron strings. Sapphira pulled her closer. "The people in this house–you know they're evil. And now they're welcoming the Rebels. What will become of you here?"

The woman appeared dazed. Then a voice emerged, low and quavering. "I got young 'uns . . . I needs the work."

"If you have children, you must go to them. The Rebels are close. Go home now. Come first light, take your children down the road. Near Boundary and Tenth Street you'll find the Church of the Holy Kingdom. Reverend Cass will do all he can for your safety. But understand this: you have worked your last night here."

As Sapphira let go of her, the maid touched her swollen cheek. "Yes, Miss," she quavered.

"Now, please tell me–are they holding a white man prisoner in there?" Sapphira's question trailed off as she held her breath. The woman nodded. Sapphira felt the heat of renewed urgency. "Where in the house are they keeping him?"

"I don't know, Miss."

"Who else is inside?"

The maid was staring at Sapphira's hip. Sapphira looked down and saw that the sides of her capuchin had parted, revealing the pistol in its holster. "Who else?!" she hissed.

The maid gazed up, her expression suddenly keen. "Miz Rav'nel," she whispered. "An' Doctor Dubray. Mister Wakefield too, with a younger fella. An' that police, Archer. An' Urs'la–her too. An' the young ladies– they upstairs, all drunk."

"Are there other servants?"

"Not tonight, Miss. Only me."

Sapphira counted off the individuals–six of them, excluding the drunk girls. Then it struck her that the most fearsome name was missing. "And Monroe?" she asked.

The maid's mouth fell slack. It was a moment before she replied. "He gone now. Be back later, I reckon . . . Miss, they's wicked, all right–but that Mister Monroe . . . You run up 'gainst him, you best use that." She nodded at the pistol. "Use it good."

Touching the holster, Sapphira felt cold at the center of her chest. "What is your name?"

"Nora, Miss."

She slipped off her capuchin. "Miss Nora, I must make a trade with you."

86

North District Perimeter
10:40 P.M.

HALFWAY ACROSS THE little plank bridge, Tucker stopped to peer over the side. In the gloom below, he discerned stumps, boulders and the faint glistening of puddles. Farther up, like a giant beaver dam, felled trees filled the ravine while others lay piled on both banks, forming a continuous bulwark. It would impede any significant Rebel movement down Rock Creek Valley. Touched with awe, Tucker pondered the expenditure of sweat, blood and will that war exacted. Death alone defined its limit, without which no tree would be left standing, no field untrampled, the whole of Earth used up.

He crossed the bridge, turned off the road and dismounted. Glad again for the moonlight, he led his horse through a maze of stumps and bushes, past the empty platforms of a gun battery, while ahead of him several low structures took shape–Fort DeRussy's outbuildings. Just beyond these, by a wooded hill, the fort itself appeared like a whale's hump tinged with firelight. To the right, on DeRussy's north side, the road looped past while a manned rifle pit ran parallel, indicated by shuffling sounds and the glint of small weaponry. Tucker wondered what reception awaited him this time. With his horse in tow, he passed between two log barracks and emerged beside the fort–mid-sized, smaller than Stevens. Several feet above him, a sentry paced in a sleepy rhythm. Tucker was about to call out when his gelding snorted.

Jerking to a stop, the militiaman swung his rifle about and called into the darkness. "Ho, there! Show yourself!"

"Ease up, soldier," said Tucker.

Lowering his weapon, the militiaman peered down. His shaggy, rangy silhouette suggested a farm boy–another gawking bumpkin. Suddenly hot with defiance, Tucker moved into a patch of fluttery torchlight and stared up. His challenger said nothing.

"Soldier," Tucker spoke, "can you tell me . . . ?"

"Sutherland–who's there?"

From behind the young sentry, a hatted shape appeared. Tucker saluted it. "Sergeant Flavius Tucker, sir–Twenty-second U.S. Colored. I'm on an errand for the District Command."

"And that would be?"

"Sir, do you know of a Lieutenant-Colonel Orlando Monks?"

"He's here," spoke the sentry, who then looked at his officer. "That's his name–ain't it, Mister . . . I mean, Cap'n, sir?"

Tucker stood motionless, his pulse thudding.

The captain gave a light cough, then leaned out over the rampart. Firelight played across his rust-colored beard. "Uh, yes–he is in command here. What do they want with him?"

"General McCook is just confirming which officers are commanding where, sir."

"You have any message for him?"

"No–no, sir. That's all."

"Well, here's one for General McCook." The captain gave another light cough. "Tell him we're in a mighty exposed position and it would please us no end to get reinforced. Tell him it's just one company here and a few provisional gunners and I'm sure he's hard-pressed himself, but if he could spare us whatever he can . . . "

The captain's voice was peculiar–abstracted, almost toneless. Tucker strained to look attentive, wishing he could tell the man to save his breath. He itched to jump back in the saddle, to ride off and find Forbes. Meanwhile, other silhouettes had materialized along the rampart, shuffling and muttering as the captain rambled on:

"We'll sure enough hold this place as best we can–tell him so–but Lord knows we could use help to man the pits and fill out the gun crews. Because if Early knocks us out of here, as I understand it, then Stevens and Reno will be outflanked and . . . "

Several paces to the captain's left, another hatted figure appeared and ambled toward him, taller than the rest. Tucker went still inside. As soldiers stepped back to make way, the officer strolled past a mounted torch and Tucker glimpsed a shoulder strap. It was regular army, its twin oak leaves indicating a major or a lieutenant-colonel.

The captain droned on: "We're all volunteers and we'll sure 'nuff do our part, but . . . "

"What's this?" asked the tall officer. It was a strong voice but smooth, almost amiable.

"A courier is all, Major," said the captain. "Seems they just wanted to confirm that Lieutenant-Colonel Monks is in charge here."

"Well, sirs," said Tucker, moving to the side of his horse. "Many thanks. I'll be . . . "

"Not so quick, there."

Tucker took his foot from the stirrup. The major loomed over the wall. Giving him a frozen salute, Tucker perceived a strong jaw and dark mustache—and though the eyes remained in shadow, he could feel their stare.

"It's a fact," spoke the major. "We're damned short on men—but I fancy that's true for the whole perimeter, eh?"

Tucker lowered his salute. "It is, sir."

The major looked at the captain. "See? We're in the same fix as everybody. So we'd best be glad for whatever's available—in this case, our dusky friend here."

Tucker licked his lips. "Sir, I have orders to return to headquarters immed . . . "

"Orders, Sergeant? Orders often conflict at a time like this. But just now I'm the ranking officer in your midst—and I'm ordering you to stay and assist in our defense. That's a touch more important than riding about and taking roll call." Hunching his broad shoulders, the major placed his hands atop the wall. "The papers say you Negroes are putting up a good enough fight down in Virginia. That's something I'd like to see first-hand, even if it's just one of you. Meanwhile . . . " With a grin in his voice, he glanced side to side. "—you can tote a few gun shells for us." Someone guffawed and a few others chuckled. The captain coughed.

"Yessir," said Tucker, his throat hardening.

Young Sutherland gestured with his rifle. "Stables are down that-a-way, by the gate."

Leading his horse in that direction, Tucker stole a last upward look. The group was dispersing, men returning to their posts. Only the major remained at the wall, towering there. In the dancing torchlight, his eyes were now visible, following Tucker's progress toward the stables. Tucker dropped his gaze.

He put his horse in one of the hay-strewn stables, two of which were already occupied–one by a sorrel, the other by a magnificent black. As he turned, he saw the major now standing at the fort's rear wall, closest to him, still staring down. With a shudder, Tucker hoped that Forbes would get here very soon.

87

Central Washington
10:40 P.M.

WAKING, BEN NOTICED how the wet bandage quivered in Anna's hands. He touched her on the elbow and felt sad, wondering if she still feared him–if she dreaded another strange, cruel utterance from his lips. Or was it still just the sight of him? Then he looked up at her face, pale and strained.

"What's the matter, Annie?"

"Let me put this on."

He held her by the forearm. "Why are you shaking?"

Her tremor worsened.

"Where's Pa?"

It seemed a heartbeat too long before she answered. "In the cellar."

"Still? What about Saph, then?"

"She . . . She's asleep. Lie back, would you?"

He eyed her more closely. "No, I think I'll go down and talk to Pa. Maybe he knows what's got you so rattled."

Dropping the bandage, she stared into a corner.

"Annie, for God's sake . . . "

"They took him."

"What?!"

Her voice fell to a mutter. "Sapphira said . . . She said someone's taken Father prisoner."

Ben struggled to sit up. "Where's Saph?!"

"Ben . . ."

"Tell me!"

"Let go of me."

He released her arm. "I'm sorry. Now please say where she is."

"She's gone. To a place called the Emperor's House. She took Father's pistol."

Extending his bad arm, Ben swung his feet over the side. In his ear a ringing began, high and thin–while in his mind, the name of the Emperor's House reverberated. Suddenly its French version echoed back: La Maison de l'Empereur–the place his father had spoken of.

"Please bring me my uniform." She quavered something about him not being well enough, but he repeated himself. "And my sidearm, too, in the second drawer."

Dull-eyed, she leaned against the bedpost.

"Annie?"

"I could lose all of you," she murmured. "All of you at once."

With his good arm he pushed himself to his feet and started toward the dresser. Anna blocked the way–her eyes clear now, glaring at him.

"Do you even know where you're going?!" she demanded.

"The Seventh Street Road, just north of Piney Branch. Pa told me."

"The roads north are jammed."

"I'll take backroads."

"On what?" she sputtered. "Do you think you'll find an open livery stable at this hour?"

"I'll get a horse one way or another. Annie . . . "

Her lips hardened. Then she made a slow turn, pulled the top drawer open and took out his folded uniform. Her cheeks had gone red.

"Whatever this infernal business is, I have to try," he said.

Wordlessly she placed the uniform on the dresser and opened the next drawer down. Taking out his cap pouch, holster belt and service revolver, she placed these beside the uniform. "You'll need a sling," she said, her tone brittle.

She left him for a moment–and in the ringing quiet, the room seemed to tilt. He looked at the side table with its medicinal jars and bottles. He could no longer detect their odors, though they surely filled the room. For him, bromine and chloride of lime would always smell of pain, just as laudanum would always taste of it. He looked over at his writing desk, the wastebasket full of his crumpled sketching efforts. Glancing down at his disfigured right arm, he tried to make a fist but could barely bend the fingers. In the fire of his first bedridden days, he had hated the arm, hated the surging pain, hated himself for feeling it. But pain and frustration had subsided for now, leaving the blank acknowledgment of his survival, his good fortune. And though the arm would likely remain a withered vestige, he might at least maintain the appearance of a whole man. Then he thought of his face. He passed his palm over the scabbed area–but just then Anna returned, jolting him back to a state of alarm.

She had brought a square of linen. Neither of them spoke as she swathed his arm, tied the sling and then helped him into his uniform. The ringing in his ear had ceased. Working his good arm into the sleeve of his jacket, Ben noted the other sleeve hanging loose; the bullet hole was patched but the bloodstain still visible, despite laundering. He thought of his cap, then remembered he had left it on the body-strewn hillside in Virginia. Anna buckled the holster around his waist. Seated on the bed, he watched as she slid his brogans onto his feet–her fingers nimble, the skittishness gone. But she was crying.

"Would you try to sleep?" he asked.

She raised her eyes; hard and glittery-green, they told him how stupid the suggestion was.

They went down to the study, where Ben opened the bottom desk drawer and, with clumsy care, began loading his pistol. Quickly frustrated, he handed the weapon to Anna. "Leave the last chamber empty," he said, "then rest the hammer against it." She completed the task with sullen efficiency. He poured some caps into his pouch, then stuffed the remaining cartridges in his inner breast pocket. Aiming the pistol at the wall, he pondered how it felt in his left hand–no more natural than his sketching pen had.

At the front door, he stopped to peer into Anna's face. He pressed her hand. For once he wanted to see some of what he had scorned in her, what he had scorned in himself: cozy delusions, storybook optimism–any bright figment to which she might cling. Yet her gaze reminded him of charred earth. Where was the ridiculous girl, the one who loved Chadwick?

"Leave, if you're leaving," she muttered.

Thinking, he barely heard her. "Annie–Chadwick's family is well off, right?"

She looked befuddled, then defensive. "They're . . . His father owns a bank. Why? What do you care about Dennis?"

"Do they have stables?"

Grasping his thought, she sighed wearily. "Yes. They're a few doors up from St. John's Church, on Sixteenth. A gray stone house with an iron fence. Go on, Ben."

He left. One block before Pennsylvania, he waved down a wagon which proved to be full of dung, bound for the city commons. Puffing a clay pipe, the grizzled old nightsoiler agreed to take a detour up Sixteenth. Awkwardly Ben hoisted himself onto the board seat, gripping it as the wagon clattered off.

Despite his pipe smoke, the old man smelled much like his cargo. "Goin' out to the forts, eh?" He gave Ben a look of fierce approval, then clapped him on the knee. "God bless you, son! To be wounded and still so full o' fight!" Suddenly light-headed, Ben almost blurted that no, he was in fact going to a fancy French whorehouse.

The nightsoiler jabbered on about the invasion while Ben kept nodding, trying to breathe through his mouth. The dizziness passed–and as they moved through the murky gaslight, he tried to fend off a swarm of fears. Ignorance spared him any mental image of his father's peril, but he could not help picturing Sapphira. He saw her hurrying down a long road–farther and farther away, until the night swallowed her.

88

Fort Derussy
11:15 P.M.

PRIVATE SUTHERLAND GESTURED to the stacked artillery shells. "Now, these here are hundred-pounders."

"Yes, they are," said Tucker.

"So it's a two-man job."

"Yes, it is."

"So we'll be stackin' 'em next to that big gun on the forward point. Addin' 'em to what's there already."

Tucker eyed the heavy cone-shaped shells and then his rangy, freckled companion–a militia recruit, of all people, addressing him as if he were the green one. In Company G of the 136th Ohio National Guard, Sutherland's youth made him an exception. Most of the others were older men whom the draft had spared, who had left their shops and fields for a state bounty and one hundred days of playing soldier. By contrast, the detachment of Pennsylvania heavy artillerymen seemed fully competent, though there were too few to man every gun.

"Private, how long have these been sitting here?"

Like his instructive tone, Sutherland's look of farm-boy bemusement was exasperating. "Since, uh . . . Since this afternoon, it was."

"Well, that's pretty damned foolish. All these shells left exposed, right next to the powder magazine? If one spark came floating off a torch, you know what the Rebs would find? Our toes, Private. Our toes and maybe our fingers."

Glancing between Tucker and the shells, Sutherland removed his cap and scratched his shaggy head. "Well, uh . . . We got interrupted, is all. We'd just started haulin' 'em over to the gun when . . . " His voice fell. "That's when Lieutenant-Colonel Monks showed up and took command. Him and that Major Spruce."

Tucker gazed along the ramparts, where militiamen sat, paced or stood in varying degrees of watchfulness. Crowded about one of the smaller guns, several Ohioans listened as an artillery lieutenant explained loading procedure. Farther along, where the wall angled to face due north, the big long-range Parrott sat on its platform while its crew stood by, scanning the moonlit terrain beyond the road. The majority of Company G filled the rifle pits along DeRussy's front and sides. Tucker had noted three sets of gun platforms outside the fort, including the one near Milkhouse Ford, and that none were occupied.

Then, up by the big gun, Tucker spied Monks. Even at a distance, there seemed an artificial bluster about the man. Gaunt and spindly in his Veteran Reserves' light blue, he moved about in a jerky imitation of a swagger–grasping his sword hilt, stopping to gesticulate or raise his binoculars or yammer at the crew. In the shadows nearby stood the slightly taller, far more imposing figure of Major Spruce.

"Anyhow," said Sutherland, "he's been tossin' orders around ever since. But these shells weren't top o' his list, I reckon . . . "

"You two–think you'll finish with that sometime tonight?" It was the captain calling. Arms crossed as he regarded them, he stood next to a siege mortar by the east wall. Despite his words and posture, his tone remained curiously mild.

The two of them bent to lift a shell. Maintaining his grip, Tucker coordinated his steps with Sutherland's as they lugged the missile, sidling their way across the packed earthen surface. He had hoped that the pain would not return–but it did, lancing him through the ribs.

Sutherland chuckled. "Know somethin'? When you come steppin' out of the dark like that, I dang near fell over. I ain't never seen a colored soldier afore."

"There are a lot of us, Private . . . Hold up for a second."

With a grunt, Tucker shifted the shell toward his good side before they moved on. Four or six men would have accomplished the whole task quickly, he thought–yet it had fallen to him and this hayseed tyke. Predictably they would make maximum use of him, sergeant's stripes or not. And where was Forbes?

They detoured around the gunnery lecture and then passed a bomb-proof, around which a half-dozen militiamen stood lounging. Tucker could feel their smirks. As he and Sutherland neared the big Parrott, the reedy voice of Monks became audible: "With this piece we have a range of over four thousand yards. Now you might find it a chore to handle but when the time comes, I'll give you some pointers. Till then, we must keep our eyes peeled." As they reached the platform, Monks pivoted to face them, motioning to the stack of hundred-pounders already beside the cannon. "Ease it down, now. Careful." Tucker was surprised to see him clean-shaven. Unquestionably, though, this was the same pinched, care-worn face as in the photograph.

The Pennsylvania gunners looked weary as Monks jabbered on. Biting back the pain, Tucker bent his knees as he and Sutherland set the shell down. He straightened up and, turning, caught sight of Major Spruce. Still in shadow, Spruce leaned back against a timber support and puffed a cigar. Tucker averted his eyes and started back toward the mound-shaped magazine. Falling in step with him, Sutherland noticed him holding onto his side.

"You hurt yourself?"

Before Tucker could reply, a jeering voice sprang from the group of loafers by the bomb-proof: "Hey, Danny-boy! You're lookin' blacker every minute, son!" Amid chortles, another man chimed in: "That's the truth, lad! Next thing, ye'll be up and dancin' on a cracker box!"

With a weak smile, Sutherland dropped his gaze and walked faster. Tucker did not bother to keep up. By the magazine entrance, he found Sutherland staring glumly at the stack of shells.

"Private, there's something I need to tell you."

"What?"

Tucker unbuttoned his jacket. Carefully pulling his shirt up, he waited until Sutherland raised his eyes and saw the ragged scar. "I got this a few weeks back. If it weren't for the invasion, I'd still be convalescing. I'm only showing you because . . . " He broke off as he saw the captain ambling toward them—a stocky man with a broad face and a sparse ruddy beard, his rolling gait more like a sea captain's.

Sutherland looked up and saluted. "Cap'n Griffith."

"Danny."

Having tucked his shirt back in, Tucker gave a laggard salute. The captain's hazy eyes matched his vocal quality. Among officers at the front,

Tucker had observed two distinct varieties of calm—one engaged, the other disengaged. It was the latter, troubling sort that seemed to possess Captain Griffith.

"What's the name again?" Griffith asked.

"Tucker, sir."

Drawing a hand up to his mouth, the captain coughed. "Well, Tucker, I couldn't help noticing that you and Sutherland seem to be stretching this out a bit. Now I know it's not the most agreeable duty, but things here could get brisk afore long and then we'll wish we'd been like the worker ant instead of the grasshopper."

"Yessir. I was just explaining . . . "

"Better now than later, you see, because who knows if the enemy's not creeping up this very minute? I may not be your career military man, but any fool can see that ant beats grasshopper at such a time . . . "

Tucker kept nodding. He wanted to lie down, to shut his ears until Griffith had finished waxing Aesop. Between Monks, Griffith and the idle catcalls, Fort DeRussy was sounding more and more like a bastion of feeble-mindedness, with blather its official tongue. When the captain's admonition rambled to its end, Tucker jumped in.

"Captain, I was just telling Private Sutherland . . . " Again he lifted his shirt. "I was wounded on the first day of Petersburg, sir. There's still some discomfort, and I was hoping that the private could take a little more of the shell's weight."

Before the scar, Griffith's gaze took on a sudden clarity and then, just as suddenly, a look of tired contemplation. Feeling awkward, Tucker covered himself.

Griffith gave another shallow cough. "Petersburg?"

"Yessir. I was with Hinks' division. We opened the assault."

"It's all right, Cap'n," said Sutherland. "I'll take more of the weight."

Without a nod or a word, Griffith wandered off.

Tucker gave a sigh of confusion. Leaving his jacket unbuttoned, he squatted to lift another shell while Sutherland squatted across from him. As they hefted the missile and began toting it, Sutherland seemed to be looking at him differently, but Tucker gave it little thought. His side still bothered him, despite the private's added help. He felt increasingly morose.

"Private, did your captain get hit on the head?"

Beneath his straining, Sutherland looked puzzled and then stung. "Did he . . . ? No. No, he didn't get hit on the head."

"He acts like it."

"Mister Grif . . . I mean, Cap'n Griffith's a good man. Back in Morrow County, he runs the feed store. Folks think a lot of him."

"I'm sure he's a fine friend and neighbor, but can you tell me what the devil's the matter with him?"

Sutherland bent lower, tightening his grip. "It's cuz of Virgil, Jr., I reckon–his eldest boy, what joined the army in the spring. I would've gone with him, 'cept I had to be home for the harvest. Anyhow, word come last week that Virgil's dead. Killed at Petersburg."

Tucker's irritation faded. "Oh."

"Cap'n Griffith ain't really been himself since then."

They passed the smaller cannon and its would-be crew, who were watching the lieutenant demonstrate the use of a muzzle swab.

"So what's it like?" said Sutherland. "Down there in Virginia?"

They were nearing the gaggle of hecklers.

"Often it's dull," said Tucker. "Not much different from garrison duty, I suppose."

"But did you get to shoot any Rebs?"

Just then the same two voices resumed sniping.

"Ho there, Danny–that don't seem right! Looks like you're doin' most of the work!"

"Sure does! I think you got it backwards, Massa Dan'l!"

Sutherland looked annoyed but made no reply. Gazing past him, Tucker spotted the most conspicuous heckler, a husky fellow with protruding ears. He imagined lugging the shell over and dropping it on the man's foot.

Arriving at the big gun, they placed the shell while Monks' oration continued–brave words in a jittery voice: "I've engineered on half the forts around Washington. Yes–including this one! You boys would be hard-pressed to find anybody who knows defense as I do–so just . . . All of you just follow orders, and we'll make our home state proud! We surely will!"

Spruce still lurked to the side, smoking his cigar. As Tucker started back with Sutherland, he saw the major turn and peer at him.

"That Monks," muttered Sutherland. "He's a queer one, that's all I can say."

"So he and Spruce just appeared out of nowhere?" Tucker asked.

"Monks didn't. He first come by a few days ago, to inspect the fort. And he comes the next day too. And yesterday, when we was choppin' trees along the creek. The fellow seems to know his stuff–but the way he carries on . . . He keeps sayin' the same things, like how good it is to be amongst Ohio boys and such. How we can all take heart, so long as he's in charge."

Tucker nodded. "That's queer, all right–since he looks more scared than anybody."

Sutherland gave a low chuckle. "Yup."

Once more they were about to pass the hecklers.

"Sergeant?" said Sutherland. "You think they could hit us tonight? The Rebs, I mean?"

In revealing his scar, Tucker had expected little–just some faint recognition of his due. Now, tardily, he appreciated the change it had brought to Sutherland's eyes. The noxious blend of presumption and fascination was gone, replaced by something very like admiration–that, and a pleading that left Tucker momentarily stuck for words. Then it occurred to him that older, experienced men were supposed to reassure younger, inexperienced ones–within reason.

"From what I hear, the Rebels' main body won't get here till tomorrow sometime. But they must know how much speed matters. Their advance troops might attempt a night march–take advantage of the dark, try to seize some part of the line and hold it till the rest of them come up. But we're supposed to get reinforcements . . . "

"Hey, Danny! After that, why don't you go water his horse for him?"

Sutherland jerked in the taunt's direction. "He's got a wound from Petersburg, dang it!"

The retort struck a callow note, more plaintive than defiant. Still, no response came until the two of them were past the group.

"How'd he sell you that story, boy?"

"He showed us!" called Sutherland. "Me and the captain!" Under his breath, he added, "And you're the hind end of a horse, Floyd."

Tucker managed a smile. He did not resume talking until they were back at the magazine. "I was saying–once our reinforcements get here, we'll be all right. But it's going to be a tight business." They lifted another shell and started hauling it. "For now we're short on numbers and fighting experience, facing the best of the Rebel army. The forts are well built, though, and well armed; their guns have a sweep of pretty much all the ground in between." Stooped and sweating, Tucker glanced at Sutherland's attentive face. He suddenly wished he could confide everything that Forbes had told him. "The main thing is, we can't afford to lose a single fort. Not this one, not any of 'em–because then they'll come pouring in like the sea."

On this pass, no jeers issued from the half-dozen idlers, and Sutherland stayed quiet until he and Tucker had almost reached the gun platform. "Well," he said, "if they come, we'll just have to fight like blazes." He spoke with slow, clumsy emphasis, as if learning a prayer.

"That's the spirit," said Tucker. "So much for a hundred days of guard duty, eh?"

Sutherland gave a tight smirk. "Yup."

Beneath the press of his own worry, Tucker hoped that Sutherland would make it back for the harvest.

On the platform, the big Parrott's crew stared northward. Monks was at last quiet, having moved several paces along the rampart. Behind him stood Spruce, no longer smoking. Depositing the shell, Tucker stole a look at the two officers–the superior rigid, the subordinate powerfully at ease. Still there was some deeper imbalance, something beyond mere posture.

Trudging back, Tucker noticed Griffith talking to the group of erstwhile mockers. By the time Tucker and Sutherland completed their next circuit, the six privates had put up their rifles and joined them in the task. Sullen-faced, they lugged one missile after another to the big Parrott. Tucker caught looks from them, some hostile and others curious. As he and Sutherland set the last shell down, he saw Monks and Spruce moving away along the east wall. Spruce lagged two paces behind the lieutenant-colonel, though his casual stride suggested nothing of deference. Tucker recalled a scene that he had witnessed a few days ago, at Franklin Square: a policeman in an attitude of bored mastery, prodding a hapless thief toward the jailhouse.

Sutherland's voice broke his concentration. "I been on my feet for hours. Let's find someplace to sit, least till Cap'n Griffith rousts us."

Tucker stretched his tired arms. "Fine with me."

The artillery instructees were conducting a mock load-and-fire sequence, stumbling about as the lieutenant looked on. Sutherland led the way past them and around the magazine, to where he had set his rifle aside. Also there, seated, were their six reluctant helpers. In a cross-legged huddle, the men ceased their low chatter and looked up. Tucker would sooner have reversed direction. Picking a spot a few yards short of the group, he sat, resting his back against the sloped wall. Sutherland hesitated, then sat halfway between his compatriots and Tucker. Trying to relax, Tucker heard a tuneful, mid-range voice that he now recognized too well:

"Ah, boys, we've come down in the world. Look at us, takin' our ease with a spade-black son of Cain."

It was the husky, jug-eared one that Sutherland had called Floyd. Tucker felt a simmering in his blood but tried to ignore it. Just for now he wanted to shut it all out–Monks, Spruce, treason, the enemy, this garrison of dolts. "Well," he said, yawning, "I'm sure an industrious gent like you could survive worse."

After a pause, there came a grunt and a dismissive chuckle.

"So do we get to see that wound of yours?" someone else asked.

"No, no–I feel shy, all of a sudden."

"Then how're we supposed to believe it?"

"Nobody's said you have to."

Sutherland stirred. "Tell us about Petersburg, will you?"

Tucker rubbed his stubbled face. Clearly he would not be left in peace. "Hinks' colored division crossed the Appomattox by night, along with Kautz's cavalry. The rest of the Eighteenth Corps followed before dawn." He told them about coming under fire, about the first charge against the high ground and being hit with canister, Captain Langstaff blown to bits. Despite his rote recitation, the images of June 15th swirled up, slicing at him. Reflexively he placed a hand to his aching side. "Our regiment captured a gun and turned it on the Rebs. Late that day we got up to their main works and took some prisoners, some rifle pits and a few redoubts."

Floyd spoke, surlier now. "Lotta good it did. Newspaper said you could've took the town that night, if you wanted."

Tucker eyed the jug-eared silhouette. "We wanted and we would have. But the order came to halt. General Smith got the jitters, is what happened. He delayed us so two corps could join us from over the James–time enough for the Rebs to get dug in and reinforced." Tucker longed to speculate aloud how this joke of a company, and this fool in particular, might perform if ordered to charge cannons.

"I heard tell about canister," said Sutherland. "They say it sounds different."

"It does," said Tucker. "Different from grape or solid shot. It's used at short range but you still hear it coming, sort of a wobbly whistle. When it goes off, the balls scatter. And for a second it's like a thousand eagles screaming overhead, swooping down."

In the gloom Floyd had turned his face away, but Tucker felt the others' somber attention. It seemed that having survived the fiercest of manly rites–an experience that they had only heard of–he had risen from object of mockery to prize exhibit. Their eyes still caged him in his skin–but for the moment, his cage sat on a pedestal. Absorbing the thought, he let a weird, heady sensation take hold of him. He could have laughed.

"But I'd guess we have a supply of canister right here in the magazine," he went on. "So if anyone's going to face that tonight, it'll be Johnny Reb. If we're attacked, it'll be a matter of staying cool and following directions from those Pennsylvania fellows."

Sutherland and a couple of others nodded, holding their rifles close.

"What bothers me most is that creek ravine," said Tucker. "Even with those trees piled in, it's our weakest spot. If we're distracted by a frontal assault, a raiding party could push through and surprise us. So it would make sense to place a gun or two at that battery station, over there by the ford."

"We done that," said one militiaman. "Two guns–but they got ordered back."

"That's right," said Sutherland. "Monks ordered 'em back into the fort. Said they were too exposed out there."

Sitting up, Tucker stared at his knees. "The whole position's exposed, for God's sake! That only makes it more so."

"Then Cap'n Griffith asked about placin' a guard detail there," the youth added. "Just a few men. But Monks said no to that too."

To Tucker, until this moment, the threat of treason had been only a dark idea. Now it loomed directly over him–an immediate presence taking shape, with fetid breath. More than ever he wished that he could reveal all that Forbes had told him, even to these dull ears.

Close by, a militia corporal stepped into the dim torchlight. "Sutherland?" he called. "Major Spruce wants to see you."

Following the corporal away, Sutherland looked apprehensive. Tucker felt the same, finding himself alone with the six huddled Ohioans. They were briefly quiet. Then one of them made a comment about Grant and the Petersburg siege, touching off a lazy discussion on the merits and demerits of the Union chieftain. Tucker made no attempt to join in. He listened for Forbes' hoofbeats, though it felt as if the captain were a hundred miles away.

Sutherland returned shortly, by which time the talk had moved to McClellan's presidential chances. Holding forth on the subject, one private interrupted himself. "So what did he want, Danny?"

The youth sat nearer the huddle this time. "Nothin' much."

"You look shook up, boy."

"I ain't shook."

"What was it, then?"

He shrugged, sending Tucker a glance. "He, uh . . . He saw me and him talkin' and . . . " Sutherland sent a steadier look. "He wanted to know if you told me anything–'bout what you come here for, and such. I told him no, cuz you didn't. That's all."

Tucker's stomach had gone hard.

"And what *is* it you come for?" said Floyd.

With an effort, Tucker kept his tone in check. "As I told the major– McCook's headquarters sent me to confirm who the front-line commanders were and report back."

"That so? Then why you figure the major's still curious?"

"You should know. The word of a colored soldier doesn't wash, I reckon."

"Reckon it don't. Heh-heh."

Ogling Tucker, one of the others shook his head. "Naw, it ain't just that. When you showed up and Spruce was leanin' over the wall, tellin' you to come inside, I was standin' close to him. He had his hand on his sidearm, like he thought you might try and skeedaddle."

Fixing his gaze on the high hunched moon, Tucker wanted it to mesmerize him, to banish these stares and voices. "Well, there you go–he was dead-set on making me a laborer."

"You know, boys," said Floyd, "I ain't sure I like what I been hearin' from this one. Maybe he's got three little stripes, but still–here he sits like a barnyard rooster, advisin' on this and that, like he knows more than white officers."

Tucker kept his eyes on the moon. He recalled the sneering sergeant at Fort Stevens, then pictured himself crushing Floyd's windpipe. The sinews of his arms drew tighter. It was a moment before he realized that the taunting voice had begun to recede, crowded out by other noise–shouts and murmurs and scuffling feet, a clatter of rifles.

"What's happenin'?" someone demanded.

Jolted anew, Tucker looked around and beheld the rising commotion. With tense inquisitive faces, gunners and militiamen were moving toward the north wall. Floyd, Sutherland and the others stood craning their necks, fumbling with their weapons. Tucker got up slowly.

Then Sutherland was at his side, looking urgent. "Rebs!" he whispered.

"Maybe," said Tucker. "And maybe something else besides."

"What? Do you know something? Come on–do you?!"

Tucker flexed his moist hands. "I know something bad's afoot, and not just outside these walls."

A rotund militia lieutenant waddled past. "To your posts!" he huffed.

Floyd's group scrambled off but Sutherland stood motionless, gripping his Springfield. "Major Spruce," he muttered, "–he looked right into my face. He said I best not be holdin' anything back, else he'd have me shot. That's what he said. But those eyes of his . . . Jesus, they cut right into me." Sutherland glanced toward the general rush, then abruptly joined it.

Looking down, Tucker watched a small lizard skitter past his shoes. Then he forced himself to move, edging around the magazine until he had a full view. Along the north wall, the mob of troops stood thickest around the big Parrott platform. There, upon the gun carriage, Monks stood with his back to the parapet, one hand clutching his binoculars while the other gesticulated. To one side, with the gun crew, Griffith stood stroking his sparse beard. On the other side, by the stacked shells, Spruce presided with his hands on his belt, watching Monks.

Tucker took a few strides into the murmuring crowd and then stopped. Panic nudged him. He looked around for Sutherland but failed to spot him. Surrounded, Tucker felt as exposed as he had on the hill near Petersburg–exposed, and even more starkly alone. The cold sensation pulled him further back in time, back to the fields where bent figures toiled. He heard the work songs.

Years after his escape to the North, he had found words to describe what even the most carefree work songs had done to him. Rising amid the flies and heat waves–from the very soil which bound him, it seemed–the straggling harmonies always struck him as a dirge. An anthem of desolation, weighing him down like stones and leaving him to yearn seaward, skyward. Yet the hope of escape had offered only vague images, while the dread of capture offered horribly vivid ones. In particular, it evoked a place he had only heard of, but whose legend still haunted him: Mount

Misery, an earthly hell somewhere in southern North Carolina. A place to which willful slaves were sent, there to be beaten and worked to death. Leading to the mountain, so the stories had it, a trail called Negro Head Road evinced that Southern penchant for the colorful and the literal, lined as it was with the heads of victims.

A sudden movement in his side-vision broke the trance. Then he saw the artillery lieutenant jostling his way forward. In the officer's purposeful wake, Tucker followed, threading and sidling through the crowd until he had reached the platform. The lieutenant was a short, wiry man with a thick black mustache. He took his place beside Griffith and the two of them looked up at Monks, who leaned down to them and blurted something. Griffith's nervous cough had worsened, hampering him as he made some respectful reply. Monks responded with an impatient slicing gesture. Hemmed in, Tucker moved closer, straining to hear through the voice-rumble. Monks looked feverish, growing hoarse as he harangued the captain:

"Can't I make myself clear?! It's a prearranged signal, understand? From our scouts!"

The lieutenant spoke up. "Beg your pardon, sir–what signal?"

Monks jabbed a finger over the wall. "There! There!"

The lieutenant hopped up on the parapet and stared into the darkness. Craning, Tucker stood on tip-toe. Down in the rifle pits, militiamen stood gazing toward the little creek bridge, whose outline Tucker could barely see. On its far side, a pair of torches waved in slow unison.

89

La Maison De l'Empereur
11:15 P.M.

WAKEFIELD COULD NOT help brooding over his missteps. He should have somehow arranged to be at DeRussy, making sure that things unfolded as they had to. Monroe and Ravenel would have opposed this, calling it interference. To them, Wakefield was now little more than a client's errand boy, a nuisance to be controlled. Yet on this of all nights, he should have been the one to define his own role.

Then there was the matter of the Monks photograph. If Truly had managed to find the critical plate before his capture, if he had already developed a print and passed it on for verification, then the whole plan was in jeopardy. Along with the box containing the Archer negatives, Wakefield had retrieved the "M" boxes from Truly's cellar–but at this point, he could not bring himself to search through them. If he discovered the Monks plate missing, mere worry would turn to useless obsession. He could only harden himself and let the minutes crawl, seated here in the deserted gaming room.

"All alone? Such a misanthrope you have become."

From the main hall, Ravenel entered. Her silver derringer hung from one hand, her key-ring from the other. She looked smaller, having taken off her marabou feathers, but an avian aspect somehow remained. Wakefield wished that he had picked a less conspicuous place to sit.

"Where is your helper?" she asked.

"I told him to go watch the back."

Drifting to the mirrored saloon-counter, she picked up the hand-bell and rang it in three casual strokes. Then she moved to Wakefield's table, where she set her keys down and took a chair. "And what are your thoughts?" she asked airily. Her posture was languid and her stare opaque, not really interested. After years of prying men open by various means, she sometimes wheedled out of mere habit.

"Perhaps you can guess," he said.

"Perhaps you should not sit facing the clock."

"Perhaps not."

Her lips drew into a wrinkled smirk. "Where is your equanimity, now that you need it so? We have done our utmost, mon ami. Calm yourself. Let events take their course."

Again he gazed over at the coffin clock, less to check its face than to avoid Ravenel's. But his tension began to ebb. He pictured the veranda of his family home and then himself beneath the hanging moss, seated with one or another of the local belles. All those ladies were in fact long since wed or widowed–his sister's smuggled letters had kept him up-to-date–but in his reverie, they retained their smiling girl faces. Then he saw himself there with Delia. And with that, he felt glad to have shed at least one layer of his upbringing.

It wearied him to think of all the courting beaus and flirting belles, their fussy postures of daintiness and chivalry. Somewhere along the way, he had come to see courtship not as a dance but as a pointless maze, a labyrinth of pretense and trickery. Trickery and pretense–he had had enough of both. Despite the bane of his secrecy, the thing he treasured most with Delia was a fundamental frankness. It stoked his love as well as his passion for her. And when they next met, he would tell her everything. At last she would understand, and the bane would lift. And no one back home would ever have to know her true story; he would fashion it to the genteel standards of Savannah. He pictured a gathering of kinfolk making his young Irish bride feel welcome–laughing, singing, tale-spinning, quaffing juleps in the dusk.

The vision dissolved and he realized how quiet it was–most strikingly, how quiet Ravenel was. He looked and saw her contemplating her hands. On the diamond-patterned tablecloth they lay before her, veined and knobby, her left one featuring a triple-set ruby ring. Her sloe eyes were half shut, the line of her mouth slightly crooked. Abruptly, as he studied her desiccated features, Ravenel seemed separate from everything–from this gaudy room, from the very finery she wore. She could have been wearing rags or buckskin or a nun's habit, sitting in a cave or a church or a frontier cabin. Wakefield felt a stunned fascination. He recalled that in his first-ever audience with Ravenel, he had wanted to take her photograph. The inspiration had soon fled, and unlike Monroe she had never requested a portrait from him. Now he wished that he had his camera here to freeze her in this moment, in this isolation. To capture her as just another mortal being.

Slowly she flexed her hands, then stared across the room at nothing. "Ursula," she murmured, "–where is that German cow?"

From the hall came the sound of quick footsteps down the stairs. Ursula hurried in and stood over the table, out of breath. "You rang, Madame?"

"I suppose I did."

"Forgive me, Madame. I vas dressing."

Ravenel beamed up at her. "Worry not, my dear. How is Archer?"

"He is resting."

"*Bien.*" Ravenel picked up the ring of keys. "Bring us a bottle of our oldest cognac."

"Ja, Madame." Ursula took the keys. "Should I look in also upon the major?"

"No need–he is well secured. Merci, Ursula."

The big girl bustled out.

Twinkling, Ravenel turned her yellowed smile on Wakefield. "Napoleon himself favored cognac, did you know? It is a most fitting way to toast victory."

He tried not to fidget. His eyes strayed to the billiard table, to the portrait of Cardinal Richelieu. "By any chance, has Monroe mentioned yet why he's so intent about Truly?"

"He has not. I fear that shall remain a mystery."

Truly had started to talk about it earlier; Wakefield now wished that he had let him speak. It struck him that he could still visit Truly in the cellar and hear him out, but aversion proved stronger than curiosity. If he could help it, he would never again set eyes on the vexatious Yankee, living or dead.

He tried to summon back his dreams of home, but to no avail. In their place was Truly–Truly in chains, in the dark. Truly awaiting Monroe. Far better it would have been to let Archer just shoot the man. Better, but impolitic. Wakefield struggled not to dwell upon it. All these regrets and anxieties and vain wishes—he had to quash them. Sensing Ravenel's prying eye, he refused to look at her.

She sighed, then spoke in that tone of hers—melodious, insinuating, cutting beneath his skin. "Poor Wakefield. In any great undertaking, remorse will hobble you. Like a pebble in your shoe, it will hobble you and bring failure, or worse. I see now how very much you needed me, how much you needed Monroe. For you we did what precious few others could have done—no others, possibly—and what you yourself could never. I find this most gratifying."

In the beginning, Wakefield recalled, Ravenel had treated him with extravagant tact and cordiality. Yet all the while, she had been doing as she did with every man—taking his measure, sniffing for weakness, reducing him to something manageable. By the time he had realized this and how well she could read him, the foul alliance had infected him to the marrow. It was for this that he hated her, as he hated Monroe—sometimes more than he could believe.

<hr/>

IN NEAR-TOTAL DARKNESS, Truly breathed the dank air. The lengths of rusty chain did not allow for a full sitting position. Anchored to the stone wall, they only let him slide his back partway down and bend his knees outward, straining against the ankle irons. He remained this way for a minute at a time, his arms stretched above him, until the wrist irons had made his hands numb. Then he pulled himself upright. His mind withstood similar exertions, by turns sagging and writhing. He could not let despair swallow him, because that would mean surrendering to the terror: Heath's impending return, Heath moving toward him in the dark.

The dark and the quiet felt like a single entity, heavy in his lungs, and he fidgeted just to hear the chains clink. Their sound told him that he was not dead yet. In his life he had seen a lot of chained men, some of whom he had personally made so, and been forced to wonder how it felt. But he had never wanted such a direct answer—this dread, this impotent fury. As in a fever, Rachel appeared to him; her lips were moving, though he could not hear her. Ben and Anna and Sapphira followed in their turns, as if death had taken them too and left him cursed, utterly alone. As each of their faces pierced him, he began to tremble. He would have tried praying then, but doubted that it would have emerged as anything but, "Please, please, please . . . "

He leaned forward, feeling yet again how solid the chains were. Next he was thrashing, rattling, snorting like a penned bull–but between the strain and the futility, he quickly grew winded. Bending over, he spat hard and let himself hang limp awhile. He kept squinting into the blackness as if something might take shape there–a serene image, maybe Rachel beckoning to him–anything to steel him when the lock turned and Heath stepped in. No matter what, he had to keep his mind until the very last. Death presented enough of a quandary–but how to meet it in darkness? To meet it shackled, at the slaughtering hands of an enemy?

THE MAID, NORA, had warned of "Mister Wakefield's young fella," who she had seen idling around the kitchen and back rooms. But having sneaked inside, Sapphira encountered no one. Crouched, she peered left into the spacious kitchen, illuminated by a lamp on the servants' table. Then she gazed straight ahead. Along the shadowy length of the back hall, nothing stirred, and all she heard was her own tight breathing. This was enemy air–thick, strange air, faintly burning in her chest. Only now did she grasp how much would be required of her. Above all, her mind would have to move like quicksilver. Her flimsy disguise, this maid's bonnet and apron, represented little more than a first step.

She started slowly along the passageway. On her right she came to a door that was cracked open. She looked inside, and the scant light from elsewhere revealed jars and boxes of foodstuffs, shelved and labeled. She closed the door and crept onward. Despite her short, careful steps, the walls seemed to move too quickly past her side-vision, as if the house were drawing her into itself. She reached a wood-and-plaster archway that seemed to section off the servants' work area, beyond which the hall became luxurious, carpeted and wainscoted. Hardly a step past this point, the ringing of a bell froze her in place. Once, twice and three times it rang from the front of the house, its cadence slow and deliberate. In the silence she stood with her ears bristling. She wondered if the summons was for the maid. Struggling to think, she told herself to move, to hide, listening for footsteps or an impatient shout. At length she heard nothing but felt no relief, aware that her momentary paralysis did not bode well.

She edged forward, then stopped at a narrow flight of stairs on her left, its upper portion angling out of view. Straining to hear, she caught the same laughter and babble that she had heard outside, although here it came down faint and echoey. She passed by and came to another door, this one with a small table beside it. On the table sat a mounted candle and a box of matches, indicating the cellar. The door proved to be locked. In the stronger light from the hall's far end, a glittering caught her eye and she looked up to see a crystal chandelier. She squinted at the hanging glass gems and then at the wallpaper. In an ornate, elongated style of old, a repetitive forest scene depicted figures both human and animal; stags bounded through the trees while hounds, archers and mounted lords pursued them. She looked down at the carpet with its rich, flowering-vine pattern. It struck her that at any other time, she would have just stood here gaping, thrilled with the alien splendor of this place.

The thought was interrupted by the sound of someone rushing down-stairs. This time she moved, rabbit-quick, ducking past the stairwell and the hall archway. Flat against the wall, she touched the pistol's lump beneath her apron. After a few panicked seconds, she realized that the footsteps came not from the nearby stairwell but some other, toward the front. She peered down the hall, then saw a large woman in a dark gown scoot across. Listening hard, she heard a fluttery, heavily accented greeting–"You rang, Madame?"–but could hear none of what followed. Alternating with the big woman's voice, an older female voice featured a different and more melodious accent, regal in tone. Sapphira inched ahead once more until she reached the stairwell. Mounting the bottom step, she faced the hall and waited. In a moment she heard the feet, this time coming in her direction. Catching her breath, she went flat against the side of the stairwell, but the brisk feet halted short of her. She heard a match being struck and then a clinking sound. Stealing a one-eyed stare around the corner, she saw the large young woman holding the lit candle. The woman slipped a ring of keys into her waistband, then pulled the cel-lar door open and stepped through. With her ears, Sapphira followed her clumping descent.

Sapphira went limp, pressing a hand to her forehead. It would do no good to keep hiding. She would have to put her ruse to the test, to see where it took her. Fleetingly she considered going after the woman in the cellar. But if she did so, what exactly would her next move be? And her next? Though she felt her nerve strengthening, sharpening by the moment, her mind had yet to catch up. So with no sense of conscious decision, she turned and started upstairs.

She kept her steps slow and silent, the racket from the second floor growing louder. Reaching the top step, she paused to gaze down a lamp-lit hall flanked with a series of shut rooms. The drunken sounds emanated from the other side of the house. She kept on. Where the rooms ended, a high-ceilinged hall overlooked the main staircase, with another corridor of rooms on the far side. She proceeded but then stopped short, staring at the plush blue carpet ahead of her. A human shadow slanted across. Sucking her breath in, she checked the impulse to draw back. Then, easing forward, she peered around the corner and beheld the shadow's owner–a pimple-faced young white man, apparently unaware of her. He wore a brown vest and a porkpie hat, tufts of dirty-blond hair rimming its underside. With a pistol held loosely at his thigh, he stood between a pair of double windows, their parted curtains giving a wide view of the rear grounds. But if he was here as a sentinel, it was no mystery why he had failed to catch Sapphira's intrusion. Gazing in the direction of the revelry, he seemed oblivious to all but that, his glum expression edged with desire.

Sapphira licked her lips. "Sir?"

The pistol twitched in his hand. Sapphira cringed. Eyeing her, the young man relaxed only a little. "Mister Wakefield send you?"

"Well, sir, I was just . . . "

"Cuz if he did, tell him I can see fine from up here. Better than in the kitchen."

After a second's hesitation, she seized upon the name. "Mistuh Wakefield, he didn' send me, suh. Ah jes' needs to ast you . . . " She sounded ridiculous to herself, alarmingly fake, though the tremor in her voice was real enough. "Dat man you got pris'nor here–ah'm s'posed to git 'im some water, 'cept now ah forgets where you done put 'im."

The youth shrugged. "He's down the cellar. Door's locked, so you gotter get the keys."

Sapphira's mind flashed to the woman she had seen downstairs. Then a girl's cackle sounded from up the opposite corridor, followed by another's high-pitched cursing. Instantly the youth's dull eyes turned eager, darting toward the noise. In him–wondrous luck–Sapphira faced the most transparent sort of enemy. But she had to get him out of the way–subtly, if possible.

She made her lips smile. "You know, suh–in dat room where de young ladies be, dere's winders too. You kin see out, jes' as good as here."

He gave her a distracted glance.

"You a gent what really like de ladies," she went on. "Oh, ah kin see dat plain as day!" Lowering her voice to a whisper, she leaned closer to him. "Why, you know–some o' dem girls, dey got a peek at you when you first come here. Put 'em right in a tizzy, you did, and dem all sayin' what a fine-lookin' fella you be, an how dey'd sho' like to see you up close."

His gaze drifted to the windows, his face a muddle of surprise, hunger and doubt.

Beaming at him, Sapphira took a few steps past him. She beckoned. "Come, suh. Young gent like you cain't waste hisself all alone. You kin watch de winders, all right, but you kin meet de ladies too. Dey sho' be wantin' to meet you."

He glanced about, tapping the pistol barrel against his leg. Sapphira's smile had begun to hurt. Praying that no one would come upon them, she yearned to seize him by the arm and lead him away. Then another giggle sounded. Beckoning once more, she took a more decisive stride. The would-be sentinel followed her.

As the magnificent main staircase came up on her right, she chanced a look down to the grand front hall. She saw no one and kept going, the youth a few paces behind. Ahead of them, the drunken voices grew more distinct–one scolding, another whimpering, two yelling over one another:

"And who'd ye be callin' a rum-bucket, ye little bitch?! Ye're the biggest rummy here!"

"Get yer bog-breath away from me, ye tub o' guts!"

Aflame with Irish rhythms, the verbal clash drew Sapphira past another series of shut paneled doors, to a set of double doors at the passageway's end. Her nerves pulled taut. Glancing back at the youth, she forced a smirk. "Dey's cuttin' up high," she whispered. "But once dey sees you, I reckon dey behave better."

Reaching for one of the brass door handles, she was startled to hear a chortling male voice within:

"Oh, oh–si vous plait, mademoiselles! Have Madame's lessons been for nothing?"

Before she could hesitate, Sapphira gripped the handle and pushed.

In the center of a large, well-furnished sitting room, two young white females stood facing each other, naked to the waist, the tops of their bright silk gowns hanging loose. Sapphira gaped at the pair, who regarded her with bleary indifference. Forcing herself to look elsewhere, she saw a card table arrayed with glasses, open bottles and a pile of playing cards. Four fully clothed girls were seated there, slouched or slumped over. Four more lounged on a sofa, holding drinks. Two more sat on a settee, one blubbering about being homesick while the other sneered, urging her to "be done with the damned snivels."

"You there!" the male voice called.

Doubly startled, Sapphira looked over by a bay window. There a bespectacled man with thinning hair and a large blunt nose sat in a rocking chair. "We are in need of more spirits," he said in his sinuous accent. Raising an empty glass, he leered at the bare-breasted duo. "A sweeter vintage, perhaps, to induce sweeter behavior."

The lamplight caught on his lenses, obscuring his eyes. Wondering if he was looking at her again, Sapphira began to stammer. Then she remembered her role. "Yessuh–ah go gits you some mo' . . . "

"And greetings to you, sir!" the man called, smiling with crowded teeth. "Voila, mademoiselles–it is our Mister Wakefield's trusty assistant!"

Sapphira eyed the young man beside her, his pimpled face slack with amazement. The bespectacled man addressed him with grand courtesy, though he did not rise from his chair.

"Young sir! Forgive me, but I have not yet learned your name."

Gawking, the youth failed to answer right away. On the settee, the weeping girl paused to gulp her drink. One of the topless two, slim and auburn-haired, started swaying on her heels while the other, an ample redhead, giggled listlessly. The youth blinked. Absently he placed his pistol atop a china cabinet, then took the hat from his scruffy head. "Name's George," he said.

"Doctor Antoine Dubray, at your service. I welcome you, Monsieur George–for I am in despair. I have been begging these lovely creatures to delight me with a little dance–a waltz, a gavotte, a rustic jig. But no, they would sooner quarrel." He gestured to the two girls. "Still, if they had a dashing partner, for whose favors they might compete . . . ?"

The auburn-haired girl stopped swaying. Pouting at George, she rose on tip-toe and spread her arms wide. The redhead stopped giggling to smile at him, but his gaze was locked upon the first girl.

"Mademoiselle Fannie," said Doctor Dubray, "–it seems our guest is willing! Mademoiselle Harriet–a pretty song, if you will, to spur their feet!"

Sapphira realized that she had been standing transfixed for a solid minute. With lowered eyes she curtsied, ready to make a discreet withdrawal. But in that same instant, the girl who had been weeping–a petite blonde in a floral-patterned gown–lurched up from the setee. Staggering to an alcove, she pulled the curtain aside to reveal three chamber pots on the floor. She sank over one of them, vomiting as expressions of disgust swept the room.

Dubray only smirked, watching the movement of the girl's pale shoulders. "Wench," he called, pointing at Sapphira. "See to Mademoiselle Wilhelmina. Or rather, to her leavings."

Sapphira crossed the room and stood over the stricken girl, whose companion on the settee had resumed cursing.

"Now, now," said Dubray, "–let nothing spoil the occasion." At the edge of Sapphira's vision, he rocked lazily, his specs gleaming as they turned to her. "Alors–black, yet comely! Perhaps she should join our games, nah?"

She stiffened, staring down at the girl.

From the table came a voice of whiney indignation. "Doctor, must you insult us so?!"

Dubray gave a sharp laugh. "Allow a gentleman his jest, my dear."

Trembling on all fours, the blonde girl spat a few times while Sapphira prayed for her to finish. Then the girl rolled onto her side. Holding her breath, Sapphira bent down and took up the fouled chamber pot.

"And now I am out of patience," said Dubray, merrily. "Sing, Mademoiselle Harriet! Sing for our charming couple! Make them prance and twirl!"

Sapphira held the pot out in front of her and headed for the door, just as the redhead began trilling a tra-la-la melody. Dropping his hat, George advanced on the auburn-haired one. With hands intertwined, they stood chest-to-chest as the girl commenced a lively drunken jig, her face averted. George scarcely moved, peering down at her bosom.

Over the redhead's high notes, Dubray again called to Sapphira. "Remember–more spirits. Tell Mademoiselle Ursula."

"Ah sho' will, suh!" she blurted.

Pressed together, the dance pair stumbled about as Dubray hunched forward, his gaze intent upon them. Sapphira stepped wide to avoid them and then backed out of the room. "Magnifique!" Dubray cooed, rocking faster. "Ah–most wonderful!"

A short distance back down the hall, Sapphira found an alcove displaying a bust of some Old World nobleman; behind its pedestal she hid the reeking chamber pot. She wiped her fingers on her apron, then continued back the way she had come. By the top of the grand staircase, she halted before a hazy, multicolored glow on the carpet. She had not noticed it the first time. Entranced, she stared down at it and then looked up to find its source, a circular stained-glass window about four feet wide. Through its geometric pieces, the moonlight fell in softly separate hues. She stepped into them and raised her arms, bathing them in bands of red, green and gold.

She recalled her dream of the angels, their bright elastic bodies passing from color to color. She recalled her father's story of the church in Mexico, of the jeweled chalice that had both named and freed her. Though still shaky, she felt clear inside. She was ready–ready for the big woman with the keys, who she guessed to be Ursula. "In the cellar," she muttered.

Returning to the back stairwell, she padded down. At the bottom, she looked both ways before proceeding to the cellar door. Again it was locked–and for one of the few times in her life, she uttered a curse. She had missed her chance. Then, from the front of the house, she heard a conversation in progress. She recognized the voice of the older woman, followed by Ursula's.

"Sit, ma cherie. You deserve to toast victory with us."

"Danke, Madame. Very kind."

The talk emanated from the room into which Ursula had disappeared earlier. With all the stealth she could manage, Sapphira crept closer.

"I regret to say that our friend Wakefield is poor company tonight," said the older one.

"Are you vell, Mister Wakefield?" said Ursula. "Please do be glad vith us."

There was a lapse and then a male voice, too low for Sapphira to catch the words.

On her left, the illustrated wall became the side of the main staircase.

"Napoleon favored cognac–did you know this, Ursula?"

"No, Madame. Most interesting."

Sapphira stopped listening. With each silent step, the big entrance hall loomed higher and wider. Going still, she concentrated on its features–the decorative shields, the broad Oriental rug. Far to the left, she spied a parlor but detected no presence within. To the right, a few feet ahead of her, the room with the voices remained out of view.

The older woman was in the midst of a languid soliloquy: "We who have quit our native shores—we suffer the pangs of memory. Yet one must endure these. In the final tally, a chaotic, ill-formed nation such as this offers greater advantage, more ways to rise and prosper . . . "

Sapphira let herself breathe. For now, she decided, it would be best to simply stay within earshot and await the right moment. She moved to step backward—but without knowing why, she crept forward instead, halting next to the foot of the staircase. Part of the room on the right was now visible, with chairs and tables. From the way the woman's voice carried, Sapphira judged that the three occupants were seated well back in the room, which was apparently a large one. She inched ahead and then moved sideways, placing her back to the staircase.

The hall seemed to expand before her eyes, gaping like a sumptuous maw. Immersed in the fear, she tried to measure herself against it. Daniel, she thought—Daniel in the lion's den. But in Daniel's lions, a spark of mercy had resided, there for his faith to summon. What mercy might she summon forth in this place? And in herself, what sort of faith? Then she thought of her father, and the thought burned its way down—through her legs, through the soles of her feet, down to the cellar.

From the big room, the woman's regal voice lectured on: "It is a matter of harnessing passions—not merely one's own, but the passions of others . . . "

In Sapphira's vision, the hall had returned to its real size. The fear too had ebbed just a little. Clenching her hands, she turned slowly about, glaring at every corner and surface until she faced the stairs. Over the middle landing, draped from the massive supporting beam, the Stars 'n' Bars of the Confederacy looked down on her. Mounted above it was a large black drum with a white emblem at its center, a hawk or an eagle. In the back of her mind, she knew that she had pushed her luck to its limit and that she had to move, to conceal herself. Yet she did not budge. Staring up at the stiff-winged white bird, she imagined herself as its prey.

90

Fort Derussy
12:15 A.M., July 11

DEEP IN THE crowd of soldiers, Tucker listened as if for rumblings in the earth. But it was only Monks he heard–Monks up on the gun carriage, more composed now but with strain in his voice, his delivery a shade too theatrical:

"Owing to breaks in communication, we've known little of the situation overall–so District Command thought it best to have a contingency plan. That signal . . . " Again he thrust a finger toward the pair of torches, a fiery metronome in the dark. "–is part of that plan. It indicates a surprise development. Regrettably, it means our position here is untenable."

Among the gunners and militiamen, there ensued a murmuring discussion over what the word "untenable" meant. But in Tucker's head, the grimmer words of Captain Forbes stuck like shrapnel: "treason," "collusion," "mortal pressure."

The artillery lieutenant jumped down from the parapet. Standing next to the big cannon, he gazed up at Monks. "But, sir–if they attack, surely we can hold them off awhile! If we . . . "

"Never mind that! What's happening is . . . the enemy has gotten here faster than expected. They must have breached the perimeter. How or why we don't know yet, but the order now is for an immediate tactical withdrawal. We're to help form a new defensive line a mile to the south."

Starting with those closest to the platform, the troops' murmuring began to subside. The lieutenant looked incredulous. "Sir, if we just place a gun or two down by the creek . . ."

"Damn it, it's an order!" Monks snapped. "We must evacuate with all due haste!"

Griffith coughed and squinted, then spoke. "Sir, uh . . . Isn't it right that there's a reserve camp close by? Couldn't that force (cough!) be moved up while we . . . ?"

"Enough of this!" Monks yelled.

From shock, the lieutenant's expression passed to full alarm. "Sir, if there was ever a time to be steadfast, it's now! We can hold out! Grant has sent reinforcements, hasn't he?"

Men herded in closer. Monks' eyes darted side to side, his sunken cheek twitching. He fired a look over his shoulder. "This . . . This is outrageous!" he sputtered. As he shook his binoculars in the lieutenant's face, his voice turned shrill. "This is my command and I intend to save it! You will assemble your platoons!"

Griffith looked befuddled, glancing about as if he had lost something.

Holding his palms out, the lieutenant grew more agitated. "Can we abandon a key position just like that?! Couldn't we at least send out a messenger to verify . . . ?" His words trailed off, his eyes shifting beyond the gun.

Spruce strode into view. Moving around the cannon, he positioned himself between Monks and the two subordinates. He loomed nearly a foot taller than the lieutenant, who he regarded with leonine ease. Tucker wanted to shout what he knew, but it stuck hard in his throat. His heart surged. In this crush of white men, how brave or mad would it be to point at a white officer and yell Treason? When their baffled attention swung from Monks to him, might it then become purest hate? The mob kind? The taunts of Private Floyd now echoed as something more–as chill warnings, the first stirrings of a nightmare.

Spruce's gaze moved briefly to Griffith, then back to the lieutenant. "Lieutenant," he said, "–I don't recall your name." The voice remained amiably supple, as if asking about the smaller man's health.

"Quinn, sir," the lieutenant answered.

"Lieutenant Quinn–Captain Griffith . . . The commanding officer alone is qualified to judge the situation. He has given an order. Any further delay on your part will amount to insubordination. Your authority will be stripped away and junior officers brevetted in your place. And worse consequences will await you, naturally. So, gentlemen, what you are hearing is your last chance to comply. You will assemble your men and march out. Immediately."

Monks' scowling lips quivered as he looked on.

Tensed before the major, Lieutenant Quinn scratched his mustache. "We should at least spike the guns," he muttered.

"March out," Spruce intoned.

Griffith fidgeted, absently stroking his beard. Quinn glanced back at him, then down at the major's boots. He exhaled through his teeth. "I do this under protest, sir."

"So long as you do it."

Blinking hard, the lieutenant jerked a salute and then nodded to one of his sergeants. "Fall in," he said in a parched voice. He stalked away, his Pennsylvanians filing after him, the Ohioans parting to let them through.

Spruce trained his stare on Griffith. The captain coughed, then glanced up. On his wide, doughy face, something definite surfaced at last–gloom, resignation. The fat militia lieutenant appeared, looking anxious as he stepped to Griffith's side. "Captain?" he said. Griffith made a shrugging gesture. "Uh . . . Yes–prepare to march." Braying the order, the lieutenant stepped to the rampart and signaled the men in the rifle pits. Sergeants took up the cry.

As the troops herded back from the wall, Tucker did not move, watching as Monks stepped down from the gun carriage. Monks had recovered something of his blustery pose–but in the next instant, it wilted as Spruce turned and gave him a cryptic look. Treason, from the murk of this night, had assumed not one but two shapes–pawn and master. This haughty scarecrow stuffed with fear, and the cold shadow that dwarfed him. The truth of it hit Tucker like a punch. Staring into the dark distance, he saw the twin tongues of flame still waving.

"You!"

Tucker stiffened. The crowd was gone and Spruce was pointing at him.

"Go ready our horses."

Tucker stared at him.

Advancing to the platform's edge, Spruce placed his hands on his belt, one by his sidearm and the other touching a sheathed bayonet. "That was a simple enough order."

Tucker twitched a salute and hurried away.

The fort's gate had been opened, Quinn's detachment set to march out. Militiamen scrambled about for their gear and rifles. Near the magazine, amid the swirl of activity, Griffith stood rocking gently on his heels. Tucker headed for him. "Captain," he called, not loud enough. "Captain!"–too loud. Griffith turned around, squinting. As Tucker stood before him, the words came in a rush. "Sir, it's vital that you listen to me. I did come here to locate Monks but I couldn't tell you the true reason. There's information that . . . "

"Slow down, there–slow down." Griffith's hazy eyes studied him. "Now, what's this?"

"You musn't obey the order, sir. You must not evacuate."

"What? I . . . " The eyes narrowed. "Well, Tucker . . . It's Tucker, isn't it? That's, um, a mite impertinent. Besides, you heard all that, didn't you? I'm new to soldiering, and some parts of it I don't care for, but . . . "

"Sir, please hear me out!" Swallowing, Tucker lowered his voice to a harsh whisper. "I was sent here by an officer of the Military Information Bureau. He should be here any minute to arrest Monks for treason. Him and Spruce."

Griffith went still. One hand resumed stroking his beard.

"Captain, does this order make any sense to you? To throw the fort?! That's an enemy signal out there, not one of ours!"

Coughing, Griffith averted his gaze. "Plenty in this world that doesn't make sense. I said my piece, but I'm not the one in charge."

"Listen, sir! Monks is not what he seems and neither is Spruce!"

"They've got fancier shoulder straps than me–that's all I know."

Growing frantic, Tucker felt as if he were talking to an addled castaway, a hollow human shell. He thought of Lieutenant Quinn–but glancing toward the gate, he saw the rear of Quinn's little column trooping out. He leaned closer to Griffith. "They are both traitors, Captain! You can't let them do this!" With a pained expression, Griffith began to turn away. Barely resisting the urge to grab his arm, Tucker spoke almost into the captain's ear. "You're being TRICKED!!"

Griffith swung about to face him, glowering. Around them, all movement ceased, stares mounting like rifle sights. Tucker's last kernel of hope dissolved. Quinn, he thought–he should have run after Quinn. Frozen, he felt a powerful need to look over his shoulder.

Griffith coughed and stammered, swollen with indignation. "Now–now–now see here! I've got . . . I've got two that rank me telling me one thing and . . . and here's you–YOU from Lord-knows-where, telling me something different and–and–and . . . Well, it's damned impertinent and what's a man to think, eh?! What the devil's a man to do?!"

The captain's fulmination went on but Tucker stopped listening. Carefully he turned around. In the play of shadow and firelight, he saw the figure of Spruce pacing toward him; closing to a few yards, Spruce halted and stood there, as dark and rooted as a hanging tree. Tucker's brain wobbled, his heart a cudgel within him. He saw the staked heads of Mount Misery.

"Come here," Spruce said.

Bolting behind the magazine, Tucker crouched there, dazed with his own speed. Griffith had gone mute. The air itself felt paralyzed, and all Tucker could think of was the heads. He had always imagined them too well–shrunken and leathery like rotten fruit, boiling with flies. His side throbbed and a bitter taste filled his mouth. Why had Forbes forsaken him? Nearby, the hefty lieutenant and a few privates stood gawking at him. He wanted to shoot them. Rage blurred his vision, fusing with despair. His fingers dug into the magazine's sod-covered wall. Gathering all of his breath, he tipped his sweaty face to the moonlight and bellowed– "THEY'RE GOING TO THROW THE FORT!!"

In the seconds of unearthly stillness that followed, it seemed that the night had until now been covered in a gauze curtain, and that Tucker's shout had torn it wide. The shadows looked blacker, the torches luridly brighter. Again he let loose–"THEY'RE GOING TO HAND IT TO THE REBS!!"

"Grab him!" Spruce shouted. "Bring him here!"

In front of Tucker, the knot of militiamen stirred, glancing at one another while their lieutenant gaped at him.

Tucker rose from his crouch. "THEY'RE TRAITORS!!" he yelled, his throat raw.

"You men!" Spruce thundered. "Grab him, I said!"

Startled to action, the big lieutenant fumbled for his sidearm while the other men budged in Tucker's direction, but by then he was running. Only one section of rampart offered him a clear path; he raced for it, his thoughts coming in shard-like flashes: leap over, roll down, pursue Quinn, plead his case. Spruce kept yelling–"Get him, damn you! Get the black bastard!"

All around his hurtling body, Tucker felt something mindless take hold: blood frenzy, pack frenzy, igniting as feet swarmed after him. Flying toward the wall, he prayed that the confusion and the murk of night would keep anyone from shooting at him. Someone clutched his left sleeve but he instantly jerked free, only to see a crouched shape block his way. The man started to raise his rifle but Tucker knocked the barrel aside and lurched around him. With the wall some five yards off, he heard other feet rushing in from his right. Knowing he could run no faster, he veered left toward a gun platform and was one stride short of it when a rifle shot rang out. He tripped as he reached the platform, pitching forward and catching himself hard against the gun carriage.

He tried to spring forward but faltered as his pain came howling back; for a second, he believed he had been shot again. He put a hand to his side–no blood. But he had lost the race, the stampede bearing down on him. Panting, his side full of pain, he pulled himself up. Militiamen crowded around the platform. From the other side of the cannon, a rifle took aim at his head; he could not discern the soldier's face but recognized the jug ears.

"Hold still, now," said Floyd. "I won't be missing twice."

Tucker gazed at the dark shapes hemming him in–his oldest nightmare, upon him at last. Despite all he had done and endured in life, it had risen from the depths to corner him. At his feet he noticed the long shaft of a gun rammer and realized that this was what he had tripped over. A minor physical object had cost him everything. Ridiculous, yes–but maybe most destinies were ridiculous. Clinging to the thought, he hoped it would help him face what followed.

At that moment, a lanky private stepped up and stood next to Floyd, though it was Tucker who he tensely addressed: "What is this? Tell me quick!"

It was Sutherland. Staring at him, Tucker tried to speak. "I was sent . . . sent to . . . "

"I think this buck's talked enough," said Floyd.

Sutherland's head twitched. "Shut it, Floyd."

Still holding his side, Tucker drew a breath and tried again. "Captain Forbes," he croaked, "–he's with Military Information. He sent me to find Monks. They know things . . . "

Lowering his rifle, Floyd turned to confront the younger private. "Boy, that mouth o' yours'll get you whipped. Bad enough, putting stock in a nigger's word over a white man's . . . "

"I didn't join up to run!" said Sutherland, his voice knotting. "To skee-daddle afore a single shot's been fired! Is that what you joined up for?!"

"You damned puppy."

"Sutherland, listen!" Tucker blurted. "Monks is a traitor. So is Spruce. And that signal over there–it's Rebel, not ours. You have to tell Griffith . . . "

The plea went unfinished as Floyd lashed out at Sutherland, striking him with his rifle butt. With a guttural sound, Sutherland dropped his own rifle and stumbled backwards, clapping a hand to his chest. For a second or two he seemed ready to keel over, but then he charged. Floyd dropped his weapon. As the two of them clinched and toppled, a riot of shouting commenced but no one moved to separate them. Just then, over the heads of the crowd, Tucker saw Spruce coming with Monks at his heels, followed by Griffith and the portly lieutenant.

Tucker sagged against the gun. Before him, Floyd and Sutherland rolled, punched and grappled. With typical militia discipline, the platoons outside the fort had broken ranks and were streaming in through the gate. Then, amid the dog-like clamor, Tucker saw Griffith barge past Spruce and begin shoving his way through the rabble.

With the look of an appalled schoolmaster, Griffith burst into the open and beheld the fistfight. "Get up!" he shouted, waving his arms. "Get up, you two, 'less you want a kick!"

The combatants wriggled apart.

Winded, Sutherland sprang to his feet. "Cap'n, sir–I didn't join up to . . . "

"Listen here, Danny . . . !"

"Sir, I . . . I didn't join up to run! Not without a fight!"

The clamor subsided. There was only shuffling and murmuring, more men pushing onto the platform. Having tottered to the side, Floyd bled from one nostril and looked dazed. Griffith scratched his beard and did not look at anyone, while behind him the swollen crowd parted wide. Spruce emerged clutching his pistol. His eyes probed about until they locked on Tucker–and in the faint torch-flicker, Tucker saw what Sutherland had meant about those eyes. They gleamed with something terrible. A pale flame–unnaturally steady, unnaturally pure, like a gas-jet.

Monks appeared beside his master. "Disgraceful!" he huffed. "Captain, I want these two on report–and the rest in formation!"

Undistracted, Spruce waved men aside with his pistol and started toward Tucker.

"Captain Griffith!" Monks barked.

Griffith replied in a soft, toneless voice. "Sir—may we please spike the guns so the Rebs can't use 'em? It wouldn't take but a moment."

"I've told you!" Monks sputtered. "There's not a moment to spare! We're needed elsewhere!" Between Tucker and the advancing Spruce, only Sutherland and the cannon remained as obstacles. Oblivious, Sutherland gazed toward his captain while Monks ranted on: "Hear me, for the last time! If you do not carry out this order . . . !"

Tucker watched Spruce draw closer.

"Yes, yes!" Griffith blurted, coughing. "All right, then! Floyd, Sutherland—you're on report! Everyone else . . . "

"Gentlemen!" Tucker boomed, his head suddenly clear. "From this night forward, the people will say it was you who failed them!!"

Spruce shoved Sutherland out of the way and raised his revolver. Tucker dove behind the cannon just as the bullet screamed off its barrel. Landing on something hard and slender, he let out a yell and then saw the rammer beneath him. "They'll say it was YOU!!" he thundered. Seizing the wooden shaft, he sprang back as Spruce loomed over the cannon and took aim. With a snarl of pain, Tucker swung the rammer. Its cylindrical end struck the pistol in the same fractional second that it fired, and the weapon flew tumbling.

Soldiers jumped back. Losing his balance, Tucker lurched sideways and used the rammer to catch himself. He had not seen where the revolver landed. Making no move to get it, Spruce blinked at him. The major's hard, well-molded face betrayed a surprise that verged on amusement, though his gas-jet stare intensified. Then came a sliding metallic sound as he unsheathed his bayonet. Moving around the gun, he resumed his advance.

Tucker inched backward, holding the rammer at a forward angle. "They'll say it was the Hundred and Thirty-Sixth Ohio!" he cried. "Company G—the ones who obeyed a couple of traitors! Who let the Rebs into Washington!!"

Spruce was yelling over him—"Take him! Go at him!" With brisk motions, the major turned and singled out a few dumbstruck privates, who then hesitantly arrayed themselves behind him. Hunching, Tucker raised the rammer high and thought of diving for the wall. He doubted that he could make it before Spruce or the others got to him. Spruce took another careful stride, his blade glinting. "Striking at an officer," he intoned, "—a fatal offense, if there ever was."

"Why was the battery pulled back from the ford?!" Tucker bawled. "Why won't they even let us spike the guns?!"

As if struck by electricity, Monks began flailing his fists. "Idiots!" he shrieked. "Kill him, goddamn it! Shoot him!"

Amid the shrill curses, a soldier on Spruce's left pointed his Springfield at Tucker. Tucker felt the hope draining out of him. Then, as abruptly as it had started, Monks' tirade ceased. The soldier lowered his rifle, turning his head in the lieutenant-colonel's direction. Spruce too pulled his eyes away from Tucker, who only then dared to look.

Monks was reeling like a drunkard, one hand pressed to his forehead while the other groped in front of him. His hat fell off. The men nearest him stepped back except for Griffith, who went to catch him but hesitated as Monks sank to his knees, moaning. Griffith looked up in bewilderment, his eyes meeting Tucker's across the cannon barrel.

Whatever was afflicting Monks, Tucker knew he could not let it distract him. Jabbed with a terrible inspiration, he called hoarsely to Griffith, trying not to yell. "If we quit this fort, sir, all the Union dead will have died for nothing. The dead of Antietam, the dead of Gettysburg . . . "

"Captain, move them out!" Spruce commanded. "I'll take care of this one!"

"The dead of Petersburg," Tucker rasped. "Petersburg, sir. Every life wasted."

On Griffith's broad pale face, a stillness took hold. At his feet, Monks let out another moan and tried to get up.

"Form ranks!" Spruce shouted.

"Petersburg!" Tucker bellowed. "All for noth . . . "

Spruce lunged blade-first at Tucker. Tucker jerked the rammer at Spruce's arm but the major skipped nimbly away. As Spruce stood fondling the bayonet, his gaze seemed to consume the air around him. Slowly he began to circle Tucker, who turned with him. The men that Spruce had ordered up had withdrawn, though Tucker knew that any one could shoot him at any moment. None of them made a move–too absorbed, perhaps, in the stealthy dance before them, the motion of predator and prey. Spruce edged forward. As Tucker edged back, his heel bumped a hard surface, and he realized that he had backed up against the gun.

In the torchlight, Spruce's sneer looked chiseled into his face. Tucker's breath had turned ragged and his hands numb, clutching the rammer, his skin suddenly cool. He sensed that only a lethal blow could stop his adversary, a blow that his weary arms and this oversized stick could not deliver. Once more he felt the pale-eyed stare, the dull stares of the multitude, the hope running out through his legs. In Spruce's bestial grace–in the broad-shouldered hunch of his silhouette, somehow taller than before–all the darkness and all the coiled savagery of night seemed concentrated. The blade gleamed as he moved in. Abruptly, from Tucker's left, a squat figure came shambling into view. Flinching, he nearly fell back against the cannon and then he was staring at Griffith's bearded profile, directly in front of him. The captain did not look at him or at Spruce but stood motionless between them, as if he had wandered there by accident. He was gazing over the parapet and the field toward a moonlit pine grove.

Equally still, Spruce looked down at Griffith, his stare cooling to puzzlement. It was a moment before he spoke. "Captain . . . Step out of the way."

Looking out on the shadowy terrain, Griffith bore the intent, quizzical look of one who had awakened in an unexpected place. The cough had left him. "You know, back home I run the feed store." He gave a lifeless chuckle. "Sort of wish I was there now."

As the troops bunched in closer, Tucker noticed Sutherland among them, transfixed.

In a tone of chill restraint, Spruce spoke again. "Step aside."

Griffith glanced up at him. "Yep–orders are orders. When I took the bounty and put on these soldier duds, I reckon that's what I agreed to."

Behind Griffith, the fat lieutenant hovered like a fretful manservant. Then Monks came tottering up. Recovering from his swoon, he pulled his hat on and stood behind Spruce.

"No, sir," Griffith went on. "–you can't pick what orders you get, or who gives 'em."

Spruce's voice went lower. "No, you cannot. Get out of the way."

Seemingly lost in the night distance, Griffith did not respond.

Tucker crouched. Holding the rammer close, he drew his heel up onto the gun carriage. He wondered if he should vault over the cannon, and how badly it might hurt his side. Or should he just charge the wall again? Over Griffith's head, Spruce's deathly eyes flashed at him.

"Captain," said Spruce, "–you are relieved of command."

Looking down at the bayonet, Griffith at last turned to face the major. "Begging your pardon, sir, but isn't that for the ranking officer to say?"

Spruce's jaw tightened. He cast an eye over his shoulder and Monks stiffened, then moved up beside him. "You are relieved, Captain!"

Tucker glanced toward the wall. Then, reconsidering, he hopped backwards onto the carriage and ducked under the cannon barrel, feeling some pain as he did so. He drew the rammer up after him and stood looking down. Between him and Spruce, several inches of iron now served as a barrier.

Monks jabbed a finger at the lieutenant. "I brevet you captain. Now—get them marching!"

Open-mouthed, the lieutenant looked pleadingly at Griffith but the captain ignored him, ambling back toward the hushed audience of militiamen. Griffith's shoulders drooped. He removed his hat, ran a hand through his hair. In the dense crossfire of eyes, he seemed more alone and oblivious than ever.

Spruce sent Tucker a barely detectable smile. Tucker felt it like steel across his throat.

Monks seemed to have finally shed his hysteria, his wrath and contempt sounding genuine as he faced the lieutenant. "March them out, I said!"

There was a ripple through the crowd, a few men shouldering arms. With an air of loutish defeat, the lieutenant turned to the troops. "Company . . . "

"I don't know what kind of order my boy Virgil got." It was Griffith, his voice suddenly clearer. With his back to Monks and Spruce, he stood kneading the brim of his hat. "Don't know who gave it, either. But he obeyed—I know that. Virgil was a good boy."

"Enough, man!" Monks spat.

"Heck, it might've been a halfway smart order, one that made sense. Lord knows, it doesn't matter now."

"Fool! I'm through with you! I could have you shot!"

"That's a fact, sir." Griffith turned, squinting down at the packed earth. "And that'd sure be a queer end, wouldn't it? Virgil obeys, his pa doesn't—and lo and behold, they both get shot."

Lowering his blade, Spruce shifted his gaze from Tucker to Monks.

Monks' teeth showed, his face twisting in a grimace. Leaning toward Griffith as if to pounce, he shook his fist. "Worthless oaf! I'll put you under arrest! I'll see you hanged! I'll . . . " The fist went still. In a rigid stoop he stood there, eyes bulging at the captain. No one moved.

Griffith gave a limp sigh and looked up. Sorrow blurred his features. "Yep . . . You could do that, sir. Or you could go to hell. Cuz it hits me that I don't really care. Maybe when the last boy's dead and buried, it'll turn out that Virgil and all of them died for nothing–but I'd rather it was for something, understand? So I'm thinking of him–he was eighteen, you know . . . " On Griffith's face, the odd, waking look had returned. He swallowed. "And I'm thinking 'bout what this buck soldier here's been saying, and I'm wondering why you're so keen to kill him. And I'm looking at you and at this major of yours and asking myself, 'Who's really top dog here?' And I smell something, sir. Cuz I might seem strange to you–and strange I might well be, these days–but I have to say, you seem *powerful* strange to me. So give whatever infernal order you want to–cuz in the end a fellow's got to decide for himself, soldier duds or no. I'm not helping you. I won't help you make things easy for the Rebs. Matter of fact, I'm aiming to make things hard for the Rebs, if I can. So l repeat, sir–you can go flying barefoot to hell. That's all."

Monks' posture was unchanged, though his stare had turned glassy.

Pulling his hat on, Griffith looked to his lieutenant. "Order the men . . . "

"FALL IN!!" Monks shrieked.

From the gawking rabble, Sutherland's voice answered–"We're with the captain!"

A rumble of affirmation swept the company.

" . . . back to their posts," said Griffith.

Resolve suddenly gripped the lieutenant as well, and he boomed the order. With a clinking and clattering of gear, the crowd began to break up. Tucker stayed put. Weak in every joint, he realized that Spruce was no longer in front of him. He looked around, startled, then saw the tall figure striding away. Amid the bustle and the troops' wary glances, the major stooped for his revolver and holstered it. Then, with the calm of one accustomed to cutting losses, he moved off. In the firelight, Monks gaped after him, his cheek twitching, hands trembling at his sides.

Tucker was still gripping the rammer. With stiff, bent fingers he propped it against the gun. He saw Floyd skulking off, wiping his nose. All around, men were positioning themselves along the walls, others trooping back out to the rifle pits. Griffith, having returned to the forward point, stood by the big Parrott and gazed through Monks' discarded binoculars. In the outer darkness by the bridge, the two points of flame still waved, faster but in a narrower arc. Tucker wondered how much time had passed since the first sighting–fifteen minutes? An hour? He was thirsty, the sweat running beneath his tunic. Then Sutherland was standing next to him.

"Thank you, soldier," Tucker said.

With a scrape on his freckled cheek, Sutherland still looked agitated. "You're welcome." He stared over at Monks. "Captain just told a few of us to keep an eye on him."

Monks leaned with both hands against the rampart, his shoulders quaking.

Tucker tapped on Sutherland's canteen. "Can a spade-black son of Cain get a swig?"

Unstopping the canteen, the youth gave it to him. Tucker took a long drink.

"Look at this."

Wiping his mouth, Tucker saw Sutherland pointing. Through the fort gate, Lieutenant Quinn's compact little column was returning at the double-quick. Tucker handed the canteen back and headed toward the artillerists. They were separating into crews, each one hastening to its assigned gun.

Griffith too went out to meet them, now with a spring in his step, and got there ahead of Tucker. "You too?" he called.

Panting, Quinn nodded. "You can credit him, yonder." He gestured toward the gate, where a lone, hobbling figure had appeared–Forbes.

"Captain!" Tucker yelled, rushing over to him.

Forbes was carrying his saddlebags, his tunic mud-splattered and unbuttoned. Winded, he limped to a stop and raised a hand. "Tucker, I'm . . . Listen, I was . . . "

"Sir–Monks tried to evacuate, but I raised a fuss and Captain Griffith refused the order. Anyhow, Monks is here for the taking. And the enemy's still out there, sending a torch signal."

Getting his breath, Forbes nodded. Briskly he explained that upon leaving Fort Bayard, his horse had stepped in a gopher hole and broken her leg, forcing him to shoot her and proceed on foot. He had stopped at Forts Reno and Kearny–no Monks. And no horse for him to beg or steal. But at last he met Quinn and his men, found out what was happening and showed them the arrest warrant.

Tucker only nodded, his attention gone dull. Despite his giant sense of relief, far more immediate was the memory of Spruce's pistol aimed at him, Spruce's bayonet ready to run him through. "There's another man here that needs arresting," he blurted. "A Major Spruce."

Forbes let the saddlebags drop. "Spruce?!"

"Yes—a real viper. He would have killed me if . . . "

"Tucker, he's the one I told you about!"

"Sir?"

"The killer, from La Maison! His main alias is Monroe, but he also goes by Spruce. Major Henry Spruce."

Pivoting, Tucker looked all around for the fearsome silhouette. "Damn it, he was here!"

Forbes muttered a curse. "As we got to the fort, Quinn placed a guard on the stables—but at the same moment, a rider flew past us in the dark." He snatched up the bags. "I'd say he's making tracks to La Maison—where Truly likely is."

Tucker winced, thinking of Sapphira. "Where is the place, sir? How far?"

"It's about a mile south of Fort Stevens, back your way. With the Rebs so close we'll have to detour, but Spruce will too. I saw a farm track back there. We can leave Monks here under guard . . . "

"No chance of that, I fear." They turned to see Griffith approaching with Sutherland behind him, the private looking troubled. "Danny here tells me the fellow just jumped the wall and made for the woods."

Sutherland gave an embarrassed shrug. "He was gone 'fore we could lift a finger."

Tucker did not care about Monks. His legs burned to move.

Glancing away, Forbes let out a sharp sigh. "Well . . . I still get his horse."

The four of them hurried out to the stable, where Griffith dismissed the two gunners standing guard. Sutherland helped Tucker saddle the horses while Forbes urged Griffith to hold fast, saying the torchbearers were probably just an advance party. With unclouded gaze, Griffith said he would give their signal a fitting reply. Forbes climbed atop Monks' bay. Tucker, already mounted, traded a salute with Griffith and a nod with Sutherland, to which the youth added a hesitant wave.

Forbes led Tucker around the wooded hill and onto a farm track. There followed an ordeal of careful trotting through the darkness, ducking pine boughs while aching for sight and speed. At one point, from the fort's direction, a cannon blast startled them. Neither man spoke. They crossed a stream bed and began to pick up speed, the track widening into a true road. With Sapphira's name drumming in his head, Tucker drew even with Forbes–and when the tree cover at last gave way to stars, they rode like demons into the moonlight.

91

La Maison De l'Empereur
12:15 A.M.

ON THE MIDDLE staircase landing, Sapphira waited beside the bust of some foreign general–"Marshal Ney," it said on the pedestal. His proud aquiline face had oppressed her at first but now she was fond of it–her lone companion, keeping her nerves in check. In the big room downstairs, the conversation went on, though she could hear little of what was said. The voice of the older woman–Nora's "Miz Rav'nel," she concluded–still dominated, its tone alternating between instruction and mockery, with fawning accompaniment from Ursula. The man called Wakefield spoke least, his voice low.

She almost jumped when she heard Ursula excuse herself and enter the main hall below. At the sound of the ascending pair of feet, she reflexively smoothed her apron. Ursula's sullen moon face rose before her–eyes lowered, the dark hair done up in sausage curls. Two steps short of the landing, Ursula saw her and stiffened.

Sapphira twitched a curtsy. "Beg yo' pardon, ma'am. Nora, she as' me come by an' finish up fo' her tonight. I her cousin."

Ursula's look passed from surprise to indignation. Remembering that the woman was foreign–German, she supposed, the accent being close to Kirschenbaum's–Sapphira made herself speak more slowly. "See, Nora got herself a sick chile. So she as' me come here so she kin git home early. You sho got a fine big house here, ma'am."

Ursula glared. "That . . . That lazy, stupid vench!"

Recalling Nora's swollen cheek, Sapphira tried to look just timid enough. "I's awful sorry, ma'am, but I do whatever you tells me. Dat doctor upstair, he say dey needs mo' liquor. He tell me to bring 'em some."

On Ursula's round face, anger merged with disdain. She stabbed a finger at Sapphira. "For this night Nora vill get no pay! And ven she next time comes, I vill teach her to not bring strange maids here!"

"Yes'm. But dat doctor, he say for me to bring dat bottle right quick."

Ursula glowered, then glanced upstairs. "Vat is your name?"

"Sapphira, ma'am."

From her waistband, Ursula drew the key-ring. "In this house, none but Madame and Mister Monroe and me may get spirits from the cellar. I vill get the bottle and you vill bring it."

Sapphira tried not to stare at the keys. "Yes'm."

Ursula turned with a huff and started back downstairs, muttering in German. Following close, Sapphira tried to grasp what she was about–and having grasped it, broke into a cold sweat. She was less aware of her concealed weapon than of the hand that would use it. As the two of them rounded the newel post and entered the dim back hall, she eyed the pinkish nape of Ursula's neck. Dread spiraled through her. And like a separate being, her hand started to quiver.

Ursula unlocked the cellar door, telling Sapphira to light the candle on the little stand. Sapphira took a match from the box and tried to light it, but her trembling foiled two attempts. Snatching the box from her, Ursula lit a match in one stroke. She lit the candle, blew out the match and took up the holder.

"You vill vait here," she snapped, opening the door.

With a rustle of crinoline, Ursula squeezed through the doorway. Sapphira watched her large, illuminated shape vanish into the cellar darkness. In her ears, her pulse mounted, rivaling the sound of Ursula's descent. Here was her one best chance. She had to seize it.

She hurried down the corridor to the kitchen. By the cupboards, on a hook-studded section of wall, several pots hung from their handles. She selected a small one and took it down, then returned to the open cellar doorway. Placing her foot on the first step, she quietly shut the door behind her, enclosing herself in darkness. Her left hand felt beneath her apron and drew the revolver–and with slow, blind caution, she descended.

The steps creaked as she eased her way downward. Then, near the foot of the stairs, a dull light appeared. She went still, breathing the musty air as the light strengthened, and she heard the rustle of Ursula's approach. Below her, only a few steps remained. She forced herself down one, down two. Then, from the bottom, Ursula's shadow thrust toward her, followed by the waddling shape itself. Sapphira froze with the pot behind her back, squeezing the handle. Unsteadily she pointed the revolver. Starting up the stairs, Ursula held the candleholder in one hand and a bottle in the other. She ascended to within two steps, then halted with a gasp. Raising the candle, she peered up, her eyes first wide with alarm and then narrowing with rage. "You!" she snarled. "I told you to . . . " Sapphira raised the muzzle to Ursula's dimpled chin. Again the eyes went wide, fixing upon the weapon. Trembling, her lips began to emit a stream of gibberish, an extended whimper. The candlelight fluttered.

Curling her finger about the trigger, Sapphira tried to speak a command of some kind, but her parched tongue would not respond. She thought of her father, then of Nora's swollen cheek. Then she remembered the pot and, with all the force she could summon, brought it down on Ursula's skull. The impact made a sharp sound, like the bark of a dog. Tottering and then reeling backwards, Ursula dropped the bottle and the candleholder, both objects thumping off the steps to the dirt floor below. The candle rolled free, and in its weakened flicker Sapphira saw Ursula at the foot of the stairs, seated upright and holding a hand to her head. The woman made no sound at first. Then, from deep in her throat, a wail began, climbing swiftly. In a spasm of alarm, Sapphira leapt down and crowned her victim a second time. Ursula went silent, though she remained upright. Placing the revolver on a step, Sapphira clutched the pot handle with both hands and struck a third, more vicious blow. The big woman slumped like a grain sack.

Sapphira crouched above the shadowed form. In her mind the blows reverberated, but at length she relaxed her grip on the pot and put it aside, then took up the revolver and holstered it. Carefully she retrieved the still-flickering candle, found the holder and stuck the candle back in, raising it over the sprawled figure. The moon face had gone slack, the eyes half-open. Shuddering, Sapphira noticed a wetness by the curly head, then saw it had leaked from the cracked wine bottle nearby. She pulled the ring of keys from Ursula's waistband, slid it onto her wrist and started forward. Then she turned around, wondering how soon Ursula might revive. Deciding not to chance it, she lifted the woman's legs and gathered them in the crook of her arm.

Straining forward, she held the candle aloft as she passed into a long, dank chamber. She halted for breath, switched arms and resumed hauling Ursula, who made no sound. Casks and tiered bottles lined the walls. Near the end of the chamber, on the right, she found an archway of sagging masonry and dragged Ursula through, entering a larger portion of the cellar. From behind, a clinking sound startled her. Dropping Ursula's legs, she whirled about. She saw nothing until she shone the candle downward, revealing a coiled length of chain. There was something attached to it. Lowering the candle, she recognized the object as a prisoner's collar, its long radial spokes plainly intended to deny all physical comfort. Her shudder went deep this time, reaching her stomach as the glow revealed other implements: a branding iron, rusted shackles, a cat o' nine-tails with lead weights. Against the wall by the archway leaned another tool, slender and cobwebbed. Bending, she saw that it was made from an animal's legbone, browned with age. Its upper end sported a leather grip while the lower had been honed to an arrow-sharp point, and she realized she was looking at a slave goad. To the mind attached to the hand that once held it, it had perhaps been something more–a proud personal symbol, like a feathered hat or an engraved walking stick.

The darkness was suddenly a physical weight pressing in on her. She could feel it gathering power, silently marshalling itself to extinguish her. Arrayed at her feet, the slaving implements seemed possessed of some hideous intelligence, ready to slink forward, seize her by the limbs and cut into her. She backed away. In the glow, the sudden sight of Ursula's hand made her throat seize, and she had to convince herself that she was not alone with a corpse. She held the candle up, watching Ursula's bosom rise and fall. Then she remembered who and what she had come here for. Praying that she had not been led wrongly, she turned and opened her mouth to call–but in the next instant, there came a shout, raspy and clenched with hatred: "Here I am, God damn you! Come on! Come look me in the eyes, you coward! You heap of shit!"

For an interminable minute, Truly had been concentrating on a story that a Russian watchmaker had told him in New York. It concerned Czar Peter the Great. Tired of his czarina, Peter had confined her to a convent so he might more freely pursue other women. Somehow, in her isolation, the czarina acquired a lover of her own, but a spy informed Peter of the affair. Visiting the cell where his wife's lover was being tortured, Peter offered the prisoner a choice: to kiss his royal ring and be mercifully dispatched, or to die in slow agony–whereupon the man spat in the despot's face. On occasion, ever since hearing the story, Truly had thought of that anonymous martyr, that doomed ferocious nobody.

Blind and shackled, Truly felt as if the pitch dark itself was holding him, pinning him like a phantom jailer. His hearing had seemingly intensified twenty-fold; so had his dread, swelling as he heard footsteps from the direction of the liquor space. Worn down to his soul, he did not try to make sense of the other noises–and as faint candlelight appeared through the door's barred window, he seized upon the tale of the czarina's lover. If this night could have but one end, he thought, it was best ended in defiance–a roar instead of a sob, a curse instead of a plea. And maybe in the final throes, a light of grace would shine and bear him off to Rachel. He started thrashing, cursing, sputtering, his voice thick with fury, his fury exalting every caged dog, bear, bull or man that had ever died so. He would spit in Heath's face.

"Father! . . . Father?!"

He fell quiet. At the cell's far end, a candle flame silhouetted the bars before fading slightly. Breathless, he listened as frantic hands fumbled with a set of keys, repeatedly trying to unlock the door. It could not be, he thought. It was an auditory mirage, a dream born of desperation–anything but what he had heard. The door swung open. The light shone in. Sapphira entered, wraithlike, dressed in a white apron and bonnet.

"Where are you?" she whispered.

Hanging from his chains, he did not answer, but then she raised the candle and hurried to him. She placed the candle at his feet and proceeded to try the keys on each shackle. The glow touched her smooth brow, her intent ebony eyes. Pinching a smaller key, she tried again. He felt the metal unclamp from one ankle and then the other. Resting against the wall, he watched her go to work on his wrists.

"Ursula's unconscious," Sapphira blurted. "I hit her. I brought your old revolver."

The last manacle snapped free. Staring into Sapphira's face, he gripped her forearms and struggled for speech. "How . . . ?"

She shook free. "We have to get out!"

Dazed and stiff, he nodded. "Yes."

Sapphira picked up the candle, took him by the elbow and guided him through the doorway. Outside the pen, she shined the candle around the walls of chipped mortar. Truly allowed himself a deep breath. "There must be a bulkhead."

"There," she said.

The glow hovered on a pair of plank doors secured with a crossbar. Truly went over and lifted the heavy bar from its slots. Pulling the doors open, Sapphira ducked through and Truly ducked after her. A half-dozen steps led up to a pair of bulkhead doors. Stooping, Truly crept up to the sturdy sloping doors, placed his palms alongside the seam and pushed. The doors gave a little and then resisted. Through a gap of a few inches, he saw a chain pulled taut. He eased the right door down while supporting the left, then reached through the gap with his free hand. Straining, he groped until he felt a padlock. He withdrew the hand, eased the other door down and peered over his shoulder. Sapphira's beautiful illuminated face bore a look he had never seen on her, that he had seen only on veteran soldiers—a feral alertness, pure as fire. How could she be here? It was sublime. It was horrible.

"I can reach the lock," he said. "Maybe the key's on the ring."

As she passed the keys up, a moan emanated from somewhere behind her. She glanced back into the dark. "Ursula," she whispered.

Truly rubbed his sore wrists. "We'd best do something about her."

They dragged Ursula into the pen. She moaned, struggling feebly as they chained her by the wrists. Still trying to grasp that he would not die in that dank chamber, Truly felt doubly anxious to leave it. He turned to do so, but Sapphira and her candle did not budge. Leaning over Ursula, she reached under her grime-streaked apron, drew the revolver and held it to the German's throat. Ursula's eyes fluttered. Truly was about to pull Sapphira away, but shock stilled him as he heard her whisper, "Not one sound—not one little noise, or I'll kill you."

WAKEFIELD POURED A second glass of cognac, but not for himself. Tired of Ravenel's barbed pleasantries and pontificating, he left her and went in search of George. He wanted simple, benign company—lame jokes, admiring attention of some sort. Perilously close to self-pity, he willed the pity in George's direction, considering what a fix this surely was for any young blockhead–to find himself in the District's most exclusive bordello, yet barred from its pleasures. Wakefield would hand him the drink, praise his loyal service and promise him rewards. They would speak with relish of Early's impending glory, of their own roles in it, of the radiant new prospects for the Confederacy.

Moving down the rear hall, he called George's name. He called it again in the kitchen. With some annoyance he put the drink on the table and checked the pantry. George was not there. Opening the back door, he called into the dark but got no answer. Unsettled, he shut the door and wandered back out to the hall. He was almost to the storeroom when, from upstairs, he heard a muffled shot and then screams.

Bounding up the back stairs and down the second-floor hall, he heard screams, yelps and curses. He caught the sound of Dubray's agitated voice trying to calm someone. Reaching the closed door of the sitting room, Wakefield drew the revolver from his shoulder holster and listened. Dubray was pleading–"Non! Non, er . . . Nein, liebchen! See how you have upset your friends!" Wakefield shoved the door open and stepped in, poised to shoot.

Glasses, bottles and playing cards were strewn around the capsized card table, its chairs knocked over. Girls cringed in corners and behind the sofa. Two of them, Fannie and Harriet, were crouched wide-eyed and half-naked by the door. On the far side of the room stood Wilhelmina, jittery as she clasped a revolver with both hands, aiming at no one in particular. Her eyes swam, tears coursing down her cheeks. The weapon looked much like the sleek Remington that Wakefield had given George. A few feet away, George faced her with raised hands and a look of tongue-tied urgency.

"Wakefield, do something!" called Dubray.

Dubray was huddled behind the rocker; above him, Wakefield spied a bullet hole in the damask wallpaper. Wakefield holstered his weapon and looked over at Wilhelmina, who only now seemed to notice him.

She started blubbering. "Mister Wakefield . . . These ones here, they do not leave me alone! They keep insulting! I vish . . . " She drooped, sobbing harder. "I vish to leave this place!"

Extending a hand, he moved toward her. "I know, Wilhelmina–it's all gone too far."

"They do not stop. Tell them to stop."

"I will. They will. Now please, give me that."

She made a series of gasping sounds. "I vant–to go–away . . . "

"Wilhelmina . . . "

Trembling, she lowered the revolver. George sprang forward and snatched it from her. Rising from behind the rocker, Dubray straightened his spectacles, scowled and then advanced upon the tottering girl. His hand drew back to slap her but Wakefield grabbed it, twisted his arm and shoved him aside. Holding Wilhelmina by the shoulders, Wakefield guided her toward the settee and she collapsed on it, still weeping, smelling faintly of vomit.

Having gotten to their feet, the other females looked on with bleary expressions. Fannie and Harriet, suddenly demure, pulled up their dress tops. Wakefield turned his gaze upon George. Eyes down, the youth scratched his shaggy head, then bent to pick his hat off the floor.

Wakefield glared. "A simple duty–and you abandon it."

Flushed, George would not look up.

"And a drunk girl ends up with your revolver."

"I'm–I'm . . . Mister Wakefield, I . . . "

"You know, George, it's a good thing you never enlisted. They'd have shot you for dereliction."

The youth winced. "Mister Wakefield–I'm sorry, I . . . That wench, that colored maid–she brung me here. She talked me into it."

"What?"

"She . . . " Kneading his beat-up hat, George fell silent.

Wakefield yanked him into the nearest corner. "All right–how'd it happen?"

George spoke in a mumble, his head still bowed. "I was keepin' watch just like you said. Then this black wench, this maid–she come 'round and asks where Truly is, says she's s'posed to bring him some water. So I tell her he's down the cellar but the cellar's locked up. Then she starts talkin' 'bout how I ought to . . . " Wakefield grabbed him by the sleeve. Jerking loose, George looked up with eyes of pained protest. "I'm sorry, Mister Wakefield! What else can I tell you, dang it?!"

"Dubray!" snapped Wakefield. "This maid who brought him in here– was she one of the usual ones?"

"I see no reason for your ill-mannered tone."

"Answer me, you quack! Was she one of the usual maids?!"

Harriet spoke up. "I never seen her before."

Others shook their heads.

"That one, Nora," said Fannie, "–she came 'round a couple o' times. But this other wench I didn't recognize. I figured her for a new one, sir."

Dubray gave an irritable sigh. "What do I know of the help? In any event, this one should be discharged. I instructed her to get us more spirits, but she has not done so."

Wakefield stared at the floor. "Ursula went to look in on you several minutes ago. You're telling me she hasn't been here?"

"No," chimed the two Irish girls.

To Wakefield, the floor's scattered objects became charged with menace–storm debris, wreckage in miniature. He looked up at George. "Come with me. Quick!"

Racing back up the hall, Wakefield stopped at Ursula's room and banged on the door. "Archer!" he yelled. "Come downstairs!" He did not wait for a response. With George at his heels, he flew back down the rear stairwell and stopped at the cellar door. Beside it, the candle was gone from the stand. He tried the knob and it turned.

Sternly inquisitive, Ravenel appeared with the derringer at her side. "What is it, Wakefield?"

"We have an infiltrator."

She frowned, eyeing George. "And did you not have this young man standing guard?"

Again George wilted.

"Leave him be," said Wakefield. "Have you seen Ursula since I left you?"

"I have not."

"Then we must assume they've gotten her, along with the keys."

Fleetingly, Ravenel's face looked more nearly innocent than Wakefield had ever seen it, too mystified for scorn. Then her gaze settled and the smirk formed, serving blame like a poison drink. He wanted to rip it off of her.

"How is the bulkhead secured?" he demanded.

"A chain and a lock," she said flatly, "on the outside."

"And that key's on your ring?"

"Of course."

"Do you think someone could get to the lock from inside?"

"That I do not know, Wakefield. For some silly reason, I never dreamed it would matter. Perhaps you should investigate?" She gestured with the derringer. "These old bones of mine will stand guard here–effectively, unlike some."

SAPPHIRA HAD PLACED the candle on the top step of the bulkhead. Hunched beside Truly, she flipped past several keys and found another smaller one.

"Third try's a charm," Truly muttered.

He pushed up against the bulkhead door, separating it from its partner until the chain pulled tight between them. Angling one thin arm around the chain, Sapphira felt for the padlock. With her other hand she worked the key-ring through the gap, pinching the little key and probing with it. Truly strained his arms, watching her. In the cramped mustiness, the quiet seemed to coil tight around them, disturbed only by the clinking and the sound of their hurried breaths. Then Truly heard the lock snap free. Sapphira pulled her hands back in, tossing the lock and the keys aside as Truly lowered the door and again shoved upward. With a groan it gave wider, the chain sliding loose but then suddenly holding. Bumping his sore head, he muttered a curse.

"It's wound tight around the handles," Sapphira whispered. "Ease down some."

He lowered the door partway, fighting for patience as Sapphira groped outside and began unwinding the chain. Licking sweat from his lips, he listened to the metallic rattle. Sapphira's movements were awkward, then frantic, then triumphant as she yanked the chain inside, casting it down the steps like a slain serpent. Truly gave a final push.

Rising into the moonlight, he rejoiced at the night air and turned around, offering his hand to Sapphira. She took it and began to emerge with the candle, just as a gleam appeared in Truly's side-vision. Jerking his eyes to the rear corner of the house, he saw a burning lamp. Abruptly it came jostling toward them, its glow outlining two male figures.

"Down!" he barked.

As Sapphira retreated and the lamp bore down on them, he seized the left bulkhead door and ducked behind it. A pistol fired, the bullet whizzing overhead. Dropping to the steps, he pulled the door shut and then scrambled back down. He slammed the other set of doors behind him and secured them with the crossbar. Panting, he placed an ear to the seam and heard Wakefield's voice, audible despite the double barrier:

"For the love of Christ, George—don't ever shoot from behind like that!"

Truly turned and saw Sapphira in her dirty apron. Staring at the barred doors, she held the candle and also the Colt.

"All right," he said. "They can't get in this way, any more than we can get out. And if they try the stairs, I'll be waiting for them." He held out his palm. It seemed to him that Sapphira hesitated a bit before handing him the revolver. Holding it up, he eyed the chambers.

"I loaded it," she said.

"So you have. Here, give me the candle."

He led her slowly through the liquor space and out to the stairs, where he placed the candle on a lower step. "There. Anyone tries to come down, I'll have a clear shot."

In the gloom, Sapphira leaned back against the wall. Truly went over and leaned beside her. With listless hands, she untied her apron and bonnet and let them drop, then removed the holster from her yellow sash-belt. She gave him the holster. From her dress pocket she dug two fistfuls of caps and cartridges and surrendered those too. Truly put most of them in his pants pocket and the remainder in his vest. Then he looped the holster onto his belt.

"Captain Forbes and Sergeant Tucker went in search of that officer," Sapphira murmured. "The traitor, I mean. He was identified from one of your photographs."

Truly had to choke off a jubilant yell. Briefly, beneath all of his ache and fear, his heart danced like a spring pony.

Sapphira's voice remained a small murmur. "Once they've done what they must, they'll be here as quickly as possible. The captain said so."

"Good, good—Bart's playing it right. Thank you, child. I can't believe you're here. Half of me doesn't want to—but thank you."

"I had no choice, Father."

She slid down into a crouch, hands resting on her knees. His finger-tips touched her hair. If they survived, he knew, the thought of this would always be a sword in him—that for no reason but his miserable hide, she had braved this house.

"We have a standoff here," he said, "but that's to our advantage. We can make it last till Forbes and Tucker show up." Beneath his fingertips, he felt her nod. "Things will get frisky then, so I'll want you to stay hidden."

"I've plenty of experience at hiding, Father."

He felt her hand curl into his, but the touch told him nothing—nothing of what she had become. He wondered if he had ever seen her clearly. Gazing at the light-fluttered stairs, he cocked his revolver. She had plucked him from death's teeth—and it had taken this, he thought, to make him see what role he cherished above all others. He yearned to feel that role again—the father's protective ferocity, his shielding power. Had this too been taken from him? What would he not sacrifice to get it back?

BACK INSIDE, WAKEFIELD replaced the socket lamp on the wall and faced Ravenel. Archer and Dubray had joined her. Pale and haggard, Archer had his hat and coat on despite being indoors and was holding his service revolver. Dubray, florid with drink, had acquired a clumsy-looking LeMat pistol.

"We kept them from escaping," said Wakefield. "Truly and a young Negress, dressed as a maid. They've sealed themselves in the cellar. I left George to watch the bulkhead."

"Young George, our sentry again? Pardonnez-moi, but I find this not so reassuring." Flinty-eyed, she glanced past his shoulder. "Mister Archer, kindly go and join the boy."

Archer left without a word.

Ravenel sighed. "So, Wakefield—what now?"

"Now, Madam, it is a simple standoff. Both ways out of the cellar are covered. They're trapped. We can wait them out—let them grow weary, inattentive. The advantage is ours."

Her eyes widened. "They are armed, then?"

"Possibly. Probably, if they're as clever as they seem."

Smiling that lizard smile, she cocked her head. "This could be swiftly ascertained, mon ami. With but a spark of courage."

Wakefield propped himself by the cellar door. He gestured to it. "Fine, Madam—ladies of courage first."

Her jaw clamped. "And I thought you an upholder of Southern chivalry."

"Oh, forgive me. Dubray—would you like to venture down?"

Toying with his weapon, the doctor looked peevish.

"No?" said Wakefield. "Then you can contribute by watching the back."

Dubray's finger shot up, wagging. "Do not take me as your lackey! I have tolerated your insults long enough!"

"Just as I tolerate your part in this episode, Doctor. You were every bit as fooled as George, were you not?"

"Go, Antoine," said Ravenel. "Let no one say we are unwilling to do our part."

With a sniff, Dubray turned on his heel and headed for the kitchen.

Ravenel leaned on the other side of the door frame. "Very well. We will wait at least for Monroe, who will no doubt have a bolder plan."

"Fair enough," said Wakefield. "And for now, we should speak low—or better, not at all."

He held her gaze just long enough and then switched to the wallpaper—the horsemen, the bounding stags. An odd, languorous detachment had come over him. He felt a passing admiration for Truly and his surprises—but however this particular surprise had been sprung, he did not care. All he wanted was news from Fort DeRussy.

IN THE DARKNESS of the pear orchard, Ben tied the bay stallion to a tree trunk. According to Chadwick's sleepy yet obliging father, the animal's name was Juniper; Ben was ready to rename it Beelzebub or perhaps Satan. It had tried repeatedly to throw him, especially after refugee traffic had forced a detour through the woods and fields. From his protracted effort to stay mounted, Ben's back and good arm felt strained and his legs bowed.

Through the moon-dappled shrubbery he observed the lit windows of the mansion, the first large house after Piney Branch—not necessarily the right one, but a prime candidate. He crept to the edge of the orchard and peered out. With a jolt he beheld an oversized Confederate battle flag above the rear veranda. His first thought was to charge inside; his second was to sag against a tree and wait for his wobbly brain to settle. He recalled Captain Langstaff's admonition: "Always reconnoiter. Do it quick, if ye must, but do it as chance allows."

Ben drew his Colt Army. On less-than-steady feet he made his way through the orchard and then along the compass of the woods. He passed a series of small, rustic outbuildings until he came to a carriage house and crouched behind it. He gazed along the far side of the mansion to the road, where wagons still clattered past; in their shifting lantern-light, he made out two male figures by the cellar bulkhead. In their hands, Ben glimpsed revolvers.

Staring at the sentries, Ben reflected that he could take the bold route or the cautious one. Laying his weapon on the grass, he shifted his arm in its sling and winced. Perhaps he could sneak up and surprise the pair. Yet he could not know how many others were inside, set to retaliate at the first shot or shout. If his father was captive here–and Sapphira, God forbid–it would be wisest to intrude silently and only then start exacting blood. He picked up his revolver and hurried back the way he had come.

Passing behind one of the sheds, he halted and looked around the corner. The moonlit grounds were brighter near the house, in which a few upper-story windows shone. Dimmer light shone from the veranda's large double window, one side of which had its sash raised–though at this distance, the curtains kept Ben from seeing inside. He crept out into the open, passing a stone well and then a flower-and-vegetable garden. Reaching a shadowy rose arbor, he stopped to listen. He heard the cricket multitude, the muffled noises of the road, Juniper nickering from the orchard–nothing more, though he could not quite trust his hearing.

He gathered himself and started obliquely for the veranda. Nearing it, he looked up at the Confederate banner, its stars and cross blaring treason to the moon. His blood simmered. Then his foot kicked something with a hollow clatter. Catching his breath, he stumbled back and squinted at the ground before him. In the weak light from the veranda, he saw a pair of pails lying there. He held still and strained his ears, teeth set in aggravation. Thinking of the two men he had observed, he eyed the far corner of the house. No one appeared. Stepping around the pails, he moved to the side of the veranda.

He placed his foot on the bottom step, raised his revolver and started up toward a door beside the window. In his gut, a savage hope ignited; like a lit fuse, it burned through him–and he knew that he would kill and smash however much he had to. But as he reached the top step, it was his luck that exploded. In the window's open half, just left of the door, he saw a man's shadow. There was scarcely time to duck before a pistol appeared through the curtains and fired, the bullet whining past his elbow. With a lurching pivot he jumped down, nearly falling as a second wild shot tore the air. Off-balance, he managed to fire his Colt. The window's far-left pane shattered. Remembering the two sentinels, Ben realized he had to take cover.

He hopped the pails, scuttled toward the well and made it there, senses whirling as another shot screamed wide of him. Hunkering against the well's cool masonry, he stared back at the veranda some dozen yards away. In neither the broken nor the unbroken side of the window could he detect any movement. The enemy—equally startled, no doubt—was no marksman; but in his own dizzy left-handed state, Ben thought, neither was he. He turned his gaze to the mansion's far corner. There he spied one of the sentries, a half-hidden silhouette in a bowler and a long coat. Maybe the man had not spotted him yet, or maybe he was trying to draw a bead on him.

Ben's heart sickened. All he had managed to do was stir up the hornets. And while the well offered fair protection, he had placed himself in a potential crossfire. It struck him that the arbor, where the moonlight barely reached, would give his foes a more difficult shooting angle. He tensed to make the dash, then flinched as a bullet struck the masonry near his head. He tipped backwards but quickly righted himself. The shot had come from the veranda. Peering around the other side of the well, he saw two stooped figures, one of them staring through the shattered pane and knocking out some remaining glass with his pistol. Ben pulled up his weapon and fired. Both figures ducked away. He took aim again, but another shot blazed from his far left. The sentry had joined in.

Crouching as low as he could, Ben felt a swoon coming on. Another shot ricocheted off the well. He shut his eyes as the dream sensation hit, sustaining the bullet's cry and bearing him off on black wings. Black wings—reeling in a blue sky, falling amid thunder. Down into the deathstorm, down to the quaking earth where men charged and men fell. It could have been Petersburg or Chancellorsville or a battle yet to come—but it was not real, he told himself. He could not surrender to it. His immediate fix—*that* was real, with bullets as true as any. Shuddering, he forced his eyes open and the dizziness was gone. Another shot rang out, sending up a tiny spout of earth by his leg.

All he could do now was divert the enemy and pray to set something in motion—a chance, a break, anything to help his father and maybe Sapphira too. He stretched his revolver hand around the well. Leaning out, he thumbed the hammer back and aimed at the broken window. A head bobbed up. He fired.

———◆———

THE BULLET CHIPPED the window frame as Wakefield ducked, slipping on the glass fragments. Catching himself against the wall, he saw Dubray crouched with his pistol by the servants' table. The doctor had sobered up in record time. Wakefield felt a swell of disgust but pushed it down, alarmed at the distraction. He had to think.

First an infiltrating Negress, then an escape attempt–now this. Something was seriously wrong. Already the sharp smell of gunpowder filled the kitchen. He had come running at the first shot but had yet to get a good glimpse of the stranger–a Union soldier, Dubray insisted.

Rising slowly, Wakefield held his Colt ready and chanced another look out at the well, a miniature fortress in the moonlight. Behind it, a foot slid out of sight. He flinched as another shot resounded, this one from the side of the house. It struck the grass near the hidden stranger, who squirmed, and in that instant Wakefield glimpsed an epaulette. An officer–Captain Forbes, perhaps, come to liberate his partner? Wakefield took quick aim and fired, hitting the rim of the well. Again the man squirmed into partial view. No, Wakefield decided–too small to be Forbes. He hopped aside as an answering shot splintered the window sill.

Wakefield rubbed his lips in thought. A spirited sort, this bluebelly, but still just one man–surely he could be dispatched with little trouble. He looked over at Dubray, now huddled beneath the table. "Well, Doctor–let me suggest a less hazardous chore for you."

Behind their specs, Dubray's dun-colored eyes were attentive.

"Go out the front. Tell Archer to creep around back through the woods and dispose of this fellow. And tell George to watch that bulkhead like a hawk, because we don't know all of what these people are up to. Off with you, then."

Clutching his LeMat and shoving chairs aside, Dubray crawled out from under the table. He straightened up but then fell to all fours as a shot struck a cupboard behind him.

Wakefield let out a laugh. "One more thing, Doctor. After you deliver the message, find an upstairs window and start firing down at our visitor. We'll make things hot for him while Archer sneaks up. Hurry, now."

Dubray nodded and then sprang for the hall, his coattails flying.

❖

FROM THE CORNER of the house, Archer saw the soldier's head poke up again. He took aim but this time the soldier fired first, missing Archer's shoulder by inches. Unflinching, the detective returned fire, striking sparks off the well as his adversary ducked. Archer stepped back into the shadows. He thought of Cecelia's letter and about his years of loathing–loathing, like flies on a carcass. All of that had ceased to affect him. Beneath the pain of his freshly scourged back, the blood sticking to his shirt, a dead calm had set in. With it had come freedom of a strange sort, as blank and white as paper–the freedom of the dead. Within that blankness, his simple function found all the space it needed–an ease of motion, machinelike as he looked, aimed and fired. He was death's emissary, nothing more. A corpse-emaker, endeavoring to make a corpse of this soldier, this intruder from nowhere. He did not care why.

A few yards behind him, George whispered. "Archer? Archer, what's he doin'?" The detective glanced over his shoulder. Trapped in his obedience, George had not moved from the bulkhead, where he stood fidgeting. "Can we switch places?" he pleaded. "I want to get a look."

Archer stared out at the well. "Stay put," he mumbled.

"What's going on?"

"Only the dead are free."

"What?"

It struck Archer that he could best answer the youth by shooting him, but then he detected movement behind the well. He raised his weapon. From the veranda, another shot made the soldier budge, exposing his hunkered shape. Archer fired. The shape rolled out of view.

A voice rang out–"Missed again, Reb!"

George cursed. "Listen to him, will you? Sir, just let me have one shot at that . . . "

The plea stopped short as Archer heard footfalls on the grass. He and George turned to meet them. From the road, passing lanterns outlined Dubray's figure as he strode up, carrying a revolver. Halting beside George, the doctor assumed his stiff majordomo posture. "Archer," he called. The policeman turned away. From the well, the soldier's weapon flared, the bullet clipping a bush to Archer's right.

Dubray cleared his throat. "Archer–I have instructions for you." Archer looked at him and saw that he had moved back a few paces.

Walking over to him, Archer recalled his first prolonged contact with Dubray–his oily pleasantries, the burning pain of his treatments. At times, during the worst of it, the doctor had seemed on the verge of smiling.

"While Wakefield keeps the soldier occupied," said Dubray, "you, Archer, are to move quietly through the trees until you can shoot him from behind." He glanced at George. "You are to stay here and keep close watch on the bulkhead. Understand?"

George nodded glumly.

Arms folded, the policeman gave no response. Dubray ogled him, then noticed the pistol pointed lazily at his thigh. "Be so kind as to aim that elsewhere."

Archer turned the muzzle toward Dubray's other thigh. "Would you like to know true freedom, Doctor?"

In his side-vision, Archer caught a baffled look from George.

Dubray peered down at the weapon, his brow glistening. "Archer?"

From the rear grounds, one shot crackled over another and the soldier yelled some other taunt. No, Archer thought–he could not sully this mission of his. As a man of principle, he could not let a mere grudge defile that blankness, that pure white void within him. Death was arbitrary, barren of grudges–and if he, its servant and emissary, could not act with indifference in a given case, then he would simply not act. Pointing his pistol at the ground, he heard himself chuckle. "Very well. I will strike with purity, sir."

With troubled eyes, Dubray retreated the way he had come.

Archer started for the woods.

"Mister Archer–let me do it. Please?"

The policeman paused to look at George, whose face he could scarcely see. The youth spoke with cramped urgency, his hand outstretched. "Listen–I went and disappointed Mister Wakefield. Should've stayed at my post, but I didn't. And I can sneak up as good as any man. Please–I got to make it up to him."

Staring at the pale blotch where George's face was, Archer contemplated the void. "Indifference," he thought–the code of the machine. It was his code now. What should he care if some rank partisan did the deed? If the fetid passions of this imbecile cried for release, let him stumble off and release them.

With a shrug, Archer ambled toward the bulkhead.

"Thanks, Mister Archer!"

Behind him he heard twigs snapping as George stole into the woods and rustled away, reeking of emotion–guilt, vengfulness, gratitude. Let the night devour it all, thought Archer. Let it join the corruption of night while he kept vigil here, pure in his blank white readiness.

Standing over the doors, he held the revolver out, pumped the ejector rod and expelled the spent cartridges. From the holster pouch beneath his coat he took a cap and cartridge and began reloading. As he finished, the swaying lights of the road drew his eye and he watched the procession–the phosphorescent dust, the encumbered rabble in flight. He picked out individual figures here and there, high in a wagon box or huddled with luggage or trudging alongside.

Once, in and out of his profession, he had routinely speculated about other people, wondering what they saw and felt. Sometimes he had wondered what it might be like to be someone else, a wholly different man. A good man, as good as others thought he was. The possibility had always been there, it seemed, like a doorway through which he might pass at any time. Now it was gone, along with his will to imagine.

Gazing at the refugees, he felt another dead chuckle rise. There was no escape, no portal to salvation. Within the curse, everything was random–randomness everywhere. Pointing his revolver toward the road, he selected one silhouette and then another, then another. Could he pick one off at this range? Not likely, he thought, and lowered the weapon.

———◆———

IN THE CELLAR's hush, Truly stood at the foot of the stairs and leaned in. This time he definitely heard a shot. "Forbes and Tucker," he whispered. "It must be them." Taking the candleholder off the step, he offered it to Sapphira.

Her face began to say no, but the word went unspoken. She took the candleholder.

"Just light my way up," he muttered, "then hide yourself. Till it's over, all right?"

Her cheeks glowed in the candlelight, her eyes lustrous. She nodded. He patted her arm, then raised his Colt and began his slow ascent.

Avoiding the stairs' creaky middle, he favored the wall side, easing his weight onto one step and then pausing, then rising to the next. Halfway up, he went still as another, more muffled shot sounded—from the rear of the house, he guessed. With all the stealth he could manage, he continued his way up, sliding along the mortared wall and ducking past a shelf. He halted again, wiped his sweaty palms on his trousers and then sank into a crouch. With his weapon held out to the side, he used his free hand for support and climbed the last few steps.

At the top, he pricked his ears, his face hovering a few inches below the doorknob. A shot sounded from down the hall, followed by a fainter report. For an excited moment, he wondered if no one was standing guard, but then he calmed himself. He could presume no such luck.

Resting his knee on the top step, he turned his head and stared down at Sapphira. She stood right where he had left her, holding the candle high and gazing up at him. He motioned her back. For a moment, she failed to respond but then started backing away. The shadows closed in around Truly, leaving just the thread of light beneath the door. He worked at keeping his breath quiet, fighting the urge to grab the knob and burst out. Yet if no clear opportunity presented itself, and very soon, he would have to do just that. And if he were killed, what would happen to Sapphira? He shut the thought out, telling himself that if he listened and kept still, his chance would come. A moment later, it did.

From the front of the house, a pair of feet came thumping; with them came Dubray's voice, addressing someone in a salvo of intricate French. Truly tensed, his every fiber on alert. Through the door and a little to the right, he heard Ravenel spin off an impatient reply. Dubray thumped past the door and stopped. He blurted something with Archer's name in it. Stirring, Truly braced one foot on the top step and the other on the third. He eared back the Colt's hammer. His fingertips touched the knob. On the other side, the exchange intensified—Dubray jumpy, Ravenel churlish, both distracted as Truly seized the knob, twisted it and launched himself against the door.

Dubray's gasp was barely out before the door's impact. Truly dropped to one knee as Ravenel yelled a Gallic oath—and with the door blocking his view, he fired through it. A shriek answered. Rolling away from the door, Truly heard it slam and saw that Dubray, thrashing on his back and squeezing a bloody forearm, had kicked it shut. Just past the doctor's spastic figure, Ravenel righted herself against the wall and glared like a gorgon. She whipped up her derringer and fired. Truly sprang to one side as the bullet tore the carpet. Slamming against the wall of the main staircase, he stumbled back and returned fire, missing as Ravenel ducked. She switched the derringer to her other hand and, from down near Dubray's kicking feet, snatched up a big LeMat. Truly's sideways leap sent him against the opposite wall, another bullet burning past his head. Recovering his balance, he took aim—but with her startling speed, Ravenel vanished into the back stairwell, his shot chipping its corner. On the floor between them, Dubray thrashed and wailed. Truly threw a glance over his shoulder, making sure there was no one behind him, then started backing up. On his left, he came to the gaming room entrance and darted inside.

In a crouching turn he held his revolver straight out, making a wide sweep of the tables. He saw no one. Standing by the threshold, he stared across the grand hall to the parlor and it too seemed unoccupied. His heart galloped. Dropping low again, he peered down the back hall. By the back stairwell, he saw Ravenel's shadow move and then the flare of her revolver. The shot splintered the wainscoting next to him, and he blazed back at her without effect. Caught beneath the diagonal line of fire, Dubray balled himself up, moaning and squirming. He had kicked over the stand with the matchbox.

Truly kept his revolver on Ravenel's position. From his pockets, he dug out some caps and cartridges to have them ready. As he did so, he glanced at Dubray. The doctor's bespectacled eyes looked back at him, big with fright; Truly fancied aiming his next shot right between them. But there were more urgent targets, worthier uses for a bullet. Aiming beyond the wounded quack, he watched Ravenel's small shadow and waited for it to move.

IN THE KITCHEN, Wakefield felt a vulnerable sensation along his back, tingling like frost. From the hallway, each thump, cry and shot told him that Truly had somehow broken out of the cellar. But he had his hands full with the derisive Billy Yank outside. Once Archer had crept up from behind and killed the soldier, Wakefield would rush to quell this other emergency. And this time, Monroe's wishes notwithstanding, Truly would die. The threat of his tenacity would end—mercifully, practically, not just to satisfy Monroe's bloodlust.

Wakefield finished reloading. He started to raise his head and the soldier fired, hitting the window frame. Taking quick aim, Wakefield fired back–and as the soldier dodged behind the well, Wakefield glimpsed an arm in a white sling. He had been trading shots with an already wounded man–wounded, fearless and about to be shot in the back. Absorbing the thought, Wakefield swallowed his repellence. He wanted this over with. Staring beyond his target, he searched the black tangle of trees and then the outbuildings. "Be quick, Archer," he said aloud. A sudden movement drew his eye. Between the stable and the smokehouse, in the partial moonlight, a figure crept from shadow to shadow. It was not Archer. In a jolt of rage, Wakefield nearly bellowed George's name–but at that instant a bullet sang past his head, making him totter and fall backwards.

The mocking voice rang out: "Careful, Reb! Pretty soon I'll try start trying to hit you!"

From out in the hall, he heard Dubray moaning. Two more shots went off. Wakefield rolled and tried to get up, the broken glass crunching beneath him. From the pit of his stomach, a sick bewilderment swirled up and drowned his rage. He rested on his elbow and steadied himself, willing his mind clear, sorting out the facts until they were his again. George, though not a clever lad, had proven his nerve on several occasions. Together they could surely vanquish the one-armed soldier. "Be quick, George," he muttered, and rose from the floor.

CREEPING TO A rear corner of the smokehouse, George stuck his head out. The well stood some twenty paces away. Huddled there, the soldier had most of his back to him, and George spied an arm swaddled in linen. The detail surprised but did not confuse him. Determination simplified everything–and having heard the Yankee's latest taunt, he felt more determined than ever. He was about to kill his first man–more important, his first bluebelly–and it was high time. Gripping the revolver, his hand bristled with power. He would redeem himself in Wakefield's eyes. With its big Stars 'n' Bars on proud display, this house was a Southern stronghold under assault–but he would save it. In one of the mansion's second-floor windows–that very room to which he had strayed–a girl's face looked down through parted curtains. From up there, fair eyes would witness his daring and see him for what he was: a trueborn Confederate, a man and not a boy. A pleasurable warmth passed through him.

He mustered just enough restraint to seek a closer spot, stealing across the moonlit gap to the sheds and then through the shadows behind them. In the midst of this he heard a rustling and went still. It had come from far back in the trees–just some scared critter, he thought. He reached the last shed and peered around it. Straight ahead he saw the well with the soldier slouched against it. Hampered by his injured arm, the Yankee fumbled with his revolver.

George felt his pulse jump. Taking a deep, silent breath, he pictured it–quiet as the air, a dozen paces toward the exposed blue back. One shot, then another and then a third for Robert E. Lee. As he imagined the shots, he was startled to hear real ones from inside the mansion. He gazed beyond the well to the broken veranda window, where he glimpsed part of Wakefield's silhouette. After a moment's puzzlement, his eyes returned to the Yankee's crouched figure. Raising his weapon, he eared back the hammer just as the rustling resumed behind him, much closer.

He turned about and stared into the gloom. Unnerved, he listened to the dense rustle, the snapping twigs and a plodding sound underneath– hooves. A big critter, then–somebody's stupid cow, lost and blundering toward him. But a short distance to his right, it was a horse that emerged, saddled but riderless. A black, rippling animal with a patch of white above its snout, its neck shiny with froth. George lowered his weapon. Huffing, the horse wheeled slowly toward him, while in the same instant a tall, hatted figure appeared alongside, as if hatched from the beast's ribcage. They halted together, man and beast, the former gripping the bridle in his right hand. In the suspended moment, the tall stranger stared, his labored breath mingling with the animal's. He let go of the bridle.

George strained his eyes to see the face. On the man's tunic, brass buttons glinted in vertical rows. Then, through the muted moonlight, color seeped like a stain: Union blue. Already the officer's hand was in motion. George brought up his revolver but the Yankee fired first. Tearing through George's chest, the bullet stunned him with the certainty that his life had ended at eighteen years. The horse let out a shrill, full-throated whinny, more like a scream as George crumpled into the high grass. He tried to cry out for his mother but made only a gurgling noise–breath gone, breath gone, pulse wild as the big Yankee loomed over him and pointed the muzzle down. As his face exploded, George's final thought was that he had been done like a pig or a rabbit, without an ounce of pity. It was not fair.

———

FOR THE PAST couple of minutes, Ben had been hearing shots from inside the house–an encouraging development, but one that inflamed his urgency. The task of reloading took every bit of his concentration. Placing the last cap on its nipple, he nearly dropped it as another shot rang out, this time not from the house. It was followed by the whinny of a horse. Stiff with alarm, he stared toward the orchard where he had left Juniper. Then another shot crackled–behind him, definitely behind him. Jerking his eyes to the sheds, he saw no one but knew that he had to take cover elsewhere. For this he would have to be both fast and lucky. Yet his chances seemed fair, since two of his three foes had mysteriously withdrawn. Perhaps it was them at his back now–something that he should have anticipated.

Holding his pistol ready, he braced himself against the well and then, at the count of three, made a clumsy beeline for the arbor. In mid-lurch he got off a shot at the veranda; surprised or distracted, the foe within was late firing back. Ben found himself in the rose-scented shadows of the arbor, on his knees and unhurt. There would be a lull now. Having placed himself here, far to one side of the grounds, he had no more of a clear shot than his enemies did.

From the mansion's interior, two more muffled shots reminded him of his principle goal. First, however, he would have to eliminate this newest threat. Through the latticework, he peered toward the outbuildings and spotted movement. From the darkness near the sheds, a large, complex shape emerged into moonlight, where it became the silhouette of a tall, hatted man leading a horse. The man paused to glance about before proceeding to the house. Though he carried a revolver, it was pointed at the ground, suggesting only moderate vigilance. He did not steer his winded horse toward the stable but kept toward the veranda. Then, as he reached the steps, the window light revealed a bearded chin, epaulettes and a tunic of federal blue.

Gaping, Ben lowered his Colt. He nearly yelled a warning but hesitated, wondering why the officer had drawn no fire–why, moreover, he betrayed no reaction to the big Rebel flag. The man holstered his weapon, tethered his horse to the railing. The light glanced off his face as he looked up, the eyes warily inquisitive. To Ben's greater astonishment, he raised his hand in a tempering gesture and spoke: "Easy, Wakefield. It's me." Before Ben could gather his wits, the officer had disappeared up the steps. He heard the door open and quickly shut.

In the quiet, Ben stared over at the black horse, magnificent despite the dust on its flanks. Through the anxious jumble of his mind, he recalled his father mentioning treason, some threat to the capital itself. There was treason afoot–and just now, he realized, he had been badly fooled. This enemy house had one more defender, perhaps more imposing than the rest.

Inside the house, another pair of shots went off, jarring him back to clarity. Slowly he emerged from the arbor and stole along the back of the mansion, ducking past a darkened window. He stopped to survey the rear grounds and the encompassing tree line, but nothing stirred. Over by the veranda, the horse snorted and swung its head toward him. Ben held his revolver high, edging closer.

<hr />

ARCHER STOOD MOTIONLESS over the bulkhead. From the silence out back, he guessed that George had carried out the instruction, but he did not care. What bothered him, what had begun to madden him, were the sounds of the ongoing duel inside the house. They announced Truly's escape from the cellar. However confounding, it was the only explanation.

Archer fought to stay indifferent–but as in so many past instances, he could not help himself. Like sparks to paper, each report singed his pure inner blankness, until at length a flame caught. He had to go inside. To the prospect of killing Truly, or at least watching him die, he could feel no indifference. Yet he had been assigned to guard this exit; to leave it unsecured would be thoroughly irresponsible. Quentin Archer remained responsible, if nothing else.

He proceeded to the moonlit fringe of the trees. Squinting at the ground, he picked out fallen branches and gathered several mid-sized ones, all of them firm but not brittle. These he jammed through the bulkhead door handles. While doing so, he thought about his particular curse, the riddle of his split nature. He loathed it as he loathed Truly. More than any harlot or deacon's robe, Truly had come to embody the torment of that riddle.

———————

RAVENEL WAS ALTERNATING between her derringer and the LeMat. Bullets had taken their toll on the plaster and the woodwork but accomplished nothing more, apart from Dubray's wounding. It seemed a question of who would run out of them first—nothing that Truly could pin his hopes on. Then, in the midst of reloading, he heard a groan and a thump from the corridor; he looked and saw Dubray on his feet, still clutching his arm as he stumbled for cover. From the back stairwell, Ravenel's arm flew out, grabbed Dubray's collar and pulled him to safety—all before Truly could act. In disgust he realized that he should have stifled his qualms and finished off the wounded man. Whatever ammunition Dubray had on his person was now Ravenel's.

It was time to press the issue. Truly tried to picture how. Then, across the cavernous main hall, one of the decorative shields by the parlor caught his eye; he recalled that other such shields adorned the side of the hall nearest him. He stepped out of the gaming room, keeping his eyes and his Colt on Ravenel's position. Backing up slowly, he let the fingers of his left hand brush the wall until they touched a shield. He lifted it down; its hanging wire, he discovered, was all he had to hold it by. The shield proved heavier than expected but smaller than he would have liked, about four feet by three. Down the corridor, Ravenel's head poked out, then darted back in as he fired. Dropping low, he jerked the shield up in time for her return shot, which screamed off the crafted metal surface. He edged forward and deflected a second shot, its impact jarring the shield and skinning a knuckle.

Truly had never imagined killing a woman, yet in Ravenel's case he felt no such inhibition. Keeping his shield up, he prepared to charge as a loud bumping noise came from behind him. He looked to see Archer appear from the front vestibule, his pistol cocked. For a startled instant, some twenty feet apart, they beheld each other. On the policeman's drawn face, Truly read the depth of hate. Speed cancelled accuracy as they fired in unison, both bullets wide of the mark. Archer sprang back into the vestibule. Now threatened fore-and-aft, Truly retreated into the gaming room.

He kept moving backwards, blundering into chairs and tables. He swung his eyes about the room. Far in the back, he spied a closed door but had no way of telling where it led. The next thing he knew, Archer and Ravenel had stationed themselves on either side of the room's entrance-way. Still backing up, he ducked as they fired at him; one bullet glanced off the shield while another shattered some glass thing behind him. He could not get a clear shot–and with two assailants so placed, the furniture lent only meager protection. So did the shield as he jerked it side to side, the hanging wire cutting into his palm. In desperation he looked behind him and saw the mirrored saloon-counter–a bulwark of polished wood, its glasses and bottles gleaming in the lamplight. It would mean fighting with his back literally to the wall. A last stand, perhaps, yet fitting for one who had always liked his whiskey.

———◆———

HEATH LOOKED DOWN at the glass shards littering the kitchen floor. Hot from his ride, he removed his hat and began unbuttoning his tunic. "So what's this, then?"

Ashen-faced, Wakefield glared at him. "Answer me first."

"He raised his piece and I shot him." Heath draped the tunic over a chair. "Now . . . "

"He was with us," croaked Wakefield. "He was sneaking up on that Yankee soldier."

Frowning, Heath peered out of the shattered pane. "What Yankee soldier?"

"He was a friend of mine."

"That news is a bit tardy." From the front of the house, another shot sounded. Heath glanced that way, then started peeling off his false beard. "Now, please answer *my* question."

Wakefield swallowed hard. "What happened at the fort?"

Heath dropped the beard by his hat on the table.

"Monroe, is DeRussy ours?! Tell me!"

Sighing, Heath rubbed his cheeks. For all his nerve and stamina, the tension of the last few hours had bitten deep. He would have enjoyed succeeding at DeRussy, as he had succeeded at most things–yet between the spineless Monks, the intemperate black sergeant and all the unforeseeables, his efforts had come to nothing. And just now it would take very little for him to strike Wakefield down, as swiftly as he had struck down the young stranger. Their mutual utility had ended. All that really mattered now—all that had come out of this mess, in fact—was the gold, safe in the cellar. The Confederate States of America would be getting no refund.

Drawn by the shots, Heath started up the hall as Wakefield shouted after him:

"Tell me, goddamn it!"

Heath did not look back. "All is well," he said. "Everything's fine, old friend."

"What the hell does that . . . ?!" Wakefield broke off, distracted by a throaty neigh from Black Marengo.

Heath sniffed the gunpowder fumes. Ahead he spied Ravenel in the main hall, standing with her thin little back to him and a shooting iron in each hand. She leaned cautiously forward, then fired into the gaming room. On the other side of the room's entranceway, Heath glimpsed Archer doing the same. Concern quickened his step, but then he heard a moan and halted by the rear stairwell. Sprawled on the bottom steps, Dubray had pulled his coat half off and rolled up his bloody sleeve to examine a wound.

"Monroe—I am shot."

"So you are. Who did it?"

Grimacing, Dubray shifted position. "Truly."

"What?"

"Truly did it! Wakefield brought him back as a prisoner but he . . . "

No longer listening, Heath gazed up the corridor. Ravenel had noticed him. Turning his way, she lowered her weapons and sent him a look of tired patience. And with a force that Heath had experienced only a handful of times, like a roar through underground caverns, his hunger surged, indistinguishable from ecstasy. Apart from the man whose name had just triggered it, this sensation was the one thing that had ever humbled him, made him feel that he might presently be torn to shreds. An anguished joy, a savage anticipation that left him mute, blinking at Ravenel. The floors, the walls, the light and even his partner's black gown had acquired a reddish tint. She was still watching him. Knowing that she understood, he kept still until the redness faded and the hunger ebbed a little, granting him that precious sense of control.

Dubray moaned on, though his wound looked minor. "Monroe, I need linen for this!"

"The key to your office—do you have it on you?"

"My arm! Mon Dieu, I have lost my profession!"

"Antoine, I'll tear your arm off unless you give me that key."

The whimpering ceased, the doctor's wet eyes gazing up. "Inside my coat," he blurted. He cringed as Heath bent down and rifled through the coat.

Heath plucked the key out, slipped it into his pants pocket and continued up the hall. Ravenel stepped up to meet him. He brought his face down close to hers.

"I'll enter from Dubray's office," he muttered. "Keep him busy." She nodded. On the far side of the entranceway, he caught a wary look from Archer. "The second I go for him, cease fire," Heath added. "Tell Archer that. I do not feel the least bit generous about this one."

She smirked. "Do you ever?"

"Just let him be mine. Mine entirely."

Her smirk vanished. Gazing up at him, she bore the same searching look as on the day they first met. "Monroe, we have gone to some trouble keeping him for you."

"Appreciated, my dear. And you may watch, of course—to your heart's content." As he spoke the words, his passion nearly choked them off. He drew a sharp breath through his nostrils.

Ravenel stepped back, as if from a cauldron ready to boil over. Eyes marveling, she beamed at him. "Sally forth, sir knight!"

The shooting resumed as he strode back down the corridor. Past the huddled Dubray, he came to the storeroom and went in, leaving the door open for light. On a shelf he found a candle and a matchbox. He lit the wick, took up the holder and proceeded to an inner door. Using the key, he entered Dubray's putrid sanctum and shined the candle about. In the darkness his excitement intensified, rising until he felt almost drunk. He had to pause, breathe, reflect.

Recalling Dubray's nervous jest—"What a surgeon you would have made!"—Heath wondered if he had indeed missed his vocation. It would have supplied him with more victims, certainly, and all on a regular basis. Almost as much as Heath himself, this room inspired terror among the young women of La Maison, to the point that some had tried to conceal their maladies. Yet Dubray usually found them out, and these cork-lined walls had absorbed their share of screaming. Most had survived his cures and experimentation, though several were of little use afterward. Each instance got Dubray a scolding from Ravenel but nothing more. For every girl lost, the immigrant docks would provide another wan and willing substitute.

On the doctor's cluttered desk lay a thick book with a long Spanish title, roughly translating to "An Index of Poisons Throughout the Known World." Beside it, open to the middle, an illustrated volume depicted methods of torture, from the rack to the man-sized frying pan. Moving on, the candle's glow revealed other features of the office: a female anatomical chart, a da Vinci vivisection print, a bookcase topped with a human skull, a table arrayed with vials, beakers and probing instruments, a raised mattress fitted with straps and buckles. But it was no time for diversion. In front of him, Heath saw the door that led into the gaming room. He went to it and squatted, placing the candle on the floor.

Barely audible through the corked wall, a shot sounded. Heath flexed his hands. Unable to see much through the keyhole, he slid the bolt and slowly cracked the door open. His gaze snaked among the chairs and tables, up to the main hall entranceway on the left. From the hall, a pair of shots chipped the saloon-counter on the other side; behind the counter, Heath glimpsed a white sleeve and then a head pulling down. A head of tousled ruddy hair.

First came the pleasureful chill and then the hunger, surging hot; quickening his blood and tightening every muscle, it threatened once more to crack his composure. If ever he needed that glacial composure, it was now. He touched his sheath and his holster and waited, eyes shut. Through a haze of red he saw the sun-baked courtyard. He saw Truly's young bantam figure–his narrowed eyes, the flash of his blade. Like brutish amulets, Heath's pistol and bayonet felt electrically charged beneath his fingertips. This, he knew, was no mere vengeance. This was destiny–a mystical rite, demanding certain proprieties; by observing these, he could achieve the savage perfection for which he longed. He would shoot only to wound. In this final act, his knife would play the main role, just as Truly's had on that day.

Behind his closed lids, the courtyard dissolved, red fading to black as his pulse settled. He was ready.

TRULY HAD SCARCELY raised his head when Archer and Ravenel fired, forcing him down. Resting against a lower shelf, he wondered why the two seemed to be anticipating his attempts to shoot back. Then he noticed a shard of mirror glass by his knee. Twisting around, he looked up at the large rectangular mirror, cracked now within its gilt frame. Slanting out a bit from the wall, it reflected most of the glossy countertop.

With one hand he seized his bullet-scored shield and thrust it top-first against the bottom of the mirror's frame. Two more bullets slammed into the wall but he kept shoving upward, tilting the mirror until one side of it slipped off its nail and scraped down the wall. Putting the shield aside, he found it easy to lift the other end of the mirror and let it drop with a crash. In this space, its size prevented it from lying flat, so he propped it next to his shield.

Though the task had taken but a moment, he felt suddenly vulnerable and snapped back into a crouch. He peered around the side of the counter, glimpsed Ravenel's revolver and ducked as she fired. Picturing Archer about to take his turn, Truly frog-hopped to the other end and caught the detective leaning out from the entranceway. Had Archer been any slower to duck, Truly's bullet would have struck his head.

Pulling back in, Truly again found himself perplexed. Neither of his foes lacked nerve or quickness, he thought–and yet neither, during his moment of distraction, had taken the opportunity to rush in close. They seemed to be biding their time.

As he moved sideways, his foot grazed the mirror and caused it to slide out from the wall. One end caught under his heel and the other against the counter's base, producing a clumsy angle. Cursing, he turned and grabbed it by its frame, ready to shove it out and away from him. At the same instant, on the fractured gleaming surface, something moved. He went still, taking in the slanted view. At the room's far end, the door that Truly had noticed earlier stood slightly ajar–while near the center, hidden except for an edge of white shirt, a large man crouched behind one of the tables.

Truly's alarm peaked, then abruptly fell away. Like the ghost of some dim acquaintance, his broken reflection looked back at him. His hair was a ruddy snarl, his face a warped mosaic. Over one blue eye, a missing sliver of glass made him appear half-blinded.

Ever since Rachel's death, life had often seemed like a twister or a locust swarm–chaotic, furious, sustained by what it destroyed. Truly saw it differently now, though as no less furious. Deep in life's wreckage lay clues that bespoke something more than chaos, something for which chance alone could not account. Patterns of union and collision, incomplete yet leading somewhere, their truth unfolding. Ordained beyond the reach of mortal vision, these patterns demanded finality. They demanded the symmetry of death. This one had begun in blood, long ago in a white stone courtyard; it would end in blood, here and now.

For a fuller view he moved the mirror a bit to the right, his foot maintaining the angle. Then he settled back against the shelves. Rotating his Colt's warm cylinder, he found one bullet left. Now was his last chance to reload. He dug out his remaining ammunition, placing it on the bottom shelf. At the same time, he kept the skewed mirror in his side-vision, stealing glances at it. Heath's stooped form emerged from its hiding place. Revolver in hand, the big man crept obliquely toward the counter, ducking behind a table some dozen feet away.

Ejecting a spent cartridge, Truly loaded a new one and fitted the firing cap. Then his time ran out. In the cracked mirror, Heath suddenly broke cover as if to charge. But almost instantly he hesitated, his jaw hard and his gaze wolflike. Truly swung around the side to fire, realizing as he did that the mirror had worked in reverse–that Heath had glimpsed it, along with Truly's poised reflection.

Lunging back to the table, Heath snarled as the shot clipped the back of his thigh. He grabbed the table and threw it over to screen himself, its chairs toppling. Truly's second shot struck the circular hardwood. From the hall, Archer and Ravenel responded together, their bullets scarring the floor and the counter's side edge. Truly recoiled as Heath bellowed–"Let him be! Hold off, damn you!"

Truly tried to resume loading but then heard a loud scraping noise. He looked to see the tabletop ramming its way toward him, shielding the killer as it knocked other furniture out of its path.

———◆———

If not for the sleek black horse, Ben might have managed to surprise the man called Wakefield. Stealing low along the veranda, he reached the steps and was about to crawl up when the horse, tethered to the railing opposite, suddenly reared and neighed. Ben ducked, cursing as Wakefield's bullet struck the post above him. He edged backward.

Then, directly behind him, someone whispered–"Ben!"

He jerked around and saw two men pressed flat against the house. Gaping at their dark profiles, he moved toward them until, with shocked joy, he recognized Forbes and Tucker. Their breathing was ragged, both of them gripping revolvers.

Slumping against the wall, Ben looked into Forbes' sweaty, unshaven face. "Promise me you'll explain all this later on."

"I'll leave that to your father," Forbes murmured. "What's the state of things?"

In an urgent whisper, Ben described the engagement thus far: Wakefield and the blue-clad officer, the separate fight inside the house.

Forbes let out a long breath. "All right–it'll be best to hit them front and back simultaneously. That door up there leads into a hallway off of the kitchen. You two wait just long enough for me to sneak around front–then, strike. Soon as I hear your shots, I'll do the same." He glanced at Tucker, who nodded. Then he looked at Ben. "By the way–that so-called Union officer? If you run into him, shoot fast." Ben nodded. Forbes hobbled away.

Pressing a hand to his side, Tucker seemed to be in some discomfort. "Lieutenant, is Sapphira in there?"

"Can't say for sure," Ben muttered. "I'm afraid she might be." He realized that the house had quieted. Wondering what it meant, he felt a chewing in his stomach.

"We left our horses up behind those sheds," Tucker whispered. "Found a dead man there, shot in the face. I got this pistol off of him."

Trading a look with him, Ben shook his head in bewilderment. He adjusted his sling.

Over by the veranda steps, the black stallion stamped and snorted.

"This man Wakefield," said Ben, "–he's only ready for me, not you. So I'll go first and then you can . . . " He broke off as he heard a muffled shot, followed by two more. The fight inside had resumed. The time for strategy was past.

———— ◆ ————

QUICK AND FRAGMENTARY, Truly's thoughts were of the frontiersmen he had known–trail scouts and mountain trappers, men hardened by sun and snow, by danger and isolation, rabidly resourceful when desperate. Attacked in the open? Shoot your horse, they said; use the carcass for cover. Your musket fails? Grab your knife. Lose your knife? Pick up a rock, a club. Saint Peter bars you at the Pearlies? Spit in his eye and run inside. Whatever's handy, use it.

Scraping and shuddering across the floor, the tabletop advanced upon him, blocking Heath almost entirely from view. Then he realized it was also blocking Heath's view of him.

Truly dropped his Colt. He grabbed the big, broken mirror and slid it out from behind the counter. As Heath's bulwark pushed to within a few feet, Truly swung the mirror out and let its end drop flat, straight into the table's path. Then, in a crouch, he shoved with all his strength, driving the frame plow-like between the floor and the table's rim. As the hardwood surface fell toward him, he let go of the mirror and lurched right, catching himself against the counter. At the same time, he glimpsed Heath pitching forward, still clutching one of the table legs–teeth bared, eyes alight, a look between rage and rapture.

The table crashed upside-down upon the mirror as Heath toppled after it, firing a wild shot, and for a second the big man lay sprawled across the table's underside. Blood darkened the back of one pant leg where Truly's bullet had nicked him. Truly seized a bottle of liquor by its neck and smashed it against the counter's edge. Struggling to rise, Heath went for the sheathed bayonet at his hip. At that instant, the resolve that Truly had made in the cellar darkness re-ignited, racing to his unshackled limbs. It was time to go mad.

Clutching the broken bottle as liquor gushed everywhere, he lunged onto Heath's back and pinned the killer's knife arm with his knee. Into the back of Heath's revolver arm he drove the glass teeth, gashing him from shoulder to elbow. Heath roared, bucking like a railcar as Truly kept stabbing. Seizing Heath by the hair, Truly glimpsed a pale, jagged scar along the scalp–and with a renewed burst of heat, he put his weapon to frenzied use, carving zig-zags across the broad, heaving back. Heath bucked and thrashed, his bellows resounding. Fleetingly, it was only the courtyard that Truly saw: the woman, the small girl and the younger Heath looking at him, his eyes the color of sooty ice. Then, under his straining knees, he saw the killer's exposed back and the shirt in rags, soaked scarlet. In the same moment, he heard a shot out in the hall, along with some new disturbance.

Then he felt Heath's left arm wrestle free. Surrendering to the fuller savagery, to the killer he had always suspected in himself, Truly raised his weapon and aimed it at the base of Heath's skull. Then he felt a crushing grip around his left leg. As Heath erupted beneath him, he let go of the hair and felt himself thrown sideways against a table leg. Rolling, he kept his grip on the bottleneck, hitting the wall as Heath surged to his feet. With the roar of a wounded grizzly, Heath stumbled back and then forward, nearly tripping over the inverted table. Truly lunged again. Heath tried to raise his revolver. Grabbing its barrel, Truly jerked the weapon upward as it discharged, while in his side-vision he saw the blade coming. He let go of the firearm, falling to his knees as the bayonet swiped overhead. Into the side of Heath's already wounded leg, he drove the glass fangs. The killer let out a thunderous howl, lurching away as Truly wobbled upright and charged after him. Catching Heath by his bloody wrist, he forced the revolver down and away. Again it fired. Snarling and sputtering, Heath halted his retreat and raised the bayonet, just as Truly lashed out with the bottle. It caught Heath on the side of the face. In the instant of Heath's ear-splitting wail, Truly yanked the revolver out of his hand, tripped backward and fell over a chair.

Breathless, Truly struggled to rise. He felt the revolver in his left hand and the bottle in his right. Thanking the latter, he let it drop and rolled onto his elbow. He retched, spat. He was lying in a strong-smelling puddle of rum, his shirt and vest splattered with Heath's blood. The killer's wailing had not ceased. "Heath!" Truly crowed. "Just like old times, eh?!"

Still holding the bayonet, Heath flailed about and bellowed like a creature possessed. His cheek was laid open, his mouth agape. His eyes rolled, blinking through blood. Below his bestial noise, the sound of shooting issued from the main hall, and Truly realized he had been hearing it for the past minute or so. Until now there had been no time to wonder about it—or why Archer and Ravenel had failed to shoot him, whatever Heath's stated wish.

On his feet now, Truly looked toward the hall. He saw nothing of the pair, though the shooting persisted. So did Heath's extended howl as he staggered from table to table, headed for the door at the far end. Stunned and queasy, Truly watched. Then he switched the revolver to his right hand and cocked the hammer.

"Nate!"

Truly looked back toward the hall.

"Nate, are you there?!" It was Forbes' voice.

"I'm coming!" Truly yelled.

From the wreckage by the saloon-counter, he retrieved the shield. He glanced to the far end of the room. Heath had vanished, his blood-trail leading to the door which was now wide open, darkness within.

Truly rushed to the hall threshold. From the vestibule doorway Forbes was firing into the parlor, where Archer huddled beside the spinet; the policeman held a hand to his thigh, his coat bloodstained. To Truly's left, more pistol-cracks came from far down the corridor. Peering through the gunpowder mist, he saw Ravenel standing flat against the wall and firing her derringer, not at him but toward the rear of the house. Dubray cowered behind her, his injured arm held stiff to his side. Scolding the doctor in French, she thrust the LeMat out grip-first and shook it at him. Unsteadily he took the weapon, just as an answering shot made both of them flinch. In his killing fever Truly would have rushed them, his revolver blazing, had a shot not sounded from the parlor. He looked to see Forbes stumble backward, his face shocked and pale.

Cursing Archer at the top of his lungs, Truly raised the shield and charged across.

FOR WAKEFIELD, ONLY the bullet was real. Everything else defied belief: the swathed arm of the soldier, his scabbed face bobbing into view; the muzzle flash as Wakefield jumped aside; Wakefield's return shot as the soldier ducked; Black Marengo stomping and whinnying by the steps; the colored soldier suddenly, stunningly there, framed in the broken section of window—all of it a too-swift dream. And then the bullet plowing into his guts—chaos, a falling apart, no answers.

Lying there, he waited for the pain to find its limit. It did not. Slowly he rolled over, the pain less but then greater. From here he could see a small portion of the back hall, just up to the storeroom. He was aware of the back door bursting open, shots being fired overhead. He heard Ravenel raving. Suddenly a large figure lurched out of the storeroom—a slashed, gouged, blood-smeared horror of a man, snarling and wailing, one hand gripping a knife. Ravenel stopped raving to let out an improbable noise, part gasp and part shriek. Wakefield closed his eyes; only then did he recognize the maimed apparition as Monroe. With disbelief bearing him away, he went completely still as the burrowed bullet screamed "All over." He saw Delia.

BEN WAS NOT sure what he had heard just before charging inside–a kind of howling, human yet barely so. He wondered if Wakefield was its source, but the man lay silent on the glass-littered kitchen floor. Ben went flat against one side of the smoky corridor; Tucker took the opposite side and the two started forward, pistols extended.

There was no sign of the two figures that Ben had seen firing at them– but from the front of the house, shots still sounded. A short way up, on the right, a door stood open with a blood-trail leading in or out. Farther up, on the left, was a stairwell, a toppled wooden stand and another door ajar. Ben's feverish mind tried to gather itself. He shut the first door, thinking that he would have to investigate later. Helping Forbes came first.

Then, from the second floor, there came an eruption of noise–screams, running, frantic female voices. It pulled the two men to the stairwell.

"I'll go up," Ben told Tucker. "There must be a main staircase out front, so you take that approach. But if you encounter Forbes, help him first."

"All right," said Tucker, already in motion.

Ben started upstairs. His ears followed the clamor and his eyes a trail of blood drops. Just below a bend in the stairs, his light-headedness returned. He rested against the wall, then tensed as the noise of a downward stampede began above him. An auburn-haired girl came reeling around the bend, her violet gown flying. She cringed to a stop, gaping as Ben lowered his weapon and other girls spilled down behind her. Shrieking and jostling, they filled the stairwell.

"Please, soldier!" the first one gasped.

"Who's up there?" he demanded.

"Doctor Dubray!" blurted another girl.

"One man, that's all?"

"Yes! Please let us by!"

Ben stepped aside. The girls streamed down as he squeezed past them, continuing his dizzy ascent. He made it to the last few blood-dotted steps. Turning his bad arm away, he used his knees and elbow to crawl toward the top landing. He raised his Colt and then his head. Down the blue-carpeted hallway, past a succession of shut doors, two people were coming toward him–a tottering blonde girl in a floral gown and, behind her, a bespectacled man in a green clawhammer coat. The latter, presumably Doctor Dubray, held a bloody arm to his side and a large revolver to the girl's head. In a strained, accented voice, he shouted, "I see you! Put down your piece, or Mademoiselle Wilhelmina will die!"

The girl made no sound. Bleary-eyed, she swayed a bit as they kept toward the landing.

"Put it down!" her captor yelled. "I am leaving this house, and you shall make way!"

Slowly they passed the head of a grand staircase.

"I'll let you withdraw and take cover," Ben called. "Let her go and I won't shoot."

Dubray sputtered a curse and kept coming, prodding his hostage before him. Ben wondered what to do but then, from the staircase beyond, saw Tucker rise and point his pistol. As the sergeant eased onto the top step, it creaked. Dubray froze, the revolver quivering in his hand. The girl halted, swaying.

"Or, on second thought," Ben called, "you could surrender right quick." Still fighting dizziness, he got to his feet. "Doctor Dubray, I'm going to tell the young lady to step aside. By the time she does, you'd better have dropped your weapon."

The girl did not wait for Ben's word; with tremulous care, she edged to one side. Dubray lowered his pistol and stood there quaking.

"Drop it!" Ben snarled.

As Tucker strode up to take the weapon, the girl abruptly turned around and snatched it from Dubray. He had only time enough to yell before she fired. Ben took a step, but his vision swirled and he had to catch himself against the wall. A series of shrieks rent the air, so high-pitched that he thought it was the girl–but straightening himself up, he saw that it was Dubray. Clutching at his groin, the man writhed as the girl stood over him. Tucker plucked the revolver from her hand. Already Dubray's cries were growing weaker.

Though steadier now, Ben felt almost completely spent.

"Lieutenant!" Tucker called. "Your father is downstairs!"

※

CROUCHED BY A sofa, Truly kept his shield up but caught a glimpse of Archer's face. The policeman's scared yet oddly distant eyes seemed fixed upon some greater threat. Clutching his bloody thigh, he hopped out of sight as Truly fired again.

"You think you can pray it away?!" Truly hollered. He saw an open door just past the spinet and, in the dim room beyond, part of a large desk. He worried that the study might have some other exit, but then spied movement behind the desk. A shot flared, striking his shield with a dull ring. He jumped to the bullet-pocked spinet, kicking its bench out of his way. From there he moved to the doorway's edge. "No, Archer!" he yelled. "There's no remedy for it! What you did to your wife! To your daughter!!" He threw the shield aside. "I'm going to take you alive, understand? And by the time they hang you, everybody will know about Archer the Preacher! They'll know every damned thing!! They'll . . . " From the other side of the doorway came a thump. Twitching, he saw Forbes sidling up along the wall. "Bart, I thought you were hit!"

"I was, after a fashion." With his Colt, Forbes indicated a neat bullet hole just under his wooden knee. He eyed Truly. "For God's sake–you're the one who's hurt!"

"That's not my blood. It's Heath's."

Forbes muttered under his breath.

Truly turned his gaze back to the study, listening hard. "It's all up, Archer!" he yelled. "You're trapped!"

"Nate," Forbes whispered. "Ben is here too."

"Ben?! What in the name of . . . ?"

"He's upstairs with Tucker, tangling with someone else. Wakefield's wounded."

He was about to tell Forbes to go help Ben and Tucker, that he could keep the injured policeman at bay, when another shot went off inside the study. Hunkering lower, he thrust his Colt through the doorway but held fire. Behind the desk, in the scant light from the parlor, he spied Archer's outstretched form.

A moment later, he raised a lamp over the body. Archer had shot himself through the temple. Wide open, his eyes seemed to encompass some final vision of doom.

Forbes leaned over the desk, staring down.

Truly looked away. In the end, he had known Archer well enough–and which ruthless lever to pull. Feeling the first real nudge of exhaustion, he put the lamp down. "So . . . Has Early grabbed himself a fort?"

"He tried," Forbes said. "We spoiled it for him."

Truly felt like lying down, his legs suddenly weak.

"Details later," said Forbes. "Now, what about Heath?"

"Still kicking–but wherever he's hidden himself, we'll root him out. Him and Ravenel."

Forbes began reloading. "You know, we were afraid that Sapphira might be here too."

"You feared right. Who do you think got me free?"

Forbes gave him a sharp glance. "Where is she now?"

"Down in the cellar. I told her to . . . Oh Christ, no."

IT WAS A sound like none that Sapphira had ever heard–a howl of limitless pain, a roar of boundless fury that filled the darkness, as if the darkness had found its own bestial voice and was turning on her. Amid the reeling of her mind, she grasped that it was not a supernatural thing but an unspeakable earthly one smashing and blundering its way toward her. Her shaking hands gripped the candleholder, the flame fluttering, her pulse imploring escape.

On numb legs she moved to the double plank doors and lifted the crossbar with one arm. She heaved it aside and yanked one door open. Placing the candle on a step, she began to shove at the bulkhead doors above her. She neither knew nor cared if one of La Maison's minions was standing guard outside. She had to flee the murderous being, the roaring entity which she could not see and did not wish to see. But the doors would not open. Mocking her desperation, they scarcely budged–and for a paralytic moment, she thought of blowing out the candle and simply huddling here, praying against discovery. Yet she was unwilling to face the full darkness.

Snatching up the candle, she forced herself back into the cellar. The hellish noises now came from somewhere in front of her and to the left, though in her terror she could not judge the distance. Beneath the sounds, she heard Ursula whimpering, then seized the idea of locking herself in the pen. She thrust her hand into her dress pocket; feeling nothing, she remembered that she had thrown the keys aside in her attempted break-out with Father. Then, as another enraged howl tore the blackness, she heard a heavy pair of feet scuffing toward her.

Faint and nearly choking, Sapphira felt as if she were being devoured, doomed already, her ears full of the predator's gnashing. With a gulp of air, she recovered and bolted right, only to feel a blow at waist level. She caught herself against a wooden surface and pushed backward, her candle revealing the large crate she had run into. The howling had fallen to wet, throaty noises as she jerked the candle around, begging it to find her a hiding place. The glow brushed the floor and walls until it silhouetted a large, stooped man lurching toward her. The candle slipped from her fingers, struck the floor. Total darkness fell.

Gasping, plunging and groping, she whirled off in some other direction, her heart rampant, praying to make a wide sweep around the man-beast. Her foot caught on something heavy; it clinked as she tripped over it and bumped her head. Sliding down a wall, she pressed her hand to the throbbing spot above her left temple. Then, on the floor, her other hand grasped a sharp-edged circular object. Instantly she realized it was the spiked slave collar. She dropped it, clawing herself erect as a snarl erupted somewhere close by, mixed with Ursula's terrified shrieks. Yet the demon sounded no closer. Though sightless, Sapphira now knew where she was–right next to the liquor storage entrance. She started groping for the archway, just as a faint glow appeared over her shoulder. She turned her head around.

The candle, having fallen upright in its holder, had not gone out. Though weak, its flame had revived enough to illuminate the creature standing near it–and to let him see her. In a listing, hulking posture he turned fully about, his bloody shirt shredded, his bloody face contorted. One hand dangled at his side, its injured arm apparently useless, but the other clutched a long knife. In the murky flux of Sapphira's brain, the name resounded: Monroe, her father's murdering incubus–Monroe, teeth bared–Monroe in the flickering light, hulking toward her.

Her heart, a frenzied drum, seemed to sap all the strength from her limbs. Sliding down the wall again, she wondered if this could be death's first sensation–her soul readying itself as the black shape moved in, leaving her limp and huddled, limp and motionless until she reached to the side and gripped something else: a protuberance, tough and smooth like a cane-stalk. Wobbling to her feet, she locked her other hand around it. Monroe was nearly upon her. With a half-suppressed moan and all the power she could manage, she swung the cat o' nine-tails in an overhead arc toward the killer's head. She heard the heavy swish, felt the lead weights strike. Lumbering backwards, Monroe let loose a wail that momentarily froze her before it broke into guttural sounds.

He swayed but then steadied himself, swiping the air with his knife. Staying clear, Sapphira lashed out again. The weighted whip-ends made a thresher-like "swack" against his arm and face, unleashing another cry. Breathless, she swung and swung again. With each pelting stroke, her body surged with a force unknown to her, as if her veins had absorbed something of the beast she was fighting; it drove her arms, propelled the rawhide tendrils. But no sooner had her terror begun to shrink than, delivering another merciless stroke, she felt a tug and found that she could not pull the whip back in. In the candlelight, the killer's blade rose silvery-sharp; one whip-end had snagged around it, and another around Monroe's wrist. He gave a powerful jerk. The weapon snapped out of her hands. Once more there was nothing between her and his rage–mad rage, thundering from his chest as he hulked forward.

Cringing, she tottered backward. Her hand pawed the shadows behind her, brushed the wall, grazed the dry shaft of bone–clutched it. With a double grip, she jabbed the goad at Monroe's upraised arm and felt it sink in. He snarled and snorted, stumbling back as Sapphira jerked the goad free and lost her balance. She fell sideways onto the coil of chain. At the same moment, light burst from the archway on her left. Caught in the yellow incandescence, Monroe stood like a ruined tower smeared red–his face a mangled horror, his one visible eye squinting into the light. Sapphira looked up and saw her father holding the lamp high, standing between her and the killer. He pointed his revolver at Monroe's chest, squeezed the trigger. There was only a brittle "click." Monroe bellowed, his single eye bulging white.

Her father threw her a look–clamp-jawed, wild-eyed. He dropped the pistol, snatched the goad from her hand. She caught the flash of Monroe's blade as he half-lunged, half-toppled in their direction. In the moment of her father's headlong thrust, there was a jostling of light and shadow and then a sound like a splitting melon. She sank onto the chain-coil. To one side, the lamp lay broken, spilling a little pool of flame. Close by, the long knife lay gleaming. She saw Monroe impaled on the goad, his brutish bulk leaning into it. He emitted a burbling noise, his shoulders twitching. In an identical hunch, her father's smaller silhouette also leaned in, straining to hold the shaft firm; with both hands he gave it a sudden twist. Blood spewed from Monroe's mouth. A choking wail escaped him, then faded as his legs buckled.

Then Sapphira saw Tucker gazing down at her. As his arms helped her up, she saw Forbes there too with another lamp. The bump on her head tingled but she felt no pain. Feeling little of anything, she watched Monroe's body heave and convulse on the floor, the goad protruding from his belly. At his feet, her father looked dazed and winded, older than she had ever seen him. She held a hand out toward him but drew it back, burying her face in Tucker's jacket. It smelled of sweat and smoke, of salvation.

TREMBLING, TRULY STAMPED out the little oil-fire around the broken lamp. He found a candle lying in its holder, still weakly burning, and picked it up. Heath lay mute but quaking in his agony. Watching his throes, Truly considered borrowing Forbes' pistol, but the thought dissolved as he gazed over at Sapphira. With her eyes closed, she rested against Tucker's side. Truly took a breath, then looked back at Heath's shadowy form. It had gone still. Only now did he recognize the protruding implement as a shank bone, probably a horse's. It registered no more than other details of the struggle: a cat o' nine-tails, splayed like a charred piece of vegetation; Heath's bayonet, dabbed with Truly's blood; his torn sleeve and the slight gash on his forearm; the rising stench of guts.

Forbes shone his lamp around. "Do you hear a whimpering?"

"Ursula," Truly rasped. "Chained up." He spat on the floor and looked at Tucker. "How's Ben?"

"He's all right." The sergeant held Sapphira closer. "Still upstairs, sir, with one of the girls. She's in a state. She shot that man Dubray."

"That leaves only Ravenel," said Forbes. "We'll find her, but let's get Sapphira outside."

As they filed out, Ursula's voice quailed after them—"Please! Do not leave me here, please!!"

Her pleading faded as Forbes led the way through the liquor area, pungent with alcohol and littered with smashed bottles. Tucker followed, supporting Sapphira and gently guiding her. Trudging behind them, Truly reached out and touched her elbow. She turned her head, too slightly to look at him.

They were headed up the stairs when, beyond the doorway above, a shot crackled. Truly stiffened, peering up. He felt his nerves reach their snapping point. Tucker pulled Sapphira aside as Truly shoved past them, tossing the candle away. Forbes drew his weapon and barreled up the remaining steps. Truly flew after him.

On the other side of the hall, a short way down, Ravenel stood by an open door. Her shoulders were hitched as if in indignation, though her arms hung limp. On the floor lay her derringer, its hammer cocked. Her shimmering sloe eyes gaped at Truly, devoid of reason–and by a strip of flesh, her jaw dangled like a ghastly ornament. Blood cascaded down her withered neck, glistened on her black satin gown. Abruptly she slid down the wall and fell forward with a soft thump.

"Here, Pa."

Truly whirled to see Ben seated near the foot of the back stairwell, a blonde girl slumped beside him. Holding his revolver in his lap, Ben seemed nearly as stupefied as the girl, staring up. Truly stepped over to him.

"She darn near got us," Ben murmured. "We came down the stairs and there's that biddy waiting, aiming at my head."

Tucker and Sapphira emerged from the cellar. Standing with Forbes, they stared down at the hag's crumpled body.

The blonde girl had dozed off. Kneeling, Truly patted Ben on the shoulder. "Well . . . you got her. You got her, and she's the last one."

Ben shook his head. "Never got to fire, Pa. The shot came from that way." He motioned.

Looking, Truly stood up. He stepped around Ravenel's corpse and crept along the corridor. He found Wakefield lying across the kitchen threshold, the smoking pistol at his side. Bending down, Truly detected shallow breathing. The Confederate's eyes were shut, his lips pressed tight. Cradling a wound in his lower left side, his hands seeped red.

Truly bent closer. "Wakefield," he whispered. "Hold on. We'll get you to a hospital."

Fluttering, the eyes peered up from a foggy depth.

Forbes said that the nearest hospital was out by the Soldiers' Home. He went out front to wave down a passing refugee wagon. Using a folded tablecloth as a compress, Sapphira knelt intently over Wakefield.

Truly went outside. By the steps, he found the black stallion pulling at its tether, tossing its fine fierce head. He managed to untie the horse, which then cantered to a water trough by the stable. Around the rose arbor, the bright-gowned girls of La Maison were gathered in an anxious covey. At his approach, their daunted stares said enough about how he looked. He heard himself addressing them in a hoarse voice, promising help of some kind. His bruised body groaned for sleep. He yearned for a tobacco chaw.

92

North District Perimeter
July 11, 1 P.M.

LATER, IF HE could, Jubal Early would determine what had gone so hideously wrong. He would pause to rue his sendoff oration to the party of rapt volunteers. He would damn the siren song of traitors and trickery and the whole stupid dime-novel scheme. He would damn V. Grayson. In his report to Lee, he would respectfully skewer the notion that anything but guts and steel could have decided the matter, and Marse Robert would likely agree. But all of that was for later. On this day, his life's flaming pinnacle, in a swelter of hope, he had to strike the enemy capital in time-honored fashion. First, however, his men would have to arrive in sufficient numbers—and therein lay the frustration.

Scaling another cloudless sky, the sun had turned devilish, disintegrating the column until its straggling men looked nothing like conquerors, more like trudging vagabonds strung out along the Seventh Street Road. No threats, curses or cajoling could spur their step. Atop his horse, through the heat waves and the roiling dust, Early watched a bunch of ragged North Carolinians shuffle past, some dragging their rifles. One of them staggered and then dropped.

Fanning himself with his black-plumed hat, Early bawled at them: "Washington, boys! It'll be ours by nightfall if you keep going! Just keep go . . . " A cannon report muffled the rest. It came from the right of the Union defenses—from DeRussy, just over Rock Creek. He had sworn not to think of it, but the fort's shelling–hundred-pounders, it sounded like, playing hell with his supply train–made that impossible.

Just before sunup, he had received a message from the distressed colonel of the Twenty-third Virginia, poised to rush in and secure DeRussy. From the fort's direction had come sounds of cannon and rifle fire, but no word from the volunteers–none until the shattered party limped out of the darkness, toting the bodies of Captain Martin Guillespie and three others. Treachery, they said–a foul ambush. Within view of the fort, Guillespie himself had raised the torch signal and been answered, after some delay, with a blast of hot iron. Who was responsible? "I," thought Early. "I, for one." But from dismay and consternation, he passed quickly to acceptance, as if all along he had secretly expected this result. Whereupon he commenced the primary plan of attack.

With light artillery, McCausland had moved southeast against Fort Reno near Tennallytown. Early with his main force had marched east to Silver Spring and then south against Fort Stevens. Falling back, the outnumbered federal cavalry offered only fitful resistance, and McCausland reported the same. Time and heat were the real enemies today. Heat and time, hammering at Early's brain. As yet, despite Washington's supposedly large pro-Southern element, no intrepid civilian had braved Union lines to bring intelligence. Were the city's defenders as under-strength as Early suspected? Or had the balance of Grant's Sixth Corps arrived? If not, when was it due? Questions, billowing with the dust.

But now, at last, it appeared that enough of Rodes' vanguard had come up. Granting the men a brief rest, Early moved onto a rise and trained his binoculars on Fort Stevens, some twenty rods distant. The stump-ridden green fields sloped gently down past isolated groves and farmhouses, past a picket line of what looked to be state militia, to a little vale with a stream bed. Just beyond that and hard by the road stood the fort–jagged with abatis, palisades and angled walls, its upper and lower tiers bristling with gun-snouts. Yet it seemed feebly garrisoned; only a few tiny figures paced or stood along the parapets. Astride the fort, some Yankee horsemen had dismounted and were filtering into the rifle pits.

To Early, over the past three years, there had occurred odd, reassuring moments of clarity. Such a moment occurred now as he focused upon the limp Stars 'n' Stripes above the roadside gate. A pitiful excuse for a flag, he had always thought–a candy-colored bedsheet, a barber's pole untwisted. He passed the binoculars to Pendleton and took the map. The sun-beaten gray infantry kept filing past and then diverging to either side of the road, forming skirmish lines. DeRussy thundered on. In the fields to the left, earth spouted high as Fort Slocum rumbled to life. Surely Stevens would soon join in and the Yankee guns would start finding their targets.

Mounted beside Early, the lantern-jawed Rodes shielded his eyes to the sun. Early fussed noisily with the map and then glared at his watch, prompting Rodes to excuse himself and confer with his line officers. Presently a burst of shouted orders signaled the advance. Early folded the map, gave it back to Pendleton and reclaimed the binoculars. As scattered musketry ensued, he watched the skirmishers fan out across the terrain and the Union picket line slowly give ground. Picking out suitable trees, Confederate sharpshooters perched themselves and took aim.

Breckinridge came riding up and Early greeted him. "Strong works, Breck. But few men, near as I can tell."

Breckinridge smiled through his sweat. "This is the city's main artery. If they're weak here, they're weak everywhere. General, my canteen's run dry–might I impose?"

Several of the retinue instantly presented their canteens, but Early thrust his into the Kentuckian's outstretched hand. Watching him drink, Early felt cheered. Breckinridge's resolve had not softened in the heat. With the prospect of glory still gaping, amid the scuffle of troops and the spreading clash of rifles, he betrayed no misgiving or muddled sentiment. Early thought of the fine celebration that awaited him and all of his top command back at the Francis P. Blair estate. Kyd Douglas, as provost marshal, had been thoughtful enough to place sentries on the mansion's wine cellar. Tonight, dining in bibulous splendor, even Breckinridge would toast the sack and ruin of Washington.

"Look there, Genr'l!" It was Pendleton, motioning toward Stevens.

Early looked. Behind and to the left of Stevens, a battalion-sized enemy mass had appeared, marching boldly forward. With well-ordered speed, two of its formations separated; one entered the fort and began lining the parapets, while the other moved out to bolster the faltering picket line. The remainder poured into the rifle pits. Despite the evident discipline of these defenders, Early's lenses revealed them as an almost comical assemblage–state militia and tan-faced army veterans, yes, but also men in civilian hats and linen dusters. Nothing shy of desperation could have produced such a mongrel force–yet its cool, quick deployment troubled Early. Given this and the artillery threat, he thought, resistance could prove stiffer than expected.

Early spied Rodes in a wheat field and trotted over to him. He had to yell above the intensifying battle noise. "Listen–I'm thinking it would be wise to let more of your men come up. It wouldn't do to send 'em in piecemeal."

Mopping his brow, Rodes looked relieved. "I concur, Genr'l. So we keep it to a skirmish for now?"

"Right. But once your whole division's up, proceed with the full assault."

A loud boom made their horses twitch. Early saw the shell strike near a farmhouse and knock several grayclads off their feet. The guns of Stevens had let loose. No Confederate batteries had yet arrived.

"I'm going to reconnoiter a bit," Early yelled. "Don't get killed, now."

Rodes gave an uncharacteristic laugh.

Early cantered back along the road and its shuffling, endless file of troops, a column in name only. Leaning out of the saddle, he harangued the stragglers: "Have you boys forgotten the Valley?! What they did to our people?! Come on, goddamn it–get up there! Remember the Shenandoah!" Not one sweaty face glanced up at him. His horse shied around one prostrate soldier, but then nearly trampled another. Coughing on the dust, Early veered away and doubled back. Then he turned west and passed over a series of knolls and dales, stopping twice to observe the action. In the smoke and fire before Stevens, he glimpsed fallen men on both sides.

He halted in a field of oat and raised his binoculars. A maple grove hid DeRussy from view–but to the south, he had a clear sweep of the ground between DeRussy and Stevens. Beyond the rifle pits, he spied no new troop formations. He scanned over the emerald woods and farmland and the yellow-brown network of roads, to the spires of Washington itself. Then, unmistakably, near the farthest reach of his vision, he beheld the Capitol Dome. His heart soared, lifting him in the saddle. Chalk-white in the sun, the dome drew his thoughts to the nation that had once claimed his loyalty.

Had he hailed from a less obscure part of Virginia, he like Breckinridge could have ended up in the United States Congress or even the Senate–attending balls, declaiming to the packed gallery, relaxing over brandy and cigars–although, given his temperament, he would likely have fought a duel or two. Still, he would not have traded this moment for any prize.

The artillery barrage mounted. Squinting harder, he stretched a hand out and touched thumb to fingertips, encompassing the faraway dome. Nestled in its fragment of blue sky, it looked as delicate as a songbird's egg. He squeezed the hand shut. Lowering his binoculars, he drew a chestful of thick summer air and crowed to the guns and musketry, the din of this Judgment Day. The rumble was such that he did not hear the hoofbeats until they had nearly reached him. He looked to see Pendleton riding up through the oat grass, his face longer than usual.

"Genr'l, a courier just arrived from . . . "

Early cupped an ear.

"From General McCausland!" Pendleton drew alongside, almost shouting. "He's run into especially strong defenses on the Georgetown Pike."

"Hell, so have we! 'Cept they're manned by a scratch force–can't he see that?!"

"He's also sighted . . . "

"Speak up, Sandie!"

The adjutant leaned in. "Large Yankee formations, Genr'l! Coming straight toward us!"

Early's gaze fell. It lingered in the deep grass before turning south again, toward the spires and the dome–his gleaming white vista, already fading. Blinking it away, his eyes settled on a particular road running diagonally from the city; just where it vanished into some wooded heights, a gauze of yellow dust had risen. He brought up the binoculars. Within the sulfurous eddies, he saw a tight blue column quick-marching toward the Seventh Street junction. Then he glimpsed one of its lead flags, bearing the Greek Cross of the Union Sixth Corps.

The heat pressed down on him. The skirmish blazed on, federal pickets now holding their ground. Handing Pendleton the binoculars, he fished a tobacco plug from his pouch and took a bite. He chewed slowly, his back hurting.

"We can still give them a good bruising!" cried Pendleton. "We can stay awhile! Once our whole force comes up . . . " From beyond the maple grove, DeRussy thundered, drowning him out completely.

PART X

Thunder

*The Confederacy is more formidable
as an enemy than ever.*
  • The Times of London,
July 25, 1864

*I am almost ready to say . . . that God wills
this contest, and wills that it shall not
end yet . . . And having begun, He could
give the final victory to either side any day.*
  • Abraham Lincoln, 1864

*Our eyes met. He stood like a statue. He gazed
at me with a kind of scared expression. I
still did not want to kill him . . . When I fired,
the Yankees broke and run, and I went up to
the boy I had killed, and the blood was
gushing out of his mouth. I was sorry.*
  • Sam Watkins,
Confederate soldier

93

Fort Stevens
July 12

*A*s FORBES SET foot on the rampart, the whistle of a sharpshooter's bullet made him flinch and then lose his balance. He fell sideways, grunting with the impact. Rolling over, he lay his binoculars down and squinted up at the hot azure sky. He was tired of being shot at.

"Forbes! Welcome to the fray!"

He looked at the crouched officer on his right, whose sharp features took a moment to register. He had not seen Wendell Holmes, Jr. since Harvard. Sitting up, Forbes reacted with a crossfire of emotion, pleased but discomfited to see an old Boston face.

"Hello, Holmes." On the near shoulder strap, Forbes saw a pair of silver oak leaves. "I mean–Lieutenant-Colonel."

The other smirked. "'Holmes' will do fine." Holmes ducked as another bullet whined overhead. Just past him, a ten-man crew huddled around a Parrott gun. "Odd to think," he said. "They say if you hear it, it's already missed you. But you duck just the same."

Forbes leaned against the staked wall. "Must mean we're not complete fatalists."

Through Holmes' open collar, a neat vertical scar showed on his neck. His patrician face seemed molded by fire, all the softness burned away. Yet the dark eyes were cool and clear; along with the suspended smirk, they lent the impression that Forbes had always had of him: a thorny iconoclast, one whose cocksureness was unsettling even in a Harvard man, let alone the son of a famed author/physician.

"Last I heard, you were convalescing," Forbes said.

"Ha! Which time?"

"After Fredericksburg."

"Got it in the heel there. Nothing too bad." Holmes rose slightly, peering toward the sputter of skirmish fire. "It's pitiful late to be saying this, but I was sorry about your brother. His company went in just before mine did."

Forbes recalled that Gerald had known Holmes better, being a fellow classman. "Thank you. It's never too late to say." He suddenly worried that Holmes might next ask him about Judith. "So what's the army doing with you now?"

"I'm aide-de-camp to General Wright."

"Really? Well–three cheers, if you had anything to do with getting him here."

Holmes huffed. "Wright didn't need any spurring, believe me. Point of fact, the real pain didn't start till we had to deal with District command. Wright had to raise hell just to get approval for yesterday's sortie."

"Which I understand was timely."

"Timely? Just before we threw that brigade in, the pickets were pushed all the way back to the rifle pits! And weren't they a sight? Noah's Ark was no more of a mix, I tell you. Veteran Reserves, hundred-day militia, citizen volunteers . . . "

Forbes felt a sudden, vague anxiety. Distracting himself, he took up his binoculars and stole a look over the palisade.

Beyond the felled trees and trickling brook of the vale, Confederate skirmishers advanced in a long, ragged line astride the road. Exchanging sporadic fire with the rifle pits, they moved through fields of oat, wheat and corn and tracts of brushwood, their gray forms blending almost to invisibility. On the brook's near side lay the smoldering ruin of a house, its chimney like a charred spinal column. Close by, another house had escaped destruction thus far, despite the efforts of federal gun crews–and from its white cupola, a marksman's long-range rifle flashed. About a mile due north, in the woods, the winking of sun on metal betrayed a substantial enemy presence. Yet Forbes knew that presence to be less than had been feared. His two surviving scouts had shown up after a week in the saddle; from them, and from his prisoner interrogations, he knew the toll that Early's month-long march had taken on Rebel ranks–heat, wounds, death and illness, whittling them down.

After some thirty hours at the city gates, Early had yet to make a full fight of it–which probably meant he never would. He had accomplished plenty for Lee, diverting men from Grant's army and embarrassing the government. But surely he knew that his chance to breach the capital defenses was gone. Hunter's troops were reportedly quick-marching from West Virginia, closing on Early's rear. And even now, in the fields behind the fort, a battle-tested brigade stood ready to attack the Confederate line. Was it daring, indecision or simple obstinacy that kept Early here, with the danger shifting hard against him?

Holmes asked to use the binoculars. Gazing through them, he asked Forbes about his present duties, and Forbes described his work with the Military Information Bureau. He spoke of the prisoners from yesterday's skirmish and of the reported cavalry raids near Baltimore–tracks torn up, telegraph lines cut, the governor's mansion burned.

Holmes handed the glasses back. "Well, this sure was a near thing, wasn't it?"

In Forbes' mind, bullets still tore through the halls of La Maison de l'Empereur. "Surely was," he muttered. Feeling an odd pressure on his tongue, he nearly blurted it out: the story of a certain other lieutenant-colonel, of the events at Fort DeRussy. But a cannon blast hushed him. Two gun platforms away, one crew had resumed trying to hit the cupola sniper's nest.

Holmes was talking: "Once Wright gives the order, those johnnies will wish they'd stayed in the Land of Corn Pone. I just wish we had a remedy for these damned sightseers."

In and around the fort, in groups and in couples and dressed as if for the theater, genteel civilian observers craned their necks to view the action. Flushed and giddy, they covered their ears and passed smiles around. Forbes thought he recognized two members of Lincoln's cabinet.

"Forbes?" Holmes said.

"Pardon me–what?"

"I said, how the devil are they getting past the provost guard?"

Forbes shrugged. "Official passes, gotten by threat or persuasion. For them, there hasn't been sport like this since First Bull Run."

Civilians, he thought. Then he recalled the sight of Octavius Duke shouldering his antiquated musket, stumbling off to test his manhood. His wave, his pie-scallop smile.

"Well," Holmes said, "I'm mustering out in a few days. By autumn I'll be back at Harvard studying law . . . " Nearby, a bullet chipped the palisade. "If I don't catch one of those first, I mean. I've had enough–and I don't care what the parlor patriots of Boston say. Point of fact, they can all take a flying . . . " Leaning back from the wall, he stared past Forbes' shoulder. "Oh, for the love of God! That is just the baldest piece of stupidity I've ever seen!"

Forbes shifted around to look. He tensed. Some fifteen yards away, a few civilians had gathered along the parapet, among them a particularly tall man in a black frock coat and stovepipe hat. As fretful soldiers tried budging them to safety, Major-General Horatio Wright appeared, waving a hand. The group dispersed, leaving only that most conspicuous figure in the high hat; oddly serene, he gazed out at the bullet-whipped spectacle while the stocky general stood at his elbow, remonstrating. Just a few feet away, a medical officer clutched himself by the thigh and crumpled; two soldiers grabbed his arms and dragged him down from the wall.

"Get down, you fool!"

Glancing back, Forbes saw that it was Holmes who had bellowed the command, hands cupped to his mouth. The tall dignitary cast a look in their direction; Forbes saw the beard. As Wright's gestures became adamant, the man at last responded and the two of them went below.

"Hard to believe," Holmes muttered.

Behind him, the stooped gunners were smiling. Forbes smiled too.

"What's the jest?" Holmes demanded.

"My friend, you just upbraided the President of the United States."

Holmes looked below. Between his eyes, a small dent appeared. "Oh."

Forbes let a chuckle escape. He let it lengthen–an unfamiliar sound but unquestionably his own, pumping from some deep inner recess. Then he remembered about Duke. Taking Holmes' loose hand, he shook it. "Say hello to the old school for me. If anyone's earned a separate peace, it's you."

He ducked down the earthen ramp as Holmes called after him: "Well, he *was* being a damned fool!"

In the barracks behind Stevens, a quick search among the wounded turned up no clerks, but a steward directed Forbes to a baggage train down the road. Headed there, he noticed how fast dusk was coming on—air cooling, shadows stretching, sky copper in the west. From the forts and outer batteries, the shelling had begun to escalate, making the air quake. Then, to Forbes' right, a solid blue-clad formation erupted from the corn and swept past him, past Stevens and the rifle pits. He paused, watched it surge toward the enemy lines and then limped onward, the din mounting at his back. Like a fingertip pressing his heart, the worry persisted. Across the road and not far ahead, the baggage train came in view, its unhitched mules grazing in the trampled corn. Teamsters dozed while male nurses attended supine or seated men in civilian garb.

On the end wagon's tailboard, a man sat slumped with both of his arms bandaged; beside him, a man in a checkered coat stood observing the battle, a pencil and tablet in his hands. At Forbes' approach, the latter turned to him and Forbes saw the red suspenders: Israel Noonan of the *Evening Star*. Noonan raised the brim of his domed hat and grinned through freckles.

"Captain Forbes," he called above the noise. "Anything for the record?"

"Nothing you can't see on your own, Mister Noonan."

"Hey, didn't we call it right? About Early? One of us should be Army Chief of Staff."

Forbes shambled up to him. "I'm looking for a friend of mine, a War Department clerk."

"Are you? Well, as I understand it, most of the War clerks were given support duties in the city. You're sure he's not back there?"

"No. Not sure at all."

"A company of them was out here yesterday. They saw a little action alongside the Quartermaster employees, which is most of what you see here. But I think all the healthy ones were ordered back to the reserve camp."

Relieved, Forbes eyed the man with the bandaged arms. In a blood-stained shirt he sat listing, bleary, threatening to roll off the tailboard. "Octavius Duke is his name," Forbes said.

Noonan consulted his tablet. "That's not one I've gotten."

"He's rather squat, with red hair. And eyeglasses."

Tucking his pencil behind a big ear, Noonan made a helpless gesture.

Forbes began picturing Duke back in the city or in camp. On guard duty, perhaps—bored, dusty and probably constipated, dozing on his musket.

To the north, cannons reverberated, the clash intensifying. Then Forbes thought he heard the wounded man mumble something. He leaned in. "What's that again?"

Feebly the man motioned with his linen-swathed arm. "Down that way," he croaked.

Some twenty paces down the line of carts and wagons, Forbes encountered an obviously drunk nurse who shrugged him toward a trio of dead bodies. The three were arranged side by side on an army gum blanket. Eyeing their pale, bloated features, Forbes saw that Duke was not among them.

Noonan had followed. "What about that one?" he said, pointing.

By a cart, half in the shade, a short figure lay covered with a dirty sheet. Forbes limped over to it. On top of the sheet lay a pair of spectacles, the lenses filmed with dust. On one side, a soft-looking white hand protruded–and at the top, a tuft of red hair. Forbes turned away. Shouldering past Noonan, he moved through the grazing mule herd to where the corn stood high, steeped in shadow.

He took his hat off, smoothed his hair. In his benumbed imagination, it was not Duke's face but Gerald's he saw, refracting into a score of others from his youth. He saw his own face too, younger, back when life had seemed a clear proposition–when hope and even certainty had come with ease. Like money from the vault, like footraces on the green. And after loss upon loss, had it been too much to ask that Octavius be spared?

Behind him, the nurse spoke with slurred impatience. "You gonna collect him, sir?"

Before Forbes could reply, Noonan called–"Hey, Captain–look here."

Forbes turned around. Standing over the sheeted form, Noonan nudged one of its feet. The form stirred. Hurrying back to it, Forbes watched as Duke pulled the grimy cover down, rolled onto his side and sat up.

"Oh . . . Oh, mercy."

"Octavius?"

Squinting hard, Duke smiled up. "Captain!" He pressed a palm to each eye. "The sun, you know–it was too much to me. The order came to fall in . . . and I just plain fell."

Forbes leaned down and retrieved the glasses. He wiped them off with his handkerchief.

Noonan chortled, slapping the tablet against his thigh. "Gentlemen, this'll make a dandy little anecdote for the *Star*!" He strutted away. "See you, Captain. Regards to Nate."

"Thanks, Noonan."

Rising, Duke steadied himself against a cart wheel. Forbes handed him the specs and he put them on. After a greedy guzzle from Forbes' canteen, he seemed to become aware of the battle noises and glanced about, looking jittery.

"What's happening?" he asked.

"Another sortie. Bigger than yesterday."

Duke rubbed his shoulder. "Yesterday . . . I tell you, Captain–the way that blunderbuss of mine kicked!"

"Got a shot off, did you?"

"Just one. Can't say if I hit anything." He shook his head. "When those Rebels closed in, I thought it was the end. The sight of them . . . I felt all alone out there. Then, when our troops appeared and went storming past–that was glorious! Like a reprieve from heaven. Like God saying, 'Here's your life back, Octavius–now see to it.'" Catching sight of the corpses, his eyes went wide. "Oh . . . Oh, Lord–I think I know one of those poor fellows!"

Forbes lay a hand on his back. "Let's be gone."

Forbes had tied his mount at the toll gate by the fort, but it was nowhere to be seen. Above the clamor, a militiaman yelled that another officer had commandeered the animal. It struck Forbes that in the past forty-eight hours he had lost two horses, both rented at Howard's Livery, from whose services he was likely banned for life. Duke stood transfixed at his side, watching the man-made tempest in front of Stevens.

Across the darkening landscape with its advancing throng of bluecoats, orange flashes marked the fight's progress. A barn and some trees had caught fire. Having cleared a peach orchard of sharpshooters, the federals had secured one knoll and were struggling to seize another. Reinforcements rushed in. Stretcher-bearers crept into the gloom of the vale while others emerged from it, toting bodies.

Forbes and Duke started away on foot. Realizing that the road would take them right past La Maison, Forbes fleetingly wished for a different route.

"Have to say," said Duke. "–I wouldn't want to repeat this experience."

"I hope you never have to," Forbes said.

"It's so queer, about yesterday. The Rebs . . . They were this wall of harm coming at us–like a bee swarm, you know? But later I saw some captured ones, and they were just men with faces. Individuals, small and mortal. All of that scary charge gone out of them."

Forbes nodded. "I know."

"Like us."

"Yes."

"I mean to say, it's a pity when you really think about it. To have to go shoot some fellow or be shot by him, when you might have met and liked him otherwise. Just because you were born to a different side. Just because of other men's greed or hate or ambition."

"Vice is a monster, Octavius."

Behind them in the reddening twilight, the sounds of carnage and the stench of gunpowder had begun to fade. Forbes limped along, his breaths labored, while Duke moved at a kind of jaunty waddle.

"How is Major Truly?" the clerk asked.

"Well enough. He'll be glad to see you."

Duke smiled up. "So, did I miss anything?"

94

Harewood Hospital, District Of Columbia

IN THE BARRACKS-LIKE building, most of the beds were occupied. The rafters were strung with garlands to fight the odor, which nevertheless seemed a solid presence; so did the quiet, disturbed only by the not-so-distant guns. Wakefield lay at the far end on the right, his mosquito netting raveled up; beside him sat Delia in a white dress and bonnet. Her lovely face was slack but her gaze steady, as if memorizing his every feature. She did not stir as Truly stood over her.

"I need time with him now," he said, softly. "You can wait in the office. They have chicory tea."

With a touch to Wakefield's hand, she rose and then padded out like a sleepwalker. Truly put his little writing case on the chair and opened it. Then he found another chair to sit on. In the light of the ceiling lantern, Wakefield's face was blanched and stubbled, his hair a sandy snarl. Yet his breathing sounded easier than before, his eyes half-open but watchful. The surgeon had applied opium powder to the wound before suturing it–and since the ether had worn off, he had given a series of morphine injections. Peritonitis had set in.

"Is there much pain?" Truly asked.

Wetting his lips, Wakefield spoke in a listless drawl. "I'm afloat on a sea of cotton."

Truly glanced around. In the bed next to Wakefield's, a leg amputee lay asleep. "I told them you're a citizen volunteer who performed valiantly. That should snuff any prejudice against your accent."

Wakefield smirked faintly.

Truly got out his tablet, jabbed his pen in the inkwell. "Listen—Early's in a tight spot. He has to withdraw or be destroyed. What I'm saying is, this whole business is done with."

"What you're saying is, certain secrets don't matter now and perhaps I should out with them. For posterity, I suppose."

"If nothing else. Ravenel revealed a lot to me, anyway. Your scheme came close—closer than I care to think about. But it failed. All that's left is your part of the story."

Wakefield let out a careful breath. "You're a true boll weevil, you know that? Persistent."

"As were . . . As are you."

Truly waited, glad to have caught Wakefield in this state of dreamy lucidity. Then, in a flat murmur, the Confederate proceeded to confirm Ravenel's version and flesh it out.

Wakefield had not asked the nature of the contract that bound the five cursed men. Yet over the months, he had learned what it was. Monroe enjoyed describing how he had fulfilled his part of the lucrative bargain: Monks' nemesis Captain Yale, laid up with wounds from Ball's Bluff—Monroe posing as a hospital orderly, applying a poisoned bandage; Underhill's former secretary Jepson out on a bender—Monroe tailing him and then bludgeoning him dead in an alley, taking his wallet to make it look like robbery; Archer's miserable wife Helen in the asylum—Monroe disguised as a night attendant, stealing into the women's ward and seizing her as she slept, forcing prussic acid down her throat; Howland, Van Gilder's impediment, working late at the *Comet-American*—Monroe cornering him in his office and forcing liquor into him until he signed the sale agreement, then dispatching him with one of Dubray's subtler poisons—and three months later, tailing the stooge attorney who had been used in the sale, then drowning him off a pier; Peavey's Uncle Solon, sailing his boat on the Patuxent—Monroe hidden below, emerging to suffocate the older man and throw him overboard.

Truly's pen scratched away until Wakefield asked for water. Getting a bucket of it from a nurse, Truly slid a hand under Wakefield's head and eased it up to the ladle. The Confederate took a few sips, his bare shoulders tensing. He sighed thanks and Truly let his head down. Without prompting, Wakefield resumed his story.

As Truly suspected, the idea for the ultimate scheme had been Wakefield's own. Ravenel and company wanted to simply pressure Monks into treason, but Wakefield argued for a different approach—one that took into account the workings and shadings of human nature, even in a specimen like Monks, and thus might prove more effective.

Here he paused. "What I mean is . . . I suspected that it could not be so direct."

"Ravenel spoke of it," said Truly. "And I believe I understood. May I tell a quick story?"

Wakefield's dim eye flickered up. "I'd welcome the distraction."

Truly put his pen down. From a shaker, he sprinkled drying sand over the page he had just written. "Back in Missouri, at the advanced age of fourteen, I found myself apprenticed to a saddler. He was a steady man and a good craftsman when sober—but that wasn't often enough, for my taste. At those other times, he would cuff me for the smallest mistake—and not being the best apprentice, I made plenty of them. But I accepted his abuse. He was a big man—but besides that, some part of me figured I deserved it. I had submitted myself to his rule, which could be summed up as, 'No mistakes, you pissant.' So like a beaver I worked to satisfy him, with mixed results."

Truly blew the excess sand off of his page. "Well, one day in the shop he was drunk again, and I knew I was in for it. But this time he didn't wait for a reason—none that I could see, anyhow. He grabbed me by the hair, threw me down and kicked me. There was no way to placate him and only one way to stop it—namely, to punch him in the privates, kick his knees out, crown him with a pail and douse him with lye. I went a little mad, understand. Within minutes I'd gathered my gear and lit out for the Santa Fe Trail, reckoning there'd be a price on my head. I spent the next few years down there in Nuevo Mexico, consorting with traders, Injuns, banditi, mountain men and such." Several beds down, a patient groaned and the nurse went to him. Truly gazed to the nearest window, the thickening gloom outside. "Come to think of it, you might say that saddler did me a good turn, drunken shit-heap though he was."

Wakefield gave a weak smile. "And down in Georgia, I grew up with the tale of a cruel master who was hacked to death by his meekest slave. When the blows fall not according to any logic, but to the master's whim, the subject may hang himself in despair. Or with nothing to lose, he may turn wild—strike back madly. Even the meekest slave. Or a scared boy."

"Or a grown coward," Truly said.

"Like Monks, yes. Given what we needed him to do, I thought it better to entrap him, tempt him into acting against us. By drawing the other men into it, we made it easy for him to take the step, going along with the group. Whatever resulted from his transgression would therefore seem a logical consequence–fair, in its way–and not as cruel whimsy on our part. In that frightened little mind of his, we would maintain our leverage."

"A leverage which was then increased," said Truly, "by reprisal against his fellow mutineers."

Wakefield blinked at the ceiling. "I'd come to hate those men, just as I'd come to hate . . . my cohorts."

Truly nodded. "But apart from that, the other men knew about Monks–and with the extortion scheme now moot, it was best to silence them. Except for Archer, who remained useful." He picked up the pen. "So on the 15th of April, the trap was sprung . . . "

"Correct. Peavey had been begging to renegotiate his payment schedule. On that pretext, he was granted an audience for the 15th. And for good measure Ravenel summoned Monks himself, with the offer of Briona Kibby's company. I went along with that, but naturally . . . I never thought the girl would come to harm, that Ravenel would let him take her from the house."

"I believe you. And if you haven't confessed your involvement to Miss McGuire, I won't tell her."

"I haven't–and thank you." Wakefield had closed his eyes. "So . . . we fooled them. The month of May passed, and none showed up with his quarterly payment. Monroe set about taking retribution. We would have spared Underhill, you know. Killing a congressman was risky enough–and besides, Ravenel enjoyed having him on a string. But when he spoke of hiring an assassin of his own and asked me to serve as go-between, that forced our hand. As for Archer–he was, as you say, too valuable for killing."

Truly thought of the letter he had found last night, on his second foray into Archer's house. Chilled, he also thought of its recipient–a man beyond redemption, foul with lies, dead by his own hand. Compassion was a limited resource, Truly decided; he would save his for cripples and orphans–and murdered wives. Applying sand once more, he closed the tablet and slid it into his inner pocket. "Have to say I'm humbled, Wakefield. With just a speck more frailty on my part, you would have won."

Wakefield was spent–ashen-faced, his voice starting to dwindle. "One frailty I would have done well to correct. The urge to . . . sign my name to photographs."

Right, Truly thought–that, and the conscientious habit of saving plate negatives.

He eyed the mosquito netting over the bed, gathered there like a bridal veil. He pondered Wakefield's biggest frailty of all: Delia–vessel of his love, unwitting party to his downfall. Truly would have to explain more of it to her–with certain omissions, for everyone's sake. Always the omissions.

From behind him came a tentative female voice. "Sir . . . ?" He looked and saw the nurse, a wan lady with earnest eyes. "Sir, you must let him sleep now."

"Of course." Quickly he put his implements back in their case. Rising, he saw Wakefield's lids flutter and then open.

"Truly . . . " As Truly bent down, Wakefield spoke just above a whisper. "There's one photograph. A sunken bridge, clouds . . . "

"I've seen it. At your shop."

"It's in my trunk, at the house. Please send it to my sister Caroline. In Savannah."

"I will. And anything else, if you like."

"What assets I have, I'd like divided evenly between Caroline and Delia."

"I'll see that they are."

Wakefield sighed, swallowed. "Delia . . . "

By the mattress, his hand hung limp–an artist's hand, uncallused and slender. Truly pressed it lightly. "She'll be with you again soon."

Back outdoors, the shelling was now more distant and sporadic. Truly took a few steps toward his rented horse but then halted, his body still sore to the bone. The dusk smelled faintly sulfurous. He stared at the signal tower, silhouetted in the distance. In his mind he suddenly beheld the Pedregal, an expanse of cooled lava near Mexico City–black, sharp, twisted rock, as far as the eye could see. For a mercifully short moment, he felt the same barrenness as when he first gazed upon that fireless hell, that blackened waste, so far from God.

95

Francis P. Blair Mansion Silver Spring, Maryland

A CANNON REPORT SHOOK the pane. Chewing hard, Early parted the damask drapes and gazed south across the District line. Random fires illuminated the woods and the road, along which men of Echols' retiring division shuffled past. Combined with the smoke, their shroud of silvery dust obscured the moon. The fight was over except for scattered shelling and picket fire. Since last night's council-of-war, which further depleted old Blair's wine cellar, Early had managed to stay philosophical.

"We got a courier from Bradley Johnson," he said. Turning from the window, he looked at Gordon, Pendleton and Breckinridge, all seated at the big dining room table with the scrolled maps. In the light from the candelabra, they looked tiredly patient. "Johnson and his horsemen will be rejoining us sometime tonight. Says he got hold of a Baltimore newspaper, which said a second Yankee corps is on its way here. That bolsters my decision."

"It's a wise choice," said Gordon, "given what the enemy showed us this evening."

Breckinridge nodded but stayed quiet, stroking his mustache. Perhaps he was still disconcerted, finding himself in the home of his erstwhile friend Blair—not as an honored guest this time, but as its opposite. Still, the Kentuckian had surprised everyone last night by proposing an assault down Rock Creek, to be followed by flanking attacks. Maybe it was the wine. Whatever the reason, it had been queer to end up preaching caution to Breckinridge, reminding him of the felled timber that obstructed the creek bed, plus the guns of DeRussy nearby–that accursed fort.

"What's more," said Early, "the paper said Hunter's racing to seal off the fords and passes in our rear. Any more delay, the jaws will close on us."

Piling on the justifications, getting nods–flatly unnecessary, but he could not help himself. He went to spit on the already well-stained carpet but then glanced at Breckinridge. Wine and spirits aside, he had promised his second-in-command to leave this house–and the neighboring one owned by Blair's son Montgomery, the U.S. Postmaster General–as unmolested as possible. He moved to the fireplace and launched a stream of tobacco juice into it, then his cud. Leaning on the mantel, he took in the room's tasteful decor. This manse would fare a lot better than the Maryland governor's had, near Baltimore. With renewed dismay, Early recalled that boastful part of Colonel Johnson's message.

Given the scuttling of the Point Lookout scheme–too far-fetched, now that Early thought of it–it was well that Johnson's havoc-raising had slowed him down. Otherwise, his eight-hundred troopers might well have been stranded. But if the North was to brand Early a barbarian, as the South had so justly branded Hunter, he wanted a worthy reason for it, something of military significance. Johnson's torching of Governor Bradford's home–sure to raise a stink in the hypocritical Yankee press–did not even come close.

"Beg your pardon, Genr'l," said Gordon, "–who is it we're waiting for?"

Stirred from his brooding, Early felt anxious again. "Major Douglas." He frowned at the mantel clock, then at Pendleton. "Sandie, do you know if Douglas was in the thick of it?"

"I believe he was, sir. Just as the Yankees attacked, I saw him riding near the center."

Early paced to another window, parted the drapes. Along the murky road, the column's movement had a pulsating quality–a slow, dusty current of men, flowing past Montgomery Blair's mansion and winding left toward Rockville. He watched it fade into the darkness. Over and done with, he thought–the great chance gone, if it had ever really existed. His back and shoulders hurt. Briefly he imagined the ache as something more–a yearning of bone and muscle, back toward the Union citadel. And where was Kyd Douglas? A glimpse of that brash young face would do him good.

At last Breckinridge spoke. "He'll be along, Genr'l. If anything had happened to him, I'm fair certain we'd have heard by now."

Early grumbled. Rubbing his left shoulder, he turned around. "Well, gentlemen–near as I can tell, we've done honor to old Stonewall's memory. We cleared the Valley. Squeezed levies out of Frederick and Hagerstown. Captured stores for Lee and livestock for the people. Mules for the teamsters, mounts and forage for the cavalry."

"Licked 'em at the Monocacy," Pendleton added, with an appreciative glance at Gordon.

Breckinridge gave a whimsical smile. "'Hear, hear,' as they say in the British Parliament. Speaking of which, this can only get us positive notice from Europe."

Early grunted. He too dared not speak the words "diplomatic recognition"–that treasured Confederate hope. He leaned by the hearth. "Most important, we drew off a good number of bluebellies, the less for Lee to tangle with. And God-a-mighty, it doesn't end here! We'll keep it up–lead 'em on a royal goose chase, for as long as we can! Not that I wouldn't have liked to get farther than this." He stared down at the fireplace, its cold ashes. "To have taken that damned candy flag of theirs and used it to wipe my horse down . . . "

Hearing footsteps, he looked up to see Douglas in the dining room entrance. "Sirs–awful sorry to have kept you." The boyish major seemed winded, his face and uniform well-smudged. He touched his hat to Early, then the others. "The messenger had trouble finding me. A lot of confusion out there."

With a long, silent breath, Early drew up straight. "No harm done," he said, shrugging toward the table. Magically his philosophical outlook had returned–bittersweet in his veins, like applejack.

Pendleton unscrolled a map and Early leaned over it, tracing the line of retreat: Rockville, Darnestown, Poolesville. Breckinridge would lead it, guarding the supply train. Ramseur and Rodes would follow with the artillery, prisoners and captured herds. The more severely wounded would have to be left behind. Early eyed Douglas. "And since you're such a hound for action, Major, you get command of the rear guard. Just a couple hundred men. When it comes your time to withdraw, the cavalry will provide cover."

"All right, Genr'l." Beneath the soot, Douglas's clean-shaven face showed an edge of strain, his usual good spirits muted.

Early indicated a bend in the Potomac. "In twenty-four hours or so, we should be across White's Ford and out of immediate danger. Then I reckon we'll get some well-deserved rest." He rapped on the tabletop. "Let's get to it, then." As they rose, he caught Douglas's eye and leaned toward him. "Major—we haven't taken Washington, but we've scared Abe Lincoln like hell!"

Douglas smirked. "Yes, Genr'l. But this afternoon when that Yankee line moved out against us, I think some other people were scared blue as hell's brimstone."

A laugh burst out of Breckinridge. Nudging the major's elbow, he regarded Early. "How about that, Genr'l?"

Early fought a smile, poking a finger at Douglas's chest. "That's true—but it won't appear in history!"

Outside, the sentries rattled to attention. Gordon and Breckinridge mounted up while Douglas and Pendleton headed away on foot, the latter with the bundled maps under this arm. As Early stood on the veranda, the steady shuffling sound from the road drew his attention. Again he watched the undulating troop column move past, its shadow-figures melding together. Like souls of the dead, he thought—souls, dust-enshrouded, marching into the beyond. An unlikely vision for him, more like one of Jackson's. Maybe some of Jackson had rubbed off on him, after all—just a bit of that warrior's mysticism. Then he noticed Breckinridge.

By the road, erect and motionless on his horse, the Kentuckian was gazing south—staring as if he could penetrate the night and dust and the smoke and flames farther on, back to Washington. Passing troops looked up at him, some doffing their hats, but he gave no sign of acknowledgment. Early left the veranda. He went to the mansion's other side, where an encampment of Georgians was breaking up, dousing its fires. Regret: Jackson would have called it sinful, an insult to Providence. And it was, in a way—a waste of spirit. Early resolved to resist its pull. He would scorn it, even if Gentleman Johnny Breckinridge did not.

"Genr'l, sir!"

From around the corner of the house, Douglas had reappeared. Three silhouettes walked shoulder to shoulder behind him, the flanking ones holding rifles. As Douglas strode up to him, Early noted the sword in his hand.

"Sir, it seems we've bagged a Yankee officer."

Early peered past the major. Guarding their prisoner, the two privates looked pleased with themselves. Between them stood the thin, slightly stooped officer with his hat askew, his light-blue uniform smeared with mud. The face was drawn and unshaven, the gaze skittish.

"These men here heard a rustling in the bushes," Douglas said. "Flushed him out like a turkey."

Early called out gruffly–"Your name and rank, sir?"

"Lieutenant-Colonel," came the voice–tense, mid-range. " . . . Griffith."

To Early's ear, the hesitation reinforced an impression of fright, unmanly and unwarranted.

"He must have been stranded by our counterattack," said Douglas. "He was unarmed, though, except for this old relic." He offered the sword. "Properly it's yours now, Genr'l."

Early glanced at the weapon. With a huff he accepted it, feeling silly about the quaint ritual. "Well–we should treat him as due his rank, I suppose. Take him inside, see if there's victuals left to feed him."

Douglas motioned to the guards, who followed him away with the prisoner.

Early paced in the other direction. Idly he watched soldiers loading a mule wagon; just as idly, he then examined the sword. It was of old manufacture, its leather scabbard soft and puckery, the brass fittings tarnished. Faintly curious, he drew it partway. Just beneath the grooved hilt, he spied lettering. He held it up, tilted it to the moonlight, read the engraved characters: MONKS 1812. The blade gleamed bright in his hands, as if from the furious heat now consuming him.

96

Old Capitol Prison

Lafayette Baker barged in, holding up Wood's note. "I need a fuller explanation."

Looking up from his requisition forms, William Wood put his pen down and smiled. "Of course. I wasn't about to write you a whole saga. I'm only surprised it took you this long to call."

"Didn't get it till half an hour ago. I've been out arresting pro-secesh all day."

"Ah, yes. Thanks to your zeal, our housing problem is worse than ever."

Baker pushed the door shut. He dropped the note on the desk and put his bowler down.

"That's a right handsome suit," said Wood. "If only Lincoln had your sartorial sense."

Baker dragged a chair up and sat with his arms crossed, his cuff links and watch fob glinting in the lamplight. "Please proceed."

"All right. It turns out Nate Truly's been busy too."

Baker's look darkened. "I suspended him. Without pay."

"Your point, Colonel?"

"Go ahead."

"Last night he came to retrieve an information source who he'd entrusted to my care–an exquisite Irish girl named Delia, who I fear has left my heart split like so much kindling."

Baker gave a sour smirk. "Which says plenty about why you took her to begin with. Aiding and abetting a man whose credentials I'd stripped away."

"Stripped away–yes, in your infinite wisdom. But harken, Mister Director, and see if the vinegar of your annoyance doesn't become the wine of gratitude. I sat with Truly a good while–the man looked worse for wear. He told me a lot."

Wood described the conspiracy between La Maison de l'Empereur and the spy Wakefield. He sketched what was known of Orlando Monks, and how Delia McGuire had identified him. He spoke of Truly's abduction, the Fort DeRussy episode and the arrest warrant for Monks, who had apparently deserted. Lastly he related the shootout at La Maison. All the while, he enjoyed the change in Baker's posture and expression–slouched to rigid, the smoldering gaze turning inward, hands kneading his broadcloth thighs.

At last Baker could not contain himself. "But this is all just Truly's version! A pinch of fact, maybe, under a heap of fabrication! Just to show me up!"

Wood's grin widened. "When it comes to shecoonery, I grant you, he could give us both a run for our money. But I fancy this is different. In the first place, wouldn't he be foolish to invent something that included so many living breathing individuals, any of whom could contradict him? Particularly in that business at DeRussy? No, Lafe, it's not that gol-darned simple." Sliding a drawer open, he took out the written statements. "In exchange for my darling Delia, Truly had with him a whole wagon full of beauties–former charges of La Maison. Regrettably, placing them all here was out of the question, so I had them taken to Sal Austin's in Marble Alley."

Baker bunched his eyebrows. "Am I hearing you correctly? That you supplied a load of harlots to a notorious brothel?"

"An *acclaimed* brothel–high-priced and well-managed. Better than leaving them to the mercy of the street. Besides, Sal's a good Unionist, unlike most of her profession in this city. At Truly's recommendation, anyhow, I did lock up one girl: Fannie O'Shea–another winsome flower of Erin, but one whose efforts to charm seemed a mite desperate. Later, Captain Forbes arrived with another, ampler-looking young lady: one Ursula Grunwald, a German. She was distraught, having been trapped a good while in La Maison's cellar. This morning I had lengthy hand-holding sessions with

Fannie and then Ursula, and obtained . . . " He patted the documents, pushed them toward Baker. " . . . signed testimony, in which they confess some wrongdoing–and, in the process, confirm much of Truly's tale."

Baker's eyes darted down at the papers.

Reaching out, Wood dragged his big key-ring across the desk. He began fingering it, picking through it like a rusted rosary. "In addition, Truly showed me a couple of items from the late Detective Archer's house."

Baker's burly shoulders hitched up. "Listen–whatever the allegations here, a dead police official is bound to raise an infernal ruckus! Now, on top of that, you're saying that Truly burgled the man's house?!"

"Twice, to be exact. On the first occasion, he snagged a signed portrait of the detective–a gift from Wakefield. Then, after the events of two nights ago, he realized he might need more evidence to protect himself. And this time he found a letter from Archer's daughter, one which seems to verify what Truly alleged about him–enough, I think, to hush any howls of condemnation from the District Police. As if that weren't enough, Truly produced another incriminating photograph, this one showing Archer engaged in a rather shocking act with the aforesaid Ursula." One by one, the keys clinked past Wood's fingers. "Truly said he's drafting a full report–augmented, he hoped, by a deathbed confession from Wakefield, plus sworn statements from the DeRussy garrison. With further corroboration from Captain Forbes and the other surviving players. All of which will produce, essentially, an epic account of your shortcomings–first and foremost, your refusal to take the matter seriously or lend adequate support. My guess is that he's writing a duplicate as well–one copy for himself, another for . . . " Wood's hand went still. "For whom, do you think? Since he's under suspension, whose desk will it likely land on instead of yours? Stanton's? The President's?"

Baker's glower shifted to a patch of exposed brick in the wall. His brow glistened.

"Not that it would be trumpeted hither and yon," said Wood. "Oh, no–not with a national election hanging over us. The government is sufficiently mortified over Early's little scare, and shaken too. Our distinguished friend Mister Stanton went so far as to hide several thousands of his own gold in a subordinate's house. Other high-placed gents did likewise. Privately, as I say, they're shaken and embarrassed–which in proud men translates to anger, plus an urgency to blame anyone but themselves. Yet none of them–Stanton, least of all–will want it known just how close

Washington came to falling. And isn't that always the way? We up here in our lofty nests, we're never as smart or all-seeing as the people hope we are, or fear we are. The illusion means everything. When it needs patching up, we waste no time doing so, preferably under cover of night. So it's not public reaction we should fret about, 'cause there won't be any." Idly Wood tapped the key ring. "Your professional future, though–that's our concern here."

Baker took a long, sullen breath. Fiddling with his silk cravat, he blinked hard. "I suppose I could cut Truly's suspension short."

Wood wagged his head. "Expunge it, you mean. And throw in his back pay." Hunching forward, he laid a hand on Baker's sleeve. "Put these other facts aside, if you like. Consider that everyone's dispensable, but that some are less so–and surely this applies to our mulish Missouri friend. Give the fellow credit, Lafe. Everything seems to indicate that he's saved the capital and maybe the Union too. Were justice anything more than a fancy notion, he would be decorated, promoted, sculpted in granite. Still, yes–you could do without him. But how well?"

"Your point's made, William. Stop touching me."

Wood eased back, stretching his arms wide. He yawned.

Still pensive, Baker fluffed his beard. "Forbes is under Colonel Sharpe's authority, not mine. He's bound to submit a report of his own."

"True. Therefore, no later than tomorrow, you should contact Sharpe and refer to the case in general terms, stressing the need for discretion. He's an agreeable man, is he not?"

Baker nodded, barely. Plucking a red silk handkerchief from his pocket, he dabbed his brow. As his stare drew back, the gray eyes betrayed a familiar flicker, as if from a candle in his head. He stuffed the handkerchief away, got up and reached for his bowler. "Well, William . . . Thank you for the word."

"You know that's not all," Wood said.

Freshly irritated, the director peered down at him. "What now?"

"Lafe–together we've interrogated any number of suspects, a good half of whom were better actors than you." Wood leered. "Or do you really think that gang out at La Maison served Richmond free of charge?"

Glancing away, Baker sat again. "I don't suppose so."

"Marvelous! Neither do I. In my session with Ursula, she did a lot of pleading and blubbering. She must have glimpsed my natural flexibility, because at one point she seized my arm and whispered, 'Mister Vood–if you let me go, there is something I vill tell you about! Something ve may share, and live vell from it afterwards!' I pretended to ignore this, though it was confirmation enough. Any fellow seeking the main chance must be judicious, Lafe—and with that in mind, I would prefer a more dependable partner than Fraulein Ursula. One who's able to keep my back covered—as I will cover his, should unseemly rumors come wafting up."

Baker clutched the bowler in his lap. In his gaze, the flicker had become a steady light.

"Bad enough," said Wood, "that these cutthroats profited from subversion. But for the profit to go unused, now that death constrains them from it? Intolerable." Wood shoved his papers back into the drawer. "You have a carriage?"

"Waiting outside," said Baker, already on his feet.

Getting up, Wood picked his worn linen jacket off the chair back. He grabbed his keys, extinguished the lamp. "Some grim sights await us, I reckon. But we'll find what we're after."

In the torch-lit yard below, a few War Department clerks personified the latest decline in guard quality, slouching on their muskets.

Wood locked his office and followed Baker along the catwalk, his keys jingling. He called to his companion's back. "Fifty-fifty—understood?"

From a shadowed corner of the prison, a voice rang out. "I see you up there, Yankee vermin! You want to escape ol' Jube, you'd best move quicker than that!"

Wood stopped to lean over the railing. "Go to sleep, Dinsmore!"

"Once Early gets us free, you'll be goin' on a mighty *long* sleep, damn your mongrel eyes!"

The rant continued. Not listening, Wood looked up at the night sky, now overcast. "For the life of me," he muttered, "I don't have the heart to tell him."

Baker called over his shoulder. "Come on."

Trailing him down the steps, Wood noted the extra vigor in Baker's stride. He cackled. "Ah, Lafe—we've always understood each other, haven't we?"

97

Louisiana Avenue

HAVING LEFT FORBES a note, Truly stepped from the boarding house just as a fancy coach pulled up. In the gaslight, Forbes' shape lumbered out and nodded to the driver, then limped toward the building. Wordlessly he and Truly acknowledged each other. They sat together on the steps as the coach rattled away.

Forbes yawned into his hand. "That was my new friend, the mayor. He was on his way back from Fort Stevens when, by happy coincidence, he spied us on the road."

"'Us'?"

"Octavius and me. I found him laid out from the heat, but unhurt."

Smiling, Truly swatted himself on the knee. "Now he'll be telling *us* war stories, eh?"

"One, maybe–over and over." With a sigh, Forbes took his hat off. "Early will likely withdraw tonight. But between Wright and Hunter and other forces closing in, we just might see him chased down and smashed."

"Yes–or merely chased. Sad to say, but the Union army has a talent for missing opportunities."

"Don't remind me." Forbes let his head droop. "So what about Wakefield?"

Truly placed his tablet on the step between them. "It's all here. I was going to give you the full account, but I see you're tired. Tomorrow, say?"

Forbes gave a slow headshake. "I got a wire from Sharpe this morning. Grant's reorganizing the Bureau, so I'm needed back at City Point."

Nodding, Truly looked at the sleeping tenements. "Thirty-seven days," he murmured.

"What?"

"Thirty-seven days–since we opened the door to Van Gilder's coach, and to the rest of this business. I just added them up."

Forbes contemplated the empty street, his face drawn in the bluish-white glow.

"About Wakefield," Truly said. "It was everything that we guessed, and more. I'm not sure whom I'll submit the report to–that depends on how things go with Lafe and me. But knowing him as I do, I'll be writing a duplicate for myself. Since you'll be having to write your own, I could come down to City Point and show you mine, to fill the blanks in."

"That I'd appreciate. Don't be surprised if the whole thing gets suppressed, though."

"I know. Oh, yes–I know." With a tepid chuckle, Truly returned the tablet to his inside pocket. They were silent for a minute. Despite his fatigue or maybe because of it, Truly wanted to go on talking. But he had kept Forbes long enough. Getting to his feet, he patted Forbes on the shoulder. "Godspeed."

"One last thing, Nate."

Truly looked down at him.

"Gold," Forbes said. "In La Maison's cellar. A crate full of it. I found it when I went back for Ursula, just a few feet from Heath's body."

Turning, Truly took a few slow strides into the avenue. "The South's payment," he muttered. Pacing back to Forbes, he pictured the glittering layers of gold. "Blood money if ever there was, eh?"

"Yes, well . . . that term applies to a lot of fortunes, doesn't it?"

From temptation to resignation, Truly's mind made a quick transit. He saw the crate full of glitter close tight. "I'll be going back to retrieve a certain photograph for Wakefield. But . . . I don't plan to set foot in that cellar again. Do you?"

"Can't think why I would." Like his tone, Forbes' gaze was oblique. "However, I did think that *you* might–for reasons that a just God would surely pardon. Because if you include this particular detail in your report, Baker will read no further. He'll make a beeline to the house."

Shuffling his feet, Truly wondered how big a fool he was being. "I'll include the detail."

"Fine, then. So will I. Listen–you're not offended, are you?"

"Constantly, but not by you. And as for Lafe . . . " Truly shrugged. "Heck—in this world, a man needs at least one other fellow to feel virtuous beside."

Forbes reached into his firing-cap pouch. He took out a shiny object and proffered it. "If he's to make his biggest-ever grab, please don't let him do it comfortably."

Truly took the object, a gold ingot.

"Blood money it may be," Forbes said, "but it's evidence too. Something to keep in reserve when the rest of it vanishes—when your boss's wardrobe suddenly triples in size."

Truly palmed the gleaming ingot, appreciating its heft. "Hm . . . That by which empires rise and fall." He slid it into his coat pocket, where it rested like any fair-sized stone.

With a lurch, Forbes got up and stretched. "Till next time, Sir Nathan." He hobbled up the steps. "And tell Sapphira . . . " Pausing, he raised a finger, then let it fall. "Never mind. Best not to encourage her."

"Let's not."

Forbes vanished into the dark building.

Starting homeward, Truly wondered if Forbes would ever marry and have children. Eventually, he concluded, though later than most. And he hoped that when the children reached a certain age, Forbes would tell them about the past thirty-seven days. A simplified version—tidy and well-lit, as in the history books. The kind that thrilled and comforted and stoked the partisan spirit, all by omitting a central fact—that the real war was fought inside a man. In his soul, in the dark, in a thousand quiet moments. Set against the immensity of this truth, everything else—armies, battles, the whole idea of side-versus-side—seemed a mere projection. Wakefield had learned it too late, whereas Heath and Ravenel had known it always. It had been their greatest advantage. In the shadows where they thrived together, no "sides" existed—just predator and prey.

As Truly walked, he felt the ingot swinging inside his coat. It brought Orlando Monks to mind. Would the wretched man ever be caught?

98

Francis P. Blair Mansion

PACING AROUND THE dining room table, Early stopped for another swallow of brandy. It only fueled his agitation–a rare sort, equal parts rage and glee. The sword, still partway out of its scabbard, stood leaning by the fireplace poker stand. He stared down at it, then kicked it over and stared at the wall. Hanging there, in oval wooden frames, were several photographic portraits of the Blair clan. By virtue of being pictures, they seemed cooly separate from the world and therefore superior to Early–him, by whose mercy this house still stood.

A knock came at the door. "Enter!" he barked.

The sergeant of the guard stepped in and saluted, then moved aside. The prisoner entered and stood there. At Early's instruction, he had been persuaded out of his muddy uniform and into clothes from an upstairs closet–a white ruffled shirt and brown pantaloons with suspenders, ill-fitting on his scrawny frame, plus a pair of ankle jacks.

Early's restlessness concentrated, his stomach suddenly a firepit. He felt a strain in his cheek muscles, then realized he was grinning at Monks. "Lieutenant-Colonel . . . Griffith!"

Monks wore the model captive's look, one of wary compliance. "General Early, sir."

With a nod, Early dismissed the sergeant.

"Must say, Griffith, you look a damned sight better. That uniform of yours had its own weight in mud and cockleburs."

"Very kind of you, General."

"You must have been stuck out there for quite a spell. Two nights, I'd wager."

"I was, sir."

"Did the guards get you fed?"

"They did, General. Most kind of you. I didn't expect such . . . "

"Well, Griffith, we observe the courtesies of rank whenever possible." Early motioned briskly to a chair. "Sit, please."

The Yankee sat. Glancing away, Early had a fleeting sense of disappointment. Monks' diction was cultivated, his high forehead lending a professorial touch. Yet with his strained posture and hollow-eyed diffidence, he could as well have been some bumpkin applying for a handyman's job—too pathetic to hate. Early took the brandy glass and bottle and placed them in front of Monks, who blinked at them and muttered thanks.

Putting his hands behind his back, Early paced to the other end of the table. "So, Griffith—you're with the Veteran Reserve Corps?"

"Yes, General."

"Seen your share of action, then—it does wear on a man. No doubt you've done good service to your own cause, and would do more. Yet even for a soldier and patriot, capture must come almost as a relief, given what you've been through."

"In a way it does, sir."

"We of the Confederacy, we've been through a lot ourselves. In this particular campaign . . . " Early stepped on something. Halting, he looked down and saw the sword under his foot, the engraved name beneath the hilt. A tremor passed through him. "My boys have endured much. I've endured much, frankly, to get this far." Stooping, he picked up the sword. He shoved the blade fully into its scabbard. "But we came so close . . . Griffith. So damned close."

Having poured himself a brandy, Monks took a jittery sip. "Your men performed admirably, General. Gave us quite a scare."

"Fine old sword, this," said Early. "Hate to deprive you of it, but we can't rightly have armed prisoners."

"I understand that, sir."

Moving to the window, Early watched the procession of dark, rifle-toting figures. The withdrawal was well under way. His eyes followed it along the road to the other Blair mansion, beyond which the night swallowed it up. The fire within him burned lower, dampened by sorrow as he felt the present already past, crumbling beneath his soldiers' feet. "My bad old man," Lee called him, and it had come to fit–as if, like an unwitting spell, the name itself had aged him. He wondered if it was truly possible to "seize" a moment, as great men were said to do–to seize and use and live in it before it crumbled, gone to dust. Stepping back, he found himself further disoriented, staring at the wall of Blair portraits–Yankee grandees and grand dames, all seated in aloof attitudes of wisdom.

From across the room, he felt his captive's festering presence. He turned to him. Monks slouched a bit, the glass empty before him. In the flickering of the candelabra, his gaunt face appeared sleepy, less watchful. Early's throat went hard. He gripped the sword tighter, his fire kindling anew.

"We came especially close at Fort DeRussy," he said. "That was a real pity, Griffith."

Glancing aside, Monks coughed slightly. "Still, sir–I . . . I'm sure your troops acquitted themselves quite well."

"Oh, they did–and got blasted for their trouble. God-a-mighty, I wish I knew what went wrong there."

Monks shifted in his seat. Almost imperceptibly, his cheek started twitching. "I don't know," he muttered.

"Speak up, Monks!"

"I don't kn . . . !" The lieutenant-colonel's mouth hung open.

"Well," said Early, "I suppose you did your best?"

Monks trembled. "Yes, General! Yes, I did! I did as required but– but . . . "

"It seemed for all the world like a deliberate trap, Monks! Isn't that what it was?!"

"No, sir! No!"

"Then you simply failed to do as promised!"

"I did as required!"

The sword made a metallic hiss as Early drew it. Dropping the scabbard, he advanced on his prisoner. "If that's so, why were my men fired upon?! Why?!"

Monks scrambled to rise but fell over in his chair. Staring up, he started writhing backward across the carpet.

Early rounded the table. Glowering, he brandished the sword as his voice struck its falsetto peak, shrill as a fife. "Why are we not in Washington, you infernal Yankee bastard?!"

Cornered, gasping, Monks struggled to his feet, jerking his hands up as Early closed in. "General, please listen! It was them, not me! They–They found out and . . . "

"Shut up! SHUT UP!!" Early stood hunched before the cowering figure. Teeth set, he aimed the quivering sword-tip between the quivering upraised hands, inches from Monks' chest. "Not just a traitor," he growled, "but a double traitor."

"A prisoner of war!" Monks cried. "You can't . . . "

"And where's the evidence of that, eh? I ordered your uniform burned, you son of a bitch! And all I see in front of me is a civilian traitor who falsely identified himself!" Glaring deep into Monks' wide eyes, he relished their terror. "Just this once, I fancy doing Yankeedom a favor and running you straight through that yellow belly!"

The lieutenant-colonel's arms went limp as his head and then the rest of him began to wobble. Moaning, he stumbled sideways and sank to his knees. Early lowered the blade. Perplexed at first, he felt a sneer twist his face and turned away. Often enough, he had imagined how it might be to impale a despised enemy–but in this case it would bring no satisfaction. Nor would anything else.

He heard a quick knock. "Yes?"

The sergeant rushed in. "Genr'l . . . " Confused, the young man looked over at Monks.

"What is it?" Early demanded.

"Sir–the other house. It's on fire."

Early's eyes snapped to the nearest window. A spasmodic orange glow silhouetted the passing men, whose shouts and cheers he now heard. Moving to the pane, he saw flames consuming the Montgomery Blair mansion. Smoke obscured part of the road, forcing the grayback column to detour into the field. By an as-yet unfired wing of the house, a soldier smashed a window and tossed a torch inside.

Early placed his hands on the sill. Resting his brow against the smooth glass, he recalled his promise to Breckinridge that both houses would be spared. "Nothing to be done about it," he mumbled.

He heard a stirring behind him and glanced over his shoulder. Crumpled against the baseboard, Monks held a hand to his head, quaking. Early looked back at the blaze. "Call the guards in," he said, and the sergeant did so. When at last Early looked around, the sergeant stood there with three privates shouldering rifles. Momentarily he forgot why he had summoned them, then poked a thumb toward Monks. "This man's a spy. Take him out and shoot him."

The sergeant tensed, his lips parting. "But Genr'l–ain't he an officer?"

"A spy, I said. And he's to be shot–immediately."

Abruptly resolute, the sergeant drew his pistol. "Yessir, Genr'l."

"No!" Monks yelped.

As Early turned back to the window, they dragged Monks kicking from the room. "No, General–please! I swear I tried! PLEASE, SIR!!" The Yankee's yelps became a full-throated howl, receding down the hallway.

Early watched the house burn. Keeping their distance, soldiers whooped and shouted as they moved past it, bathed in its shuddering brilliance. A section of roof caved in, billowing sparks. From somewhere amid the night's chaos, Early thought he heard a burst of musketry, followed by a pistol shot.

"To hell with it," he muttered. "To hell with it all."

He pulled a chair out and sat staring across the room. In their little oval frames, the collection of lofty Blair faces again confronted him. He wanted to shout a question at them but did not know precisely what.

99

Truly Residence

THE SOUND HELD Truly motionless on the doorstep. It was strange to hear at such an hour: Sapphira's piano, its tune like pungent blossoms on the night. Quietly he hummed to the melody's gliding descent, then stopped as a high, clear voice began singing:

> *'Twas early in the month of May*
> *When green buds they were swellin'*
> *Sweet William on his deathbed lay*
> *For the love of Barbry Ellen . . .*

When had he last heard Anna sing? When had she last pierced him with that voice, that sound of Rachel's legacy? For an aching moment, he dared to imagine that it was Rachel in there, just beyond the door. He wanted it to last. Despite his weariness, he wanted to stay here indefinitely on the threshold, in this trance as voice and piano intertwined, sailing high and swooping low, telling the tale:

> *Upon her grave there grew a rose*
> *On William's grave, a briar . . .*

And so it ended, the way it always ended. Sapphira's playing ceased. Truly turned the knob and stepped inside. Not bothering to hang his hat and coat, he entered the parlor. Greeting him, Anna and Sapphira stood there in their nightclothes.

Ben, in his nightshirt, sat cradling a whiskey on the settee, a fresh bandage on his face. He squinted a smile. "Have a drink, Pa?"

"No. That would finish me off, methinks." Truly flopped into his chair.

Anna took a cane chair while Sapphira returned to the piano bench.

"Tucker and I spent the night in the rifle pits at Fort Slocum," said Ben. "By this morning enough reinforcements had come up, so we were dismissed. I've slept about ten hours." He sipped his whiskey. "I left Tucker at Reverend Cass's place. He'll likely stop by tomorrow."

Truly sent a glance to Sapphira, who lowered her eyes. "Well, you've done a heap of service," he told Ben. "You and Tucker both."

"Seems you and Forbes have too."

Yawning, Truly rubbed his rough cheeks. "The fuller story of which I'll save for later."

"We'll be all ears, Pa."

"We certainly will!" said Anna. Her gaze verged on a glare. Unable to meet it, Truly looked down and saw a shiny brass object by his chair. His spittoon.

As a wave of generosity swept through him, he gave Anna a sleepy smile. "So tell me, sweet girl–how's young Chadwick doing in all of this?"

"Oh–my poor Dennis! He's wounded again."

"What?"

"I visited him this evening. A cannon rolled over his foot." Blinking tears away, Anna brightened. "But at least we'll still be close while he recovers. Truth be told, I was dreading his return to frontline duty."

"You know, I believe I will have that drink."

"I'll get it," said Sapphira.

He watched her move to the side table and measure out a glass of whiskey from the decanter. Absently he reached into his coat pocket for his tobacco; instead he touched the gold ingot. He withdrew his hand and accepted the glass from Sapphira. Thanking her, he stared at the fireplace mantel. There between the flower vases, his own sour-looking portrait sat beside Rachel's tranquil one.

"Why in tarnation is that up there?"

"I found it in the cellar," said Sapphira. "Since you bothered to have it taken . . . "

He looked up at her and then at Ben and Anna, then back at the portraits. He took a warming sip. "Saph–you know 'Lorena,' don't you?"

"Oh, yes."

"Annie, do you know the words?"

"Most of them."

"Would you mind?"

While Anna took her place by the piano, Sapphira reseated herself and played a gentle progression, feeling it out. She stopped to flex her hands before starting again. Anna closed her eyes and sang:

> *The years creep slowly by, Lorena*
> *The snow is on the grass again;*
> *The sun's low down the sky, Lorena*
> *The frost gleams where the flowers have been . . .*

Truly put his glass aside. Caressed by the song, he was soon dozing. He saw himself on a speckled pony he had once owned, riding the plains of his youth. He saw Rachel and himself at the Missouri homestead, seated together atop the flour barrel. Then he saw some other young couple, whirling in a graceful dance as the music played; through curtains of light and shadow they came waltzing toward him and then all around him, their faces obscure. He wondered who they could be. It seemed a good while before he became aware of a larger sound–rolling and cavernous, overpowering the music and then quashing it. The dancing pair whirled out of sight.

Startled awake, he saw Ben craning his neck to the window, where Anna and Sapphira stood peering out. A deep rumble shook the house. "Artillery?" he muttered. "This close?"

Jerking out of his seat, he left the parlor and strode down the hall. He wanted to look in the direction of the President's Park, hoping that it was just an ill-timed fireworks or perhaps an extra-large cannon salute. In the kitchen he lit a hand lamp before venturing onto the back porch. He strained his ears. Again the night rumbled–and as he raised the lamp, its halo revealed misty threads of rain, the grass glistening.

The roof overhang kept the top step dry so he eased down onto it, placing the lamp at his side. He listened to the rain. Then, resting on his elbows, he noticed a domed black object by the steps, half-hidden in a clump of tall grass. He leaned down and picked it up. It was the bowler that Baker had sent him, now smudged and mildewed. He held it, twirled it, then flung it into the rainy darkness. Reaching into his coat pocket, he touched the ingot and squeezed it. The thunder boomed.

Heath and Ravenel were vanquished, he thought, but not the vast dark beast that had spawned them. Against that beast, any victory was small and short-lived, little more than a holding action. Wherever people surged, its darkness surged with them, as it had with the first slave ships and fugitive vessels. From the squalor of the cities, it had pushed ever westward with the settlements, boomtowns and cavalry outposts, to the buffalo plains where lone Indians gazed east, keeping vigil. Amid the bugles of war, its pulse resounded as a deep drum, while at other times it came as a fainter, more subterranean sound, no less maddening or insistent–in the rhetoric of the soapbox and the jabber of mansion drawing rooms; in pulpit orations and the clamor of immigrant throngs; beneath the ringing of hammers and the roar of factory furnaces; in the rattle of wagon trains and the rumble of orphan trains, all bound for destinations too far for any homeward cry to carry, or for an answering cry to reach.

On the nation's self-proclaimed march to glory, the dark beast would follow close behind, largely ignored and frequently unsuspected, even as it conjured madness in every shape. While noble laws were enacted, worthy dreams accomplished, good deeds done and gleaming spires erected, it would exact its share of tribute, fueled by lies, greed and betrayal. There would be untold wreckage. Lanterns would flicker out while mob torches lit the night. Bells and choirs would go silent while howls of vengeance rent the air. Hope would shrivel while hate poisoned the rivers. Singly or en masse, honest lives would break while evil ones prospered. These things would happen, as surely as they had happened before–and all to that timeless demonic thrum, working its way into the current of men's blood.

Truly heard the porch door open. Then Sapphira was standing beside him, staring out at the rain.

"Drought's over," he said.

She moved to the bottom step. He watched her stand there, a white-robed figure in the lamplight, hands and face upturned to the rain. Reaching out, he pulled her gently by the sleeve until she stepped back up and settled next to him. Water beaded her brow, sparkled in her hair.

"Storms don't trouble me," she said. "Not this kind."

The thunder sounded again, receding now, though the rain held steady.

"'A tale told by an idiot,'" Truly murmured, "'–full of sound and fury, signifying . . .'"

"Signifying *something*, Father. Something, surely."

"Oh . . . I reckon that's so. I used to be more convinced, is all." Truly gazed to the upper fringe of the lamp glow, where the rain was just a murky veil. He sighed. "Lord, we do give ourselves a heap of credit, don't we? Just for being born in time. Even while we're busy smashing the world to pieces, we fancy ourselves the Children of Light–wiser, smarter, freer than any that came before. But how do you guess we'll look to future folk? Like trolls, I figure. A queer race of trolls–wallowing in ignorance, chasing our shadows around."

Sapphira wiped a droplet from her cheek. "Well . . . It's only God's verdict that's supposed to count. Why else would people pray?"

He muffled a yawn. "Let me tell you about me and praying, missy. Try as I might, I can't get past the word 'Please.'"

Slowly she got to her feet. "As I understand it, the words matter less than the thought." Fluffing her robe, she looked down at him. "You need sleep, Father."

"I won't be long."

She went back inside.

Truly watched the rain. The day would come, he told himself–it had to come–when no one would confuse real thunder with the man-made sort. He rubbed his eyes. Drowsing, he saw the two dancers again–the entwined young man and woman, blurred of feature yet graceful of form, gliding toward him. Who were they? Somehow he cherished them. But had he a single prayer to say, it would have been for them to return whence they came. To whirl away beautifully, back into the warm fold of the past and the known.

THE END

Historical Epilogue

JUBAL EARLY'S ARMY of the Valley evaded the clumsy federal pursuit and returned to the Shenandoah, where Lee ordered it to stay on and maintain its threat. Soon it made another foray. On July 30, cavalry chief John McCausland reluctantly burned the town of Chambersburg, Pennsylvania, when Early's ransom demand ("levy") proved impossible. Again Union forces chased the Confederates back to the Valley.

Early could not have had better subordinates than Breckinridge, Echols, Gordon, Pendleton, Ramseur and Rodes. But following Chambersburg, his luck steadily ran out. In the first week of August, Grant sent General Philip H. Sheridan to "follow [Early] to the death." Famously, Grant also directed him to make the Shenandoah "a barren waste . . . so that crows flying over it for the balance of the season will have to carry their own provender."

On September 19, after weeks of small-scale actions, Sheridan struck at Opequon Creek near Winchester. Division commander Robert Rodes was killed in the fighting, which wiped out a quarter of Early's force. Early retreated to Fisher's Hill but, three days later, was attacked and demolished once more, forced to retreat sixty miles. This time he lost Alexander "Sandie" Pendleton, who had been called the finest staff officer in the Confederacy. At this worst possible moment, Breckinridge's corps was called away to face another Union threat, this one in southwestern Virginia.

Back at Petersburg, the siege ground on, with United States Colored Troops increasingly seeing action. On July 30, many of them met disaster at the Battle of the Crater, which commenced when four tons of gunpowder were detonated beneath Confederate lines. Coal miners from a Pennsylvania regiment had dug a 500-foot tunnel for this purpose, while a black division of General Ambrose Burnside's underwent tactical training

so it could lead the subsequent assault. The plan could well have led to Petersburg's capture and shortened the war, had General George Meade's all-too-typical doubts concerning black soldiery not intervened. At the eleventh hour, he ordered the lead division replaced by an ill-prepared white one. (Grant approved the order, explaining afterward that he had not wanted to appear careless of black lives, given the operation's peril.) The attack that followed the great explosion was completely bungled, with federals trapped in the giant crater and Confederates firing down. The lead Union officer, Brigadier-General James Ledlie, was found drunk and hiding in a trench and was later cashiered. When the black troops were at last sent in, they ran straight into a ferocious counterattack and suffered heavily, some being cut down after surrendering.

The 22nd U.S. Colored Regiment, featured in this novel, was spared participation in the Crater fiasco but not in the Battle of New Market Heights two months later. On the march to the battle site, the 22nd and other USCT regiments endured jeers from white troops who accompanied them. There were no such jeers on the return march, the black federals having charged and smashed the Confederate position. By this time, the political and military outlook on the war had changed dramatically. On September 2, news that General William Sherman had captured Atlanta resounded like a thunderclap and virtually ensured Lincoln's reelection– a possibility that the President himself had doubted. In the Shenandoah, meanwhile, Phil Sheridan's scorched-earth policy terrorized the largely pro-Southern populace. David Hunter's depredations of the past spring looked mild by comparison. Homes and barns were burned by the hundreds and livestock borne off by the thousands, depriving Lee's army of much-needed food.

But Early still had some fight in him. On October 19, at Cedar Creek, he surprised Sheridan's force in a dawn attack and initially routed much of it. But Sheridan himself came galloping from nearby Winchester, rallying his men for a counterattack. When John B. Gordon pointed out a dangerous gap in the Confederate line, Early failed to close it and the Yankees came crashing through, turning their defeat into a major victory. During this action, the Southern "boy general" Stephen D. Ramseur fell, wearing a white rose to celebrate the birth of his first child.

Lee deemed Early's Washington raid a success. The Southern press and public did not–and with ultimate defeat looming, they heaped recriminations on Early. Through the miserable winter, rumors of his hard drinking and unfitness were circulated as fact. Illness, transfers and desertion reduced his badly mauled "army" to about 2,000. On March 2, 1865, at Waynesboro, a Union cavalry division under Brigadier-General George A. Custer finally crushed this remnant. Early, barely escaping capture, was relieved of all command.

Breckinridge had been assigned a mountainous military district that sprawled across three state lines. With scant resources, he fended off Northern encroachment and governed the region with fairness, winning admiration even from its Tory (pro-Union) element. This part of his career began on a dark note, however. On October 2, he had scarcely arrived in the vicinity when a federal column that included black cavalrymen struck at Saltville, Virginia. Regular and Home Guard troops turned it back. The next morning, Breckinridge rode out to find victorious Confederates shooting the Negro wounded. He angrily brought a halt to the massacre, but it resumed as soon as he rode to another part of the battlefield. The exact number of executed black prisoners and wounded remains unknown, but estimates have ranged from 45 to over a hundred.

Lee condemned the atrocity and ordered the arrest of Brigadier-General Felix Robertson, who Breckinridge had declared most responsible. Robertson was by then in Georgia. Severely wounded soon afterward, he dropped out of sight and escaped punishment. Only one known perpetrator ever paid for his deeds at Saltville–the ruthless Confederate guerilla Champ Ferguson. Captured and tried by Union authorities, he was hanged inside a square of black troops.

In January, 1865, Breckinridge was called to serve as Secretary of War. Given his administrative talents–and the mediocrity of his predecessor James Seddon–one wonders how the war might have turned out, had he been the original appointee. He sacked the notoriously uncooperative commissary-general Lucius Northrop. He backed a plan (as he had when the late General Pat Cleburne first proposed it) to free slaves in return for their joining the Confederate forces. But everything he did came far too late. When Richmond fell in April, he went to North Carolina and helped General Joseph Johnston negotiate surrender terms with Sherman. News that federal marshals were on his trail sent him on an arduous journey of escape–to Florida and then Cuba, then to Europe and finally Canada.

Well before the war's end, Breckinridge had begun to question the strict states-rights doctrine that he had once so potently symbolized. Unlike

Early, he retained a sentimental fondness for the Stars 'n' Stripes, which he could see flying across the Falls at Niagara. Early, now a good friend and fellow exile, was a frequent visitor at Breckinridge's Niagara home. In 1869, through the efforts of Northern publisher Horace Greeley, a general amnesty program brought home scores of ex-Confederates, including Early and Breckinridge. Of the two men's contrasting personalities, a mutual friend observed, "In large part [Breckinridge] was within, what Early was without." Yet their post-exile lives could hardly have differed more.

Back in 1851, as a young attorney, Early had successfully represented a young ex-slave woman named Indiana Choice. (Choice had been freed by her widowed mistress, whose second husband later tried to negate the manumission.) Ten years later, Early showed little patience for the rabid pro-slavery element and opposed Virginia's secession. But the war left him bitter and recalcitrant. He returned to Virginia and resumed his law practice. The mid-1870's found him virulently white-supremacist, refusing to participate in any commemorative ceremony that included Negro veterans. In word and in writing, he also did much to promote the cult of Robert E. Lee, which raised that great, now-deceased general to godlike status (much as the cult of Lincoln did for that greatest, most mysterious of Presidents.) Early never married, though he sired four children by Julia McNealey of Rocky Mount. Disdaining the loyalty oath, he died "unreconstructed" in 1894, aged 77.

Welcomed back to Kentucky, Breckinridge took the loyalty oath and, along with Lee, became a major force for moderation and reconciliation. His extensive and lifelong dealings with black Americans set him apart from other white leaders, North and South. This and his native kindliness did much to mitigate his rather conventional views on race in general. (Bolstering his deeply conservative grasp of the U.S. Constitution, these views helped spawn the tragic irony of his 1860 presidential bid, with its pro-slavery platform.) Some American descendents of the slave-owning class still rhapsodize over how wonderfully their forebears treated the help. However self-serving these claims may be, Breckinridge did in fact show an unusual degree of consideration toward his slaves, though by the late 1850's he had ceased to own any. He did frequent business with free blacks, lending and borrowing money. He defended black clients in court. The steward of the U.S. Senate, a black man, presented him with a gold-headed ebony cane as a token of regard. In the post-war years, he supported the admission of black testimony in cases that involved white defendants. He also took a highly public stand against the Ku Klux Klan. Denouncing it as a collection of "idiots and villains," he helped stifle its power in Kentucky for a generation.

Apart from practicing law, he served as branch president for a life insurance company. He also backed a railroad construction project—but in the Panic of 1873, this venture went bankrupt. The consequent worry and humiliation wore his health down. He died two years later at the age of 54, mourned throughout his home state.

Of two other Early subordinates who lived to tell the tale: At Appomattox, by then a lieutenant-general, the incomparable John Brown Gordon was chosen to surrender the Southern colors. He went on to serve one term as governor of Georgia and two as U.S. senator. Henry Kyd Douglas eventually made brigadier-general (perhaps the youngest on either side) and was also at Appomattox, where his brigade fired the last shot and was last to surrender. His memoir *I Rode With Stonewall* ranks among the best-written and most vivid of the war.

Of some Union officers depicted or mentioned in this novel: Horatio Wright and Christopher Augur were career military men. Augur, a brave if not especially talented general, turned 43 on the day that he and the capital braced for Early—surely one of the most uncomfortable birthdays on record. Wright led the final assault at Petersburg on April 2, 1865, capturing that city and precipitating Richmond's fall the next day. Lew Wallace, whose stand at the Monocacy delayed Early for a precious twenty-four hours, went on to become governor of New Mexico Territory and U.S. minister to Turkey; a writer of historical novels, he won immortality with *Ben Hur*. Oliver Wendell Holmes became one of the most celebrated legal minds in U.S. history, serving thirty years as an associate justice on the Supreme Court. Barton Alexander, one of Washington's cooler and more competent authorities, made brigadier-general in early '65; he supervised the post-war dismantling of General Barnard's fortifications, the most extensive in the world at that time.

George Sharpe, organizer and chief of the Bureau of Military Information, would have been an asset to any army in any war. Well-traveled, multi-lingual and classically educated, he had served as a low-level diplomat in Rome and Vienna before starting a law practice in his hometown of Kingston, NY. At the war's outbreak, he went to the front as captain of a militia company. A year later, he raised the 120th New York Regiment with his own funds and became its colonel. In February, 1863, he took up General Joseph Hooker's challenge to form a secret service bureau for the Army of the Potomac. The Army's overall intelligence capability was inferior to that of the Confederates and had figured into its string of major defeats. After three arduous months, Sharpe had assembled a stable of highly competent scouts and agents, both military and civilian, and was cross-checking intelligence from a wide variety of sources. In this he had invaluable help from his immediate subordinates, Captain John McEntee and the civilian scout "Captain" John Babcock. The Bureau's greatest triumph occurred in the weeks preceding Gettysburg, when its web of informants and diligent sifting of reports revealed the enemy's size, composition and direction. In time, however, General Meade absorbed the Bureau into his command structure, curtailing its independence and interfering with its methodology. In part because of this, Early's Raid went undetected until it was almost too late. The near-calamity prompted Grant, the supreme commander, to reorganize the Bureau and restore its full effectiveness.

Sharpe was promoted to brigadier-general in February, 1865. At Appomattox, he had the job of issuing paroles to every Confederate soldier, including Lee himself. In 1867, having resumed his happy life in Kingston, Sharpe was dispatched by Secretary of State Seward to Europe, where he vainly pursued the alleged Lincoln assassination conspirator John Surratt. President Grant appointed him federal marshal for the Southern District of New York in 1869. Against great resistance, he conducted an accurate census and thereby revealed election fraud, helping to break the power of the Tweed Ring. He then served as New York's surveyor of customs until 1878, after which he remained active in the law and in state politics. He died in 1900.

Of William Wood's strange hold over Edwin Stanton, it was often said, "Stanton is head of the War Department and Wood is head of Stanton." But in the aftermath of Lincoln's murder, the relationship came apart. Wood took up the cause of accused conspirator Mary Surratt, whose innocence he proclaimed, and sought an audience with President Andrew Johnson. In this Stanton allegedly thwarted him, breaking a promise that Surratt would be spared the gallows. The woman hanged along with three male conspirators. That same year, Wood severed his ties with the War Department and become chief of the Treasury's Secret Service division.

In 1867-68, Johnson's efforts to fire Stanton touched off a political crisis. It culminated in Johnson's impeachment and near-removal from office, after which Stanton resigned. He died in late 1869, just days after President Grant nominated him for the Supreme Court. In an 1883 series of articles, Wood stated that Stanton had committed suicide, haunted to the last by the ghost of Mary Surratt. This claim was widely believed, though never proven. (Amid the aftershocks of the assassination, instances of personal disaster and despair make the period seem truly cursed. Senators James Lane of Kansas and Preston King of New York, for two examples, committed suicide within months of each other. The pair had blocked the White House stairs when Surratt's daughter Anna came to beg a presidential pardon.)

Wood made another startling claim, this one dating from the outset of his and Stanton's acquaintance. In an 1854 patent infringement trial that involved the McCormick reaping machine, defense attorney Stanton had called Wood as an expert witness. Wood now said that he had perjured himself, altering an early model of the reaper and helping to win the case. He did not say whether Stanton knew of the deception–but to many, the story explained how Wood had come to secure the powerful man's sponsorship. (Another member of the defense team was Illinois lawyer Abraham Lincoln, toward whom Stanton was rudely dismissive; Lincoln nevertheless appointed him as War Secretary eight years later–a tribute to the President's pragmatic ego, as well as his eye for talent.) Wood died in 1903 at the age of 83, a more durable scoundrel than his friend Lafayette Baker.

For his role in running down the assassin John Wilkes Booth, Baker received $3,750 in reward money and got a promotion to brigadier-general. From that point, his fortunes took a steep dive. Johnson banned him from the White House in early 1866, having discovered that Baker was spying on him. With the war safely over, newspapers savaged Baker for excessive zeal, and his relations with Stanton soured as well. Sacked from the War Department, he took revenge in his less-than-reliable *History of the United States Secret Service* (1867), wherein he revealed the existence of Booth's suppressed diary. He was called before the House Judiciary Committee, to whom he implied that Stanton had removed pages from the diary. In the Johnson impeachment investigation, he testified against the President.

Baker died in 1868, aged 41, supposedly of meningitis. It is thought that he was working on another memoir, this one portraying Stanton as the mastermind behind Lincoln's murder. Like many such theories, this one has proven stubborn despite being roundly discredited. Yet it must be added that in the 1960's, Professor Ray A. Neff of Indiana State University used an atomic absorption spectrophotometer to analyze Baker's hair and cited arsenic poisoning as the cause of death. Baker's brother-in-law Wally Pollack, who had periodically been bringing him imported beer, is the chief suspect. Pollack was a War Department employee.

A word on the District of Columbia Metropolitan Police: Few police departments have had to face the challenges that this one did from its 1861 inception, when the capital's crime and population began to surge. Under Superintendents William Webb and A.C. Richards, the DCMP did a remarkable job overall. It screened its applicants well and remained largely free of corruption. One fictional bad officer should not obscure these facts.

Acknowledgments

OVER THE MARATHON course of writing *Lucifer's Drum* and researching its historical basis, I received help from friends, relatives and strangers who gave feedback, shared expertise, sent materials and offered simple encouragement. Any inaccuracy or other blemish exists despite their generosity. Of the experts I consulted, many or most have no doubt moved on from the positions cited here. My lasting thanks go to:

F. Terry Hambrecht, M.D., of the National Museum of Civil War Medicine, Frederick, MD; Civil War re-enactor Frank Coukaroula of the National Park Service, Lee Mansion, Arlington, VA; Paul Plamann of the National Park Service, Fort McHenry, Baltimore, MD; Jim Aguirre of the Maryland Historical Survey, Crownsville, MD; re-enactors Mike Kraus and Doug Hungell; Fred Waters and Cynthia Sarkis of Photo Antiquities, Pittsburgh, PA; Mark Osterman, International Museum of Photography at the George Eastman House, Rochester, NY; Ken and Sharon Hansgen of the White Elephant B & B Inn, Savannah, TN; Dr. Marilyn Zoidis of the Smithsonian Institution; Don Kennon and Betty Coed of the U.S. Capitol and U.S. Senate Historical Societies, respectively; all the good people at the Historical Society of Washington, D.C.

Also: Dana Hay, for her unfailing help and faith; Becky Argall, for her generosity and sharp editorial eye; Susan Day, whose maps and other D.C. information were of constant benefit; Anita Samuelsen and the late Dr. Tom Samuelsen, whose kindly interest resonates in the great books he left me; Josh Russell, the best traveling buddy I ever had, thanks to whom I experienced Gettysburg National Battlefield; Barbara Raisbeck and the late Tobey Raisbeck, for their graciousness and patient ears; Lee Snow and the late Roger Snow, for the same; Shara McCallum and Steve Shwartzer, for their invaluable friendship; Mike LeSage and Leigh Anne Duck, for keeping life in the South fun; the Merlin-like Geoff Sauer, for his computer-related gifts; Tim Umland, the most hospitable man in Washington, with whom I stood on the overgrown ramparts of Fort DeRussy; my late father Bernard MacKinnon and my mother Loretta MacKinnon; Robert Fisher, for years of useful/tactful feedback; Jim Veraldi, whose conversation and love of history were a regular boost back in Pittsburgh; Al Varel, loyal correspondent and an example of true dedication; Debbie Noack, loyal correspondent and source of precious encouragment; Sandra Kane, for her faith and thoughtfulness; the late and much-loved Carol Burdick, who stoked my confidence in the callow years; Howard Bahr, for his kindly insights and for writing *The Black Flower*, the most transcendent work of Civil War fiction I have ever read; Jamie Gildard, for his grasp of military history and his layered skills as a reader; Anne and Dale Rugieri, for their years of graciousness; George Smithers, for his abundant help; Peter Ceren, for his smart and generous advice; Lois Lowry, for her vast kindness way back when.

Also, for similar good reasons: Cheryl Ripsom Massey, Jervon Stuart, Beth Espy, Victor Coonin, Alan Glenn, Kathy Mills, Dan Rosen, the late Jodi Brown, the late Herman Butler, Patty Lasky, Steve Strom, Paul Austin, George Fifield, Scott Harris, Steve Sparks, Irwin Rumler, Mandy Young, Rosemary Lemmis, Tom Hajduk, Ann Chenoweth, Eric Bliman, Bert Hitt, Bill Elliott, Nathan Tipton, Jimmy Powell, Raka Nandi and Robert Saxe, Ken Ward and Kerrie Rogers, Chris Werry and Vidya Dinamani, Peter and Maureen Goggin, Patti Wojahn and Pat Morandi, George and Donna Brennen, Ellie and Josh Hardison, Philip and Alyce Guichelaar, my father-in-law Chang Kyo Kim and my late mother-in-law Hazel Kim; my sibs– John, Mary Rose, Carol Ann, Paula, Ellen and Ron. Last but really topping the list is my wife Loel, whose patience, perceptiveness, computer skills, et al, were priceless from start to finish. Whatever I've managed to win here is hers too.

Among the works of historical scholarship that inform this novel (despite its many acts of fictive license), the following figure prominently: *Reveilee In Washington, 1860-1865* by Margaret Leech (a Pulitzer winner that deserves perpetual rediscovery); *Capital Losses: A Cultural History of Washington's Destroyed Buildings* by James M. Goode; *Mr. Lincoln's Forts* by Cooling & Owen; *This Hallowed Ground* by Bruce Catton; *Battle Cry of Freedom: The Civil War Era* by James M. McPherson; *So Far From God: The U.S. War With Mexico, 1846-48* by John S. D. Eisenhower; *Jubal's Raid: General Early's Famous Attack on Washington in 1864* by Frank E. Vandiver;

The Shenandoah Valley in 1864 by George E. Pond; *A Photographic History of the Civil War*, ed.-in-chief Francis Trevelyan Miller; *The Secret War for the Union: The Untold Story of Military Intelligence in the Civil War* by Edwin C. Fishel; *Spies for the Blue and Gray* by Harnett T. Kane; *The War Between the Spies: A History of Espionage during the American Civil War* by Alan Axelrod; *Abraham Lincoln and the Fifth Column* by George Fort Milton; *The Eyes and Ears of the Civil War* by G. Allen Foster; *Lincoln* by David Herbert Donald; *Jubal: The Life and Times of General Jubal Early, CSA* by Charles C. Osborne; *Breckinridge: Statesman, Soldier, Symbol* by William C. Davis; *The Sable Arm: Negro Troops in the Union Army* by Dudley Taylor Cornish; *Forged In Battle: The Civil War Alliance of Black Soldiers and White Officers* by Joseph T. Glatthaar; *The Birth of Photography: The Story of the Formative Years, 1800-1900* by Brian Coe, Curator of the Kodak Museum; the excellent series on Civil War medicine by Alfred J. Bollet, M.D., in *Resident and Staff Physician* magazine.

Other valuable sources were: *The Blue and the Gray* by Henry Steele Commager; *Lee's Lieutenants* by Douglas Southall Freeman; *A Treasury of Civil War Tales* by Webb Garrison; *The Civil War* by Harry Hansen; *Battles and Leaders of the Civil War*, ed. R. U. Johnson and C. C. Buel; *Battlefields of the Civil War* by Roger W. Hicks and Frances E. Schultz; *The Look of the Old West* by Foster-Harris, illus. by Evelyn Curro; *America Moves West* by Robert E. Riegel; *Spies and Spymasters of the Civil War* by Donald E. Markle; *Secret Missions of the Civil War* by Philip Van Doren Stern; *The Civil War Notebook of Daniel Chisholm: A Chronicle of Daily Life in the Union Army, 1864-65*, ed. W. Springer Menge and J. August Shimrack; *Co. Aytch: A Side Show of the Big Show* by Sam R. Watkins; *All For The Union: The Civil War Diary and Letters of Elisha Hunt Rhodes*, ed. Robert Hunt Rhodes; *Blue-eyed Child of Fortune: The Civil War Letters of Robert Gould Shaw*, ed. Russell Duncan; *Grant: A Biography* by William S. McFeely; *Kit Carson: A Pattern For Heroes* by Thelma S. Guild and Harvey L. Carter; *A History of Negro Troops in the War of the Rebellion, 1861-1865* by George W. Williams, LL.D. (which includes a first-hand account of the Battle of Baylor's Farm, depicted in Chap. 29); *Black Cargoes: A History of the Atlantic Slave Trade, 1518-1865* by Daniel P. Mannix in collaboration with Malcolm Cowley; *Roll, Jordan, Roll: The World the Slaves Made* by Eugene D. Genovese; *Brass-Pounders: Young Telegraphers of the Civil War* by Alvin F. Harlow; *District of Columbia Police* by Richard Sylvester; *The Writer's Guide to Everyday Life in the 1800's* by Marc McCutcheon; *Everyday Life During the Civil War* by Michael J. Varhola.

B. MacKinnon, April 2013

31933942R20445

Made in the USA
Charleston, SC
03 August 2014